Consuelo

SHE MOTIONED HIM, WITH AN IMPERIOUS GESTURE, BACK TO THE GONDOLA.

[Page 116

Consuelo

A Romance of Venice

By George Sand

A DA CAPO PAPERBACK

Library of Congress Cataloging in Publication Data

Sand, George, pseud. of Mme. Dudevant, 1804-1876.
  Consuelo: a romance of Venice.

  Reprint of the ed. published by A. L. Burt Co., New
York, in series: Burt's library of the world's best
books.
  I. Title.
PZ3.S21Co 1979 [PQ2400] 843'.7   79-15632
ISBN 0-306-80102-7 (pbk.)

PQ
2400
. C 3
1979

ISBN 0-306-80102-7
First Da Capo Paperback Edition 1979

This Da Capo Press paperback edition of *Consuelo:
A Romance of Venice* is an unabridged
republication of the edition published by
A. L. Burt Company in New York (n.d.)

Published by Da Capo Press, Inc.
A Subsidiary of Plenum Publishing Corporation
227 West 17th Street, New York, N.Y. 10011

CONSUELO.

CHAPTER I.

"Yes, yes, young ladies; toss your heads as much as you please; the wisest and best among you is —— But I shall not say it; for she is the only one of my class who has a particle of modesty, and I should fear, were I to name her, that she should forthwith lose that uncommon virtue which I could wish to see in you——"

"In nomine Patris, et Filii, et Spiritus Sancti,"

sang Costanza, with an air of effrontery.

"Amen!" exclaimed all the other girls in chorus.

"Naughty man!" said Clorinda, pouting out her pretty lips, and tapping with the handle of her fan the wrinkled and bony fingers which the singing-master had left stretched on the keys of the silent instrument.

"Go on, young ladies—go on," said the old professor, with the resigned and submissive air of one who for forty years had had to suffer for six hours daily the airs and contradictions of successive generations of female pupils. "It is not the less true," added he, putting his spectacles into their case, and his snuff-box into his pocket, without raising his eyes toward the angry and mocking group, "that this wise, this docile, this studious, this attentive, this good child, is not you, Signora Clorinda; nor you, Signora Costanza; nor you, either, Signora Zulietta; neither is it Rosina; and still less Michela——"

"In that case, it is I!"

"No; it is I!"

"By no means; it is I!"

"'Tis I!"

"'Tis I!" screamed out all at once, with their clear and thrilling voices, some fifty fair or dark-haired girls, darting like a flock of sea-birds on some poor shell-fish left stranded by the waves.

The shell-fish, that is to say, the maestro — and I maintain that no other metaphor could so well express his angular movements, his filmy eyes, his red-streaked cheeks, and more especially the innumerable stiff, white and pointed curls of his professional wig — the maestro, I say, forced back three times upon his seat, after having risen to go away, but calm and indifferent as the shell-fish itself, rocked and hardened by the storms, had long to be entreated to declare which of his pupils deserved the praises of which he was usually so sparing, but of which he now showed himself so prodigal. At last, yielding as if with regret to the entreaties, which his sarcasms had provoked, he took the roll with which he was in the habit of marking the time, and made use of it to separate and range in two lines his unruly flock. Then, advancing with a serious air between the double row of these light-headed creatures, he proceeded toward the organ-loft, and stopped before a young person who was seated, bent down, on one of the steps. She, with her elbows on her knees, and her fingers in her ears, in order not to be distracted by the noise, and twisted into a sort of coil like a squirrel sinking to sleep, conned over her lesson in a low voice, so as to disturb no one. He, solemn and triumphant, with leg advanced and outstretched arm, seemed like the shepherd Paris awarding the apple, not to the most beautiful, but to the wisest.

"Consuelo! the Spaniard!" exclaimed all the young choristers, struck at first with the utmost surprise, but almost immediately joining in a general burst of laughter, such as Homer attributes to the gods of Olympus, and which caused a blush of anger and indignation on the majestic countenance of the professor.

Little Consuelo, with her closed ears, had heard nothing of this dialogue. Her eyes were bent on vacancy, and, busied with her task, she remained some moments unconscious of the uproar. Then, perceiving herself the object of general attention, she dropped her hands on her knees, allowed her book to fall on the floor, and, petrified with astonishment not unmixed with fear, rose at length and looked around in order to see what ridiculous person or thing afforded matter for such noisy gaiety.

"Consuelo," said the maestro, taking her hand without

further explanation, " come, my good child, and sing me the *'Salve Regina'* of Pergolese, which thou hast learned but a fortnight, and which Clorinda has been studying for more than a year."

Consuelo, without replying and without evincing either anger, shame, or embarassment, followed the singing-master to the organ, where, sitting down, he struck with an air of triumph, the key-note for his young pupil. Then Consuelo, with unaffected simplicity and ease, raised her clear and thrilling voice, and filled the lofty roof with the sweetest and purest notes with which it had ever echoed. She sang the *' Salve Regina'* without a single error—without venturing one note which was not perfectly just, full, sustained, or interrupted at the proper place; and following with unvarying precision the instructions which the learned master had given her, fulfilling with her clear perceptions his precise and correct intentions, she accomplished, with the inexperience and indifference of a child, that which science, practice, and enthusiasm had not perhaps done for the most perfect singer. In a word, she sang to admiration.

" It is well, my child," said the good old master, always chary of his praise. " You have studied with attention that which you have faithfully performed. Next time you shall repeat the cantata of Scarlatti which I have taught you."

" *Si, Signor Professor*," replied Consuelo — " now may I go?"

" Yes, my child. Young ladies, the lesson is over."

Consuelo placed in her little basket her music and her crayons, as well as her black fan — the inseparable companion alike of Spaniard and Venetian — which she never used, although she never went without it. Then, disappearing behind the fretwork of the organ, she flew as lightly as a bird down the mysterious stairs which led to the body of the cathedral, knelt for a moment in crossing the nave, and, when just on the point of leaving the church, found beside the font a handsome young man who, smiling, presented the holy water to her. She took some of it, looking at him all the time with the self-possession of a little girl who knows and feels that she is not yet a woman, and mingling her thanks and her devotional gesture in so agreeable a fashion that the signor could not help laughing outright. Consuelo began to laugh like wise, but, all at once, as if she had recollected that some one was waiting for her, she cleared the porch and the steps in a bound, and was off in a twinkling.

In the meantime, the professor again replaced his spectacles in his huge waistcoat pocket, and thus addressed his silent scholars:

"Shame upon you, my fair pupils!" said he. "This little girl, the youngest of you all—the latest comer in the class—is the only one of you capable of executing a solo, Even in the choruses, no matter what errors are made on every side of her, I always find her firm and steady as a note of the harpsichord. It is because she has zeal, patience, and — what you will never have, no, not one of you—a conscience!"

"Ah! now the murder is out," cried Costanza, as soon as the professor had left the church. "He only repeated it some thirty-nine times during the lesson, and now, I verily believe, he would fall ill if he did not get saying it the fortieth."

"A great wonder, indeed, that this Consuelo should get on!" exclaimed Zulietta; "she is so poor that she must work to learn something whereby to earn her bread."

"They tell me her mother was a gipsy," said Michelina, "and that the little one sang about the streets and highways before she came here. To be sure, she has not a bad voice; but then she has not a particle of intelligence, poor child! She learns merely by rote; she follows to the letter the professor's instructions—and her lungs do the rest."

"If she had the best lungs in the world, and the best brains into the bargain," said the handsome Clorinda, "I would not give my face in exchange for hers."

"I do not know that you would lose so much," replied Costanza, who had not a very exalted opinion of Clorinda's beauty.

"She is not handsome either," said another; "she is as yellow as a paschal candle. Her great eyes say just nothing at all, and then she is always so ill dressed! She is decidedly ugly.

"Poor girl! she is much to be pitied — no money — no beauty!"

Thus finished the praises of Consuelo. They comforted themselves by their contemptuous pity for having been forced to admire her singing.

CHAPTER II.

THE scene just related took place in Venice about a hundred years ago, in the church of the Mendicanti, where the celebrated maestro Porpora had just rehearsed the grand vespers which he was to direct on the following Assumption-day. The young choristers whom he had so smartly scolded were pupils of the state schools, in which they were instructed at the expense of government and afterwards received a dowry preparatory to marriage or the cloister, as Jean Jacques Rousseau, who admired their magnificent voices at the same period and in the same church, has observed. He mentions the circumstance in the charming episode in the eighth book of his "Confessions." I shall not here transcribe those two admirable pages, lest the friendly reader, whose example under similar circumstances I should certainly imitate, might be unable to resume my own. Hoping, then, that the aforesaid confessions are not at hand, I continue my narrative.

All these young ladies were not equally poor. Notwithstanding the strictness of the administration, it is certain that some gained admission, to whom it was a matter of speculation rather than necessity to receive an artistic education at the expense of the republic. For this reason it was that some permitted themselves to forget the sacred laws of equality, thanks to which they had been enabled to take their seats clandestinely along with their poorer sisters. All, therefore, did not fulfil the intentions of the austere republic respecting their future lot. From time to time there were numbers who, having received their gratuitous education, renounced their dowry to seek a more brilliant fortune elsewhere. The administration, seeing that this was inevitable, had sometimes admitted to the course of instruction the children of poor artists, whose wandering existence did not permit them a long stay in Venice. Among this number was the little Consuelo, born in Spain, and arriving from thence in Italy by the route of St. Petersburg, Constantinople, Mexico, Archangel, or any other still more direct after the eccentric fashion of the Bohemians.

Nevertheless, she hardly merited this appellation ; for she was neither Hindoo nor gipsy, and still less of any of the tribes of Israel. She was of good Spanish blood—

doubtless with a tinge of the Moresco ; and though some-what swarthy, she had a tranquillity of manner which was quite foreign to any of the wandering races. I do not wish to say any thing ill of the latter. If I had invented the character of Consuelo, I do not pretend that I would have traced her parentage from Israel, or even further ; but she was altogether, as everything about her organi-zation betrayed, of the family of Ishmael. To be sure I never saw her, not being a century old, but I was told so and I cannot contradict it. She had none of the feverish petulance, alternated by fits of apathetic languor, which distinguishes the *zingarella ;* neither had she the insinu-ating curiosity nor the frontless audacity of Hebrew mendicancy. She was calm as the water of the lagunes, and at the same time active as the light gondolas that skimmed along their surface.

As she was growing rapidly and as her mother was very poor, her clothes were always a year too short, which gave to her long legs of fourteen years' growth, accustomed to show themselves in public, a sort of savage grace which one was pleased and at the same time sorry to see. Whether her foot was large or not, it was impossible to say, her shoes were so bad. On the other hand, her figure, confined in narrow stays ripped at every seam, was elastic and flexible as a palm-tree, but without form, fulness, or attraction. She, poor girl ! thought nothing about it, ac-customed as she was to hear herself called a gipsy and a wanderer by the fair daughters of the Adriatic. Her face was round, sallow, and insignificant, and would have struck nobody, if her short thick hair fastened behind her ears, and at the same time her serious and indifferent demeanor, had not given her a singularity of aspect which was but little attractive. Faces which do not please at first, by degrees lose still more the power of pleasing. The beings to whom they belong, indifferent to others, become so to themselves, and assume a negligence of aspect which repels more and more. On the contrary, beauty observes, admires, and decks itself as it were in an imag-inary mirror which is always before its eyes. Ugliness forgets itself and is passed by. Nevertheless, there are two sorts of ugliness : one which suffers, and protests against the general disapprobation by habitual rage and envy — this is the true, the only ugliness. The other, ingenuous, careless, which goes quietly on its way, neither inviting nor shunning comparisons, and which wins the heart while it shocks the sense—such was the ugliness of Consuelo. Those who were sufficiently generous to interest themselves about her, at first regretted that she was not pretty ; and then, correcting themselves, and patting her head with a familiarity which beauty does not permit, added —"After all, you are a good creature ;" and Consuelo was perfectly satisfied, although she knew very well that that meant, "You are nothing more."

In the meantime, the young and handsome signor who had offered her the holy water at the font, stayed behind till he had seen all the scholars disappear. He looked at them with attention, and when Clorinda, the handsomest, passed near him, he held out his moistened fingers that he might have the pleasure of touching hers. The young girl blushed with pride, and passed on, casting as she did so one of those glances of shame mixed with boldness, which are expressive neither of self-respect nor modesty.

As soon as they had disappeared in the interior of the convent, the gallant patrician returned to the nave, and addressed the preceptor, who was descending more slowly the steps of the tribune.

"*Corpo di bacco!* dear maestro," said he, " will you tell me which of your pupils sang the ' *Salve Regina ?*'"

"And why do you wish to know, Count Zustiniani?" said the professor, accompanying him out of the church.

"To compliment you on your pupil," replied the patrician. "You know how long I have attended vespers, and even the exercises ; for you are aware what a dilettante I am in sacred music. Well, this is the first time that I have heard Pergolese sung in so perfect a manner, and as to the voice, it is the most beautiful that I have ever listened to.

"I believe it well," replied the professor, inhaling a large pinch of snuff with dignity and satisfaction.

"Tell me then the name of this celestial creature who has thrown me into such an ecstasy. In spite of your severity and your continual fault-finding, you have created the best school in all Italy. Your choruses are excellent, and your solos very good ; but your music is so severe, so grand, that young girls can hardly be expected to express its beauties."

" They do not express them," said the professor mourn-fully, " because they do not feel them. Good voices, God be thanked, we do not want; but as for a good musical organization, alas, it is hardly to be met with !"

" You possess at least one admirably endowed. Her organ is magnificent, her sentiment perfect, her skill re-markable—name her, then."

" Is it not so?" said the professor, evading the question ; " did it not delight you?"

" It took my heart by storm—it even drew tears from me—and that by means so simple, combinations so little sought after, that at first I could hardly understand it. Then I remembered what you had so often told me touch-ing your divine art, my dear master, and for the first time I understood how much you were in the right."

" And what did I say to you?" said the maestro, with an air of triumph.

" You told me," replied the count, " that simplicity is the essence of the great, the true, the beautiful in art."

" I also told you that there was often reason to observe and applaud what was clever, and brilliant, and well com-bined."

" Doubtless ; but between these secondary qualities and the true manifestations of genius, there was an abyss, you said. Very well, dear maestro : your cantatrice is alone on one side, while all the rest are on the other."

" It is not less true than well expressed," observed the professor, rubbing his hands.

" Her name?" replied the count.

" What name?" rejoined the malicious professor.

" Oh, *per Dio Santo!* that of the siren whom I have just been hearing."

" What do you want with her name, Signor Count?" replied Porpora, in a tone of severity.

" Why should you wish to make a secret of it, maestro?"

" I will tell you why, if you will let me know what object you have in finding out."

" Is it not a natural and irresistible feeling to wish to see and to know the objects of our admiration?"

" Ah! that is not your only motive. My dear Count, pardon me for thus contradicting you, You are a skillful amateur and a profound connoisseur in music, as every body knows; but you are, over and above all, proprietor of the theater of San Samuel. It is your glory and your interest alike, to encourage the loftiest talent and the finest voices of Italy. You know that our instruction is good, and that with us alone those studies are pursued which form great musicians. You have already carried off Corilla from me, as she will one day be carried off from you by an engagement in some other theater ; so you are come to spy about, to see if you can't get a hold of some other Corilla—if, indeed, we have formed one. That is the truth, Signor Count, you must admit."

"And were it even so, dear maestro," replied the count, smiling, "what would it signify to you?—where is the harm?"

"It is a great deal of harm, Signor Count. Is it nothing to corrupt, to destroy these poor creatures?"

"Ha! my most austere professor, how long have you been the guardian angel of their tender virtues?"

"I know very well, Signor Count, I have nothing to do with them, except as regards their talent, which you disfigure and disgrace in your theaters by giving them inferior music to sing. Is it not heart-rending—is it not shameful—to see Corilla, who was just beginning to understand our serious art, descend from the sacred to the profane—from prayer to badinage—from the altar to the boards—from the sublime to the absurd—from Allegri and Palestrina to Albinoni and the barber Apollini?"

"So you refuse, in your severity, to name a girl respecting whom I can have no intention, seeing that I do not know whether she has the necessary qualifications for the theater?"

"I absolutely refuse."

"And do you suppose I shall not find it out?"

"Alas! you will do so if you are bent upon it, but I shall do my utmost to prevent you from taking her from us."

"Very well, maestro, you are half conquered, for I have seen her—I have divined your mysterious divinity."

"So, so," replied the master, with a reserved and distrustful air; "are you sure of that?"

"My eyes and my heart have alike revealed her to me, and, that you may be convinced, I shall describe her to you. She is tall—taller, I think, than any of your pupils—fair as the snow on Friuli, and rosy as the dawn

CONSUELO.

of a summer morn; she has flaxen hair, azure eyes, an exquisitely rounded form, with a ruby on her finger which burned my hand as I touched it, like sparks from a magic fire."

" Bravo!" exclaimed Porpora, with a cunning air; " in that case I have nothing to conceal. The name of your beauty is Clorinda. Go and pay your court to her; gain her over with gold, with diamonds, and gay attire. You will easily conclude an engagement with her. She will help you to replace Corilla; for the public of your theater always prefer fine shoulders to sweet sounds, flashing eyes to a lofty intellect."

" Am I then mistaken, my dear maestro?" said the count, a little confused; " and is Clorinda but a commonplace beauty?"

" But suppose my siren, my divinity, my angel, as you are pleased to call her," resumed the maestro, maliciously, " was anything but a beauty?"

" If she be deformed, I beseech you not to name her, for my illusion would be too cruelly dissipated. If she were only ugly, I could still adore her; but I should not engage her for the theater, because talent without beauty is a misfortune, a struggle, a perpetual torment for a woman. What are you looking at, maestro, and why do you pause?"

" Why? because we are at the water-steps, and I see no gondola. But you, Count, what do you look at?"

" I was looking to see if that young fellow on the steps there, beside that plain little girl, was not my protegé, Anzoleto, the handsomest and most intelligent of all our little plebeians. Look at him, dear maestro. Do you not, like me, feel interested in him? That boy has the sweetest tenor in Venice, and he is passionately fond of music, for which he has an incredible aptitude. I have long wished to speak to you about it, and to ask you to give him lessons. I look upon him as the future support of my theater, and hope in a few years to be repaid for all my trouble. Hola, Zoto! come hither, my child, that I may present you to the illustrious master Porpora."

Anzoleto drew his naked legs out of the water, where they hung carelessly while he amused himself stringing those pretty shells which in Venice are poetically termed *fioro di mare.* His only garments were a pair of well-worn pantaloons and a fine shirt, through the rents of which one could see his white shoulders, modeled like those of a youthful Bacchus. He had all the grace and beauty of a young Fawn, chiseled in the palmiest days of Grecian art; and his features displayed that singular union, not unfrequent in the creations of Grecian statuary, of careless irony with dreamy melancholy. His fine fair hair, somewhat bronzed by the sun, clustered in Antinöus-like curls about his alabaster neck; his features were regular and beautifully formed; but there was something bold and forward in the expression of his jet-black eyes which displeased the maestro. The boy promptly rose when he heard the voice of Zustiniani, pitched his shells into the lap of the little girl beside him, who without raising her eyes went on with her occupation of stringing them along with golden beads, and coming forward, kissed the count's hand, after the fashion of the country.

"Upon my word, a handsome fellow!" said the professor, giving him a tap on the cheek; "but he seems occupied with amusements rather childish for his time of life: he is fully eighteen years old, is he not?"

"Nineteen shortly, *Sior Professor,*" replied Anzoleto in the Venetian dialect; "but if I amuse myself with shells it is to help little Consuelo here to make her necklaces."

"Consuelo," said the master, advancing toward his pupil with the count and Anzoleto, "I did not imagine that you cared for ornaments."

"Oh, it is not for myself, Signor," replied Consuelo, rising cautiously to prevent the shells falling from her lap; "I make them for sale in order to procure rice and Indian corn."

"She is poor and supports her mother," said Porpora. "Listen, Consuelo: should you find yourself in any difficulty, be sure to come and see me: but I absolutely forbid you to beg, remember."

"Oh, you need not forbid her, *Sior Professor,*" replied Anzoleto with animation; "she will never do so; and beside I would prevent her."

"But you have nothing," said the count.

"Nothing but your liberality, Eccellenza; but we share together, the little one and myself."

"She is a relative, then?"

"No; she is a stranger—it is Consuelo."

"Consuelo! what a singular name!" said the count.

"A beautiful name, Eccellenza," resumed Anzoleto; "it means Consolation."

"Oh, indeed? She is your friend then, it appears?"

"She is my betrothed, Signor."

"So soon? Such children! to think of marriage already!"

"We shall marry on the day that you sign my engagement at San Samuel, Eccellenza."

"In that case you will have to wait a long time, my little ones."

"Oh, we shall wait," replied Consuelo, with the cheerful gaiety of innocence."

The count and the maestro amused themselves for some time longer with the frank remarks and repartees of the young couple; then having arranged that Anzoleto should give the professor an opportunity of hearing his voice in the morning, they separated, leaving him to his serious occupations.

"What do you think of that little girl?" said the professor to Zustiniani.

"I saw her but an instant, and I find her sufficiently ugly to justify the maxim, that in the eyes of a youth of eighteen every woman is handsome."

"Very good," rejoined the professor; "now permit me to inform you that your divine songstress, your siren, your mysterious beauty, was no other than Consuelo."

"What! that sooty creature? that dark and meager grasshopper? Impossible, maestro!"

"No other, Signor Count. Would she not make a fascinating *prima donna?*"

The count stopped, looked back, and clasping his hands while he surveyed Consuelo at a distance, exclaimed in mock despair, "Just Heaven! how canst thou so err as to pour the fire of genius into heads so poorly formed?"

"So you give up your culpable intentions?" said the professor.

"Most certainly."

"You promise me?" added Porpora.

"Oh, I swear it," replied the count.

CHAPTER III.

BORN in sunny Italy, brought up by chance like a sea-bird sporting on its shores, poor, an orphan, a castaway, and nevertheless happy in the present and confiding in the future, foundling as he doubtless was — Anzoleto, the handsome youth of nineteen who spent his days with little Consuelo in perfect freedom on the footways of Venice, was not as might be supposed in his first love. Too early initiated, he would perhaps have been completely corrupted and worn out, had he dwelt in our somber climate, or had nature endowed him with a feebler organization. But early developed and destined to a long and powerful career, his heart was pure and his senses were restrained by his will. He had met the little Spaniard by chance, singing hymns before the Madonette; and for the pleasure of exercising his voice he had joined her for hours together beneath the stars. Then they met upon the sands of the Lido to gather shell-fish, which he eat, and which she converted into chaplets and other ornaments. And then again they had met in the churches, where she prayed with all her heart, and where he gazed with all his eyes at the fine ladies. In all these interviews Consuelo had appeared to him so good, so sweet, so obliging, and so gay, that she had become his inseparable friend and companion —he knew not very well how or why. Anzoleto had known the joys of love. He felt friendship for Consuelo; and as he belonged to a country and a people where passion reigns over every other feeling, he knew no other name for this attachment than that of love. Consuelo admitted this mode of speaking after she had addressed Anzoleto as follows: "If you are my lover, it is then with the intention of marrying me?" To which he replied: "Certainly, if you wish it we shall marry each other." From that moment it was a settled affair. Possibly Anzoleto was amusing himself, but to Consuelo it was matter of firm conviction. Even already his young heart experienced those contradictory and complicated emotions which agitate and discompose the existence of those who love too early.

Given up to violent impulses, greedy of pleasure, loving only what promoted his happiness, hating and avoiding every thing which opposed his gratifications, at heart an artist—that is to say, feeling and reveling in life with frightful intensity — he soon found that his transient attachments imposed on him the sufferings and dangers of a passion which he did not really feel; and he experienced the want of sweet companionship and of a chaste and tranquil outlet to his feelings. Then, without understanding the charm which drew him to Consuelo—having little experience of the beautiful—hardly knowing whether she was handsome or ugly—joining for her sake in amusements beneath his age—he led with her in public, on the marble floors and on the waters of Venice, a life as happy, as pure, as retired, and almost as poetic, as that of Paul and Virginia in the recesses of the forest. Although they enjoyed unrestrained liberty—no watchful, tender parents to form them to virtue—no devoted attendant to seek them and bring them back to the bosom of their homes—not even a dog to warn them of danger—they never experienced harm. They skimmed over the waters of the lagunes in all times and seasons in their open boat, without oars or pilot; they wandered over the marshes without guide, without watch, and heedless of the rising waters ; they sang before the vine-covered chapels at the corners of the streets without thinking of the hour, and sometimes with no other couch than the white tiles, still warm with the summer rays. They paused before the theater of Punchinello, and followed with riveted attention the fantastic drama of the beautiful Corisanda, queen of the puppet show, without thinking of their breakfast or the little probability there was of supper. They enjoyed the excesses of the carnival, he with his coat turned inside out, she with a bunch of old ribbons placed coquettishly over her ear. They dined sumptuously — sometimes on the balustrades of a bridge or on the steps of a palace—on shell-fish, fennel stalks, and pieces of citron. In short, they led a free and joyous life, without incurring more risk, or feeling more emotion, than might have been experienced by two young people of the same age and sex. Days, years passed away. Anzoleto formed other connections, while Consuelo never imagined that he could love any one but her. She became a young woman without feeling it necessary to exercise any further reserve with her betrothed; while he saw her undergo this transformation without feeling any impatience, or desiring to change this intimacy, free as it was at once from scruple, mystery, or remorse.

It was already four years since Professor Porpora and Zustiniani had mutually introduced their little musicians, and during this period the count had never once thought of the young chorister. The professor had likewise forgotten the handsome Anzoleto, inasmuch as he had found him endowed with none of the qualities desirable in a pupil —to wit, a serious, patient disposition, absolute submission to his teacher, and complete absence of all musical studies before the period of his instruction. "Do not talk to me," said he, "about a pupil whose mind is any thing else than a *tabula rasa*, or virgin wax, on which I am to make the first impression. I cannot afford to give up a year to unteach what has been learned before. If you want me to write, give me a clear surface, and that too of a good quality. If it be too hard I can make no impression on it, if too soft I shall destroy it at the first stroke." In short, although he acknowledged the extraordinary talents of the young Anzoleto, he told the count with some temper and ironical humility, at the end of his first lesson, that his method was not adapted to a pupil so far advanced, and that a master could only embarrass and retard the natural progress and invincible development of so superior an organization.

The count sent his protegé to Professor Mellifiore, who with roulades and cadences, modulations and trills, so developed his brilliant qualities, that at twenty-three he was considered capable, in the opinion of all those who heard him in the saloons of the court, of coming out at San Samuel in the first parts. One evening the dilettanti, nobility, and artists of repute then in Venice, were requested to be present at a final and decisive trial. For the first time in his life Anzoleto doffed his plebeian attire, put on a black coat, a satin vest, and with curled and powdered hair and buckles in his shoes, glided over with a composed air to the harpsichord, where amid the glare of a hundred wax-lights and under the gaze of two or three hundred persons, he boldly distended his chest, and made the utmost display of powers that were to introduce him into a career where not one judge alone, but a whole public, held the palm in one hand and downfall in the other.

We need not ask whether Anzoleto was secretly agitated.

Nevertheless, he scarcely allowed his emotion to be apparent; and hardly had his piercing eyes divined by a stealthy glance the secret approbation which women rarely refuse to grant to so handsome a youth—hardly had the amateurs, surprised at the compass of his voice and his facility of expression, uttered a few faint murmurs of applause—when joy and hope flooded his whole being. For the first time Anzoleto, hitherto ill-instructed and undervalued, felt that he was no common man; and transported by the necessity and the consciousness of success, he sang with an originality, an energy, and skill, that were altogether remarkable. His taste to be sure was not always pure, nor his execution faultless; but he was always able to extricate himself by his boldness, his intelligence, and enthusiasm. He failed in effects which the composer had intended, but he realized others which no one ever thought of—neither the author who composed, the professor who interpreted, nor the virtuoso who rehearsed them. His originality took the world by storm. For one innovation his awkwardness was pardoned, and for an original sentiment they excused ten rebellions against method. So true it is that in point of art the least spark of genius—the smallest flight in the direction of new conquests—exercises a greater fascination than all the resources and lights of science within known limits.

Nobody, perhaps, was able to explain these matters, and nobody escaped the common enthusiasm. Corilla began by a grand aria, well sung and loudly applauded : yet the success of the young débutant was so much greater than her own, that she could not help feeling an emotion of anger. But when Anzoleto, loaded with caresses and praises, returned to the harpsichord where she was seated, he said, with a mixture of humility and boldness, "And you, queen of song and queen of beauty! have you not one encouraging look for the poor unfortunate who fears and yet adores you?" The prima donna, surprised at so much assurance, looked more closely at the handsome countenance which till then she had hardly deigned to notice—for what vain and triumphant woman cares to cast a glance on the child of obscurity and poverty ? She looked, and was struck with his beauty. The fire of his glances penetrated her soul ; and, vanquished, fascinated in her turn, she directed toward him a long and earnest gaze, which served to seal his celebrity. In this memorable meeting Anzoleto had led the public, and disarmed his most redoubtable adversary; for the beautiful songstress was not only queen of the stage, but at the head of the management, and of the cabinet of Count Zustiniani.

CHAPTER IV.

In the midst of the general and somewhat exaggerated applause which the voice and manner of the débutant had drawn forth, a single auditor, seated on the extreme edge of his chair, his legs close together and his hands motionless on his knees, after the fashion of the Egyptian gods, remained dumb as a sphinx and mysterious as a hieroglyphic. It was the able professor and celebrated composer Porpora. While his gallant colleague Professor Mellifiore, ascribing to himself all the honor of Anzoleto's success, plumed himself before the women and saluted the men, as if to thank them even for their looks, the master of sacred song, with eyes bent on the ground, silent and severe, seemed lost in thought. When the company, who were engaged to a ball at the palace of the Doge, had slowly departed, and the most enthusiastic dilettanti, with some ladies, alone remained, Zustiniani approached the severe maestro.

"You are too hard upon us poor moderns, my dear professor," said he; "but your silence does not impose upon me. You would exclude this new and charming style which delights us all. But your heart is open in spite of you, and your ears have drunk in the seductive poison."

"Come, *Sior Professor*," said the charming Corilla, resuming with her old master the infantine manners of the *scuola*, "you must grant me a favor."

"Away, unhappy girl!" said the master, partly smiling and partly displeased at the caresses of his inconstant pupil: "there is no further communion between us. I know you no more. Take your sweet smiles and perfidious warblings elsewhere."

"There, now; he is coming round," said Corilla, taking with one hand the arm of the débutant, without letting go her hold of the white and ample cravat of the professor.

"Come hither, Zoto, and bow the knee before the most learned maestro in all Italy. Submit thyself, my child, and disarm his rigor; One word from him, if thou couldst obtain it, would be more to thee than all the trumpets of renown."

"You have been severe toward me, Signor Professor," said Anzoleto, bending before him with mock humility; "nevertheless, my only wish for four years has been to induce you to reverse your cruel judgment; and if I have not succeeded to-night, I fear I shall never have the courage to appear before the public, loaded with your anathema."

"Child!" said the professor, rising hastily and speaking with an earnestness which imparted something noble to his unimpressive figure, "leave false and honied words to women. Never descend to the language of flattery, even to your superiors—much less to those whose suffrage you disdain. It is but an hour ago since, poor, unknown, timid, in this little corner, all your prospects hung upon a hair—on a note from your throat—a moment's failure of your resources, or the caprice of your audience. Chance, and the effort of an instant, have made you rich, celebrated, insolent. Your career is open before you, and you have only to go on, so long as your strength sustains you. Listen, then; for the first, and perhaps for the last time, you are about to hear the truth. You are in a false direction; you sing badly, and love bad music. You know nothing, and have studied nothing thoroughly. All you have is the facility which exercise imparts. You assume a passion which you do not feel; you warble and shake like those pretty coquettish damsels whom one pardons for simpering where they know not how to sing. You know not how to combine your phrases; you pronounce badly; you have a vulgar accent, a false and common style. Do not be discouraged, however, with all these defects. You have wherewith to combat them. You have qualities which neither labor nor instruction can impart. You have that which neither bad advice nor bad example can take away. You have the sacred fire—you have genius! Alas! it is a fire which will shine upon nothing grand, a genius that will remain forever barren; for I have seen it in your eyes, as I have felt it in your breast. You have not the worship of art; you have not faith in the great masters, nor respect for their grand conceptions; you love glory, and glory for yourself alone. You might—you could—but, no! it is too late! Your destiny will be as the flash of a meteor—like that of——"

And the professor, thrusting his hat over his brows, turned his back, and without saluting any one, left the apartment, absorbed in mentally completing his enigmatic sentence.

Every one tried to laugh at the sententious professor ; but his words left a painful impression, and a melancholy feeling of doubt, which lasted for some moments. Anzoleto was the first who apparently ceased to think of them, though they had occasioned him an intense feeling of joy, pride, anger, and emulation, which was destined to influence all his after life. He appeared exclusively engaged in pleasing Corilla, and he knew so well how to flatter her, that she was very much taken with him at this first meeting. Count Zustiniani was not jealous, and perhaps had his reasons for taking no notice of them. He was interested in the fame and success of his theater more than in any thing else in the world ; not that he cared about money, but because he was a real fanatic in all that related to what are termed the *fine arts*. This, in my opinion, is a phrase which is generally employed in a very vulgar sense, and being altogether Italian, is consequently enthusiastic and without much discernment. The *culture of art*, a modern expression, which the world did not make use of a hundred years ago, has a meaning altogether different from *a taste for the fine arts*. The count was a man of taste in the common acceptation of the word—an amateur, and nothing more ; but the gratification of this taste was the great business of his life. He loved to be busy about the public, and to have the public busy about him—to frequent the society of artists—to rule the fashion—to have his theater, his luxury, his amiability, and his magnificence made the subject of conversation. He had, in short, the ruling passion of the great noblemen of his country— namely, ostentation. To possess and direct a theater was the best means of occupying and amusing the whole city. He would have been happy if he could have seated the whole republic at his table. When strangers asked Professor Porpora who was the Count Zustiniani, he was accustomed to reply—" He is one who loves to give entertainments, and who serves up music at his theater as he would pheasants on his table."

It was one in the morning before the company separated. "Anzoleto," said Corilla, when alone with him in the embrasure of the balcony, "where do you live?" At this unexpected inquiry, Anzoleto grew pale and red almost at the same moment; for how could he confess to the rich and fascinating beauty before him, that he had in a manner neither house nor home? Even this response would have been easier than to mention the miserable den where he was in the habit of taking refuge, when neither inclination nor necessity obliged him to pass the night in the open air.

"Well, what is there so extraordinary in my question?" said Corilla, laughing.

"I am asking myself," replied Anzoleto, with much presence of mind, "what royal or fairy palace were fitting home for the happy mortal who is honored by a glance from Corilla."

"What does all this flattery mean?" said she, darting on him one of the most bewitching glances contained in the storehouse of her charms.

"That I have not that honor," replied the young man; "but that, if I had, I should be content only to float between earth and sky, like the stars."

"Or like the *cuccali*," said the songstress, bursting into a fit of laughter. 'It is well known that gulls (*cuccali*) are proverbially simple, and to speak of their awkwardness in the language of Venice, is equivalent to saying, in ours, "As stupid as a goose."

"Ridicule me—despise me," replied Anzoleto; "I would rather you should do so than not think of me at all."

"Well, then," said she, "since you must reply in metaphors, I shall take you with me in my gondola; and if I take you away from your abode, instead of taking you to it, it will be your own fault."

"If that be your motive for inquiry, my answer is brief and explicit; my home is on the steps of your palace."

"Go, then, and await me on the stairs below," said Corilla, lowering her voice; "for Zustiniani may blame the indulgence with which I have listened to your nonsense."

In the first impulse of his vanity Anzoleto disappeared, and darting toward the landing-place of the palace, to the prow of Corilla's gondola, counted the moments by the beating of his fevered pulse. But before she appeared on the steps of the palace, many thoughts had passed through the anxious and ambitious brain of the débutant. "Corilla," said he to himself, "is all powerful; but if by pleasing her I were to displease the count, or if, in virtue of my too easy triumph, I were to destroy her power, and disgust him altogether with so inconstant a beauty——"

In the midst of these perplexing thoughts, Anzoleto measured with a glance the stair, which he might yet re-mount, and was planning how to effect his escape, when torches gleamed from under the portico, and the beautiful Corilla, wrapped in an ermine cloak, appeared upon the upper steps, amid a group of cavaliers anxious to support her rounded elbow in the hollow of their hand, and in this manner to assist her to descend, as is the custom in Venice.

"Well," said the gondolier of the prima donna to the undecided Anzoleto, "what are you doing there? Make haste into the gondola, if you have permission; if not, proceed on your way, for my lord count is with the signora."

Anzoleto threw himself into the bottom of the gondola, without knowing what he did. He was stupified. But scarcely did he find himself there, when he fancied the amazement and indignation which the count would feel, should he enter into the gondola with Corilla, and find there his insolent protegé. His cruel anxiety was pro-tracted for several minutes. The signora had stopped aboul half-way down the staircase; she was laughing and talking with those about her, and, in discussing a musical phrase, she repeated it in several different ways. Her clear and thrilling voice died away amid the palaces and cupolas of the canal, as the crow of the cock before the dawn is lost in the silence of the open country.

Anzoleto, unable to contain himself, resolved to escape by the opening of the gondola which was furthest from the stair. He had already thrust aside the glass in its panel of black velvet, and had passed one leg through the opening, when the second rower of the prima donna, who was stationed at the stern, leaning over the edge of the little cabin, said in a low voice, "They are singing—that is as much as to say, 'You may wait without being afraid.'"

"I did not know the usual custom," thought Anzoleto, who still tarried, not without some mixture of consternation. Corilla amused herself by bringing the count as far as the side of the gondola, and kept him standing there, while she repeated the "*felicissima notte*" until she had left the shore. She then came and placed herself beside her new admirer, with as much ease and self-possession as if his life and her own fortune had not been at stake.

"Look at Corilla," said Zustiniani to the Count Barberigo. "Well, I would wager my head that she is not alone in yonder gondola."

"And why do you think so?" replied Barberigo.

"Because she asked me a thousand times to accompany her to her palace."

"Is that your jealousy?"

"Oh, I have been long free from that weakness. I should be right glad if our prima donna would take a fancy to some one who would prevent her from leaving Venice, as she sometimes threatens. I could console myself for her desertion of me, but I could neither replace her voice nor her talents, nor the ardor with which she inspires the public at San Samuel."

"I understand; but who, then, is the happy favorite of this mad princess!"

The count and his friend enumerated all whom Corilla appeared to encourage during the evening. Anzoleto was absolutely the only one whom they failed to think of.

CHAPTER V.

A VIOLENT struggle arose in the breast of the happy lover, who, agitated and palpitating, was borne on the waters through the tranquil night, with the most celebrated beauty of Venice. Anzoleto was transported by his ardor, which gratified vanity rendered still more powerful. On the other hand, the fear of displeasing, of being scornfully dismissed and impeached, restrained his impetuosity. Prudent and cunning, like a true Venetian as he was, he had not aspired to the theater for more than six years, without being well informed as to the fantastic and imperious women who governed all its intrigues. He was well assured that his reign would be of short duration, and if he did not withdraw from this dangerous honor, it was because he was taken in a measure by surprise. He had merely wished to gain tolerance by his courtesy; and, behold! his youth, his beauty, and budding glory, had inspired love! "Now," said Anzoleto, with the rapid perception which heads of his wonderful organization enjoy, "there is nothing but to make myself feared, if to-morrow I would not be ridiculous. But shall a poor devil like myself accomplish this with a haughty beauty like Corilla?" He was soon decided. He began a system of distrust, jealousy, and bitterness, of which the passionate coquetry astonished the prima donna. Their conversation may be resumed as follows:

Anzoleto.—"I know that you do not love me—that you will never love me; therefore am I sad and constrained beside you."

Corilla.—"And suppose I were to love you?"

Anzoleto.—"I should be wretched, because that were to fall from heaven into the abyss, and lose you perchance an hour after I had gained you, at the price of all my future happiness?"

Corilla.—"And what makes you think me so inconstant?"

Anzoleto.—"First, the want of desert on my part; second, the ill that is said of you."

Corilla.—"And who dares to asperse me?"

Anzoleto.—"Every body, because every body adores you."

Corilla.—"Then, if I were mad enough to like you, and to tell you so, would you repel me?"

Anzoleto.—"I know not if I should have the power to fly; but if I had, I know that I should never behold you again."

"Very well," said Corilla, "I have a fancy to try the experiment—Anzoleto, I love you."

"I do not believe it," replied he. "If I stay, it is because I think you are only mocking me. That is a game at which you shall not frighten me, and still less shall you pique me."

"You wish to try an encounter of wit, I think."

"No, indeed; I am not in the least to be dreaded, since I give you the means of overcoming me; it is to freeze me with terror, and to drive me from your presence, in telling me seriously what you have just now uttered in jest."

"You are a knowing fellow, and I see that one must be careful what one says to you. You are one of those who not only wish to breathe the fragrance of the rose, but would pluck and preserve it. I could not have supposed you so bold and so decided at your age."

"And do you despise me therefore?"

"On the contrary, I am the more pleased with you. Good-night, Anzoleto; we shall see each other again."

She held out her white hand, which he kissed passionately. "I have got off famously," said he, as he escaped by the passages leading from the canaletto.

Despairing of gaining access to his nest at so late an hour he thought he would lie down at the first porch, to gain the heavenly repose which infancy and poverty alone know; but for the first time in his life, he could not find a slab sufficiently smooth for his purpose. The pavement of Venice is the cleanest and whitest in the world; still the light dust scattered over it hardly suited a dark dress of elegant material and latest fashion. And then the propriety of the thing! The boatmen who would have carefully stepped over the young plebeian, in the morning would have insulted him, and perhaps soiled his parasitic livery during his repose. What would they have thought of one reposing in the open air in silk stockings, fine linen, and lace ruffles? Anzoleto regretted his good woollen cap, worn and old, no doubt, but thick, and well calculated to resist the unhealthy morning fogs of Venice. It was now toward the latter end of February; and although the days at this period were warm and brilliant, the nights at Venice were still very cold. Then he thought he would gain admission into one of the gondolas fastened to the bank, but they were all secured under lock and key. At last he found one of which the door yielded; but in getting in he stumbled over the legs of the baracole, who had retired for the night. "*Per diavolo!*" said a rough voice from the bottom of the cabin, "who are you, and what do you want?"

"Is it you, Zanetto?" replied Anzoleto, recognizing the man, who was generally very civil to him; "let me stretch myself beside you, and dream awhile within your cabin."

"And who are you?" said Zanetto.

"Anzoleto; do you not know me?"

"*Per diavolo*, no! You have garments which Anzoleto never wore, unless he stole them. Be off! Were you the

Doge in person I would not open my bark to a man who strutted about in fine clothes when he had not a corner to rest in."

"So, so," thought Anzoleto; "the protection and favor of the Count Zustiniani have exposed me to greater danger and annoyances than they have procured me advantages. It is time that my fortune should correspond with my success, and I long to have a few sequins to enable me to support the station I have assumed."

Sufficiently out of sorts, he sauntered through the deserted streets, not daring to pause a moment, lest the perspiration should be checked which anger and fatigue had caused to flow freely forth. "It is well if I do not grow hoarse," said he to himself; "to-morrow the count will show me off to some foolish Aristarchus, who, if I have the least little feather in the throat in consequence of this night's want of rest, will say that I have no voice; and the Signor Count, who knows better, will repeat, 'If you had but heard him last night!' 'He is not equal, then,' the other will observe; 'or perhaps he is not in good health;' 'Or perhaps,' as a third will aver, 'he was tired last night. The truth is, he is very young to sing several days in succession. Had you not better wait till he is riper and more robust?' And the count will say, 'Diavolo! if he grow hoarse after a couple of songs, he will not answer me.' Then, to make sure that I am strong and well, they will make me exercise every day till I am out of breath, and break my voice to prove that I have lungs. To the devil with their protection, I say! Ah! if I were only free of these great folk, and in favor with the public, and courted by the theaters, I could sing in their saloons, and treat with them as equal powers.

Thus plotting, Anzoleto reached one of those little spots termed *corti* in Venice. Courts indeed they were not, but an assemblage of houses opening on a common space, corresponding with what, in Paris, is called *cité*. But there is nothing in the disposition of these pretended courts like the elegant and systematic arrangements of our modern squares. They are obscure spots, sometimes impassible, at other times allowing passage; but little frequented, and dwelt in by persons of slender fortune—laborers, workmen, or washerwomen, who stretch their linen across the road, somewhat to the annoyance of the passengers, who put up with it in return for permission to go across. Woe to the poor artist who is obliged to open the windows of his apartment in these secluded recesses, where rustic life, with its noisy unclean habits, reappears in the heart of Venice, not two steps from large canals and sumptuous edifices! Woe to him if silence be necessary to his occupation! for, from morn till night, there is an interminable uproar, with children, fowls, and dogs, screaming and playing within the narrow space, the chatter of women in the porches, and the songs of workmen, which do not leave him a moment of repose. Happy, too, if *Improvisatori* do not bawl their sonnets till they have gathered a coin from every window; or Brighella do not fix her station in the court, ready to begin her dialogue afresh with the *avocato, " Il tedesco e il diavolo,"* until she has exhausted in vain her eloquence before the dirty children—happy spectators, who do not scruple to listen and to look on, although they have not a farthing in their possession.

But at night, when all is silent, and when the quiet moon lights up the scene, this assemblage of houses of every period, united to each other without symmetry or pretension, divided by deep shadows full of mystery in their recesses, and of a wild spontaneous beauty, presents an infinitely picturesque assemblage. Every thing is beautiful under the light of the moon. The least architectural effect assumes force and character, and the meanest balcony, with its clustering vine, reminds you of Spain and of romantic adventures with the cloak and sword. The clear atmosphere in which the distant cupolas rising above the dark mass are bathed, sheds on the minutest details of the picture a vague yet harmonious coloring, which invites one to reveries without end.

It was in the Corte Minelli, near the church of San Fantin, that Anzoleto found himself when the clocks of the different churches tolled the hour of two. A secret instinct had led his devious steps to the dwelling of one of whom he had not thought since the setting of the sun. Hardly had he entered the court, when he heard a sweet voice call him by the last syllables of his name ; and raising his head he saw for an instant a faint profile shadow itself on one of the most miserable abodes of the place. A moment afterward a door opened, and Consuelo, in a muslin petticoat and wrapped in an old black silk mantle, which had served as adornment for her mother, extended one hand to him, while at the same time she placed her finger on her lip to enforce silence. They crept up the ruined stair, and, seated at length on the terrace, they began one of those long whispering conversations, interrupted by kisses, which one hears by nights along the level roofs, like the converse of wandering spirits wafted through the mist, amid the strange chimneys hooded with red turbans of all the houses of Venice.

"How, my poor friend!" said Anzoleto; "have you waited for me until now?"

"Did you not say you would give me an account of the evening, and tell me if you sang well—if you afforded pleasure—if they applauded you—if they signed your engagement?"

"And you, my best Consuelo," said Anzoleto, struck with remorse on seeing the confidence and sweetness of this poor girl, "tell me if my long absence has made you impatient—if you are not tired—if you do not feel chill on this cold terrace—if you have already supped—if you are not angry with me for coming so late—if you are uneasy—if you found fault with me."

"No such thing," she replied, throwing her arms about his neck. "If I have been impatient, it was not with you; if I felt wearied—if I was cold—I am no longer so, since you are here. Whether I have supped or not I do not know; whether I have found fault with you?—why should I find fault with you?—if I have been disquieted?—why should I have been so?—if I have been angry with you?—never!"

"You are an angel!" said Anzoleto, returning her caress. "Ah, my only consolation! how cold and perfidious are all other hearts!"

"Alas! what has happened?—what have they done to the sun of my soul?" exclaimed Consuelo, mixing with the sweet Venetian dialect the passionate expressions of her native tongue.

Anzoleto told her all that had happened—even his moonlight sail with Corilla, and more especially the encouragement which she had held out to him; only he smoothed matters over somewhat, saying nothing that could vex Consuelo, since in point of fact he had been faithful—and he told *almost* all. But there is always some minute particle of truth on which judical inquiry has never thrown light—which no client has revealed to his advocate—which no sentence has ever aimed at except by chance—because in these few secret facts or intentions is the entire cause, the motive, the aim—the object in a word—of these great suits, always so badly pleaded and always so badly judged, whatever may be the ardor of the speakers or the coolness of the magistrate.

To return to Anzoleto. It is not necessary to say what peccadilloes he omitted, what emotions in public he translated in his own fashion, what secret palpitations in the gondola he forgot to mention. I do not think he even spoke of the gondola at all, and as to his flatteries to the cantatrice, why they were adroit mystifications by means of which he escaped her perilous advances without making her angry. Wherefore being unwilling, and I may add unable, to mention all the temptations which he had surmounted by his prudence and caution, why, dear lady reader, should the young rogue awaken jealousy in the bosom of Consuelo? Happily for the little Spaniard she knew nothing of jealousy. This dark and bitter feeling only afflicts souls that have greatly suffered, and hitherto Consuelo had been happy in her affection as she was good. The only thing that made a profound impression upon her was the severe yet flattering denunciation of Professor Porpora on the adored head of Anzoleto. She made him repeat all the expressions which the maestro had used, and when he had done so, pondered on them long and earnestly.

"My little Consuelo," said Anzoleto without remarking her abstraction, "it is horribly cold here. Are you not afraid of getting cold? Think, my dear, that our prospects depend much more upon your voice than upon mine."

"I never get cold," said she; "but you are so lightly dressed with your fine clothes. Here now, put on this mantle."

"What would you have me do with this fine bit of torn taffeta? I would rather take shelter for half an hour in your apartment.'

"'Tis well," said Consuelo, "but then we must not speak, the neighbors would hear us and we should be to blame. They are not ill-disposed; they see us together without tormenting me about it, because they know **very**

well you do not come here at night. You would do better
to sleep at home."

"Impossible! They will only open at daylight and
there are still three hours to watch. See, my teeth chatter with the cold!"

"Well," said Consuelo getting up, "I shall let you into
my room and return to the terrace, so that if any body
should observe it, it will be seen there is nothing wrong."

She brought him into a dilapidated apartment, where
under flowers and frescoes on the wall appeared a second
picture, almost in a worse condition than the first. A large
square bed with a mattress of seaweed, and a spotted muslin coverlet, perfectly clean but patched with fragments of
every-imaginable color; a straw chair, a little table, an
antique guitar, a filagree cross — the only wealth her
mother had left — a spinet, a great heap of worm-eaten
music, which Professor Porpora was kind enough to lend
—such was the furniture of the young artist, daughter of
a poor Bohemian, the pupil of a celebrated master, and
the beloved of a handsome adventurer. As there was but
one chair, and as the table was covered with music, there
was no seat for Anzoleto but the bed, on which he placed
himself without hesitation. Hardly was he seated, when,
overwhelmed with fatigue, his head fell upon the woollen
cushion which served as a pillow; but almost immediately,
starting up again by a violent effort, he exclaimed:

"And you, my poor girl, are you going to take no rest?
Ah! I am a wretch—I shall go and lie in the streets."

"No," said Consuelo, gently thrusting him back—"you
are ill and I am not. My mother died a good Catholic;
she is now in heaven, and sees us at this very hour. She
knows you have kept the promise you made to her, never
to abandon me. She knows that our affection has been
pure since her death as before. She sees at this moment
that I neither do nor think what is wrong—that her soul
may repose in the Lord!" And here Consuelo made the
sign of the cross. Anzoleto already slumbered. "I am
going to tell my beads," continued Consuelo, moving
away, "that you may not take the fever."

"Angel that you are!" faintly murmured Anzoleto, and
he did not even perceive that he was alone. She had gone
in fact to the terrace. In a short time she returned to assure herself that he was not ill, and, finding that he slept

tranquilly, she gazed long and earnestly at his beautiful face, as it lay lighted by the moon.

Then, determined to resist drowsiness herself, and finding that the emotions of the evening had caused her to neglect her work, she lighted the lamp, and, seated before the little table, she noted a composition which Master Porpora had required of her for the following day.

CHAPTER VI.

THE Count Zustiniani, notwithstanding his philosophical composure, was not so indifferent to the insolent caprices of Corilla as he pretended. Good-natured, weak, frivolous, Zustiniani was only a rake in appearance and by his social position. He could not help feeling at the bottom of his heart the ungrateful return which this insolent and foolish girl had made to his generosity; and though at that period it was considered the worst possible taste, as well at Venice as at Paris, to seem jealous, his Italian pride revolted at the absurd and miserable position in which Corilla had placed him. So, the same afternoon that had seen Anzoleto shine at the Palazzo Zustiniani, the count, after having laughed with Barberigo over the tricks of Corilla, his saloons being emptied and the wax-lights extinguished, took down his cloak and sword, and, in order to ease his mind, set off for the palazzo inhabited by the poor singer.

He found that she was alone, but still ill at ease, he began to converse in a low voice with the barcarole who was mooring the gondola of the prima donna under the arch reserved for that purpose, and, by virtue of a few sequins, he easily convinced himself that he was not mistaken, and that Corilla had not been alone in the gondola; but who it was that had accompanied her he could not ascertain—the gondolier knew not. He had met Anzoleto a hundred times in the passages of the theater, or near the Palazzo Zustiniani, but failed to recognize him when powdered and in his dark attire.

This inscrutable mystery completed the count's annoyance. He consoled himself with ridiculing his rival, the only vengeance which good breeding permitted, and not less cruel in a gay and frivolous age than murder at more serious periods. He could not sleep ; and at the hour when Porpora began his instructions, he set out for the *Scuola di Mendicanti*, and the hall where the young pupils were wont to assemble.

The position of the count with regard to the learned professor was for some years past much changed. Zustiniani was no longer the musical antagonist of Porpora, but in some sort his associate and leader. He had advanced considerable sums to the establishment over which the learned maestro presided, and out of gratitude the directors had invested him with the supreme control. The two associates then were as good friends as could be expected from the intolerance of the maestro with regard to the music in vogue—an intolerance, however, which was considerably softened by the assistance and resources lavished by the count in behalf of the propagation of serious music. Besides, the latter had brought out at San Samuel an opera which the maestro had written.

" My dear master," said Zustiniani, drawing Porpora aside, " you must not only give me one of your pupils for the theater, but say which of them is best calculated to replace Corilla. That artist is wearied, her voice has decayed, her caprices ruin us, and the public will be disgusted. Truly we must obtain a *succeditrice*." Pardon, dear reader, for this was said in Italian, and the count made no mistake.

" I have not got what you require," replied Porpora, drily.

" What! my dear maestro," exclaimed the count, "you are not going to fall back into your dark moods? Is it after all the sacrifices and all the devotion which I have manifested toward you, that you are going to deny me a slight favor when I ask your assistance and advice in my own behalf?"

" I would not be justified in granting it," replied the professor, " and what I have just said is the truth, told you by a friend, and with the desire to oblige you. I have not in my school a single person capable of replacing Corilla. I do not estimate her higher than she deserves; yet in declaring that the talent of this girl has no real worth in my eyes, I am forced to acknowledge that she possesses an experience, a skill, a facility, and a sympathy with the public, which can only be acquired by years of practice, and which could not be attained by other début-antes for a long time."

"That is true," said the count; "but we made Corilla, we saw her begin, we procured the approbation of the public; her beauty gained her three-fourths of her success, and you have individuals equally agreeable in your school. You cannot deny that, master. Come, admit that Clorinda is the most beautiful creature in the universe."

"Yes, but saucy, mincing, insupportable. The public perhaps may find her grimaces charming—but she sings false, she has neither soul nor intelligence. It is true that the public has only ears; but then she has neither memory nor address, and she could only save herself from condemnation by the happy charlatanism that succeeds with so many others."

Thus saying, the professor cast an involuntary glance upon Anzoleto, who, under favor of the count, and on pretense of listening to the class, had kept a little apart, attending to the conversation.

"It matters not," said Zustiniani, who heeded little the master's rancor; "I shall not give up my project. It is long since I have heard Clorinda. Let her come with five or six others, the prettiest that can be found. Come, Anzoleto," said he, smiling, "you are well enough attired to assume the grave air of a young professor. Go to the garden and speak to the most striking of these young beauties, and tell them that the professor and I expect them here."

Anzoleto obeyed, but whether through malice or address, he brought the ugliest, so that Jean Jacques might have said for once with truth, "Sofia was one-eyed, and Cattina was a cripple."

This *quid pro quo* was taken in good part; and after they had laughed in their sleeves, they dismissed them, in order to send those of their companions whom the professor named. A charming group soon made their appearance, with Clorinda at their head.

"What magnificent hair!" exclaimed the count, as the latter passed him with her superb tresses.

"There is much more *on* than *in* that head," said the professor, without deigning to lower his voice.

After an hour's trial the count could stand it no longer, but with courteous expressions to the young ladies, retired

full of consternation, after saying in the professor's ear,
" We must not think of these cockatoos!"

" Would your Excellency permit me to say a word respecting the subject which occupies you," said Anzoleto in a low voice to the count as they descended the steps.

" Speak," said the count; " do you know this marvel whom we seek?"

" Yes, Eccellenza."

" In what sea will you fish up this precious pearl?"

" At the bottom of the class, where the jealous Porpora placed her on the day when you passed your female battalion in review."

" What! is there a diamond in the school whose splendor has never reached my eyes? If Master Porpora has played me such a trick——"

" Illustrious, the diamond of which I speak is not strictly part of the school; she is only a poor girl who sings in the choruses when they require her services, and to whom the professor gives lessons partly through charity, but still more from love of his art."

" In that case her abilities must be extraordinary, for the professor is not easily satisfied, and is no way prodigal of his time and labor. Could I have heard her perchance without knowing it?"

" Your Excellency heard her long ago when she was but a child. Now she is a young woman—able, studious, wise as the professor himself, and capable of extinguishing Corilla on the first occasion that she sings a single air beside her in the theater."

" Does she never sing in public? Did she not sing sometimes at vespers?"

" Formerly, your Excellency, the professor took pleasure in hearing her sing in the church; but since then the *scolari*, through jealousy and revenge, have threatened to chase her from the tribune if she reappears there by their side."

" She is a girl of bad conduct then?"

" Oh Heavens! she is a virgin, pure as the newly fallen snow! But she is poor and of mean extraction—like myself, Eccellenza, whom you yet deign to elevate by your goodness—and these wicked harpies have threatened to complain to you of bringing into their class a pupil who did not belong to it."

"Where can I hear this wonder?"

"Let your Highness order the professor to make her sing before you, and you can then judge of her voice and the amount of her talent."

"Your confidence inclines me to believe you. You say I heard her long since? I cannot remember when?"

"In the church of the Mendicanti, on a general rehearsal of the ' *Salve Regina* ' of Pergolese."

"Oh, I remember now," exclaimed the count; "voice, accent, and intelligence equally admirable!"

"She was then but fourteen, my Lord—no better than a child."

"Yes—but now I think of it, I remember she was not handsome."

"Not handsome, Eccellenza!" exclaimed Anzoleto, quite astounded.

"She was called — let me see — was it not a Spanish name—something out of the way?"

"It was Consuelo, my Lord."

"Yes, that is the name ; you were to marry her then, a step which made the professor and myself laugh a little. Consuelo—yes, it is the same; the favorite of the professor, an intelligent girl, but very ugly."

"Very ugly ?" repeated Anzoleto, as if stupified.

"Yes, my child. Do you still admire her ?"

"She is my friend, Illustrissimo."

"Friend! that is to say sister or sweetheart—which of the two ?"

"Sister, my master."

"In that case I can give you an answer without paining you; your idea is devoid of common sense. To replace Corilla it would require an angel of beauty, and your Consuelo, if I remember rightly, was not only ugly, but frightful !"

The count was accosted at this moment by one of his friends, and left Anzoleto, who was struck dumb with amazement, and who repeated with a sigh, "She is frightful !"

CHAPTER VII.

It may appear rather astonishing, dear reader, and yet it is very certain, that Anzoleto never had formed an opinion of the beauty or the ugliness of Consuelo. Consuelo was a being so solitary, so unknown in Venice, that no one had thought of seeking whether, beneath this veil of isolation and obscurity, intelligence and goodness had ended by showing themselves under an agreeable or insignificant form. Porpora, who had no senses but for his art, had only seen in her the artist. Her neighbors of the Corte Minelli observed, without attaching any blame to it, her innocent love for Anzoleto. At Venice they are not particular on this score. They predicted indeed very often, that she would be unhappy with this youth without business or calling, and they counseled her rather to seek to establish herself with some honest workman. But she replied to them that, as she herself was without friends or support, Anzoleto suited her perfectly, and as for six years no day had passed without their seeing them together, never seeking any concealment and never quarreling, they had ended by accustoming themselves to their free and apparently indissoluble union, and no neighbor had ever paid court to the *amica* of Anzoleto. Whether was this owing to her supposed engagement or to her extreme poverty?—or was it, perhaps, that her person had no attractions for them ? This last supposition is the most probable.

Every one knows, however, that from fourteen to fifteen, girls are generally thin, out of sorts, without harmony either as to proportions or movements. Toward fifteen, to use a common expression, they undergo a sort of fusion, after which they become, if not pretty, at least agreeable. It has even been remarked that it is not desirable that a young girl should grow good-looking too early.

Consuelo, like others, had gained all the benefits of adolescence; she was no longer called ugly, simply because she had ceased to be so. And as she was neither Dauphine nor Infanta, however, there were no crowds of courtiers to proclaim that her royal highness grew day by day more beautiful; and no one was sufficiently solicitous to tell Anzoleto that he should have no occasion to blush for his bride.

Since Anzoleto had heard her termed ugly at an age when the word had neither sense nor meaning, he had forgotten to think about it; his vanity had taken another direction. The theater and renown were all his care, and he had no time to think of conquests. His curiosity was appeased—he had no more to learn. At twenty-two he was in a measure *blasé;* yet his affection for Consuelo was tranquil as at eighteen, despite a few chaste kisses, taken as they were given, without shame.

Let us not be astonished at this calmness and propriety on the part of a youth in other respects not over-particular. Our young people had ceased to live as described at the beginning of this history. Consuelo, now nearly sixteen, continued her somewhat wandering life, leaving the conservatory to eat her rice and repeat her lesson on the steps of the Piazetta with Anzoleto. When her mother, worn out by fatigue, ceased to sing for charity in the coffee-houses in the evening, the poor creature sought refuge in one of the most miserable garrets of the Corte Minelli, to die upon a pallet. Then the good Consuelo, quitting her no more, entirely changed her manner of life. Exclusive of the hours when the professor deigned to give his lessons, she labored sometimes at her needle, sometimes at counterpoint, but always at the bedside of her imperious and despairing mother, who had cruelly ill-treated her in her infancy, and who now presented the frightful spectacle of a last struggle without courage and without virtue. The filial piety and devotion of Consuelo never flagged for a single instant. The pleasures of youth and of her free and wandering life —even love itself—all were sacrificed without a moment's hesitation or regret. Anzoleto made bitter complaints, but finding reproaches useless, resolved to forget her and to amuse himself; but this he found impossible. He had none of the industry of Consuelo; he learned quickly but imperfectly the inferior lessons which his teacher, to gain the salary promised by Zustiniani, gave him equally quickly and equally ill. This was all very well for Anzoleto, in whom prodigal nature made up for lost time and the effects of inferior instruction, but there were hours of leisure during which the friendly and cheerful society of Consuelo were found sadly wanting. He tried to addict himself to the habits of his class ; he frequented public-houses, and wasted with young scape-graces the trifling bounties he enjoyed through the favor of Count Zustiniani. This sort of life pleased him for some weeks; but he soon found that his health and his voice were becoming sensibly impaired— that the *far-niente* was not excess, and that excess was not his element. Preserved from bad passions through a higher species of self-love, he retired to solitude and study ; but they only presented a frightful mixture of gloom and difficulty. He saw that Consuelo was no less necessary to his talents than to his happiness. She was studious and persevering—living in an atmosphere of music as a bird in the air or a fish in the wave—loving to overcome difficulties without inquiring into their nature any more than a child —but impelled to combat the obstacles and penetrate the mysteries of art, by an instinct invisible as that which causes the germ to penetrate the soil and seek the air. Consuelo enjoyed one of those rare and happy temperaments for which labor is an enjoyment, a sort of repose, a necessary condition, and to which inaction would be an effort, a waste, in short a disease—if inaction indeed to such natures were possible. But they know nothing of the kind; in apparent idleness they still labor, but it is not so much reverie as meditation. In seeing them act, one would suppose that they were creating, whereas they but give expression to what has been already created. You will tell me, gentle reader, that you have never known such rare temperaments; to which I shall reply, dearly beloved reader, that I have met with but one. If so, am I older than you? Why can I not tell you that I have analyzed in my own poor brain the divine mystery of this intellectual activity? But alas! friendly reader, it is neither you nor I who shall study this in ourselves.

Consuelo worked on, amusing herself the while. She persisted for hours together, either by free and capricious flights of song or by study on the book, to vanquish difficulties which would have repelled Anzoleto if left to himself; and without any idea of emulation or premeditated design, she forced him to follow her, to second her, to comprehend and to reply to her—sometimes, as it were, in the midst of almost childish bursts of laughter — sometimes borne away by the poetic and creative *fantasia*, which pervades the popular temperament of Italy and Spain! During the many years in which he was influenced by the genius of Consuelo—drinking at a source which he did not comprehend—copying her without knowing it, Anzoleto, held besides in chains by his indolence, had become a strange compound of knowledge and ignorance, of inspiration and frivolity, of power and weakness, of boldness and awkwardness, such as had plunged Porpora at the last rehearsal into a perfect labyrinth of meditation and conjecture. The maestro did not know the secret of the riches which he had borrowed from Consuelo; for having once severely scolded the little one for her intimacy with this great idler, he had never again seen them together. Consuelo, bent upon maintaining the good-will of her master, took care whenever she saw him at a distance, if in company with Anzoleto, to hide herself with agile bounds behind a column, or to disappear in the recesses of some gondola.

These precautions were still continued, when, Consuelo having become a nurse, Anzoleto, unable to support her absence, and feeling life, hope, inspiration, and even existence failing him, returned to share her sedentary life, and to bear with her the sourness and angry whims of the dying woman. Some months before the close of her life, the unhappy creature, broken down by her sufferings, and vanquished by the filial piety of her daughter, felt her soul opened to milder emotions. She habituated herself to the attentions of Anzoleto, who, although little accustomed to acts of friendship and self-denial, displayed a zealous kindness and good-will toward the feeble sufferer. Anzoleto had an even temper and gentle demeanor. His perseverance toward her and Consuelo at length won her heart, and in her last moments she made them promise never to abandon each other. Anzoleto promised, and even felt in this solemn act a depth of feeling to which he had been hitherto a stranger. The dying woman made the engagement easier to him by saying: "Let her be your friend, your sister, or your wife, only leave her not; she knows none, has listened to none, but you."

Consuelo, now an orphan, continued to ply her needle and study music, as well to procure means for the present as to prepare for her union with Anzoleto. During two years he continued to visit her in her garret, without experiencing any passion for her, or being able to feel it for others, so much did the charm of being with her seem preferable to all other things.

Without fully appreciating the lofty faculties of his companion, he could see that her attainments and capabilities were superior to those of any of the singers at San Samuel, or even to those of Corilla herself. To his habitual affection were now added the hope, and almost the conviction, that a community of interests would render their future existence at once brilliant and profitable. Consuelo thought little of the future ; foresight was not among her good qualities. She would have cultivated music without any other end in view than that of fulfilling her vocation; and the community of interest which the practice of that art was to realize between her and her friend, had no other meaning to her than that of an association of happiness and affection. It was therefore without apprising her of it, that he conceived the hope of realizing their dreams ; and learning that Zustiniani had decided on replacing Corilla, Anzoleto, sagaciously divining the wishes of his patron, had made the proposal which has already been mentioned.

But Consuelo's ugliness — this strange, unexpected, and invincible drawback, if the count indeed were not deceived —had struck terror and consternation to his soul. So he retraced his steps to the Corte Minelli, stopping every instant to recall to his mind in a new point of view, the likeness of his friend, and to repeat again and again "Not pretty?—ugly?—frightful?"

CHAPTER VIII.

"WHY do you stare at me so?" said Consuelo, seeing him enter her apartment, and fix a steady gaze upon her, without uttering a word, "One would think you had never seen me before."

"It is true, Consuelo," he replied ; "I have never seen you."

"Are you crazy?" continued she ; "I know not what you mean."

"Ah, Heavens! I fear I am," exclaimed Anzoleto. "I have a dark, hideous spot in my brain, which prevents me from seeing you."

"Holy Virgin! you are ill, my friend!"

"No, dear girl ; calm yourself, and let us endeavor to

see clearly. Tell me, Consuelo, do you think me handsome?"

"Surely I do, since I love you."

"But if you did not love me, what would you think of me then?"

"How can I know?"

"But when you look at other men, do you know whether they are handsome or ugly?"

"Yes; but I find you handsomer than the handsomest."

"Is it because I am so or because you love me?"

"Both one and the other, I think. Every body calls you handsome, and you know that you are so. But why do you ask?"

"I wish to know if you would love me were I frightful?"

"I should not be aware of it perhaps."

"Do you believe, then, that it is possible to love one who is ugly?"

"Why not, since you love me?"

"Are you ugly, then, Consuelo? Tell me truly — are you indeed ugly?"

"They have always told me so—do you not see it?"

"No; in truth, I see no such thing."

"In that case, I am handsome enough, and am well satisfied."

"Hold there, Consuelo. When you look at me so sweetly, so lovingly, so naturally, I think you prettier far than Corilla; but I want to know if it be an illusion of my imagination or reality. I know the expression of your countenance; I know that it is good, and that it pleases me. When I am angry, it calms me; when sorrowful, it cheers me; when I am cast down, it revives me. But your features, Consuelo, I cannot tell if they are ugly or not."

"But I ask you once more, what does it concern you?"

"I must know; tell me, therefore, if it be possible for a handsome man to love an ugly woman."

"You loved my poor mother, who was no better than a specter, and I loved her so dearly!"

"And did you think her ugly?"

"No; did you?"

"I thought nothing about it. But to love with passion, Consuelo—for, in truth, I love you passionately, do I not? I cannot live without you—cannot quit you. Is not that love, Consuelo?"

" Could it be anything else?"

" Could it be friendship?"

" Yes, it might, indeed, be friendship ——"

Here the much surprised Consuelo paused and looked attentively at Anzoleto, while he, falling into a melancholy reverie, asked himself for the first time whether it was love or friendship which he felt for Consuelo ; or whether the moderation and propriety of his demeanor were the result of respect or indifference. For the first time he looked at the young girl with the eyes of a youth ; analyzed, not without difficulty, her face, her form, her eyes—all the details in fine of which he had had hitherto but a confused ideal in his mind. For the first time Consuelo was embarrassed by the demeanor of her friend. She blushed, her heart beat with violence, and she turned aside her head, unable to support Anzoleto's gaze. At last, as he preserved a silence which she did not care to break, a feeling of anguish took possession of her heart, tears rolled down her cheeks, and she hid her face in her hands.

" Oh, I see it plainly," said she; " you have come to tell me that you will no longer have me for your friend."

" No, no ; I did not say that—I did not say that!" exclaimed Anzoleto, terrified by the tears which he caused her to shed for the first time ; and, restored to all his brotherly feeling, he folded Consuelo in his arms. But as she turned her head aside, he kissed, in place of her calm, cool check, a glowing shoulder, ill-concealed by a handkerchief of black lace.

" I know not well what ails me," exclaimed Consuelo, tearing herself from his arms ; " I think I am ill ; I feel as if I were going to die."

" You must not die," said Anzoleto, following and supporting her in his arms; " you are fair, Consuelo — yes, you are fair!"

In truth, she was then very fair. Anzoleto never inquired how, but he could not help repeating it, for his heart felt it warmly.

" But," said Consuelo, pale and agitated, " why do you insist so on finding me pretty to-day?"

" Would you not wish to be so, dear Consuelo?"

" Yes, for you!"

" And for others too?"

"It concerns me not."

"But if it influenced our future prospects?" Here Anzoleto, seeing the uneasiness which he caused his betrothed, told her candidly all that had occurred between the count and himself. And when he came to repeat the expressions, any thing but flattering, which Zustiniani had employed when speaking of her, the good Consuelo, now perfectly tranquil, could not restrain a violent burst of laughter, drying at the same time her tear-stained eyes.

"Well?" said Anzoleto, surprised at this total absence of vanity, "do you take it so coolly? Ah! Consuelo, I can see that you are a little coquette. You know very well that you are not ugly."

"Listen," said she, smiling; "since you are so serious about trifles, I find I must satisfy you a little. I never was a coquette, and not being handsome, do not wish to seem ridiculous. But as to being ugly, I am no longer so."

"Indeed! Who has told you?"

"First it was my mother, who was never uneasy about my ugliness. I heard her often say that she was far less passable than I in her infancy, and yet when she was twenty she was the handsomest girl in Burgos. You know that when the people looked at her in the cafés where she sang, they said, 'This woman must have been once beautiful.' See, my good friend, beauty is fleeting; when its possessor is sunk in poverty it lasts for a moment and then is no more. I might become handsome—who knows?—if I was not to be too much exhausted, if I got sound rest, and did not suffer too much from hunger."

"Consuelo, we will never part. I shall soon be rich. You will then want for nothing, and can be pretty at your ease."

"Heaven grant it; but God's will be done!"

"But all this is nothing to the purpose; we must see if the count will find you handsome enough for the theater."

"That hard-hearted count! Let us trust that he will not be too exacting."

"First and foremost then, you are not ugly?"

"No; I am not ugly. I heard the glass-blower over the way there say not long ago to his wife, 'Do you know that little Consuelo is not so much amiss. She has a fine figure, and when she laughs she fills one's heart with joy; but when she sings, oh, how beautiful she is!'"

"And what did the glass-blower's wife say?"

"She said: 'What is it to you? Mind your business. What has a married man to do with young girls?'"

"Did she appear angry?"

"Oh, very angry."

"It is a good sign. She knew that her husband was not far wrong. Well, what more?"

"Why, the Countess Moncenigo, who gives out work and has always been kind to me, said last week to Dr. Ancillo, who was there when I called: 'Only look, doctor, how this *Zitella* has grown, how fair she is and how well made!'"

"And what did the doctor say?"

"'Very true, madam,' said he; '*per Bacco!* I should not have known her: she is one of those constitutions that become handsome when they gain a little fat. She will be a fine girl, you will see that.'"

"And what more?"

"Then the superior of Santa Chiara, for whom I work embroidery for the altars, said to one of the sisters: 'Does not Consuelo resemble Santa Cecilia? Every time that I pray before her image I cannot help thinking of this little one, and then I pray for her that she may never fall into sin and that she may never sing but for the church.'"

"And what said the sister?"

"The sister replied: 'It is true, mother—it is quite true.' As for myself, I hastened to the church and looked at their Cecilia, which is painted by a great master, and is very, very beautiful."

"And like you?"

"A little."

"And you never told me that?"

"I never thought of it."

"Dear Consuelo, you are beautiful then?"

"I do not think so; but I am not so ugly as they say. One thing is certain—they no longer call me ugly. Perhaps they think it would give me pain to hear it.'"

"Let me see, little Consuelo; look at me. First, you have the most beautiful eyes in the world."

"But my mouth is large," said Consuelo, laughing, and taking up a broken bit of looking-glass which served her as a *pysche*.

"It is not very small indeed, but then what glorious

teeth!" said Anzoleto; "they are as white as pearls, and when you smile you show them all."

"In that case you must say something that will make me laugh, when we are with the count."

"You have magnificent hair, Consuelo."

"Oh yes; would you like to see it?" and she loosed the pins which fastened it, and her dark shining locks fell in flowing masses to the floor.

"Your chest is broad, your waist small, your shoulders —ah, they are beautiful, Consuelo!"

"My feet," said Consuelo, turning the conversation, "are not so bad;" and she held up a little Andalusian foot, a beauty almost unknown in Venice.

"Your hand is beautiful, also," said Anzoleto, kissing for the first time that hand which he had hitherto clasped only in compassion. "Let me see your arms."

"But you have seen them a hundred times," said she, removing her long gloves.

"No; I have never seen them," said Anzoleto, whose admiration every moment increased, and he again relapsed into silence, gazing with beaming eyes on the young girl, in whom each moment he discovered new beauties.

All at once Consuelo, embarrassed by this display, endeavored to regain her former quiet enjoyment, and began to pace up and down the apartment, gesticulating and singing from time to time in a somewhat exaggerated fashion, several passages from the lyric drama, just as if she were a performer on the stage.

"Magnificent!" exclaimed Anzoleto, ravished with surprise at finding her capable of a display which she had not hitherto manifested.

"It is any thing but magnificent," said Consuelo, reseating herself; "and I hope you only spoke in jest."

"It would be magnificent on the boards at any rate. I assure you there would not be a gesture too much. Corilla would burst with jealousy, for it is just the way she gets on when they applaud her to the skies."

"My dear Anzoleto, I do not wish that Corillo should grow jealous about any such nonsense; if the public were to applaud me merely because I knew how to ape her, I would never appear before them."

"You would do better then?"

"I hope so, or I should never attempt it."

" Very well ; how would you manage ?"

" I cannot say."

" Try."

" No; for all this is but a dream; and until they have decided whether I am ugly or not, we had better not plan any more fine projects. Perhaps we are a little mad just now, and after all, as the count has said, Consuelo may be frightful."

This last supposition caused Anzoleto to take his leave.

CHAPTER IX.

At this period of his life, though almost unknown to biographers, Porpora, one of the best Italian composers of the eighteenth century, the pupil of Scarlatti, the master of Hasse, Farinelli, Cafariello, Mingotti, Salimbini, Hubert (surnamed the Porporino), of Gabrielli, of Monteni— in a word, the founder of the most celebrated school of his time — languished in obscurity at Venice, in a condition bordering on poverty and despair. Nevertheless, he had formerly been director of the conservatory of the *Aspedaletto* in the same city, and this period of his life had been even brilliant. He had there written and performed his best operas, his most beautiful cantatas, and his finest church music. Invited to Vienna in 1728, he had there after some effort gained the favor of the Emperor Charles VI. Patronized at the court of Saxony, where he gave lessons to the electoral princess, Porpora from that repaired to London, where he rivaled for nine or ten years the glory of Handel, the master of masters, whose star at that period had begun to pale. The genius of the latter, however, obtained the supremacy, and Porpora, wounded in pride and purse, had returned to Venice to resume the direction of another conservatory. He still composed operas, but found it difficult to get them represented. His last, although written in Venice, was brought out in London, where it had no success. His genius had incurred these serious assaults, against which fortune and glory might perhaps have sustained him ; but the neglect and ingratitude of Hasse, Farinelli, and Cafariello, broke his heart, soured his character, and poisoned his old age. He is known to have died miserable and neglected in his eightieth year at Naples.

At the period when Count Zustiniani, foreseeing and almost desiring the defection of Corillo, sought to replace her, Porpora was subject to violent fits of ill humor, not always without foundation; for if they preferred and sang at Venice the music of Jomilli, of Lotti, of Carissimi, of Gaspirini, and other excellent masters, they also adopted without discrimination the productions of Cocchi, of Buini, of Salvator Apollini, and other local composers, whose common and easy style served to flatter mediocrity. The operas of Hasse could not please a master justly dissatisfied. The worthy but unfortunate Porpora, therefore, closing his heart and ears alike to modern productions, sought to crush them under the glory and authority of the ancients. He judged too severely of the graceful compositions of Galuppi, and even the original fantasias of Chiozzetto, a favorite composer at Venice. In short, he would only speak of Martini, Durante, Monte Verde, and Palestrina; I do not know if even Marcello and Leo found favor in his eyes. It was therefore with reserve and dissatisfaction that he received the first overtures of Zustiniani concerning his poor pupil, whose good fortune and glory he nevertheless desired to promote; for he had too much experience not to be aware of her abilities and her deserts. But he shook his head at the idea of the profanation of a genius so pure, and so liberally nurtured on the sacred manna of the old masters, and replied—" Take her if it must be so—this spotless soul, this stainless intellect—cast her to the dogs, hand her over to the brutes, for such seems the destiny of genius at the period in which we live."

This dissatisfaction, at once grave and ludicrous, gave the count a lofty idea of the merit of the pupil from the high value which the severe master attached to it.

"So, so, my dear maestro," he exclaimed ; " is that indeed your opinion? is this Consuelo a creature so extraordinary, so divine ?"

" You shall hear her," said Porpora, with an air of resignation, while he murmured, " It is her destiny."

The count succeeded in raising the spirits of the master from their state of depression, and led him to expect a serious reform in the choice of operas. He promised to exclude inferior productions so soon as he should succeed in getting rid of Corilla, to whose caprices he attributed their admission and success. He even dexterously gave him to understand that he would be very reserved as to Hasse ; and declared that if Porpora would write an opera for Consuelo, the pupil would confer a double glory on her master in expressing his thoughts in a style which suited them, as well as realize a lyric triumph for San Samuel and for the count.

Porpora, fairly vanquished, began to thaw, and now secretly longed for the coming out of his pupil, as much as he had hitherto dreaded it from the fear that she should be the means of adding fresh luster to the productions of his rivals. But as the count expressed some anxiety touching Consuelo's appearance, he refused to permit him to hear her in private and without preparation.

"I do not wish you to suppose," said he, in reply to the count's questions and entreaties, "that she is a beauty. A poorly dressed and timid girl, in presence of a nobleman and a judge—a child of the people, who has never been the object of the slightest attention—cannot dispense with some preparatory toilet. And besides Consuelo is one whose expression genius ennobles in an extraordinary degree. She must be seen and heard at the same time. Leave it all to me ; if you are not satisfied you may leave her alone, and I shall find out means of making her a good nun, who will be the glory of the school and the instructress of future pupils." Such in fact was the destiny which Porpora had planned for Consuelo.

When he saw his pupil again, he told her that she was to be heard and an opinion given of her by the count ; but as she was uneasy on the score of her looks, he gave her to understand that she would not be seen—in short, that she would sing behind the organ-screen, the count being merely present at the service in the church. He advised her, however, to dress with some attention to appearance, as she would have to be presented, and though the noble master was poor he gave her money for the purpose. Consuelo, frightened and agitated, busied for the first time in her life with attention to her person, hastened to see after her toilet and her voice. She tried the last, and found it so fresh, so brilliant, and so full, that Anzoleto, to whom she sung, more than once repeated with ecstasy, " Alas ! why should they require more than that she knows how to sing?"

CHAPTER X.

On the eve of the important day, Anzoleto found Con‧
suelo's door closed and locked, and after having waited for
a quarter of an hour on the stairs, he finally obtained per‑
mission to see his friend in her festal attire, the effect of
which she wished to try before him. She had on a hand‑
some flowered muslin dress, a lace handkerchief, and pow‑
der. She was so much altered, that Anzoleto was for some
moments uncertain whether she had gained or lost by the
change. The hesitation which Consuelo read in his eyes
was as the stroke of a dagger to her heart.

" Ah !" said she, " I see very well that I do not please
you. How can I hope to please a stranger, when he who
loves me sees nothing agreeable in my appearance?"

" Wait a little," replied Anzoleto. " I like your elegant
figure in those long stays, and the distinguished air which
this lace gives you. The large folds of your petticoat suit
you to admiration, but I regret your long black hair.
However, it is the fashion, and to-morrow you must be a
lady."

" And why must I be a lady? For my part I hate this
powder, which fades one, and makes even the most beauti‑
ful grow old before her time. I have an artificial air under
all these furbelows ; in short I am not satisfied with
myself, and I see you are not so either. Oh! by the bye,
I was at rehearsal this morning, and saw Clorinda, who
also was trying on a new dress. She was so gay, so fear‑
less, so handsome (oh! she must be happy — you need not
look twice at her to be sure of her beauty), that I feel
afraid of appearing beside her before the count."

" You may be easy ; the count has seen her, and has
heard her too."

" And did she sing badly?"

" As she always does."

" Ah, my friend, these rivalries spoil the disposition. A
little while ago, if Clorinda, who is a good girl notwith‑
standing her vanity, had been spoken of unfavorably by a
judge, I should have been sorry for her from the bottom
of my heart ; I should have shared her grief and humili‑
ation ; and now I find myself rejoicing at it! To strive,
to envy, to seek to injure each other, and all that for a

man whom we do not love, whom we do not even know! I feel very low-spirited, my dear love, and it seems to me as if I were as much frightened by the idea of succeeding as by that of failing. It seems as if our happiness was coming to a close, and that to-morrow after the trial, whatever may be the result, I shall return to this poor apartment a different person from what I have hitherto lived in it."

Two large tears rolled down Consuelo's cheeks.

"What! are you going to cry now?" said Anzoleto. "Do you think of what you are doing? You will dim your eyes and swell your eyelids. Your eyes, Consuelo! do not spoil your eyes, with are the most beautiful feature in your face."

"Or rather the least ugly," said she, wiping away her tears. "Come, when we give ourselves up to the world we have no longer any right to weep."

Her friend tried to console her, but she was exceedingly dejected all the rest of the day; and in the evening, as soon as she was alone, she carefully brushed out the powder, combed and smoothed her ebon hair, tried on a little dress of black silk, still fresh and well preserved, which she usually wore on Sundays, and recovered some portion of her confidence on once more recognizing herself in her mirror. Then she prayed fervently and thought of her mother, until, melted to tears, she cried herself to sleep. When Anzoleto came to seek her the next day in order to conduct her to the church, he found her seated before her spinet, dressed as for a holyday, and practicing her trial piece. "What!" cried he, "your hair not dressed! not yet ready! It is almost the hour. What are you thinking of, Consuelo?"

"My friend," answered she resolutely, "my hair is dressed, I am ready, I am tranquil. I wish to go as I am. Those fine robes do not suit me. You like my black hair better than if it were covered with powder. This waist does not impede my breathing. Do not endeavor to change my resolution; I have made up my mind. I have prayed to God to direct me, and my mother to watch over my conduct. God has directed me to be modest and simple. My mother has visited me in my dreams, and she said what she has always said to me; 'Try to sing well—Providence will do the rest.' I saw her take my fine dress, my laces and my ribbons, and arrange them in the wardrobe; and then she put my black frock and my mantilla of muslin on the chair at the side of my bed. As soon as I awoke I put past my costume as she had done in the dream, and I put on the black frock and mantilla which you see. I feel more courage since I have renounced the idea of pleasing by means which I do not know how to use. Now, hear my voice; everything depends on that, you know " She sounded a note.

"Just Heavens! we are lost," cried Anzoleto ; "your voice is husky and your eyes are red. You have been weeping yesterday evening, Consuelo; here's a fine business! I tell you we are lost; you are foolish to dress yourself in mourning on a holyday—it brings bad luck and makes you ugly. Now quick! quick! put on your beautiful dress, while I go and buy you some rouge. You are as pale as a specter."

This gave rise to a lively discussion between them. Anzoleto was a little rude. The poor girl's mind was again agitated, and her tears flowed afresh. Anzoleto was irritated still more, and in the midst of their debate the hour struck—the fatal hour (a quarter before two), just time enough to run to the church and reach it out of breath. Anzoleto cursed and swore. Consuelo, pale and trembling as the star of the morning which mirrors itself in the bosom of the lagunes, looked for the last time into her little broken mirror; then turning, she threw herself impetuously into Anzoleto's arms. "Oh, my friend," cried she, "do not scold me—do not curse me. On the contrary press me to your heart, and drive from my cheek this deathlike paleness. May your kiss be as the fire from the altar upon the lips of Isaiah, and may God not punish us for having doubted his assistance."

Then she hastily threw her mantilla over her head, took the music in her hand, and dragging her dispirited lover after her, ran toward the church of the Mendicanti, where the crowd had already assembled to hear the magnificent music of Porpora. Anzoleto, more dead than alive, proceeded to join the count, who had appointed to meet him in his gallery; and Consuelo mounted to the organ loft, where the choir was already arranged, and the professor seated before his desk. Consuelo did not know that the gallery of the count was so situated as to command a full view of the organ loft, that he already had his eyes fixed upon her, and did not lose one of her movements.

But he could not as yet distinguish her features, for she knelt on arriving, hid her face in her hands, and began to pray with fervent devotion. "My God," said she, in the depths of her heart, "thou knowest that I do not ask Thee to raise me above my rivals in order to abase them. Thou knowest that I do not wish to give myself to the world and to profane arts, in order to abandon Thy love, and to lose myself in the paths of vice. Thou knowest that pride does not swell my soul, and that it is in order to live with him whom my mother permitted me to love, never to separate myself from him, to ensure his enjoyment and happiness, that I ask Thee to sustain me, and to ennoble my voice and my thoughts when I shall sing Thy praise!"

When the first sound of the orchestra called Consuelo to her place, she rose slowly, her mantilla fell from her shoulders, and her face was at length visible to the impatient and restless spectators in the neighbouring tribune. But what marvelous change is here in this young girl, just now so pale, so cast down, so overwhelmed by fatigue and fear! The ether of heaven seemed to bedew her lofty forehead, while a gentle languor was diffused over the noble and graceful outlines of her figure. Her tranquil countenance expressed none of those petty passions which seek, and as it were exact, applause. There was something about her, solemn, mysterious, and elevated—at once lovely and affecting.

"Courage, my daughter!" said the professor in a low voice. "You are about to sing the music of a great master, and he is here to listen to you."

"Who?—Marcello?" said Consuelo, seeing the professor lay the Hymns of Marcello open on the desk.

"Yes—Marcello," replied he. "Sing as usual—nothing more and nothing less—and all will be well."

Marcello, then in the last year of his life, had in fact come once again to revisit Venice, his birth-place, where he had gained renown as composer, as writer, and as magistrate. He had been full of courtesy toward Porpora, who had requested him to be present in his school, intending to surprise him with the performance of Consuelo, who knew his magnificent "*I cieli immensi narrano*" by heart. Nothing could be better adapted to the religious glow that now animated the heart of this noble girl. So soon as the first words of this lofty and brilliant production shone be-

fore her eyes, she felt as if wafted into another sphere.
Forgetting Count Zustiniani — forgetting the spiteful
glances of her rivals — forgetting even Anzoleto — she
thought only of God and of Marcello, who seemed to interpret those wondrous regions whose glory she was about
to celebrate. What subject so beautiful! what conception
so elevated!

> I cieli immensi narrano
> Del grandi Iddio la gloria;
> Il firmamento lucido
> All' universo annunzia
> Quanto sieno mirabili
> Della sua destra le opere.

A divine glow overspread her features, and the sacred
fire of genius darted from her large black eyes, as the
vaulted roof rang with that unequaled voice, and with those
lofty accents which could only proceed from an elevated
intellect, joined to a good heart. After he had listened
for a few instants, a torrent of delicious tears streamed
from Marcello's eyes. The count, unable to restrain his
emotion, exclaimed: "By the Holy Rood this woman is
beautiful! She is Santa Cecilia, Santa Teresa, Santa Consuelo! She is poetry, she is music, she is faith personi-
fied!" As for Anzoleto, who had risen, and whose
trembling knees barely sufficed to sustain him with the aid
of his hands, which clung convulsively to the grating of
the tribune, he fell back upon his seat ready to swoon, intoxicated with pride and joy.

It required all the respect due to the locality, to prevent
the numerous dilettanti in the crowd from bursting into
applause as if they had been in the theater. The count
would not wait till the close of the service to express his
enthusiasm to Porpora and Consuelo. She was obliged to
repair to the tribune of the count to receive the thanks
and gratitude of Marcello. She found him so much
agitated as to be hardly able to speak.

"My daughter," said he, with a broken voice, "receive
the blessing of a dying man. You have caused me to forget for an instant the mortal sufferings of many years. A
miracle seems exerted in my behalf, and the unrelenting,
frightful malady appears to have fled forever at the sound
of your voice. If the angels above sing like you, I shall
long to quit the world in order to enjoy that happiness

which you have made known to me. Blessings then be on you, oh my child, and may your earthly happiness correspond with your deserts! I have heard Faustina, Romanina, Cuzzoni, and the rest; but they are not to be named along with you. It is reserved for you to let the world hear what it has never yet heard, and to make it feel what no man has ever yet felt."

Consuelo, overwhelmed by this magnificent eulogium, bowed her head, and almost bending to the ground, kissed, without being able to utter a word, the livid fingers of the dying man ; then rising she cast a look upon Anzoleto which seemed to say, "Ungrateful one, you knew not what I was!"

CHAPTER XI.

DURING the remainder of the service, Consuelo displayed energy and resources which completely removed any hesitation Count Zustiniani might have felt respecting her. She led, she animated, she sustained the choir, displaying at each instant prodigious powers, and the varied qualities of her voice rather than the strength of her lungs. For those who know how to sing do not become tired, and Consuelo sang with as little effort and labor as others might have in merely breathing. She was heard above all the rest, not because she screamed like those performers without soul and without breath, but because of the unimaginable sweetness and purity of her tones. Beside, she felt that she was understood in every minute particular. She alone, amid the vulgar crowd, the shrill voices and imperfect trills of those around her, was a musician and a master. She filled therefore instinctively and without ostentation, her powerful part, and as long as the service lasted she took the prominent place which she felt was necessary. After all was over, the choristers imputed it to her as a grievance and a crime; and those very persons who, failing and sinking, had as it were implored her assistance with their looks, claimed for themselves all the eulogiums which were given to the school of Porpora at large. At these eulogiums the master smiled and said nothing; but he looked at Consuelo, and Anzoleto understood very well what his look meant.

After the business of the day was over, the choristers partook of a select collation which the count had caused to be
served up in one of the parlors of the convent. Two immense tables in the form of a half moon were separated by
the grating, in the center of which, over an immense paté,
there was an opening to pass the dishes, which the count
himself gracefully handed round to the principal nuns and
pupils. The latter, dressed as Beguines, came by dozens
alternately to occupy the vacant places in the interior of
the cloisters. The superior, seated next the grating, was
thus at the right hand of the count as regarded the outward hall; the seat on his left was vacant. Marcello, Porpora, the curate of the parish, and the officiating priests,
some dilletanti patricians, and the lay administrators of
the school, together with the handsome Anzoleto with his
black coat and sword, had a place at the secular table.
The young singers, though usually animated enough on
such occasions, what with the pleasure of feasting, of conversing with gentlemen, the desire of pleasing, or at least
of being observed—were on that day thoughtful and constrained. The project of the count had somehow transpired—for what secret can be kept in a convent without
oozing out?—and each of these young girls secretly flattered herself that she should be presented by Porpora in
order to succeed Corilla. The professor was even malicious
enough to encourage their illusions, whether to induce
them to perform better before Marcello, or to revenge himself for the previous annoyance during their course of instruction. Certain it is that Clorinda, who was one of the
out-pupils of the conservatory, was there in full attire,
waiting to take her place beside the count; but when she
saw the despised Consuelo, with her black dress and tranquil mien, the ugly creature whom she affected to despise,
henceforth esteemed a musician and the only beauty of
the school, she became absolutely frightful with anger—
uglier than Consuelo had ever been—ugly as Venus herself
would become were she actuated by a base and degrading
motive. Anzoleto, exulting in his victory, looked attentively at her, seated himself beside her, and loaded her
with absurd compliments which she had not sense to understand, but which, nevertheless, consoled her. She
imagined she would revenge herself on her rival by attracting her betrothed, and spared no pains to intoxicate him

with her charms. She was no match, however, for her companion, and Anzoleto was acute enough to load her with ridicule.

In the meantime Count Zustiniani, upon conversing with Consuelo, was amazed to find her endowed with as much tact, good sense, and conversational powers, as he had found in her talent and ability at church. Absolutely devoid of coquetry, there was a cheerful frankness and confiding good nature in her manner which inspired a sympathy equally rapid and irresistible. When the repast was at an end, he invited her to take the air in his gondola with his friends. Marcello was excused on account of his failing health; but Porpora, Barberigo, and other patricians were present, and Anzoleto was also of the party. Consuelo, who felt not quite at home among so many men, entreated the count to invite Clorinda; and Zustiniani, who did not suspect the badinage of Anzoleto with this poor girl, was not sorry to see him attracted by her. The noble count, thanks to the sprightliness of his character, his fine figure, his wealth, his theater, and also the easy manners of the country and of the time, had a strong spice of conceit in his character. Fired by the wine of Greece and by his musical enthusiasm, and impatient to revenge himself on the perfidious Corilla, he thought there was nothing more natural than to pay his court to Consuelo. Seating himself therefore beside her in the gondola, and so arranging that the young people should occupy the other extremity, he began to direct glances of a very significant character on his new flame. The simple and upright Consuelo took no notice. Her candor and good principle revolted at the idea that the protector of her friend could harbor ill designs; indeed, her habitual modesty, in no way affected by the splendid triumph of the day, would have made it impossible for her to believe it. She persisted therefore in respecting the illustrious signor, who adopted her along with Anzoleto, and continued to amuse herself with the party of pleasure, in which she could see no harm.

So much calmness and good faith surprised the count, who remained uncertain whether it was the joyous submission of an unresisting heart or the unsuspiciousness of perfect innocence. At eighteen years of age, however, now as well as a hundred years ago, especially with a friend such as Anzoleto, a girl could not be perfectly ignorant. Every probability was in favor of the count; nevertheless, each time that he seized the hand of his protegée, or attempted to steal his arm round her waist, he experienced an indefinable fear, and a feeling of uncertainty—almost of respect—which restrained him, he could not tell how.

Barberigo found Consuelo sufficiently attractive, and he would in his turn gladly have maintained his pretensions, had he not been restrained by motives of delicacy toward the count. "Honor to all," said he to himself, as he saw the eyes of Zustiniani swimming in an atmosphere of voluptuous delight; "my turn will come next." Meanwhile the young Barberigo, not much accustomed to look at the stars when on excursions with ladies, inquired by what right Anzoleto should appropriate the fair Clorinda; and approaching he endeavored to make him understand that his place was rather to take the oar than to flirt with ladies. Anzoleto, notwithstanding his acuteness, was not well bred enough to understand at first what he meant; besides, his pride was fully on a par with the insolence of the patricians. He detested them cordially, and his apparent deference toward them merely served to disguise his inward contempt. Barberigo, seeing that he took a pleasure in opposing them, bethought himself of a cruel revenge. "By Jove!" said he to Clorinda, "your friend Consuelo is getting on at a furious rate; I wonder where she will stop. Not contented with setting the town crazy with her voice, she is turning the head of the poor count. He will fall madly in love, and Corilla's affair will soon be settled."

"Oh, there is nothing to fear," exclaimed Clorinda, mockingly; "Consuelo's affections are the property of Anzoleto here, to whom in fact she is engaged. They have been waiting for each other, I don't know how many years."

"I do not know how many years may be swept away in the twinkling of an eye," said Barberigo, "especially when the eyes of Zustiniani take it upon them to cast the mortal dart. Do you not think so, beautiful Clorinda?"

Anzoleto could bear it no longer. A thousand serpents already found admission into his bosom. Hitherto such a suspicion had never entered into his mind. He was transported with joy at witnessing his friend's triumph, and it was as much to give expression to his transports as to amuse his vanity, that he occupied himself in rallying the unfortunate victim of the day. After some cross-purposes with Barberigo, he feigned a sudden interest in a musical discussion which Porpora was keeping up with some of the company in the center of the bark, and thus leaving a situation which he had now no longer any wish to retain, he glided along unobserved almost to the prow. He saw at the first glance that Zustiniani did not relish his attempt to interrupt his tête-à-tête with his betrothed, for he replied coolly, and even with displeasure. At last, after several idle questions badly received, he was advised to go and listen to the instructions which the great Porpora was giving on counterpoint.

"The great Porpora is not my master," said Anzoleto, concealing the rage which devoured him. "He is Consuelo's master; and if it would only please your Highness," said he in a low tone, bending toward the count in an insinuating manner, "that my poor Consuelo should receive no other lessons than those of her old teacher."

"Dear and well beloved Zoto," replied the count caressingly, but at the same time with profound malice, "I have a word for your ear;" and leaning toward him he added: "your betrothed has doubtless received lessons from you that must render her invulnerable; but if I had any pretension to offer her others, I should at least have the right to do so during one evening."

Anzoleto felt a chill run through his frame from head to foot.

"Will your gracious Highness deign to explain yourself?" said he, in a choking voice.

"It is soon done, my good friend," replied the count in a clear tone—"*gondola for gondola.*"

Anzoleto was terrified when he found that the count had discovered his tête-à-tête with Corilla. The foolish and audacious girl had boasted to Zustiniani in a violent quarrel that they had been together. The guilty youth vainly pretended astonishment. "You had better go and listen to Porpora about the principle of the Neapolitan schools," said the count, "you will come back and tell me about it, for it is a subject that interests me much."

"I perceive, your Excellency," replied Anzoleto, frantic with rage, and ready to dash himself into the sea.

"What?" said the innocent Consuelo, astonished at his hesitation, "will you not go? Permit me, Signor Count; you shall see that I am willing to serve you." And before the count could interpose, she bounded lightly over the seat which separated her from her old master, and sat down close beside him.

The count, perceiving that matters were not far enough advanced, found it necessary to dissemble. "Anzoleto," said he, smiling, and pulling the ear of his protegé a little too hard, "my revenge is at an end. It has not proceeded nearly so far as your deserts; neither do I make the slightest comparison between the pleasure of conversing in the presence of a dozen persons with your betrothed, and the tête-à-tête which you have enjoyed in a well-closed gondola with mine."

"Signor Count!" exclaimed Anzoleto, violently agitated "I protest on my honor——"

"Where is your honor?" resumed the count; "is it in your left ear?" and he menaced the unfortunate organ with an infliction similar to that with which he had just visited the right.

"Do you suppose your protegé has so little sense," said Anzoleto, recovering his presence of mind, "as to be guilty of such folly?"

"Guilty or not," rejoined the count, drily, "it is all the same to me." And he seated himself beside Consuelo.

CHAPTER XII.

THE musical dissertation was continued until they reached the palace of Zustiniani, where they arrived toward midnight, to partake of coffee and sherbet. From the technicalities of art they had passed on to style, musical ideas, ancient and modern forms; from that to artists and their different modes of feeling and expressing themselves. Porpora spoke with admiration of his master Scarlatti, the first who had imparted a pathetic character to religious compositions; but there he stopped, and would not admit that sacred music should trespass upon profane, in tolerating ornaments, trills and roulades.

"Does your Highness," said Anzoleto, "find fault with

these and other difficult additions, which have nevertheless constituted the glory and success of your illustrious pupil Farinelli?"

"I only disapprove of them in the church," replied the maestro; "I would have them in their proper place, which is the theater. I wish them of a pure, sober, genuine taste, and appropriate in their modulations, not only to the subject of which they treat, but to the person and situation that are represented, and the passion which is expressed. The nymphs and shepherds may warble like any birds; their cadences may be like the flowing fountain; but Medea or Dido can only sob and roar like a wounded lioness. The coquette, indeed, may load her silly cavatina with capricious and elaborate ornament. Corilla excels in this description of music; but once she attempts to express the deeper emotions, the passions of the human heart, she becomes inferior even to herself. In vain she struggles, in vain she swells her voice and bosom —a note misplaced, an absurd roulade, parodies in an instant the sublimity which she had hoped to reach. You have all heard Faustina Bordoni, now Madame Hasse : in situations appropriate to her brilliant qualities, she had no equal ; but when Cuzzoni came, with her pure, deep feeling, to sing of pain, of prayer, or tenderness, the tears which she drew forth banished in an instant from your heart the recollection of Faustina. The solution of this is to be found in the fact that there is a showy and superficial cleverness, very different from lofty and creative genius. There is also that which amuses, which moves us, which astonishes, and which completely carries us away. I know very well that sudden and startling effects are now in fashion ; but if I taught them to my pupils as useful exercises, I almost repent of it when I see the majority so abuse them — so sacrifice what is necessary to what is superflous—the lasting emotion of the audience to cries of surprise and the darts of a feverish and transitory pleasure."

No one attempted to combat conclusions so eternally true with regard to all the arts, and which will be always applied to their varied manifestations by lofty minds. Nevertheless, the count, who was curious to know how Consuelo would sing ordinary music, pretended to combat a little the severe notions of Porpora ; but seeing that the modest girl, instead of refuting his heresies, ever turned her eyes to her old master as if to solicit his victorious replies, he determined to attack herself, and asked her "if she sang upon the stage with as much ability and purity as at church?"

"I do not think," she replied, with unfeigned humility, "that I should there experience the same inspirations or acquit myself nearly so well."

"This modest and sensible reply satisfies me," said the count; "and I feel assured that if you will condescend to study those brilliant difficulties of which we every day become more greedy, you will sufficiently inspire an ardent, curious, and somewhat spoiled public."

"Study!" replied Porpora, with a meaning smile.

"Study!" cried Anzoleto, with superb disdain.

"Yes, without doubt," replied Consuelo, with her accustomed sweetness. "Though I have sometimes labored in this direction, I do not think I should be able to rival the illustrious performers who have appeared in our time."

"You do not speak sincerely," exclaimed Anzoleto, with animation. "Eccelenza, she does not speak the truth. Ask her to try the most elaborate and difficult airs in the repertory of the theater, and you will see what she can do."

"If I did not think she were tired," said the count, whose eyes sparkled with impatience and curiosity. Consuelo turned hers artlessly to Porpora, as if to await his command.

"Why, as to that," said he, "such a trifle could not tire her; and as we are here a select few, we can listen to her talent in every description of music. Come, Signor Count, choose an air, and accompany it yourself on the harpsichord."

"The emotion which the sound of her voice would occasion me," replied Zustiniani, "would cause me to play falsely. Why not accompany her yourself, maestro?"

"I should wish to *see* her sing," continued Porpora; "for between us be it said I have never seen her sing. I wish to know how she demeans herself, and what she does with her mouth and with her eyes. Come, my child, arise; it is for me as well as for you that this trial is to be made."

"Let me accompany her, then," said Anzoleto, seating himself at the instrument.

"You will frighten me, O my master!" said Consuelo to Porpora.

"Fools alone are timid," replied the master.   "Whoever is inspired with the love of art need fear nothing.   If you tremble, it is because you are vain ; if you lose your resources, it is because they are false ; and if so, I shall be one of the first to say—'Consuelo is good for nought.'"

And without troubling himself as to what effect these tender encouragements might produce, the professor donned his spectacles, placed himself before his pupil, and began to beat the time on the harpsichord to give the true movement of the ritornella.   They chose a brilliant, strange and difficult air from an opera buffa of Galuppi,— *The Diavolessa,*—in order to test her in a species of art the most opposite to that in which she had succeeded in the morning.   The young girl enjoyed a facility so prodigious as to be able, almost without study and as if in sport, to overcome, with her pliable and powerful voice, all the difficulties of execution then known.   Porpora had recommended and made her repeat such exercises from time to time, in order to see that she did not neglect them ; but he was quite unaware of the ability of his wonderful pupil in this respect.   As if to revenge herself for the bluntness which he had displayed, Consuelo was roguish enough to add to *The Diavolessa* a multitude of turns and ornaments until then esteemed impracticable, but which she improvised with as much unconcern and calmness as if she had studied them with care.

These embellishments were so skillful in their modulations, of a character so energetic, wild, and startling, and mingled in the midst of their most impetuous gaiety with accents so mournful, that a shudder of terror replaced the enthusiasm of the audience, and Porpora, rising suddenly, cried out with a loud voice—"You are the devil in person !"

Consuelo finished her air with a *crescendo di forza* which excited shouts of admiration, while she reseated herself upon her chair with a burst of laughter.

"Wicked girl !" said Porpora to her, "you have played me a trick which deserves hanging.   You have mocked me.   You have hidden from me half your studies and your powers.   It is long since I could teach you any thing, and you have received my lessons from hypocrisy ; perhaps to steal from me the secrets of composition and of teaching, in order to surpass me in every thing, and make me pass afterwards for an old pedant."

"Dear master," replied Consuelo, "I have done no more than imitate your roguery toward the Emperor Charles. Have you not often told me that adventure ?—how his imperial majesty did not like trills, and had forbidden you to introduce a solitary one into your oratorio ; and how, having scrupulously respected his commands even to the end of the work, you gave him a tasteful *diverti-mento* in the final fugue, commencing it by four ascending trills, repeated *ad finitum* afterward in the *stretto* by all the parts? You have this evening been pleading against the abuse of embellishments, and yet you ordered me to use them. I have made use of too many, in order to prove to you that I likewise can be extravagant, a fault of which I am quite willing to plead guilty."

"I tell you that you are Beelzebub in person," returned Porpora. "Now sing us something human, and sing as you understand it, for I see plainly that I can no longer be your master."

"You will always be my respected and well-beloved master," cried she, throwing herself upon his neck and pressing him to her heart ; "it is to you that I owe my bread and my instruction for ten years. Oh, my master! they say that you have formed only ingrates ; may God deprive me on the instant of my love and my voice, if I carry in my heart the poison of pride and ingratitude!"

Porpora turned pale, stammered some words, and imprinted a paternal kiss upon the brow of his pupil ; but he left there a tear, and Consuelo, who did not dare to wipe it off, felt that cold and bitter tear of neglected old age and unhappy genius slowly dry upon her forehead. She felt deeply affected with a sort of religious terror, which threw a shade over all her gaiety, and extinguished all her fancy for the rest of the evening. An hour afterward, when they had lavished upon her all the usual phrases of admiration, surprise, and rapture, without being able to draw her from her melancholy, they asked for a specimen of her dramatic talent. She sang a grand air of Jomelli, from the opera of *Didone Abandonata.* Never had she felt in so great a degree the necessity of breathing forth her sadness ; she was sublime in pathos, in simplicity, in grandeur, and her features and expression were even more beautiful than they had been at the church. Her complexion was flushed with a feverish glow ; her eyes shot forth lurid lightnings; she was no longer a saint, she was even more — she was a woman consumed by love. The count, his friend Barberigo, Anzoleto, and I believe even the old Porpora himself, were almost out of their senses. Clorinda was suffocated with despair. Consuelo, to whom the count announced that on the morrow her engagement should be drawn up and signed, begged of him to promise her a second favor, and to engage his word to her after the manner of the ancient chevaliers, without knowing to what it referred. He did so, and the company separated, overpowered by that delicious emotion which is caused by great events and swayed at pleasure by great geniuses.

CHAPTER XIII.

WHILE Consuelo was achieving all these triumphs, Anzoleto had lived so completely in her as to forget himself; nevertheless, when the count in dismissing him mentioned the engagement of his betrothed, without saying a word of his own, he called to mind the coolness with which he had been treated during the evening, and the dread of being ruined without remedy poisoned all his joy. The idea darted across his mind to leave Consuelo on the steps, leaning on Porpora's arm, and to return to cast himself at the feet of his benefactor; but as at this moment he hated him, we must say in his praise that he withstood the temptation to humiliate himself. When he had taken leave of Porpora, and prepared to accompany Consuelo along the canal, the gondoliers of the count informed him that by the commands of their master the gondola waited to conduct the signora home. A cold perspiration burst upon his forehead. "The signora," said he, rudely, "is accustomed to use her own limbs; she is much obliged to the count for his attentions."

"By what right do you refuse for her?" said the count, who was close behind him. Anzoleto turned and saw him, not with uncovered head as a man who dismissed his guests, but with his cloak thrown over his shoulders, his hat in one hand, and his sword in the other, as one who seeks adventures. Anzoleto was so enraged, that a thought of stabbing him with the long narrow knife which a Venetian always carried about concealed on his person, flashed across his mind. "I hope, madam," said the count, in a firm voice, "that you will not offer me the affront of refusing my gondola to take you home, and cause me the vexation of not permitting me to assist you to enter it."

Consuelo, always confiding, and suspecting nothing of what passed around her, accepted the offer, thanked him, and placing her pretty rounded elbow in the hand of the count, she sprang without ceremony into the gondola. Then a dumb but energetic dialogue took place between the count and Anzoleto. The count, with one foot on the bank and one on the bark, measured Anzoleto with his eye, who, standing on the last step of the stairs leading from the water's edge to the palace, measured him with a fierce air in return, his hand in his breast and grasping the handle of his knife. A single step, and the count was lost. What was most characteristic of the Venetian disposition in this rapid and silent scene, was, that the two rivals watched each other without either hastening the catastrophe. The count was determined to torture his rival by apparent irresolution, and he did so at leisure, although he saw and comprehended the gesture of Anzoleto. On his side Anzoleto had strength to wait, without betraying himself, until it would please the count to finish his malicious pleasantry or give up his life. This pantomine lasted two minutes, which seemed to Anzoleto an age, and which the count supported with stoical disdain. The count then made a profound bow to Consuelo, and turning toward his protegé, "I permit you also," said he, "to enter my gondola; in future you will know how a gallant man conducts himself;" and he stepped back to allow Anzoleto to pass into the boat. Then he gave orders to the gondolier to row to the Corte Minelli, while he remained standing on the bank, motionless as a statue. It almost seemed as if he awaited some new attempt at murder on the part of his humiliated rival.

"How does the count know your abode?" was the first word which Anzoleto addressed to his betrothed, when they were out of sight of the palace of Zustiniani.

"Because I told him," replied Consuelo.

"And why did you tell him?"

"Because he asked me."

"You do not guess then why he wished to know?"

"Probably to convey me home."

" Do you think so ? Do you think he will not come to see you?"

" Come to see me ? what madness ! And in such a wretched abode! That would be an excess of politeness which I should never wish."

" You do well not to wish it, Consuelo ; for excess of shame might ensue from this excess of honor."

" Shame! and why shame to me ? In good faith I do not understand you to-night, dear Anzoleto; and I think it rather odd that you should speak of things I do not comprehend, instead of expressing your joy at our incredible and unexpected success."

" Unexpected indeed," returned Anzoleto, bitterly.

" It seemed to me that at vespers, and while they applauded me this evening, you were even more intoxicated than I was. You looked at me with such passionate eyes that my happiness was doubled in seeing it reflected from you. But now you are gloomy and out of sorts, just as when we wanted bread and our prospects were uncertain."

" And now you wish that I should rejoice in the future? Possibly it is no longer uncertain, but assuredly it presents nothing cheering for me."

" What more would we have? It is hardly a week since you appeared before the count and were received with enthusiasm."

" My success was infinitely eclipsed by yours—you know it well."

" I hope not; besides, if it were so, there can be no jealousy between us."

These ingenuous words, uttered with the utmost truth and tenderness, calmed the heart of Anzoleto. " Ah, you are right," said he, clasping his betrothed in his arms ; " we cannot be jealous of each other, we cannot deceive each other;" but as he uttered these words he recalled with remorse his adventure with Corilla, and it occurred to him that the count, in order to punish him, might reveal his conduct to Consuelo whenever he had reason to suppose that she in the least encouraged him. He fell into a gloomy reverie, and Consuelo also became pensive.

" Why," said she, after a moment's silence, " did you say that we could not deceive each other ? It is a great truth surely, but why did you just then think of it?"

" Hush! let us not say another word in this gondola,"

said Anzoleto; "they will hear what we say and tell it to the count. This velvet covering is very thin, and these palace gondolas have recesses four times as deep and as large as those for hire. Permit me to accompany you home," said he, when they had been put ashore at the entrance of the Corte Minelli.

"You know that it is contrary to our agreement and custom," replied she.

"Oh, do not refuse me," said Anzoleto, "else you will plunge me into fury and despair."

Frightened by his tone and his words, Consuelo dared no longer refuse; and when she had lighted her lamp and drawn the curtains, seeing him gloomy and lost in thought, she threw her arms around him. "How unhappy and disquieted you seem this evening!" said she; "what is the matter with you?"

"Do you not know, Consuelo? do you not guess?"

"No, on my soul!"

"Swear that you do not guess it. Swear it by the soul of your mother—by your hopes of heaven!"

"Oh, I swear it!"

"And by our love?"

"By our love."

"I believe you, Consuelo, for it would be the first time you ever uttered an untruth!"

"And now will you explain yourself?"

"I shall explain nothing. Perhaps I may have to explain myself soon; and when that moment comes, and when you have too well comprehended me, woe to us both, the day on which you know what I now suffer!"

"O Heaven! what new misfortune threatens us? What curse assails us, as we re-enter this poor chamber, where hitherto we had no secrets from each other? Something too surely told me when I left it this morning that I should return with death in my soul. What have I done that I should not enjoy a day that promised so well? Have I not prayed God sincerely and ardently? Have I not thrust aside each proud thought? Have I not suffered from Clorinda's humiliation? Have I not obtained from the count a promise that he should engage her as *seconda donna* with us? What have I done, must I again ask, to incur the sufferings of which you speak—which I already feel since you feel them?"

"And did you indeed procure an engagement for Clorinda?"

"I am resolved upon it, and the count is a man of his word. This poor girl has always dreamed of the theater, and has no other means of subsistence."

"And do you think that the count will part with Rosalba, who knows something, for Clorinda who knows nothing?"

"Rosalba will follow her sister Corilla's fortunes: and as to Clorinda we shall give her lessons, and teach her to turn her voice, which is not amiss, to the best account. The public, besides, will be indulgent to a pretty girl. Were she only to obtain a third place, it would be always something—a beginning—a source of subsistence."

"You are a saint, Consuelo; you do not see that this dolt, in accepting your intervention, although she should be happy in obtaining a third, or even a fourth place, will never pardon you for being first."

"What signifies her ingratitude? I know already what ingratitude and the ungrateful are."

"You!" said Anzoleto, bursting into a laugh, as he embraced her with all his old brotherly warmth.

"Oh," replied she, enchanted at having diverted him from his cares, "I should always have before my eyes the image of my noble master Porpora. Many bitter words he uttered which he thought me incapable of comprehending; but they sank deep into my heart and shall never leave it. He is a man who has suffered greatly, and is devoured by sorrow. From his grief and his deep indignation, as well as what has escaped from him before me, I have learned that artists, my dear Anzoleto, are more wicked and dangerous than I could suppose—that the public is fickle, forgetful, cruel and unjust—that a great career is but a heavy cross, and that glory is a crown of thorns. Yes, I know all that, and I have thought and reflected upon it so often, that I think I should neither be astonished nor cast down were I to experience it myself. Therefore it is that you have not been able to intoxicate me by the triumph of to-day—therefore it is your dark thoughts have not discouraged me. I do not yet comprehend them very well; but I know that with you, and provided you love me, I shall strive not to hate and despise mankind like my poor unhappy master, that noble yet simple old man."

CHAPTER XIV.

IN LISTENING to his betrothed, Anzoleto recovered his serenity and his courage. She exercised great influence over him, and each day he discovered in her a firmness and rectitude which supplied every thing that was wanting in himself. "I am only afraid," said he, "that the count will find you so superior that he shall judge me unworthy to appear with you before the public. He seemed this evening to have forgotten my very existence. He did not even perceive that in accompanying you I played well. In fine, when he told you of your engagement, he did not say a word of mine. How is it that you did not remark that?"

"It never entered my head that I should be engaged without you. Does he not know that nothing would persuade me to it? that we are betrothed? that we love each other? Have you not told him all this?"

"I have told him so, but perhaps he thinks that I wish to boast, Consuelo."

"In that case I shall boast myself of my love, Anzoleto; I shall tell him so that he cannot doubt it. But you are deceived, my friend; the count has not thought it necessary to speak of your engagement, because it was a settled thing since the day that you sung so well at his house."

"But not yet ratified, and your engagement he has told you will be signed to-morrow."

"Do you think I shall sign the first? Oh, no! you have done well to put me on my guard. My name shall be written below yours."

"You swear it?"

"Oh, fie! Do you ask oaths for what you know so well? Truly you do not love me this evening, or you would not make me suffer by seeming to imagine that I did not love you."

At this thought Consuelo's eyes filled with tears, and she sat down with a pouting air, which rendered her charming. "I am a fool—an ass!" thought Anzoleto. "How could I for one instant suppose that the count could triumph over a soul so pure—an affection so full and entire?

He is not so inexperienced as not to perceive at a glance that Consuelo is not for him, and he would not have been so generous as to offer me a place in his gondola, had he not known that he would have played the part of a fool there. No, no; my lot is well assured—my position unassailable. Let Consuelo please him or not, let him love, pay court to her—all that can only advance my fortunes, for she will soon learn to obtain what she wishes without incurring any danger. Consuelo will soon be better informed on this head than myself. She is prudent, she is energetic. The pretensions of the dear count will only turn to my profit and glory."

And thus abjuring all his doubts, he cast himself at the feet of his betrothed, and gave vent to that passionate enthusiasm which he now experienced for the first time, and which his jealousy had served for some hours to restrain.

"O my beauty—my saint—my queen!" he cried, "excuse me for having thought of myself in place of prostrating myself before you, as I should have done, on finding myself again with you in this chamber. I left it this morning in anger with you. Yes, yes; I should have re-entered it upon my knees. How could you love and smile upon a brute like me? Strike me with your fan, Consuelo; place your pretty foot upon my neck. You are greater than I am by a hundredfold, and I am your slave for ever from this day."

"I do not deserve these fine speeches," said she, abandoning herself to his transports; "and I excuse your doubts because I comprehend them. It was the fear of being separated from me—of seeing our lot divide—which caused you all this unhappiness. You have failed in your faith in God, which is much worse than having accused me. But I shall pray for you, and say, 'Lord, forgive as I forgive him.'"

While thus innocently and simply expressing her love, and mingling with it that Spanish feeling of devotion so full of human affection and ingenuous candor, Consuelo was beautiful. Anzoleto gazed on her with rapture.

"Oh, thou mistress of my soul!" he exclaimed, in a suffocated voice, "be mine for evermore?"

"When you will — to-morrow," said Consuelo, with a heavenly smile.

" To-morrow? and why to-morrow?"

" You are right : it is now past midnight—we may be
married to-day.   When the sun rises let us seek the priest.
We have no friends, and the ceremony need not be long.
I have the muslin dress, which I have never yet worn.
When I made it, dear Anzoleto, I said to myself, ' Perhaps I may not have money to purchase my wedding
dress, and if my friend should soon decide on marrying
me, I would be obliged to wear one that I have had on already.'   That, they say, is unlucky.   So, when my mother
appeared to me in a dream, to take it from me and lay it
past, she knew what she did, poor soul!   Therefore, by
to-morrow's sun we shall swear at San Samuel fidelity for
ever.   Did you wish to satisfy yourself first, wicked one,
that I was not ugly?"

" O Consuelo !" exclaimed Anzoleto, with anguish,
" you are a child.   We could not marry thus, from one
day to another, without its being known.   The count and
Porpora, whose protection is so necessary to us, would be
justly irritated if we took this step without consulting or
even informing them.   Your old master does not like me
too well, and the count, as I know, does not care much for
married singers.   We cannot go to San Samuel where every
body knows us, and where the first old woman we met
would make the palace acquainted with it in half an hour.
We must keep our union secret."

" No, Anzoleto," said Consuelo, " I cannot consent to
so rash—so ill-advised a step.   I did not think of the objections you have urged to a public marriage : but if they
are well founded they apply with equal force to a private
and clandestine one.   It was not I who spoke first of it,
Anzoleto, although I thought more than once that we
were old enough to be married ; yet it seemed right to
leave the decision to your prudence, and, if I must say it,
to your wishes ; for I saw very well that you were in no
hurry to make me your wife, nor had I any desire to remind you.   You have often told me that before settling
ourselves, we must think of our future family, and secure
the needful resources.   My mother said the same, and
it is only right.   Thus, all things considered, it would be
too soon.   First, our engagement must be signed—is not
that so?   Then we must be certain of the good-will of the
public.   We can speak of all this after we make our debut.

But why do you grow pale, Anzoleto? Why do you wring your hands? O Heaven! are we not happy? Does it need an oath to insure our mutual love and reliance?"

"O Consuelo! how calm you are! how pure! how cold!" exclaimed Anzoleto, with a sort of despair.

"Cold!" exclaimed the young Spaniard, stupified, and crimson with indignation. "God, who reads my heart, knows whether I love you!"

"Very well," retorted Anzoleto, angrily; "throw yourself into his bosom, for mine is no safe refuge; and I shall fly lest I become impious."

Thus saying he rushed toward the door, believing that Consuelo, who had hitherto never been able to separate from him in any quarrel, however trifling, would hasten to prevent him, and in fact she made an impetuous movement as if to spring after him, then stopped, saw him go out, ran likewise to the door, and put her hand on the latch in order to call him back. But summoning up all her resolution by a superhuman effort, she fastened the bolt behind him, and then, overcome by the violent struggle she had undergone, she swooned away upon the floor, where she remained motionless till daybreak.

CHAPTER XV.

"I MUST confess that I am completely enchanted with her," said the Count Zustiniani to his friend Barberigo, as they conversed together on the balcony of his palace about two o'clock the same night.

"That is as much as to say that I must not be so," replied the young and brilliant Barberigo, "and I yield the point, for your rights take precedence of mine. Nevertheless, if Corilla should mesh you afresh in her nets, you will have the goodness to let me know, that I may try and win her ear."

"Do not think of it, if you love me. Corilla has never been other than a plaything. I see by your countenance that you are but mocking me."

"No, but I think that the amusement is somewhat serious which causes us to commit such follies and incur such expense."

"I admit that I pursue my pleasures with so much ar-

door that I spare no expense to prolong them; but in
this case it is more than fancy—it is passion which I feel.
I never saw a creature so strangely beautiful as this Consuelo: she is like a lamp that pales from time to time, but
which at the moment when it is apparently about to expire,
sheds so bright a light that the very stars are eclipsed."

"Ah!" said Barberigo, sighing, "that little black dress
and white collar, that slender and half devout toilet, that
pale, calm face, at first so little striking, that frank address and astonishing absence of coquetry—all become
transformed, and, as it were, grow divine when inspired
by her own lofty genius of song. Happy Zustiniani, who
hold in your hands the destinies of this dawning star!"

"Would I were secure of the happiness which you envy!
But I am discouraged when I find none of those passions
with which I am acquainted, and which are so easy to
bring into play. Imagine, friend, that this girl remains
an enigma to me even after a whole day's study of her.
It would almost seem from her tranquility and my awkwardness, that I am already so far gone that I cannot see
clearly."

"Truly you are captivated, since you already grow blind.
I, whom hope does not confuse, can tell you in three words
what you do not understand. Consuelo is the flower of
innocence; she loves the little Anzoleto, and will love him
yet for some time; but if you affront this attachment of
childhood, you will only give it fresh strength. Appear
to consider it of no importance, and the comparison which
she will not fail to make between you and him will not fail
to cool her preference."

"But the rascal is as handsome as Apollo; he has a
magnificent voice, and must succeed. Corilla is already
crazy about him; he is not one to be despised by a girl who
has eyes."

"But he is poor, and you are rich—he is unknown, and
you are powerful. The needful thing is to find out
whether they are merely betrothed, or whether a more intimate connection binds them. In the latter case Consuelo's eyes will be soon opened; in the former there will
be a struggle and uncertainty which will but prolong her
anguish."

"I must then desire what I horribly fear, and which
maddens me with rage when I think of it. What do you
suppose?"

"I think they are merely betrothed."

"But it is impossible. He is a bold and ardent youth, and then the manners of those people!"

"Consuelo is in all respects a prodigy. You have had experience to little purpose, dear Zustiniani, if you do not see in all the movements, all the looks, all the words of this girl, that she is pure as the ocean gem."

"You transport me with joy."

"Take care—it is folly, prejudice. If you love Consuelo, she must be married to-morrow, so that in eight days her master may make her feel the weight of her chain, the torments of jealousy, the *ennui* of a troublesome, unjust, and faithless guardian; for the handsome Anzoleto will be all that. I could not observe him yesterday between Consuelo and Clorinda without being able to prophesy her wrongs and misfortunes. Follow my advice, and you will thank me. The bond of marriage is easy to unloose between people of that condition, and you know that with women love is an ardent fancy which only increases with obstacles."

"You drive me to despair," replied the count; "nevertheless, I feel that you are right."

Unhappily for the designs of Count Zustiniani, this dialogue had a listener upon whom they did not reckon, and who did not lose one syllable of it. After quitting Consuelo, Anzoleto, stung with jealousy, had come to prowl about the palace of his protector, in order to assure himself that the count did not intend one of those forcible abductions then so much in vogue, and for which the patricians had almost entire impunity. He could hear no more; for the moon, which just then rose over the roofs of the palace, began to cast his shadow on the pavement, and the two young lords, perceiving that a man was under the balcony, withdrew and closed the window.

Anzoleto disappeared in order to ponder at his leisure on what he had just heard; it was quite enough to direct him what course to take in order to profit by the virtuous counsels of Barberigo to his friend. He slept scarcely two hours, and immediately when he awoke, ran to the Corte Minelli. The door was still locked, but through the chincks he could see Consuelo, dressed, stretched on the bed and sleeping, pale and motionless as death. The coolness of the morning had roused her from her swoon, and she threw herself on the bed without having strength to undress. He stood for some moments looking at her with remorseful disquietude, but at last becoming uneasy at this heavy sleep, so contrary to the active habits of his betrothed, he gently enlarged an opening through which he could pass his knife and slide back the bolt. This occasioned some noise; but Consuelo, overcome with fatigue, was not awakened. He then entered, knelt down beside her couch, and remained thus until she awoke. On finding him there Consuelo uttered a cry of joy, but instantly taking away her arms, which she had thrown round his neck, she drew back with an expression of alarm.

" You dread me now, and instead of embracing, fly me," said he with grief. " Oh, I am cruelly punished for my fault; pardon me, Consuelo, and see if you have ever cause to mistrust your friend again. I have watched you sleeping for a whole hour; pardon me, sister—it is the first and last time you shall have to blame or repulse your brother; I shall never more offend you by my hastiness and ill-temper. Leave me, banish me, if I fail in my oath. Are you satisfied, dear and good Consuelo?"

Consuelo only replied by pressing the fair head of the Venetian to her heart and bathing it with tears. This outburst comforted her; and soon after falling back upon her pillow, "I confess," said she, "that I am overcome; I hardly slept all night, we parted so unhappily."

"Sleep, Consuelo; sleep, dear angel," replied Anzoleto. "Do you remember the night that you allowed me to sleep on your couch; while you worked and prayed at your little table? It is now my turn to watch and protect you. Sleep, my child; I shall turn over your music and read it to myself whilst you repose an hour or two; no one will disturb us before the evening. Sleep, then, and prove by this confidence that you pardon and trust me."

Consuelo replied by a heavenly smile. He kissed her forehead and placed himself at the table, while she enjoyed a refreshing sleep, mingled with sweet dreams.

Anzoleto had lived calmly and innocently too long with this young girl, to render it difficult after one day's agitation to regain his usual demeanour. This brotherly feeling was, as it were, the ordinary condition of his soul; besides, what he had heard the preceding night under the balcony of Zustiniani, was well calculated to strengthen his faltering purpose. "Thanks, my brave gentleman," said he to himself; "you have given me a lesson which the *rascal* will turn to account just as much as one of your own class. I shall abstain from jealousy, infidelity, or any weakness which may give you an advantage over me. Illustrious and profound Barberigo! your prophecies bring counsel; it is good to be of your school."

Thus reflecting, Anzoleto, overcome by a sleepless night, dozed in his turn, his head supported on his hand and his elbows on the table; but his sleep was not sound, and the daylight had begun to decline as he rose to see if Consuelo still slumbered. The rays of the setting sun streaming through the window, cast a glorious purple tinge on the old bed and its beautiful occupant. Her white mantilla she had made into a curtain, which was secured to a filagree crucifix nailed to the wall above her head. Her veil fell gracefully over her well-proportioned and admirable figure; and, bathed in this rose-colored light as a flower which closes its leaves together at the approach of evening, her long tresses falling upon her white shoulders, her hands crossed on her bosom as a saint on her marble tomb, she looked so chaste and heavenly that Anzoleto mentally exclaimed, "Ah, Count Zustiniani, that you could see her this moment, and behold the prudent and jealous guardian of a treasure you vainly covet, beside her!"

At this moment a faint noise was heard outside, and Anzoleto, whose faculties were kept on the stretch, thought he recognized the splashing of water at the foot of Consuelo's ruined dwelling, although gondolas rarely approached the Corte Minelli. He mounted on a chair, and was by this means able to see through a sort of loophole near the ceiling, which looked toward the canal. He distinctly saw Count Zustiniani leave his bark, and question the half-naked children who played on the beach. He was uncertain whether he should awaken his betrothed or close the door; but, during the ten minutes which the count occupied in finding out the garret of Consuelo, he had time to regain the utmost self-possession and to leave the door ajar, so that any one might enter without noise or hindrance; then reseating himself, he took a pen and pretended to write music. He appeared perfectly calm and tranquil although his heart beat violently.

The count slipped in, rejoicing in the idea of surprising his protegée, whose obvious destitution he conceived would favor his corrupt intentions. He brought Consuelo's engagement ready signed along with him, and he thought with such a passport his reception could not be very discouraging; but at the first sight of the strange sanctuary in which this sweet girl slept her angelic sleep under the watchful eye of her contented lover, Count Zustiniani lost his presence of mind, entangled his cloak which he had thrown with a conquering air over his shoulders, and stopped between the bed and the table, utterly uncertain whom he should address. Anzoleto was revenged for the scene at the entrance of the gondola.

"My lord," he exclaimed, rising as if surprised by an unexpected visit, "shall I awaken my betrothed?"

"No," replied the count, already at his ease, and affecting to turn his back that he might contemplate Consuelo; "I am so happy to see her thus, I forbid you to awaken her."

"Yes, you may look at her," thought Anzoleto; "it is all I wished for."

Consuelo did not awaken, and the count, speaking in a low tone and assuming a gracious and tranquil aspect, expressed his admiration without restraint. "You were right, Zoto," said he with an easy air; "Consuelo is the first singer in Italy, and I was wrong to doubt that she was the most beautiful woman in the world."

"Your highness thought her frightful, however," said Anzoleto, maliciously.

"You have doubtless complained to her of all my folly; but I reserve to myself the pleasure of obtaining pardon by so honorable and complete an apology that you shall not again be able to injure me in recalling my errors."

"Injure you, Signor Count!—how could I do so even had I the wish?"

Consuelo moved. "Let us not awaken her too suddenly," said the count, "and clear this table that I may place on it and read her engagement. Hold!" said he when Anzoleto had obeyed him; "cast your eyes over this paper while we wait for hers to open."

"An engagement before trial!—it is magnificent, my noble patron. And she is to appear at once, before Corilla's engagement has expired?"

"That is nothing; there is some trifling debt of a thousand sequins or so due her, which we shall pay off."

"But what if Corilla should cabal?"

"We will confine her under the leads."

"'Fore Heaven! nothing stops your highness."

"Yes, Zoto," replied the count coldly; "thus it is: what we desire we do, toward one and all."

"And the conditions are the same as for Corilla—the same conditions for a débutante without name or reputation as for an illustrious performer adored by the public?"

"The new singer shall have even more; and if the conditions granted her predecessor do not satisfy her, she has only to say a word and they shall be doubled. Every thing depends upon herself," continued he, raising his voice a little as he perceived that Consuelo was awake: "her fate is in her own hands."

Consuelo had heard all this partially, through her sleep. When she had rubbed her eyes and assured herself that she was not dreaming, she slid down into the space between the bed and the wall, without considering the strangeness of her position, and after arranging her hair, came forward with ingenuous confidence to join in the conversation.

"Signor Count," said she, "you are only too good; but I am not so presumptuous as to avail myself of your offer. I will not sign this engagement until I have made a trial of my powers before the public. It would not be delicate on my part. I might not please—I might incur a *fiasco* and be hissed. Even should I be hoarse or unprepared, or even ugly that day, your word would be still pledged—you would be too proud to take it back and I to avail myself of it."

"Ugly on that day, Consuelo!—you ugly!" said the count, looking at her with burning glances; "come now," he added, taking her by the hand and leading her to the mirror, "look at yourself there. If you are adorable in this costume, what would you be, covered with diamonds and radiant with triumph?"

The count's impertinence made Anzoleto gnash his teeth; but the calm indifference with which Consuelo received his compliments restrained his impatience. "Sir," said she, pushing back the fragment of looking-glass which he held in his hand, "do not break my mirror; it is the only one I ever had, and it has never deceived me. Ugly or pretty,

I refuse your liberality; and I may tell you frankly that I shall not appear unless my betrothed be similarly engaged. I will have no other theater nor any other public except his; we cannot be separate, being engaged to each other."

This abrupt declaration took the count a little unawares, but he soon regained his equanimity.

"You are right, Consuelo," replied he; "I never intended to separate you; Zoto shall appear with yourself. At the same time I cannot conceal from you that his talents, although remarkable, are much inferior to yours."

"I do not believe it, my lord," said Consuelo, blushing as if she had received a personal insult.

"I hear that he is your pupil, much more than that of the maestro I gave him. Do not deny it, beautiful Consuelo. On learning your intimacy, Porpora exclaimed, 'I am no longer astonished at certain qualities he possesses which I was unable to reconcile with his defects.'"

"Thanks to the Signor Professor" said Anzoleto with a forced smile.

"He will change his mind," said Consuelo, gaily; "besides the public will contradict this dear good master."

"The good dear master is the best judge of music in the world," replied the count. "Anzoleto will do well to profit by your lessons; but we cannot arrange the terms of his agreement before we have ascertained the sentiments of the public. Let him make his appearance, and we shall settle with him according to justice and our own favorable feelings toward him, on which he has every reason to rely."

"Then let us both make our appearance," replied Consuelo; "but no signature—no agreement before trial; on that I am determined."

"You are not satisfied with my terms, Consuelo; very well, then you shall dictate them yourself; here is the pen—add—take away—my signature is below."

Consuelo seized the pen; Anzoleto turned pale, and the count, who observed him, chewed with pleasure the end of the ruffle which he twisted on his fingers. Consuelo erased the contract and wrote upon the portion remaining above the signature of the count:

"Anzoleto and Consuelo severally agree to such conditions as it shall please Count Zustiniani to impose after their first appearance, which shall take place during the ensuing month at the theater of San Samuel."

She signed rapidly, and passed the pen to her lover.

"Sign without looking," said she. "You can do no less to prove your gratitude, and your confidence in your benefactor."

Anzoleto had glanced over it in a twinkling; he signed —it was but the work of a moment. The count read over his shoulder.

"Consuelo," said he, "you are a strange girl—in truth an admirable creature. You will both dine with me," he continued, tearing the contract and offering his hand to Consuelo, who accepted it, but at the same time requested him to wait with Anzoleto in his gondola while she should arrange her toilet.

"Decidedly," said she to herself when alone, "I shall be able to buy a new marriage robe." She then arranged her muslin dress, settled her hair, and flew down the stairs, singing with a voice full of freshness and vigor. The count, with excess of courtesy, had waited for her with Anzoleto at the foot of the stair. She believed him further off, and almost fell into his arms, but suddenly disengaging herself, she took his hand and carried it to her lips, after the fashion of the country, with the respect of an inferior who does not wish to infringe upon the distinctions of rank ; then turning, she clasped her betrothed, and bounded with joyous steps toward the gondola, without awaiting the ceremonious escort of her somewhat mortified protector.

CHAPTER XVI.

THE count, seeing that Consuelo was insensible to the stimulus of gain, tried to flatter her vanity by offering her jewels and ornaments; but these she refused. Zustiniani at first imagined that she was aware of his secret intentions; but he soon saw that it was but a species of rustic pride, and that she would receive no recompense until she conceived she had earned it by working for the prosperity of his theater. He obliged her, however, to accept a white satin dress, observing that she could not appear with propriety in her muslin robe in his saloon, and adding that he would consider it a favor if she would abandon the attire of the people. She submitted her fine figure to the fashionable milliners, who turned it to good account, and did not spare the material. Thus transformed in two days into a woman of the world, and induced to accept a necklace of fine pearls which the count presented to her as payment for the evening when she sang before him and his friends, she was beautiful, if not according to her own peculiar style of beauty, at least as she should be to be admired by the vulgar. This result, however, was not perfectly attained. At the first glance Consuelo neither struck nor dazzled any body; she was always pale, and her modest, studious habits took from her look that brilliant glance which we witness in the eyes of women whose only object is to shine. The basis of her character, as well as the distinguishing peculiarity of her countenance, was a reflective seriousness. One might see her eat, and talk, and weary herself with the trivial concerns of daily life, without even supposing that she was pretty; but once the smile of enjoyment, so easily allied to serenity of soul, came to light up her features, how charming she became! And when she was further animated—when she interested herself seriously in the business of the piece—when she displayed tenderness, exaltation of mind, the manifestation of her inward life and hidden power—she shone resplendent with all the fire of genius and love, she was another being, the audience were hurried away—passion-stricken as it were—annihilated at pleasure—without her being able to explain the mystery of her power.

What the count experienced for her therefore astonished and annoyed her strangely. There were in this man of the world artistic chords which had never yet been struck, and which she caused to thrill with unknown emotions; but this revelation could not penetrate the patrician's soul sufficiently to enable him to discern the impotence and poverty of the means by which he attempted to lead away a woman so different from those he had hitherto endeavored to corrupt.

He took patience and determined to try the effects of emulation. He conducted her to his box in the theater that she might witness Corilla's success, and that ambition might be awakened in her; but the result was quite different from what might have been anticipated. Consuelo left the theater, cold, silent, fatigued, and in no way excited by the noise and applause. Corilla was deficient in

solid talent, noble sentiment, and well-founded power; and
Consuelo felt quite competent to form an opinion of this
forced, factitious talent, already vitiated at its source by
selfishness and excess. She applauded unconsciously,
uttered words of formal approval, and disdained to put on
a mask of enthusiasm for one whom she could neither fear
nor admire. The count for a moment thought her under
the influence of secret jealousy of the talents, or at least
of the person, of the prima donna. "This is nothing,"
said he, "to the triumphs which you will achieve when
you appear before the public as you have already appeared
before me. I hope that you are not frightened by what
you see."

"No, Signor Count," replied Consuelo, smiling; "the
public frightens me not, for I never think of it. I only
think of what might be realized in the part which Corilla
fills in so brilliant a manner, but in which there are many
defects which she does not perceive."

"What! you do not think of the public?"

"No; I think of the piece, of the intentions of the composer, of the spirit of the part, and of the good qualities
and defects of the orchestra, from the former of which we
are to derive advantage, while we are to conceal the latter
by a louder intonation at certain parts. I listen to the
choruses, which are not always satisfactory, and require a
more strict direction; I examine the passages on which all
one's strength is required, and also those of course where
it may advantageously be reserved. You will perceive,
Signor Count, that I have many things to think of besides
the public, who know nothing about all that I have mentioned, and can teach me nothing."

This grave judgment and serious inquiry so surprised
Zustiniani that he could not utter a single question, and.
asked himself, with some trepidation, what hold a gallant
like himself could have on a genius of this stamp.

The appearance of the two débutants was preceded by
all the usual inflated announcements; and this was the
source of continual discussion and difference of opinion between the Count and Porpora, Consuelo and her lover. The
old master and his pupil blamed the quack announcements
and all those thousand unworthy tricks which have driven
us so far into folly and bad faith. In Venice, during those
days, the journals had not much to say as to public affairs;

they did not concern themselves with the composition of the audience; they were unaware of the deep resources of public advertisements, the gossip of biographical announcements, and the powerful machinery of hired applause. There was plenty of bribing, and not a few cabals, but all this was concocted in coteries, and brought about through the instrumentality of the public, warmly attached to one side, or sincerely hostile to the other. Art was not always the moving spring ; passions, great and small, foreign alike to art and talent, then as now, came to do battle in the temple; but they were not so skillful in concealing these sources of discord, and in laying them to the account of pure love for art. At bottom, indeed, it was the same vulgar, worldly spirit, with a surface less complicated by civilization.

Zustiniani managed these affairs more as a nobleman than as the conductor of a theater. His ostentation was a more powerful impulse than the avarice of ordinary speculators. He prepared the public in his saloons, and warmed up his representations beforehand. His conduct, it is true, was never cowardly or mean, but it bore the puerile stamp of self-love, a busy gallantry, and the pointed gossip of good society. He therefore proceeded to demolish, piece by piece, with considerable art, the edifice so lately raised by his own hands to the glory of Corilla. Every body saw that he wanted to set up in its place the miracle of talent; and as the exclusive possession of this wonderful phenomenon was ascribed to him, poor Consuelo never suspected the nature of his intentions toward her, although all Venice knew that the count, disgusted with the conduct of Corilla, was about to introduce in her place another singer; while many added, " Grand mystification for the public, and great prejudice to the theater; for his favorite is a little street singer, who has nothing to recommend her except her fine voice and tolerable figure."

Hence arose fresh cabals for Corilla, who went about playing the part of an injured rival, and who implored her extensive circle of adorers and their friends to do justice to the insolent pretensions of the *zingarella*. Hence, also new cabals in favor of Consuelo, by a numerous party, who, although differing widely on other subjects, united in a wish to mortify Corilla, and elevate her rival in her place.

As to the veritable dilettanti of music, they were equally

divided between the opinion of the serious masters—such as Porpora, Marcello, and Jomelli, who predicted, with the appearance of an excellent musician, the return of the good old usages and casts of performance — and the anger of second-rate composers, whose compositions Corilla had always preferred, and who now saw themselves threatened with neglect in her person. The orchestra, dreading to set to work on scores which had been long laid aside, and which consequently would require study, all those retainers of the theater, who in every thorough reform always foresaw an entire change of the performers, even the very scene-shifters, the tirewomen, and the hairdressers—all were in movement for or against the débutante at San Samuel. In point of fact the début was much more in every body's thoughts than the new administration or the acts of the Doge, Pietro Grimaldi, who had just then peaceably succeeded his predecessor, Luigi Pisani.

Consuelo was exceedingly distressed at these delays and the petty quarrels connected with her new career ; she would have wished to come out at once, without any other preparation than what concerned herself and the study of the new piece. She understood nothing of those endless intrigues which seemed to her more dangerous than useful, and which she felt she could very well dispense with. But the count, who saw more clearly into the secrets of his profession and who wished to be envied his imaginary happiness, spared nothing to secure partisans, and made her come every day to his palace to be presented to all the aristocracy of Venice. Consuelo's modesty and reluctance ill supported his designs; but he induced her to sing, and the victory was at once decisive—brilliant—incontestible.

Anzoleto was far from sharing the repugnance of his betrothed for these secondary means. His success was by no means so certain as hers. In the first place the count was not so ardent in his favor, and the tenor whom he was to succeed was a man of talent, who would not be easily forgotten. It is true he also sang nightly at the count's palace and Consuelo in their duets brought him out admirably; so that, urged and sustained by the magic of a genius superior to his own, he often attained great heights. He was on these occasions both encouraged and applauded; but when the first surprise excited by his fine voice was over, more especially when Consuelo had revealed herself, his deficiency was apparent and frightened even himself. This was the time to work with renewed vigor; but in vain Consuelo exhorted him and appointed him to meet her each morning in the Corte Minelli—where she persisted in remaining spite of the remonstrances of the count, who wished to establish her more suitably—Anzoleto had so much to do—so many visits, engagements and intrigues on hand — such distracting anxieties to occupy his mind—that neither time nor courage was left for study.

In the midst of these perplexities, seeing that the greatest opposition would be given by Corilla, and also that the count no longer gave himself any trouble about her, Anzoleto resolved to visit her himself in order to deprecate her hostility. As may easily be conceived, she had pretended to take the matter very lightly, and treated the neglect and contempt of Zustiniani with philosophical unconcern. She mentioned and boasted everywhere that she had received brilliant offers from the Italian opera at Paris, and calculating on the reverse which she thought awaited her rival, laughed outright at the illusions of the count and his party. Anzoleto thought that with prudence and by employing a little deceit, he might disarm this formidable enemy; and having perfumed and adorned himself, he waited on her at one in the afternoon —an hour when the siesta renders visits unusual, and the palaces silent.

CHAPTER XVII.

ANZOLETO found Corilla alone in a charming boudoir, reclining on a couch in a becoming undress ; but the alteration in her features by daylight, led him to suspect that her security with regard to Consuelo was not so great as her faithful partisans asserted. Nevertheless she received him with an easy air, and tapping him playfully on the cheek, while she made a sign to her servant to withdraw, exclaimed—" Ah, wicked one, is it you?—are you come with your tales, or would you make me believe you are no dealer in flourishes, nor the most intriguing of all the postulants for fame? You were somewhat conceited, my handsome friend, if you supposed that I should be disheartened by your sudden flight after so many tender declarations; and still more conceited was it to suppose that you were wanted, for in four-and-twenty hours I had forgotten that such a person existed."

"Four-and-twenty hours!—that is a long time," replied Anzoleto, kissing the plump and rounded arm of Corilla. "Ah! if I believed that, I should be proud indeed; but I know that if I was so far deceived as to believe you when you said——"

"What I said, I advise you to forget also. Had you called you would have found my door shut against you. What assurance to come to-day!"

"Is it not good taste to leave those who are in favor, and to lay one's heart and devotion at the feet of her who——"

"Well, finish—to her who is in disgrace. It is most generous and humane on your part, most illustrious friend!" And Corilla fell back upon the satin pillow with a burst of shrill and forced laughter.

Although the disgraced prima donna was no longer in her early freshness—although the mid-day sun was not much in her favor, and although vexation had somewhat taken from the effect of her full-formed features—Anzoleto, who had never been on terms of intimacy with a woman so brilliant and so renowned, felt himself moved in regions of the soul to which Consuela had never descended, and whence he had voluntarily banished her pure image. He therefore palliated the raillery of Corilla by a profession of love which he had only intended to feign, but which he now actually began to experience. I say love for want of a better word, for it were to profane the name to apply it to the attraction awakened by such women as Corilla. When she saw the young tenor really moved, she grew milder, and addressed him after a more amiable fashion. "I confess," said she, "you selected me for a whole evening, but I did not altogether esteem you. I know you are ambitious, and consequently false, and ready for every treason. I dare not trust to you. You pretended to be jealous on a certain night in my gondola, and took upon you the airs of a despot. That might have disenchanted me with the insipid gallantries of our patricians, but you deceived me, ungrateful one! you were engaged to another, and are going to marry—whom?—oh? I know very well—

my rival, my enemy, the débutante, the new protegée of Zustiniani. Shame upon us two—upon us three—upon us all !" added she, growing animated in spite of herself, and withdrawing her hand from Anzoleto. .

"Cruel creature !" he exclaimed, trying to regain her fair fingers, "you ought to understand what passed in my heart when I first saw you, and not busy yourself with what occupied me before that terrible moment. As to what happened since, can you not guess it, and is there any necessity to recur to the subject ?"

"I am not to be put off with half words and reservations ; do you love the *zingarella,* and are you about to marry her ?"

"And if I loved her, how does it happen I did not marry her before ?"

"Perhaps the count would have opposed it. Every one knows what he wants now. They even say that he has ground for impatience, and the little one still more so."

The color mounted to Anzoleto's face when he heard language of this sort applied to the being whom he venerated above all others.

"Ah, you are angry at my supposition," said Corilla ; "it is well—that is what I wished to find out. You love her. When will the marriage take place ?"

"For the love of Heaven, madam, let us speak of nobody except ourselves."

"Agreed," replied Corilla. "So, my former lover and your future spouse——"

Anzoleto was enraged ; he rose to go away, but what was he to do ? Should he enrage still more the woman whom he had come to pacify ? He remained undecided, dreadfully humiliated, and unhappy at the part he had imposed on himself.

Corilla eagerly desired to win his affections, not because she loved him, but because she wished to be revenged on Consuelo, whom she had abused without being certain that her insinuations were well founded.

"You see," said she, arresting him on the threshold with a penetrating look, "that I have reason to doubt you ; for at this moment you are deceiving some one—either her or myself."

"Neither one nor the other," replied he, endeavoring to justify himself in his own eyes. "I am not her lover, and

I never was so. I am not in love with her, for I am not jealous of the count."

" Oh ! indeed ? You are jealous even to the point of denying it, and you come here to cure yourself or distract your attention from a subject so unpleasant. Many thanks!"

"I am not jealous, I repeat ; and to prove that it is not mortification which makes me speak, I tell you that the count is no more her lover than I am ; that she is virtuous, child as she is, and that the only one guilty towards you is Count Zustiniani."

" So, so ; then I may hiss the *zingarella* without afflicting you. You shall be in my box on the night of her début, and you shall hiss her. Your obedience shall be the price of my favor—take me at my word, or I draw back."

" Alas! madam, you wish to prevent me appearing myself, for you know I am to do so at the same time as Consuelo. If you hiss her, I shall fall a victim to your wrath, because I shall sing with her. And what have I done, wretch that I am, to displease you? Alas! I had a delicious but fatal dream. I thought for a whole evening that you took an interest in me, and that I should grow great under your protection. Now I am the object of your hatred and anger — I, who have so loved and respected you as to fly you! Very well, madam ; satiate your enmity. Overthrow me—ruin me—close my career. So that you can here tell me, in secret, that I am not hateful to you, I shall accept the public marks of your anger."

" Serpent!" exclaimed Corilla, " where have you imbibed the poison which your tongue and your eyes distil? Much would I give to know, to comprehend you, for you are the most amiable of lovers and the most dangerous of enemies."

" I your enemy! how could I be so, even were I not subdued by your charms? Have you enemies then, divine Corilla? Can you have them in Venice, where you are known and where you rule over no divided empire? A love quarrel throws the count into despair ; he would remove you, since thereby he would cease to suffer. He meets a little creature in his path who appears to display resources, and who only asks to be heard. Is this a crime on the part of a poor child, who only hears your name with terror, and who never utters it herself without respect? And you ascribe to this little one insolent pretensions which she does not entertain. The efforts of the count to recommend her to his friends, the kindness of these friends, who exaggerate her deserts, the bitterness of yours, who spread calumnies which serve but to annoy and vex you, while they should but calm your soul in picturing to you your glory unassailable and your rival all trembling — these are the prejudices which I discover in you, and at which I am so confounded that I hardly know how to assail them."

"You know but too well, with that flattering tongue of yours," said Corilla, looking at him with tenderness mixed with distrust; "I hear the honeyed words which reason bids me disclaim. I wager that this Consuelo is divinely beautiful, whatever may have been said to the contrary, and that she has merits, though opposed to mine, since the severe Porpora has proclaimed them."

"You know Porpora; you know all his crotchety ideas. An enemy of all originality in others, and of every innovation in the art of song, he declares a little pupil, who listens to his dotage, submissive to his pedantry, and who runs over the scale decently, to be preferable to all the wonders which the public adores. How long have you tormented yourself about this crazy old fool?"

"She afraid? I was told, on the contrary, that she was gifted with rare impudence."

"Alas, poor girl! they do wish to ruin her then. You shall hear her, noble Corilla; you will be moved by a generous pity, and you will encourage instead of hissing her as you said just now in jest."

"Either you deceive me, or my friends have greatly deceived me with regard to her."

"Your friends have allowed themselves to be deceived. In their indiscreet zeal they have been terrified at seeing a rival raised up against you — terrified by a child! — terrified for you! Ah! those persons cannot love you much, since they appreciate you so little. Oh! if I had the happiness to be your friend, I should know better what you are, and I should not do you the injustice to be affrighted by any rivalry, were it even that of a Faustina or a Molteni."

"Do not believe that I have been frightened. I am neither jealous nor malicious; the success of others having never injured mine, I have never troubled myself about them. But when I think that they endeavor to brave me and to make me suffer "

"Do you wish me to bring the little Consuelo to your feet? If she had dared, she would already have come to ask your advice and your assistance. But she is so timid a child! and then they had calumniated you to her. They said to her also that you were cruel, vindictive, and that you reckoned confidently on her fall."

"Did they say that? Then I understand why you are here."

"No, madam, you do not understand; for I did not believe it an instant — I never shall believe it. Oh no, madam! you do not understand why."

In speaking thus, Anzoleto made his black eyes sparkle, and bent his knee before Corilla with an expression of profound respect and love.

"She is without talent then?"

"Why, she has a passable voice, and sings decently at church, but she can know nothing of the theater; and besides, she is so paralyzed with fear, that it is much to be dreaded she will lose the few resources that Heaven has given her."

Corilla was destitute neither of acuteness nor ill-nature; but as happens to women excessively taken with themselves, vanity sealed her eyes and precipitated her into the clumsy trap.

She thought she had nothing to apprehend as regarded Anzoleto's sentiments for the débutante. When he justified himself, and swore by all the gods that he had never loved this young girl, save as a brother should love, he told the truth, and there was so much confidence in his manner that Corilla's jealousy was overcome. At length the great day approached, and the cabal was annihilated. Corilla, on her part, thenceforth went on in a different direction, fully persuaded that the timid and inexperienced Consuelo would not succeed, and that Anzoleto would owe her an infinite obligation for having contributed nothing to her downfall. Besides, he had the address to embroil her with her firmest champions, pretending to be jealous, and obliging her to dismiss them rather rudely.

While he thus labored in secret to blast the hopes of a woman whom he pretended to love, the cunning Venetian played another game with the count and Consuelo. He boasted to them of having disarmed this most formidable enemy by dexterous management, interested visits, and bold falsehoods. The count, frivolous and somewhat of a gossip, was extremely amused by the stories of his protegé. His self-love was flattered at the regret which Corilla was said to experience on account of their quarrel, and he urged on this young man, with the levity which one witnesses in affairs of love and gallantry, to the commission of cowardly perfidy. Consuelo was astonished and distressed. "You would do better," said she, "to exercise your voice and study your part. You think you have done much in propitiating the enemy, but a single false note, a movement badly expressed, would do more against you with the impartial public than the silence of the envious. It is of this public that you should think, and I see with pain that you are thinking nothing about it."

"Be calm, little Consuelo," said he ; "your error is to believe a public at once impartial and enlightened. Those best acquainted with the matter are hardly ever in earnest, and those who are in earnest know so little about it, that it only requires boldness to dazzle and lead them away."

CHAPTER XVIII.

IN the **midst of** the anxieties awakened by the desire of success and by the ardor of Corilla, the jealousy of Anzoleto with regard to the count slumbered. Happily Consuelo did not need a more watchful or more moral protector. Secure in innocence, she avoided the advances of Zustiniani, and kept him at a distance precisely by caring nothing about it. At the end of a fortnight this Venetian libertine acknowledged that she had none of those worldly passions which lead to corruption, though he spared no pains to make them spring up. But even in this respect he had advanced no further than the first day, and he feared to ruin his hopes by pressing them too openly. Had Anzoleto annoyed him by keeping watch, anger might have caused him to precipitate matters; but Anzoleto left him at perfect liberty. Consuelo distrusted nothing, and he only tried to make himself agreeable, hoping in time to become necessary to her. There was no sort of delicate attentions, or refined gallantries, that he omitted. Consuelo placed them all to the account of the liberal and elegant manners of his class, united with a love for art and a natural goodness of disposition. She displayed toward him an unfeigned regard, a sacred gratitude, while he, happy and yet dissatisfied with this pure-hearted unreserve, began to grow uneasy at the sentiment which he inspired until such period as he might wish to break the ice.

While he gave himself up with fear, and yet not without satisfaction, to this new feeling—consoling himself a little for his want of success by the opinion which all Venice entertained of his triumph—Corilla experienced the same transformation in herself. She loved with ardor, if not with devotion; and her irritable and imperious soul bent beneath the yoke of her young Adonis. It was truly the queen of beauty in love with the beautiful hunter, and for the first time humble and timid before the mortal of her choice. She affected, with a sort of delight, virtues which she did not possess. So true it is that the extinction of self-idolatry in favor of another, tends to raise and ennoble, were it but for an instant, hearts the least susceptible of pure emotions.

The emotion which she experienced reacted on her talents, and it was remarked at the theater that she performed pathetic parts more naturally and with greater sensibility. But as her character and the essence of her nature were thus as it seemed inverted, as it required a sort of internal convulsion to effect this change, her bodily strength gave way in the combat, and each day they observed—some with malicious joy, others with serious alarm—the failure of her powers. Her brilliant execution was impeded by shortness of breath and false intonations. The annoyance and terror which she experienced weakened her still further, and at the representation which took place previous to the début of Consuelo, she sang so false, and failed in so many brilliant passages, that her friends applauded faintly, and were soon reduced to silence and consternation by the murmurs of her opponents.

At length the great day arrived ; the house was filled to suffocation. Corillo, attired in black, pale, agitated, more dead than alive, divided between the fear of seeing her lover condemned and her rival triumph, was seated in the recess of her little box in the theater. Crowds of the aristocracy and beauty of Venice, tier above tier, made a brilliant display. The fops were crowded behind the scenes, and even in the front of the stage. The lady of the Doge took her place along with the great dignitaries of the republic. Porpora directed the orchestra in person; and Count Zustiniani waited at the door of Consuelo's apartment till she had concluded her toilet, while Anzoleto, dressed as an antique warrior, with all the absurd and lavish ornament of the age, retired behind the scenes to swallow a draught of Cyprus wine, in order to restore his courage.

The opera was neither of the classic period nor yet the work of an innovator. It was the unknown production of a stranger. To escape the cabals which his own name or that of any other celebrated person would have caused, Porpora, above all things anxious for the success of his pupil, had brought forward *Ipermnestra*, the lyrical production of a young German, who had enemies neither in Italy nor elsewhere, and who was styled simply Christopher Gluck.

When Anzoleto appeared on the stage a murmur of admiration burst forth. The tenor to whom he succeeded—an admirable singer, who had had the imprudence to continue on the boards till his voice became thin and age had changed his looks—was little regretted by an ungrateful public; and the fair sex, who listened oftener with their eyes than with their ears, were delighted to find, in place of a fat elderly man, a fine youth of twenty-four, fresh as a rose, fair as Phœbus, and formed as if Phidias himself had been the artist—a true son of the lagunes, *Bianco, crespo e grassotto.*

He was too much agitated to sing his first air well, but his magnificent voice, his graceful attitudes, and some happy turns, sufficed to propitiate the audience and satisfy the ladies. The débutant had great resources; he was applauded threefold, and twice brought back before the scenes, according to the custom of Italy, and of Venice in particular.

Success gave him courage, and when he re-appeared with Ipermnestra, he was no longer afraid. But all the effect of this scene was for Consuelo. They only saw, only listened to her. They said to each other, "Look at her—yes, it is she!" "Who? the Spaniard?" "Yes—the débutante, *l'amante del Zustiniani.*"

Consuelo entered, self-possessed and serious. Casting her eyes around she received the plaudits of the spectators with a propriety of manner equally devoid of humility and coquetry, and sang a recitative with so firm a voice, with accents so lofty, and a self-possession so victorious, that cries of admiration from the very first resounded from every part of the theater. "Ah! the perfidious creature has deceived me," exclaimed Corilla, darting a terrible look toward Anzoleto, who could not resist raising his eyes to hers with an ill-disguised smile. She threw herself back upon her seat, and burst into tears.

Consuelo proceeded a little further; while old Lotti was heard muttering with his cracked voice from his corner, "*Amici miei, questo è un portento!*"

She sang a bravura, and was ten times interrupted. They shouted "Encore!" they recalled her to the stage seven times amid thunders of applause. At length the furor of Venetian dilettantism displayed itself in all its ridiculous and absurd excess. "Why do they cry out thus?" said Consuelo, as she retired behind the scenes only to be brought back immediately by the vociferous applause of the pit. "One would think that they wished to stone me."

From that moment they paid but a secondary attention to Anzoleto. They received him very well indeed, because they were in a happy vein; but the indulgence with which they passed over the passages in which he failed, without immediately applauding those in which he succeeded, showed him very plainly, that however he might please the women, the noisy majority of males held him cheaply, and reserved their tempestuous applause for the prima donna. Not one among all those who had come with hostile intentions, ventured a murmur, and in truth there were not three among them who could withstand the irresistible inclination to applaud the wonder of the day.

The piece had the greatest success, although it was not listened to, and nobody was occupied with the music in itself. It was quite in the Italian style—graceful, touching, and gave no indication of the author of *Alcestes* and *Orpheus*. There were not many striking beauties to astonish the audience. After the first act, the German maestro was called for, with Anzoleto, the débutante, and Clorinda, who, thanks to the protection of Consuelo, had sung through the second part with a flat voice and an inferior tone, but whose beautiful arms propitiated the spectators—Rosalba, whom she had replaced, being very lean.

In the last act, Anzoleto, who secretly watched Corilla and perceived her increasing agitation, thought it prudent to seek her in her box, in order to avert any explosion. So soon as she perceived him she threw herself upon him like a tigress, bestowed several vigorous cuffs, the least of which was so smart as to draw blood, leaving a mark that red and white could not immediately cover. The angry tenor settled matters by a thrust on the breast, which threw the singer gasping into the arms of her sister Rosalba. "Wretch! traitor!" she murmured in a choking voice, "your Consuelo and you shall perish by my hand!"

"If you make a step, a movement, a single gesture, I will stab you in the face of Venice," replied Anzoleto, pale and with clenched teeth, while his faithful knife, which he knew how to use with all the dexterity of a man of the lagunes, gleamed before her eyes.

"He would do as he says," murmured the terrified Rosalba; "be silent—let us leave this: we are here in danger of our lives."

Although this tragi-comic scene had taken place after the manner of the Venetians, in a mysterious and rapid *sotto voce*, on seeing the débutant pass quickly behind the scenes to regain his box, his cheek hidden in his hand, they suspected some petty squabble. The hairdresser, who was called to adjust the curls of the Grecian prince and to plaster up his wound, related to the whole band of choristers that an armorous cat had sunk her claw into the face of the hero. The aforesaid barber was accustomed to this kind of wounds, and was no new confident of such adventures. The anecdote made the round of the stage, penetrated, no one knew how, into the body of the house, found its way into the orchestra, the boxes, and, with some additions, descended to the pit. They were not yet aware of the position of Anzoleto with regard to Corilla; but some had noticed his apparent devotion to Clorinda, and the general report was, that the *seconda donna*, jealous of the *prima donna*, had just blackened the eye and broken three teeth of the handsomest of tenors.

This was sad news for some, but an exquisite bit of

scandal for the majority. They wondered if the representation would be put off, or whether the old tenor, Stefanini, should have to appear, roll in hand, to finish the part. The curtain rose, and every thing was forgotten on seeing Consuelo appear, calm and sublime as at the beginning. Although her part was not extremely tragical, she made it so by the power of her acting and the expression of her voice. She called forth tears, and when the tenor reappeared, the slight scratch only excited a smile; but this absurd incident prevented his success from being so brilliant, and all the glory of the evening was reserved for Consuelo, who was applauded to the last with frenzy.

After the play, they went to sup at the Palace Zustiniani, and Anzoleto forgot Corilla, whom he had shut up in her box, and who was forced to burst it open in order to leave it. In the tumult which always follows so successful a representation, her retreat was not noticed ; but the next day, this broken door coincided so well with the torn face of Anzoleto, that the love affair, hitherto so carefully concealed, was made known.

Hardly was he seated at the sumptuous banquet which the count gave in honour of Consuelo, and while all the Venetian dilettanti handed to the triumphant actress sonnets and madrigals composed the evening before, when a valet slipped under his plate a little billet from Corilla, which he read aside, and which was to the following effect:

"If you do not come to me this instant, I shall go to seek you openly, were you even at the end of the world—were you even at the feet of your Consuelo, thrice accursed."

Anzoleto pretended to be seized with a fit of coughing, and retired to write an answer with a pencil on a piece of ruled paper which he had torn in the antechamber of the count from a music-book:

" Come if you will. My knife is ready, and with it my scorn and hatred."

The despot was well aware that with such a creature fear was the only restraint—that threats were the only expedient at the moment; but in spite of himself he was gloomy and absent during the repast, and as soon as it was over he hurried off to go to Corilla.

He found the unhappy girl in a truly pitiable condition,

Convulsions were followed by torrents of tears. She was seated at the window, her hair dishevelled, her eyes swollen with weeping, and her dress disordered. She sent away her sister and maid, and in spite of herself, a ray of joy overspread her features, at finding herself with him whom she had feared she might never see again. But Anzoleto knew her too well to seek to comfort her. He knew that at the first appearance of pity or repentance he would see her fury revive, and seize upon revenge. He resolved to keep up the appearance of inflexible harshness; and although he was moved with her despair, he overwhelmed her with cruel reproaches, declaring that he was only come to bid her an eternal farewell. He suffered her to throw herself at his feet, to cling by his knees even to the door, and to implore his pardon in the anguish of grief. When he had thus subdued and humbled her, he pretended to be somewhat moved, and promising to return in the morning, he left her.

CHAPTER XIX.

WHEN Anzoleto awoke the following morning, he experienced a reverse of the jealousy with which Count Zustiniani had inspired him. A thousand opposing sentiments divided his soul. First, that other jealousy which the genius and success of Consuelo had awakened in his bosom. This sank the deeper in his breast in proportion as he measured the triumph of his betrothed with what in his blighted ambition he was pleased to call his downfall. Again the mortification of being supplanted in reality, as he was already thought to be, with her, now so triumphant and powerful, and of whom the preceding evening he was so pleased to believe himself the only lover. These two feelings possessed him by turns, and he knew not to which to give himself up in order to extinguish the other. He had to chose between two things, either to remove Consuelo from the count and from Venice, and along with her to seek his fortune elsewhere, or to abandon her to his rival, and take his chance alone in some distant country with no drawback to his success. In this poignant uncertainty, in place of endeavoring to recover his calmness with his true friend, he returned to Corilla, and plunged back into the storm. She added fuel to the flame, by showing him, in even stronger colors than he had imagined the preceding night, all the disadvantages of his position. "No person," said she, "is a prophet in his own country. This is a bad place for one who has been seen running about in rags, and where every one may say—(and God knows the nobles are sufficiently given to boast of the protection, even when it is only imaginary, which they accord to artists)—' I was his protector; I saw his hidden talent; it was I who recommended and gave him a preference.' You have lived too much in public here, my poor Anzoleto. Your charming features struck those who knew not what was in you. You astonished people who have seen you in their gondolas singing the stanzas of Tasso, or doing their errands to gain the means of support. The plain Consuelo, leading a retired life, appears here as a strange wonder. Besides she is a Spaniard, and uses not the Venetian accent; and her agreeable, though somewhat singular pronunciation, would please them, even were it detestable. It is something of which their ears are not tired. Your good looks have contributed mainly to the slight success you obtained in the first act, but now people are accustomed to you."

"Do not forget to mention that the handsome scratch you gave me beneath the eye, and for which I ought never to pardon you, will go far to lessen the last-mentioned trifling advantage."

"On the contrary, it is a decided advantage in the eyes of women, but frivolous in those of men. You will reign in the saloons with the one party; without the other you would fall at the theater. But how can you expect to occupy their attention, when it is a woman who disputes it with you—a woman who not only enthrals the serious dilettanti, but who intoxicates by her grace and the magic of her sex, all who are not connoisseurs in music. To struggle with me, how much talent did Stefanini, Savario —all indeed who have appeared with me on the stage require."

"In that case, dear Corilla, I should run as much risk in appearing with you as with Consuelo. If I were inclined to follow you to France, you have given me fair warning."

These words which escaped from Anzoleto were as a ray

of light to Corilla. She saw that she had hit the mark more nearly than she had supposed, for the thought of leaving Venice had already dawned in the mind of her lover. The instant she conceived the idea of bearing him away with her, she spared no pains to make him relish the project. She humbled herself as much as she could, and even had the modesty to place herself below her rival. She admitted that she was not a great singer, nor yet sufficiently beautiful to attract the public; and as all this was even truer than she cared to think, and as Anzoleto was very well aware of it, having never been deceived as to the immense superiority of Consuelo, she had little trouble in persuading him. Their partnership and flight were almost determined upon at this interview, and Anzoleto thought seriously of it, although he always kept a loop-hole for escape if necessary.

Corilla, seeing his uncertainty, urged him to continue to appear, in hopes of better success; but quite sure that these unlucky trials would disgust him altogether with Venice and with Consuelo.

On leaving his fair adviser, he went to seek his only real friend, Consuelo. He felt an unconquerable desire to see her again. It was the first time he had begun and ended a day without receiving her chaste kiss upon his brow; but as, after what had passed with Corilla, he would have blushed for his own instability, he persuaded himself that he only went to receive assurance of her unfaithfulness, and to undeceive himself as to his love for her. "Doubtless," said he, "the count has taken advantage of my absence to urge his suit, and who can tell how far he has been successful?" This idea caused a cold perspiration to stand upon his forehead; and the thought of Consuelo's perfidy so affected him that he hastened his steps, thinking to find her bathed in tears. Then an inward voice, which drowned every other, told him that he wronged a being so pure and noble, and he slackened his pace, reflecting on his own odious conduct, his selfish ambition, and the deceit and treachery with which he had stored his life and conscience, and which must inevitably bear their bitter fruit.

He found Consuelo in her black dress seated beside her table, pure, serene, and tranquil, as he had ever beheld her. She came forward to meet him with the same affection as ever, and questioned him with anxiety, but without distrust or reproach, as to the employment of his time during his absence.

"I have been suffering," said he, with the very deep despondency which his inward humiliation had occasioned. "I hurt my head against a decoration, and although I told you it was nothing, it so confused me that I was obliged to leave the Palazzo Zustiniani last night lest I should faint and have to keep my bed all morning."

"Oh, Heavens!" said Consuelo, kissing the wound inflicted by her rival; "you have suffered, and still suffer."

"No, the rest has done me good; do not think of it; but tell me how you managed to get home all alone last night."

"Alone? Oh, no; the count brought me in his gondola."

"Ah, I was sure of it," cried Anzoleto, in a constrained voice. "And of course he said a great many flattering things to you in this interview."

"What could he say that he had not already said a hundred times? He would spoil me and make me vain were I not on my guard against him. Beside, we were not alone; my good master accompanied me—ah! my excellent friend and master."

"What master?—what excellent friend?" said Anzoleto, once more reassured, and already absent and thoughtful.

"Why, Porpora, to be sure. What are you thinking of?"

"I am thinking, dear Consuelo, of your triumph yesterday evening; are you not thinking of it too?"

"Less than of yours, I assure you."

"Mine! ah, do not jest, dear friend; mine was so meager that it rather resembled a downfall."

Consuelo grew pale with surprise. Notwithstanding her remarkable self-possession, she had not the necessary coolness to appreciate the different degree of applause bestowed on herself and her lover. There is in this sort of ovation an intoxication which the wisest artists cannot shun, and which deceives some so widely as to induce them to look upon the support of a cabal as a public triumph. But instead of exaggerating the delight of her audience, Consuelo, terrified by so frightful a noise, had hardly understood it, and could not distinguish the preference awarded to her over Anzoleto. She artlessly chid him for his unreasonable expectations; and seeing that she could not persuade him nor conquer his sadness, she gently re-proached him with being too desirous of glory, and with attaching too much value to the favor of the world. "I have always told you," said she, "that you prefer the re-sults of art to art itself. When we do our best—when we feel that we have done well—it seems to me that a little more or less of approbation can neither add to nor dimin-ish our inward satisfaction. Recollect what Porpora said to me the first time I sang at the Zustiniani palace: 'Who-ever is penetrated with a true love of his art need fear nothing——.'"

"You and your Porpora," interrupted Anzoleto, with some heat, "can very easily satisfy yourselves with these fine maxims. Nothing is so easy as to philosophize on the evils of life when you know only its sweets. Porpora, although poor and oppressed, has an illustrious name. He has gathered so many laurels that his old head may whiten peaceably under their shade. You, who feel yourself in-vincible, are inaccessible to fear. At the first leap you raise yourself to the highest round of the ladder, and blame those who have no legs for their dizziness. That is not only uncharitable, Consuelo, but decidedly unjust. And besides, your argument is not applicable to me; you say that we should despise the approbation of the public when we have our own; but if I possess not that inward testimony of having done well, what then? Can you not see that I am horribly dissatisfied with myself? Did you not hear that I was detestable? Did you not hear that I sang miserably?"

"No; for it was not so. You neither exceeded nor fell short of yourself. The emotion which you experienced hardly at all diminished your powers. Besides, it was quickly dissipated, and those things which you knew well you expressed well."

"And those which I did not know?" said Anzoleto, fixing upon her his large black eyes, rendered hollow by fatigue and anxiety.

She sighed and remained for an instant silent; then she said, embracing him: "Those which you do not know you must learn. If you had been only willing to study be-tween the rehearsals, as I recommended—but this is not the time to reproach you; on the contrary, it is the time to repair all. Come, let us take only two hours a day, and you will see how soon we shall triumph over the obstacles which oppose your success."

"Will it then be the work of one day?"

"It will be the work of some months at most."

"And I play to-morrow! I continue to appear before an audience which judges me by my defects much more than by my good qualities."

"But which will quickly perceive your progress."

"Who knows? If they take an aversion to me?"

"They have proved the contrary."

"So then you think they have been indulgent to me?"

"Well, yes; they have, my friend. In those places where you were weak, they were kind; where you were strong, they did you justice."

"But, in the meanwhile, I shall have a miserable engagement."

"The count is magnificent in all his dealings, and does not spare money. Besides, has he not offered me more than enough to maintain us both in opulence?"

"Ah! there it is! I shall live by your success!"

"I have lived long enough by your favor."

"But it is not money that I refer to. If he does engage me at a small salary, that is of little consequence; but he will engage me for the second and third parts."

"He has no other *primo uomo* * at hand. For a long time past he has relied and depended upon you. Besides, he is all in your favor. You said he would be opposed to our marriage. Far from that, he seems to wish it, and often asks me when I will invite him to my wedding."

"Ah, very good! very good, indeed! Many thanks, Signor Count."

"What do you mean by that?"

"Nothing. Only, Consuelo, you were very wrong not to prevent my appearance until my faults, with which you were so well acquainted, were corrected by more mature study. For, I repeat it, you knew my faults."

"Did I not speak openly to you? Have I not often warned you? But you always told me that the public did not understand; and when I saw the success you had at the count's palace the first time you sang there, I thought——"

First man as *prima donna* is *first lady*.

"That the people of fashion knew no more than the vulgar public."

"I thought that your good qualities would be more striking than your faults; and it has been so, it seems to me, with one as well as with the other."

"In fact," thought Anzoleto, "she speaks truly, and if I could put off my engagement—but then I run the risk of seeing a tenor take my place who would not give it back to me."

"Let me see," said he, after taking several turns up and down the apartment; "what are my faults?"

"What I have often told you : too much boldness, and not sufficient preparation ; an energy more feverish than sustained ; dramatic effects, which are the work of the will rather than of emotion. You were not imbued with the feeling of your part as a whole. You learned it by fragments. You saw in it only a succession of pieces more or less brilliant, and you did not seize either the gradation, or the development, or the aggregate. In your anxiety to display your fine voice and the facility which you possess in certain respects, you exhibit the whole extent of your powers almost on your entrance upon the scene. On the slightest opportunity you endeavored after effect, and all your effects were alike. At the end of the first act they knew you—ay, knew you by heart ; but they did not know that that was all, and still expected something prodigious for the end. That something was not in you. Your emotion was expended, and your voice had no longer the same freshness. You felt this, you forced both the one and the other; the audience felt it likewise, and to your great surprise remained unmoved when you considered yourself most pathetic. The reason was, that at that moment they did not see the artist inspired by passion, but the actor laboring for success."

"And how do others do?" cried Anzoleto, stamping his foot. "Have I not heard them all—all who have been applauded at Venice during the last ten years? Did not old Stefanini scream when his voice failed him? And yet they applauded him with transport."

"It is true, and I do not understand how the people could be so deceived. Without doubt they recollected the time when he had more power, and did not wish to hurt his feelings in his old age."

"And Corilla too, that idol whom you overthrew, did not she strain after effect?—did she not make efforts which were painful to see and to hear? Was she really excited when they applauded her to the skies?"

"It was because I considered her method factitious, her effects detestable, her playing as well as her singing destitute of taste and grandeur, that I presented myself so calmly upon the stage, persuaded, like you, that the public knew little about it."

"Ah!" said Anzoleto, with a deep sigh, "there you put your finger upon my wound, my poor Consuelo."

"How is that, my well beloved?"

"How is that? do you ask me? We deceived ourselves, Consuelo. The public does know. The heart teaches what ignorance conceals. It is an overgrown child, who requires to be amused and excited. It is contented with what is given it, but show it something better, and then it compares and understands. Corilla could charm it last week, although she sung false and wanted breath. You appear, and Corilla is lost, effaced, buried. Let her re-appear, and she would be hissed. If I had made my *début* after her, I should have had complete success, as I had at the count's the first time I sang after her. But beside you I was eclipsed. It ought to be so, and it always will be so. The public had a taste for tinsel—it mistook paste for precious stones—it was dazzled by it. It is shown a diamond of the first water, and already it cannot understand how it could have been so grossly deceived. It can no longer endure false diamonds, and holds them at their true value. This is my misfortune, Consuelo, that I was brought in comparison with you, like a piece of Venetian glass beside a pearl of the fathomless ocean."

Consuelo did not understand all the bitterness and truth contained in these observations. She placed them to the account of her betrothed's affection, and answered to what she considered soft flatteries only by smiles and caresses. She pretended that he would surpass her if he would only take pains, and raised his courage by persuading him that nothing was easier than to sing like her. In this she was perfectly sincere, having never been retarded by any difficulty, and not knowing that labor itself is the first of obstacles for him who has not the love of it united with perseverance.

CHAPTER XX.

ENCOURAGED by Consuelo's frankness and by the faithless Corilla's perfidy, to present himself once more in public, Anzoleto began to work vigorously, so that at the second representation of *Ipermnestra* he sang much better. But as the success of Consuelo was proportionably greater, he was still dissatisfied, and began to feel discouraged by this confirmation of his inferiority. Every thing from this moment wore a sinister aspect. It appeared to him that they did not listen to him—that the spectators who were near him were making humiliating observations upon his singing—and that benevolent amateurs, who encouraged him behind the scenes, did so with an air of pity. Their praises seemed to have a double meaning, of which he applied the less favorable to himself. Corilla, whom he went to consult in her box between the acts, pretended to ask him with a frightened air if he were not ill.

" Why?" said he, impatiently.

" Because your voice is dull, and you seem overcome. Dear Anzoleto, strive to regain your powers, which were paralyzed by fear or discouragement."

" Did I not sing my first air well?"

" Not half so well as on the first occasion. My heart sank so that I found myself on the point of fainting."

"But the audience applauded me, nevertheless."

" Alas ! what does it signify? I was wrong to dispel your illusion. Continue then; but endeavor to clear your voice."

" Consuelo," thought he, " meant to give me good advice. She acts from instinct, and succeeds. But where could I gain the experience which would enable me to restrain the unruly public? In following her counsel I lose my own natural advantages: and they reckon nothing on the improvement of my style. Come, let me return to my early confidence. At my first appearance at the count's, I saw that I could dazzle those whom I failed to persuade. Did not old Porpora tell me that I had the blemishes of genius. Come, then, let me bend this public to my dictation, and make it bow to the yoke."

He exerted himself to the utmost, achieved wonders in

the second act, and was listened to with surprise. Some clapped their hands, others imposed silence, while the majority inquired whether it were sublime or detestable.

A little more boldness, and Anzoleto might perhaps have won the day; but this reverse affected him so much that he became confused, and broke down shamefully in the remainder of his part.

At the third representation he had resumed his confidence, and resolved to go on in his own way. Not heeding the advice of Consuelo, he hazarded the wildest caprices, the most daring absurdities. Cries of "oh, shame!" mingled with hisses, once or twice interrupted the silence with which these desperate attempts were received. The good and generous public silenced the hisses, and began to applaud; but it was easy to perceive the kindness was for the person, the blame for the artist. Anzoleto tore his dress on re-entering his box, and scarcely had the representation terminated, than he flew to Corilla, a prey to the deepest rage, and resolved to fly with her to the ends of the earth.

Three days passed without his seeing Consuelo. She inspired him neither with hatred nor coldness, but merely with terror; for in the depths of a soul pierced with remorse, he still cherished her image, and suffered cruelly from not seeing her. He felt the superiority of a being who overwhelmed him in public with her superiority, but who secretly held possession of his confidence and his good-will. In his agitation he betrayed to Corilla how truly he was bound to his noble-hearted betrothed, and what an empire she held over his mind. Corilla was mortified, but knew how to conceal it. She pitied him, elicited a confession, and so soon as she had learned the secret of his jealousy, she struck a grand blow, by making Zustiniani aware of their mutual affection, thinking that the count would immediately acquaint Consuelo, and thus render a reconciliation impossible.

Surprised to find another day pass away in the solitude of her garret, Consuelo grew uneasy; and as still another day of mortal anguish and vain expectation drew to its close, she wrapped herself in a thick mantle, for the famous singer was no longer sheltered by her obscurity, and ran to the house occupied for some weeks by Anzoleto, a more comfortable abode than what he had before enjoyed, and one of the numerous houses which the count possessed in the city. She did not find him, and learned that he was seldom there.

This did not enlighten her as to his infidelity. She knew his wandering and poetic habits, and thought that, not feeling at home in these sumptuous abodes, he had returned to his old quarters. She was about to continue her search, when, on returning to pass the door a second time, she found herself face to face with Porpora.

"Consuelo," said he in a low voice, "it is useless to hide from me your features. I have just heard your voice, and cannot be mistaken in it. What do you here at this hour, my poor child, and whom do you seek in this house?"

"I seek my betrothed," replied Consuelo, while she passed her arm within that of her old master; "and I do not know why I should blush to confess it to my best friend. I see very well that you disapprove of my attachment, but I could not tell an untruth. I am unhappy; I have not seen Anzoleto since the day before yesterday at the theater; he must be unwell."

"He unwell!" said the professor, shrugging his shoulders. "Come, my poor girl, we must talk over this matter; and since you have at last opened your heart to me, I must open mine also. Give me your arm; we can converse as we go along. Listen, Consuelo, and attend earnestly to what I say. You cannot—you ought not—to be the wife of this young man. I forbid you, in the name of God, who has inspired me with the feelings of a father toward you."

"Oh, my master," replied Consuelo, mournfully, "ask of me the sacrifice of my life, but not that of my love."

"I do not ask it—I command it," said Porpora, firmly. "The lover is accursed—he will prove your torment and your shame, if you do not forswear him for ever."

"Dear master," replied she, with a sad and tender smile, "you have told me so very often—I have endeavored in vain to obey you. You dislike this poor youth; you do not know him, and I am certain you will alter your mind."

"Consuelo," said the master, more decidedly, "I have till now, I know, made vain and useless objections. I spoke to you as an artist, and as to an artist, as I only saw one in your betrothed. Now I speak to you as a man—I speak to you of a man—and I address you as a woman. This woman's love is wasted; the man is unworthy of it, and he who tells you so knows he speaks the truth."

"Oh, Heavens! Anzoleto—my only friend, my protector, my brother—unworthy of my love! Ah, you do not know what he has done for me; how he has cared for me since I was left alone in the world. I must tell you all;" and Consuelo related the history of her life and of her love, and it was one and the same history.

Porpora was affected, but not shaken from his purpose.

"In all this," said he, "I see nothing but your innocence, your virtue, your fidelity. As to him, I see very well that he has need of your society and your instructions, to which, whatever you may think, he owes the little that he knows and the little he is worth. It is not, however, the less true, that this pure and upright lover is no better than a castaway—that he spends his time and money in low dissipation—and only thinks of turning you to the best account in forwarding his career."

"Take heed to what you say," replied Consuelo, in suffocating accents. "I have always believed in you, O my master! after God; but as to what concerns Anzoleto, I have resolved to close my heart and my ears. Ah, suffer me to leave you," she added, taking her arm from the professor—"it is death to listen to you."

"Let it be death then to your fatal passion, and through the truth let me restore you to life," he said, pressing her arm to his generous and indignant breast. "I know that I am rough, Consuelo—I cannot be otherwise; and therefore it is that I have put off as long as I could the blow which I am about to inflict. I had hoped that you would open your eyes, in order that you might comprehend what was going on around you. But in place of being enlightened by experience, you precipitate yourself blindly into the abyss. I will not suffer you to do so — you, the only one for whom I have cared for many years. You must not perish—no, you must not perish."

"But, my kind friend, I am in no danger. Do you believe that I tell an untruth when I assure you by all that is sacred that I have respected my mother's wishes? I am not Anzoleto's wife, but I am his betrothed."

"And you were seeking this evening the man who may not and cannot be your husband."

" Who told you so?"

" Would Corilla ever permit him?"

"Corilla!—what has he to say to Corilla?"

" We are but a few paces from this girl's abode. Do you seek your betrothed ? If you have courage you will find him there."

" No, no! a thousand times no!" said Consuelo, tottering as she went, and leaning for support against the wall. " Let me live, my master—do not kill me ere I have well begun to live. I told you that it was death to listen to you."

"You must drink of the cup," said the inexorable old man ; " I but fulfill your destiny. Having only realized ingratitude, and consequently made the objects of my tenderness and attention unhappy, I must say the truth to those I love. It is the only thing a heart long withered and rendered callous by suffering and despair can do. I pity you, poor girl, in that you have not a friend more gentle and humane to sustain you in such a crisis. But such as I am I must be ; I must act upon others, if not as with the sun's genial heat, with the lightning's blasting power. So then, Consuelo, let there be no paltering between us. Come to this palace. You must surprise your faithless lover at the feet of the treacherous Corilla. If you cannot walk, I must drag you along — if you cannot stand, I shall carry you. Ah, old Porpora is yet strong, when the fire of Divine anger burns in his heart!"

" Mercy, mercy!" exclaimed Consuelo, pale as death. " Suffer me yet to doubt. Give me a day, were it but a single day, to believe in him — I am not prepared for this infliction."

" No, not a day—not a single hour!" replied he inflexibly. " Away! I shall not be able to recall the passing hour, to lay the truth open to you ; and the faithless one will take advantage of the day which you ask, to place you again under the dominion of falsehood. Come with me— I command you—I insist on it."

" Well, I will go!" exclaimed Consuelo, regaining strength, through a violent reaction of her love. " I will go, were it only to demonstrate your injustice and the truth of my lover ; for you deceive yourself unworthily, as you would also deceive me. Come, then, executioner as you are, I shall follow, for I do not fear you."

Porpora took her at her word; and seizing her with a hand of iron, he conducted her to the mansion which he inhabited. Having passed through the corridors and mounted the stairs, they reached at last a terrace whence they could distinguish over the roof of a lower building, completely unhabited, the palace of Corilla, entirely darkened with the exception of one lighted window, which opened upon the somber and silent front of the deserted house. Any one at this window might suppose that no person could see them; for the balcony prevented any one from seeing up from below. There was nothing level with it, and above, nothing but the cornice of the house which Porpora inhabited, and which was not placed so as to command the palace of the singer. But Corilla was ignorant that there was at the angle a projection covered with lead, a sort of recess concealed by a large chimney, where the maestro with artistic caprice came every evening to gaze at the stars, shun his fellows, and dream of sacred or dramatic subjects. Chance had thus revealed to him the intimacy of Anzoleto with Corilla, and Consuelo had only to look in the direction pointed out, to discover her lover in a tender tête-à-tête with her rival. She instantly turned away; and Porpora, who, dreading the effects of the sight upon her, had held her with superhuman strength, led her to a lower story into his apartments, shutting the door and window to conceal the explosion which he anticipated.

CHAPTER XXI.

But there was no explosion. Consuelo remained silent, and as it were stunned. Porpora spoke to her. She made no reply, and signed to him not to question her. She then rose, and going to a large pitcher of iced water which stood on the harpsichord, swallowed great draughts of it, took several turns up and down the apartment, and sat down before her master without uttering a word.

The austere old man did not comprehend the extremity of her sufferings.

"Well," said he, "did I deceive you? What do you think of doing?"

A painful shudder shook her motionless figure — she passed her hand over her forehead.

"I can think of nothing," said she, "till I understand
what has happened to me."

"And what remains to be understood?"

"Every thing! because I understand nothing. I am
seeking for the cause of my misfortune without finding
any thing to explain it to me. What have I done to
Anzoleto that he should cease to love me? What fault
have I committed to render me unworthy in his eyes?
You cannot tell me, for I search into my own heart and can
find there no key to the mystery. O! it is inconceivable.
My mother believed in the power of charms. Is Corilla a
magician?"

"My poor child," said the maestro, "there is indeed a
magician, but she is called Vanity; there is indeed a poison,
which is called Envy. Corilla can dispense it, but it was
not she who molded the soul so fitted for its reception.
The venom already flowed in the impure veins of Anzoleto.
An extra dose has changed him from a knave into a traitor
—faithless as well as ungrateful."

"What vanity, what envy?"

"The vanity of surpassing others. The desire to excel,
and rage at being surpassed by you."

"Is that credible? Can a man be jealous of the advantages of a woman? Can a lover be displeased with the
success of his beloved? Alas! there are indeed many
things which I neither know nor understand."

"And will never comprehend, but which you will experience every hour of your existence. You will learn that
a man can be jealous of the superiority of a woman, when
this man is an ambitious artist; and that a lover can loathe
the success of his beloved when the theater is the arena of
their efforts. It is because an actor is no longer a man,
Consuelo—he is turned into a woman. He lives but
through the medium of his sickly vanity, which alone he
seeks to gratify, and for which alone he labors. The
beauty of a woman he feels a grievance; her talent extinguishes or competes with his own. A woman is his
rival, or rather he is the rival of a woman; he has all the
littleness, all the caprice, all the wants, all the ridiculous
airs of a coquette. This is the character of the greatest
number of persons belonging to the theater. There are
indeed grand exceptions, but they are so rare, so admirable,
that one should bow before them and render them homage,

as to the wisest and best. Anzoleto is no exception ; he is the vainest of the vain. In that one word you have the explanation of his conduct."

"But what unintelligible revenge ! What poor and insufficient means ! How can Corilla recompense him for his losses with the public ? Had he only spoken openly to me of his suffering (alas ! it needed only a word for that), I should have understood him perhaps—at least I would have compassionated him, and retired to yield him the first place."

"It is the peculiarity of envy to hate people in proportion to the happiness of which it deprives them ; just as it is the peculiarity of selfish love to hate in the object which we love, the pleasures which we are not the means of procuring him. While your lover abhors the public which loads you with glory, do you not hate the rival who intoxicates him with her charms ?

"My master, you have uttered a profound reflection, which I would fain ponder on."

"It is true. While Anzoleto detests you for your happiness on the stage, you hate him for his happiness in the boudoir of Corilla."

"It is not so. I could not hate him ; and you have made me feel that it would be cowardly and disgraceful to hate my rival. As to the passion with which she fills him, I shudder to think of it—why I know not. If it be involuntary on his part, Anzoleto is not guilty in hating my success."

"You are quick to interpret matters, so as to excuse his conduct and sentiments. No ; Anzoleto is not innocent or estimable in his suffering like you. He deceives, he disgraces you, while you endeavor to justify him. However, I did not wish to inspire you with hatred and resentment, but with calmness and indifference. The character of this man influences his conduct. You will never change him. Decide, and think only of yourself."

"Of myself—of myself alone ! Of myself, without hope or love !"

"Think of music, the divine art, Consuelo ; you would not dare to say that you love it only for Anzoleto ?"

"I have loved art for itself also ; but I never separated in my thoughts these inseparable objects—my life and that of Anzoleto. How shall I be able to love any thing when the half of my existence is taken away ?"

"Anzoleto was nothing more to you than an idea, and this idea imparted life. You will replace it by one greater, purer, more elevating. Your soul, your genius, your entire being, will no longer be at the mercy of a deceitful, fragile form; you shall contemplate the sublime ideal stripped of its earthly covering; you shall mount heavenward, and live in holy unison with God himself."

"Do you wish, as you once did, that I should become a nun?"

"No; this were to confine the exercise of your artistic faculties to one direction, whereas you should embrace all. Whatever you do, or wherever you are, in the theater or in the cloister, you may be a saint, the bride of heaven."

"What you say is full of sublimity, but shrouded in a mysterious garb. Permit me to retire, dear master; I require time to collect my thoughts and question my heart."

"You have said it, Consuelo; you need insight into yourself. Hitherto in giving up your heart and your prospects to one so much your inferior, you have not known yourself. You have mistaken your destiny, seeing that you were born without an equal, and consequently without the possibility of an associate in this world. Solitude, absolute liberty, are needful for you. I would not wish you husband, or lover, or family, or passions, or bonds of any kind. It is thus I have conceived your existence, and would direct your career. The day on which you give yourself away, you lose your divinity. Ah, if Mingotti and Moltini, my illustrious pupils, my powerful creations, had believed in me, they would have lived unrivaled on the earth. But woman is weak and curious; vanity blinds her, vain desires agitate, caprices hurry her away. In what do these disquietudes result?—what but in storms and weariness, in the loss, the destruction, or vitiation, of their genius. Would you not be more than they, Consuelo? Does not your ambition soar above the poor concerns of this life? or would you not appease these vain desires, and seize the glorious crown of everlasting genius?"

Porpora continued to speak for a long time with an eloquence and energy to which I cannot do justice. Consuelo listened, her looks bent upon the ground. When he had finished, she said: "My dear master, you are profound; but I cannot follow you sufficiently throughout. It seems to me as if you outraged human nature in proscribing its most noble passions—as if you would extinguish the instincts which God himself had implanted, for the purpose of elevating what would otherwise be a monstrous and anti-social impulse. Were I a better Christian I should perhaps better understand you; I shall try to become so, and that is all I can promise."

She took her leave, apparently tranquil, but in reality deeply agitated. The great though austere artist conducted her home, always preaching but never convincing. He nevertheless was of infinite service in opening to her a vast field of serious thought and inquiry, wherein Anzoleto's particular crime served but as a painful and solemn introduction to thoughts of eternity. She passed long hours, praying, weeping, and reflecting; then lay down to rest, with a virtuous and confiding hope in a merciful and compassionate God.

The next day Porpora announced to her that there would be a rehearsal of *Ipermnestra* for Stefanini, who was to take Anzoleto's part. The latter was ill, confined to bed, and complained of a loss of voice. Consuelo's first impulse was to fly to him and nurse him. "Spare yourself this trouble," said the professor, "he is perfectly well; the physician of the theater has said so, and he will be this evening with Corilla. But Count Zustiniani, who understands very well what all that means, and who consents without much regret that he should put off his appearance, has forbidden the physician to unmask the pretense, and has requested the good Stefanini to return to the theater for some days."

"But, good Heavens! what does Anzoleto mean to do? Is he about to quit the theater?"

"Yes—the theater of San Samuel. In a month he is off with Corilla for France. That surprises you? He flies from the shadow which you cast over him. He has entrusted his fate to a woman whom he dreads less, and whom he will betray so soon as he finds he no longer requires her.

Consuelo turned pale, and pressed her hands convulsively on her bursting heart. Perhaps she had flattered herself with the idea of reclaiming Anzoleto, by reproaching him gently with his faults, and offering to put off her appearance for a time. This news was a dagger stroke to her, and she could not believe that she should no more see him whom she had so fondly loved. "Ah," said she, "it is but an uneasy dream; I must go and seek him; he will explain every thing. He cannot follow this woman; it would be his destruction. I cannot permit him to do so; I will keep him back; I will make him aware of his true interests, if indeed he be any longer capable of comprehending them. Come with me, dear master; let us not forsake him thus."

"I will abandon you," said the angry Porpora, "and for ever, if you commit any such folly. Entreat a wretch— dispute with Corilla? Ah, Santa Cecilia! distrust your Bohemian origin, extinguish your blind and wandering instincts. Come! they are waiting for you at rehearsal. You will feel pleasure in singing with a master like Stefanini, a modest, generous, and well-informed artist."

He led her to the theater, and then for the first time she felt an abhorrence of this artist life, chained to the wants of the public, and obliged to repress one's own sentiments and emotions to obey those of others. This very rehearsal, the subsequent toilet, the performance of the evening, proved a frightful torment. Anzoleto was still absent. Next day there was to be an opera buffa of Galuppi's— *Arcifanfano Re de' Matti.* They had chosen this farce to please Stefanini, who was an excellent comic performer. Consuelo must now make those laugh whom she had formerly made weep. She was brilliant, charming, pleasing to the last degree, though plunged at the same time in despair. Twice or thrice sobs that would force their way found vent in a constrained gaiety, which would have appeared frightful to those who understood it. On retiring to her box, she fell down insensible. The public would have her return to receive their applause. She did not appear; a dreadful uproar took place, benches were broken, and people tried to gain the stage. Stefanini hastened to her box half dressed, his hair disheveled, and pale as a specter. She allowed herself to be supported back upon the stage, where she was received with a shower of bouquets, and forced to stoop to pick up a laurel crown. "Ah, the pitiless monsters!" she murmured as she retired behind the scenes.

"My sweet one," said the old singer, who gave her his hand, "you suffer greatly; but these little things," added he, picking up a bunch of brilliant flowers, "are a specific for all our woes; you will become used to it, and the time perhaps will arrive when you will only feel fatigue and uneasiness when they forget to crown."

" Oh, how hollow and trifling they are!" thought poor Consuelo. When she returned to her box she fainted away, literally upon a bed of flowers, which had been gathered on the stage and thrown pell-mell upon the sofa. The tirewoman left the box to call a physician. Count Zustiniani remained for some instants alone by the side of his beautiful singer, who looked pale and broken as the beautiful jasmines which strewed her couch. Carried away by his admiration, Zustiniani lost his reason, and yielding to his foolish hopes, he seized her hand and carried it to his lips. But his touch was odious to the pure-minded Consuelo. She roused herself to repel him as if it had been the bite of a serpent. " Ah! far from me," said she, excited into a sort of delirium; " far from me, all love, all caresses, and all honeyed words!—no love—no husband—no lover—no family for me! my dear master has said it—liberty, the ideal, solitude, glory!" and she burst into such an agony of tears, that the count, terrified, threw himself upon his knees before her, and strove to calm her. But he could say nothing healing to that wounded soul, and his passion, which at that moment reached its highest paroxysm, expressed itself in spite of him. He understood but too well in her emotion the despair of the betrayed lover. He gave expression to the enthusiasm of a hopeful one. Consuelo appeared to hear him, and withdrew her hand from his with a vacant smile, which the count took for a slight encouragement.

Some men, although possessing great tact and penetration in the world, are absurd in such conjectures. The physician arrived and administered a sedative in the style which they called *drops.* Consuella was then enveloped in her mantle and carried to her gondola. The count entered with her, supporting her in his arms, and always talking of his love, even with a certain eloquence which it seemed to him must carry conviction. At the end of a quarter of an hour, obtaining no response, he implored a word, a look.

" To what then shall I answer?" said Consuelo, rousing herself as from a dream; " I have heard nothing."

Zustiniani, although at first discouraged, thought there could not be a better opportunity, and that this afflicted

soul would be more accessible than after reflection and reason. He spoke again, but there was the same silence, the
same abstraction, only that there was a not-to-be-mistaken
effort, though without any angry demonstration, to repel
his advances. When the gondola touched the shore, he
tried to detain Consuelo for an instant, to obtain a word of
encouragement. "Ah, signor," said she, coldly, "excuse
my weak state. I have heard badly, but I understand. Oh
yes, I understand perfectly. I ask this night, this one
night to reflect, to recover from my distress. To-morrow,
yes, to-morrow, I shall reply without fail."

"To-morrow! dear Consuelo, oh, it is an age! But I
shall submit—only allow me at least to hope for your friendship."

"Oh, yes, yes! there is hope," replied Consuelo, in a
constrained voice, placing her foot upon the bank; "but
do not follow me," said she, as she motioned him with an
imperious gesture back to the gondola; "otherwise there
will be no room for hope."

Shame and anger restored her strength, but it was a nervous, feverish strength, which found vent in hysteric
laughter as she ascended the stairs.

"You are very happy, Consuelo," said a voice in the
darkness, which almost stunned her; "I congratulate you
on your gaiety."

"Oh, yes," she replied, while she seized Anzoleto's arm
violently, and rapidly ascended with him to her chamber.
"I thank you, Anzoleto. You were right to congratulate
me. I am truly happy—oh, so happy!"

Anzoleto, who had been waiting for her, had already
lighted the lamp, and when the bluish light fell upon their
agitated features, they both started back in affright.

"We are very happy, are we not, Anzoleto?" said she
with a choking voice, while her features were distorted
with a smile that covered her cheeks with tears. "What
think you of our happiness?"

"I think, Consuelo," replied he, with a calm and bitter
smile, "that we have found it troublesome, but we shall
get on better by and bye."

"You seemed to me to be much at home in Corilla's
boudoir."

"And you, I find, very much at your ease in the gondola
of the count."

" The count! You knew, then, Anzoleto, that the count wished to supplant you in my affection?"

" And in order not to annoy you, my dear, I prudently kept in the background."

" Ah, you knew it; and this is the time you have taken to abandon me!"

" Have I not done well? are you not content with your lot? The count is a generous lover, and the poor condemned singer would have no business, I fancy, to contend with him."

" Porpora was right: you are an infamous man. Leave my sight! You do not deserve that I should justify myself. It would be a stain were I to regret you. Leave me, I tell you; but first know that you can come out at Venice and re-enter San Samuel with Corilla. Never shall my mother's daughter set foot upon the vile boards of a theater again."

" The daughter of your mother the *zingara* will play the great lady in the villa of Zustiniani, on the shores of the Brenta. It will be a fair career, and I shall be glad of it."

" O my mother!" exclaimed Consuelo, turning toward the bed and falling on her knees, as she buried her face in the counterpane, which had served as a shroud for the *zingara*.

Anzoleto was terrified and affected by this energetic movement, and the convulsive sobs which burst from the breast of Consuelo. Remorse seized on his heart, and he approached his betrothed to raise her in his arms; but she rose of herself, and pushing him from her with wild strength, thrust him toward the door, exclaiming, as she did so, "Away—away! from my heart, from my memory! farewell forever!"

Anzoleto had come to seek her with a low and selfish design, nevertheless it was the best thing he could have done. He could not bear to leave her, and he had struck out a plan to reconcile matters. He meant to inform her of the dangers she ran from the designs of Zustiniani, and thus remove her from the theater. In this resolution he paid full homage to the pride and purity of Consuelo. He knew her incapable of tampering with a doubtful position, or of accepting protection which ought to make her blush. His guilty and corrupt soul still retained unshaken

faith in the innocence of this young girl, whom he was
certain of finding as faithful and devoted as he had left her
days before. But how reconcile this devotion with the
preconceived design of deceiving her, and, without a
rupture with Corilla, of remaining still her betrothed, her
friend? He wished to re-enter the theater with the latter,
and could not think of separating at the very moment
when his success depended on her. This audacious and
cowardly plan was nevertheless formed in his mind, and
he treated Consuelo as the Italian women do those madonnas whose protection they implore in the hour of repentance, and whose faces they veil in their erring moments.

When he beheld her so brilliant and so gay in her buffa
part at the theater, he began to fear that he had lost too
much time in maturing his design. When he saw her
return in the gondola of the count, and approach with a
joyous burst of laughter, he feared he was too late, and
vexation seized him; but when she rose above his insults,
and banished him with scorn, respect returned with fear,
and he wandered long on the stair and on the quay, expecting her to recall him. He even ventured to knock and
implore pardon through the door; but a deep silence reigned
in that chamber, whose threshold he was never to cross
with Consuelo again. He retired, confused and chagrined,
determining to return on the morrow, and flattering himself
that he should then prove more successful. "After
all," said he to himself, "my project will succeed; she
knows the count's love, and all that is requisite is half
done."

Overwhelmed with fatigue, he slept; long in the afternoon he went to Corilla.

"Great news?" she exclaimed, running to meet him
with outstretched arms; "Consuelo is off."

"Off! gracious Heaven! whither, and with whom?"

"To Vienna, where Porpora has sent her, intending to
join her there himself. She has deceived us all, the little
cheat. She was engaged for the emperor's theater, where
Porpora purposes that she should appear in his new
opera."

"Gone! gone without a word!" exclaimed Anzoleto,
rushing toward the door.

"It is of no use seeking her in Venice," said Corilla,
with a sneering smile and a look of triumph. "She set

out for Palestrina at daybreak, and is already far from this on the mainland. Zustiniani, who thought himself beloved, but who was only made a fool of, is furious, and confined to his couch with fever; but he sent Porpora to me just now, to try and get me to sing this evening; and Stefanini, who is tired of the stage, and anxious to enjoy the sweets of his retirement in his casino, is very desirous to see you resume your performances. Therefore prepare for appearing to-morrow in *Ipermnestra.* In the meantime, as they are waiting for me, I must run away. If you do not believe me, you can take a turn through the city, and convince yourself that I have told you the truth."

"By all the furies!" exclaimed Anzoleto, "you have gained your point, but you have taken my life along with it."

And he swooned away on the Persian carpet of the false Corilla.

CHAPTER XXI.

THE person most embarrassed respecting the part he had to play after the flight of Consuelo, was Count Zustiniani. After having allowed it to be said, and led all Venice to believe, that the charming singer favored his addresses; how could he explain, in a manner flattering to his self-love, the fact that, at the first declaration, she had abruptly and mysteriously disappeared, and thus thwarted his wishes and his hopes? Many thought that, jealous of his treasure, he had hidden her in one of his country houses. But when they heard Porpora, with that blunt openness which never deceived, say that he had advised his pupil to precede and wait for him in Germany, nothing remained but to search for the motives of so strange a resolution. The count, indeed, to put them off the track, pretended to show neither vexation nor surprise; but his disappointment betrayed itself in spite of him, and they ceased to attribute to him that good fortune on which he had been so much congratulated. The greater portion of the truth became clear to all the world—viz.: the infidelity of Anzoleto, the rivalry of Corilla, and the despair of the poor Spaniard, whom they pitied and sincerely regretted. Anzoleto's first impulse had been to run to Porpora; but the latter repulsed him sternly. "Cease to question me, ambitious young man, without heart and without truth," the indignant master replied; "you never merited the affection of that noble girl, and you shall never know from me what has become of her. I will take every care that you shall not find a trace of her; and if by chance you should one day meet with her, I hope that your image will be effaced from her heart and memory as fully as I desire and labor to accomplish it."

From Porpora, Anzoleto went to the Corte Minelli. He found Consuelo's apartment already surrendered to a new occupant, and encumbered with the materials of his labor. He was a worker in glass, long since installed in the house, and who transferred his workshop to her room with much glee.

"Ah, ha! it is you, my boy?" said he to the young tenor; "you have come to see me in my new shop? I shall do very well here, and my wife is very glad that she can lodge all the children below. What are you looking for? Did little Consuelo forget any thing? Look, my child, search; it will not annoy me."

"Where have they put her furniture?" said Anzoleto, agitated and struck with despair at not finding any vestige of Consuelo in this place which had been consecrated to the purest enjoyments of his life.

"The furniture is below in the court; she made a present of it to mother Agatha, and she did well. The old woman is poor, and will make a little money out of it. Oh! Consuelo always had a good heart. She has not left a farthing of debt in the Corte, and she made a small present to every body when she went away. She merely took her crucifix with her. But it was very odd her going off in the middle of the night without telling any one! Master Porpora came this morning to arrange all her affairs; it was like the execution of a will. It grieved all the neighbors; but they consoled themselves at last with the thought that she is no doubt going to live in a fine palace on the canalazzo, now that she is rich and a great lady. As for me, I always said she would make a fortune with her voice, she worked so hard. And when will the wedding be, Anzoleto? I hope that you will buy something from me to make presents to all the young girls of the quarter."

" Yes, yes," replied Anzoleto wildly. He fled with
death in his soul, and saw in the court all the gossips of
the place holding an auction of Consuelo's bed and table—
that bed on which he had seen her sleep, that table at
which he had seen her work ! " Oh, Heavens ! already
nothing left of her!" cried he involuntarily, wringing his
hands. He felt almost tempted to go and stab Corilla.

After an interval of three days he reappeared on the
stage with Corilla. They were both outrageously hissed,
and the curtain had to be lowered before the piece was
finished. Anzoleto was furious, Corilla perfectly uncon-
cerned. " This is what your protection procures me,"
said he, in a threatening tone, as soon as he was alone with
her. The prima donna answered him with great coolness:
" You are affected by trifles, my poor child ; it is easily
seen that you know little of the public, and have never
borne the brunt of its caprices. I was so well prepared
for the reverse of this evening, that I did not even take
the pains to look over my part; and if I did not tell you
what was to happen, it was because I knew very well you
would not have had courage enough to enter upon the
stage with the certainty of being hissed. Now, however,
you must know what you have to expect. The next time
we shall be treated even worse. Three, four, six, eight
representations perhaps, will pass thus; but during these
storms an opposition will manifest itself in our favor.
Were we the most stupid blockheads in the world, the
spirit of contradiction and independence would raise up
partisans for us, who will become more and more zealous.
There are so many people who think to elevate themselves
by abusing others, that there are not wanting those who
think to do the same by protecting them. After a dozen
trials, during which the theater will be a field of battle
between the hissers and the applauders, our opponents will
be fatigued, the refractory will look sour, and we shall
enter upon a new phase. That portion of the public which
has sustained us, without well knowing why, will hear us
coldly; it will be like a new début for us, and then it will
depend upon ourselves, thank Heaven! to subdue the audience and remain masters of them. I predict great success for you from that moment, dear Anzoleto ; the spell
which has hitherto weighed you down will be removed.
You will breathe an atmosphere of encouragement and

sweet praises, which will restore your powers. Remember the effect which you produced at Zustiniani's the first time you were heard there. You had not time to complete your conquest—a more brilliant star came too soon to eclipse you; but that star has allowed itself to sink below the horizon, and you must be prepared to ascend with me into the empyrean."

Every thing happened as Corilla had predicted. The two lovers had certainly to pay dearly, during some days, for the loss the public had sustained in the person of Consuelo. But their constancy in braving the tempest wearied out an anger which was too excessive to be lasting. Zustiniani encouraged Corilla's efforts. As for Anzoleto, the count, after having made vain attempts to draw a *primo uomo* to Venice at so advanced a season, when all the engagements were already made with the principal theaters in Europe, made up his mind, and accepted him for his champion in the struggle which was going on between the public and the administration of his theater. That theater had a reputation too brilliant to be periled by the loss of one performer. Nothing like this could overcome fixed habits. All the boxes were let for the season, and the ladies held their levees there, and met as usual. The real dilettanti kept up their dissatisfaction for a time, but they were too few in number to be cared for. Besides, they were at last tired of their own animosity, and one fine evening, Corilla, having sung with power, was unanimously recalled. She reappeared, leading with her Anzoleto, who had not been called for, and who seemed to yield to a gentle violence with a modest and timid air. He received his share of the applauses, and was reengaged the next day. In short, before a month had passed, Consuelo was as much forgotten as is the lightning which shoots athwart a summer sky. Corilla excited enthusiasm as formerly, and perhaps merited it more ; for emulation had given her more earnestness, and love sometimes inspired her with more feeling and expression. As for Anzoleto, though he had not overcome his defects, he had succeeded in displaying his incontestible good qualities. They had become accustomed to the first and admired the last. His charming person fascinated the women, and he was much sought after for the saloons, the more so because Corilla's jealousy increased the piquancy of coquetting with him. Clorinda also developed her powers upon the stage; that is to say, her heavy beauty and the easy nonchalance of unequaled dulness, which was not without its attraction for a portion of the spectators. Zustiniani, partly to relieve his mind after his deep disappointment, covered her with jewels, and pushed her forward in the first parts, hoping to make her succeed Corilla, who was positively engaged at Paris for the coming season.

Corilla saw without vexation this competition, from which she had nothing to fear either present or future : she even took a malicious pleasure in bringing out that cool and impudent incapacity which recoiled before nothing. These two creatures lived therefore in a good understanding and governed the administration imperiously. They put aside every serious piece, and revenged themselves upon Porpora by refusing his operas, to accept and bring forward those of his most unworthy rivals. They agreed together to injure all who displeased them, and to protect all who humbled themselves before their power. During that season, thanks to them, the public applauded the compositions of the *decadence,* and forgot that true and grand music had formerly flourished in Venice.

In the midst of his success and prosperity (for the count had given him a very advantageous engagement) Anzoleto was overwhelmed with profound disgust, and drooped under the weight of a melancholy happiness. It was pitiful to see him drag himself to the rehearsals hanging on the arm of the triumphant Corilla, pale, languishing, handsome as Apollo, but ridiculously foppish in his appearance, like a man wearied of admiration, crushed and destroyed under the laurels and myrtles he had so easily and so largely gathered. Even at the performances, when upon the stage with Corilla, he yielded to the necessity he felt of protesting against her by his superb attitude and his impertinent languor. While she devoured him with her eyes, he seemed by his looks to say to the audience: " Do not think that I respond to so much love! On the contrary, whoever will deliver me from it will do me a great service."

The fact was that Anzoleto, spoiled and corrupted by Corilla, turned against her the instincts of selfishness and ingratitude which she had excited in his heart against the whole world. There remained to him but one sentiment which was true and pure in its nature ; the imperishable love which, in spite of his vices, he cherished for Consuelo. He could divert his attention from it, thanks to his natural frivolity ; but he could not cure himself of it, and that love haunted him like remorse, like a torture, in the midst of his most culpable excesses. In the midst of them all, a specter seemed to dog his steps ; and deep-drawn sighs escaped from his breast when in the middle of the night he passed in his gondola along the dark buildings of the Corte Minelli. Corilla, for a long time subdued by his bad treatment, and led, as all mean souls are, to love only in proportion to the contempt and out-rages she received, began at last to be tired of this fatal passion. She had flattered herself that she could conquer and enchain his savage independence. She had worked for that end with a violent earnestness, and she had sacri-ficed every thing to it. When she felt and acknowledged the impossibility of ever succeeding, she began to hate him, and to search for distractions and revenge. One night when Anzoleto was wandering in his gondola about Venice with Clorinda, he saw another gondola rapidly glide off, whose extinguished lantern gave notice of some clandestine rendezvous. He paid little attention to it ; but Clorinda, who, in her fear of being discovered, was always on the look-out, said to him, "Let us go more slowly. It is the count's gondola ; I recognise the gon-dolier."

"In that case we will go more quickly," replied An-zoleto; "I wish to rejoin him, and to know with whom he is enjoying this fresh and balmy evening."

"No, no; let us return," cried Clorinda. "His eye is so piercing and his ear so quick. We must be careful not to annoy him."

"Row, I say!" cried Anzoleto, to his gondolier; "I wish to overtake that bark which you see before us."

Notwithstanding Clorinda's prayers and terror, this was the work of but an instant. The two barks grazed each other, and Anzoleto heard a half-stifled burst of laughter proceed from the other gondola. "Ha!" said he, "this is fair play—it is Corilla who is taking the air with the signor count." So saying, Anzoleto leaped to the bow of his gondola, took the oar from the hands of the bacarole, and following the other gondola rapidly, overtook it and grazed it a second time, exclaiming aloud as he passed, "Dear Clorinda, you are without contradiction the most beautiful and the most beloved of all women."

"I was just saying as much to Corilla," immediately replied the count, coming out of his cabin and approaching the other bark with consummate self-possession; "and now that our excursions on both sides are finished, I propose that we make an exchange of partners."

"The signor count only does justice to my loyalty," replied Anzoleto in the same tone. "If he permit me, I will offer him my arm, that he may himself escort the fair Clorinda into his gondola."

The count reached out his arm to rest upon Anzoleto's; but the tenor, inflamed by hatred, and transported with rage, leaped with all his weight upon the count's gondola and upset it, crying with a savage voice: "Signor Count, *gondola for gondola!*" Then abandoning his victims to their fate, and leaving Clorinda speechless with terror and trembling for the consequences of his frantic conduct, he gained the opposite bank by swimming, took his course through the dark and tortuous streets, entered his lodging, changed his clothes in a twinkling, gathered together all the money he had, left the house, threw himself into the first shallop which was getting under way for Trieste, and snapped his fingers in triumph as he saw, in the dawn of morning, the clock-towers and domes of Venice sink beneath the waves.

CHAPTER XXIII.

IN the western range of the Carpathian mountains, which separate Bohemia from Bavaria, and which receives in these countries the name of the Boehmer Wald, there was still standing, about a century ago, an old country seat of immense extent, called, in consequence of some forgotten tradition, the Castle of the Giants. Though presenting at a distance somewhat the appearance of an ancient fortress, it was no more than a private residence, furnished in the taste, then somewhat antiquated but always rich and sumptuous, of Louis XIV. The feudal style of architecture had also undergone various tasteful modifications in the parts of the edifice occupied by the Lords of Rudolstadt, masters of this rich domain.

The family was of Bohemian origin, but had become naturalized in Germany on its members changing their name, and abjuring the principles of the Reformation, at the most trying period of the Thirty Years' War. A noble and valiant ancestor, of inflexible Protestant principles, had been murdered on the mountain in the neighborhood of his castle, by the fanatic soldiery. His widow, who was of a Saxon family, saved the fortune and the life of her young children by declaring herself a Catholic, and entrusting to the Jesuits the education of the heirs of Rudolstadt. After two generations had passed away, Bohemia being silent and oppressed, the Austrian power permanently established, and the glory and misfortunes of the Reformation at last apparently forgotten, the Lords of Rudolstadt peacefully practiced the Christian virtues, professed the Romish faith, and dwelt on their estates in unostentatious state, like good aristocrats and faithful servants of Maria Theresa. They had formerly displayed their bravery, in the service of their emperor Charles VI ; but it was strange that young Albert, the last of this illustrious and powerful race, and the only son of Count Christian Rudolstadt, had never borne arms in the War of Succession, which had just terminated; and that he had reached his thirtieth year without having sought any other distinction than what he inherited from his birth and fortune. This unusual course had inspired his sovereign with suspicion of collusion with her enemies; but Count Christian, having had the honor to receive the empress in his castle, had given such reasons for the conduct of his son as seemed to satisfy her. Nothing, however, had transpired of the conversation between Maria Theresa and Count Rudolstadt. A strange mystery reigned in the bosom of this devout and beneficent family, which for ten years a neighbor had seldom visited; which no business, no pleasure, no political agitation, induced to leave their domains; which paid largely and without a murmur all the subsidies required for the war, displaying no uneasiness in the midst of public danger and misfortune ; which in fine seemed not to live after the same fashion as the other nobles, who viewed them with distrust, although knowing nothing of them but their praiseworthy deeds and noble

conduct. At a loss to what to attribute this unsocial and
retired mode of life, they accused the Rudolstadts sometimes of avarice, sometimes of misanthropy; but as their
actions uniformly contradicted these imputations, their
maligners were at length obliged to confine their reproaches to their apathy and indifference. They asserted
that Count Christian did not wish to expose the life of his
son—the last of his race—in these disastrous wars, and
that the empress had, in exchange for his services, accepted a sum of money sufficient to equip a regiment of
hussars. The ladies of rank who had marriageable daughters admitted that Count Christian had done well; but
when they learned the determination that he seemed to
entertain of providing a wife for his son in his own family,
in the daughter of the Baron Frederick, his brother—
when they understood that the young Baroness Amelia had
just quitted the convent at Prague where she had been
educated, to reside henceforth with her cousin in the
Castle of the Giants—these noble dames unanimously pronounced the family of Rudolstadt to be a den of wolves,
each of whom was more unsocial and savage than the
others. A few devoted servants and faithful friends alone
knew the secret of the family, and kept it strictly.

This noble family was assembled one evening round a
table profusely loaded with game, and those substantial
dishes with which our ancestors in Slavonic states still continued to regale themselves at this period, notwithstanding
the refinements which the court of Louis XV had introduced into the aristocratic customs of a great part of
Europe. An immense hearth on which burned huge
billets of oak, diffused heat throughout the large and
gloomy hall. Count Christian in a loud voice had just
said grace, to which the other members of the family
listened standing. Numerous aged and grave domestics,
in the costume of the country—viz. large mameluke
trousers, and long mustachios—moved slowly to and fro in
attendance on their honored masters. The chaplain of the
castle was seated on the right of the count, the young
Baroness Amelia on his left—"next his heart," as he was
wont to say with austere and paternal gallantry. The
Baron Frederick, his junior brother, whom he always
called his "*young* brother," from his not being more than
sixty years old, was seated opposite. The Canoness Wen-

ceslawa of Rudolstadt, his eldest sister, a venerable lady of
seventy, afflicted with an enormous hump and a frightful
leanness, took her place at the upper end of the table ;
while Count Albert, the son of Count Christian, the betrothed of Amelia, and the last of the Rudolstadts, came
forward, pale and melancholy, to seat himself on the other
end, opposite his noble aunt.

Of all these silent personages, Albert was certainly the
one least disposed and least accustomed to impart animation
to the others. The chaplain was so devoted to his masters,
and so reverential toward the head of the family in
particular, that he never opened his mouth to speak unless
encouraged to do so by a look from Count Christian; and
the latter was of so calm and reserved a disposition, that
he seldom required to seek from others a relief from his
own thoughts.

Baron Frederick was of a less thoughtful character and
more active temperament, but he was by no means remarkable for animation. Although mild and benevolent as his
eldest brother, he had less intelligence and less enthusiasm.
His devotion was a matter of custom and politeness. His
only passion was a love for the chase, in which he spent
almost all his time, going out each morning and returning
each evening, ruddy with exercise, out of breath, and
hungry. He ate for ten, drank for thirty, and even
showed some sparks of animation when relating how his
dog Sapphire had started the hare, how Panther had un-
kenneled the wolf, or how his falcon Attila had taken
flight; and when the company had listened to all this with
inexhaustible patience, he dozed over quietly near the fire
in a great black leathern arm-chair, and enjoyed his nap
until his daughter came to warn him that the hour for
retiring was about to strike.

The canoness was the most conversable of the party.
She might even be called chatty, for she discussed with
the chaplain, two or three times a week, for an hour at a
stretch, sundry knotty points touching the genealogy of
Bohemian, Hungarian, and Saxon families, the names and
biographies of whom, from kings down to simple gentlemen, she had on her finger ends.

As for Count Albert, there was something repelling and
solemn in his exterior, as if each of his gestures had been
prophetic, each of his sentences oracular to the rest of the

family. By a singular peculiarity inexplicable to any one not acquainted with the secret of the mansion, as soon as he opened his lips, which did not happen once in twenty-four hours, the eyes of his friends and domestics were turned upon him; and there was apparent on every face a deep anxiety, a painful and affectionate solicitude; always excepting that of the young Amelia, who listened to him with a sort of ironical impatience, and who alone ventured to reply, with the gay or sarcastic familiarity which her fancy prompted.

This young girl, exquisitely fair, of a blooming complexion, lively, and well formed, was a little pearl of beauty; and when her waiting-maid told her so, in order to console her for her cheerless mode of life, "Alas!" the young girl would reply, "I am a pearl shut up in an oyster of which this frightful Castle of the Giants is the shell." This will serve to show the reader what sort of petulant bird was shut up in so gloomy a cage.

On this evening the solemn silence which weighed down the family, particularly during the first course (for the two old gentlemen, the canoness, and the chaplain, were possessed of a solidity and regularity of appetite which never failed) was interrupted by Count Albert.

"What frightful weather!" said he, with a profound sigh.

Every one looked at him with surprise ; for if the weather had become gloomy and threatening during the hour they had been shut up in the interior of the castle, nobody could have perceived it, since the thick shutters were closed. Every thing was calm without and within, and nothing announced an approaching tempest.

Nobody, however, ventured to contradict Albert; and Amelia contented herself with shrugging her shoulders, while the clatter of knives and forks, and the removal of the dishes by the servants, proceeded, after a moment's interruption, as before.

"Do not you hear the wind roaring amid the pines of the Boehmer Wald, and the voice of the torrent sounding in your ears?" continued Albert in a louder voice, and with a fixed gaze at his father.

Count Christian was silent. The baron, in his quiet way, replied, without removing his eyes from his venison. which he hewed with athletic hand as if it had been a lump of granite: "Yes, we had wind and rain together at sunset, and I should not be surprised were the weather to change to-morrow."

Albert smiled in his strange manner, and every thing again became still; but five minutes had hardly elapsed when a furious blast shook the lofty casements, howled wildly around the old walls, lashing the waters of the moat as with a whip, and died away on the mountain tops with a sound so plaintive, that every face, with the exception of Count Albert's, who again smiled with the same indefinable expression, grew pale.

"At this very instant," said he, "the storm drives a stranger toward our castle. You would do well, Sir Chaplain, to pray for those who travel beneath the tempest amid these rude mountains."

"I hourly pray from my very soul," replied the trembling chaplain, "for those who are cast on the rude paths of life amid the tempest of human passions."

"Do not reply, Mr. Chaplain," said Amelia, without regarding the looks or signs which warned her on every side not to continue the conversation. "You know very well that my cousin likes to torment people with his enigmas. For my part I never think of finding them out."

Count Albert paid no more attention to the railleries of his cousin than she appeared to pay to his discourse. He leaned an elbow on his plate, which almost always remained empty and unused before him, and fixed his eyes on the damask table-cloth, as if making a calculation of the ornaments on the pattern, though all the while absorbed in a reverie.

CHAPTER XXIV.

A FURIOUS tempest raged during the supper; which meal lasted just two hours, neither more nor less, even on fast-days, which were religiously observed but which never prevented the count from indulging his customary habits, no less sacred to him than the usages of the Romish Church. Storms were too frequent in these mountains, and the immense forests which then covered their sides imparted to the echoes a character too well known to the inhabitants of the castle, to occasion them even a passing emotion. Nevertheless, the unusual agitation of Count Albert communicated itself to the rest of the family, and the baron, disturbed in the usual current of his reflections, might have evinced some dissatisfaction, had it been possible for his imperturbable placidity to be for a moment ruffled. He contented himself with sighing deeply, when a frightful peal of thunder, occurring with the second remove, caused the carver to miss the choice morsel of a boar's ham which he was just then engaged in detaching.

"It cannot be helped," said the baron, directing a compassionate smile towards the poor carver, who was quite downcast with his mishap.

"Yes, uncle, you are right," exclaimed Count Albert in a loud voice and rising to his feet; "it cannot be helped. The Hussite is down; the lightning consumes it; spring will revisit its foliage no more!"

"What say you, my son?" asked the old count, in a melancholy tone. "Do you speak of the huge oak of the Schreckenstein?"*

"Yes, father; I speak of the great oak to whose branches we hung up some twenty monks the other day."

"He mistakes centuries for weeks just now," said the canoness in a low voice, while she made the sign of the cross. "My dear child," she continued, turning to her nephew, "if you have really seen what has happened, or what is about to happen, in a dream, as has more than once been the case, this miserable withered oak, considering the sad recollections associated with the rock it shaded, will be no great loss."

"As for me," exclaimed Amelia, "I am delighted that the storm has rid us of that gibbet, with its long, frightful skeleton arms, and its red trunk which seemed to ooze out blood. I never passed beneath it when the breeze of evening moved amid its foliage, without hearing sighs as if of agony, and commending my soul to God while I turned away and fled."

"Amelia," replied the count, who just now appeared to hear her words for the first time perhaps for days, "you did well not to remain beneath the Hussite as I did for

---

* "Stone of Terror," — a name not unfrequently used in these regions.

hours, and even entire nights. You would have seen and heard things which would have chilled you with terror and never have left your memory."

"Pray, be silent," cried the young baroness, starting and moving from the table where Albert was leaning : "I cannot imagine what pleasure you take in terrifying others every time you open your lips."

"Would to Heaven, dear Amelia," said the old baron, mildly, "it were indeed but an amusement which your cousin takes in uttering such things."

"No, my father; I speak in all seriousness. The oak of the Stone of Terror is overthrown, cleft in pieces. You may send the wood-cutters to-morrow to remove it. I shall plant a cypress in its place, which I shall name, not the Hussite, but the Penitent, and the Stone of Terror shall be called the Stone of Expiation."

"Enough, enough, my son!" exclaimed the agonized old man. "Banish these melancholy images, and leave it to God to judge the actions of men."

"They have disappeared, father—annihilated, with the implements of torture which the breath of the storm and the fire of heaven have scattered in the dust. In place of pendent skeletons, fruits and flowers rock themselves amid the zephyrs on the new branches, and in place of the man in black who nightly lit up the flames beside the stake, I see a pure celestial soul which hovers over my head and yours. The storm is gone, the danger over : those who traveled are in shelter ; my soul is in peace, the period of expiation draws nigh, and I am about to be born again."

"May what you say, O well-beloved child, prove true!" said Christian, with extreme tenderness; "and may you be freed from the phantoms which trouble your repose! Heaven grant me this blessing, and restore peace, and hope, and light to my son!"

Before the old man had finished speaking, Albert leaned forward, and appeared to fall into a tranquil slumber.

"What means this?" broke in the young baroness; "what do I see?—Albert sleeping at table? Very gallant, truly!"

"This deep and sudden sleep," said the chaplain, surveying the young man with intense interest, "is a favorable crisis, which leads me to look forward to a happy change, for a time at least, in his situation."

"Let no one speak to him, or attempt to rouse him," exclaimed Count Christian.

"Merciful Heaven," prayed the canoness, with clasped hands, "realize this prediction, and let his thirtieth year be that of his recovery!"

"Amen!" added the chaplain, devoutly. "Let us raise our hearts with thanks to the God of Mercy for the food which he has given us, and entreat him to deliver this noble youth, the object of so much solicitude."

They rose for grace, and every one remained standing, absorbed in prayer for the last of the Rudolstadts. As for the old count, tears streamed down his withered cheeks. He then gave orders to his faithful servants to convey his son to his apartment, when Baron Frederick, considering how he could best display his devotion toward his nephew, observed with childish satisfaction: "Dear brother, a good idea has occurred to me. If your son awakens in the seclusion of his chamber, while digestion is going on, bad dreams may assail him. Bring him to the saloon, and place him in my large arm-chair. It is the best one for sleeping in in the whole house. He will be better there than in bed, and when he awakens he will find a good fire and friends to cheer his heart."

"You are right, brother;" replied Christian, "let us bear him to the saloon and place him on the large sofa."

"It is wrong to sleep lying, after dinner," continued the baron; "I believe, brother, that I am aware of that from experience. Let him have my arm-chair—yes, my arm-chair is the thing."

Christian very well knew that were he to refuse his brother's offer, it would vex and annoy him; the young count was therefore propped up in the hunter's leathern chair, but he remained quite insensible to the change, so sound was his sleep. The baron placed himself on another seat, and warming his legs before a fire worthy of the times of old, smiled with a triumphant air whenever the chaplain observed that Albert's repose would assuredly have happy results. The good soul proposed to give up his nap as well as his chair, and to join the family in watching over the youth; but after some quarter of an hour, he was so much at ease that he began to snore after so lusty a fashion as to drown the last faint and now far distant gusts of the storm.

The castle bell, which only rang on extraordinary occasions, was now heard, and old Hans, the head domestic, entered shortly afterward with a letter which he presented to Count Christian without saying a word. He then retired into an adjoining apartment to await his master's commands. Christian opened the letter, cast his eye on the signature, and handed the paper to the young baroness, with a request that she would peruse the contents. Curious and excited, Amelia approached a candle, and read as follows:

"ILLUSTRIOUS AND WELL-BELOVED LORD COUNT,

"Your Excellency has conferred on me the favor of asking a service at my hands. This indeed, is to confer a greater favor than all those which I have already received, and of which my heart fondly cherishes the remembrance. Despite my anxiety to execute your esteemed orders, I did not hope to find so promptly and suitably the individual that was required; but favorable circumstances having concurred to an unforeseen extent in aiding me to fulfill the desires of your Highness, I hasten to send a young person who realizes, at least in part, the required conditions. I therefore send her only provisionally, that your amiable and illustrious niece may not too impatiently await a more satisfactory termination to my researches and proceedings.

"The individual who has the honor to present this is my pupil, and in a measure my adopted child; she will prove, as the amiable baroness has desired, an agreeable and obliging companion, as well as a most competent musical instructress. In other respects, she does not possess the necessary information for a governess. She speaks several languages, though hardly sufficiently acquainted with them perhaps to teach them. Music she knows thoroughly, and she sings remarkably well. You will be pleased with her talents, her voice, her demeanor, and not less so with the sweetness and dignity of her character. Your Highness may admit her into your circle without risk of her infringing in any way on etiquette, or affording any evidence of low tastes. She wishes to remain free as regards your noble family, and therefore will accept no salary. In short, it is neither as a duenna nor as a servant, but as companion and friend to the amiable baroness, that she appears; just as that lady did me the honor to mention in the gracious *post-scriptum* which she added to your Excellency's communication.

"Signor Corner, who has been appointed ambassador to Austria, awaits the orders for his departure; but these he thinks will not arrive before two months. Signora Corner, his worthy spouse, and my generous pupil, would have me accompany them to Vienna, where she thinks I should enjoy a happier career. Without perhaps agreeing with her in this, I have acceded to her kind offers, desirous as I am to abandon Venice, where I have only experienced annoyance, deception and reverses. I long to revisit the noble German land where I have seen so many happy days, and renew my intimacy with the venerable friends I left there. Your Highness holds the first place in this old, wornout, yet not wholly chilled heart, since it is actuated by eternal affection and deepest gratitude. To you, therefore, illustrious signor, do I commend and confide my adoptive child, requesting on her behalf hospitality, protection and favor. She will repay your goodness by her zeal and attention to the young baroness. In three months I shall come for her, and offer in her place a teacher who may contract a more permanent engagement.

" Awaiting the day on which I may once more press the hand of one of the best of men, I presume to declare myself, with respect and pride, the most humble and devoted of the friends and servants of your Highness, *chiarissima, stimatissima, illustrissima,*

" NICHOLAS PORPORA,

" Chapel Master, Composer, and Professor of

" Vocal Music.

" Venice, the —— of —— 17—."

Amelia sprang up with joy on perusing this letter, while the old count, much affected, repeated — " Worthy Porpora! respectable man! excellent friend !"

" Certainly, certainly," exclaimed the Canoness Wenceslawa, divided between the dread of deranging their family usages and the desire of displaying the duties of hospitality toward a stranger, " we must receive and treat her well, provided she do not become weary of us here."

" But, uncle, where is this precious mistress and future friend ?" exclaimed the young baroness, without attending to her aunt's reflections. " Surely she will shortly be here in person. I await her with impatience."

Count Christian rang. " Hans," said he, " by whom was this delivered ?"

" By a lady, most gracious lord and master."

" Here already !" exclaimed Amelia. " Where?—oh where ?"

" In her post carriage at the drawbridge."

" And you have left her to perish outside, instead of introducing her at once ?"

" Yes, madam ; I took the letter, but forbade the postilion to slacken rein or take foot out of the stirrup. I also raised the bridge behind me until I should have delivered the letter to my master."

" But it is unpardonable, absurd, to make guests wait outside in such weather. Would not any one think we were in a fortress, and that we take every one who comes for an enemy ? Speed away then, Hans."

Hans remained motionless as a statue. His eyes alone

expressed regret that he could not obey the wishes of his young mistress ; but a cannon-ball whizzing past his ear would not have deranged by a hair's breath the impassive attitude with which he awaited the sovereign orders of his old master.

" The faithful Hans, my child," said the baron slowly, " knows nothing but his duty and the word of command. Now then, Hans, open the gates and lower the bridge. Let every one light torches, and bid the stranger welcome."

Hans evinced no surprise in being ordered to usher the unknown into a house where the nearest and best friends were only admitted after tedious precautions. The canoness proceeded to give directions for supper. Amelia would have set out for the drawbridge ; but her uncle, holding himself bound in honor to meet his guest there, offered his arm to his niece, and the impatient baroness was obliged to proceed majestically to the castle gate, where the wandering fugitive Consuelo had already alighted.

CHAPTER XXV.

DURING the three months that had elapsed since the Baroness Amelia had taken it into her head to have a companion, less to instruct her than to solace her weariness, she had in fancy pictured to herself a hundred times the form and features of her future friend. Aware of Porpora's crusty humor, she feared he would send some severe and pedantic governess. She had therefore secretly written to him to say (as if her desires were not law to her doting relatives), that she would receive no one past twenty-five. On reading Porpora's answer she was so transported with joy that she forthwith sketched in imagination a complete portrait of the young musician—the adopted child of the professor, young, and a Venetian — that is to say, in Amelia's eyes, made expressly for herself, and after her own image.

She was somewhat disconcerted, therefore, when, instead of the blooming, saucy girl that her fancy had drawn, she beheld a pale, melancholy, and embarrassed young person ; for, in addition to the profound grief with which her poor heart was overwhelmed, and the fatigue of a long and rapid journey, a fearful and almost fatal impression had been made on Consuelo's mind by the vast pine forests tossed by the tempest, the dark night illuminated at intervals by livid flashes of lightning, and, above all, by the aspect of this grim castle, to which the howlings of the baron's kennel and the light of the torches borne by the servants lent a strange and ghastly effect. What a contrast with the *firmanento lucido* of Marcello — the harmonious silence of the nights at Venice—the confiding liberty of her former life, passed in the bosom of love and joyous poesy! When the carriage had slowly passed over the drawbridge, which sounded hollow under the horses' feet, and the portcullis fell with a startling clang, it seemed to her as if she had entered the portals of the "Inferno" of Dante; and, seized with terror, she recommended her soul to God.

Her countenance therefore showed symptoms of extreme agitation when she presented herself before her hosts; and the aspect of Count Christian, his tall, wasted figure, worn at once by age and vexation, and dressed in his ancient costume, completed her dismay. She imagined she beheld the specter of some ancient nobleman of the middle ages; and looking upon every thing that surrounded her as a dream, she drew back, uttering an exclamation of terror.

The old count, attributing her hesitation and paleness to the jolting of the carriage and the fatigue of the journey, offered his arm to assist her in mounting the steps, endeavoring at the same time to utter some kind and polite expressions. But the worthy man, on whom nature had bestowed a cold and reserved exterior, had become, during so long a period of absolute retirement, such a stranger to the usages and conventional courtesies of the world, that his timidity was redoubled; and under a grave and severe aspect he concealed the hesitation and confusion of a child. The obligation which he considered himself under to speak Italian, a language which he had formerly known tolerably well but which he had almost forgotten, only added to his embarrassment; and he could merely stammer out a few words, which Consuelo heard with difficulty, and which she took for the unknown and mysterious language of the Shades.

Amelia, who had intended to throw herself upon Consuelo's neck, and at once appropriate her to herself, had nothing to say—such is the reserve imparted, as if by contagion, even to the boldest natures, when the timidity of others seems to shun their advances.

Consuelo was introduced into the great hall where they had supped. The count, divided between the wish to do her honor and the fear of letting her see his son while buried in his morbid sleep, paused and hesitated, and Consuelo, trembling and feeling her knees give way under her, sank into the nearest seat.

"Uncle," said Amelia, seeing the embarrassment of the count, "I think it would be better to receive the signora here. It is warmer than in the great saloon, and she must be frozen by the wintry wind of our mountains. I am grieved to see her so overcome with fatigue, and I am sure that she requires a good supper and a sound sleep much more than our ceremonies. Is it not true, my dear signora?" added she, gaining courage enough to press gently with her plump and pretty fingers the powerless arm of Consuelo.

Her lively voice, and the German accent with which she pronounced her Italian, reassured Consuelo. She raised her eyes to the charming countenance of the young baroness, and, looks once exchanged, reserve and timidity were alike banished. The traveler understood immediately that this was her pupil, and that this enchanting face at least was not that of a specter. She gratefully received all the attentions offered her by Amelia, approached the fire, allowed her cloak to be taken off, accepted the offer of supper, although she was not the least hungry; and more and more reassured by the kindness of her young hostess, she found at length the faculties of seeing, hearing, and replying.

While the domestics served supper, the conversation naturally turned on Porpora, and Consuelo was delighted to hear the old count speak of him as his friend, his equal, almost as his superior. Then they talked of Consuelo's journey, the route by which she had come, and the storm which must have terrified her. "We are accustomed at Venice," replied Consuelo, "to tempests still more sudden and perilous; for in our gondolas, in passing from one part of the city to another, we are often threatened with shipwreck even at our very thresholds. The water which serves us instead of paved streets, swells and foams like the waves of the sea, dashing our frail barks with such violence against the walls, that they are in danger of destruction before we have time to land. Nevertheless, although I have frequently witnessed such occurrences, and am not naturally very timid, I was more terrified this evening than I have ever been before, by the fall of a huge tree, uprooted by the tempest in the mountains and crashing across our path. The horses reared upright, while the postilion in terror exclaimed—'It is the Tree of Misfortune!—it is the Hussite which has fallen!' Can you explain what that means, *Signora Baronessa?*"

Neither the count nor Amelia attempted to reply to this question; they trembled while they looked at each other. "My son was not deceived," said the old man! "Strange! strange in truth!"

And excited by his solicitude for Albert, he left the saloon to rejoin him, while Amelia, clasping her hands, murmured—"There is magic here, and the devil in presence bodily."

These strange remarks reawakened the superstitious feeling which Consuelo had experienced on entering the castle of Rudolstadt. The sudden paleness of Amelia, the solemn silence of the old servants in their red liveries—whose square bulky figures and whose lack-luster eyes, which their long servitude seemed to have deprived of all sense and expression, appeared each the counterpart of his neighbors—the immense hall wainscoted with black oak, whose gloom a chandelier loaded with lighted candles did not suffice to dissipate; the cries of the screech-owl, which had recommenced its flight round the castle, the storm being over; even the family portraits and the huge heads of stags and boars carved in relief on the wainscoting—all awakened emotions of a gloomy cast that she was unable to shake off. The observations of the young baroness were not very cheering. "My dear signora," said she, hastening to assist her, "you must be prepared to meet here things strange, inexplicable, often unpleasant, sometimes even frightful; true scenes of romance which no one would believe if you related them, and on which you must pledge your honor to be silent forever."

While the baroness was thus speaking the door opened

slowly, and the Canoness Wenceslawa, with her hump, her angular figure, and severe attire, the effect of which was heightened by the decorations of her order which she never laid aside, entered the apartment with an air more affably majestic than she had ever worn since the period when the Empress Maria Theresa, returning from her expedition to Hungary, had conferred on the castle the unheard-of honor of taking there a glass of hippocras and an hour's repose. She advanced toward Consuelo, and after a couple of courtesies and a harangue in German, which she had apparently learned by heart, proceeded to kiss her forehead. The poor girl, cold as marble, received what she considered a death salute, and murmured some inaudible reply.

When the canoness had returned to the saloon, for she saw that she rather frightened the stranger than otherwise, Amelia burst into laughter long and loud.

" By my faith," said she to her companion, " I dare swear you thought you saw the ghost of Queen Libussa ; but calm yourself; it is my aunt, the best and most tiresome of women."

Hardly had Consuelo recovered from this emotion when she heard the creaking of great Hungarian boots behind her. A heavy and measured step shook the floor, and a man with a face so massive, red, and square, that those of the servants appeared pale and aristocratic beside it, traversed the hall in profound silence, and went out by the great door which the valets respectfully opened for him. Fresh agitation on the part of Consuelo, fresh laughter on that of Amelia.

" This," said she, " is Baron Rudolstadt, the greatest hunter, the most unparalleled sleeper, and the best of fathers. His nap in the saloon is concluded. At nine he rises from his chair, without on that account awakening, walks across this hall without seeing or hearing any thing, retires to rest, and wakes with the dawn, alert, active, vigorous as if he were still young, and bent on pursuing the chase anew with falcon, hound, and horse."

Hardly had she concluded when the chaplain passed. He was stout, short, and pale as a dropsical patient. A life of meditation does not suit the dull Slavonian temperament, and the good man's obesity was no criterion of robust health. He made a profound bow to the ladies, spoke in an under tone to a servant, and disappeared in the track of the baron. Forthwith, old Hans and another of these automatons, which Consuelo could not distinguish, so closely did they resemble each other, took their way to the saloon. Consuelo, unable any longer even to appear to eat, followed them with her eyes. Hardly had they passed the door, when a new apparition, more striking than all the rest, presented itself at the threshold. It was a youth of lofty stature, and admirable proportions, but with a countenance of corpse-like paleness. He was attired in black from head to foot, while a velvet cloak, trimmed with sable and held by tassels and clasps of gold, hung from his shoulders. Hair of ebon blackness fell in disorder over his pale cheeks, which were further concealed by the curls of his glossy beard. He motioned away the servants who advanced to meet him, with an imperative gesture, before which they recoiled as if his gaze had fascinated them. Then he turned toward Count Christian who followed him.

"I assure you, father," said he, in a sweet voice and winning accents, "that I have never felt so calm. Something great is accomplished in my destiny, and the peace of Heaven has descended on our house."

"May God grant it, my child !" exclaimed the old man, extending his hand to bless him.

The youth bent his head reverently under the hand of his father ; then raising it with a mild and sweet expression, he advanced to the center of the hall, smiled faintly, while he slightly touched the hand which Amelia held out to him, and looked earnestly at Consuelo for some seconds. Struck with involuntary respect, Consuelo saluted him with downcast eyes; but he did not return the salutation, and still continued to gaze on her.

"This is the young person," said the canoness in German, "whom——" But the young man interrupted her with a gesture which seemed to say, "Do not speak to me, do not disturb my thoughts." Then slowly turning away, without testifying either surprise or interest, he deliberately retired by the great door.

"You must excuse him, my dear young lady," said the canoness; "he——"

"I beg pardon, aunt, for interrupting you," exclaimed Amelia; "but you are speaking German, which the signora does not understand."

"Pardon me, dear signora!" replied Consuelo, in Italian; "I have spoken many languages in my childhood, for I have traveled a good deal. I remember enough of German to understand it perfectly. I dare not yet attempt to speak it, but if you will be so good as to give me some lessons, I hope to regain my knowledge of it in a few days."

"I feel just in the same position," replied the canoness, in German. "I comprehend all the young lady says, yet could not speak her language. Since she understands me, I may tell her that I hope she will pardon my nephew the rudeness of which he has been guilty in not saluting her, when I inform her that this young man has been seriously ill, and that after his fainting fit he is so weak that probably he did not see her. Is not this so, brother?" asked the good Wenceslawa, trembling at the falsehoods she had uttered, and seeking her pardon in the eyes of Count Christian.

"My dear sister," replied the old man, "it is generous in you to excuse my son. The signora, I trust, will not be too much surprised on learning certain particulars which we shall communicate to her to-morrow, with all the confidence which we ought to feel for a child of Porpora, and, I hope I may soon add, a friend of the family."

It was now the hour for retiring, and the habits of the establishment were so uniform, that if the two young girls had remained much longer at table, the servants would doubtless have removed the chairs and extinguished the lights, just as if they had not been there. Besides, Consuelo longed to retire, and the baroness conducted her to the elegant and comfortable apartment which had been set apart for her accommodation.

"I should like to have an hour's chat with you," said she, as soon as the canoness, who had done the honors of the apartment, had left the room. "I long to make you acquainted with matters here, so as to enable you to put up with our eccentricities. But you are so tired that you must certainly wish, in preference, to repose."

"Do not let that prevent you, signora," replied Consuelo; "I am fatigued, it is true, but I feel so excited that I am sure I shall not close my eyes during the night. Therefore talk to me as much as you please, with this stipulation only, that it shall be in German. It will serve as a lesson for me; for I perceive that the Signor Count and the canoness as well, are not familiar with Italian."

"Let us make a bargain," said Amelia. " You shall go
to bed and rest yourself a little, while I throw on a dressing-gown and dismiss my waiting-maid. I shall then
return, seat myself by your bed-side, and speak German so
long as we can keep awake. Is it agreed?"

" With all my heart," replied Consuelo.

CHAPTER XXVI.

"Know, then, my dear," said Amelia, when she had
settled herself as aforesaid—" but, now that I think of it,
I do not know your name," she added, smiling. " It is
time, however, to banish all ceremony between us; you
will call me Amelia, while I shall call you——"

"I have a singular name, somewhat difficult to pronounce," replied Consuelo. " The excellent Porpora,
when he sent me hither, requested me to assume his name,
according to the custom which prevails among masters
toward their favorite pupils. I share this privilege, therefore, with the great Huber, surnamed Porporina; but, in
place of Porporina, please to call me simply Nina."

" Let it be Nina, then, between ourselves," said Amelia.
"Now, listen, for I have a long story to tell you; and if
I do not go back a little into the history of the past, you
will never understand what took place in this house to-
day."

"I am all attention," replied the new Porporina.

"Of course, my dear Nina," said the young baroness,
"you know something of the history of Bohemia."

"Alas!" replied Consuelo, "as my master must have
informed you, I am very deficient in information. I know
somewhat of the history of music, indeed; but as to that
of Bohemia, or any other country, I know nothing."

"In that case," replied Amelia, " I must tell you enough
of it to render my story intelligible. Some three hundred
years ago, the people among whom you now find yourself,
were great, heroic, and unconquerable. They had, indeed,
strange masters, and a religion which they did not very
well understand, but which their rulers wished to impose
by force. They were oppressed by hordes of monks, while
a cruel and abandoned king insulted their dignity, and

crushed their sympathies. But a secret fury and deep-seated hatred fermented below; the storm broke out; the strangers were expelled; religion was reformed; convents were pillaged and razed to the ground; while the drunken Wenceslas was cast into prison, and deprived of his crown. The signal of the revolt had been the execution of John Huss and Jerome of Prague, two wise and courageous Bohemians, who wished to examine and throw light upon the mysteries of Catholicism, and whom a council cited, condemned, and burned, after having promised them safe conduct and freedom of discussion. This infamous treason was so grating to national honor, that a bloody war ravaged Bohemia, and a large portion of Germany, for many years. This exterminating war was called the war of the Hussites. Innumerable and dreadful crimes were committed on both sides. The manners of the times were fierce and cruel over the whole earth. Party spirit and religious fanaticism rendered them still more dreadful; and Bohemia was the terror of Europe. I shall not shock your imagination, already unfavorably impressed by the appearance of this savage country, by reciting the horrible scenes which then took place. On the one side, it was nothing but murder, burnings, destructions; churches profaned, and monks and nuns mutilated, hung, and thrown into boiling pitch. On the other side, villages were destroyed, whole districts desolated, treasons, falsehoods, cruelties, abounded on every side. Hussites were cast by thousands into the mines, filling abysses with their dead bodies, and strewing the earth with their own bones and those of their enemies. These terrible Hussites were for a long time invincible; even yet their name is not mentioned without terror; and yet their patriotism, their intrepid constancy, and incredible exploits, have bequeathed to us a secret feeling of pride and admiration, which young minds, such as mine, find it somewhat difficult to conceal."

"And why conceal it?" asked Consuelo, simply.

"It is because Bohemia has fallen back, after many struggles, under the yoke of slavery. Bohemia is no more, my poor Nina. Our masters were well aware that the religious liberty of our country was also its political freedom; therefore they have stifled both."

"See," replied Consuelo, "how ignorant I am! I never

heard of these things before, and I did not dream that men could be so unhappy and so wicked."

"A hundred years after John Huss, another wise man, a new sectarian, a poor monk called Martin Luther, sprang up to awaken the national spirit, and to inspire Bohemia, and all the independent provinces of Germany, with hatred of a foreign yoke and revolt against popedom. The most powerful kings remained Catholics, not so much for love of religion, as for love of absolute power. Austria united with them in order to overwhelm us, and a new war, called the Thirty Years' War, came to shake and destroy our national independence. From the commencement of this war, Bohemia was the prey of the strongest; Austria treated us as conquered; took from us our faith, our liberty, our language, and even our name. Our fathers resisted courageously, but the imperial yoke has weighed more and more heavily upon us. For the last hundred and twenty years, our nobility, ruined and decimated by exactions, wars, and torments, have been forced to expatriate themselves, or turn renegades by abjuring their origin, germanising their names (pay attention to this), and renouncing the liberty of professing their religious opinions. They have burned our books, destroyed our schools—in a word, made us Austrians. We are but a province of the empire, and you hear German spoken in a Slavonic state—that is saying enough."

"And you now suffer and blush for this slavery? I understand you, and I already hate Austria with all my heart."

"Oh! speak low," exclaimed the young baroness. "No one can, without danger, speak thus under the black sky of Bohemia; and in this castle there is but one person, my dear Nina, who would have the boldness or the folly to say what you have just said: that is my cousin Albert."

"Is this, then, the cause of the sorrow which is imprinted on his countenance? I felt an involuntary sensation of respect on looking at him."

"Ah, my fair lioness of St. Mark," said Amelia, surprised at the generous animation which suddenly lighted up the pale features of her companion; "you take matters too seriously. I fear that in a few days my poor cousin will inspire you rather with pity than with respect."

"The one need not prevent the other," replied Consuelo, "but explain yourself, my dear baroness."

"Listen," said Amelia; "we are a strictly Catholic family, faithful to church and state. We bear a Saxon name, and our ancestors, on the Saxon side, were always rigidly orthodox. Should my aunt, the canoness, some day undertake to relate, unhappily for you, the services which the counts and German barons have rendered to the holy cause, you will find that, according to her, there is not the slightest stain of heresy on our escutcheon. Even when Saxony was Protestant, the Rudolstadts preferred to abandon their Protestant electors, rather than the communion of the Romish church. But my aunt takes care never to dilate on these things in presence of Count Albert; if it were not for that, you should hear the most astonishing things that ever human ears have listened to."

"You excite my curiosity without gratifying it. I understand thus much, that I should not appear, before your noble relatives, to share your sympathy and that of Count Albert for old Bohemia. You may trust to my prudence, dear baroness; besides, I belong to a Catholic country, and the respect which I entertain for my religion, as well as that which I owe your family, would ensure my silence on every occasion."

"It will be wise; for I warn you once again that we are terribly rigid upon that point. As to myself, dear Nina, I am a better compound—neither Protestant nor Catholic. I was educated by nuns, whose prayers and paternosters wearied me. The same weariness pursues me here, and my aunt Wenceslawa, in her own person, represents the pedantry and superstition of a whole community. But I am too much imbued with the spirit of the age, to throw myself, through contradiction, into the not less presumptuous controversies of the Lutherans: as for the Hussites, their history is so ancient that I have no more relish for it than for the glory of the Greeks and Romans. The French way of thinking is to my mind; and I do not believe there can be any other reason, philosophy, or civilization, than that which is practiced in charming and delightful France, the writings of which I sometimes have a peep at in secret, and whose liberty, happiness, and pleasures, I behold from a distance, as in a dream, through the bars of my prison."

"You each moment surprise me more," said Consuelo, innocently. "How does it come that just now you appeared full of heroism, in recalling the exploits of your ancient Bohemians? I believed you a Bohemian, and somewhat of a heretic."

"I am more than heretic, and more than Bohemian," replied Amelia, laughing; "I am the least thing in life incredulous altogether; I hate and denounce every kind of despotism, spiritual or temporal; in particular I protest against Austria, which of all old duennas is the most wrongheaded and devout."

"And is Count Albert likewise incredulous? Is he also imbued with French principles? In that case, you should suit each other wonderfully?"

"Oh, we are the furthest in the world from suiting each other, and now, after all these necessary preambles, is the proper time to speak of him.

"Count Christian, my uncle, was childless by his first wife. Married again at the age of forty, he had five girls, who, as well as their mother, all died young, stricken with the same malady—a continual pain, and a species of slow brain fever. This second wife was of pure Bohemian blood, and had beside great beauty and intelligence. I did not know her. You will see her portrait in the grand saloon, where she appears dressed in a bodice of precious stones and scarlet mantle. Albert resembles her wonderfully. He is the sixth and last of her children, the only one who has attained the age of thirty; and this not without difficulty: for without apparently being ill, he has experienced rude shocks and strange symptoms of disease of the brain, which still cause fear and dread as regards his life. Between ourselves, I do not think that he will long outlive this fatal period which his mother could not escape. Although born of a father already advanced in years, Albert is gifted with a strong constitution, but, as he himself says, the malady is in his soul, and has ever been increasing. From his earliest infancy, his mind was filled with strange and superstitious notions. When he was four years old, he frequently fancied he saw his mother beside his cradle, although she was dead, and he had seen her buried. In the night he used to awake and converse with her, which terrified my aunt Wenceslawa so much that she always made several women sleep in his chamber near the child, while the chaplain used I do not know how much holy water, and said masses by the dozen, to oblige the specter to keep quiet. But it was of no avail, for the child, although he had not spoken of his apparitions for a long time, declared one day in confidence to his nurse, that he still saw his own dear mother; but he would not tell, because Mr. Chaplain had said wicked words in the chamber to prevent her coming back.

"He was a silent and serious child. They tried to amuse him; they overwhelmed him with toys and playthings, but these only served for a long time to make him more sad. At last they resolved not to oppose the taste which he displayed for study, and in effect this passion being satisfied, imparted more animation to him, but only served to change his calm and languishing melancholy into a strange excitement, mingled with paroxysms of grief, the cause of which it was impossible to foresee or avert. For example, when he saw the poor, he melted into tears, stripped himself of his little wealth, even reproaching himself that he had not more to bestow. If he saw a child beaten, or a peasant ill-used, he became so indignant that he would swoon away, or fall into convulsions for hours together. All this displayed a noble disposition and a generous heart; but the best qualities, pushed to extremes, become defective or absurd. Reason was not developed in young Albert in proportion to feeling and imagination. The study of history excited without enlightening him. When he learned the crimes and injustice of men, he felt an emotion like that of the barbarian monarch, who, listening to the history of Christ's passion and death, exclaimed while he brandished his weapon, 'Ah! had I been there, I should have cut the wicked Jews into a thousand pieces!'

"Albert could not deal with men as they have been and are. He thought Heaven unjust in not having created them all kind and compassionate like himself; he did not perceive that, from an excess of tenderness and virtue, he was on the point of becoming impious and misanthropic. He did not understand what he felt, and at eighteen was as unfit to live among men, and hold the place which his position demanded in society, as he was at six months old. If any person expressed in his presence a selfish thought, such as our poor world abounds with, and without which it could not exist, regardless of the rank of the person, or the feelings of the family toward him, he displayed immediately an invincible dislike to him, and nothing could induce him to make the least advance. He chose his society from among the most humble, and those most in disfavor with fortune and even nature. In the plays of his child-hood he only amused himself with the children of the poor, and especially with those whose stupidity or infirmities had inspired all others with disgust or weariness. This strange inclination, as you will soon perceive, has not abandoned him.

"As in the midst of these eccentricities he displayed much intelligence, a good memory, and a taste for the fine arts, his father and his good aunt Wenceslawa, who tenderly cherished him, had no cause to blush for him in society. They ascribed his peculiarities to his rustic habits; and when he was inclined to go too far, they took care to hide them under some pretext or other from those who might be offended by them. But in spite of his ad-mirable qualities and happy dispositions, the count and the canoness saw with terror this independent, and in many respects insensible nature, reject more and more the laws of polite society and the amenities and usages of the world."

"But as far as you have gone," interrupted Consuelo, "I see nothing of the unreasonableness of which you speak."

"Oh," replied Amelia, "that is because you are your-self, so far as I can see, of an open and generous disposi-tion. But perhaps you are tired of my chatter, and would wish to sleep?"

"Not at all, my dear Baroness," replied Consuelo. "I entreat you to continue."

Amelia resumed her narrative in these words:

CHAPTER XXVII.

"You say, dear Nina, that hitherto you discover noth-ing extravagant in the actions or manner of my poor cousin. I am about to give you better proofs of it. My uncle and aunt are without doubt the best Christians and the most charitable souls in the world. They liberally dispense alms to all around them, and it would be impos-sible to display less pomp or pride in the use of riches than do these worthy relatives of mine. Well, my cousin made the discovery that their manner of living was altogether opposed to the spirit of the Gospel. He wished that, after the example of the early Christians, they should sell all they had and become beggars, after having distributed the proceeds among the poor. If, restrained by the respect and love which he bore them, he did not exactly use words to this effect, he showed plainly what he thought, in bitterly deploring the lot of the poor, who are only born to toil and suffer, while the rich live in luxury and idleness. When he had given away in charity all his pocket-money, it was in his estimation but as a drop of water in the sea, and he demanded yet larger sums, which they dared not refuse him, and which flowed through his hands as water. He has given so much, that you will no longer see a poor person in all the country which surrounds us, and I must add that we find our position nothing the better for it; inasmuch as the wants and demands of the lower orders increase in proportion to the concessions made to them, and our good peasants, formerly so mild and humble, begin to give themselves airs, thanks to the prodigality and fine speeches of their young master. If we had not the power of the imperial government to rely upon, which affords us protection on one hand, while it oppresses us on the other, I believe that, more especially since the succession of the Emperor Charles, our estates and castles might have been pillaged twenty times over by the bands of war-famished peasants which the inexhaustible benevolence of Albert, celebrated for thirty leagues round, has brought upon our backs.

"When Count Christian attempted to remonstrate with young Albert, telling him that to give all in one day was to deprive us of the means of giving any thing the next, 'Why, my beloved father,' he replied, 'have we not a roof to shelter us which will last longer than ourselves, while thousands of unfortunates have only the cold and inclement sky above their heads? Have we not each more clothes than would suffice for one of these ragged and shivering families? Do I not see daily upon our table more meats and good Hungarian wine than would suffice to refresh and comfort these poor beggars, exhausted with fatigue and hunger? Have we a right to refuse when we have so much more than we require? Are we even permitted to use what is necessary while others are in want? Has the law of Christ changed?'"

" What reply could the count, the canoness, and the chaplain, who had educated this young man in the austere principles of religion, make to these fine words? They were accordingly embarrassed when they found him take matters thus literally, and hold no terms with those existing arrangements on which, as it appears to me, is founded the whole structure of society.

" It was another affair as regarded political matters. In Albert's eyes, the social arrangements which permitted sovereigns, in conformity with their pride and vainglory, to destroy millions of men and ruin entire countries, were nothing less than monstrous. This intolerance in these respects might have entailed dangerous consequences, so that his relatives no longer ventured to bring him to Vienna, Prague, or any other city where his virtuous fanaticism might have proved fatal to him. They were not even certain as to his religious views; but they knew that there was quite enough in his exalted notions to bring a heretic to the stake. He hated popes, inasmuch as these apostles of Jesus Christ leagued themselves with kings against the peace and majesty of the people. He blamed the luxury, worldly spirit, and ambition of bishops, abbés, and churchmen generally. He repeated sermons of Luther and John Huss to the poor chaplain, and in the meantime passed hours together prostrate on the chapel floor, plunged in ecstasies worthy of a saint. He observed fasts beyond the rigid prescriptions of the Church; it was even said he wore a haircloth shirt; and it required all his father's influence and his aunt's tenderness to induce him to renounce austerities which were only calculated to turn his head.

" When these wise and affectionate parents saw that he was in a fair way to dissipate his patrimony in a few years, and perhaps be thrown into prison as a rebel to the Holy Church and empire, they at last decided on making him travel, hoping that, by seeing men and the laws of nations, which are nearly the same all over the civilized world, he would become accustomed to live like them and with them. They therefore confided him to the care of a tutor, a subtle Jesuit, a man of the world and of tact, if there ever was one, who understood his part at once, and pledged himself in his conscience to undertake all that which they did not even dare to ask of him. To speak plainly, it was thought desirable to corrupt and blunt this untamed soul, and to form it to the social yoke, by infusing drop by drop the sweet and necessary poisons of ambition, of vanity, of religious, political, and social indifference. Do not knit your brows, dear Porporina. My worthy uncle is a simple and upright man, who from his youth has taken all these things as he has found them, and, without hypocrisy and without examination, has learned how to reconcile tolerance and religion, the duties of a Christian and those of a noble. In a world and in an age where, for millions like ourselves, one man like Albert is found, he who keeps with the age and with the world, is a wise man, and he who wishes to go back two thousand years into the past, is a fool, who gives offense to his neighbors and converts nobody.

"Albert traveled for eight years. He visited Italy, France, England, Prussia, Poland, Russia, and even the Turks, and returned through Hungary, Southern Germany, and Bavaria. He conducted himself most prudently during these long excursions, spending no more than the handsome income which his parents allowed him, writing to them numerous and affectionate letters, in which he spoke merely of what he saw, without making any profound observations upon any subject whatever, and without giving his tutor any cause for complaint or ingratitude. Having returned here about the beginning of last year, after the first salutations were over, he retired, as I was informed, to the chamber which his mother had formerly occupied, remained shut up there several hours, and came out very pale to wander alone upon the mountain.

"During this time the abbé spoke confidentially with the Canoness Wenceslawa and the chaplain, who had requested him to give them full particulars respecting the physical and moral condition of the young count. 'Count Albert,' said he, 'whether the effects of travel have produced a complete change in his character, or whether, from what your lordships had related to me of his childhood, I had formed a false idea of him, has shown himself to me, from the first day of our connection, just the same as you have seen him to-day — gentle, calm, forbearing, patient, and exquisitely polite. This amiable conduct has never varied for a single instant, and I should be the most unjust of men if I advanced a single complaint against him. Nothing of what I feared as to his extravagant expenses, his abruptness, his declamations, or his exalted asceticism, has happened. He has not even once requested to manage for himself the little fortune you confided to me, and has never expressed the least dissatisfaction with my guardianship. It is true that I always anticipated his wishes, and that whenever I saw a poor man approach our carriage, I hastened to send him away satisfied, before he had even time to extend his hand. This method of proceeding succeeded completely ; and I may observe, that as the spectacle of misery and infirmity has never saddened his lordship's sight, he has not once seemed to remember his old prepossessions on this point. I have never heard him find fault with any one, blame any custom, or express an unfavorable opinion respecting any institution! That ardent devotion, the excess of which you feared, has apparently given way to a regularity of conduct every way becoming a man of the world. He has seen the most brilliant courts and the highest society of Europe, without appearing either intoxicated or offended at any thing which met his eye. Everywhere he has been remarked for his beauty, his noble bearing, his unobtrusive politeness, and the good taste that distinguished his conversation, which was always well timed and appropriate. His habits have remained as pure as those of a well-educated young girl, and this without showing any prudery or bad taste. He has seen theaters, museums, and monuments; he has conversed calmly and judiciously upon the arts. In fact, I cannot in any way understand the uneasiness he has caused your lordships, having for my part never seen a more reasonable man. If there be any thing extraordinary about him, it is his prudence, his steadiness, and the entire absence of strong desires and passions, which I have never met with in a young man so advantageously endowed by nature, birth, and fortune.'

"All this was in fact only a confirmation of the frequent letters which the abbé had written to the family; but they had always feared some exaggeration on his part, and were only really easy when they found that he could assert the moral restoration of my cousin, without fear of being contradicted by his conduct under the eyes of his parents. They loaded the abbé with presents and caresses, and waited with patience for Albert's return from his walk. It lasted a long time, however; and when at last he arrived at supper hour, they were struck by his paleness and the gravity of his expression. In the first joyful moments of their meeting, his features had expressed a sweet and heartfelt satisfaction which were no longer to be found in them. They were astonished, and spoke of it anxiously in a low voice to the abbé. He looked at Albert, and turning with surprise to those who questioned him, 'I see nothing extraordinary in the count's face,' said he; 'he has the calm and dignified expression which I have always observed during the eight years I have had the honor to accompany him.'

"Count Christian was satisfied with this answer. 'He left us still adorned with the roses of youth,' said he to his sister, 'and often, alas! the victim of a sort of internal fever which gave strength to his voice and brilliancy to his appearance; he returns embrowned by the sun of southern countries, somewhat worn by fatigue perhaps, and with that gravity of manner which becomes a full grown man. Do you not think, my dear sister, that it is better so?'

"'I think, with all this gravity, he looks very sad,' replied my good aunt; 'and I have never seen a young man of twenty-eight so phlegmatic, and with so little to say. He answers us merely in monosyllables.'

"'The count has always been very sparing of his words,' replied the abbé.

"'He was not so formerly,' said the canoness. 'If he spent weeks together in silence and meditation, he had also his days of gaiety and even of eloquence.'

"'I have never,' returned the abbé, 'seen him depart from the reserve which your ladyship remarks at this moment.'

"'Were you better pleased when he talked too much, and said things which made us tremble?' said Count Christian to his alarmed sister. 'That is just the way with women.'

"'He was at least alive then,' said she, 'and now he looks like an inhabitant of the other world, who takes no part in the affairs of this one.'

"'That is the unvarying character of the count,' replied the abbé; 'he is reserved; he is a man who never communicates his impressions to others, and who, if I must speak the whole of what I think, is not much impressed by any external objects. Such is the case with cold, sensible, and reflective persons. He is so constituted; and I should fear that in seeking to excite him, the result would be to unhinge a mind so inimical to all action, and to all dangerous undertakings.'

" 'Oh! I am certain such is not his true character!' cried the canoness.

" 'Madam, I am sure, will overcome the prejudices she has formed against so rare an advantage.'

" 'In fact, dear sister,' said the count, 'I think that the abbé speaks very wisely. Has he not by his care and attention produced the result we so much desired? Has he not turned aside the misfortunes which we feared? Albert threatened to be a prodigy, a hair-brained enthusiast. He returns to us such as he should be, to merit the esteem, the confidence, and the consideration of his fellow-men.'

" 'But as senseless as a musty volume,' said the canoness; 'or perhaps prejudiced against all things, and disdaining whatever does not agree with his secret instincts. He does not even seem happy to see us, who expected him with so much impatience.'

" 'The count was very impatient to return,' answered the abbé; 'I could plainly perceive it, although he did not manifest it openly, He is so timid and reserved!'

" 'He is not naturally reserved,' replied she quickly. 'He was sometimes violent, and sometimes tender to excess. He often vexed me; but immediately when that was the case, he threw himself upon my bosom and I was disarmed.'

" 'With me,' said the abbé, 'he has never had any fault to repair.'

" 'Believe me, sister, it is much better so,' said my uncle.

" 'Alas,' said the canoness, 'then he will always have that expression which terrifies me and oppresses my heart!'

" 'It is the dignified and noble countenance which becomes a man of his rank,' replied the abbé.

" 'It is a countenance of stone!' cried the canoness. 'He is the very image of my mother, not as I knew her, sensible and benevolent, but as she is painted, motionless and frozen in her frame of oak.'

" 'I repeat to your ladyship,' said the abbé, ' that this

has been Count Albert's habitual expression for eight years.'

" ' Alas! then, there have been eight mortal years during which he has not smiled on any one,' said the good aunt, the tears flowing down her cheeks ; 'for during the last two hours that I have fixed my eyes upon him, I have not seen the slightest smile animate his closed and colorless lips. Ah! I am almost tempted to rush toward him, and press him to my heart, reproaching him with his indifference, and scolding him, as I used to do, to see if he will not as of old throw himself upon my neck with sobs.'

" ' Beware of any such imprudence, my dear sister,' said Count Christian, compelling her to turn away from Albert, whom she still looked at with moistened eyes. ' Do not hearken to the weakness of your loving heart ; we have proved sufficiently that excessive sensibility was the bane both of the life and strong reason of our child. By distracting his thoughts, by removing him from every emotion, the abbé, conformably to our advice and that of the physicians, has succeeded in calming that agitated soul; do not now destroy his work, from the caprices of childish tenderness.'

" The canoness yielded to these reasons, and tried to accustom herself to Albert's frigid exterior, but she could not succeed, and frequently said to her brother privately, ' You may say what you please, Christian, but I fear he has been stupified, by treating him not like a man, but like a sick child.'

" When about to separate in the evening they embraced each other. Albert received his father's blessing respectfully, and when the canoness pressed him to her heart, he perceived that she trembled, and that her voice faltered. He began to tremble also, and tore himself quickly from her arms, as if a sharp sense of suffering had been awakened within him.

" ' You see, sister,' said the count in a low voice, ' he has long been accustomed to these emotions, and you have caused him pain.' At the same time, uneasy and agitated himself, he followed his son with his eyes, to see if, in his manner toward the abbé, he could perceive any exclusive preference to that person. But Albert saluted his tutor with cold politeness.

" ' My son,' said the count, ' I believe I have only fulfilled your intentions and satisfied your wishes by requesting the abbé not to leave you, as he had already proposed, and by obtaining from him a promise to remain with us as long as possible. I did not wish that the happiness of finding our family circle once more reassembled, should be poisoned by any regret on your part, and I hope that your respected friend will aid us in securing that happiness to you without any drawback.'

" Albert answered only by a low bow, and at the same time a strange smile passed over his lips.

" ' Alas!' said the canoness, as soon as he had left the room. ' Is that the smile he gives now?'

CHAPTER XXVIII.

" During Albert's absence, the count and the canoness had formed innumerable projects for the future welfare of their dear child, among which, that of marrying him occupied a prominent place. With his fine person, his illustrious name, and his still considerable fortune, Albert could have aspired to a connection with the noblest families in the kingdom. But in case his indolence and shy, retiring disposition should make him unwilling to bring himself forward and push his fortune in the world, they kept in reserve for him a young person of equally high birth with himself, since she was his cousin-germain, and bore the same name; she was not so rich, indeed, but was young, handsome, and an only daughter. This young person was Amelia, Baroness of Rudolstadt, your humble servant and new friend.

" ' She,' said they, when conversing together by the fireside, ' has as yet seen nobody. Brought up in a convent, she will be only too happy to exchange the cloister for a husband. She cannot hope for a better match; and as to the eccentricities of her cousin, the old associations of their childhood, the ties of relationship, and a few months' intimacy with us, will go far to overcome her repugnance to them, and bring her round to tolerate, were it only for the sake of family feeling, what might be unendurable to a stranger.' They were sure of the consent of my father, who never had any will but that of his elder brother and his sister Wenceslawa; and who, to say the truth, has never had a will of his own.

" When, after a fortnight's careful observation of his manners, the constant melancholy and reserve, which appeared to be the confirmed character of my cousin, became evident to them, my uncle and aunt concluded that the last scion of their race was not destined to win renown by great or noble deeds. He displayed no inclination for a bright career in arms, diplomacy, or civil affairs. To every proposal he mildly replied that he should obey the wishes of his relations, but that for his own part he desired neither luxury or glory. After all, this indolent disposition was but an exaggerated copy of his father's, a man of such calm and easy temperament that his imperturbability borders on apathy, and his modesty is a kind of self-denial. What gives to my uncle's character a tone which is wanting in his son's, is his strong sense, devoid of pride, of the duties he owes to society. Albert seemed formerly to understand domestic duties, but public ones, as they were regarded by others, concerned him no more than in his childhood. His father and mine had followed the career of arms, under Montecuculli, against Turenne. They had borne with them into the war a kind of religious enthusiasm, inspired by the example of the emperor. A blind obedience to their superiors was considered the duty of their time. This more enlightened age, however, strips the monarch of his false halo, and the rising generation believe no more in the divine right of the crown than in that of the tiara. When my uncle endeavored to stir up in his son's bosom the flame of ancient chivalric ardor, he soon perceived that his arguments had no meaning for a reasoner who looked on such things with contempt.

" ' Since it is thus,' my uncle observed to my aunt, ' we will not thwart him. Let us not counteract this melancholy remedy, which has at least restored to us a passionless, in place of an impetuous man. Let his life, in accordance with his desire, be tranquil, and he may become studious and philosophic as were many of his ancestors, an ardent lover of the chase like our brother Frederick, or a just and beneficent master, as we ourselves try to be. Let him lead from henceforward the untroubled and inoffensive life of an old man; he will be the first Rudolstadt whose life shall have known no youth. But as he must not be the last of his race, let us marry him, so that the heirs of our name may fill up this blank in the glory of our house. Who knows but it may be the will of Providence that the generous blood of his ancestors now sleeps in his veins only to reawaken with a fresh impulse in those of his descendants?'

"So it was decided that they should break the ice on this delicate subject to my cousin Albert.

"They at first approached it gently; but as they found this proposal quite as unpalatable as all previous ones had been, it became necessary to reason seriously with him. He pleaded bashfulness, timidity, and awkwardness in female society.

"'Certainly,' said my aunt, 'in my young days I would have considered a lover so grave as Albert more repulsive than otherwise; and I would not have exchanged my hump for his conversation.'

"'We must then,' said my uncle, 'fall back upon our last resource, and persuade him to marry Amelia. He has known her from infancy, looks upon her as a sister, and will be less timid with her; and, as to firmness of character, she unites animation and cheerfulness, she will by her good humor dissipate those gloomy moods into which he so frequently relapses.'

"Albert did not condemn this project, and, without openly saying so, consented to see and become acquainted with me. It was agreed that I should not be informed of the plan, in order to save me the mortification of being rejected, which was always possible on his part. They wrote to my father, and as soon as they had secured his consent, they took steps to obtain the dispensation from the Pope which our consanguinity rendered necessary. At the same time my father took me from the convent, and one fine morning we arrived at the Castle of the Giants—I very well pleased to breathe the fresh air, and impatient to see my betrothed; my good father full of hope, and fancying that he had ingeniously concealed from me a project which he had unconsciously betrayed in every sentence he uttered in the course of the journey.

"The first thing which struck me in Albert was his fine figure and noble air. I confess, dear Nina, that my heart beat almost audibly when he kissed my hand, and that for some days I was charmed by his look, and delighted by the most trifling word that fell from his lips. His serious, thoughtful manner was not displeasing to me. He seemed to feel no constraint in my society: on the contrary, he was unreserved as in the days of our childhood; and when, from a dread of failing in politeness, he wished to restrain his attention, our parents urged him to continue his ancient familiarity with me. My cheerfulness sometimes caused him to smile involuntarily, and my good aunt, transported with joy, attributed to me the honor of this improvement, which she believed would be permanent. At length he came to treat me with the mildness and gentleness one displays toward a child, and I was content— satisfied that he would shortly pay more attention to my little animated countenance, and to the handsome dresses by which I studied to please him. But I had soon the mortification to discover that he cared little for the one, and that he did not even appear to see the other. One day my good aunt wished to direct his attention to a beautiful blue dress, which suited my figure admirably. Would you believe it?—he declared its color to be a bright red! His tutor, the abbé, who had honeyed compliments ever ready on his lips, and who wished to give his pupil a lesson in gallantry, insinuated that he could easily guess why Count Albert could not distinguish the color of my dress. Here was a capital opportunity for Albert to address to me some flattering remarks on the roses of my cheeks or the golden hue of my hair. He contented himself, however, with drily telling the abbé that he was as capable of distinguishing colors as he was, and with repeating his assertion that my robe was as red as blood. I do not know why this rudeness of manner and eccentricity of expression made me shudder. I looked at Albert, and his glance terrified me. From that day I began to fear him more than I loved him. In a short time I ceased to love him at all, and now I neither love nor fear him; I merely pity him. You will by degrees understand why.

"The next day we were to go to Tauss, the nearest village, to make some purchases. I had promised myself much pleasure from this excursion as Albert was to accompany me on horseback. When ready to set out, I of course expected that he would offer me his arm. The carriages were in the court, but he did not make his appearance, although

his servant said that he had knocked at his door at the
usual hour. They sent again to see if he were getting
ready. Albert always dressed by himself, and never permitted a servant to enter his chamber until he had quitted
it. They knocked in vain; there was no reply. His
father, becoming uneasy at this continued silence, went
himself to the room; but he could neither open the door,
which was bolted inside, nor obtain a reply to his questions. They began to be frightened, when the abbé observed in his usual placid manner, that Count Albert was
subject to long fits of sleep, which might almost be termed
trances, and if suddenly awakened, he was agitated, and
apparently suffered for many days, as if from a shock.
'But that is a disease,' said the canoness, anxiously.

"'I do not think so,' said the abbe. 'He has never complained of any thing. The physicians whom I brought to
see him when he lay in this state, found no feverish symptoms, and attributed his condition to excess of application
or study; and they earnestly advised that this apparently
necessary repose and entire forgetfulness should not be
counteracted by any mode of treatment.'

"'And is it frequent?' asked my uncle.

"'I have observed it only five or six times during eight
years; and not having annoyed him by my attentions, I
have never found any unpleasant consequences.'

"'And does it last long?' I demanded in my turn, very
impatiently.

"'Longer or shorter, according to the want of rest
which precedes or occasions these attacks; but no one can
know, for the count either does not himself recollect the
cause, or does not wish to tell it. He is extremely studious, and conceals it with unusual modesty.'

"'He is very learned then?' I replied.

"'Extremely learned.'

"'And he never displays it?'

"'He makes a secret of it—nay, does not himself suspect it.'

"'Of what use is it, in that case?'

"'Genius is like beauty,' replied this Jesuit courtier,
casting a soft look upon me; 'both are favors of Heaven
which occasion neither pride nor agitation to those who
enjoy them.'

"I understood the lesson, and only felt the more annoyed, as you may suppose. They resolved to defer the drive until my cousin should awake; but when at the end of two hours I saw that he did not stir, I laid aside my rich riding-dress, and commenced to my embroidery, not without spoiling a good deal of silk and missing many stitches. I was indignant at the neglect of Albert, who over his books in the evening had forgotten his promised ride with me, and who had now left me to wait, in no very pleasant humor, while he quietly enjoyed his sleep. The day wore on, and we were obliged to give up our proposed excursion. My father, confiding in the assurance of the abbé, took his gun, and strolled out to kill a few hares. My aunt, who had less faith in the good man's opinion, went upstairs more than twenty times to listen at her nephew's door, but without being able to hear the faintest breathing. The poor woman was in an agony of distress. As for my uncle, he took a book of devotion, to try its effect in calming his inquietude, and began to read in a corner of the saloon with a resignation so provoking that it half tempted me to leap out of the window with chagrin. At length toward evening, my aunt, overjoyed, came to inform us that she had heard Albert rise and dress himself. The abbé advised us to appear neither surprised nor uneasy, not to ask the count any questions, and to endeavor to divert his mind and his thoughts, if he evinced any signs of mortification at what had occurred.

"'But if my cousin be not ill, he is mad!' exclaimed I, with some degree of irritation.

"I observed my uncle change countenance at this harsh expression, and I was struck with sudden remorse. But when Albert entered without apologizing to any one, and without even appearing to be aware of our disappointment, I confess I was excessively piqued and gave him a very cold reception, of which, however, absorbed as he was in thought, he took not the slightest notice.

"In the evening, my father fancied that a little music would raise his spirits. I had not yet sung before Albert, as my harp had only arrived the preceding evening. I must not, accomplished Porporina, boast of my musical acquirements before you; but you will admit that I have a good voice, and do not want natural taste. I allowed them to press me, for I had at the moment more inclination to cry than to sing, but Albert offered not a word to draw me out. At last I yielded, but I sang badly, and Albert, as if I had tortured his ears, had the rudeness to leave the room after I had gone through a few bars. I was compelled to summon all my pride to my assistance to prevent me from bursting into tears, and to enable me to finish the air without breaking the strings of my harp. My aunt followed her nephew; my father was asleep ; my uncle waited near the door till his sister should return, to tell him something of his son. The abbé alone remained to pay me compliments, which irritated me yet more than the indifference of the others. 'It seems,' said I to him, ' that my cousin does not like music.'

" ' On the contrary, he likes it very much,' replied he, ' but it is according——'

" ' According to the manner in which one performs,' said I, interrupting him.

" ' Yes,' replied he, in no wise disconcerted, ' and to the state of his mind. Sometimes music does him good, sometimes harm. You have, I am certain, agitated him so much that he feared he should not be able to restrain his emotion. This retreat is more flattering to you than the most elaborate praise.'

" The compliments of this Jesuit had in them something so sinister and sarcastic that it made me detest him. But I was soon freed from his annoyance, as you shall presently learn.

CHAPTER XXIX.

" On the following day my aunt, who never speaks unless when strongly moved, took it into her head to begin a conversation with the abbé and the chaplain, and as, with the exception of her family affections, which entirely absorb her, she is incapable of conversing on any topic but that of family honor, she was ere long deep in a dissertation on her favorite subject, genealogy, and laboring to convince the two priests that our race was the purest and the most illustrious, as well as the most noble, of all the families of Germany, on the female side particularly. The abbé listened with patience, the chaplain with profound respect, when Albert, who apparently had taken no interest in the old lady's disquisition, all at once interrupted her.

" 'It would seem, my dear aunt,' said he, 'that you are laboring under some hallucination as to the superiority of our family. It is true that their titles and nobility are of sufficient antiquity, but a family which loses its name, abjures it in some sort in order to assume that of a woman of foreign race and religion, gives up its right to be considered ancient in virtue and faithful to the glory of its country.'

"This remark somewhat disconcerted the canoness, but as the abbé had appeared to lend profound attention to it, she thought it incumbent on her to reply.

" 'I am not of your opinion, my dear child,' said she; 'we have often seen illustrious houses render themselves still more so, and with reason, by uniting to their name that of a maternal branch, in order not to deprive their heirs of the honor of being descended from a woman so illustriously connected.'

" 'But this is a case to which that rule does not apply,' answered Albert, with a pertinacity for which he was not remarkable. 'I can conceive the alliance of two illustrious names. It is quite right that a woman should transmit to her children her own name joined with that of her husband; but the complete extinction of the latter would appear to me an insult on the part of her who would exact it, and an act of baseness on the part of him who would submit to it.'

" 'You speak of matters of very remote date, Albert,' said the canoness, with a profound sigh, 'and are even less happy than I in the application of the rule. Our good abbé might from your words suppose that some one of our ancestors had been capable of such meanness. And since you appear to be so well informed on subjects of which I supposed you comparatively ignorant, you should not have made a reflection of this kind relative to political events, now, thank God, long passed away !'

" 'If my observation disturb you, I shall detail the facts, in order to clear the memory of our ancestor Withold, the last Count of Rudolstadt, of every imputation injurious to it. It appears to interest my cousin,' he added, seeing that my attention had become riveted upon him, astonished as I was to see him engage in a discussion so contrary to his philosophical ideas and silent habits. 'Know, then, Amelia, that our great-great-grandfather, Wratislaw, was

only four years old when his mother, Ulrica, of Rudolstadt, took it into her head to inflict upon him the insult
of supplanting his true name—the name of his fathers,
which was Podiebrad—by this Saxon name which you and
I bear to-day—you without blushing for it, and I without
being proud of it.'

" 'It is useless, to say the least of it,' said my uncle,
who seemed ill at ease, 'to recall events so distant from the
time in which we live.'

" 'It appears to me,' said Albert, 'that my aunt has
gone much further back, in relating the high deeds of the
Rudolstadts, and I do not know why one of us, when he
recollects by chance that he is of Bohemian and not of
Saxon origin—that he is called Podiebrad, and not Rudolstadt—should be guilty of ill-breeding in speaking of
events which occurred not more than twenty-five years
ago.'

" 'I know very well,' replied the abbé, who had listened to Albert with considerable interest, 'that your illustrious family was allied in past times to the royal line of
George Podiebrad; but I was not aware that it had descended in so direct a line as to bear the name.'

" 'It is because my aunt, who knows how to draw out
genealogical trees, has thought fit to forget the ancient and
venerable one from which we have sprung. But a genealogical tree, upon which our glorious but dark history has
been written in characters of blood, stands yet upon the
neighboring mountains.'

" As Albert became very animated in speaking thus,
and my uncle's countenance appeared to darken, the abbé,
much as his curiosity was excited, endeavored to give the
conversation a different turn. But mine would not suffer
me to remain silent when so fair an opportunity presented
itself for satisfying it. 'What do you mean, Albert?' 1
exclaimed, approaching him.

" 'I mean that which a Podiebrad should not be ignorant of,' he replied; 'that the old oak of the Stone of
Terror, which you see every day from your window, Amelia,
and under which you should never sit down without raising your soul to God, bore, some three hundred years ago,
fruit rather heavier than the dried acorns it produces
to-day.'

" 'It is a shocking story,' said the chaplain, horror·

struck, 'and I do not know who could have informed the count of it.'

" 'The tradition of the country, and perhaps something more certain still,' replied Albert. ' You have in vain burned the archives of the family, and the records of history, Mr. Chaplain; in vain have you brought up children in ignorance of the past ; in vain imposed silence on the simple by sophistry, on the weak by threats : neither the dread of despotic power, however great, nor even that of hell itself, can stifle the thousand voices of the past which awaken on every side. No, no ! they speak too loudly, these terrible voices, for that of a priest to hush them ! They speak to our souls in sleep, in the whisperings of spirits from the dead ; they appeal to us in every sound we hear in the external world ; they issue even from the trunks of the trees, like the gods of the olden time, to tell us of the crimes, the misfortunes, and the noble deeds of our ancestors !'

" 'And why, my poor child,' said the canoness, ' why cherish in your mind such bitter thoughts—such dreadful recollections ?'

" 'It is your genealogies, dear aunt—it is your recurrence to the times that are gone—which have pictured to my mind those fifteen monks hung to the branches of the oak by the hand of one of my ancestors—the greatest, the most terrible, the most persevering—he who was surnamed the Terrible—the blind, the invincible John Ziska of the Chalice !'

" The exalted yet abhorred name of the chief of the Taborites, a sect which during the war of the Hussites surpassed all other religionists in their energy, their bravery, and their cruelty, fell like a thunderbolt on the ears of the abbé and the chaplain. The latter crossed himself, and my aunt drew back her chair, which was close to that of Albert. 'Good Heaven !' she exclaimed, ' of what and of whom does this child speak ? Do not heed him, Mr. Abbé ! Never—no, never—was our family connected by any ties, either of kindred or friendship, with the odious reprobate whose name has just been mentioned !'

" 'Speak for yourself, aunt,' said Albert with energy ; ' you are a Rudolstadt to the heart's core, although in reality a Podiebrad. As for myself, I have more Bohemian blood in my veins — all the purer too for its having less foreign admixture. My mother had neither Saxons, Bavarians, nor Prussians, in her genealogical tree; she was of pure Slavonic origin. And since you appear to care little for nobility, I, who am proud of my descent, shall inform you of it, if you are ignorant, that John Ziska left a daughter who married the lord of Prachalitz, and that my mother herself, being a Prachalitz, descends in a direct line from John Ziska, just as you yourself, my aunt, descend from the Rudolstadts.'

" ' It is a dream, a delusion, Albert !'

" ' Not, so, dear aunt; I appeal to the chaplain, who is a God-fearing man and will speak the truth. He has had in his hands the parchments which prove what I have asserted.'

" ' I ?' exclaimed the chaplain, pale as death.

" ' You may confess it without blushing before the abbé,' replied Albert with cutting irony, ' since you only did your duty as an Austrian subject and a good Catholic in burning them the day after my mother's death.'

" ' That deed, which my conscience approved, was witnessed by God alone,' falteringly replied the chaplain, terror-stricken at the disclosure of a secret of which he considered himself the sole human repository. ' Who, Count Albert, could have revealed it to you?'

" ' I have already told you, Mr. Chaplain—a voice which speaks louder than that of a priest.'

" ' What voice, Albert ?' I exclaimed, with emotion.

" ' The voice which speaks in sleep,' replied Albert.

" ' But that explains nothing, my son,' said Count Christian, sighing.

" ' It is the voice of blood, my father,' said Albert, in a tone so sepulchral that it made us shudder.

" ' Alas !' said my uncle, clasping his hands, ' these are the same reveries, the same phantoms of the imagination, which haunted his poor mother. She must have spoken of it to our child in her last illness,' he added, turning to my aunt, ' and such a story was well calculated to make a lively impression on his memory.'

" ' Impossible, brother !' replied the canoness. ' Albert was not three years old when he lost his mother !'

" ' It is more likely,' said the chaplain in a low voice, ' that there must have remained in the house some one of those cursed heretical writings, filled with lies and impieties, which she had preserved from family pride, but which nevertheless she had the courage and virtue to surrender to me in her last moments.'

" 'No, not one remained,' replied Albert, who had not lost a single word of what the chaplain said, although he had spoken in a low voice, and although he was walking about, much agitated, at that moment at the other end of the saloon. 'You know very well, sir, that you destroyed them all; and moreover, that the day after her death you searched and ransacked every corner of her chamber.'

" 'Who has thus aided, or rather misled, your memory, Albert?' asked Count Christian in a severe tone; 'what faithless or imprudent servant has dared to disturb your young mind by an exaggerated account of these domestic events?'

" 'No one, my father; I swear it to you by my religion and my conscience!'

" 'The enemy of the human race has had a hand in it,' said the terrified chaplain.

" 'It would probably be nearer the truth,' observed the abbé, 'and more Christian, to conclude that Count Albert is endowed with an extraordinary memory, and that occurrences, the recital of which does not usually strike a child of tender years, have remained engraved upon his mind. What I have seen of his rare intelligence, induces me readily to believe that his reason must have had a wonderfully precocious development; and as to his faculty of remembering events, I know that it is in fact prodigious.'

" 'It seems prodigious to you, only because you are entirely devoid of it,' replied Albert, drily. 'For example, you cannot recollect what you did in 1619, after Withold Podiebrad the Protestant, the valiant, the faithful (your grandfather, my dear aunt), and the last who bore our name, had dyed with his blood the Stone of Terror. You have forgotten your conduct under those circumstances, I would wager, Mr. Abbé.'

" 'I confess I have entirely forgotten it,' replied the abbé with a sarcastic smile, which was not in very good taste at a moment when it was evident to us that Albert's mind was wandering.

" 'Well, I will remind you,' returned Albert, without being at all disconcerted. 'You immediately went and advised those soldiers of the empire who had struck the blow, to fly or hide, because the laborers of Pilsen, who had the courage to avow themselves Protestants, and who adored Withold, were hastening to avenge their master's death, and would assuredly have cut them in pieces. Then you came to find my ancestress Ulrica, Withold's terrified and trembling widow, and promised to make her peace with the Emperor Ferdinand II, and preserve her estate, her title, her liberty, and the lives of her children if she would follow your advice, and purchase your services at the price of gold. She consented; her maternal love prompted that act of weakness. She forgot the martyrdom of her noble husband. She was born a Catholic, and had abjured that faith only from love for him. She knew not how to endure misery, proscription, and persecution, in order to preserve to her children a faith which Withold had sealed with his blood, and a name which he had rendered more illustrious than even those of his ancestors, who had been *Hussites, Calixtins, Taborites, Orphans, Brethren of the Union, and Lutherans.'* (All these names, my dear Porporina, are those of different sects, which united the heresy of John Huss to that of Luther, and which the branch of the Podiebrads from which we descend had probably followed.) 'In fine,' continued Albert, 'the Saxon woman was afraid, and yielded. You took possession of the château, you turned aside the imperial troops, you caused our lands to be respected, and you made an immense *auto-da-fè* of our titles and our archives. That is why my aunt, happily for her, has not been able to re-establish the genealogical tree of the Podiebrads, and has resorted to the less indigestible pasture of the Rudolstadts. As a reward for your services you were made rich, very rich. Three months afterward Ulrica was permitted to go and embrace the emperor's knees at Vienna, and graciously allowed by him to denationalize her children, to have them educated by you in the Romish religion, and to enrol them afterward under the standard against which their father and their ancestors had so valiantly fought. We were incorporated, my sons and I, in the ranks of Austrian tyranny.'

" 'Your sons and you!' said my aunt in despair, seeing that he wandered more and more.

" 'Yes, my sons Sigismond and Rodolph,' replied Albert, very seriously.

"'Those are the names of my father and uncle!' said Count Christian. 'Albert, where are your senses? Recall them, my son. More than a century separates us from those sad occurrences, which took place by the order of Providence.'

"Albert would not desist. He was fully persuaded, and wished to persuade us, that he was the same as Wratislaw, the son of Withold, and the first of the Podiebrads who had borne the maternal name of Rudolstadt. He gave us an account of his childhood, of the distinct recollection he had of Count Withold's execution (the odium of which he attributed to the Jesuit Dithmar, who, according to him, was no other than the abbé, his tutor), the profound hatred which during his childhood he had felt for this Dithmar, for Austria, for the Imperialists, for the Catholics. After this his recollections appeared confused, and he added a thousand incomprehensible things about the eternal and perpetual life, about the reappearance of men upon the earth, supporting himself upon that article of the Hussite creed which declared that John Huss was to return to Bohemia one hundred years after his death, and complete his work—a prediction which it appeared had been accomplished, since, according to him, Luther was John Huss resuscitated. In fine, his discourse was a mixture of heresy, of superstition, of obscure metaphysics, and of poetic frenzy; and it was all uttered with such an appearance of conviction, with recollections, so minute, so precise, and so interesting, of what he pretended to have seen, not only in the person of Wratislaw, but also in that of John Ziska, and I know not of how many other dead persons, who he maintained had been his own appearances in the past, that we remained listening to him with open mouths, and without the power of interrupting or contradicting him. My uncle and aunt, who were dreadfully afflicted at this insanity, which seemed to them impious, endeavored to discover its origin; for this was the first time that it displayed itself openly, and it was necessary to know its source in order to be able to combat it. The abbé tried to turn it all off as a jest, and to make us believe that Count Albert had a very witty and sarcastic disposition, and took pleasure in mystifying us with his amazing learning. 'He had read so much,' said he, ' that he could in the same manner relate the history of all ages, chapter by chapter, with such details and such precision as to make us believe, if we were ever so little inclined to the marvelous, that he had in fact been present at the scenes he relates.' The canoness, who in her ardent devotion is not many degrees removed from superstition, and who began to believe her nephew on the faith of his recital, received the abbé's insinuations very badly, and advised him to keep his jests for a more fitting occasion; then she made a strong effort to induce Albert to retract the errors with which he was imbued. 'Take care, aunt,' cried Albert, impatiently, 'that I do not tell you who you are. Hitherto I have not wished to know, but something warns me at this moment that the Saxon Ulrica is near.'

"'What! my poor child!' replied she; 'that prudent and devout ancestress, who knew how to preserve for her children their lives, and for her descendants the independence, the fortune, and the honors they now enjoy? Do you think she lives again in me? Well, Albert, so dearly do I love you, that I would do even more for you than she did; I would even sacrifice my life, if by so doing I could calm your troubled soul.'

"Albert looked at her a moment with an expression at once severe and tender. 'No, no,' said he at last, approaching her and kneeling at her feet, 'you are an angel, and you used to receive the communion in the wooden ·cup of the Hussites. But the Saxon woman is here, nevertheless, and her voice has reached my ear several times to-day.'

"'Allow her to be me, Albert,' said I exerting myself to cheer him, 'and do not think too ill of me for not having delivered you up to the executioners in 1619.'

"'You my mother!' said he, looking at me with flaming eyes; 'do not say that, for if so I cannot forgive you. God caused me to be born again in the bosom of a stronger woman; he retempered me in the blood of Ziska—in my own substance, which had been misled, I know not how. Amelia, do not look at me! above all, do not speak to me! It is your voice, Ulrica, which has caused me all the suffering I endure to-day.'

"On saying this, Albert hastily left the room, and we remained overpowered by the sad discovery we had made of the alienation of his mind.

"It was then two o'clock in the afternoon; we had dined

quietly, and Albert had drunk only water. There was nothing therefore which could lead us to suppose that this frenzy could be occasioned by intoxication. The chaplain and my aunt immediately rose to follow and nurse him, thinking him seriously ill. But, inconceivable as it may seem, Albert had already disappeared, as if by enchantment. They could not find him in his own apartment, nor in his mother's, where he frequently used to shut himself up, nor in any corner of the château. They searched for him in the garden, in the warren, in the surrounding woods, and among the mountains. No one had seen him, far or near. No trace of his steps was anywhere to be found. The rest of the day and the succeeding night were spent in the same manner. No one went to bed in the house; our people were on foot until dawn, and searching for him with torches.

" All the family retired to pray. The next day and the following night were passed in the same consternation. I cannot describe the terror I felt—I, who had never suffered any uneasiness, who had never experienced in my life domestic events of such importance. I seriously believed that Albert had either killed himself or fled forever. I was seized with convulsions, and finally with a malignant fever. I still felt for him some remains of love, in the midst of the terror with which so fatal and so strange a character inspired me. My father had strength enough to pursue his usual sport of hunting, thinking that in his distant excursions he might possibly happen on Albert in the midst of the woods. My poor aunt, a prey to anguish, but still active and courageous, nursed me, and tried to comfort every body. My uncle prayed night and day. When I saw his faith and his pious submission to the will of Heaven, I regretted that I was not devout.

" The abbé feigned some concern, but affected to feel no apprehension. It was true, he said, that Albert had never thus disappeared from his presence, but he required seasons of solitude and reflection. His conclusion was that the only remedy for these singularities was never to thwart them, and not to appear to remark them much. The fact is, that this intriguing and profoundly selfish underling cared for nothing but the large salary attached to his situation of tutor, which he had made to last as long as possible by deceiving the family respecting the result of his good offices. Occupied by his own affairs and his own pleasures, he had abandoned Albert to his extravagant inclinations. Possibly he had often seen him ill and frequently excited, and had, without doubt, allowed free scope to his fancies. Certain it is that he had had the tact to conceal them from every one who could have given us notice; for in all the letters which my uncle received respecting his son, there was nothing but eulogiums upon his appearance and congratulations upon the beauty of his person. Albert had nowhere left the impression that he was ill or devoid of sense. However this may have been, his mental life during those eight years of absence has always remained an impenetrable mystery to us. The abbé, after three days had elapsed, seeing that he did not make his appearance, and fearing that his own position had been injured by this accident, departed, with the intention as he said of seeking for him at Prague, whither the desire of searching for some rare book might, according to him, have drawn him. 'He is,' said he, 'like those learned men who bury themselves in their studies, and forget the whole world when engaged in their harmless pursuits.' Thereupon the abbé departed, and did not return.

"After seven days of mortal anguish, when we began at last to despair, my aunt, in passing one evening before Albert's chamber, saw the door open, and Albert seated in his arm-chair, caressing his dog, who had followed him in his mysterious journey. His garments were neither soiled nor torn; only the gold ornaments belonging to them were somewhat blackened, as if he had come from a damp place or had passed the nights in the open air. His shoes did not appear as if he had walked much; but his beard and hair bore evidence to a long neglect of the care of his person. Since that day he has constantly refused to shave himself, or to wear powder like other men, and that is why he had to you the appearance of a ghost.

"My aunt rushed toward him with a loud cry. 'What is the matter, my dear aunt?' said he, kissing her hand. 'One would imagine you had not seen me for ages.'

"'Unhappy child!' cried she, 'it is now seven days since you left us without saying a word ; seven long, weary days, seven dreadful nights, during which we have searched for you, wept for you, and prayed for you.'

" ' Seven days?' said Albert, looking at her with surprise. ' You must mean to say seven hours, my dear aunt, for I went out this morning to walk, and I have come back in time to sup with you. How can I have occasioned you so much anxiety by so short an absence?'

" ' I must have made a slip of the tongue,' said she, fearing to aggravate his disease by mentioning it ; ' I meant to say seven hours. I was anxious because you are not accustomed to take such long walks, and besides I had an unpleasant dream last night ; I was foolish!'

" ' Good, excellent aunt!' said Albert, covering her hands with kisses, ' you love me as if I were still a little child. I hope my father has not shared your anxiety.'

" ' Not at all; he is expecting you at supper. You must be very hungry.'

" ' Not very. I dined well.'

" ' Where and when, Albert?'

" ' Here, this morning, with you, my good aunt ; you have not yet recovered your senses, I perceive. Oh, I am very unhappy at having caused you such a fright! How could I foresee it?'

" ' You know that such is my character. But allow me to ask you then where you have eaten and slept since you left us?'

" ' How could I have had any inclination either to eat or sleep since this morning?'

" ' Do you not feel ill?'

" ' Not the least in the world.'

" ' Nor wearied? You must no doubt have walked a great deal, and scaling the mountains is so fatiguing. Where have you been?'

" Albert put his hand to his forehead, as if to recollect, but he could not tell.

" ' I confess to you,' said he, ' that I know nothing about it. I was much preoccupied. I must have walked without seeing, as I used to do in my childhood ; you know I never could answer you when you questioned me.'

" ' And during your travels, did you pay any more attention to what you saw?'

" ' Sometimes, but not always. I observed many things, but I have forgotten many others, thank God.'

" ' And why *thank God?*'

" ' Because there are such horrible things to be seen on

the face of the earth!' replied he, rising with a gloomy expression which my aunt had not yet observed in him. She saw that it would not do to make him talk any more, and she ran to announce to my uncle that his son was found. No one yet knew it in the house ; no one had seen him enter. His return had left no more trace than his departure.

" My poor uncle, who had shown so much courage in enduring misfortune, had none in the first moments of joy. He swooned away ; and when Albert reappeared before him, his face was more agitated than his son's. Albert, who since his long journey had not seemed to notice any emotion in those around him, appeared entirely renewed and different from what he had been before. He lavished a thousand caresses on his father, was troubled at seeing him so changed, and wished to know the cause. But when they ventured to acquaint him with it, he never could comprehend it, and all his answers were given with a good faith and earnestness, which proved his complete ignorance of where he had been during the seven days he had disappeared."

"What you have told me seems like a dream, my dear baroness," said Consuelo, "and has set me thinking rather than sleeping. How could a man live seven days without being conscious of any thing?"

" That is nothing compared to what I have yet to relate ; and until you have seen for yourself, that, far from exaggerating, I soften matters in order to abridge my tale, you will, I can conceive, have some difficulty in believing me. As for me, who am relating to you what I have seen, I still ask myself sometimes if Albert is a sorcerer, or if he makes fools of us. But it is late, and I really fear that I have imposed upon your patience."

" It is I who impose upon yours," replied Consuelo ; "you must be tired of talking. Let us put off till to-morrow evening, if you please, the continuation of this incredible history."

" Till to-morrow then," said the young baroness, embracing her.

CHAPTER XXX.

THE incredible history which she had just heard, kept Consuelo, in fact, long awake. The dark, rainy, and tempestuous night also contributed to fill her with superstitious fancies which she had never before experienced. "Is there then some incomprehensible fatality," said she to herself, "which impends over certain individuals? What crime against God could that young girl have committed, who was telling me so frankly just now of her wounded self-love and the vanishing of her fairest dreams? What evil have I myself done, that the sole affection of my heart should be torn from my bleeding bosom? But, alas! what fault has this savage Albert of Rudolstadt been guilty of, that he should thus lose his consciousness and the power of governing his life? What hatred has Providence conceived for Anzoleto, thus to abandon him as it has done, to wicked and perverse inclinations."

Overcome at last by fatigue, she slept, and lost herself in a succession of dreams without connection and without end. Two or three times she awoke and fell asleep again, without being able to understand where she was, and thinking she was still traveling. Porpora, Anzoleto, Count Zustiniani, Corilla, all passed in turn before her eyes, saying sad and strange things to her, and reproaching her with some unknown crime, for which she was obliged to undergo punishment, without being able to remember that she had ever committed it. But all these visions disappeared to give place to that of Count Albert, who passed continually before her with his black beard, his fixed and motionless eyes, and his suit of mourning trimmed with gold, and sometimes sprinkled with tears like a funeral pall.

On opening her eyes in the morning, fully awake, she found Amelia already dressed with elegance, fresh and smiling, beside her bed.

"Do you know, my dear Porporina," said the young baroness, as she imprinted a kiss upon her brow, "that there is something strange about you? I must be destined to live with extraordinary beings, for you also are certainly one. I have been looking at you asleep for the last quarter of an hour, to see by daylight if you are handsomer than I am. I confess to you that this matter is of some consequence to me, and that notwithstanding I have entirely abjured my love for Albert, I should be somewhat piqued if he looked upon you with interest. Do you think that strange? The reason is, he is the only man here, and hitherto I have been the only woman. Now we are two, and we shall pull caps if you extinguish me completely."

" You are pleased to jest," replied Consuelo, " and it is not generous on your part. But will you leave aside your raillery, and tell me what there is extraordinary in my appearance? Perhaps all my ugliness has come back. Indeed that must be the case."

" I will tell you the truth, Nina. At the first glimpse I caught of you this morning, your paleness, your large eyes only half closed and rather fixed than asleep, and your thin arm which lay stretched on the coverlet, gave me a moment's triumph. And then, looking at you longer, I was almost terrified by your immobility and your truly regal attitude. Your arm I will maintain is that of a queen, and your calmness has in it something commanding and overpowering, for which I cannot account. Now, I think you are fearfully beautiful, and yet there is a sweetness in your countenance. Tell me who you are. You attract and intimidate me. I feel ashamed of the follies I related of myself last night. You have not yet told me anything of yourself, and yet you are acquainted with nearly all my defects."

" If I have the air of a queen, of which I never was aware," replied Consuelo, smiling sadly, " it must be the piteous air of a dethroned one. As to my beauty, it has always seemed to me very problematical; and as to the opinion I have of you, dear Baroness Amelia, it is all in favor of your frankness and good nature."

" I am indeed frank—but are you so, Nina ? Yes, you have an air of grandeur and royalty. But are you confiding? I do not believe that you are."

" It was not my place to be so first—that you will allow. It was for you, protectress and mistress of my destiny as you are at this moment, to make the first advances."

" You are right. But your strong sense terrifies me. If I seem a scatter-brain, you will not lecture me too much, will you?"

" I have no right to do so. I am your mistress in music,

and in nothing else. Beside, a poor daughter of the people, like me, will always know how to keep her place."

" You a daughter of the people, high-spirited Porporina ! Oh ! you deceive me ; it is impossible. I should sooner believe you the mysterious offspring of some family of princes. What was your mother?"

" She sang, as I do."

" And your father?"

Consuelo was struck dumb. She had not prepared all her answers to the rather indiscreet questions of the little baroness. In truth she had never heard her father spoken of, and had never even thought of asking if she had one.

" Come," said Amelia, bursting into a laugh, " I was sure I was right; your father is some grandee of Spain, or some doge of Venice."

This style of speaking seemed to Consuelo trifling and offensive.

" So," said she, with some displeasure, " an honest mechanic or a poor artist has no right to transmit natural distinction to his child ? Is it absolutely necessary that the children of common people should be coarse and misshapen?"

" That last word is an epigram for my aunt Wenceslawa," replied the baroness, laughing still more loudly. " Come, my dear, forgive me if I do plague you a little, and permit me to fashion in my own brain a more attractive romance about you. But dress yourself quickly, my child; for the bell will soon ring, and my aunt would let the family die of hunger rather than have breakfast served without you. I will help you to open your trunks; give me the keys. I am sure that you have brought the prettiest dresses from Venice, and I am dying to see all the new fashions—I have lived so long in this country of savages."

Consuelo, in a hurry to arrange her hair, gave the keys, without hearing what had been said, and Amelia hastened to open a trunk which she imagined was full of dresses; but to her great surprise she found only a mass of old music, printed rolls worn out by long use, and apparently illegible manuscripts.

" Ah? what is all this?" cried she, hastily shaking the dust from her pretty fingers. " You have a droll wardrobe there, my dear child."

" They are treasures; treat them with respect, my dear

baroness," replied Consuelo. "There are among them the autographs of the greatest masters, and I would rather lose my voice than not return them safely to Porpora, who has confided them to me." Amelia opened a second trunk, and found it full of ruled paper, treatises on music, and other books on composition, harmony, and counterpoint.

"Ah! I understand," said she laughing; "this is your jewel-box."

"I have no other," replied Consuelo, "and I hope you will use it often."

"Very well: I see you are a severe mistress. But may one ask, without offending you, my dear Nina, where you have put your dresses?"

"At the bottom of this little box," replied Consuelo, opening it, and showing the baroness a little dress of black silk, carefully and freshly folded.

"Is that all?" said Amelia.

"That is all," replied Consuelo, "with my traveling dress. In a few days I shall make a second black dress, for a change."

"Ah! my dear child, then you are in mourning?"

"Perhaps so, signora," replied Consuelo, gravely.

"In that case forgive me. I ought to have known from your manner that you had some sorrow at your heart, and I shall love you quite as well for it. We shall sympathize even sooner; for I also have many causes of sadness, and might even now wear mourning for my intended husband. Ah! my dear Nina, do not be provoked at my gaiety; It is often merely an effort to conceal the deepest suffering." They kissed each other, and went down to breakfast, where they found the family waiting for them.

Consuelo saw, at the first glance, that her modest black dress and her white neckerchief, closed even to the chin by a pin of jet, gave the canoness a very favorable opinion of her. Old Christian was a little less embarrassed and quite as affable toward her as the evening before. Baron Frederick, who through courtesy had refrained that day from going to the chase, could not find a word to say, although he had prepared a thousand fine speeches to thank her for the attentions she would pay to his daughter. But he took a seat beside her at the table, and set himself to help her with an importunity so child-like and minute, that he had no time to satisfy his own appetite. The chaplain asked her in what order the patriarch arranged the procession at Venice, and questioned her upon the appearance and ornaments of the churches. He saw by her answers that she had visited them frequently; and when he knew that she had learned to sing in the divine service, he testified the utmost respect for her.

As for Count Albert, Consuelo hardly dared to raise her eyes to him, precisely because he was the only one who inspired her with a lively feeling of curiosity. She did not even know what sort of a reception he had given her. Once only she looked at him in a mirror as she crossed the saloon, and saw that he was dressed with some care, although still in black. But although possessing all the distinguished appearance of a man of high birth, his un-trimmed beard and hair, and pallid complexion, gave him rather the pensive and neglected air of a handsome fisher-man of the Adriatic, than that of a German noble.

Still, the harmony of his voice, which pleased the musical ear of Consuelo, gave her courage by degrees to look at him, and she was surprised to find in him the air and manners of a very sensible man. He spoke little, but judiciously; and when she rose from the table, he offered her his hand, without looking at her it is true (he had not done her that honor since the day before), but with much ease and politeness. She trembled in every limb on placing her hand in that of the fantastic hero of the tales and dreams of the preceding evening, and expected to find it cold as that of a corpse. But it was soft and warm as that of a healthy man. Consuelo could hardly conceal her amazement. Her emotion gave her a sort of vertigo; and the glances of Amelia, who followed her every motion, would have completed her embarrassment, if she had not called all her powers to her aid, in order to preserve her dignity in presence of the mischievous young girl. She returned Count Albert the profound bow which he made after conducting her to a chair; but not a word, not a look, was exchanged between them.

"Do you know, perfidious Porporina," said Amelia to her companion, seating herself near her in order to whisper freely in her ear, "that you have produced a wonderful effect upon my cousin?"

"I have not perceived much of it yet," replied Consuelo.

"That is because you have not deigned to notice his

manner toward me. For a whole year he has not once offered me his hand to lead me to or from the table, and now he conducts himself toward you with the most marked attention. It is true that he is in one of his most lucid moments, and one might say that you have brought him health and reason. But do not trust to appearances, Nina. It will be the same with you as it was with me: after three days of cordiality he will not even remember your existence."

"I see that I must accustom myself to your jesting," said Consuelo.

"Is it not true, my dear aunt," said Amelia, in a low voice, to the canoness, who came forward and took a seat near her and Consuelo, "that my cousin is extremely amiable toward our dear Porporina?"

"Do not jest about him, Amelia," said Wenceslawa, gently; "the young lady will soon enough perceive the cause of our sorrows."

"I am not jesting, good aunt. Albert is perfectly well this morning, and I rejoice to see him as I have never before seen him since I came here. If he were shaved and powdered like other people, you would think he had never been ill."

"His air of calmness and health strikes me very agreeably in truth," said the canoness; "but I dare not flatter myself that so happy a state of things will last."

"What a noble and benevolent expression he has!" said Consuelo, wishing to touch the heart of the canoness in its most tender point.

"Do you think so?" said Amelia, transfixing her with a saucy and incredulous look.

"Yes, I do think so," replied Consuelo firmly; "and as I told you yesterday evening, never did a human face inspire me with more respect."

"Ah! my dear daughter," said the canoness, suddenly casting off her constrained air, and pressing Consuelo's hand tenderly, "good hearts at once understand each other! I feared lest my poor child should terrify you. It is a source of great pain to me to read in the countenances of others the aversion inspired by such maladies. But you have great sensibility, I perceive, and have at once comprehended that in his wasted and diseased frame dwells a sublime soul, well worthy of a happier lot,"

Consuelo was moved even to tears by the words of the excellent canoness, and kissed her hand affection. ately. She already felt more confidence and sympathy with that old deformed lady than with the brilliant and frivolous Amelia.

They were interrupted by Baron Frederick, who, relying more upon his courage than his conversational powers, approached with the intention of asking a favor from the Signora Porporina. Even more awkward in the presence of ladies than his elder brother (this awkwardness was, it would seem, a family complaint, which one need not be much astonished to find developed, even to boorishness, in Albert), he stammered out some words, which Amelia undertook to comprehend and translate to Consuelo.

" My father asks you," said she, " if you feel courage enough to think of music after so painful a journey, and if it would not be an imposition on your good nature, to request you to hear my voice and judge of my style?"

" With all my heart;" replied Consuelo, rising immediately, and opening the harpsichord.

" You will see," said Amelia to her in a low voice, as she arranged her music on the stand, " that this will put Albert to flight, notwithstanding your good looks and mine." In fact, Amelia had hardly played a few bars, when Albert rose and went out on tip-toe, like a man who flatters himself that he is not perceived.

" It is astonishing," said Amelia, still talking in a low voice while she played out of time, " that he did not slam the door furiously after him, as he sometimes does when I sing. He is quite amiable, one might almost say, gallant, to-day."

The chaplain, thinking to cover Albert's departure, approached the harpsichord and pretended to listen attentively. The rest of the family formed a half-circle at a little distance, waiting respectfully for the judgment which Consuelo should pronounce upon her pupil.

Amelia courageously chose an air from the *Achille in Scyro* of Pergolese, and sang it with assurance from beginning to end in a shrill, piercing voice, accompanied by so comical a German accent, that Consuelo, who had never heard any thing of the kind, was scarcely able to keep from smiling at every word. It was hardly necessary to hear four bars, to be convinced that the young baroness had no true idea and no knowledge whatever of music. She had a flexible voice, and perhaps had received good instruction; but her character was too frivolous to allow her to study any thing conscientiously, For the same reason she did not mistrust her own powers, and, with German *sang froid*, attempted the boldest and most difficult passages. She failed in all, and thought to cover her unskillfulness by forcing her intonation and thundering the accompaniment, eking out the measure as best she could, by adding time to the bars which followed those in which she had diminished it, and changing the character of the music to such an extent, that Consuelo could hardly recognize what she heard, although the pages were before her eyes.

Yet Count Christian, who was a perfect connoisseur, but who attributed to his niece all the timidity he would have felt in her place, exclaimed from time to time to encourage her: "Very well, Amelia, very well indeed! beautiful music." The canoness, who did not know very much about it, looked anxiously into the eyes of Consuelo, in order to anticipate her opinion; and the baron, who loved no other music than the flourishes of the hunting-horn, believing that his daughter sang too well for him to understand, waited in confidence for the expression of the judge's satisfaction. The chaplain alone was charmed by these *gargouillades*, which he had never heard before Amelia's arrival at the château.

Consuelo very clearly saw that to tell the plain truth would distress the whole family. Resolving to enlighten her pupil in private upon all these matters which she had to forget before she could learn any thing, she praised her voice, asked about her studies, approved the choice of masters whose works she had been made to study, and thus relieved herself of the necessity of declaring that she had studied them incorrectly.

The family separated, well pleased with a trial which had been painful only to Consuelo. She was obliged to go and shut herself up in her apartments with the music she had just heard profaned, and read it with her eyes, singing it mentally; in order to efface the disagreeable impression she had received.

CHAPTER XXXI.

WHEN the family reassembled toward evening, Consuelo, feeling more at ease with all these people whom she now began to get acquainted with, replied with less reserve and brevity to the questions, which on their part they felt more courage to address to her, respecting her country, her art, and her travels. She carefully avoided, as she had determined, speaking of herself, and she related the events in the midst of which she had lived, without ever mentioning the part she had taken in them. In vain did the curious Amelia strive to lead her to enlarge on her personal adventures. Consuelo did not fall into the snare, nor for an instant betray the incognito she had resolved to maintain. It would be difficult to say precisely why this mystery had a peculiar charm for her. Many reasons induced her to observe it. In the first place, she had promised, even sworn to Porpora, to keep herself so completely hidden and concealed in every manner, that it would be impossible for Anzoleto to discover her route, if he should attempt to pursue her — a very useless precaution, for Anzoleto, at this time, after a few quickly smothered wishes of the kind, was occupied only with his débuts and his success at Venice.

In the second place, Consuelo, wishing to conciliate the esteem and affection of the family who gave her a temporary refuge in her friendless and melancholy situation, understood very well that they would much more readily receive her as a simple musician, a pupil of Porpora, and teacher of vocal music, than as prima donna, a performer on the stage, and a celebrated cantatrice. She knew that among these unpretending and pious people, an avowal of such a position would impose upon her a difficult part ; and it is probable that, notwithstanding Porpora's recommendation, the arrival of Consuelo, the débutante, and the wonder of San Samuel, would have somewhat startled them. But even if these powerful motives had not existed, Consuelo would still have experienced the necessity of silence, and of keeping secret the brilliancy and the sufferings of her career. Every thing was linked together in her life—her power and her weakness, her glory and her love. She could not raise the smallest corner of the veil, without laying bare one of the wounds of her soul ; and these wounds were still too recent, too painfnl, too deep, to be healed by kindness or sympathy. She found relief only in the barrier which she had raised between the sorrowful memories of the past and the calm energy of her new existence. This change of country, of scene, and of name, transported her at once into an unknown region, where, by assuming a new character, she hoped to become a new being.

This renunciation of vanities, which might have solaced another woman, proved the salvation of this courageous being. In renouncing all compassion, as well as all human glory, she felt celestial strength come to her aid. " I must regain some portion of my former happiness," she said ; " that which I so long enjoyed, and which consisted in loving and in being beloved. The moment I sought their admiration, they withdrew their love, and I have paid too dear for the honors they bestowed in place of their good-will. Let me begin again, obscure and insignificant, that I may be subjected neither to envy, nor ingratitude, nor enmity on the earth. . The least token of sympathy is sweet, and the highest testimony of admiration is mingled with bitterness. If there be proud and strong hearts to whom praise suffices, and whom triumph consoles, I have cruelly experienced that mine is not of the number. Alas ! glory has torn my lover's heart from me ; let humility yield me in return at least some friends."

It was not thus that Porpora meant. In removing Consuelo from Venice, and from the dangers and agonies of her love, he only intended to 'procure her some repose before recalling her to the scene of ambition, and launching her afresh into the storms of artistic life. He did not know his pupil. He believed her more of a woman—that is to say, more impressionable than she was. In thinking of her he did not fancy her as calm, affectionate, and busied with others, as she had always been able to become, but plunged in tears and devoured with vain regret. But he thought at the same time that a reaction would take place, and that he should find her cured of her love, and anxious to recommence the exercise of her powers, and enjoy the privileges of her genius.

The pure and religious feeling conceived by Consuelo of the part she was to play in the family of Rudolstadt, spread from this day a holy serenity over her words, her actions, and her countenance. Those who had formerly seen her dazzling with love and joy beneath the sun of Venice, could not easily have understood how she could become all at once calm and gentle in the midst of strangers, in the depths of gloomy forests, with her love blighted, both as regarded the past and the future. But goodness finds strength where pride only meets despair. Consuelo was glorious that evening, with a beauty which she had not hitherto displayed. It was not the half-developed impulse of sleeping nature waiting to be roused, nor the expansion of a power which seizes the spectators with surprise or delight; neither was it the hidden, incomprehensible beauty of the *scolare zingarella:* no, it was the graceful penetrating charm of a pure and self-possessed woman, governed by her own sacred impulses.

Her gentle and simple hosts needed no other than their generous instincts to drink in, if I may use the expression, the mysterious incense which the angelic soul of Consuelo exhaled in their intellectual atmosphere. They experienced, even in looking at her, a moral elevation which they might have found it difficult to explain, but the sweetness of which filled them as with a new life. Albert seemed for the first time to enjoy the full possession of his faculties. He was obliging and good-natured with every one. He was suitably so with Consuelo, and spoke to her at different times in such terms as showed that he had not relinquished, as might be supposed, the elevated intellect and clear judgment with which nature had endowed him. The baron did not once fall asleep, the canoness ceased to sigh, and Count Christian, who used to sink at night into his arm-chair, bent down under the weight of old age and vexation, remained erect with his back to the chimney, in the center of his family, and sharing in the easy and pleasant conversation, which was prolonged till nine in the evening.

"God has at length heard our prayers," said the chaplain to Count Christian and the canoness, who remained in the saloon after the departure of the baron and the young people. "Count Albert has this day entered his thirtieth year, and this solemn day, so dreaded by him and by ourselves, has passed over calmly and with unspeakable happiness."

"Yes, let us return thanks to God," said the old count. "It may prove but a blessed dream, sent for a moment to comfort us, but I could not help thinking all this day, and this evening in particular, that my son was perfectly cured."

"Brother," replied the canoness, "and you, worthy chaplain, I entreat pardon, but you have always believed Albert to be tormented by the enemy of human kind. For myself, I thought him at issue with opposing powers which disputed the possession of his poor soul, for often when he repeated words of the bad angel, Heaven spoke from his mouth the next moment. Do you recollect what he said yesterday evening during the storm, and his words on leaving us? 'The peace of God has come down on this house.' Albert experienced the miracle in himself, and I believe in his recovery as in the divine promise."

The chaplain was too timid to admit all at once so bold a proposition. He extricated himself from his embarrassment by saying : "Let us ascribe it to Eternal Goodness ;" "God reads hidden things ;" "The soul should lose itself in God ;" and other sentences more consolatory than novel.

Count Christian was divided between the desire of conforming to the somewhat exaggerated asceticism of his good sister, and the respect imposed by the prudent and unquestioning orthodoxy of his confessor.

He endeavored to turn the conversation by speaking of the charming demeanor of Porporina. The canoness, who loved her already, praised her yet more ; and the chaplain sanctioned the preference which they experienced for her. It never entered their heads to attribute the miracle which had taken place among them to Consuelo. They accepted the benefit without recognizing its source. It was what Consuelo would have asked of God could she have been consulted.

Amelia was a close observer. It soon became evident to her that her cousin could conceal the disorder of his thoughts from persons whom he feared, as well as from those whom he wished to please. Before relations and friends of the family whom he either disliked or esteemed, he never betrayed by any outward demonstration the eccentricity of his character. When Consuelo expressed her surprise at what had been related the preceding evening, Amelia, tormented by a secret uneasiness, tried to make her afraid of Count Albert by recitals which had already terrified herself. "Ah, my poor friend," said she, "distrust this deceitful calm ; it is a pause which always intervenes between a recent and an approaching crisis. You see him to-day as I first saw him, when I arrived here in the beginning of last year. Alas ! if you were destined to become the wife of such a visionary, and if, to combat your reluctance they had determined to keep you prisoner for an indefinite period in this frightful castle, with surprises, terrors, and agitations for your daily fare—nothing to be seen but tears, exorcisms and extravagances—expecting a cure which will never happen—you would be quite disenchanted with the fine manners of Albert, and the honeyed words of the family."

"It is not credible," said Consuelo, "that they would unite you against your will to a man whom you do not love. You appear to be the idol of your relatives."

"They will not force me ; they know that would be impossible. But they forget that Albert is not the only husband who would suit me, and God knows when they will give up the foolish hope that the affection with which I at first regarded him will return. And then my poor father, who has here wherewith to satisfy his passion for the chase, finds himself so well off in this horrible castle, that he will always discover some pretext for retarding our departure. Ah ! if you only knew some secret, my dear Nina, to make all the game in the country perish in one night, you would render me an inestimable service."

"I can do nothing, unfortunately, but try to amuse you by giving you lessons in music, and chatting with you in the evenings when you are not inclined to sleep. I shall do my utmost to soothe and to compose you."

"You remind me," said Amelia, "that I have not related the remainder of the story. I shall begin at once, that I may not keep you up too late.

"Some days after his mysterious absence, which he still believed had only lasted seven hours, Albert remarked the absence of the abbé, and asked where he had gone.

"'His presence was no longer necessary,' they replied ; 'he returned to his own pursuits. Did you not observe his absence ?'

"'I perceived,' replied Albert, 'that something was needful to complete my suffering, but I did not know what it was.'

" ' You suffer much then, Albert ?' asked the canoness.

" ' Much ;' he replied, in the tone of a man who had been asked if he had slept well.

" ' And the abbé was obnoxious to you ?' said Count Christian.

" ' Very,' he replied, in the same tone.

" ' And why, my son, did you not say so sooner ? Why have you borne for so long a time the presence of a man whom you so much disliked, without informing me of it? Do you doubt, my dear child, that I should have quickly terminated your sufferings ?'

" ' It was but a feeble addition to my grief,' said Albert, with frightful tranquility; ' and your goodness, which I do not doubt, my dear father, would have but slightly relieved it, by giving me another superintendent.'

" ' Say another traveling companion, my son ; you employ an expression injurious to my tenderness.'

" ' Your tenderness was the cause of your anxiety, my father. You could not be aware of the evil you inflicted on me in sending me from this house, where it was designed by Providence I should remain till its plans for me should be accomplished. You thought to labor for my cure and repose; but I knew better what was good for us both—I knew that I should obey you—and this duty I have fulfilled.'

" ' I know your virtue and your affection, Albert ; but can you not explain yourself more clearly ?'

" ' That is very easy,' replied Albert; ' and the time is come that I should do so.'

" Albert spoke so calmly that we thought the fortunate moment had arrived when his soul should cease to be a melancholy enigma. We pressed around him, and encouraged him by our looks and caresses to open his heart for the first time in his life. He appeared at length inclined to do so, and spoke as follows:

" ' You have always looked upon me,' said he, ' and still continue to look upon me, as in ill-health and a madman. Did I not feel for you all infinite respect and affection, I should, perhaps, have widened the abyss which separates us, and I should have shown you that you are in a world of errors and prejudices, while Heaven has given me access to a sphere of light and truth. But you could not understand me without giving up what constitutes your

tranquillity, your security, and your creed. When, borne
away by my enthusiasm, imprudent words escaped me, I
soon found I had done you harm in wishing to root up
your chimeras and display before your enfeebled eyes the
burning flame which I bore about with me. All the details
and habits of your life, all the fibers of your heart, all the
springs of your intellect, are so bound up together, so
trammeled with falsehood and darkness, that I should but
seem to inflict death instead of life. There is a voice,
however, which cries to me in watching and in sleep, in
calm and in storm, to enlighten and convert you. But I
am too loving and too weak a man to undertake it. When
I see your eyes full of tears, your bosoms heave, your fore-
heads bent down—when I feel that I bring only sorrow and
terror—I fly, I hide myself, to resist the cry of conscience
and the commands of destiny. Behold the cause of my
illness ! Behold my torment, my cross, my suffering! Do
you understand me now ?'

"My uncle, my aunt, and the chaplain, understood this
much — that Albert had ideas of morality and religion
totally different from their own ; but, timid as devout,
they feared to go too far, and dared not encourage his
frankness. As to myself, I was only imperfectly acquainted
with the peculiarities of his childhood and youth, and I
did not at all understand it. Besides, I was at this time
like yourself, Nina, and knew very little of this Hussitism
and Lutheranism which I have since heard so much of,
while the controversies between Albert and the chaplain
overwhelmed me with weariness. I expected a more
ample explanation, but it did not ensue. 'I see,' said
Albert, struck with the silence around him, 'that you do
not wish to understand me, for fear of understanding too
much. Be it so, then. Your blindness has borne bitter
fruits. Ever unhappy, ever alone, a stranger among those
I love, I have neither refuge nor stay but in the consolation which has been promised me.'

"'What is this consolation, my son ?' said Count Christian, deeply afflicted. 'Could it not come from us? Shall
we never understand each other ?'

"'Never, my father; let us love each other, since that
alone is permitted. Heaven is my witness, that our immense and irreparable disagreement has never diminished
the love I bear you.'

" 'And is not that enough ?' said the canoness, taking one hand, while her brother pressed Albert's other hand in his own. 'Can you not forget your wild ideas, your strange belief, and live fondly in the midst of us ?'

" 'I do live on affection,' replied Albert. 'It is a blessing which produces good or evil, according as our faith is a common one or otherwise. Our hearts are in union, dear Aunt Wenceslawa, but our intellects are at war ; and this is a great misfortune for us all. I know it will not end for centuries. Therefore I await the happiness that has been promised me, and which gives me power to hope on.'

" 'What is that blessing, Albert ? can you not tell me ?'

" 'No, I cannot tell you, because I do not know. My mother has not allowed a week to pass without announcing it to me in my sleep, and all the voices of the forest have repeated it to me as often as I have questioned them. An angel often hovers above the Stone of Terror, and shows me his pale and luminous face, at that ominous place, under the shade of that oak, where, when my contemporaries called me Ziske, I was transported with the anger of the Lord, and became for the first time the instrument of his vengeance; at the foot of that rock, where, when I called myself Wratislaw, I saw the mutilated and disfigured head of my father Withold stricken off by one blow of a saber—a fearful expiation, which taught me to know sorrow and pity—a day of fatal retribution, when the Lutheran blood washed away the Catholic blood, and made me a weak and tender man in the place of the man of fanaticism and destruction, which I had been a hundred years before——'

" 'Divine goodness!' said my aunt, crossing herself, 'his madness has seized him again!'

" 'Do not interrupt him, sister,' said Count Christian, making a great effort, 'let him explain himself. Speak, my son, what did the angel say to you upon the Stone of Terror?'

" 'He told me that my consolation was near,' replied Albert, his face glowing with enthusiasm, 'and that it would descend upon my heart as soon as I had completed my twenty-ninth year!'

" My uncle dropped his head upon his breast. Albert seemed to allude to his death, in designating the age at

which his· mother died, and it appears she had often predicted that neither she nor her son would reach the age
of thirty.   It seems that my aunt Wanda was also somewhat visionary, to say the least; but I have never been able
to obtain any precise information on this subject.   It is a
very sad recollection to my uncle, and no one about him
dares to awaken it.

"The chaplain endeavored to banish the unpleasant feeling which this prediction had occasioned, by leading
Albert to explain himself respecting the abbé.   It was on
that point the conversation had begun.

"Albert on his side made a great effort to answer him.
'I speak to you of things divine and eternal,' replied he,
after a little hesitation, 'and you recall to my mind the
short and fleeting concerns of time—those childish and
ephemeral cares, the record of which is almost effaced
within me.'

"'Speak, my son, speak!' returned Count Christian;
'we must strive to know you this day.'

"'You have never known me, father,' replied Albert,
'and you will not know me in what you call this life.   But
if you wish to know why I traveled, why I endured that
unfaithful and careless guardian, whom you had attached
to my steps like a greedy and lazy dog to the arm of a blind
man, I will tell you in a few words.   I had caused you
enough of suffering.   It was my duty to withdraw from
your sight, a son rebellious to your teachings and deaf to
your remonstrances.   I knew well that I should not be
cured of what you called my insanity, but you required
both repose and hope, and I consented to remove myself.
You exacted from me a promise that I would not separate,
without your consent, from the guide you had given me,
and that I would permit myself to be conducted by him
over the world.   I wished to keep my promise.   I wished
also that he should sustain your hope and your confidence,
by giving you an account of my gentleness and patience.
I was gentle and patient.   I closed my heart and my ears
against him; he had the sagacity not even to think of
opening them.   He led me about, dressed me, and fed me
like a child.   I renounced the idea of fulfilling the duties
of life as I thought they ought to be fulfilled.   I accustomed myself to see misery, injustice, and folly reign upon
the earth.   I have seen men and their institutions, and

indignation has given place to pity in my heart, for I have seen that the misfortunes of the oppressed were less than those of their oppressors. In my childhood I loved only the victims: now I feel charity for the executioners—melancholy penitents, who endure in this generation the punishment of crimes which they have committed in former existences, and whom God condemns to be wicked, a suffering which is a thousand times more cruel than that of being their innocent prey. This is why I now give alms only to relieve myself personally from the weight of riches, without tormenting you with my sermonizing—knowing, as I now do, that the time has not yet come for happiness, since the time for being good, to speak the language of men, is still far off.'

"'And now that you are delivered from this superintendent, as you call him, now that you can live tranquilly, without having before your eyes the spectacle of miseries which you extinguish one by one about you, without being restrained by any one in your generous disposition, can you not make an effort to banish these mental disquietudes?'

"'Do not ask me any more questions, my dear parents,' replied Albert; 'I shall not speak any more to-day.'

"He kept his word and even more; for he did not open his lips for a whole week.

CHAPTER XXVIII.

"ALBERT'S history will be concluded in a few words, my dear Porporina, because, unless I repeat what you have already heard, I have not much more to tell you. The conduct of my cousin during the eighteen months which I have passed here, has been a continual repetition of the extravagancies of which I have informed you. Only Albert's pretended recollection of what he had been, and what he had seen, in past ages, assumed an appearance of frightful reality, when he began to manifest a peculiar and truly wonderful faculty of which you may have heard, but in which I did not believe until I saw the proofs he gave of it. This faculty is called, I am told, in other countries, the second sight; and those who possess it are objects of great veneration among superstitious people. As for me, who know not what to think of it, and will not undertake to give you a reasonable explanation, it only adds an additional motive to deter me from becoming the wife of a man who could see all my actions, even if I were a hundred leagues off, and who could almost read my thoughts. Such a wife ought to be at least a saint, and how could she be one with a man who seems to have made a compact with Satan?"

" You have the happy privilege of being able to jest on every subject," said Consuelo; "I wonder at the cheerfulness with which you speak of things which make my hair stand on end. In what does this second sight consist?"

" Albert sees and hears what no one else can see and hear. When a person whom he loves is coming, although no one expects him, Albert announces his approach, and goes to meet him an hour beforehand. In the same way also he retires and shuts himself up in his chamber, when he feels that any one whom he dislikes is about to visit us.

" One day when he was walking with my father in a by-path on the mountains, he suddenly stopped and made a wide circuit through rocks and brushwood, in order not to pass near a certain place, which nevertheless presented nothing peculiar in its appearance. They returned by the same path a few moments after, and Albert again took the same precaution. My father, who observed this movement, pretended to have lost something, and endeavored to draw him to the foot of a cedar which appeared to be the object of his repugnance. Not only did Albert avoid approaching it, but he affected even not to walk upon the shadow which the tree cast over the path; and while my father passed and repassed under it, he manifested extraordinary uneasiness and anguish. At last, my father having stopped altogether at the foot of the tree, Albert uttered a cry and hastily called him back. But he refused for a long time to explain himself respecting this fancy, and it was only when overcome by the prayers of the whole family, that he declared that the tree marked the place of a burial, and that a great crime had been committed on this spot. The chaplain thought that if Albert knew of any murder which had formerly been committed in that place, it was his duty to inform him of it, in order to give Christian burial to the abandoned bones.

" ' Take care what you do,' said Albert, with an air at

the same time sad and ironical, which he often assumes. 'The man, woman, and child whom you will find there were Hussites, and it was the drunkard Wenceslas who had their throats cut by his soldiers one night when he was concealed in our woods, and was afraid of being observed and betrayed by them.'

"Nothing more was said to my cousin respecting this circumstance. But my uncle, who wished to know if it was an inspiration, or merely a caprice on his part, caused a search to be made during the night at the place which my father pointed out. They found the skeletons of a man, a woman, and a child. The man was covered with one of those enormous wooden shields which the Hussites carried, and which are easily recognized by the chalice engraved upon them, with this device in Latin around it : ' *O Death, how bitter is thy coming to the wicked ; but refreshing to him whose actions have been just, and directed with reference to thee !'* *

"The bones were transferred to a more retired spot in the forest, and when, several days after, Albert passed the foot of the cedar a second time, my father remarked that he manifested no repugnance at walking on the place, which nevertheless had been again covered with stones and sand, and in which nothing appeared changed. He did not even remember the emotion he experienced on that occasion, and had some difficulty in recalling it to his mind on its being mentioned.

"'You must be mistaken,' said he to my father, 'and I must have been *warned* in some other place. I am certain there is nothing here, for I feel no cold, nor pain, nor shivering!'

"My aunt was inclined to attribute this power of divination to the special favor of Providence; but Albert is so melancholy, so tormented, so unhappy, that one can hardly think Providence would have bestowed on him so fatal a gift. If I believed in the devil, I should much sooner embrace the supposition of our chaplain, who charges all Albert's hallucinations to his account. My uncle Christian, who is a more sensible man, and firmer

---

* "*O Mors quam est amara memoria tua hominibus injustis, viro quieto sujus omnes res flunt ordinate et ad hoc.*" This sentence is taken from the Bible. But there the rich are named instead of the wicked, and the poor instead of the just.

in his religious belief than any of the rest of us, explains many of these things very reasonably. He believes that, notwithstanding the pains taken by the Jesuits during and after the Thirty Years' War, to burn all the heretical writings in Bohemia, and particularly those which were found at the Castle of the Giants, notwithstanding the minute searches made by the chaplain in every corner after the death of my aunt Wanda, some historical documents of the time of the Hussites must have remained concealed in a secret place unknown to every body, and Albert must have found them. He thinks that the reading of those dangerous papers has vividly impressed his diseased imagination, and that he attributes to a supernatural recollection of previous existences upon earth, the impression which he then received of many details now unknown, but minutely detailed in these manuscripts. The stories he relates to us can thus be naturally explained, as well as his otherwise inexplicable disappearances for days and whole weeks; for it is as well to inform you that these have been repeated several times, and it is impossible to suppose they can be accomplished out of the château. Every time he has so disappeared it has been impossible to discover him, and we are certain that no peasant has ever given him refuge or nourishment. We know to a certainty that he has fits of lethargy which keep him confined to his chamber whole days. Whenever the door is broken open and much noise made around him, he falls into convulsions. Therefore they take good care not to do this, but leave him to his trance. At such moments extraordinary things certainly take place in his mind; but no sound, no outward agitation betrays them, and we are only informed of them afterward by his conversations. When he recovers from this state, he appears relieved and restored to reason; but by degrees the agitation returns and goes on increasing, until it overpowers him. It would seem that he foresees the duration of these crises; for when they are about to be long, he goes to a distance, or conceals himself in some lurking-place, which, it is supposed, must be a grotto of the mountain, or a subterranean chamber in the château, known to him alone. Hitherto no one has been able to discover it, and any attempt to do so is the more difficult, as we cannot watch him, and he is made dangerously ill if any one follows him, observes him, or even questions him. It has been therefore thought best to leave him entirely free, since we have come to regard these absences, which were at the commencement so terrifying, as favorable crises in his malady. When they occur, my aunt suffers the most acute anxiety, and my uncle prays, but nobody stirs ; and as to myself, I can assure you I am growing very insensible on the subject. Anxiety has been succeeded by ennui and disgust, and I would rather die than marry this maniac. I admit his noble qualities ; but though it may seem to you that I ought to disregard his phantasies, since they are the effect of his malady, I confess that they irritate me, and are a thorn in my life and that of my family."

" That seems to me somewhat unjust, dear baroness," said Consuelo. " That you have a repugnance to becoming Count Albert's wife I can now understand very well ; but that you should lose your interest in him, I confess I do not understand at all."

" It is because I cannot drive from my mind the idea that there is something voluntary in the poor man's madness. It is certain that he has great force of character, and that on a thousand occasions he has considerable control over himself. He can put off the attacks of his malady at will. I have seen him master them with much power, when those around him did not seem inclined to consider them in a serious light. On the contrary, whenever he sees us disposed to credulity and fear, he appears to wish to produce an effect on us by his extravagancies, and to abuse our weakness toward him. This is why I feel annoyed, and frequently long for his patron Beelzebub to come for him at once, that we may be freed from his presence."

" These are very severe witticisms," said Consuelo, " respecting so unhappy a being, and one whose mental malady seems to me more poetical and marvelous than repulsive."

" As you please, dear Porporina," returned Amelia. " Admire these sorceries as much as you will, if you can believe in them. As for me, I look upon such things in the same light as our chaplain, who recommends his soul to God, and does not take any pains to understand them. I take refuge in the arms of reason, and excuse myself from explaining what I am sure must be capable of a very natural explanation, though at present unknown to us. The only thing certain in my cousin's miserable lot is, that his reason has entirely disappeared, and that imagination has whirled him to such a distance from earth that all his sight and sense are gone. And since I must speak plainly, and use the word which my poor uncle Christian was obliged to utter with tears, at the knees of the Empress Maria-Theresa, who is not to be satisfied with half answers or half explanations — in one word, Albert of Rudolstadt is MAD ; or insane, if you consider that epithet more polite."

Consuelo only answered by a deep sigh. At that instant Amelia seemed to her to be a very hateful person, and to have a heart of iron. She tried to excuse her in her own eyes, by reflecting upon what she must have suffered during eighteen months of a life so sad, and filled with such painful emotions. Then returning to her own misfortune, "Ah!" thought she, "why cannot I place Anzoleto's fault to the score of madness? If he had fallen into delirium in the midst of the intoxications and deceptions of his first appearance on the stage, I feel that I should not have loved him any less ; I should only require to know that his unfaithfulness and ingratitude proceeded from insanity, to adore him as before and fly to his assistance."

Several days passed without Albert's giving, either by his manner or his conversation, the least confirmation of his cousin's assertions respecting the derangement of his mind ; but one day the chaplain having unintentionally contradicted him, he began to utter some incoherent sentences, and then, as if he were himself sensible of it, rushed hastily out of the saloon and ran to shut himself up in his chamber. They thought he would remain there a long time ; but an hour afterward, he re-entered, pale and languishing, dragged himself from chair to chair, moved around Consuelo without seeming to pay any more attention to her than on other days, and ended by seeking refuge in the deep embrasure of a window, where he leaned his head on his hands, and remained perfectly motionless.

It was the hour of Amelia's music lesson, and she expressed a wish to take it, in order, as she said in a low voice to Consuelo, to drive away that gloomy figure which destroyed all her gaiety, and diffused a sepulchral odor through the apartment.

"I think," replied Consuelo, "that we had better go up to your apartment; your spinet will do for the accompaniment. If it be true that Count Albert does not like music, why augment his sufferings, and consequently those of his family?"

Amelia yielded to this last consideration, and they ascended together to her apartment, the door of which they left open, because they found it a little smoky. Amelia, as usual, wished to go on in her own way, with showy and brilliant cavatinas, but Consuelo, who began to show herself strict, made her try several simple and serious airs, taken from the religious songs of Palestrina. The young baroness yawned, became impatient, and declared that the music was barbarous, and would send her to sleep.

"That is because you do not understand it," said Consuelo. "Let me sing some passages, to show you that it is admirably written for a voice, besides being sublime and lofty in its character."

She seated herself at the spinet, and began to sing. It was the first time she had awakened the echoes of the old château, and she found the bare and lofty walls so admirably adapted for sound, that she gave herself up entirely to the pleasure which she experienced. Her voice, long mute, since the last evening when she sang at San Samuel —that evening when she fainted, broken down by fatigue and sorrow—instead of being impaired by so much suffering and agitation, was more beautiful, more marvelous, more thrilling than ever. Amelia was at the same time transported and affrighted. She was at length beginning to understand that she did not know any thing, and that perhaps she never could learn any thing, when the pale and pensive figure of Albert suddenly appeared, in the middle of the apartment, in front of the two young girls, and remained motionless and apparently deeply moved until the end of the piece. It was only then that Consuelo perceived him, and was somewhat terrified. But Albert, falling on his knees, and raising toward her his large dark eyes, swimming in tears, exclaimed in Spanish, without the least German accent, "O Consuelo! Consuelo! I have at last found thee!"

"Consuelo?" cried the astonished girl, expressing herself in the same language, "Why, señor, do you call me by that name?"

"I call you Consolation," replied Albert, still speaking in Spanish, "because a consolation has been promised to my desolate life, and because you are that consolation which God at last grants to my solitary and gloomy existence."

"I did not think," said Amelia, with suppressed rage, "that music could have produced so prodigious an effect on my dear cousin. Nina's voice is formed to accomplish wonders, I confess; but I may remark to both of you, that it would be more polite toward me, and more according to general etiquette, to use a language which I can understand."

Albert appeared not to have heard a word of what his betrothed had said. He remained on his knees, looking at Consuelo with indescribable surprise and transport, and repeating in a tender voice, "Consuelo! Consuelo!"

"But what is it he calls you?" said Amelia, somewhat pettishly, to her companion.

"He is asking me for a Spanish air, which I do not know," said Consuelo, much agitated; "but I think we had better stop, for music seems to affect him deeply today." And she rose to retire.

"Consuelo!" repeated Albert, in Spanish, "if you leave me, my life is at an end, and I will never return to earth again!" Saying this, he fell at her feet in a swoon, and the two young girls, terrified, called the servants to carry him to his apartment, and endeavor to restore him to consciousness.

CHAPTER XXXIII.

Count Albert was laid softly upon his bed; and while one of the two domestics who had carried him searched for the chaplain, who was a sort of a family physician, and the other for Count Christian, who had given orders that he should always be called at the least indisposition of his son, the two young girls, Amelia and Consuelo, went in quest of the canoness. But before either of these persons could reach the bedside of the invalid, although they made all possible haste, Albert had disappeared. They found his door open, his bed scarcely marked by the momentary repose he had taken, and his chamber in its accustomed order. They sought him everywhere, but, as always happened in similar cases, without the slightest success; after which the family sank into the sort of gloomy resignation of which Amelia had spoken to Consuelo, and seemed to await with that silent terror which they had learned to suppress, the always hoped for and always uncertain return of this singular young man.

Although Consuelo could have wished to avoid informing Albert's parents of the strange scene which had accurred in Amelia's apartment, the latter did not fail to relate the whole, and to depict in vivid colors the sudden and violent effects which Porporina's singing had produced upon her cousin.

"Then it is very certain that music affects him unfavorably," replied the chaplain.

"In that case," replied Consuelo, "I will take good care he shall not hear me; and when I am engaged with the young baroness, we will shut ourselves up so closely that no sound can reach Count Albert's ears."

"That will be a great annoyance to you, my dear young lady," said the canoness; "ah! it is not my fault that your residence here is not more agreeable."

"I wish to share both your sorrows and your joys," returned Consuelo, "and I ask no higher satisfaction than to be made a partaker of them by your confidence and your friendship."

"You are a noble girl!" said the canoness, extending to her a long hand, dry and polished as yellow ivory. "But listen," added she; "I do not believe that music really does harm to my dear Albert. From what Amelia has related of this morning's occurrence, I imagine on the contrary that he experienced too vivid a delight, and perhaps his suffering arose from the too sudden cessation of your lovely melodies. What did he say to you in Spanish? That is a language which he speaks perfectly well, as he does many others which he learned in his travels with surprising facility. When we ask him how he can retain so many different languages, he answers that he knew them before he was born, and that he merely recalls them — this one, because he spoke it twelve hundred years ago, and another, alas! for aught I know, when he was at the Crusades. As we must conceal nothing from you, dear signora, you will hear strange accounts of what he calls his anterior existences. But translate to me in our German, which you already speak so well, the meaning of the words which he said to you in your language, with which none of us here are acquainted."

Consuelo at that moment felt an embarrassment for which she could not account. Nevertheless she thought it best to tell nearly the whole truth, and explained that Albert had requested her to go on playing, and not to leave him, since she gave him much consolation.

"Consolation!" cried the quick-witted Amelia. "Did he use that word? You know, aunt, how significant it is in my cousin's mouth."

"It is, in fact, a word which he has frequently on his lips," replied Wenceslawa, "and which seems to have a prophetic meaning for him ; but I see nothing on this occasion which could render the use of such a word other than perfectly natural."

"But what was that which he repeated so often, dear Porporina ?" returned Amelia, pertinaciously. "He seemed to repeat a particular word to you many times, but from my agitation I am not able to remember what it was."

"I did not understand it myself," replied Consuelo, making a great effort to tell a falsehood.

"My dear Nina," said Amelia to her in a whisper, "you are quick-witted and prudent: as for me, who am not altogether stupid, I think I understand very well that you are the mystic consolation promised by the vision to Albert in his thirtieth year. Do not think to conceal from me that you understood this even better than I did; it is a celestial mission of which I am not jealous."

"Listen, dear Porporina," said the canoness, after having reflected for a few minutes; "we have always thought that Albert, when he disappeared from among us in a manner which might almost be called magical, was concealed in some place not far off—in the house perhaps— thanks to some retreat of which he alone has the secret. I know not why, but it seems to me that if you would sing at this moment he would hear you and come to us."

"If I thought so——" said Consuelo, ready to obey.

"But if Albert is near us, and the effect of music should be to increase his aberration ?" remarked the jealous Amelia.

"Well," said Count Christian, "we must make the trial,

I have heard that the incomparable Farinelli had the power of dissipating by his voice the gloomy melancholy of the king of Spain, as young David had that of calming the fury of Saul by his harp. Try, generous Porporina; so pure a soul as yours must exercise a salutary influence on all around it."

Consuelo, much moved, seated herself at the harpsichord and sang a Spanish hymn in honor of Our Lady of Consolation, which her mother had taught her when a child, and which began with these words, *Consuelo de mi alma,* "Consolation of my soul," etc. She sang with so pure a voice, and with so much unaffected piety, that her hosts of the old manor-house almost forgot the object of their anxieties, and gave themselves up to sentiments of hope and of faith. A profound silence reigned both within and without the château; the doors and windows had been opened in order that Consuelo's voice might reach as far as possible, and the moon with her pale and trembling light illumined the embrasures of the vast windows. All was calm, and a sort of religious serenity succeeded to the anguish they had felt, when a deep sigh, as if breathed forth from a human breast, responded to the last sounds uttered by Consuelo. The sigh was so distinct and so prolonged, that all present, even Baron Frederick, who, half awake, turned his head as if some one had called him, heard it. All turned pale and looked at each other, as if to say, "It was not I; was it you?" Amelia could not repress a cry, and Consuelo, to whom it seemed as if the sigh proceeded from some one at her very side, though she was seated at the harpsichord apart from the rest of the family, felt so alarmed that she could not utter a word.

"Divine goodness!" said the terrified canoness, "did you hear that sigh which seemed to come from the depths of the earth?"

"Say rather, aunt," cried Amelia, "that it passed over our heads like the breath of night."

"Some owl, attracted by the light, must have flown across the apartment while we were absorbed by the music, and we have heard the fluttering of its wings at the moment it flew out through the window." Such was the opinion put forward by the chaplain, whose teeth nevertheless chattered with fear.

"Perhaps it was Albert's dog," said Count Christian.

"Cynabre is not here," replied Amelia. "Wherever Albert is, Cynabre is always with him. Some one certainly sighed here strangely. If I dared to go to the window, I would see if any one were listening in the garden; but even if my life depended on it, I have not strength sufficient.

"For a person so devoid of prejudices," said Consuelo to her in a low voice, and forcing a smile, "for a little French philosopher, you are not very brave, my dear baroness; I will try to be more so."

"Do not go, my dear," replied Amelia aloud, "nor pretend to be valiant, for you are as pale as death, and will be ill."

"What childish fancies, my dear Amelia!" said Count Christian, advancing toward the window with a grave and firm step. He looked out, saw no one, closed the sash calmly, and said, "It seems that real evils are not keen enough for the ardent imaginations of women; they must add to them the creations of their own brains, always too ingenious in searching for causes of suffering. Certainly that sigh had nothing mysterious in it; some one of us, affected by the beautiful voice and the wonderful talent of the signora, must have breathed forth his admiration unwittingly. Perhaps it was myself, and yet I was not sensible of it. Ah? Porporina, if you should not succeed in curing Albert, at least you know how to pour celestial balm on wounds as deep as his."

The words of this pious old man, always wise and calm in the midst of the domestic misfortunes which overwhelmed him, were in themselves a celestial balm, and Consuelo felt their healing effect. She was tempted to throw herself on her knees before him, and ask his blessing; as she had received that of Porpora on leaving him, and that of Marcello on that bright and sunny day of her life, which had been the commencement of an uninterrupted succession of misfortunes.

CHAPTER XXXIV.

SEVERAL days passed over without their hearing any news of Count Albert; and Consuelo, to whom this position of things appeared dismal in the extreme, was astonished to see the Rudolstadt family bear so frightful a state of uncertainty without evincing either despair or even impatience. Familiarity with the most cruel anxieties produces a sort of apparent apathy, or else real hardness of heart, which wounds and almost irritates those minds whose sensibility has not yet been blunted by long-continued misfortune. Consuelo, a prey to a sort of nightmare in the midst of these doleful impressions and inexplicable occurrences, was astonished to see that the order of the house was hardly disturbed, that the canoness was equally vigilant, the baron equally eager for the chase, the chaplain regular as ever in the same devotional exercises, and Amelia gay and trifling as usual. The cheerful vivacity of the latter was what particularly offended Consuelo. She could not conceive how the baroness could laugh and play, while she herself could hardly read or work with her needle. The canoness, however, employed herself in embroidering an altar front for the chapel of the castle. It was a masterpiece of patience, exquisite workmanship, and neatness. Hardly had she made the tour of the house, when she returned to seat herself at her work, were it only to add a few stitches, while waiting to be called by new cares to the barns, the kitchens, or the cellars. One should have seen with how much importance these little concerns were treated, and how that diminutive creature hurried along, at a pace always regular, always dignified and measured, but never slackened, through all the corners of her little empire; crossing a thousand times each day in every direction the narrow and monotonous surface of her domestic domain. What also seemed strange to Consuelo was the respect and admiration which the family and country in general attached to this indefatigable housekeeping — a pursuit which the old lady seemed to have embraced with such ardor and jealous observance. To see her parsimoniously regulating the most trifling affairs, one would have thought her covetous and distrustful; and yet on important occasions she displayed a soul deeply imbued with noble and generous sentiments. But these excellent qualities, especially her maternal tenderness, which gave her in Consuelo's eyes so sympathizing and venerable an air. would not of themselves have been sufficient in the eyes of the others to elevate her to the rank of the heroine of the family. She required, besides, the far more important qualification of a scrupulous attention to the trifling details of the household, to cause her to be appreciated for what she really was, notwithstanding what has been said, a woman of strong sense and high moral feeling. Not a day passed that Count Christian, the baron, or the chaplain, did not repeat every time she turned her back, "How much wisdom, how much courage, how much strength of mind does the canoness display!" Amelia herself, not distinguishing the true and ennobling purpose of life, in the midst of the puerilities which, under another form, constituted the whole of hers, did not venture to disparage her aunt under this point of view, the only one that, in Consuelo's eyes, cast a shadow upon the bright light which shone from the poor and loving soul of the hunchback Wenceslawa. To the *zingarella*, born upon the highway and thrown helpless on the world, without any other master or any other protection than her own genius, so much care, so much activity and intensity of thought to produce such miserable results as the preservation and maintenance of certain objects and certain provisions, appeared a monstrous perversion of the understanding. She, who possessed none and desired none of the world's riches, was grieved to see a lovely and generous soul voluntarily extinguish itself in the business of acquiring wheat, wine, wood, hemp, cattle, and furniture. If they had offered her all these goods, so much desired by the greater part of mankind, she would have asked, instead, a moment of her former happiness, her rags, the clear and lovely sky above her head, her fresh young love and her liberty upon the lagunes of Venice—all that was stamped on her memory in more and more glowing colors, in proportion as she receded from that gay and laughing horizon to penetrate into the frozen sphere which is called real life!

She felt her heart sink in her bosom when at nightfall she saw the old canoness, followed by Hans, take an immense bunch of keys, and make the circuit of all the buildings and all the courts, closing the least openings, and examining the smallest recesses into which an evildoer could have crept; as if no one could sleep in security within those formidable walls, until the water of the torrent, which was restrained behind a neighboring parapet, had rushed roaring into the trenches of the château, while in addition the gates were locked and the drawbridge raised. Consuelo had so often slept, in her distant wanderings by the roadside, with no covering save her mother's torn cloak thrown over her for shelter ! She had so often welcomed the dawn upon the snowy flagstones of Venice, washed by the waves, without having a moment's fear for her modesty, the only riches she cared to preserve! "Alas !" said she, "how unhappy are these people in having so many things to take care of ! Security is the aim of their pursuits by day and night, and so carefully do they seek it, that they have no time to find or enjoy it." Like Amelia, therefore, she already pined in her gloomy prison—that dark and somber Castle of the Giants, where the sun himself seemed afraid to penetrate. But while the young baroness only thought of fêtes, of dresses, and whispering suitors, Consuelo dreamed of wandering beside her native wave-washed shores—a thicket or a fisher-boat for her palace, the boundless heavens for her covering, and the starry firmament to gaze on!

Forced by the cold of the climate and the closing of the castle gates to change the Venetian custom which she had retained, of watching during a part of the night and rising late in the morning, she at last succeeded, after many hours of sleeplessness, agitation, and melancholy dreams, in submitting to the savage law of the cloister, and recompensed herself by undertaking, alone, several morning walks in the neighboring mountain. The gates were opened and the bridges lowered at the first dawn of day, and while Amelia, secretly occupied in reading novels during a part of the night, slept until awakened by the first breakfast bell, Porporina sallied forth to breathe the fresh air and brush the early dew from the herbage of the forest. One morning as she descended softly on tiptoe, in order to awaken no one, she mistook the direction she ought to take among the numberless staircases and interminable corridors of the château, with which she was hardly yet acquainted. Lost in a labyrinth of galleries and passages, she traversed a sort of vestibule, which she did not recognize, imagining she should find an exit to the garden by that way. But she merely reached the entrance of a little chapel built in a beautiful but antique style, and dimly lighted from above by a circular window of stained glass in the vaulted ceiling, which threw a feeble light upon the center of the pavement, and left the extremities of the building in mysterious gloom. The sun was still below the horizon, and the morning gray and foggy. At first Consuelo thought herself in the chapel of the château, where she had heard mass the preceding Monday. She knew that the chapel opened upon the gardens; but before crossing it to go out, she wished to honor the sanctuary of prayer, and knelt upon the first step of the altar. But, as it often happens to artists to be preoccupied with outward objects in spite of their attempts to ascend into the sphere of abstract ideas, her prayer could not absorb her sufficiently to prevent her casting a glance of curiosity around her; and she soon perceived that she was not in the chapel, but in a place to which she had not before penetrated. It was neither the same shrine nor the same ornaments. Although this unknown chapel was very small, she could hardly as yet distinguish objects around her; but what struck Consuelo most was a marble statue kneeling before the altar, in that cold and severe attitude in which all figures on tombs were formerly represented. She concluded that she was in a place reserved for the sepulchers of some distinguished ancestors, and, having become somewhat fearful and superstitious since her residence in Bohemia, she shortened her prayer and rose to retire.

But at that moment when she cast a last timid look at the figure which was kneeling ten paces from her, she distinctly saw the statue unclasp its hands of stone, and slowly make the sign of the cross, as it uttered a deep sigh.

Consuelo almost fell backward, and yet she could not withdraw her haggard eyes from that terrible statue. What confirmed her in the belief that it was a figure of stone was that it did not appear to hear the cry of terror which escaped from her, and that it replaced its two large white hands one upon the other, without seeming to have the least connection with the outer world.

CHAPTER XXXV.

IF the ingenious and imaginative Anne Radcliffe had found herself in the place of the candid and unskillful narrator of this veracious history, she would not have allowed so good an opportunity to escape, of leading you, fair reader, through corridors, trap-doors, spiral staircases, and subterranean passages, for half a dozen flowery and attractive volumes, to reveal to you only at the seventh, all the arcana of her skillful labors. But the strong-minded reader, whom it is our duty to please, would not probably lend herself so willingly, at the present period, to the innocent stratagem of the romancer. Besides, as it might be difficult to make her believe them, we will tell her as soon as possible the solution of all our enigmas. And to explain two of them at once, we will confess that Consuelo, after some moments of cool observation, recognized in the animated statue before her eyes, the old Count Christian, who was mentally reciting his morning prayers in his oratory, and in the sigh of compunction which unwittingly escaped from him, the same unearthly sigh which she thought she had heard close beside her, on the evening when she sang the hymn to Our Lady of Consolation.

A little ashamed of her terror, Consuelo remained rooted to her place by respect, and by the fear of disturbing so fervent a prayer. Nothing could be more solemn or more touching than to see that old man, prostrate upon the stone pavement, offering his heart to God at the opening of the day, and plunged in a sort of celestial ecstasy which appeared to close his senses to all perception of the outward world. His noble features did not betray any emotion of grief. A gentle breeze penetrating by the door which Consuelo had left open, agitated the semi-circle of silvery hair which still remained upon the back part of his head, and his broad forehead, bald to the very summit, had the yellow and polished appearance of old marble. Clothed in an old-fashioned dressing-gown of white woolen stuff, which somewhat resembled a monk's frock, and which fell in large, stiff, heavy folds about his attenuated person, he had all the appearance of a monumental statue; and after he had resumed his immovable position, Consuelo was obliged to look at him a second time, in order not to fall again into her former illusion.

After having contemplated him for some time with attention, placing herself a little on one side to see him better, she asked herself, as if involuntarily, while still lost in admiration and emotion, if the kind of prayer which this old man addressed to God was efficacious for the restoration of his unhappy son, and if a soul so passively submissive to the letter of his religious tenets, and to the rough decrees of destiny, had ever possessed the warmth, the intelligence, and the zeal which Albert required from a father's love. Albert too had a mystic soul; he also had led a devout and contemplative life; but from all that Amelia had related to Consuelo, and from what she had remarked with her own eyes during the few days she had passed at the château, Albert had never found the counsel, the guide, the friend, who could direct his imagination, diminish the vehemence of his feelings, and soften the burning sternness of his virtue. She guessed that he must feel isolated, and look upon himself as a stranger in the midst of this family so determined not to contradict him, but to grieve for him in silence either as a heretic or a madman. She felt so herself from the kind of impatience she experienced at that wearying and interminable prayer addressed to Heaven, as if to transfer to it entirely the care which they themselves ought to have employed in searching for the fugitive, in finding him, in persuading him, and bringing him home. For it must have required a fearful amount of despair and grief, to withdraw so affectionate and good a young man from the bosom of his relatives, to bury him in a complete forgetfulness of self, and to deprive him even of the recollection of the uneasiness and anxiety he might occasion to those who were dearest to him.

The resolution they had taken of never opposing him, and of feigning calmness while overcome with terror, seemed to Consuelo's lofty and well-regulated mind a species of culpable negligence or gross error. There was in such a course a sort of pride and selfishness which a narrow faith inspires in those persons who consent to wear the badge of intolerance, and who believe in only one path by which they can attain to heaven, and that path rigidly marked out by the finger of the priest. " Heavenly Father," said Consuelo, with fervent devotion, " can this lofty soul,

so warm, so charitable, so free from human passions, be
less precious in thy sight than the patient and slothful
spirits which submit to the injustice of the world, and see
without indignation justice and truth forgotten upon the
earth? Was that young man possessed by the evil one,
who in his childhood gave all his toys and ornaments to the
children of the poor, and who, at the first awakening of
his reflective powers, wished to deprive himself of all his
wealth, in order to solace human miseries? And are they,
these kind and benevolent lords who weep for misfortune
with barren tears, and comfort it with trifling gifts — are
they wise in thinking that they are to attain to heaven by
prayers and acts of submission to the emperor and the pope,
rather than by righteous works and great sacrifices? No,
Albert is not mad; a voice cries to me from the inmost recesses of my heart, that he is the fairest type of the just
man and of the saint that has issued from the hands of
nature. And if painful dreams and strange illusions have
obscured the clearness of his vision — if, in short, he has
become deranged as they think, it is their blind contradiction, it is the absence of sympathy, it is the loneliness of
his heart, which has brought about this deplorable result.
I have seen the cell in which Tasso was confined as mad,
and felt that he was perhaps only exasperated by injustice.
In the saloons of Venice I have heard those great saints of
Christendom, whose histories have haunted my dreams in
childhood, and wrung tears from my aching heart, treated
as madmen; their miracles called juggleries, and their
revelations frenzied dreams. But by what right do these
people, this pious old man, this timid canoness, who believe in the miracles of the saints and the genius of the
poets, pronounce upon their child this sentence of shame
and reprobation, which should be borne only by the diseased and the wicked. Mad! no, madness is horrible and
repulsive! It is a punishment from God for great crimes,
and can a man become mad by the very consequence of
his virtue? I thought that it was enough to suffer under the
weight of undeserved evil, in order to have a claim upon
the respect as well as on the pity of men. And if I myself
had gone mad, if I had blasphemed on that terrible day
when I saw Anzoleto at another's feet, would I, therefore,
have lost all title to the counsels, to the encouragements,
to the spiritual cares of my Christian brethren? Would

they have driven me forth or left me wandering upon the highways, saying: "There is no remedy for her; let us give her alms, and not speak to her; for since she has suffered so much she can understand nothing?' Well! it is thus that they treat this unfortunate Count Albert! They feed him, they clothe him, they take care of him, and, in a word, bestow upon him the alms of a childish solicitude. But they do not speak to him; they are silent when he questions them; they droop their heads or turn them away when he strives to persuade them. They let him fly, when the horror of solitude drives him into solitude still more profound, and wait till he returns, praying to God to watch over him and bring him back safe and well, as if the ocean were between him and the objects of his affection. And yet they think he is not far off; they make me sing to awaken him, as if he were buried in a lethargic sleep in the thickness of some wall, or in the hollow and aged trunk of some neighboring tree. And yet they have never even thought of exploring all the secrets of this old building, they have never dug into the bowels of this excavated soil! Ah! if I were Albert's father or his aunt, I would not have left one stone upon another until I had found him; not a tree of the forest should have remained standing until they had restored him to me."

Lost in her reflections, Consuelo departed noiselessly from Count Christian's oratory, and found, without knowing how, an exit from the castle leading toward the open country. She wandered through the forest paths, and sought out the rudest and most difficult, guided by a romantic hope of discovering Albert. No common attraction, no shadow of imprudent fancy carried her onward in this venturous design.

Albert filled her imagination, and occupied her waking dreams, it is true; but in her eyes it was not a handsome young man, enthusiastically attracted toward her, whom she was seeking in those desert places, in the hope of seeing and enjoying an interview with him unobserved by spectators; it was a noble and unfortunate being whom she imagined she could save, or at least calm by the purity of her zeal. She would in the same manner have sought out a venerable hermit, who required her care and assistance, or a lost child, in order to restore him to his mother.

She was a child herself, and yet she enjoyed as it were a foretaste of maternal love in her simple faith, ardent charity, and exalted courage. She dreamed of and undertook this pilgrimage, as Joan of Arc had dreamed of and undertaken the deliverance of her country. It did not even occur to her that the resolution she had taken could be a subject for ridicule or blame ; she could not conceive how it happened that Amelia, bound to him by the ties of blood, and in the commencement by the stronger bonds of love, should not have formed the same project and succeeded in carrying it out.

She walked forward rapidly; no obstacle deterred her. The silence of that vast forest no longer affected her mind with sadness or fear. She saw the track of wolves upon the sand, and felt no uneasiness lest she should meet the famished pack. It seemed to her that she was urged on by a divine hand which rendered her invulnerable. She knew Tasso by heart from having sung his verses every night upon the lagunes, and imagined that she was walking under the protection of his talisman, as did the generous Ubaldo to the discovery of Rinaldo, through the snares of the enchanted forest. She threaded her way through the rocks and brushwood with a firm and elastic step, her brow glowing with a secret pride, and her cheeks tinged with a delicate carnation. Never had she seemed lovelier upon the stage in her heroic characters, and yet she thought no more of the stage at this moment than she had thought of herself when she entered the theater.

From time to time she stopped, thoughtful and reflective. "And if I should meet him suddenly," thought she, "what could I say to convince and tranquilize him ? I know nothing of those mysterious and profound subjects which agitate him. I merely guess their nature, through the veil of poetry which my excited imagination, unused to their contemplation, has raised around them. I ought to possess more than mere zeal and charity, I ought to have science and eloquence, to find words worthy to be listened to by a man so much my superior—by a madman so wise when compared with all the reasonable beings among whom I have lived. I will go on; God will inspire me when the moment comes; for as to myself, I might search for ever, and should only lose myself more and more in the darkness of my ignorance. Ah! if I had read

numberless books of religion and history, like Count
Christian and Canoness Wenceslawa! If I knew by heart
all the prayers of the Church, I should, no doubt, be able
to apply some one of them appropriately to his unfortunate
situation; but all my acquirements of this nature are lim-
ited to a few phrases of the catechism, imperfectly understood, and consequently imperfectly remembered, and I
know not how to pray except through the medium of an
anthem or a hymn.   However sensitive he may be to
music, I fear I shall not be able to persuade this learned
theologian by a cadence or a sweet strain.   No matter ; it
seems to me there is more power in my persuaded and resolute heart, than in all the doctrines studied by his
parents, who are indeed both good and kind, but at the
same time cold and wavering as the fogs and snows of
their native mountains."

CHAPTER XXXVI.

AFTER many turnings and windings through the inex-
tricable mazes of the forest, which extended over a rough
and hilly tract of country, Consuelo found herself on an
elevation covered over with a confused heap of rocks and
ruins, very difficult to be distinguished from each other,
so destructive had been the hand of man, jealous of that
of time.   It now presented nothing but the appearance of
a mountain of ruins, but had been formerly the site of a
village, burned by order of the redoubtable blind man, the
celebrated Calixtin chief John Ziska, from whom Albert
believed himself to have descended, and perhaps was so in
reality.

This ferocious and indefatigable captain having commanded his troops, one dark and dismal night, to attack the
Fortress of the Giants, then guarded for the emperor by the
Saxons, overheard his soldiers murmur, and one among them
not far from him, say—" This cursed blind man supposes
that all can do without light as well as he."   Thereupon
Ziska, turning to one of the four devoted disciples who
accompanied him everywhere, guiding his horse and
chariot and giving him a precise account of the position
and movements of the enemy, said to him, with that extraordinary accuracy of memory, or principle of second

sight, which in him supplied the place of vision : " There is a village near this, is there not?" " Yes, father," replied the Taborite guide, " to your right, upon a hill in front of the fortress." Ziska then summoned the discontented soldier whose murmurs had reached his ear : " My child," said he to him, " you complain of the darkness ; go immediately and set fire to the village upon the hill to my right, and by the light of the flames we can march and fight." This terrible order was executed. The burning village lighted the march and attack of the Taborites. The Castle of the Giants was carried in two hours, and Ziska took possession of it.

At dawn the next day it was observed and made known to him, that in the midst of the ruins of the village, and at the very summit of the hill which had served the soldiers as a platform for observing the movements of the enemy, a young oak, rare in those countries and already vigorous, had remained standing and unscathed, apparently preserved from the heat of the flames around it by the water of a cistern which bathed its roots. " I know the cistern well," replied Ziska. " Ten of our number were cast into it by the accursed inhabitants of that village, and since that time the stone which covers it has not been removed. Let it remain and serve as their monument, since we are not among those who believe that wandering souls are driven from the gates of heaven by the Roman patron (Peter, the key-bearer, whom they have made a saint), because their bodies rot in ground unconsecrated by the hands of the priests of Belial. Let the bones of our brothers rest in peace in that cistern. Their souls are living. They have already assumed other bodies, and those martyrs fight among us although we know them not. As to the inhabitants of the village, they have received their reward, and as to the oak, it has done well in defying the conflagration ; a more glorious destiny than that of sheltering miscreants was reserved for it. We needed a gallows, and there it stands. Go and bring me those twenty Augustine monks whom we took yesterday in their convent, and who make a difficulty about following us. We will hang them high and dry on the branches of that brave oak, whose health such an ornament will quite restore."

It was done as soon as said. The oak from that time

was called the *Hussite,* the stone of the cistern, the *Stone of Terror,* and the ruined village on the deserted hill, *Schreckenstein.*

Consuelo had heard this frightful chronicle related in all its details by the Baroness Amelia. But as she had as yet seen the theater of it only from a distance, or by night at the time of her arrival at the château, she would not have recognised it, if, on casting her eyes below, she had not seen at the bottom of the ravine which the road crossed, the large fragments of the oak rent by the lightning, which no inhabitant of the country, and no servant of the château, had dared to cut or carry away; a superstitious fear being still attached in their minds, although after the lapse of several centuries, to this monument of horror, this contemporary of John Ziska; while the visions and predictions of Albert had invested this tragical spot with a still more repulsive character.

Thus Consuelo, on finding herself alone and unexpectedly before the Stone of Terror, upon which, overcome with fatigue, she had even seated herself, felt her courage shaken and her heart strangely oppressed. According, not only to Albert, but all the mountaineers of the country, terrible apparitions haunted the Schreckenstein, and drove from it all hunters rash enough to frequent its neighborhood in search of game. Consequently this hill, though very near the château, was often the abode of wolves and wild animals, who found there a secure refuge against the pursuits of the baron and his hounds.

The imperturbable Frederick did not on his own account much fear being assailed by the devil, with whom moreover he would not have feared to measure himself hand to hand; but superstitious in his own way, and in cases where his favorite occupations were concerned, he was persuaded that a pernicious influence there threatened his dogs, and attacked them with unknown and incurable disorders. He had lost several of them, from having suffered them to slake their thirst in the rills of water which escaped from the veins of the hill, and which perhaps sprang from the condemned cistern, the ancient tomb of the Hussites. So he recalled, with all the authority of his whistle, his greyhound Panther, or his slow-hound Sapphire, whenever they wandered in the neighborhood of the Schreckenstein.

Consuelo, blushing at this feeling of cowardice which she had resolved to combat, determined to rest a moment on the fatal stone, and to retire from it only at the slow and steady pace which marks a tranquil mind in the midst of trial. But just as she turned her eyes from the blighted oak which she saw two hundred feet below her, to cast them upon surrounding objects, she saw that she was not alone upon the Stone of Terror, and that a mysterious figure had seated itself at her side, without announcing its approach by the slightest noise. The figure had a large, round, and staring face, fixed on a deformed body, thin and crooked as a grasshopper's, and was dressed in an indescribable costume belonging to no age or country, the ragged condition of which amounted almost to slovenliness. Nothing in this being, save the strangeness and suddenness of its appearance, was calculated to inspire terror, for its looks and gestures were friendly. A kind and gentle smile played around the large mouth, and an infantile expression softened the wandering of mind which was betrayed by its vague look and hurried gestures. Consuelo, on finding herself alone with a madman, in a place where no one could come to her assistance, certainly felt alarmed, notwithstanding numerous bows and kind smiles which the insane being addressed to her. She thought it prudent to return his salutations and motions of the head in order to avoid irritating him, but she rose as quickly as possible, and left the place, pale and trembling.

The maniac did not follow her, and made no movement to recall her; he merely climbed upon the Stone of Terror to look after her, and saluted her by waving his cap with various fantastic gestures, all the while uttering a Bohemian word which Consuelo did not understand. When she found herself at a considerable distance, she recovered sufficient courage to look at and listen to him. She already reproached herself for having felt terrified in the presence of one of those unfortunates, whom a moment before she had pitied in her heart, and vindicated from the contempt and desertion of mankind. " He is a gentle maniac," said she to herself, " perhaps made crazy by love. He has found no refuge from coldness and contempt but on this accursed rock, on which no other person would dare to dwell, and where demons and specters are kinder to him than his fellow-men, since they do not drive him away nor trouble him in the indulgence of his moody temper. Poor creature! who laughest and playest like a child, with gray beard and a round and shapeless back! God doubtless protects and blesses thee in thy misfortune, since He sends thee only pleasing thoughts, and has not made thee misanthropical and violent, as thou hadst a right to be!" The maniac, seeing that she walked more slowly, and seeming to understand her kind look, began to speak to her in Bohemian with great volubility; and his voice had an exceeding sweetness, a touching charm which contrasted forcibly with his ugliness. Consuelo, not understanding him, and supposing that he wanted alms, drew from her pocket a piece of money which she placed upon a large stone, after raising her arm to show it to him, and to point to him the spot where she placed it. But he only laughed louder than ever, rubbing his hands and exclaiming in bad German: "Useless, useless! Zdenko needs nothing, Zdenko is happy, very happy! Zdenko has consolation, consolation, consolation!" Then, as if he had remembered a word which he had sought for a long time in vain, he shouted with a burst of joy, and so as to be understood, though he pronounced very badly, " *Consuelo, Consuelo, Consuelo, de mi alma.*"

Consuelo stopped, astounded, and addressing him in Spanish: "Why do you call me thus?" said she, "who has taught you that name? Do you understand the language which I speak to you?" At all these questions, to which Consuelo waited in vain for an answer, the maniac did nothing but jump and rub his hands, like a man enchanted with himself; and as long as she could distinguish the sound of his voice, she heard him repeat her name in different tones, accompanied with laughter and exclamations of joy, like a speaking bird, when he tries to articulate a word which he has been taught, and which he interrupts with the warbling of his natural song.

On returning to the château, Consuelo was lost in thought "Who, then," said she to herself, "has betrayed the secret of my disguise, so that the first savage I meet in these solitudes calls me by my own name? Can this crazy being have seen me anywhere? Such people travel; perhaps he has been in Venice at the same time as myself." She tried in vain to recall the faces of all the beggars and vagabonds she had been accustomed to see on the quays and on the Place of St. Mark, but that of the maniac of the Stone of Terror did not present itself to her memory. But as she once more crossed the draw-bridge, a more logical and interesting association of ideas occurred to her mind. She resolved to clear up her suspicions, and secretly congratulated herself on not having altogether failed in her purpose in the expedition she had just concluded.

CHAPTER XXXVII.

WHEN she again found herself full of animation and hope in the midst of the downcast and silent family, she reproached herself for the severity with which she had secretly blamed the apathy of these deeply afflicted people. Count Christian and the canoness eat almost nothing at breakfast, and the chaplain did not venture to satisfy his appetite, while Amelia appeared to be the victim of a violent fit of ill-humor. When they rose from table, the old count stopped for an instant at the window, as if to look at the gravel-walk leading to the rabbit-warren, by which Albert might return, and drooped his head sadly as if to say, " Yet another day has begun badly, and will end in the same manner !" Consuelo endeavored to cheer them by playing on the harpsichord some of the latest religious compositions of Porpora, to which they always listened with peculiar admiration and interest.

She was distressed at seeing them so overwhelmed with grief, and at not being able to tell them that she felt some hope. But when she saw the count take his book, and the canoness her needle, and when she was summoned to the embroidery-frame of the latter to decide whether a certain figure should have blue stitches or white in the center, she could not prevent her thoughts from wandering to Albert, who was perhaps dying from fatigue and exhaustion in some corner of the forest, without knowing how to find his way back, or lying on some cold stone, overcome by the fearful attacks of catalepsy, and exposed to the assaults of wolves and snakes ; while under the skillful and persevering fingers of the tender Wenceslawa, the most brilliant flowers seemed to grow in thousands on the canvas, watered some-times by a secret but fruitless tear. As soon as she could exchange a few words with the pouting Amelia, she inquired from her who was that deformed and crazy being who traversed the country, dressed in singular costume, laughing like a child at every one whom he met. "Ah! it is Zdenko," replied Amelia. "Did you never meet him before in your walks? One is sure of meeting him everywhere, for he has no fixed dwelling."

"I saw him this morning for the first time," said Consuelo, "and thought that he must be the tutelary genius of the Schreckenstein."

"It is there, then, that you have been walking since dawn? I begin to think you are slightly crazed yourself, my dear Nina, to wander thus at break of day through desert places, where you may encounter worse beings than the inoffensive Zdenko."

"Some hungry wolf, for instance?" replied Consuelo, laughing; "it seems to me that the carbine of the baron, your father, should shield all the country with its protection."

"I speak not merely of wild beasts," said Amelia; "the country is not so free as you imagine from the worst animals in creation, viz. brigands and vagabonds. The wars which have just ended have ruined so many families that whole tribes of beggars prowl about, sometimes going so far as to solicit alms, pistol in hand. There are also swarms of those Egyptian Zingari, whom the French have done us the honor to call Bohemians, as if they were aborigines of our mountains, instead of merely infesting them at the commencement of their appearance in Europe. These people, driven away and repulsed everywhere, although cowardly and obsequious before an armed man, might well be bold with a young girl like you; and I fear that your fancy for adventurous walks will expose you more than becomes so proper a person as my dear Porporina affects to be."

"Dear baroness," replied Consuelo, "though you seem to consider the tusks of a wolf as a slight danger compared with those which threaten me, I confess to you that I fear them much more than I do the Zingari. The latter are old acquaintance of mine, and in general I feel it almost impossible to be afraid of poor, weak, and persecuted beings. It seems to me that I shall always know how to address those people in a way which will secure me their confidence and their sympathy; for, ugly, badly dressed, and despised as they are, it is impossible for me not to be particularly interested in them."

"Bravo, my dear!" cried Amelia, with increasing bitterness. "I see you completely share Albert's fine sentiments with regard to beggars, robbers, and foreigners; and I shall not be astonished to see you one of these mornings walking, as he does, and leaning on the rather dirty and very infirm arm of the agreeable Zdenko!"

These words were as a ray of light to Consuelo, which she had sought from the commencement of the conversation, and which consoled her for the raillery of her companion. "Count Albert then lives on good terms with Zdenko?" she asked, with an air of satisfaction which she did not even think of concealing.

"He is his most intimate, his most valued friend," replied Amelia, with a disdainful smile. "He is the companion of his walks, the confidant of his secrets, the messenger, it is said, of his correspondence with the devil. Zdenko and Albert are the only persons who would venture to repair at all hours to the Stone of Terror, and there converse on the most knotty points of divinity. Albert and Zdenko are the only persons who are not ashamed to seat themselves upon the grass with the Zingari who halt beneath our fir-trees, and partake with them the disgusting meal which those people prepare in their wooden porringers. They call that holding communion, and a very low sort of communion it certainly is. Ah! what a husband, what a fascinating lover would my cousin Albert be, when he seized the hand of his betrothed with a hand that had just pressed that of a pestiferous Zingaro, and carried it to those lips which had just drunk the wine of the chalice from the same cup with Zdenko!"

"All this may be very witty," said Consuelo, "but for my part I understand nothing of it."

"That is because you have no taste for history," returned Amelia, "and because you did not listen attentively to all that I related about the Hussites and the Protestants, during the last few days that I have been making myself hoarse explaining scientifically to you the enigmas and absurd practices of my cousin. Did I not tell you that the great quarrel between the Hussite and the Roman Church arose respecting the communion in both elements?

The council of Bale decided that there was profanation in giving the blood of Christ to the laity in the element of wine, alleging—mark the beautiful reasoning! that his body and his blood were contained equally in both elements, and that whoever eat the one drank the other. Do you comprehend?"

"It seems to me that the fathers of the council themselves did not comprehend very well. They ought to have said, if they wished to be logical, that the communion of wine was useless; but profanation? how could that be, if in eating the bread you drank the blood also?"

"It was because the Hussites had a terrible thirst for blood, and the fathers of the council knew it well. The fathers also thirsted for the blood of the people, but they wished to drink it under the element of gold. The poor people revolted, and seized, as the price of their sweat and their blood, the treasures of the abbeys and the copes of the bishops. This was the origin of the quarrel, in which mingled afterward, as I have told you, the sentiment of national independence and the hatred of foreigners. The dispute respecting the communion was the symbol of it. Rome and her priests officiated in chalices of gold and jewels; the Hussites affected to officiate in vases of wood, in order to censure the luxury of the church and to imitate the poverty of the apostles. This is why Albert, who has taken it into his head to become a Hussite, after these occurrence of the past have lost all value and signification, and who pretends to understand the true doctrine of John Huss better than John Huss himself, invents all sorts of communions, and goes communing on the highways with beggars and simpletons. It was the mania of the Hussites to commune everywhere, at all hours, and with all the world."

"All this is very strange," replied Consuelo, "and can only be explained to my mind by an exalted patriotism, carried in Count Albert, I must confess, even to the extent of fanaticism. The thought is perhaps profound, but the forms he clothes it in, seem to be very puerile for so serious and so learned a man. Is not the true communion more properly alms-giving? What meaning can there be in those vain ceremonies which have gone out of use, and which those whom he associates with them, certainly do not comprehend?"

"As to alms-giving, Albert is not wanting in that; and if they would give him free scope, he would soon rid himself of those riches which for my part I should be very glad to see melt away in the hands of his beggars."

"And why so?"

"Because my father would no longer entertain the fatal idea of enriching me by making me the wife of this maniac. For it is well you should know, my dear Porporina," added Amelia, maliciously, "that my family has not yet renounced that agreeable design. During these last few days, when my cousin's reason shone like a fleeting ray of sunshine from between the clouds, my father returned to the attack with more firmness than I thought him capable of exhibiting toward me. We had a very animated quarrel, the result of which seems to be that they will endeavor to overcome my resistance by the weariness of retirement, like a citadel which an enemy endeavors to reduce by famine. Therefore if I fail, if I yield to their attacks, I shall be obliged to marry Albert in spite of himself, in spite of myself, and in spite of a third person who pretends not to care the least in the world about it."

"Oh! indeed?" replied Consuelo, laughing; "I expected that epigram, and you only granted me the honor of conversing with you this morning in order to arrive at it. I receive it with pleasure, because I see in this little pretense of jealousy, the remains of a warmer affection for Count Albert than you are willing to acknowledge."

"Nina!" cried the young baroness, energetically, "if you imagine you see that, you have but little penetration, and if you see it with pleasure, you have but little affection for me. I am violent, perhaps proud, but certainly not in the habit of dissembling. I have already told you the preference which Albert gives to you irritates me against him, not against you. It wounds my self-love, but it flatters my hope and my inclination. It makes me long that he would, for your sake, commit some great folly which would free me from all circumspection with regard to him, by justifying the aversion against which I have long struggled, and which I now feel for him without any mixture of pity or love."

"May God grant," replied Consuelo, gently, "that this is the language of passion and not of truth! For it would be a very harsh truth in the mouth of a very cruel person."

The bitterness which Amelia testified in these conversations made little impression upon Consuelo, generous mind. A few seconds afterward, she thought only of her enterprise, and the dream which she cherished of restoring Albert to his family diffused a kind of pure-hearted joy over the monotony of her occupations. She required this excitement to dissipate the *ennui* which threatened her, and which being the malady most opposed and hitherto most unknown to her active and energetic nature, would certainly have been fatal to it. In fact, when she had given her unruly and inattentive pupil a long and tiresome lesson, she had nothing more to do but to exercise her voice and to study her ancient authors. But this consolation, which hitherto had never failed her, was now obstinately disputed. Amelia, with her restless frivolity, came every moment to interrupt and trouble her by childish questions and unseasonable observations. The rest of the family were in deep dejection. Already five long weary days had passed without the reappearance of the young count, and every day of his absence added to the gloom and depression of the preceding one.

In the afternoon, Consuelo, while wandering through the garden with Amelia, saw Zdenko on the other side of the moat which separated them from the open country. He seemed busy talking to himself, and from the tone of his voice one would have said he was relating a history. Consuelo stopped her companion, and asked her to translate what the strange personage was saying.

"How can you expect me to translate reveries without connection and without meaning?" said Amelia, shrugging up her shoulders. "This is what he has just mumbled, if you are very desirous of knowing: 'Once there was a great mountain, all white, all white, and by its side a great mountain, all black, all black, and by its side a great mountain, all red, all red.' Does that interest you very much?"

"Perhaps it might, if I could know what follows. Oh! what would I not give to understand Bohemian! I must learn it."

"It is not nearly so easy as Italian or Spanish, but you are so studious that you will quickly master it if you wish; I will teach you, if that will at all gratify you."

"You are an angel. On the condition, however, that

you are more patient as a mistress than as a pupil. And now what does Zdenko say?"

"Now the mountains are speaking:

"'Why, O red, all red mountain, hast thou crushed the mountain all black? And why, O white, all white mountain, hast thou permitted the black, the all black mountain to be crushed?'"

Here Zdenko began to sing with a thin and broken voice, but with a correctness and sweetness which penetrated Consuelo's very soul. His song was as follows:

"O black mountains and white mountains, you will need much water from the red mountain to wash your robes.

"Your robes, black with crimes and white with idleness; your robes stained with lies and glittering with pride.

"Now they are both washed, thoroughly washed, your robes that would not change color; they are worn, well worn, your robes that would not drag along the road.

"Now all the mountains are red, very red! It will need all the water of heaven, all the water of heaven, to wash them."

"Is that improvised, or is it an old Bohemian air?" asked Consuelo of her companion.

"Who knows?" replied Amelia; "Zdenko is either an inexhaustible improvisatore or a very learned rhapsodist. Our peasants are passionately fond of hearing him, and respect him as a saint, considering his madness rather as a gift from Heaven than as a malady of the mind. They feed and cherish him, and it depends upon himself alone to be the best lodged and the best dressed man in the country, for every one desires the pleasure and the advantage of having him for a guest. He passes for a bearer of good luck, a harbinger of fortune. When the weather is threatening, if Zdenko happen to pass they say, 'Oh! it will be nothing; the hail will not fall here.' If the harvest is bad, they ask Zdenko to sing; and as he always promises years of abundance and fertility, they are consoled for the present by the expectation of a more favorable future. But Zdenko is unwilling to dwell anywhere; his wandering nature carries him to the deepest recesses of the forests. No one knows where he is sheltered at night, nor where he finds a refuge against the cold and the storms. Never, for the last ten years, has he been seen to enter under any other roof than that of the Castle of the Giants, because he pretends that his ancestors are in all the other houses of the country, and that he is forbidden to present himself before them. Nevertheless, he follows Albert to his apartment, for he is as devoted and submissive to Albert as his dog Cynabre. Albert is the only living being who can at will enchain his savage independence, and by a word put a stop to his unquenchable gaiety, his eternal songs, and his indefatigable babble. Zdenko formerly had, it is said, a very fine voice, but he has worn it out by talking, singing, and laughing. He is not older than Albert, though he looks like a man of fifty, and they were companions in childhood. At that time Zdenko was only half crazed. Descended from an ancient family (one of his ancestors makes a considerable figure in the war of the Hussites), he evinced sufficient memory and quickness to induce his parents, taking into view his want of physical strength, to destine him for the cloister. For a long time he wore the dress of a novice in one of the mendicant orders, but they could never succeed in making him submit to their rules, and when he was sent on a circuit with one of the brothers of his convent, and an ass to be loaded with the gifts of the faithful, he would leave the wallet, the ass, and the brother in the lurch, and wander off to take a long vacation in the depths of the forest. When Albert departed on his travels, Zdenko fell into a low and melancholy state, threw off his frock, and became a complete vagabond. His melancholy disappeared by degrees, but the glimmering ray of reason, which had always shone amid the oddities of his character, was entirely extinguished. He no longer talked except incoherently, displayed all sorts of incomprehensible manias, and became really crazy. But as he always continued sober, mild, and inoffensive, he may be termed rather idiotic than mad. Our peasants call him nothing else but *the innocent.*"

"What you tell me of this poor man inspires me with a warm sympathy for him," said Consuelo; "I wish I could talk to him. He knows a little German, does he not?"

"He understands it, and can speak it tolerably well. But, like all Bohemian peasants, he has a horror of the language; and beside, when he is absorbed in his reveries, as he is now, it is very doubtful if he will answer when you question him."

" Then make an effort to speak to him in his own language, and to attract his attention to us," said Consuelo.

Amelia called Zdenko several times, asking him in Bohemian if he were well, and if he were in need of any thing ; but she could not once induce him to raise his head, which was bent toward the earth, nor to interrupt a little play he was carrying on with three pebbles, one white, one red, and one black, which he threw at each other, laughing with great glee every time he knocked them down.

" You see it is quite useless," said Amelia. " When he is not hungry, or is not looking for Albert, he never speaks to us. In one or the other of those cases, he comes to the gate of the castle, and if he is only hungry he remains at the gate. They then give him what he wants ; he thanks them and goes away. If he wishes to see Albert, he enters, goes and knocks at the door of his chamber, which is never closed to him, and there he will remain for whole hours, silent and quiet as a timid child if Albert is at work, talkative and cheerful if Albert is disposed to listen to him, but never irksome, it would seem, to my amiable cousin, and more fortunate in that respect than any member of the family."

" And when Count Albert is invisible, as he is at this moment for instance, does Zdenko, who loves him so ardently—Zdenko, who lost all his gaiety when the count set out on his travels—Zdenko, his inseparable companion, remain tranquil? Does he show no uneasiness?"

" None whatever. He says that Albert has gone to see the great God, and that he will soon return. That was what he said when Albert was traveling over Europe, and when he had become reconciled to his absence."

" And do you not suspect, dear Amelia, that Zdenko may have a better foundation than all of you for this apparent security ? Has it never occurred to you that he might be in Albert's confidence, and that he watches over him in his delirium or lethargy?"

" We did indeed think so, and for a long time watched all his proceedings; but like his patron, Albert, he detests all watching, and, more crafty than a fox when hunted by the dogs, he circumvented all our efforts, baffled all our attempts, and rendered useless all our observations. It would seen that he has, like Albert, the gift of making

himself invisible when he pleases.   Sometimes he has disappeared instantaneously from the eyes which were fixed
upon him, as if he had cloven the earth that it might
swallow him up, or as if a cloud had wrapped him in its
impenetrable veil.   At least this is what is affirmed by our
people, and by my aunt Wenceslawa herself, who, notwithstanding all her piety, has not a very strong head as
regards Satanic influences."

"But you, my dear baroness, cannot believe in these
absurdities?"

"For my part, I agree with my uncle Christian.   He
thinks that if Albert, in his mysterious sufferings, relies
solely on the succor and help of this idiot, it would be very
dangerous to interfere with him in any way, and that by
watching and thwarting Zdenko's movements, there is a
risk of depriving Albert for hours, and perhaps for whole
days, of the care and even of the nourishment which he
may receive from him.   But for mercy's sake let us go on,
dear Nina; we have bestowed sufficient time on this matter, and yonder idiot does not excite in me the same interest that he does in you.   I am tired of his romances and
his songs, and his cracked voice almost gives me a sore
throat from sympathy."

"I am astonished," said Consuelo, as she suffered herself to be drawn away by her companion, "that his voice
has not an extraordinary charm in your ears.   Broken as
it is, it makes more impression on me than that of the
greatest singers."

"Because you are sated with fine voices, and novelty
amuses you."

"The language which he sings has to my ears a peculiar
sweetness," returned Consuelo, "and his melodies have not
the monotony you seem to imagine; on the contrary, they
contain very refined and original ideas."

"Not for me, who have been beset by them," replied
Amelia.   "At first I took some interest in the words,
thinking, as do the country people, that they were ancient
national songs, and curious in a historical point of view;
but as he never repeats them twice in the same manner, I
feel certain they are improvisations, and I was soon convinced that they were not worth listening to, although our
peasants imagine they find in them a symbolical sense
which pleases them."

As soon as Consuelo could get rid of Amelia, she ran back to the garden, and found Zdenko in the same place, on the outside of the moat and absorbed in the same play. Convinced that this unfortunate being had secret relations with Albert, she had stealthily entered the kitchen and seized a cake make of honey and fine flour, carefully kneaded by the canoness with her own hands. She remembered having seen Albert, who eat very sparingly, show an instinctive preference for this dainty, which his aunt always prepared for him with the greatest care. She wrapped it up in a white handkerchief, and meaning to throw it across the moat to Zdenko, she called to him. But as he appeared not to wish to listen to her, she remembered the vivacity with which he had uttered her name, and she therefore pronounced it in German. Zdenko seemed to hear it; but he was at that moment in one of his melancholy moods, and without looking up, he repeated in German, shaking his head and sighing, " Consolation! Consolation!" as if he would have said, " I have no further hope of consolation."

" Consuelo !" then said the young girl, wishing to see if her Spanish name would reawaken the joy he had shown on pronouncing it in the morning.

Immediately Zdenko abandoned his pebbles, and began to leap and gambol upon the bank of the moat, throwing up his cap into the air, and stretching out his arms to her, uttering some very animated Bohemian words with a face radiant with pleasure and affection.

" Albert," cried Consuelo to him again, as she threw the cake across the moat.

Zdenko seized it, laughing, and did not unfold the handkerchief; but he said many things which Consuelo was in despair at not being able to understand. She tried to remember one phrase in particular, which he repeated several times, accompanying it by numerous bows and greetings. Her musical ear helped her to seize the exact pronunciation, and as soon as she lost sight of Zdenko, who ran off at full speed, she wrote it upon her tablets, with the Venetian orthography, intending to ask Amelia for its meaning. But before leaving Zdenko she wished to give him something that would testify in the most delicate manner to Albert the interest she felt for him, and having recalled the crazy being, who came back obedient to her voice, she threw him a bouquet of flowers which she had gathered an hour before in the green-house, and which, still fresh and fragrant, were fastened to her girdle. Zdenko seized it, repeated his salutations, renewed his exclamations and gambols, and then burying himself in the dense thicket, where it would have seemed that only a hare could force a passage, disappeared entirely. Consuelo followed his rapid flight for a few moments with her eyes, by marking the tops of the branches as they moved in a southeasterly direction; but a light wind which sprang up rendered her observation useless, by agitating all the branches of the coppice, and she re-entered the château, more than ever bent upon the prosecution of her design.

CHAPTER XXXVIII.

When Amelia was asked to translate the phrase which Consuelo had written upon her tablets and engraved in her memory, she replied that she did not understand it at all, although she could render it literally by these words:

" *May he who has been wronged salute thee.*"

" Perhaps," added she, " he refers to Albert or himself, and means that wrong has been done them in accusing them of madness, as they consider themselves the only sensible men on the face of the earth. But what good can it do to seek for the meaning of a madman's talk? This Zdenko occupies your imagination much more than he deserves."

" It is the custom of the peasantry in all countries," replied Consuelo, " to attribute to the insane a kind of inspiration, higher than that enjoyed by cold and settled minds. I have a right to retain the prejudices of my class, and I confess I can never believe that a madman speaks at random when he utters words which are unintelligible to us."

" Let us see," said Amelia, " if the chaplain, who is deeply versed in all the ancient and modern sayings which our peasants use, knows the meaning of this." And running to the good man, she asked him for an explanation of Zdenko's words.

But these obscure words seemed to strike the chaplain with

a frightful light. "In the name of the living God," cried he, turning pale, "where can your ladyship have heard such blasphemy?"

"If it be such, I cannot understand its meaning," replied Amelia, laughing; "and therefore I await your explanation."

"Word for word, it is in good German exactly what you have just said, madam: '*May he who has been wronged salute thee.*' But if you wish to know the meaning (and I hardly dare to utter it), it is, in the thought of the idolater who pronounced it: '*May the devil be with thee.*'"

"In other words," returned Amelia, laughing still more heartily, "'*Go to the devil.*' Well, it is a pretty compliment; and this is what you gain, my dear Nina, from talking with a fool. You did not think that Zdenko, with so affable a smile and such merry grimaces, would utter so ungallant a wish."

"Zdenko!" cried the chaplain. "Ah! then it is that unfortunate idiot who makes use of such sayings? I am glad it is no worse—I trembled lest it should be some other person. But I was wrong—it could proceed only from a brain crammed with the abominations of the ancient heresies. Whence can he have learned things almost unknown and forgotten nowadays? The spirit of evil alone can have suggested them to him."

"But, after all, it is only a very vulgar oath which the common people use in all countries," returned Amelia; "and Catholics are no more shocked by it than others."

"Do not think so, baroness," said the chaplain. "It is not a malediction in the wandering mind of him who uses it; on the contrary, it is a homage, a benediction—and there is the sin. This abomination comes from the Lollards, a detestable sect, which engendered that of the Vaudois, which engendered that of the Hussites——"

"Which engendered many others," said Amelia, assuming a grave air to mock the good priest. "But come, Mr. Chaplain, explain to us how it can be a compliment to recommend one's neighbor to the devil."

"The reason is, that in the opinion of the Lollards, Satan was not the enemy of the human race, but on the contrary its protector and patron. They held that he was a victim to injustice and jealousy. According to them the

Archangel Michael, and the other celestial powers who had precipitated him into the abyss, were the real demons, while Lucifer, Beelzebub, Ashtaroth, Astarte, and all the monsters of hell, were innocence and light themselves. They believed that the reign of Michael and his glorious host would soon come to an end, and that the devil would be restored and reinstated in heaven, with his accursed myrmidons. In fine, they paid him an impious worship, and accosted each other by saying, ' *May he who has been wronged* '—that is to say, he who has been misunderstood and unjustly condemned—' *salute thee* '—that is, protect and assist thee."

" Well," said Amelia, bursting into a fit of laughter, " my dear Nina is certainly under very favorable guardianship, and I should not be astonished if we should soon have to apply exorcisms to destroy the effect of Zdenko's incantations upon her."

Consuelo was somewhat disturbed at this raillery. She was not quite certain that the devil was a chimera and hell a poetic fable. She would have been induced to share the chaplain's indignation and affright, if, provoked at Amelia's laughter, he had not been at the moment perfectly ridiculous. Confused and disturbed in all her earliest belief by the contest between the superstition of the one party and the incredulity of the other, Consuelo that evening could hardly say her prayers. She inquired into the meaning of all those forms of devotion which she had hitherto received without examination, and which no longer satisfied her alarmed mind. " From what I have been able to see," thought she, " there are two kinds of devotion at Venice—that of the monks, the nuns, and the people, which goes perhaps too far; for it accepts, along with the mysteries of religion, all sorts of additional superstitions, such as the *orco* (the demon of the lagunes), the sorceries of Melamocco, the gold-seekers, the horoscope and vows to saints for the success of designs, far from pious, and often far from honest. Then there is that of the higher clergy and of the fashionable world, which is only a pretense ; for these people go to church as they go to the theater—to hear the music and show themselves ; They laugh at every thing and examine nothing, in religion, thinking that there is nothing serious or binding on the conscience in it, and that it is all a matter of form and habit. Anzoleto was not in the least religious; that was one source of grief to me, and I was right to look upon his unbelief with terror. My master Porpora, again—what did he believe? I know not. He never explained himself on that point, and yet he spoke to me of God and of Divine things at the most sorrowful and the most solemn moments of my life. But though his words struck me forcibly, the only impression they left was one of terror and uncertainty. He seemed to believe in a jealous and absolute God, who sends inspiration and genius only to those who are separated by their pride from the sufferings and the joys of their race. My heart regrets this fierce religion, and could not adore a God who should forbid me to love. Which then is the true God? Who will show him to me? My poor mother was a believer, but with how many childish idolatries was her worship mingled! What am I to believe?—what am I to think? Shall I say, like the thoughtless Amelia, that reason is the only God? But she does not know even that God, and cannot show him to me, for there is no one less reasonable than she. Can one live without religion? Of what use then would life be? For what object could I labor? To what purpose should I cherish pity, courage, generosity, a sense of right—I, who am alone in the universe—if there be not in that universe a Supreme Being, omniscient and full of love, who judges, who approves, who aids, preserves and blesses me? What strength, what excitement, can those have in life, who can dispense with a hope and a love beyond the reach of human illusions and worldly vicissitudes?

"Supreme Being!" cried she in her heart, forgetting the accustomed form of her prayer, "teach me what I ought to do. Infinite Love! teach me what I ought to love. Infinite Wisdom! teach me what I ought to believe."

While thus praying and meditating, she forgot the flight of time, and it was past midnight, when before retiring to bed she cast a glance over the landscape now lighted by the moon's pale beams. The view from her window was not very extensive, owing to the surrounding mountains, but exceedingly picturesque. A narrow and winding valley, in the center of which sparkled a mountain stream, lay before her, its meadows gently undulating until they reached the base of the surrounding hills, which shut in the horizon, except where at intervals they opened to permit the eye to discover still more distant and steeper ranges, clothed to the very summit with dark green firs. The last rays of the setting moon shone full on the principal features of this somber but striking landscape, to which the dark foliage of the evergreens, the pent-up water, and the rocks covered with moss and ivy, imparted a stern and savage aspect.

While comparing this country with all those she had traversed in her childhood, Consuelo was struck with an idea that had not before occurred to her; viz., that the landscape before her was not altogether new to her, whether she had formerly passed through this part of Bohemia, or seen elsewhere places very similar. "We traveled so much, my mother and I," said she to herself, "that it would not be astonishing if I had already been here. I have a distinct recollection of Dresden and Vienna, and we may have crossed Bohemia in going from one of those cities to the other. Still it would be strange if we had received hospitality in one of the out-houses of this very castle in which I am now lodged as a young lady of consequence; or if we had by our ballads earned a morsel of bread at the door of some one of those cabins, where Zdenko now stretches out his hand for alms and sings his ancient songs—Zdenko, the wandering artist, who is my equal and fellow, although he no longer seems so."

Just at this moment her eyes were directed toward the Schreckenstein, the summit of which could be perceived above a nearer eminence, and it seemed to her that this fearful spot was crowned by a reddish light which faintly tinged the transparent azure of the sky. She fixed her attention upon it, and saw the flickering light increase, become extinct, and reappear, until at last it shone so clear and decided that she could not attribute it to an illusion of her senses. Whether it was the temporary retreat of a band of Zingari, or the haunt of some brigand, it was not the less certain that the Schreckenstein was occupied at that moment by living beings ; and Consuelo, after her simple and fervent prayer to the God of truth, was no longer disposed to believe in the existence of the fantastic and evil-minded spirits with which the popular tradition peopled the mountain. But was it not more probably Zdenko who had kindled the fire, to shield himself from the cold of the night? And if it were Zdenko, was it not to warm Albert that the dry branches of the forest were burning at that moment? This luminous appearance was often seen upon the Schreckenstein; it was spoken of with terror, and attributed to something supernatural. It had been said a thousand times that it emanated from the enchanted trunk of Ziska's old oak. But the *Hussite* no longer existed; at least it lay at the bottom of the ravine, and the red light still shone on the summit of the mountain. Why did not this mysterious light-house induce them to institute a seach there for the supposed retreat of Albert?

"Oh, apathy of devout minds!" thought Consuelo; "are you a boon of Providence, or an infirmity of weak and imperfect natures?" She asked herself at the same time if she should have the courage to go alone at that hour to the Schreckenstein; and she decided that, actuated by benevolence and charity, she could dare all. But she could adopt this flattering conclusion with perfect safety, as the strict closing of the château left her no opportunity of executing her design.

In the morning she awoke full of zeal, and hurried to the Schreckenstein. All was silent and deserted. The grass was untrodden around the Stone of Terror; there was no trace of fire, no vestige of the presence of last night's guests. She wandered over the mountain in every direction, but found nothing which could indicate their presence. She called Zdenko on every side; she tried to whistle, in order to see if she could awaken the barkings of Cynabre, and shouted her own name several times. She uttered the word "consolation" in all the languages she knew; she sang some strains of her Spanish hymn, and even of Zdenko's Bohemian air, which she remembered perfectly. But in vain. The crackling of the dried lichens under her feet, and the murmuring of the mysterious waters which ran beneath the rocks, were the only sounds that answered her.

Fatigued by this useless search, she was about to retire after having taken a moment's rest upon the stone, when she saw at her feet a broken and withered rose-leaf. She took it up, examined it, and after a moment's reflection felt convinced that it must be a leaf of the bouquet she had thrown to Zdenko, for the mountain did not produce wild roses, even if it had been the season for them, and as yet there were none in flower except in the green-house of the château. This faint indication consoled her for the apparent fruitlessness of her walk, and left her more than ever convinced that it was at the Schreckenstein they must hope to find Albert.

But in what cave of this impenetrable mountain was he concealed? He was not then always there, or perhaps he was at that moment buried in a fit of cataleptic insensibility; or rather, perhaps, Consuelo had deceived herself when she attributed to her voice some power over him, and the veneration he had professed for her was but a paroxysm of his madness which had left no trace in his memory. Perhaps at this very moment he saw and heard her, laughed at her efforts, and despised her useless attempts.

At this last thought Consuelo felt a burning blush mount to her cheeks, and she hastily left the Schreckenstein, almost resolving never to return there. However, she left a little basket of fruit which she had brought with her.

But on the morrow she found the basket in the same place, untouched. Even the leaves which covered the fruit had not been disturbed by any curious hand. Her offering had been disdained, or else neither Albert nor Zdenko had been there; and yet the ruddy light of a fire of fir branches had again shone the previous night upon the summit of the mountain. Consuelo had watched until daylight in order to observe it closely. She had several times seen the brightness diminish, and then increase, as if a vigilant hand had supplied nourishment to the flame. No one had seen any Zingari in the neighborhood. No stranger had been remarked in the paths of the forest; and all the peasants whom Consuelo questioned respecting the luminous appearance of the Stone of Terror, answered her in bad German, that it was not good to search into those things, and that people ought not to interfere in the affairs of the other world.

Nine days had now elapsed since Albert had disappeared. This was the longest absence of the kind that had ever taken place, and this protracted delay, united to the gloomy omen which had ushered in his thirtieth birthday, was not calculated to revive the hopes of the family. At last they began to be seriously alarmed ; Count Christian did nothing but utter heart-breaking sighs; the baron went to hunt without a thought of killing any thing; the chaplain offered up an extra number of prayers; Amelia no longer dared to laugh or converse as usual; and the canoness, pale and weak, unable to pursue her household cares, and forgetful of her tapestry work, told her beads from morning till night, kept little tapers burning before the image of the Virgin, and seemed stooped lower by a foot than usual. Consuelo ventured to propose a thorough and careful examination of the Schreckenstein, related what researches she had made there, and mentioned to the canoness privately the circumstance of the rose-leaf, and the careful watch which she had kept all night on the luminous summit of the mountain. But the preparations which Wenceslawa preposed to make for the search, soon caused Consuelo to repent of having spoken so frankly. The canoness wished to have Zdenko seized and terrified by threats, to equip and provide fifty men with torches and muskets, and while the chaplain should pronounce his most terrible exorcisms upon the fatal stone, that the baron, followed by Hans and his most courageous attendants, should institute a regular siege of the Schreckenstein in the middle of the night. To surprise Albert in this manner would be the sure way to throw him into a state of derangement, and perhaps even of violent frenzy; and Consuelo, therefore, by force of arguments and prayers, prevailed upon Wenceslawa not to take any step without her advice. What she proposed was, to leave the château the following night, and accompanied only by the canoness, and followed at a distance by Hans and the chaplain only, to examine the fire of the Schreckenstein on the spot. But this resolution was beyond the strength of the canoness. She was firmly persuaded that an assembly of demons was held on the Stone of Terror, and all that Consuelo could obtain was, that the drawbridge should be lowered at midnight, and that the baron with some other volunteers should follow her, without arms and in the greatest silence. It was agreed that this attempt should be concealed from Count Christian, whose great age and feeble health unfitted him for such an expedition in the cold and unwholesome night air, and who would yet wish to join it if he were informed. All was executed as Consuelo desired. The baron, the chaplain and Hans accompanied her. She advanced alone, a hundred steps in front of her escort, and ascended the Schreckenstein with a courage worthy of Bradamante. But in proportion as she approached, the brightness which seemed to issue in rays from the fissures of the rock was extinguished by degrees, and when she reached the summit, profound darkness enveloped the mountain from the summit to the base. A deep silence and gloomy solitude reigned all around. She called Zdenko, Cynabre, and even Albert, although in uttering the latter name her voice trembled. All was mute, and echo alone answered her unsteady voice.

She returned toward her companions, completely disheartened. They praised her courage to the skies, and ventured in their turn to explore the spot she had just quitted, but without success; and all returned in silence to the château, where the canoness, who waited for them at the gate, felt her last hope vanish at their recitals.

CHAPTER XXXIX.

CONSUELO, after receiving the thanks of the good Wenceslawa, and the kiss which she imprinted upon her forehead, proceeded toward her apartment cautiously, in order not to awaken Amelia, from whom the enterprise had been concealed. She slept on the first floor, while the chamber of the canoness was in the basement story. But in ascending the stairs she let her light fall, and it was extinguished before she could recover it. She thought she could easily find her way without it, especially as the day began to dawn; but whether from absence of mind, or that her courage, after an exertion too great for her sex, abandoned her of a sudden, she was so much agitated that on reaching the story on which her apartment was situated, she did not stop there, but continued to ascend to the upper story, and entered the gallery leading to Albert's chamber, which was situated almost immediately over hers. But she stopped, chilled with affright, at the entrance of the gallery, on seeing a thin dark form glide along before her, as if its feet did not touch the floor, and enter the chamber toward which Consuelo was hastening under the idea that it was her own. In the midst of her terror she had presence f mind enough to examine this figure and to ascertain by a rapid glance in the indistinct light of the dawn that it wore the form and dress of Zdenko. But what was he going to do in Consuelo's apartment at such an hour, and with what message could he have been entrusted for her? She did not feel disposed to encounter such a tête-à-tête, and descended the stairs to seek the canoness; but upon reaching the flight below she recognized her corridor and the door of her apartment, and perceived that it was Albert's into which she had just seen Zdenko enter.

Then a thousand conjectures presented themselves to her mind, which had now become somewhat composed. How could the idiot have penetrated at night into a castle so well guarded and so carefully examined every evening by the canoness and the domestics? The apparition of Zdenko confirmed her in the idea which she had always entertained, that there was some secret outlet from the château, and perhaps a subterranean communication with the Schreckenstein. She ran to the door of the canoness, who was shut up in her gloomy cell, and who uttered a loud cry on seeing her appear without a light, and somewhat pale. "Be not disturbed, my dear madam," said the young girl; "I have just met with a strange occurrence, but one which need not terrify you in the least. I have just seen Zdenko enter Count Albert's chamber."

"Zdenko! you must be dreaming, my child; how could he have got in? I closed all the gates with the same care as usual, and during the whole of your trip to the Schreckenstein I kept good guard; the bridge was raised, and when you had all crossed it on your return, I remained behind to see it raised again."

"However that may be, madam, Zdenko is nevertheless in Count Albert's chamber. You have only to go there to be convinced of it."

"I will go immediately," replied the canoness, "and drive him out as he deserves. The wretched creature must have come in during the day. But what object could he have in coming here? Most probably he is looking for Albert, or has come to wait for him—a sure proof, my poor child, that he knows no more where he is than we do ourselves."

"Well, let's question him, however," said Consuelo.

"In one instant," said the canoness, who in preparing

for bed, had taken off two of her petticoats, and who considered herself too lightly dressed with the remaining three; "I cannot present myself thus before a man, my dear. Go and look for the chaplain or my brother the baron, whichever you can find first — we must not expose ourselves alone before this crazy man. But what am I thinking of? A young person like you cannot go and knock at the doors of these gentlemen. Wait a moment, I will hurry; I shall be ready in an instant."

And she began to rearrange her dress, the more slowly because she was hurried, and because, her regular habits being deranged, she hardly knew what she was about. Consuelo, impatient at so long a delay, during which Zdenko might have time to leave Albert's chamber, and hide himself in the castle so that he could not be found, recovered all her energy. "Dear madam," said she, lighting a candle, "will you please to call the gentlemen? I will go in the meantime and see that Zdenko does not escape us."

She mounted the two flights hastily, and with a courageous hand opened Albert's door, which yielded without resistance; but she found the apartment deserted. She entered a neighboring cabinet, raised all the curtains, and even ventured to look under the bed and behind the furniture. Zdenko was no longer there, and had left no trace of his entrance.

"There is no one here," said she to the canoness, who came trotting along followed by Hans and the chaplain: the baron was already in bed and asleep, and they could not awaken him.

"I begin to fear," said the chaplain, a little dissatisfied at the fright they had given him, "that the Signora Porporina may have been the dupe of her own illusions——"

"No, Mr. Chaplain," replied Consuelo quickly, "no one here is less so than I am."

"And in truth no one has more courage and steady friendship," replied the good man; "but in your ardent hope you imagine, signora, that you see indications where unhappily none exist."

"Father," said the canoness, "the Porporina has the courage of a lion united to the wisdom of a sage. If she has seen Zdenko, Zdenko has been here. We must search for him through the whole house; and as, thank God! every outlet is well closed, he cannot escape us."

They roused the domestics and searched everywhere. Not a chest of drawers did they leave unopened, nor a piece of furniture unmoved. They displaced all the forage in the graneries, and Hans had even the simplicity to look into the baron's great boots. But Zdenko was not found there, any more than elsewhere. They began to think that Consuelo must have been dreaming; but she remained more than ever convinced of the necessity of discovering the secret outlet from the château, and resolved to employ all her energy in the attempt. She had taken but a few hours' repose when she commenced her examination. The wing of the building containing her apartment (in which was Albert's also) rested against, and was as it were supported by the hill. Albert himself had chosen this picturesque situation, which enabled him to enjoy a fine view toward the south, and to have on the eastern side a pretty little garden, occupying a terrace on a level with the cabinet in which he studied. He had a great taste for flowers, and cultivated some very rare species upon this square of soil which had been brought to the barren summit of the eminence. The terrace was surrounded by a heavy freestone wall about breast-high, built upon the shelving rock, and from this elevated post the eye commanded the precipice on the other side, and a portion of the vast serrated outline of the Boehmer Wald. Consuelo, who had not before visited this spot, admired its beautiful situation and picturesque arrangement, and requested the chaplain to explain to her what use was formerly made of the terrace, before the castle had been transformed from a fortress into a baronial residence.

"It was," said he, "an ancient bastion, a sort of fortified platform, whence the garrison could observe the movements of troops in the valley and the surrounding mountains. There is no pass through the mountains which cannot be discovered from this spot. Formerly a high wall with loopholes on all sides surrounded the platform, and protected its occupants from the arrows and balls of an enemy."

"And what is this?" asked Consuelo, approaching a cistern which was in the center of the parterre, and into which there was a descent by means of a narrow, steep, and winding staircase.

"That is a cistern which always furnished an abundant

supply of excellent rock-water to the besieged—a resource of incalculable value to a stronghold."

"Then this water is good to drink?" said Consuelo, examining the greenish and moss-covered water of the cistern. "It seems to me quite muddy."

"It is no longer good, or at least it is not always so, and Count Albert only uses it to water his flowers. I must tell you that for two years an extraordinary phenomenon has occurred in this cistern. The spring—for it is one, the source of which is more distant in the heart of the mountain—has become intermittent. For whole weeks the level is extraordinarily low, and when that is the case Count Albert has water drawn by Zdenko from the well in the great court, to refresh his cherished plants. Then, all of a sudden, in the course of a single night and sometimes even in an hour, the cistern is filled with a lukewarm water, muddy as you now see it. Sometimes it empties rapidly; at others the water remains a long time, and is purified by degrees, until it becomes cold and limpid as rock-crystal. A phenomenon of this kind must have taken place last night, for even yesterday I saw the cistern clear and quite full, and now it looks muddy as if it had been emptied and filled anew."

"Then these phenomena do not occur at regular intervals?"

"By no means, and I should have examined them with care, if Count Albert, who prohibits all entrance to his apartments and garden, with that gloomy reserve which characterizes all his actions, had not forbidden me the amusement. I have thought, and still think, that the bottom of the cistern is choked up by mosses and wall plants, which at times close the entrance of the subterranean waters, and afterward yield to the force of the spring."

"But how do you explain the sudden disappearance of the water at other times?"

"By the great quantity which the count uses to water his flowers."

"But it seems to me that it would require great labor to empty this cistern. It cannot be very deep, then?"

"Not deep! It is impossible to find the bottom."

"In that case, your explanation is not satisfactory," said Consuelo, struck by the chaplain's stupidity.

"Well, find a better," returned he, somewhat confused, and a little piqued at his own want of sagacity.

"Certainly I will find a better," thought Consuelo, who felt deeply interested in the capricious changes of the fountain.

"If you ask Count Albert what it signifies," continued the chaplain, desirous to display a little witty incredulity, in order to recover his superiority in the eyes of the clear-sighted stranger, "he will tell you that these are his mother's tears, which dry up and are renewed again in the bosom of the mountain. The famous Zdenko, to whom you attribute so much penetration, would swear to you that there is a siren concealed therein, who sings most exquisitely to those who have ears to hear her. Between them they have baptized this well the *Fountain of Tears.* It is a very poetic explanation, and those who believe in pagan fables may be satisfied with it."

"I shall not be satisfied with it," thought Consuelo; "I will know how these tears are dried."

"As for myself," pursued the chaplain, "I have thought there must be an escape of the water in some corner of the cistern."

"It seems to me," replied Consuelo, "that unless that were so, the cistern, being supplied by a spring, would constantly overflow."

"Doubtless, doubtless," said the chaplain, not wishing to appear as if he had thought of that for the first time; "very little consideration must make that apparent. But there must be some remarkable derangement in the channels of the water, since it no longer preserves the same level it did formerly."

"Are they natural channels, or aqueducts made by the hands of men?" asked the persevering Consuelo; "that is what I should wish to know."

"That is what no one can ascertain," replied the chaplain, "since Count Albert does not wish to have his precious fountain touched, and has absolutely forbidden that it should be cleaned out."

"I was certain of it," said Consuelo, retiring; "and I think you would do well to respect his wishes, for God knows what misfortune would happen to him if any one attempted to thwart his siren!"

"I am beginning to be convinced," said the chaplain, on quitting Consuelo, "that this young person's mind is no less deranged than the count's. Can insanity be contagious? Or did Master Porpora send her to us, in order that the country air might restore her brain to a healthy condition? To see the pertinacity with which she made me explain the mystery of the cistern, one would suppose that she was the daughter of some engineer of the Venetian canals, and wished to appear well informed on the matter ; but I see by her last words, as well as by the hallucinations she had respecting Zdenko this morning, and the pleasant excursion she led us last night to the Schreckenstein, that it is a phantasy of the same nature. Can it be possible that she expects to find Count Albert at the bottom of this well? Unfortunate young people! would that you could find there reason and truth!" Thereupon the good chaplain proceeded to repeat his breviary while waiting for the dinner-hour.

"It must be," thought Consuelo on her side, "that idleness and apathy engender a singular weakness of mind, since this holy man, who has read and learned so much, has not the least suspicion of my presentiment respecting that fountain. And yet they call Zdenko imbecile!" So saying, Consuelo went to give the young baroness a music lesson until the time should arrive when she could renew her examination.

CHAPTER XL.

"HAVE you ever been present at the falling of the water, or seen it reascend?" said Consuelo in a low voice to the chaplain, as he sat comfortably digesting his dinner during the evening.

"What! what did you say?" cried he, bounding up in his chair, and rolling his great round eyes.

"I was speaking to you of the cistern," returned she, without being disconcerted ; "have you ever yourself observed the occurrence of the phenomenon?"

"Ah! yes—the cistern—I remember," replied he with a smile of pity. "There!" thought he, "her crazy fit has attacked her again."

"But you have not answered my question, my dear chaplain," said Consuelo, who pursued her object with that kind of eagerness which characterized all her thoughts and actions, and which was not prompted in the least by any malicious feeling toward the worthy man.

" I must confess, mademoiselle," replied he coldly, "that I was never fortunate enough to observe that to which you refer, and I assure you I never lost my sleep on that account."

"Oh ! I am very certain of that," replied the impatient Consuelo.

The chaplain shrugged his shoulders, and with a great effort rose from his chair in order to escape from so very ardent an inquirer.

" Well ! since no one here is willing to lose an hour's sleep for so important a discovery, I will devote my whole night to it if necessary," thought Consuelo ; and while waiting for the hour of retiring, she wrapped herself in her mantle and proceeded to take a turn in the garden.

The night was cold and bright, and the mists of evening dispersed in proportion as the moon, then full, ascended toward the empyrean. The stars twinkled more palely at her approach, and the atmosphere was dry and clear. Consuelo, excited but not overpowered by the mingled effects of fatigue, want of sleep, and the generous but perhaps rather unhealthy sympathy she experienced for Albert, felt a slight sensation of fever which the cool evening air could not dissipate. It seemed to her as if she touched upon the fulfillment of her enterprise, and a romantic presentment, which she interpreted as a command and encouragement from Providence, kept her mind uneasy and agitated. She seated herself upon a little grassy hillock studded with larches, and began to listen to the feeble and plaintive sound of the streamlet at the bottom of the valley. But it seemed to her as if another voice, still more sweet and plaintive, mingled with the murmurings of the water, and by degrees floated upward to her ears. She stretched herself upon the turf, in order, being nearer the earth, to hear better those light sounds which the breeze wafted toward her every moment. At last she distinguished Zdenko's voice. He sang in German, and by degrees she could distinguish the following words, tolerably well arranged to a Bohemian air, which was characterized by the same simple and plaintive expression as those she had already heard.

" There is down there, down there, a soul in pain and in labor, which awaits her deliverance.

" Her deliverance, her consolation, so often promised.

" The deliverance seems enchained, the consolation seems pitiless.

" There is down there, down there, a soul in pain and in labor, which is weary of waiting."

When the voice ceased singing, Consuelo rose, looked in every direction for Zdenko, searched the whole park and garden to find him, called him in various places, but was obliged to return to the castle without having seen him.

But an hour afterward, when the whole household had joined in a long prayer for Count Albert, and when everybody had retired to rest, Consuelo hastened to place herself near the Fountain of Tears, and seating herself upon the margin amid the thick mosses and water plants which grew there naturally, and the irises which Albert had planted, she fixed her eyes upon the motionless water, in which the moon, then arrived at the zenith, was reflected as in a mirror.

After waiting almost an hour, and just as the courageous maiden, overcome by fatigue, felt her eyelids growing heavy, she was aroused by a slight noise at the surface of the water. She opened her eyes, and saw the spectarum of the moon agitated, broken, and at last spread in luminous circles upon the mirror of the fountain. At the same time a dull rushing sound, at first imperceptible but soon impetuous, became apparent, and she saw the water gradually sink, whirling about as in a funnel, and in less than a quarter of an hour disappear in the depths of the abyss.

She ventured to descend several steps. The spiral staircase, which appeared to have been built for the purpose of permitting the household to reach at pleasure the varying level of the water, was formed of granite blocks half buried in the rock, or hewn out of it. These slimy and slippery steps afforded no means of support, and were lost in the frightful depth. The darkness, and the noise of the water which still splashed at the bottom of the immeasurable precipice, joined to the impossibility of treading securely with her delicate feet upon the stringy ooze, arrested Consuelo in her mad attempt; she ascended backward with great difficulty, and seated herself, terrified and trembling, upon the first step.

In the meantime, the water still seemed to be continually receding into the bosom of the earth. The noise became more and more remote, till at last it ceased entirely, and Consuelo pondered on the propriety of getting a light in order to examine the interior of the cistern as far as possible from above; but she feared to miss the arrival of him whom she expected, and remained patient and motionless for nearly an hour longer. At last she thought she perceived a feeble glimmer at the bottom of the well, and leaning anxiously forward, saw that the wavering light ascended little by little. In a short time she was no longer in doubt; Zdenko was ascending the spiral staircase, aided by an iron chain which was secured to the rocky sides. The noise which he made in raising the chain from time to time and again letting it fall, made Consuelo aware of the existence of this species of balustrade, which ceased at a certain height, and which she could neither see nor suspect. Zdenko carried a lantern which he hung on a hook set apart for this purpose and inserted in the rock about twenty feet below the surface of the soil; then he mounted the rest of the staircase lightly and rapidly, without any chain or apparparent means of support. However, Consuelo, who observed every thing with the greatest attention, saw that he helped himself along by catching hold of certain projecting points in the rock, of some wall plants more vigorous than the rest, and of some bent nails which stood out from the sides, and with which he seemed perfectly familiar. As soon as he had ascended high enough to see Consuelo, she concealed herself from his view by stooping behind the semi-circular stone wall which bordered the well, and which was interrupted only at the entrance of the steps. Zdenko emerged into the light, and began slowly to gather flowers in the garden with great care and as if making a selection, until he had formed a large bouquet. Then he entered Albert's study, and through the glass door Consuelo saw him for a long while moving the books, and searching for one which he appeared at last to have found; for he returned toward the cistern, laughing and talking to himself in a satisfied tone, but in a low and almost inaudible voice, so much did he seem divided between the necessity of muttering to himself according to his usual custom, and the fear of wakening the family in the castle.

Consuelo had not yet asked herself whether she should address him, and request him to conduct her to Albert;

and it must be confessed, at that moment, confounded by what she saw, discouraged in the midst of her enterprise, joyous at having discovered what she so much longed to know, but at the same time dismayed at the thoughts of descending into the entrails of the earth and the abyss of water, she did not feel sufficient courage to go forward to the end, but allowed Zdenko to descend as he had mounted, resume his lantern and disappear, singing in a voice which gained confidence as he sank into the depths of his retreat.

"The deliverance is enchained, the consolation is pitiless."

With outstretched neck and palpitating heart, Consuelo had his name ten times upon her lips to recall him. She was about to decide by a heroic effort, when she suddenly reflected that such a surprise might make the unfortunate man stagger upon the difficult and dangerous staircase, and perhaps lose his footing. She refrained therefore, promising herself that she would be more courageous on the next day at the right time.

She waited some time longer to see the water again ascend, and this time the phenomenon took place much more speedily. Hardly fifteen minutes had elapsed from her losing the sound of Zdenko's voice and the light of his lantern, before a dull noise like the distant rumbling of thunder was heard, and the water, rushing with violence, ascended, whirling and dashing against the walls of its prison like a seething caldron. This sudden irruption of water had something so frightful in its appearance, that Consuelo trembled for poor Zdenko, asking herself if, in sporting with such dangers and governing thus the forces of nature, there was no risk of his being overpowered by the violence of the current, and of her seeing him float to the surface of the fountain, drowned and bruised like the slimy plants which were tossed on its waves.

Still the means of accomplishing this must be very simple! it only needed perhaps to lower or raise a floodgate, perhaps only to place a stone on his arrival and remove it on his return. But might not this man, always so absent and lost in his strange reveries, be mistaken, and remove the stone a little too soon? Could he have come by the subterranean path which gave passage to the water of the spring? "Nevertheless I must pass it with him, or without him," said Consuelo, "and that no later than the coming night; *for there is down there a soul in labor and in pain, which waits for me, and which is weary of waiting.* These words were not sung unintentionally, and it was not without some object that Zdenko, who detests German and pronounces it with difficulty, made use of that language to-day."

At last she retired to rest, but she had terrible dreams all the rest of the night. Her fever was gradually gaining ground. She did not perceive it, so strong did she feel her courage and resolution; but every moment she started out of her sleep, imagining herself still upon the steps of that frightful staircase, and unable to reascend, while the water rose below her with the roar of thunder and the rapidity of lightning. She was so changed the next day that every body remarked the alteration in her features. The chaplain was unable to refrain from confiding to the canoness, that *this agreeable and obliging person* appeared to him to have her brain somewhat deranged; and the good Wenceslawa, who was not accustomed to see so much courage and devotion, began to fear that the Porporina was a very imaginative young lady, and had a very excitable nervous temperament. She relied too much on her good doors cased in iron, and her faithful keys always jingling in her girdle, to give credence for any length of time to the entrance and escape of Zdenko the night before the last. She therefore spoke to Consuelo in affectionate and compassionate terms, beseeching her not to identify herself with the unhappiness of the family so as to destroy her health, and made an effort to inspire her with hopes of her nephew's speedy return, which she herself in the secret recesses of her heart began to lose.

But she was agitated at once by sentiments of fear and hope, when Consuelo, with a look glowing with satisfaction and a smile of gentle pride, replied, "You have good reason to hope, dear madam, and to wait with confidence. Count Albert is alive and as I hope not very ill; for in his retreat he is still interested in his books and flowers. I am certain of it, and could give you proofs."

"What do you mean to say, my dear child?" cried the canoness, struck by her air of conviction. "What have you learned? what have you discovered? Speak, in the name of Heaven! restore life to a despairing family!"

"Say to Count Christian that his son lives and is not far from this. This is as true as that I love and respect you."

The canoness rose for the purpose of hastening to her brother, who had not yet descended to the saloon; but a look and a sigh from the chaplain arrested her steps.

"Let us not inconsiderately inspire such joyful hopes in my poor Christian's breast," said she, sighing in her turn. "If the fact should contradict your sweet promises, my dear child, we should give a death-blow to his unhappy father."

"Then you doubt my words?" replied the astonished Consuelo.

"God forbid, noble Nina! But you may be under an illusion. Alas, this has happened so often to ourselves! You say that you have proofs, my dear daughter—can you not mention them?"

"I cannot—at least it seems to me I ought not," said Consuelo, somewhat embarrassed. "I have discovered a secret to which Count Albert evidently attaches great importance, and I do not think I can reveal it without his permission."

"Without his permission?" cried the canoness, looking at the chaplain irresolutely. "Can she have seen him?" The chaplain shrugged his shoulders imperceptibly, not comprehending the pain his incredulity inflicted on the poor canoness.

"I have not seen him," returned Consuelo; "but I shall see him soon, and so will you, I hope. But I fear I should retard his return if I thwarted his wishes by my indiscretion."

"May Divine truth dwell in your heart, generous creature, and speak through your lips!" said Wenceslawa, looking at her with anxious and pitying eyes. "Keep your secret if you have one, and restore Albert to us if it be in your power. All that I know is, that if this be realized I will embrace your knees, as at this moment I kiss your poor forehead — which is moist and burning," added she, turning toward the chaplain with an air of great emotion, after having pressed her lips to the fevered forehead of the young girl.

"Even if she be mad," said she to the latter, as soon as they were alone, "she is still an angel of goodness, and she seems more interested in our sufferings than we are ourselves. Ah, father, there seems to be a curse upon this house! Every one who has a lofty and noble heart seems struck here with derangement, and our life is passed in pitying what we are constrained to admire."

"I do not deny the good intentions of this young stranger," replied the chaplain. "But that there is delirium in her actions you cannot doubt, madam. She must have dreamed of Count Albert last night, and imprudently gives us her visions as certainties. Be careful not to agitate the pious and resigned spirit of your venerable brother by such unfounded assertions. Perhaps also it would be more prudent not to encourage too much the rash enterprises of Signora Porporina. They might lead her into dangers of a different nature from those she has been willing to encounter hitherto ——"

"I do not comprehend you," said the Canoness Wenceslawa, with great simplicity.

"I feel much embarrassed how to explain myself," returned the worthy man, "still it seems to me that—if a secret understanding, very honorable and very disinterested without doubt, should be established between this young artist and the noble count ——"

"Well?" said the canoness, opening her eyes very wide.

"Well, madam! do you not think that sentiments of interest and solicitude, entirely innocent in their origin, might in a little time, with the aid of circumstances and romantic ideas, become dangerous to the repose and dignity of the young musician?"

"I never would have thought of that," said the canoness, struck by this observation. "But do you think, father, that the Porporina could forget her humble and precarious position so far as to become attached to one so much her superior as my nephew Albert of Rudolstadt?"

"The Count Albert of Rudolstadt might himself contribute unintentionally to such a feeling, by the inclination he evinces to treat as prejudices the time-honored advantages of rank and birth."

"You make me seriously uneasy," said Wenceslawa, whose pride of family constituted her chief and almost only failing. "Can this unfortunate feeling have already taken root in the child's heart? Can her agitation and her earnest desire to discover Albert, conceal any motive

less pure than her natural generosity of soul and attachment to us?"

"I flatter myself not as yet," replied the chaplain,
whose only desire was to play an important part in the
affairs of the family by his advice and his counsels, while
preserving at the same time the appearance of timid respect and submissive obsequiousness.   "Still, my dear
daughter, you must have your eyes open to passing events,
and not allow your vigilance to slumber in the presence of
such dangers.   This delicate part it is your duty to perform, and it demands all the prudence and penetration
with which Heaven has endowed you."

After this conversation the canoness' thoughts were in a
state of the utmost confusion, and her anxiety took entirely a new direction.   She almost forgot that Albert was
as it were lost to her, perhaps dying, perhaps even dead,
and thought only of preventing the effects of an affection,
which in her secret heart she called *disproportionate;* like
the Indian in the fable, who, pursued into a tree by *terror*
under the form of a tiger, amuses himself by contending
with *annoyance* in the form of a fly buzzing about his head.

All day long she kept her eyes fixed upon the Porporina,
watching all her steps and anxiously analyzing every
word she uttered.   Our heroine, for the courageous Consuelo was one at that moment in all the force of the term,
easily perceived this anxiety, but was far from attributing
it to any other feeling than the doubt of her fulfilling her
promise to restore Albert.   She never thought of concealing her agitation, so much was she convinced, by
the tranquility and firmness of her conscience, that
she ought to be proud of her project rather than
blush for it.   The modest confusion which the young
count's enthusiastic expression of attachment for her had
excited in her mind a few days before, gradually faded
away before her serious resolution, free as it was from the
least shade of vanity.   The bitter sarcasms of Amelia,
who had a suspicion of the nature of her enterprise without knowing its details, did not move her in the least.
She hardly heard them, and only answered by smiles;
leaving to the canoness, whose ears were opened wider
every hour, the care of recording them, of commenting
upon them, and finding in them a terrible meaning.

CHAPTER XLI.

NEVERTHELESS, seeing that she was watched by Wenceslawa with more vigilance than ever, Consuelo feared that she might be thwarted by a mistaken zeal, and composed herself to a more restrained demeanor; thanks to which precaution she was enabled during the day to escape from the canoness's attention, and with nimble feet to take the direction of the Schreckenstein. She had no other project in view at the moment, than to meet Zdenko, to lead him to an explanation, and ascertain positively if he was willing to conduct her to Albert. She found him quite close to the castle on the path which led to the Schreckenstein. He seemed on his way to meet her, and addressed her with great volubility in Bohemian. "Alas! I do not comprehend you," said Consuelo, as soon as she could find an opportunity of speaking; "I hardly know German, that harsh language which you hate like slavery, and which to me is as sad as exile. But since we cannot otherwise understand each other, consent to speak it with me; we speak it each as badly as the other. I promise you to learn Bohemian, if you will teach it to me."

At these friendly words Zdenko became serious, and stretching out to Consuelo his dry and callous hand, which she did not hesitate to clasp in hers, "Sweet daughter of God," said he, in German, "I will teach you my language and my songs. Which do you wish me to begin with?"

Consuelo thought it better to yield to his fancies, and employ the vehicle of song in questioning him. "I wish that you would sing to me," said she, "the ballad of Count Albert."

"There are," replied he, "more than two hundred thousand ballads about my brother Albert. I cannot teach them to you, as you would not comprehend them. Every day I make new ones, which do not in the least resemble the old. Ask me for anything else."

"Why should I not comprehend them? I am the consolation. I am called Consuelo for you—do you understand? and for Count Albert who alone knows me here."

"You Consuelo?" said Zdenko with a mocking laugh. "Oh, you do not know what you say. *The deliverance is enchained——*"

"I know—*The consolation is pitiless.* But it is you who are ignorant, Zdenko. The deliverance has broken its chains, the consolation has freed itself from its shackles."

"False! false! madness, German talk!" returned Zdenko, ceasing his laugh and his gambols; "you do not know how to sing."

"Yes, I do know," said Consuelo; "listen." And she sang the first phrase of his song of the three mountains, which she had fixed in her memory, with the words which Amelia had assisted her to recollect and pronounce. Zdenko heard her with transports of delight, and said with a deep sigh, "I love you dearly, my sister—much, very much! Shall I teach you another song."

"Yes, that of Count Albert, but first in German; afterward you shall teach it to me in Bohemian."

"How does it begin?" said Zdenko, looking at her roguishly.

Consuelo began the air of the song she had heard the day before, " *There is down there, down there, a soul in labor and in pain——*"

"O, that was yesterday's; I do not recollect it to-day," said Zdenko, interrupting her.

"Well, tell me to-day's."

"The first words? you must tell me the first words."

"The first words? Here they are—listen: Count Albert is down yonder, down yonder in the grotto of Schreckenstein——"

Hardly had she pronounced these words when Zdenko suddenly changed his countenance and attitude; and his eyes flashed with indignation. He made three steps backward, raised his hands as if to curse Consuelo, and began to talk Bohemian to her with all the energy of anger and menace. Frightened at first, but reassured on seeing that he retired from her, Consuelo wished to recall him, and made a movement as if to follow him. He turned infuriated, and seizing an enormous stone, which he seemed to raise without difficulty in his weak and fleshless arms: "Zdenko has never done harm to any one," cried he in German; "Zdenko would not break the wing of a poor fly, and if a little child wished to kill him, he would allow himself to be killed by a little child. But if you look at me again, if you say another word to me, daughter of evil! liar! Austrian! Zdenko will crush you like an earthworm, if he should afterward be obliged to throw himself into the torrent to cleanse his body and his soul from the human blood which he had shed !"

Consuelo, terrified, took to flight, and at the bottom of the hill met a countryman, who, astonished at seeing her running, pale, and as if pursued by some one, asked her if she had met a wolf. Consuelo, wishing to know if Zdenko was subject to fits of furious madness, said that she had met the *innocent*, and that he had frightened her.

" You must not be afraid of the innocent," said the countryman, smiling at what he considered the cowardice of a fine lady. " Zdenko is not wicked ; he is always singing or laughing, or reciting stories which nobody understands, and which are very beautiful."

" But sometimes he gets angry, and then he threatens and throws stones?"

" Never, never," replied the countryman; " that never has happened. You need never be afraid of Zdenko. Zdenko is as innocent as an angel."

When she had recovered from her fright, Consuelo felt that the countryman must be right, and that she had provoked by an imprudent word the first and only attack of fury which the innocent Zdenko had ever experienced. She reproached herself bitterly. " I was too hasty," said she to herself; " I have awakened in the peaceful mind of this man, deprived as he is of what is proudly called reason, a suffering to which until this moment he was a stranger, and which may now seize upon him on the slightest occasion. He was formerly only partially deranged, perhaps I have made him a confirmed madman."

But she became still more dejected in thinking of the motives for Zdenko's anger. It was beyond all doubt that she had guessed rightly in naming the Schreckenstein as the place of Albert's retreat. But with what jealous and anxious care did Albert and Zdenko wish to hide this secret even from her! She, it was plain, was not excepted from this proscription; she had then no influence over Count Albert; and the feeling which prompted him to call her his consolation, the pains he had taken the day before to cause Zdenko to invoke her aid by a symbolic song, his confiding to his crazy follower the name of Consuelo—was all this solely the fantasy of the moment, and did no true and constant aspiration point out to him one person more than another as his liberator and his consolation? Even the name of Consolation, uttered, and as it were divined, by him, was a matter of pure chance. She had not concealed from any one that she was of Spanish birth, and that her mother tongue was still more familiar to her than the Italian; and Albert, excited to a pitch of enthusiasm by her song, and knowing of no expression more energetic than that which embodied the idea for which his soul thirsted, and with which his imagination was filled, had addressed her in a language which he knew perfectly, and which no one about him except herself could understand.

Consuelo had never been much deceived in this respect. Still, so fanciful and so ingenious a coincidence had seemed to her something providential, and her imagination had seized upon it without much examination.

But now every thing was once more doubtful. Had Albert, in some new phase of his mania, forgotten the feeling he had experienced for her? Was she henceforth useless for his relief, powerless for his welfare? or was Zdenko, who had appeared so intelligent and earnest in seconding Albert's designs, more hopelessly deranged than Consuelo had been willing to suppose? Did he merely execute the orders of his friend, or did he completely forget them, when he furiously forbade to the young girl all approach to the Schreckenstein, and all insight into the truth?

" Well," whispered Amelia, on her return, " did you see Albert this evening floating in the sunset clouds? or will you make him come down the chimney to-night by some potent spell?"

" Perhaps so," replied Consuelo, a little provoked. It was the first time in her life that she felt her pride wounded. She had entered upon her enterprise with so pure and disinterested a feeling, so earnest and high-minded a purpose, that she suffered deeply at the idea of being bantered and despised for want of success.

She was dejected and melancholy all the evening; and the canoness, who remarked the change, did not fail to attribute it to her fear of having disclosed the fatal attachment which had been born in her heart.

The canoness was strangely deceived. If Consuelo had nourished the first seeds of a new passion, she would have been an entire stranger to the fervent faith and holy confidence which had hitherto guided and sustained her. But so far from this, she had perhaps never experienced the poignant return of her former passion more strongly, than under these circumstances, when she strove to withdraw herself from it by deeds of heroism and a sort of exalted humanity.

On entering her apartment in the evening, she found on her spinet an old book, gilt and ornamented, which she immediately thought she recognized as that which she had seen Zdenko carry away from Albert's study the night before. She opened it at the page where the tassel was placed; it was at that penitential psalm which commences: *De profundis clamavi ad te.* And these Latin words were underlined with ink which appeared to have been recently written, for it stuck a little to the opposite page. She turned over the leaves of the whole volume, which was a famous ancient Bible, called Kralic's, printed in 1579, but found no other indication, no marginal note, no letter. But this simple cry, rising as it were from the depths of the earth, was it not sufficiently significant, sufficiently eloquent? What a contradiction there was then between the expressed and constant desire of Albert, and the recent conduct of Zdenko.

Consuelo was convinced of the truth of her last supposition. Albert, weak and helpless at the bottom of the subterranean cavern which she supposed to be under the Schreckenstein, was perhaps detained there by Zdenko's senseless tenderness. He was perhaps the victim of that idiot, who watched over and cherished him after his own fashion, kept him a close prisoner, although yielding sometimes of his own desire to see the light of day while he executed Albert's messages to Consuelo, but opposing himself entirely to the success of her attempts from fear or inexplicable caprice. "Well," said she, "I will go, even if I should have to encounter real dangers; I will go, though I should seem ridiculously imprudent in the eyes of stupid and selfish persons; I will go, though I should be humiliated by the indifference of him who summons me. Humiliated! and how can I be so, if he be himself really as crazy as poor Zdenko? I can have no feeling but one of pity toward either of them. I shall have done my duty. I shall have obeyed the voice of God which inspires me, and His hand which impels me forward with irresistible force."

The feverish excitement in which she had been during the whole of the preceding days, and which, since her last unfortunate meeting with Zdenko, had given place to a painful languor, once more manifested itself both in her mind and body. She felt all her strength restored, and hiding from Amelia the book, her enthusiasm, and her design, she exchanged some cheerful words with her, waited till she had gone to sleep, and then hastened to the Fountain of Tears, furnished with a little dark lantern which she had procured that same morning.

She waited a long while, and was several times obliged to enter Albert's study in order to revive her chilled limbs by a warmer air. While there, she cast a glance upon the enormous mass of books, not arranged in rows as in a library, but thrown pell-mell upon the floor in the middle of the chamber, as if with a sort of contempt and disgust. She ventured to open some of them. They were almost all written in Latin, and Consuelo could only presume that they were works of religious controversy, emanating from the Romish Church or approved by it. She was endeavoring to comprehend their titles, when she at last heard the bubbling of the water. She closed her lantern, hastened to hide herself behind the balustrade, and awaited Zdenko's arrival. This time he did not stop either in the garden or the study, but passed through both, and crossing Albert's apartment, proceeded, as Consuelo learned afterward, to listen at the door of the oratory, and of Count Christian's chamber, in order to see whether the old man was praying in distress or sleeping tranquilly. This was a step which his own anxiety often prompted him to take without Albert's suggestion, as will be seen by what follows.

Consuelo did not hesitate as to the part she had to take; her plan was already arranged. She no longer trusted to the reason or the good-will of Zdenko; she wished to reach, alone and without guard, him whom she supposed a prisoner. Most probably there was but one path which led under-ground from the cistern of the château to that of the Schreckenstein. If this path was difficult or dangerous, at least it was practicable, since Zdenko passed through it every night. It certainly must be so with a light; and Consuelo was provided with tapers, with steel, tinder, and flint, to strike fire in case of accident. What inspired her with the greatest confidence of arriving at the

Schreckenstein by this subterranean route, was an ancient story she had heard the canoness relate, of a siege formerly sustained by the Teutonic Order. " Those knights," said Wenceslawa, " had in their very refectory a cistern which supplied them with water from the neighboring mountain, and when their spies wished to make a sortie to observe the enemy, they dried the cistern, traversed its subterranean passages, and came out at a village at some distance which was subject to them." Consuelo remembered that, according to the tradition of the country, the village which had covered the hill, called Schreckenstein since its destruction by fire, had been subject to the Fortress of the Giants, and had had secret communication with it in the time of siege. She was strengthened, therefore, both by reason and by tradition, in seeking this communication and outlet.

She profited by the absence of Zdenko to descend into the well. Before doing so, however, she fell upon her knees, commended herself to God, and, with simple and unaffected piety, made a sign of the cross, as she had done in the wing of the theater of San Samuel before appearing upon the stage for the first time. Then she courageously descended the steep and winding stairs, searching in the wall for the points of support which she had seen Zdenko make use of, and not looking beneath her for fear of dizziness. She reached the iron chain without accident, and as soon as she had seized hold of it, felt more assured, and had sufficient coolness to look down toward the bottom of the well. There was still some water, and this discovery caused her a moment's agitation. But a little reflection reassured her immediately. The well might be very deep, but the opening in the subterranean passage by which Zdenko came, must be placed at a certain distance below the surface of the soil. She had already descended fifty steps, with that address and agility which young ladies educated in drawing-rooms can never attain, but which the children of the people acquire in their sports and pastimes, and gives them a confidence and courage which they ever afterward retain. The only real danger was that of slipping on the wet steps; but Consuelo had found in a corner an old slouched hat with large brims, which Baron Frederick had long worn in the chase, and this she had cut up and fastened to her shoes after the manner of

buskins. She had remarked a similar contrivance on the
feet of Zdenko in his last nocturnal expedition. With
these felt soles Zdenko walked through the corridors of the
château without making any noise, and it was on this
account he had seemed to her rather to glide like a ghost
than to walk like a human being. It was also the custom
of the Hussites thus to shoe their spies, and even their
horses, when they attempted a surprise upon the enemy.

At the fifty-second step, Consuelo found a sort of platform and a low arched passage-way leading from it. She
did not hesitate to enter, and to advance in a low, narrow,
and subterranean gallery, still dripping with the water
which had just left it, and hewed out and arched by the
hand of man with great solidity. She walked forward,
without meeting any obstacle or feeling any emotion of
fear for about five minutes, when she imagined she heard a
slight noise behind her.

It was perhaps Zdenko, who had descended, and was
taking the road to the Schreckenstein. But she was in
advance of him, and she quickened her pace in order not
to be overtaken by so dangerous a traveling companion.
He had no reason to suppose she was before him, and of
course could not be in pursuit of her; and while he amused
himself with singing and muttering his interminable
stories, she would have time to reach Albert and put herself under his protection.

But the noise which she heard increased, and seemed
like that of water which roars and strives and rushes
forward. What could have happened? Had Zdenko perceived her design? Had he raised the sluice-gate to inter-
cept her and swallow her up? But he could not do this
before passing it himself, and he was behind her. This
reflection was not very comforting. Zdenko was capable
of devoting himself to death and drowning with her, rather
than betray Albert's retreat. Still Consuelo saw no gate,
no sluice-way, no stone in her path, which could have
retained the water and afterward given it vent. In this
case the water could only be before her, and the noise
came from behind. It still increased, it mounted, it approached with a roar like thunder.

Suddenly Consuelo, struck by a horrible idea, perceived
that the gallery, instead of rising, descended, at first with
a gentle inclination, and afterward more and more rapidly.

The unfortunate girl had mistaken the way. In her hurry, and confused by the thick vapor which arose from the bottom of the cistern, she had not seen a second arch, much larger, and directly opposite that which she had taken. She had entered the canal which served to carry away the surplus water of the well, instead of that which ascended to the reservoir or spring. Zdenko, returning by the opposite path, had quietly raised the gate; the water had fallen in a cascade to the bottom of the cistern, which was already filled to the height of the waste passage, and was now rushing into the gallery in which Consuelo fled, almost expiring with terror. In a short period the gallery — which was so proportioned that the cistern lost less water by this outlet than it received by the corresponding one on the opposite side, and could thus be filled—would in its turn be overflowed. In an instant, in the twinkling of an eye, the gallery would be inundated, and the inclination was still downward toward the abyss whither the water tended to precipitate itself. The vault, dripping from the roof, announced clearly that the water filled it entirely, that there was no possible means of safety, and that all the speed she could employ would not save the unhappy victim from the impetuosity of the torrent. The air was already pent up by the great mass of water which hurried onward with a deafening noise; a suffocating heat impeded her respiration and produced a sort of deadening effect on all her faculties. Already the roaring of the unchained flood sounded in her very ear—already a red foam, threatening precursor of the coming, wave flowed over the path, and outstripped the uncertain and feeble steps of the terrified victim.

CHAPTER XLII.

"O MY mother!" she cried, "open thine arms to receive me! O Anzoleto, I love thee! O my God, receive my soul into a better world!"

Hardly had she uttered this cry of agony to Heaven, when she tripped and stumbled over some object in her path. O surprise! O divine goodness! It is a steep and narrow staircase, opening from one of the walls of the gallery, and up which she rushes on the wings of fear and of hope! The vault rises before her—the torrent dashes forward—strikes the staircase which Consuelo has had just time to clear—engulfs the first ten steps— wets to the ankle the agile feet which fly before it, and filling at last to the vaulted roof the gallery which Consuelo has left behind her, is swallowed up in the darkness, and falls with a horrible din into a deep reservoir, which the horoic girl looks down upon from a little platform she has reached on her knees and in darkness.

Her candle has been extinguished. A violent gust of wind had preceded the irruption of the mass of waters. Consuelo fell prostrate upon the last step, sustained hitherto by the instinct of self-preservation, but ignorant if she was saved—if the din of this cataract was not a new disaster which was about to overtake her — if the cold spray which dashed up even to where she was kneeling, and bathed her hair, was not the chilling hand of death extended to seize her.

In the meantime, the reservoir is filled by degrees to the height of other deeper waste ways, which carry still further in the bowels of the earth the current of the abundant spring. The noise diminishes, the vapors are dissipated, and a hollow and harmonious murmur echoes through the caverns. With a trembling hand Consuelo succeeds in relighting her candle. Her heart still beats violently against her bosom, but her courage is restored, and throwing herself on her knees she thanks God. Lastly, she examines the place in which she is, and throws the trembling light of her lantern upon the surrounding objects. A vast cavern, hollowed by the hand of nature, is extended like a roof over an abyss into which the distant fountain of the Schreckenstein flows, and loses itself in the recesses of the mountain. This abyss is so deep that the water which dashes into it cannot be seen at the bottom; but when a stone is thrown in, it is heard falling for a space of two minutes with a noise resembling thunder. The echoes of the cavern repeat it for a long time, and the hollow and frightful dash of the water is heard still longer, and might be taken for the howlings of the infernal pack. At one side of this cavern a narrow and dangerous path, hollowed out of the rock, runs along the margin of the precipice, and is lost in another gallery where the labor of man ceases, and which takes an upward direction and leaves the course of the current.

This is the road which Consuelo must take. There is no other—the water has closed and entirely filled that by which she came. It is impossible to await Zdenko's return in the grotto; its dampness would be fatal, and already the flame of her candle grows pale, flickers, and threatens to expire, without the possibility of being relighted.

Consuelo is not paralyzed by the horror of her situation. She thinks indeed that she is no longer on the road to the Schreckenstein, but that these subterranean galleries which open before her are a freak of nature, and conduct to places which are impassable, or to some labyrinth whence there is no issue. Still she will venture, were it only to seek a safer asylum until the next night. The next night, Zdenko will return and stop the current, the gallery will be again emptied, and the captive can retrace her steps and once more behold the blue vault of heaven.

Consuelo therefore plunged into the mysterious recesses of the cavern with fresh courage, attentive this time to all the peculiarities of the soil, and always careful to follow the ascending paths, without allowing her course to be diverted by the different galleries, apparently more spacious and more direct, which presented themselves every moment. By this means she was sure of not again meeting any currents of water, and of being able to retrace her steps.

She continued to advance in the midst of a thousand obstacles. Enormous stones blocked up her path ; gigantic bats, awakened from their slumbers by the light of the lantern, came striking against it in squadrons, and whirling around the traveler like spirits of darkness. After the first emotions of surprise were over, she felt her courage increase at each fresh danger. Sometimes she climbed over immense blocks of stone which had been detached from the huge vault overhead, where other enormous masses hung from the cracked and disjointed roof, as if every moment about to fall and overwhelm her. At other times the vault became so low and narrow that Consuelo was obliged to creep on her hands and knees amid a close and heated atmosphere, in order to force a passage. She proceeded thus for half an hour, when on turning a sharp angle which her light and agile form could hardly pass, she fell from Charybdis into Scylla, on finding herself face to face with Zdenko—Zdenko, at first petrified by surprise and frozen by terror, but soon indignant, furious, and menacing, as she had previously seen him.

In this labyrinth, surrounded by such numberless obstacles, and aided only by a light which the want of air threatened to stifle every moment, Consuelo felt that flight was impossible. For a moment she had the idea of defending herself hand to hand against his murderous attempts; for Zdenko's wandering eyes and foaming mouth sufficiently announced that this time he would not confine himself to threats. Suddenly he took a strange and ferocious resolution, and began to gather huge stones and build them one upon the other between himself and Consuelo, in order to wall up the narrow gallery in which she was. In this way he was certain, by not emptying the cistern for several days, to cause her to perish with hunger, like the bee which incloses the incautious hornet in his cell by stopping up the mouth with wax.

But it was not with wax, but with granite, that Zdenko built, and he carried on his work with astonishing rapidity. The amazing strength which this man, although emaciated and apparently so weak, displayed in collecting and arranging the blocks, proved to Consuelo that all resistance would be vain, and that it was better to trust to finding another exit by retracing her steps, than to drive him to extremity by irritating him. She used her utmost powers of entreaty and persuasion to endeavor to move him. "Zdenko," said she, "what are you doing there, foolish one? Albert will reproach you with my death. Albert expects and calls me. I am his friend, his consolation, his safety. In destroying me, you destroy your friend and your brother."

But Zdenko, fearing to be persuaded, and resolved to continue his work, commenced to sing in his own language a lively and animated air, still continuing to build his cyclopean wall with an active and powerful hand.

One stone only was wanting to complete the edifice. Consuelo, with a feeling of terror, saw him fix it in its place. "Never," thought she, "shall I be able to demolish this wall; I should require the hands of a giant." The wall was now finished, and immediately she saw Zdenko commence building another, behind the first. It was a quarry, a whole fortress, which ne meant to heap up between her and Albert. He continued to sing, and seemed to take extreme pleasure in his work.

A fortunate idea at last occurred to Consuelo. She remembered the famous heretical formula she had requested Amelia to explain to her, and which had so shocked the chaplain. "Zdenko!" cried she in Bohemian, through one of the openings of the badly joined wall which already separated them ; "Friend Zdenko, *may he who has been wronged salute thee !*"

Hardly had she pronounced these words, when they operated upon Zdenko like a charm : he let fall the enormous block which he held, uttered a deep sigh, and began to demolish his wall with even more promptitude than he had displayed in building it. Then reaching his hand to Consuelo, he assisted her in silence to surmount the scattered fragments, after which he looked at her with attention, sighed deeply, and giving her three keys tied together with a red ribbon, pointed out the path before her, and repeated, "May he who has been wronged salute thee !"

"Will you not serve me as a guide?" said she. "Conduct me to your master." Zdenko shook his head. "I have no master," said he ; "I had a friend, but you deprive me of him. Our destiny is accomplished. Go whither God directs you ; as for me, I shall weep here till you return."

And seating himself upon the ruins, he buried his head in his hands, and would not utter another word. Consuelo did not stop long to console him. She feared the return of his fury, and profiting by this momentary respect, and certain at last of being on the route to the Schreckenstein, she hurried forward on her way. In her uncertain and perilous journey, Consuelo had not made much advance ; for Zdenko, who had taken a much longer route, but one which was inaccessible to the water, had met her at the point of junction of the two subterranean passages, which made the circuit of the château, its vast outbuildings, and the hill on which it stood—one, by a well-arranged winding path, excavated in the rock by the hand of man — the other frightful, wild, and full of dangers. Consuelo did not in the least imagine that she was at that moment under the park, and yet she passed its gates and moat by a path which all the keys and all the precautions of the canoness could no longer close against her.

After having proceeded some distance on this new route, she almost resolved to turn back and renounce an enterprise which had already proved so difficult and almost fatal to her. Perhaps fresh obstacles awaited her. Zdenko's ill-will might be excited afresh. And if he should pursue and overtake her? If he should raise a second wall to prevent her return? Whereas, on the other hand, by abandoning her project, and asking him to clear the way to the cistern and empty it again that she might ascend, she had every chance of finding him gentle and benevolent. But she was still too much under the influence of her recent emotion, to think of once more facing that fantastic being. The terror he had caused her increased in proportion to the distance which separated them, and after having escaped his vengeance by almost miraculous presence of mind, she felt herself utterly overcome on thinking of it. She therefore continued her flight, having no longer the courage to attempt what might be necessary to render him favorable, and only wishing to find one of those magic doors, the keys of which he had given her, in order to place a barrier between herself and the possible return of his fury.

But might she not find Albert — that other madman whom she rashly persisted in thinking kind and tractable —actuated by feelings toward her similar to those which Zdenko had just manifested? There was a thick veil of doubt and uncertainty over all this adventure; and stripped it of the romantic attraction which had served as an inducement for her to undertake it. Consuelo asked herself if she was not the most crazy of the three, to have precipitated herself into this abyss of dangers and mysteries, without being sure of arriving at a favorable result.

Nevertheless, she followed the gallery, which was spacious, and admirably excavated by the athletic heroes of the middle ages. All the rocks were cut through by an elliptic arch of much character and regularity. The less compact portions, the chalky veins of the soil, and all those places where there was any danger of the roof falling in, were supported by finely worked arches of freestone, bound together by square keystones of granite. Consuelo did not stop to admire this immense work, executed with a solidity which promised to defy the lapse of many ages; neither did she ask herself how the present owners of the château could be ignorant of the existence of so important a construction.

She might have explained it by remembering, that all the historical documents of the family and estate had been destroyed more than a century before, at the epoch of the Reformation in Bohemia; but she no longer looked around her, and hardly bestowed a thought upon any thing except her own safety, satisfied with simply finding a level floor, an air which she could breathe, and a free space in which to move. She had still a long distance to traverse, although the direct route to the Schreckenstein was much shorter than the winding path through the mountain. She found the way very tedious, and no longer able to determine in what direction she was proceeding, she knew not if it led to the Schreckenstein, or to some more distant termination.

After walking for about a quarter of an hour, she found the vault gradually increase in height, and the work of the architect cease entirely. Nevertheless these vast quarries, and these majestic grottoes through which she passed, were still the work of man; but trenched upon by vegetation, and receiving the external air through numberless fissures, they had a less gloomy aspect than the galleries, and contained a thousand hiding-places and means of escape from the pursuit of an irritated adversary. But a noise of running water, which was now heard, made Consuelo shudder; and if she had been able to jest in such a situation, she might have confessed to herself that Baron Frederick on his return from the chase had never expressed a greater horror of water than she experienced at that instant.

But reflection soon reassured her. Ever since she had left the precipice where she had been so nearly overwhelmed with the rush of water, she had continued to ascend, and unless Zdenko had at his command a hydraulic machine of inconceivable power and extent, he could not raise to that height his terrible auxiliary, the torrent. Besides, it was evident that she must somewhere encounter the current of the fountain, the sluice, or the spring itself, and if she had reflected further, she would have been astonished that she had not yet found in her path this mysterious source, this Fountain of Tears which supplied the cistern. The fact was, that the spring pursued its way through unknown regions of the mountain, and that the gallery, cutting it at right angles, did not encounter it except just near the cistern, and afterward under the Schreckenstein, as happened to Consuelo. The sluice-gate was far behind her, on the path which Zdenko had passed alone, and Consuelo approached the spring, which for ages had been seen by no one except Albert and Zdenko. In a short time she met with the current, and this time she walked along its bank without fear and without danger.

A path of smooth fresh sand bordered the course of the limpid and transparent stream, which ran with a pleasant murmur between carefully formed banks. There the handiwork of man once more reappeared. The path sloped down to the margin of the rivulet, and wound its way through beautiful aquatic plants, enormous wall-flowers, and wild brambles, which flourished in this sheltered place without injury from the rigor of the season. Enough of the external air penetrated through cracks and crevices to support the vegetation, but these crevices were too narrow to afford passage to the curious eye which sought to pry into them from without. It was like a natural hot-house, preserved by its vaults from cold and snow, but sufficiently aired by a thousand imperceptible breathing-holes. It seemed as if some careful and discriminating hand had protected the lives of those beautiful plants, and freed the sand which the torrent threw upon its banks of any stones that could have hurt the feet, and this supposition would have been correct. It was Zdenko who had made the neighborhood of Albert's retreat so lovely, pleasant and secure.

Consuelo already began to feel the grateful influence which the less gloomy and poetic aspect of external objects produced upon her imagination. When she saw the pale rays of the moon glance here and there through the openings of the rocks, and reflect themselves upon the moving water; when she saw the motionless plants, which the water did not reach, agitated at intervals by the wind of the forest ; when she perceived herself ascending nearer and nearer to the surface of the earth, she felt her strength renovated, and the reception which awaited her at the end of her heroic pilgrimage was depicted to her mind in less somber colors. At last she saw the path turn abruptly from the margin of the stream, enter a short gallery newly built, and terminate at a little door, which seemed of metal, it was so cold, and which was encircled, and as it were framed, by an enormous ground-ivy.

When she saw herself at the end of all her fatigues and uncertainty—when she rested her weary hand upon this last obstacle, which would yield to her touch in a moment (for she held the key of the door in her other hand)—Consuelo hesitated, and felt a timidity take possession of her, which was more difficult to conquer than all her terrors. She was about to penetrate alone into a place closed to every eye, to every human thought, and there to surprise, in sleep or reverie, a man whom she hardly knew; who was neither her father, nor her brother, nor her husband ; who perhaps loved her, but whom she neither could love nor wished to love. "God has conducted me here," thought she, "through the most frightful dangers. It is by his will and by his protection that I have reached this spot. I come with a fervent mind, a resolution full of charity, a tranquil heart, a disinterestedness proof against every assault. Perhaps death awaits me, and yet the thought does not terrify me. My life is desolate, and I could lose it without much regret; I felt this an instant since, and for the last hour I have seen myself doomed to a frightful death, with a tranquillity for which I was not prepared. This is, perhaps, a favor which God sends to me in my last moments. Perhaps I am about to perish under the blows of a madman, and I advance to meet this catastrophe with the firmness of a martyr. I believe with ardent faith in an eternal life, and feel that if I perish here, victim to a friendship, perhaps useless, but at least conscientious, I shall be recompensed in a happier life. What delays me ? and why do I experience an inexplicable dread, as if I were about to commit a fault, and to have to blush before him I have come to save?" Thus did Consuelo, too modest to understand her modesty, struggle with her feelings, and almost reproach herself for the delicacy of her scruples. Nevertheless she put the key into the lock of the door; but she tried to turn it ten times before she could resolve to do so. A sensation of overpowering lassitude took possession

of her frame, and threatened to incapacitate her from proceeding with her enterprise, at the very moment when success seemed to crown her efforts.

CHAPTER XLIII.

HOWEVER, she made up her mind. She had three keys,
and she therefore must pass through three doors and two
apartments, before reaching that in which she supposed
Albert to be a prisoner. She would thus have sufficient
time to stop, if her strength failed her.

She entered a vaulted hall, which had no other furniture
than a bed of dried fern on which was thrown a sheep-skin
as coverlet. A pair of ancient-looking sandals, very much
worn, served as an indication by which she recognized it as
Zdenko's chamber. She recognized also the little basket
which she had carried filled with fruit to the Stone of
Terror, and which after two days had disappeared. She
resolved upon opening the second door, after having carefully closed the first, for she still thought with terror of
the possible return of the wayward owner of this dwelling.
The second apartment which she entered was vaulted like
the first, but the walls were protected by mats and trellises
covered with moss. A stove diffused a pleasant heat
through it, and it was doubtless its funnel opening in the
rock, which produced the fleeting light seen by Consuelo
on the summit of the Schreckenstein. Albert's bed, like
Zdenko's, was formed of a heap of leaves and dried herbs;
but Zdenko had covered it with magnificent bear-skins, in
spite of the absolute equality which Albert exacted in all
their habits, and which Zdenko observed in every thing
that did not interfere with the passionate tenderness
he felt for him, and with the care which he bestowed
upon him in preference to himself. Consuelo on entering this chamber was received by Cynabre, who hearing the key turn in the lock, had posted himself upon
the threshold, with raised ear and anxious eye. But
Cynabre had received a peculiar education from his
master; he was a friend, and not a guardian. When young
he had been so strictly forbidden to howl and to bark, that he
had entirely lost the habit so natural to all animals of his

species. If any one had approached Albert with evil intentions, he would have found his voice; if any one had attacked him he would have defended him. But prudent and circumspect as a hermit, he never made the slightest noise without being sure of what he was about, and without having carefully examined and smelled those who approached him. He walked up therefore to Consuelo with a look that had something almost human in it; smelled her dress, and especially her hand, which had held for a long time the keys touched by Zdenko; and completely reassured by this circumstance, he abandoned himself to the grateful recollection he had retained of her, and placed his great velvet paws upon her shoulders with silent joy, while he slowly swept the earth with his long and feathery tail. After this grave but sincere welcome, he returned to his bed on the corner of the skin which covered his master's couch, and stretched himself upon it with the apparent weariness of old age, although he still followed with his eyes Consuelo's every step and movement.

Before venturing to approach the third door, Consuelo cast a glance around this hermitage, in order to gather from it some indication of the moral condition of him who occupied it. She found no trace of madness or despair. An extreme neatness and order prevailed throughout. A cloak and other garments were hanging from the horns of the urus, a curiosity which Albert had brought from the forests of Lithuania, and which served for clothes-pegs. His numerous books were regularly arranged in a bookcase of rough boards, supported by great branches admirably fashioned by a rude but ingenious hand. The table and the two chairs were of the same workmanship. A hortus siccus and some old books of music, entirely unknown to Consuelo, with titles and words in the Slavonic language, served to reveal more completely the peaceful, simple, and studious habits of the anchorite. An iron lamp, curious from its antiquity, was suspended from the middle of the vault, and burned in the eternal night of this melancholy sanctuary.

Consuelo remarked that there were no fire-arms in the place. Notwithstanding the taste of the wealthy inhabitants of those forests for the chase and for the objects of luxury which accompany its enjoyment, Albert had no gun, not even a hunting-knife, and his old dog had never learned the *grande science;* for which reason Cynabre was an object of Baron Frederick's contempt and pity. Albert had a horror of blood ; and though he appeared to enjoy life less than any one, he had a religious and boundless respect for the idea of life in general. He could neither himself kill, nor see killed, even the lowest animals of creation. He would have delighted in all the natural sciences, but he contented himself with mineralogy and botany. Even entomology seemed to him too cruel a science, and he never could have sacrificed the life of an insect to gratify his curiosity. Consuelo knew these particulars, and she now remembered them on seeing the evidences of Albert's peaceful occupations. "No, I will not be afraid," said she to herself, "of so gentle and peaceful a being. This is the cell of a saint and not the dungeon of a madman." But the more she was reassured as to the nature of his mental malady, the more did she feel troubled and confused. She almost regretted that she was not to find a deranged or dying man ; and the certainty of presenting herself before a real man made her hesitate more and more.

Not knowing how to announce herself, she sunk into a reverie which had lasted some minutes when the sound of an admirable instrument struck her ear ; it was a violin of Stradivarius, giving birth to a solemn and sublime strain, under a chaste and skillful hand. Never had Consuelo heard so perfect a violin, so touching and at the same time so simple a performance. The air was unknown to her ; but from its strange and simple forms, she judged it to be more ancient than any ancient music she was acquainted with. She listened with rapture, and now comprehended how Albert could have so well appreciated her from the first phrase he heard her sing. It was because he had the revelation of the true, the grand music. He might not be acquainted possibly with all the wonderful resources of the art ; but he had within him the divine *afflatus,* the intelligence, and the love of the beautiful. When he had finished, Consuelo, entirely reassured, and animated by a more lively sympathy, was about to venture to knock at the door which still separated her from him, when it opened slowly, and she saw the young count advance, his head bowed down, his eyes fixed upon the earth, and his violin and bow hanging loosely in his nerveless hands. His paleness was frightful, and his hair and dress in a disorder which Consuelo had not before witnessed. His absent air, his broken and dejected attitude, and the despairing apathy of his movements, announced, if not entire alienation, at least the disorder and abandonment, of human reason. He seemed one of those mute and oblivious specters, in which the Slavonian people believe, who enter mechanically into the houses at night, and are seen to act without connection and without aim, obeying as if by instinct the former habits of their lives, without recognizing and without seeing their friends and terrified servants, who fly from or look at them in silence, frozen with astonishment and fear. Such was Consuelo on meeting Count Albert, and perceiving that he did not see her, although he was not two paces distant. Cynabre had risen and licked his master's hand. Albert said some friendly words to him in Bohemian ; then following with his eyes the movements of the dog, who carried his discreet caresses to Consuelo, he gazed attentively at the feet of the young girl, which were shod at this moment much like those of Zdenko, and without raising his head, spoke in Bohemian some words which she did not understand, but which seemed a question, and ended with her name. On seeing him in this state, Consuelo felt her timidity disappear. Yielding entirely to her compassion, she saw only the unfortunate man with his bleeding heart, who still invoked without recognizing her, and placing her hand upon the young man's arm confidently and firmly, she said to him in Spanish, with her pure and penetrating voice, " Consuelo is here!"

CHAPTER XLIV.

HARDLY had Consuelo uttered her name, when Count Albert, raising his eyes and looking in her face, immediately changed his attitude and expression. He let his violin fall to the ground with as much indifference as if he had never known its use, and clasping his hands with an air of profound tenderness and respectful sadness, " It is thou then whom I see at last in this place of exile and suffering, O my poor Wanda?" cried he, uttering a sigh

which seemed to rend his breast. " Dear—dear—and unhappy sister! Unfortunate victim, whom I avenged too
late, and whom I knew not how to defend! Ah! thou
knowest that the villain who outraged thee, perished in
torments, and that my pitiless hand was bathed in the
blood of his accomplices. I opened the deep veins of the
accursed church. I washed thy dishonor and my own and
that of my people, in rivers of blood. What more dost
thou desire, O restless and revengeful spirit? The times
of zeal and anger have passed away; we live now in the
days of repentance and of expiation. Ask from me tears
and prayers—ask no more for blood. I have henceforth a
horror for blood, and will shed no more. No, no, not a
single drop! John Ziska will henceforth fill his chalice
only with inexhaustible tears and bitter sobs!"

While speaking thus with wandering eyes and features
animated by a sudden phrenzy, Albert moved around Consuelo, and recoiled with a kind of horror each time she
made a movement to interrupt this strange adjuration.
Consuelo did not require much reflection to understand
the turn which her host's insanity had taken. She had
heard the history of John Ziska related often enough to
know that a sister of that formidable fanatic, who had been
a nun before the breaking out of the war of the Hussites,
had died of sorrow and shame in her convent, from a
forced breach of her vows; and that the life of Ziska had
been one long and solemn vengeance of that crime. At
that moment, Albert, recalled by some association of ideas
to his ruling fancy, believed himself John Ziska, and
addressed her as the shade of Wanda, his unfortunate
sister.

She resolved not to contradict his illusion too abruptly.

"Albert," said she, " for your name is no longer John,
as mine is no longer Wanda, look at me well, and see that
I, as well as you, am changed in features and character.
What you have just said, I came to recall to your mind.
Human justice is more than satisfied, and it is the day of
divine justice which I now announce to you. God commands us to forgive and to forget. These fatal recollections, this pertinacity of yours in exercising a faculty
which he has not given to other men, this scrupulous and
gloomy remembrance which you retain of your anterior
existences, God is offended at, and withdraws from you,

because you have abused them. Do you hear me, Albert, and do you understand me now?"

"O my mother!" replied Albert, pale and trembling, falling on his knees and looking at Consuelo with an extraordinary expression of terror, "I do hear thee, and understand thy words. I see that thou transformest thyself, to convince and subdue me. No, thou art no longer Wanda of Ziska, the violated virgin, the weeping nun. Thou art Wanda of Prachalitz, whom men call Countess of Rudolstadt, and who bore in thy bosom the wretched being they now call Albert."

"It is not by the caprice of men that you are so called," returned Consuelo, with firmness; "for it is God who has caused you to live again under other conditions and with new duties. Those duties, Albert, you either do not know or you despise them. You travel back the course of ages with an impious pride; you aspire to penetrate the secrets of destiny; you think to equal yourself with God, by embracing in your view the present and the past. It is I who tell you this, and it is truth, it is faith which inspires me; this always looking backward is rash and criminal. This supernatural memory which you attribute to yourself is an illusion. You have taken some vague and feeble glimmerings for certainty, and your imagination has deceived you. Your pride has built up an empty and unsubstantial edifice, when you assign to yourself the most important parts in the history of your ancestors. Beware lest you are not what you suppose. Fear lest, to punish you, eternal wisdom should open your eyes for an instant, and cause you to perceive in your former life, less illustrious faults and less glorious objects of remorse, than those on which you dare to pride yourself."

Albert heard this discourse with timid attention, his face hidden in his hands, and his knees buried in the earth.

"Speak! speak! O voice of Heaven! which I hear, but which I no longer recognize," murmured he, in stifled accents. "If thou art the angel of the mountain—if thou art, as I believe, the celestial figure which has so often appeared to me upon the Stone of Terror—speak—command my will, my conscience, my imagination. Thou well knowest that I seek for the light with anguish, and that if I lose myself in the darkness, it is from my desire to dissipate it in order to reach thee."

"A little humility, a little confidence and submission to the eternal decrees of wisdom, which are incomprehensible to man—that is the path of truth for you, Albert. Renounce from your heart, and renounce firmly, once for all, any wish to know any thing beyond this passing existence which is imposed upon you; and you will again become acceptable to God, useful to man, tranquil in yourself. Humble your proud intellect; and without losing faith in your immortality, without doubting the divine goodness, which pardons the past and watches over the future, apply yourself to render humane and full of good fruits, this present life which you despise, when you ought to respect it and give yourself to it, with all your strength, your self-denial, and your charity. Now, Albert, look at me, and may your eyes be unsealed. I am no longer your sister nor your mother; I am a friend whom Heaven has sent to you, and whom it has conducted by miraculous means to snatch you from pride and from insanity. Look at me, and tell me, on your soul and on your conscience, who I am and what is my name."

Albert, trembling and confused, raised his head and looked at her again, but with less wildness and terror than before.

" You cause me to leap over abysses," said he to her; "by your deep and searching words you confound my reason, which (for my misfortune) I thought superior to that of other men, and you order me to know and understand the present time and human affairs. I cannot. To lose the remembrance of certain phases of my life, I must pass through a terrible crisis ; and to seize the sense of a new phase, I must transform myself by efforts which lead me to the gates of death. If you command me, in the name of a power which I feel superior to mine, to assimulate my thoughts to yours, I must obey ; but I know those horrible struggles, and I know that death is their termination. Pity me, you who operate upon me by a sovereign charm ; aid me, or I sink. Tell me who you are, for I do not know. I do not remember ever to have seen you before ; I do not know your sex, and you are there before me like a mysterious statue, the type of which I vainly strive to find in my memory. Help me! help me! for I feel that I am dying."

While speaking thus, Albert, whose face was at first

flushed with a feverish brightness, became again of a frightful paleness. He stretched out his hands toward Consuelo; but immediately lowered them to the ground to support himself, as if he had been overpowered by an irresistible faintness. Consuelo, becoming by degrees initiated into the secrets of his mental malady, felt herself reanimated, and as if inspired by new strength and intelligence. She took his hands, and obliging him to rise, she conducted him toward the chair which was near the table. He let himself fall into it, overpowered by unsufferable fatigue, and bent forward as if about to faint. The struggle of which he spoke was but too real. Albert had the faculty of recovering his reason, and repelling the suggestions of the fever which consumed his brain; but he did not succeed without efforts and sufferings which exhausted his powers. When this reaction was produced of its own accord, he issued from it refreshed, and as it were renewed, but when he induced it by a resolution of his still powerful will, his body sank under the effort, and all his limbs were affected by catalepsy. Consuelo understood what was passing within him. "Albert," said she, placing her cold hand upon his head, "I know you, and that suffices. I am interested in you, and that also must be sufficient for you at present. I forbid your making any effort of your will to recognize or to speak to me. Only listen; and if my words seem obscure to you, wait till I explain myself, and be in no haste to discover their meaning. I ask of you a passive submission and an entire abandonment of your reflective powers. Can you descend into your heart, and there concentrate all your existence?"

"Oh, how much good you do me!" replied Albert. "Speak to me again—speak to me always thus. You hold my soul in your hands. Whoever you may be, keep it—do not let it escape—for it would go and knock at the gates of eternity, and would there be broken. Tell me who you are—tell me quickly; and if I do not comprehend, explain it to me; for, in spite of myself, I seek to know and am agitated."

"I am Consuelo," replied the young girl; "and you know it, since you instinctively speak to me in a language which I alone, of all those near you, can comprehend. I am the friend whom you have expected for a long while, and whom you recognized one day as she was singing Since that day you have left your family and hidden yourself here. Since that day I have sought for you; you have appealed to me several times through Zdenko; but Zdenko, who executed your orders in certain respects, was not willing to conduct me to you. I have succeeded, through a thousand dangers——"

"You could not have succeeded had Zdenko been unwilling," interrupted Albert, raising his body, which was weighed down and resting upon the table. "You are a dream, I see it well, and all that I hear is simply passing in my imagination. Oh, my God! you lull me with deceitful joys, and suddenly the disorder and incoherence of my dreams are revealed to me, and I find myself alone—alone in the world with my despair and my madness! O Consuelo! Consuelo! fatal and delicious dream! where is the being that bears your name, and is sometimes clothed with your form? No, you exist only in me, and it is my delirium which has created you."

Albert again let his head fall on his extended arms, which became cold and rigid as marble.

Consuelo saw him approach his lethargic crisis, and felt herself so exhausted and so ready to faint, that she feared she could not avert it. She endeavored to reanimate Albert's hands in her own, which were hardly more alive. "My God," said she, with a choking voice, her heart sinking within her, "succor two unfortunate beings who can hardly do any thing for each other!"

She saw herself alone, shut up with a dying man, dying herself, and expecting no help for herself or for him, except from Zdenko, whose return seemed to her more to be dreaded than desired.

Her prayer seemed to strike Albert with an unexpected emotion. "Some one is praying by my side," said he, trying to raise his overburdened head. "I am not alone. Oh, no! I am not alone," added he, looking at Consuelo's hand clasped in his. "Succoring hand, mysterious pity, human, fraternal sympathy! You render my agony very gentle, my heart very grateful!" And he imprinted his frozen lips on Consuelo's hand, and remained thus for a long while.

A feeling of modesty restored to Consuelo the sense of life. She did not dare to withdraw her hand from the unfortunate young man; but divided between her embarrassment and her weariness, and no longer able to remain standing, she was compelled to rest upon Albert, and to place her other hand upon his shoulder.

"I feel myself restored," said Albert, after a few moments. "It seems to me that I am in my mother's arms. O my aunt Wenceslawa, if it be you who are near me, forgive me for having forgotten you—you, and my father, and all my family—whose very names had escaped my memory. I return to you—do not leave me; but restore to me Consuelo—Consuelo, whom I had so long expected, whom I had at last found, and whom I find no more, and without whom I can no longer exist."

Consuelo endeavored to speak to him; but in proportion as Albert's memory and strength seemed restored to him, Consuelo's life seemed to desert her. So much terror and fatigue, so many emotions and superhuman efforts, had so broken her down, that she could struggle no longer. The words expired upon her lips, she felt her limbs bend under her, and every object swam before her eyes. She fell upon her knees by the side of Albert, and her swooning form struck the breast of the young man.

Immediately Albert, as if awaking from a dream, saw her—recognized her—uttered a deep cry, and arousing himself, pressed her in his arms with wild energy. Through the veil of death which seemed to spread over her eyelids, Consuelo saw his joy and was not terrified. It was a holy joy radiant with purity. She closed her eyes and fell into a state of utter prostration, which was not sleep nor waking, but a kind of indifference and insensibility to all present things.

CHAPTER XLV.

WHEN Consuelo recovered the use of her faculties, finding herself seated upon a hard bed, and not yet able to raise her eyelids, she endeavoured to collect her thoughts. But the prostration had been so complete that her powers returned but slowly; and as if the sum of the fatigues and emotions which she had latterly experienced had surpassed her strength, she tried in vain to remember what

had happened to her since she left Venice. Even her departure from that adopted country, where she had passed
such happy days, appeared to her like a dream; and it was a
solace (alas, too fleeting!) to her to be able to doubt for
an instant her exile, and the misfortunes which caused it.
She therefore imagined that she was still in her poor
chamber in the Corte Minelli, on her mother's pallet, that
after having had a violent and trying scene with Anzoleto, the confused recollection of which floated in her
memory, she returned to life and hope on feeling him near
her, on hearing his interrupted breathing, and the tender
words he addressed to her in a low and murmuring voice.
A languishing and delicious joy penetrated her heart at
this thought, and she raised herself with some exertion to
look at her repentant friend, and to stretch out her hand
to him. But she pressed a cold and unknown hand; and
in place of the smiling sun, whose rosy brilliancy she
was accustomed to see through her white curtain, she
saw only a sepulchral light, falling from the roof of a
gloomy vault, and swimming in a humid atmosphere; she
felt under her arm the rude spoils of savage animals, and
amid a horrible silence the pale face of Albert bent toward
her like that of a specter.

Consuelo thought she had descended living to the tomb;
she closed her eyes, and fell back upon the bed of dried
leaves with a deep groan. It was some minutes before she
could remember where she was, and to what gloomy host
she was confided. Terror, which the enthusiasm of her
devotion had hitherto combated and subdued, seized upon
her, so that she feared to open her eyes lest she should
see some horrible spectacle—the paraphernalia of death
—a sepulcher—open before her. She felt something upon
her brow, and raised her hand to it. It was a garland of
leaves with which Albert had crowned her. She took it
off to look at it, and saw a branch of cypress.

"I believed you dead, O my soul, O my consolation!"
said Albert, kneeling beside her; "and before following
you to the tomb, I wished to adorn you with the emblems
of marriage. Flowers do not grow around me, Consuelo.
The black cypress offered the only branches from which
my hand could gather your coronet of betrothal. There it
is; do not despise it. If we must die here, let me swear
to you that, if restored to life, I would never have had any

other spouse than you ; that I die united with you by an indissoluble oath."

"Betrothed! united!" cried Consuelo, casting terrified glances around her; "who has pronounced that decree? who has celebrated that marriage?"

"It is destiny, my angel," replied Albert, with an inexpressible gentleness and sadness. "Think not to escape from it. It is a strange destiny for you, and even more so for me. You forbade me a short time since to search into the past; you prohibited to me the remembrance of those bygone days which are called the night of ages. My being has obeyed you, and henceforth I know nothing of my anterior life. But my present life, I have questioned it, I know it. I have seen it entire with one glance; it appeared to me during the instant in which you reposed in the arms of death. Your destiny, Consuelo, is to belong to me, and yet you will never be mine. You do not love me, you never will love me as I love you. Your love for me is only charity, your devotion only heroism. You are a saint whom God sends, but you will never be a woman to me. I must die, consumed by a love you cannot partake; and yet, Consuelo, you will be my wife as you are now my betrothed, whether we perish now, and your pity consents to give me that title of husband, which no kiss will ever confirm, or whether we again see the sun, and your conscience commands you to accomplish the designs of God toward me."

"Count Albert," said Consuelo, endeavoring to rise from her bed covered with bear-skins, which resembled a funereal couch, "I know not if it be the enthusiasm of a heated imagination, or the continuance of your delirium, which make you speak thus. I have no longer the strength to dispel your illusions; and if they must turn against me —against me, who have come at the peril of my life to succor and console you—I feel that I can no longer contend with you for my life or my liberty. If the sight of me irritates you, and if God abandons me, may His will be done! You, who think you know so many things, do not know how my life has been poisoned, and with how little regret I should sacrifice it."

"I know that you are very unhappy, my poor saint. I know that you wear on your brow a crown of thorns, which I cannot tear away. The cause and the consequences of your misfortunes I do not know, neither do I ask you for them. But I should love you very little, I should be little worthy of your compassion, if from the day when I first met you I had not felt and recognized in you the sorrow which fills your soul and embitters your life. What can you fear from me, Consuelo ?—from my soul ? You, so firm and so wise, whom God has inspired with words which subdued and restored me in an instant, you must feel the light of your faith and your reason strangely weakened, since you fear your friend, your servant, your slave. Rouse yourself, my angel ; look at me. See me here at your feet, and forever, my forehead in the dust. What do you wish—what do you command ? Do you wish to leave this place on the instant, without my following you, without my ever appearing before you again ? What sacrifice do you exact? What oath do you wish me to take? I can promise you every thing, and obey you in every thing. Yes, Consuelo, I can even become a tranquil man, submissive, and in appearance as reasonable as other men. Should I thus be less repulsive, less terrifying to you ? Hitherto I have never been able to do as I wished, but hereafter every thing you desire will be granted me. Perhaps I may die in transforming myself according to your will ; but I tell you in my turn that my life has ever been embittered, and that I should not regret losing it for you."

" Dear, generous Albert!" said Consuelo, reassured and greatly affected, "explain yourself more clearly, and let me at last understand the depths of your impenetrable soul. You are in my eyes superior to all other men; and from the first moment that I saw you, I felt for you a respect and a sympathy which I have no cause to conceal. I have always heard it said that you were insane, but I have not been able to believe it. All that has been related to me of you only added to my esteem and to my confidence. Still I could not help seeing that you were overpowered by a deep and strange mental disease. I persuaded myself, presumptuously perhaps, but sincerely, that I could relieve your malady. You yourself have aided in making me think so. I have come to seek you, and now you tell me things respecting myself and you which would fill me with a boundless veneration, if you did not mix up with them strange ideas drawn from a spirit of fatalism which I cannot share. Can I say all without wounding you and making you suffer?"

" Say all, Consuelo; I know beforehand what you have to say."

" Well, I will say it, for I had so promised myself. All those who love you despair of you. They think they must respect, that is to say, spare, what they call your insanity; they fear to exasperate you by letting you see that they know it, lament it, and fear it. For myself, I cannot believe them, and cannot tremble in asking you why, being so wise, you have sometimes the appearance of an insane person; why, being so good, you perform deeds of ingratitude and pride; why, being so enlightened and religious, you abandon yourself to the reveries of a diseased and despairing mind; and lastly, why you are here alone, buried alive in a gloomy cavern—far from your family, who weep and search for you—far from your fellow-men, whom you cherish with an ardent zeal—far from me, too, whom you invoked, whom you say you love, and who has been able to reach you only by miracles of resolution and the divine protection?"

" You ask of me the secret of my life, the solution of my destiny, and yet you know it better than I do, Consuelo. It is from you I expected the revelation of my being, and you question me! Oh! I understand you; you wish to lead me to a confession, to an efficacious repentance, to a victorious resolution. You shall be obeyed. But it is not at this instant that I can know, and judge, and transform myself in this manner. Give me some days, some hours at least, to learn for myself and for you if I am mad, or if I enjoy the use of my reason. Alas! alas! both are true, and it is my misery not to be able to doubt it ; but, to know if I must lose my judgment and my will entirely, or if I shall be able to triumph over the demon who besieges me, that is what I cannot do at this instant. Have pity upon me, Consuelo; I am still under the influence of an emotion more powerful than myself. I know not what I have said to you; I know not how many hours you have been here; I know not how you could be here without Zdenko, who did not wish to bring you ; I know not even in what region my thoughts were wandering when you first appeared to me. Alas! I know not how many ages I have been shut up here, struggling with unheard-of sufferings against the scourge which destroys me. Even these sufferings I remember no longer when they have passed; there remains in their place only a terrible fatigue, a sort of stupor, a terror which I long to banish. Let me forget myself, Consuelo, if it be only for a few moments; my ideas will become clearer, my tongue will be loosened. I promise, I swear it to you. Let the light of truth beam softly and by degrees on my eyes, long shrouded in fearful darkness and unable to endure the full strength of its rays. You have ordered me to concentrate all my life in my heart. Yes; those were your words; my reason and my memory date no further back than from the moment you spoke them. Well! these words have diffused an angelic calm over my spirit. My heart lives now once more, though my spirit still sleeps. I fear to speak to you of myself; I might wander, and again terrify you by my ravings. I wish to live only in feeling, and it is an unknown life to me; it would be a life or delight if I could abandon myself to it without displeasing you. Ah, Consuelo! why did you tell me to concentrate all my life in my heart? Explain your meaning; let me think only of you, see and comprehend only you—in a word, love you. O my God, I love—I love a living being!—a being like myself! I love her with all the strength of my heart and soul! I can concentrate upon her all the ardor, all the holiness of my affections. It is happiness enough for me to be allowed this, and I have not the madness to ask for more."

"Well, dear Albert, let your wearied soul repose in this sweet sentiment of a peaceful and brotherly tenderness. God is my witness that you can do so without fear and without danger; for I feel a strong and sincere friendship for you—a kind of veneration which the frivolous observations and vain judgments of the world cannot shake. You have become aware, by a sort of divine and mysterious intuition, that my whole life is broken by sorrow; you said so, and it was divine truth which prompted your words. I cannot love you otherwise than as a brother; but do not say that it is charity, pity alone, which influences me. If humanity and compassion have given me courage to come here, sympathy and a heartfelt esteem for your virtues gave me also the courage and the right to speak to you as I do. Banish, therefore, from this moment and forever, the illusion under which you labor respecting your own feelings. Do not speak of love, do not speak of marriage. My past life, my recollections, make the first impossible; the difference in our conditions would render the second humiliating and insupportable to me. By indulging in such dreams you will render my devotion to you rash, perhaps culpable. Let us seal by a sacred promise the engagement which I make, to be your sister, your friend, your consoler, whenever you are disposed to open your heart to me; your nurse, when suffering renders you gloomy and taciturn. Swear that you will not look on me in any other light, and that you will never love me otherwise."

"Generous woman!" said Albert, turning pale, "you reckon largely on my courage, and you know well the extent of my love, in asking of me such a promise. I should be capable of lying for the first time in my life—I could even debase myself so far as to pronounce a false oath—if you required it of me. But you will not require it of me, Consuelo; you know that this would be to introduce a new source of agitation into my life, and into my conscience a remorse which has not yet stained it. Do not be uneasy at the manner in which I love you. First of all I am ignorant of it; I only know that to deprive this affection of the name of love would be to utter a blasphemy. I submit myself to all the rest; I accept your pity, your care, your goodness, your peaceful friendship; I will speak to you only as you permit; I will not say a single word which could trouble you, nor give you a single look which could make you veil your eyes; I will not even touch your dress, if you fear being sullied by my breath. But you would be wrong to treat me with such mistrust, and you would do better to encourage in me those gentle emotions which restore us to life, and from which you can fear nothing. I can well understand that your modesty might be alarmed at the expression of a love which you do not share; I know that your pride would reject the marks of a passion which you do not wish either to excite or to encourage. Therefore be calm, and swear without fear to be my sister and my consoler, as I swear to be your brother and servant. Do not ask of me more; I will neither be indiscreet nor importunate. It is sufficient for me that you know you can command me and govern me despotically—not as you would govern a brother, but as you would dispose of a being who has given himself to you entirely and forever "

CHAPTER XLVI.

THIS language reassured Consuelo for the present, but did not leave her without apprehension for the future. That Albert's fanatical self-denial had its source in a deep and unconquerable passion, the serious nature of his character and the solemnity of his countenance could leave no doubt. Consuelo, perplexed, though at the same time moved with compassion, asked herself if she could continue to consecrate her cares to this man, so unreservedly and unchangeably in love with her. She had never treated this sort of relation lightly in her thoughts, and she saw that with Albert no woman could enter upon it without serious consequences. She did not doubt his devotedness; but the calmness which she had flattered herself she should restore to him must be irreconcilable with the existence of so ardent a love and the impossibility she felt of responding to it. She held out her hand to him with a sigh, and remained pensive, with her eyes fixed on the ground, and plunged in a melancholy reverie.

"Albert," said she at last, raising her eyes, and finding his anxiously fixed upon her with an expression of anguish and sorrow, "you do not know me, when you wish to impose upon me a character for which I am so ill fitted. None but a woman who would abuse it could accept it. I am neither proud nor a coquette; I think I am not vain, and I have no passion for sway. Your love would flatter me, if I could share it; and if it were so, I would tell you instantly. To afflict you in the situation in which I find you, by the reiterated assurance of the contrary, would be an act of cold-blooded cruelty which you ought to have spared me, and which is nevertheless imposed upon me by my conscience, though my heart detests it, and is deeply grieved in accomplishing it. Pity me for being obliged to afflict you, to offend you perhaps, at a moment when I would willingly give my life to restore you to happiness and health."

"I know it, high souled maiden," said Albert, with a melancholy smile. "You are so good, so great, that you would give your life for the meanest creature; but I know that your conscience will bend to no one. Do not then fear to offend me in displaying this sternness which I admire—this stoical coldness, which your virtue maintains along with the most moving pity. It is not in your power to afflict me, Consuelo. I am not the sport of illusion; I am accustomed to bitter grief; my life has been made up of painful sacrifices. Do not then treat me as a visionary, as a being without heart and without self-respect, in repeating what I already know, that you will never love me. Consuelo, I am acquainted with the circumstances of your life, although I know neither your name, nor family, nor any important fact concerning you. I know the history of your soul; the rest does not concern me. You loved, you still love, and you will always love, one of whom I know nothing, whom I do not wish to know, and with whom I shall never compete. But know, Consuelo, that you shall never be his, or mine, or even your own. God has reserved for you a separate existence, of which the events are hidden from me, but of which I foresee the object and end. The slave and victim of your own greatness of soul, you will never receive in this life other recompense than the consciousness of your own power and goodness. Unhappy in the world's estimation, you will yet be the most serene and the most fortunate of human creatures, because you will ever be the best and the most upright; for the wicked and the base, dearest sister, are alone to be pitied, and the words of Christ will remain true as long as men continue blind and unjust: 'Happy are those who are persecuted; happy those who weep, and who labor in trouble.'"

The power and dignity which were at this moment stamped upon the lofty and majestic forehead of Albert, exercised over Consuelo so great a fascination that she forgot the part of proud sovereign and austere friend, which she had imposed upon herself, to bow to the spell of this man's influence, so inspired by faith and enthusiasm. She supported herself with difficulty, still overwhelmed with fatigue and emotion, and trembling from excess of weariness, she sank on her knees, and, clasping her hands, began to pray fervently and aloud. "If Thou, my God," she exclaimed, "dost put this prophecy in the mouth of a saint, Thy holy will be done! In my infancy I besought from Thee an innocent and childlike happiness; but Thou hast reserved for me happiness under a severe and rude form, which I am unable to comprehend. Open Thou mine eyes—grant me an humble and contrite heart. I am willing, O my God! to submit to this destiny, which seems so adverse, and which so slowly revealed itself, and only ask from Thee that which any of Thy creatures is entitled to expect from Thy loving justice — faith, hope, and charity!"

While praying thus, Consuelo was bathed in tears, which she did not seek to restrain. After such feverish agitation, this paroxysm served to calm her troubled feelings, while it weakened her yet more. Albert prayed and wept along with her, blessing the tears which he had so long shed in solitude, and which now mingled with those of a pure and generous being.

"And now," said Consuelo, rising, "we have thought long enough of what concerns ourselves; it is time to think of others, and to recollect our duties to them. I have promised to restore you to your family, who already mourn and pray for you as for one dead. Do you not desire, my dear Albert, to restore joy and peace to your afflicted relatives? Will you not follow me?"

"So soon!" exclaimed the young count in despair; "separate so soon, and leave this sacred asylum, where God alone is with us—this cell, which I cherish still more since you have appeared to me in it—this sanctuary of a happiness which I shall perhaps never again experience—to return to the false and cold world of prejudices and customs. Ah! not yet, my soul, my life! Suffer me to enjoy yet a day, yet an age of delight. Let me here forget that there exists a world full of deceit and sorrow, which pursues me like a dark and troubled dream; permit me to return by slow degrees to what men call reason. I do not yet feel strong enough to bear the light of their sun and the spectacle of their madness. I require to gaze upon your face and listen to your voice yet longer. Besides, I have never left my retreat from a sudden impulse, or without long reflection—my endeared yet frightful retreat, this terrific yet salutary place of expiation, whither I am accustomed to hasten as with a wild joy, without once looking back, and which I leave with doubts but two well founded, and with lasting regret. You know not, Consuelo, what powerful ties attach me to this voluntary prison—you know not that there is here a second self, the true Albert, who will not leave it—a self which I ever find when I return, and yet which besets me like a specter when I leave it. Here I have conscience, faith, light, strength—in a word, life. In the world there are fear, madness, despair—passions which sometimes invade my peaceful seclusion, and engage with me in a deadly struggle. But, behold! behind this door there is an asylum where I can subdue them and become myself again. I enter sullied with their contact; and giddy from their presence—I issue purified, and no one knows what tortures purchase this patience and submission. Force me not hence, Consuelo, but suffer me gradually and by prayer to wean my attachment from the place."

"Let us then enter and pray together," said Consuelo; "we shall set out immediately afterward. Time flies; the dawn is perhaps already near. They must remain ignorant of the path which leads to the castle, they must not see us enter together; for I am anxious not to betray the secret of your retreat, and hitherto no one suspects my discovery. I do not wish to be questioned, or to resort to falsehoods. I must be able to keep a respectful silence before your relatives, and suffer them to believe that my promises were but presentiments and dreams. Should I be seen to return with you, my absence would seem disobedience; and although, Albert, I would brave every thing for you, I would not rashly alienate the confidence and affection of your family. Let us hasten then; I am exhausted with fatigue, and if I remain here much longer I shall lose all my remaining strength, so necessary for this new journey. We shall pray, and then depart."

"Exhausted, say you? Repose here then, beloved one. I will guard you religiously, or if my presence disturb you, you shall shut me up in the adjacent grotto; close this iron door between us, and while, sunk in slumber, you forget me, I shall, until recalled by you, pray for you in *my church.*"

"But reflect that while you are praying and sunk in repose, your father suffers long hours of agony, pale and motionless as I once saw him, bowed down with age and grief, pressing with feeble knees the floor of his oratory, and apparently only awaiting the news of your death to resign his last breath. And your poor aunt's anxiety will throw her into a fever, incessantly ascending, as she does, the highest towers of the castle, vainly endeavoring to trace the paths to the mountain, by one of which it is supposed you departed. This very morning the members of your family, when they assemble together in the château, will sorrowfully accost each other with fruitless inquiries and conjectures, and again separate at night with despair and anguish in their hearts. Albert, you do not love your relatives, otherwise you would not thus, without pity or remorse, permit them to suffer and languish."

"Consuelo! Consuelo!" exclaimed Albert, as if awaking from a dream, "do not speak to me thus; your words torture me. What crime have I committed? — what disasters have I caused? Why are my friends thus afflicted? How many hours have passed since I left them?"

"You ask how many hours! Ask rather how many days—how many nights—nay, now many weeks!"

"Days! — nights! Hush! Consuelo, do not reveal to me the full extent of my misfortune. I was aware that I here lost correct ideas of time, and that the remembrance of what was passing on the earth did not descend with me into this tomb; but I did not think that the duration of this unconsciousness could be measured by days and weeks."

"Is it not, my friend, a voluntary obliviousness? Nothing in this place recalls the days which pass away and begin again; eternal darkness here prolongs the night. You have not even a glass to reckon the hours. Is not this precaution to exclude all means of measuring time, a wild expedient to escape the cries of nature and the voice of conscience?"

"I confess that when I come here, I feel it requisite to abjure every thing merely human. But, O God! I did not know that grief and meditation could so far absorb my soul as to make long hours appear like days, or days to pass away as hours. What am I, and why have they never informed me of this sad change in my mental organization?"

"This misfortune is, on the contrary, a proof of great intellectual power, but diverted from its proper use, and given up to gloomy reverie. They try to hide from you the evils of which you are the cause. They respect your sufferings while they conceal their own. But in my opinion it was treating you with little esteem; it was doubting the goodness of your heart. But, Albert, *I* do not doubt you, and *I* conceal nothing from you."

"Let us go, Consuelo, let us go," said Albert, quickly

throwing his cloak over his shoulders. "I am a wretch! I have afflicted my father whom I adore, my aunt whom I dearly love. I am unworthy to behold them again. Ah! rather than again be guilty of so much cruelty, I would impose upon myself the sacrifice of never revisiting this retreat. But, no; once more I am happy, for I have found a friend in you, Consuelo, to direct my wandering thoughts, and restore me to my former self. Some one has at length told me the truth, and will always tell it to me. Is it not so, my dear sister?"

"Always, Albert; I swear to you that you shall ever hear the truth from me."

"Power Divine! and the being who comes to my aid is she to whom alone I can listen—whom alone I can believe. The ways of God are known but to himself. Ignorant of my own mental alienation, I have always blamed the madness of others. Alas Consuelo! had my noble father himself told me of that which you have just disclosed, I would not have believed him. But you are life and truth; you can bring conviction, and give to my troubled soul that heavenly peace which emanates from yourself."

"Let us depart," said Consuelo, assisting him to fasten his cloak, which his trembling hand could not arrange upon his shoulders.

"Yes, let us go," said he, gazing tenderly upon her as she fulfilled this friendly office; "but first, swear to me, Consuelo, that if I return hither you will not abandon me, swear that you will come again to seek me, were it only to overwhelm me with reproaches—to call me ingrate, parricide—and to tell me that I am unworthy of your solicitude. Oh! leave me not a prey to myself, now that you see the influence you have over my actions, and that a word from your lips persuades and heals, where a century of meditation and prayer would fail."

"And will you, on your part," replied Consuelo, leaning on his shoulder, and smiling expressively, "swear never to return hither without me?"

"Will you indeed return with me!" he rapturously exclaimed, looking earnestly in her face, but not daring to clasp her in his arms; "only swear this to me, and I will pledge myself by a solemn oath never to leave my father's roof without your command or permission."

"May God hear and receive our mutual promise!"

ejaculated Consuelo, transported with joy. "We will come back to pray in your church; and you, Albert, will teach me to pray, as no one has taught me hitherto; for I have an ardent desire to know God. You, my friend, will reveal heaven to me, and I when requisite will recall your thoughts to terrestrial things and the duties of human life."

"Divine sister!" exclaimed Albert, his eyes swimming in tears of delight, "I have nothing to teach you. It is you who must be the agent in my regeneration. It is from you I shall learn all things, even prayer. I no longer require solitude to raise my soul to God. I no longer need to prostrate myself over the ashes of my fathers, to comprehend and feel my own immortality. To look on you is sufficient to raise my soul to heaven in gratitude and praise."

Consuelo drew him away, she herself opening and closing the doors. "Here, Cynabre!" cried Albert to his faithful hound, giving him a lantern of better construction than that with which Consuelo was furnished, and better suited to the journey they were about to undertake. The intelligent animal seized the lamp with an appearance of pride and satisfaction, and preceded them at a measured pace, stopping when his master stopped, increasing or slackening his speed as he did, and sagaciously keeping the middle of the path, in order to preserve his precious charge from injury by contact with the rocks or brushwood.

Consuelo walked with great difficulty, and would have fallen twenty times but for Albert's arm, which every moment supported and raised her up. They once more descended together the course of the stream, keeping along its fresh and verdant margin.

"Zdenko," said Albert, "delights in tending the Naiad of these mysterious grottoes. He smooths her bed when encumbered as it often is with gravel and shells: he fosters the pale flowers which spring up beneath her footsteps, and protects them against her kisses, which are sometimes rather rude."

Consuelo looked upward at the sky through the clefts of the rock, and saw a star glimmer in its blue vault. "That," said Albert, "is Aldebaran, the star of the Zingari. The day will not dawn for an hour yet."

"That is my star," replied Consuelo, "for I am, my

dear count, though not by race, by calling, a kind of
Zingara. My mother bore no other name at Venice,
though, in accordance with her Spanish prejudices, she
disclaimed the degrading appellation. As for myself, I
am still known in that country by the name of the
Zingarella."

"Are you indeed one of that persecuted race," replied
Albert; "if so, I should love you yet more than I do, were
that possible."

Consuelo, who had thought it right to recall Count
Rudolstadt to the disparity of their birth and condition,
recollected what Amelia had said of Albert's sympathy for
the wandering poor, and, fearing lest she had involuntarily
yielded to an instinctive feeling of coquetry, she kept
silence.

But Albert thus interrupted it in a few moments:

"What you have just told me," said he, "awakens in
me, I know not by what association of ideas, a recollection
of my youth, childish enough it is true, but which I must
relate to you: for since I have seen you, it has again and
again recurred to my memory. Lean more on me, dear
sister, while I repeat it.

"I was about fifteen, when, returning late one evening
by one of the paths which border on the Schreckenstein,
and which wind through the hills in the direction of the
castle, I saw before me a tall thin woman, miserably clad,
who carried a burthen on her shoulders, and who paused
occasionally to seat herself, and to recover breath. I
accosted her. She was beautiful, though embrowned by
the sun and withered by misery and care. Still there was
in her bearing, mean as was her attire, a sort of pride and
dignity, mingled, it is true, with an air of melancholy.
When she held out her hand to me, she rather commanded
pity than implored it. My purse was empty. I entreated
her to accompany me to the castle, where she could have
help, food, and shelter for the night.

"'I would prefer remaining here,' replied she, with a
foreign accent, which I conceived to be that of the
wandering Egyptians, for I was not at that time acquainted
with the various languages which I afterward learned in my
travels. 'I could pay you,' she added, 'for the hospitality
you offer, by singing songs of the different countries which
I have traversed. I rarely ask alms unless compelled to do
so by extreme distre.

" ' Poor creature !' said I, ' you bear a very heavy burden ; your feet are wounded and almost naked. Entrust your bundle to me ; I will carry it to my abode, and you will thus be able to walk with more ease.'

" ' This burden daily becomes heavier,' she replied, with a melancholy smile, which imparted a charm to her features; ' but I do not complain of it. I have borne it without repining for years, and over hundreds of leagues. I never trust it to any one besides myself; but you appear so good and so innocent, that I shall lend it to you until we reach your home.'

" She then unloosed the clasp of her mantle, which entirely covered her, the handle of her guitar alone being visible. This movement discovered to me a child of five or six years old, pale and weather-beaten like its mother, but with a countenance so sweet and calm that it filled my heart with tenderness. It was a little girl, quite in tatters, lean, but hale and strong, and who slept tranquilly as a slumbering cherub on the bruised and wearied back of the wandering songstress. I took her in my arms, but had some trouble in keeping her there; for, waking up and finding herself with a stranger, she struggled and wept. Her mother, to soothe her, spoke to her in her own language; my caresses and attentions comforted her, and on arriving at the castle we were the best friends in the world. When the poor woman had supped, she put her infant in a bed which I had prepared, attired herself in a strange dress, sadder still than her rags, and came into the hall, where she sang Spanish, French, and German ballads, with a clearness and delicacy of voice, a firmness of intonation, united to a frankness and absence of reserve in her manner, which charmed us all. My good aunt paid her every attention, which the Zingara appeared to feel ; but she did not lay aside her pride, and only gave evasive answers to our questions. The child interested me even more than its mother; and I earnestly wished to see her again, to amuse her, and even to keep her altogether. I know not what tender solicitude awoke in my bosom for this little being, poor, and a wanderer on the earth. I dreamed of her all night long, and in the morning I ran to see her. But already the Zingara had departed, and I traversed the whole mountain around without being able to discover her. She had risen before the dawn, and, with

her child, had taken the way toward the south, carrying
with her my guitar, which I had made her a present of,
her own, to her great sorrow, being broken.

"Albert! Albert?" exclaimed Consuelo, with extraordinary emotion; "that guitar is at Venice with Master
Porpora, who keeps it for me, and from whom I shall re-
claim it, never to part with it again. It is of ebony, with
a cipher chased on silver—a cipher which I well remember,
'A. R.' My mother, whose memory was defective, from
having seen so many things, neither remembered your
name nor that of your castle, nor even the country where
this adventure had happened; but she often spoke of the
hospitality she had received from the owner of the guitar,
of the touching charity of the young and handsome signor,
who had carried me in his arms for half a league, chatting
with her the while as with an equal. Oh, my dear Albert,
all that is fresh in my memory also. At each word of
your recital, these long slumbering images were awakened
one by one; and this is the reason why your mountains
did not appear absolutely unknown to me, and why I
endeavored in vain to discover the cause of these confused
recollections which forced themselves upon me during my
journey, and especially why, when I first saw you, my
heart palpitated and my head bowed down respectfully, as
if I had just found a friend and protector, long lost and
regretted.

"Do you think, then, Consuelo," said Albert, pressing
her to his heart, "that I did not recognize you at the
first glance? In vain have years changed and improved
the lineaments of childhood. I have a memory wonderfully retentive, though often confused and dreamy, which
needs not the aid of sight or speech to traverse the
space of days and of ages. I did not know that you were
my cherished Zingarella, but I felt assured I had already
known you, loved you, and pressed you to my heart—a
heart which, although unwittingly, was from that instant
bound to yours forever."

CHAPTER XLVII.

THUS conversing, they arrived at the point where the two paths divided, and where Consuelo had met Zdenko. They perceived at a distance the light of his lantern, which was placed on the ground beside him. Consuelo, having learned by experience the dangerous whims, and almost incredible strength of the idiot, involuntarily pressed close to Albert, on perceiving the indication of his approach.

" Why do you fear this mild and affectionate creature?" said the young count, surprised, yet secretly gratified at her terror. " Poor Zdenko loves you, although since yesternight a frightful dream has made him refractory and rather hostile to your generous project of coming to seek me. But he is, when I desire it, as submissive as a child, and you shall see him at your feet if I but say the word."

" Do not humiliate him before me," replied Consuelo; " do not increase the aversion which he already entertains for me. I shall by and bye inform you of the serious reasons I have to fear and avoid him for the future."

" Zdenko," replied Albert, " is surely an ethereal being, and it is difficult to conceive how he could inspire any one whatever with fear. His state of perpetual ecstasy confers on him the purity and charity of angels."

" But this state of ecstasy when it is prolonged becomes a disease. Do not deceive yourself on this point. God does not wish that man should thus abjure the feeling and consciousness of his real life, to elevate himself—often by vague conceptions—to an ideal world. Madness, the general result of these hallucinations, is a punishment for his pride and indolence."

Cynabre stopped before Zdenko, and looked at him affectionately, expecting some caresses, which his friend did not deign to bestow upon him. He sat with his head buried in his hands, in the same attitude and on the same spot as when Consuelo left him. Albert addressed him in Bohemian, but he hardly answered. He shook his head with a disconsolate air ; his cheeks were bathed in tears, and he would not even look at Consuelo. Albert raised his voice and addressed him with a determined air ; but there was more of exhortation and tenderness than of command and reproach, in the tones of his voice. Zdenko rose at last, and offered his hand to Consuelo, who clasped it, trembling.

"From henceforward," said he in German, looking at her kindly, though sadly, "you must no longer fear me; but you have done me a great injury, and I feel that your hand is full of misfortune for us."

He walked before them, exchanging a few words with Albert from time to time. They followed the spacious and solid gallery which Consuelo had not yet traversed at this extremity, and which led them to a circular vault, where they again met the water of the fountain, flowing into a vast basin, formed by the hand of man and bordered with hammered stone. It escaped thence by two currents, one of which was lost in the caverns, the other took the direction toward the cistern of the château. It was this which Zdenko had closed by replacing with his Herculean hand three enormous stones which he removed when he wished to dry the cistern to the level of the arcade, and the staircase which led to Albert's terrace.

"Let us seat ourselves here," said the count to his companion, "in order to give the water of the cistern time to drain off by a waste way——"

"Which I know but too well," said Consuelo, shuddering from head to foot.

"What do you mean?" asked Albert, looking at her with surprise.

"I will tell you by and bye," said Consuelo, "I do not wish to grieve and agitate you now by the relation of the perils which I have surmounted——"

"But what does she mean?" cried Albert, looking at Zdenko.

Zdenko replied in Bohemian with an air of indifference, while kneading with his long brown hands lumps of clay, which he placed in the interstices of his sluice, in order to hasten the draining of the cistern. "Explain yourself, Consuelo," said Albert, much agitated. "I can comprehend nothing of what he says. He pretends that he did not conduct you to this place, but that you came by subterranean passages which I know to be impassable, and where a delicate female could never have dared to venture, nor have been able to find her way. He says (Great God! what does the unfortunate not say?) that it was destiny which conducted you, and that the archangel Michael, whom he calls the proud and domineering, caused you to pass safely through the water and the abyss."

"It is possible," said Consuelo, with a smile, "that the archangel Michael had something to do with it; for it is certain that I came by the waste-way of the fountain, that I fled before the torrent, that I gave myself up for lost two or three times, that I traversed caverns and abysses where I expected at every step to be swallowed up or suffocated; and yet these dangers were not more fearful than Zdenko's anger, when chance or Providence caused me to find the true route." Here Consuelo, who always expressed herself in Spanish with Albert, related to him in a few words the reception which his pacific Zdenko had given her, and his attempt to bury her alive which he had almost succeeded in accomplishing at the moment when she had the presence of mind to appease him by the singular watchword of the heretics. A cold perspiration burst out upon Albert's forehead on hearing these incredible details, and he often darted terrible glances at Zdenko, as if he would have annihilated him. Zdenko, on meeting them, assumed a strange expression of revolt and disdain. Consuelo trembled to see these two insane persons excited against each other; for notwithstanding the profound wisdom and lofty sentiments which characterized the greater part of Albert's conversation, it was evident to her that his reason had sustained a severe shock, from which perhaps it would never entirely recover. She tried to reconcile them by addressing affectionate words to each. But Albert, rising and giving the keys of his hermitage to Zdenko, said a few cold words to him, to which Zdenko submitted on the instant. He then resumed his lantern and went his way, singing his strange airs with their incomprehensible words.

"Consuelo," said Albert, as soon as he had retired out of sight, "if this faithful animal which lies at your feet should become mad — yes, if my poor Cynabre should endanger your life by an involuntary fury, I should certainly be obliged to kill him; and do not think that I would hesitate, though my hand has never shed blood, even that of beings inferior to man. Be tranquil, therefore, no danger will menace you hereafter."

"Of what are you speaking, Albert?" replied the young girl, agitated at this unlooked-for allusion. "I fear nothing now. Zdenko is still a man, though he has lost his reason by his own fault perhaps, and partly also by yours. Speak not of blood and punishment. It is your duty to restore him to the truth, and to cure him, instead of encouraging his insanity. Come, let us go; I tremble lest the day should dawn, and surprise us on our arrival."

" You are right," said Albert, continuing his route. " Wisdom speaks by your lips, Consuelo. My insanity has smitten that unfortunate as if by contagion, and it was quite time for you to arrive, and save us from the abyss to which we were both hastening. Restored by you, I will endeavor to restore Zdenko. And yet if I do not succeed, if his insanity again puts your life in danger, although Zdenko be a man in the sight of God, and an angel in his tenderness for me—though he be the only true friend I have hitherto had upon the earth—be assured, Consuelo, I will tear him from my heart, and you shall never see him again."

" Enough, enough, Albert?" murmured Consuelo, incapable after so many terrors of supporting a fresh one; " do not let such ideas dwell upon your mind. I would rather lose my life a hundred times, than inflict upon yours such a fearful necessity and such a cause for despair."

Albert did not heed her, and seemed absent. He forgot to support her, and did not perceive that she faltered and stumbled at every step. He was absorbed by the idea of the dangers she had incurred for his sake; and in his terror at picturing them to himself, in his ardent solicitude and excited gratitude, he walked rapidly, making the gallery resound with his hurried exclamations, and leaving her to drag herself after him with efforts which became every moment more painful. In this cruel situation, Consuelo thought of Zdenko who was behind her, and who might follow them; of the torrent which he always held, as it were, in his hand, and which he could again unchain at the moment when she was ascending the well alone, deprived of Albert's assistance; for the latter, a prey to a new fancy, thought he saw her before him, and followed a deceitful phantom, while he abandoned her to darkness. This was too much for a woman, and even for Consuelo herself. Cynabre trotted on as fast as his master, and bounded before him carrying the lantern. Consuelo had left hers in the cell. The road made numerous turns behind which the light disappeared every instant. Consuelo struck against one of those angles, fell, and could not rise again. The chill of death ran through all her limbs. A last apprehension presented itself to her mind. Zdenko had probably received orders to open the sluice-gate after a certain time, in order to conceal the staircase and the issue of the cistern, so that even if hatred did not inspire him, he would obey this necessary precaution from habit. "It is accomplished then," thought Consuelo, making vain attempts to drag herself forward on her knees. "I am the victim of a pitiless destiny. I shall never escape from this cavern—my eyes will never again behold the light of day."

Already a thicker veil than that of the outward darkness spread itself over her sight; her hands became numb, and an apathy, which resembled the sleep of death, suspended her terror. Suddenly she felt herself caught and raised by a powerful arm, which drew her toward the cistern. A burning bosom beats against hers, and warms it; a friendly and caressing voice addresses her with tender words; Cynabre bounds before her, shaking the light. It is Albert, who, restored to himself, seizes and saves her, with the passionate tenderness of a mother who has lost and found her child. In three minutes they arrived at the canal which the water of the fountain had left dry, and reached the archway and the staircase. Cynabre, accustomed to this dangerous ascent, leaped forward first, as if he feared to encumber his master's steps by remaining too near him.

Albert, carrying Consuelo on one arm, and clinging with the other to the chain, ascended the spiral staircase, at the foot of which the water already began to mount also. This was not the least of the dangers which Consuelo had encountered: but she felt no fear. Albert was endowed with a herculean strength, in comparison with which Zdenko's was as a child's, and at this moment he was animated with supernatural power. When he had deposited his precious burden upon the margin of the well in the light of the breaking dawn, Consuelo, at last breathing freely, and rising from his panting breast, wiped with her veil his broad forehead bathed in perspiration. "My friend," said she, tenderly, "without you I should have died, and you have repaid all that I have done for you; but I now feel your fatigue more than you do yourself, and it seems to me that in your place I should sink under it."

"O my little Zingarella!" said Albert to her with enthusiasm, kissing the veil which she rested upon his face, "you are as light in my arms as on the day when I descended from the Schreckenstein to carry you to the château."

"Which you will not again leave without my permission, Albert; do not forget your oath."

"Nor you yours," replied he, kneeling before her. He then assisted her to wrap herself in the veil, and to cross his chamber, from which she escaped stealthily to regain her own. The family began to awake in the castle. Already from the lower story a dry and piercing cough, the signal of her rising, was heard from the canoness. Consuelo was fortunate enough not to be seen or heard by any one. Fear gave her wings to regain the shelter of her apartment. With a trembling hand she freed herself from her soiled and torn clothes, and hid them in a trunk, from which she removed the key. She retained sufficient strength and recollection to conceal every trace of her mysterious journey, but hardly had she let her wearied head fall upon the pillow, when a heavy yet troubled sleep, full of fanciful dreams and horrible adventures, chained it there, under the weight of an overpowering and raging fever.

CHAPTER XLVIII.

IN the meantime the Canoness Wenceslawa, after spending half an hour at her devotions, ascended the staircase, and according to her custom devoted the first care of the day to her dear nephew. She approached the door of his chamber, and bent her ear to the keyhole, though with less hope than ever of hearing the slight noise which would announce his return. What was her surprise and her joy on distinguishing the regular sound of his breathing during sleep? She made a great sign of the cross, and ventured to unlatch the door and enter gently on tiptoe. She saw Albert peacefully slumbering in his bed, and Cynabre curled up on a neighboring arm-chair. She did not wake either of them, but ran to find Count Christian, who, prostrate in his oratory, prayed with his accustomed resignation that his son might be restored to him, either in heaven or upon earth.

"My brother," said she to him in a low voice, and kneeling beside him, "cease your prayers, and search your heart for the most fervent thanksgiving. God has heard you."

There was no need that she should explain herself further. The old man, turning toward her, and meeting her little sparkling eyes, animated with a profound and sympathetic joy, raised his shriveled hands toward the altar, and cried with a smothered voice: "O my God, Thou hast restored to me my son!"

Then both simultaneously began to recite in a low voice alternate verses of the beautiful song of Simeon—"*Now lettest thou thy servant depart in peace.*"

They resolved not to awaken Albert. They summoned the baron, the chaplain, and all the servants, and devoutly heard mass, and returned thanksgiving in the chapel of the château. Amelia learned the return of her cousin with sincere joy; but she considered it very unjust that in order to celebrate this event piously she should be obliged to undergo a mass during which she had to stifle many yawns.

"Why has not your friend, the good Porporina, joined with us in thanking Providence?" said Count Christian to his niece, when the mass was ended.

"I have tried in vain to awaken her," replied Amelia. "I called her, shook her, and used every means; but I could not succeed in making her understand, or even open her eyes. If she were not burning hot, and red as fire, I should think her dead. She must have slept very badly last night, and she certainly has a fever."

"Then the sweet girl is ill!" returned the old count. "My dear Wenceslawa, you should go and administer such remedies as her condition may require. God forbid that so happy a day should be saddened by the suffering of that noble girl!"

"I will go, my brother," replied the canoness, who no longer said a word nor took a step respecting Consuelo without consulting the chaplain's looks. "But do not be uneasy, Christian; it will be of no consequence. The Signora Nina is very nervous; she will soon be well."

"Still, is it not a very singular thing," said she to the chaplain an instant after, when she could take him aside, "that this girl should have predicted Albert's return with so much confidence and accuracy? Dear chaplain, possibly we have been mistaken respecting her. Perhaps she is a kind of saint who has revelations."

"A saint would have come to hear mass, instead of having the fever at such a moment," objected the chaplain with a profound air.

This judicious remark drew a sigh from the canoness. She nevertheless went to see Consuelo, and found her in a burning fever, accompanied by an unconquerable lethargy. The chaplain was called, and declared that she would be very ill if the fever continued. He questioned the young baroness as to whether her neighbor had not passed a very disturbed night.

"On the contrary," replied Amelia, "I did not hear her move. I expected from her predictions and the fine stories she has been telling for some days past, to have heard the *sabbat* danced in her apartment. But the devil must have carried her a great ways off, or she must have had to deal with very well-educated imps, for she did not move, so far as I know, and my sleep was not disturbed a single instant."

These pleasantries appeared to the chaplain to be in very bad taste; and the canoness, whose heart made amends for the failings of her mind, considered them misplaced at the bedside of a friend who was seriously ill. Still she said nothing, attributing her niece's bitterness to a too well-founded jealousy, and asked the chaplain what medicines ought to be administered to the Porporina.

He ordered a sedative, which they could not make her swallow. Her teeth were locked, and her livid lips rejected all liquid. The chaplain pronounced this to be a bad sign. But with an apathy which was unfortunately too contagious in that house, he deferred until a second examination the judgment he should have pronounced upon the patient. "We will see; we must wait; we can decide on nothing as yet;" such were the favorite sentences of the tonsured Esculapius. "If this continues," repeated he, on quitting Consuelo's chamber, "we must consider about the propriety of calling in a physician, for I would not take upon myself the responsiblity of treating an extraordinary case of nervous affection. I will pray for this young lady, and perhaps in the state of mind which she has manifested during these last few days, we must expect from God alone assistance more efficacious than that of art."

They left a maid-servant by the bedside of Consuelo, and went to prepare for breakfast. The canoness herself kneaded the sweetest cake that had ever been produced by her skillful hands. She flattered herself that Albert, after his long fast, would eat this favorite dish with pleasure. The lovely Amelia made a toilet charming in its freshness, hoping that her cousin might feel some regret at having offended and irritated her, when he saw her so bewitching. Every one thought of preparing some agreeable surprise for the young count, and they forgot the only one who ought to have interested them—the poor Consuelo—to whom they were indebted for his return, and whom Albert would be impatient to see again.

Albert soon awoke, and instead of making useless attempts to recall the occurrences of the preceding night, as was always the case after those fits of insanity which drove him to his subterranean abode, he promptly recovered the recollection of his love, and of the happiness which Consuelo had bestowed upon him. He rose quickly, dressed and perfumed himself, and ran to throw himself into the arms of his father and his aunt. The joy of those good relatives was at its height when they saw that Albert had full possession of his reason, that he had a consciousness of his long absence, and that he asked their forgiveness with an ardent tenderness, promising never again to cause them so much trouble and uneasiness. He saw the transports excited by his return to the knowledge of the reality; but he remarked the care they persisted in taking to conceal his situation from him, and he was somewhat humbled at being treated like a child, when he felt that he had again become a man. He submitted, however, to this punishment—too trifling in proportion to the evil he had caused—saying to himself that it was a salutary warning, and that Consuelo would be pleased at his comprehending and accepting it.

As soon as he was seated at table, in the midst of the caresses, the tears of happiness, and the earnest attentiou of his family, he anxiously looked around for her who had now become necessary to his life and his peace. He saw her place empty, and dared not ask why the Porporina did not appear. Still the canoness, who saw him turn his head and start every time the door opened, thought herself obliged to relieve him from all anxiety by saying that their young guest had slept badly, that she was now quiet, and expected to keep her bed a part of the day.

Albert knew very well that his liberator must be overpowered by fatigue, and yet terror was depicted on his countenance at this news. "My dear aunt," said he, no longer able to restrain his emotion. "I think that if the adopted daughter of Porpora were seriously indisposed, we should not all be here at table, quietly engaged in eating and talking."

"Comfort yourself, Albert," said Amelia, reddening with vexation, "Nina is busy dreaming of you, and predicting your return, which she awaits, sleeping, while we here celebrate it in joy."

Albert turned pale with indignation, and darting a withering glance at his cousin, "If any one here has slept during my absence," said he, "it is not the person whom you name, who should be reproached with it; the freshness of your cheeks, my fair cousin, testifies that you have not lost an hour of sleep during my absence, and that you have at this moment no need of repose. I thank you with all my heart, for it would be very painful for me to ask your forgiveness, as I do that of all the other members and friends of my family."

"Many thanks for the exception," returned Amelia, crimson with anger; "I will endeavor always to deserve it, by keeping my watchings and anxieties for some one who will feel obliged for them, and not turn them into a jest."

This little altercation, which was by no means a new thing between Albert and his betrothed, but which had never been so bitter on either one side or the other, threw an air of gloom and restraint over the rest of the morning, notwithstanding all the efforts which were made to divert Albert's attention.

The canoness went to see her patient several times, and found her each time more feverish and more oppressed. Amelia, whom Albert's anxiety wounded as if it had been a personal affair, went to weep in her chamber. The chaplain ventured so far as to say to the canoness that a physician must be sent for in the evening, if the fever did not abate. Count Christian kept his son near him, to distract his thoughts from an anxiety which he did not comprehend, and which he believed still to be the result of disease. But while chaining him to his side by affectionate words, the good old man could not find the least subject for conversation and intimacy with that spirit which he had never wished to sound, from the fear of being conquered and subdued by an intellect superior to his own in matters of religion. It is true that Count Christian called by the names of madness and rebellion, that bright light which pierced through the eccentricities of Albert, and the splendor of which the feeble eyes of a rigid Catholic could not endure ; but he resisted the feeling which impelled him to question him seriously. Every time he had tried to correct his heresies, he had been reduced to silence by arguments full of justice and firmness. Nature had not made him eloquent. He had not that ease and animation which maintains a controversy, and still less that charlatanism of discussion which, in default of logic, imposes by an air of science and pretended certainty. Simple and modest, he allowed his lips to be closed ; he reproached himself with not having turned his younger days to better account, by studying those profound arguments which Albert opposed to him; and certain that there were, in theological science, treasures of truth by means of which one more learned and skillful than himself could have crushed Albert's heresy, he clung to his shaken faith, and in order to excuse himself from acting more energetically, took refuge in his ignorance and simplicity, and thereby emboldened the rebel, and did him more harm than good.

Their conversation, interrupted twenty times by a kind of mutual fear, and twenty times resumed with effort on both sides, at last failed of itself. Old Christian fell asleep in his arm-chair, and Albert left him to go and obtain information respecting Consuelo's condition, which alarmed him the more, the more they tried to conceal it from him.

He spent more than two hours wandering about the corridors of the château, watching for the canoness and the chaplain on their passage to and fro to ask them for news. The chaplain persisted in answering him concisely and briefly; the canoness put on a smiling face as soon as she perceived him, and affected to speak of other things, in order to deceive him by an appearance of security. But Albert saw that she began to be seriously alarmed, and that she continually made more and more frequent visits to Consuelo's chamber, and he remarked that they did not fear to open and close the doors every moment, as if that sleep, which they pretended was quiet and necessary, could not be disturbed by noise and agitation. He ventured so far as to approach that chamber into which he would have given his life to penetrate for a single instant. The entrance was through another room, which was separated from the corridor by two thick doors through which neither sight nor sound could penetrate. The canoness, remarking this attempt, shut and locked both, and no longer visited the patient except by passing through Amelia's chamber, which was adjoining, and where Albert would not have sought information without extreme repugnance. At last, seeing him exasperated, and fearing the return of his disease, she ventured on a falsehood; and while asking forgiveness of God in her heart, she announced to him that the invalid was much better, and that she promised to come down and dine with the family.

Albert did not mistrust his aunt's words, whose pure lips had never sinned against truth so openly as they had just done; and he rejoined the old count, praying with fervor for the hour which was to restore to him Consuelo and happiness.

But the hour struck in vain. Consuelo did not appear. The canoness, making a rapid progress in the art of lying, told him that she had risen, but that she found herself still somewhat weak, and preferred dining in her apartment. She even pretended to send up choice portions of the most delicate dishes. These artifices triumphed over Albert's terror. Although he experienced an overpowering sadness, and as it were a presentiment of some misfortune, he submitted, and made great efforts to appear calm.

In the evening, Wenceslawa came with an air of satisfaction which was hardly at all assumed to say that the Porporina was better; that her skin was no longer burning; that her pulse was rather weak than full, and that she would certainly pass an excellent night. "Why then am I frozen with terror, notwithstanding these good tidings?"

thought the young count, as he took leave of his relatives
at the accustomed hour.

The fact was that the good canoness, who, notwithstanding her emaciation and deformity, had never been ill in
her life, understood nothing of the maladies of others.
She saw Consuelo pass from a fiery redness to a livid paleness, her feverish blood congeal in her arteries, and her
chest, too much oppressed to be raised under the effort of
respiration, appear calm and motionless. For an instant
she thought her relieved, and had announced this news
with a childlike confidence. But the chaplain, who was
rather better informed, saw plainly that this apparent
repose was the forerunner of a violent crisis. As soon as
Albert had retired, he gave the canoness notice that the
hour had come to send for a physician. Unfortunately
the city was far distant, the night dark, the roads detestable, and Hans very slow, notwithstanding his zeal. The
storm rose, the rain fell in torrents. The old horse which
carried the aged servant stumbled twenty times, and
finished by losing himself in the woods with his terrified
rider, who took every hill for the Schreckenstein, and
every flash of lightning for the flaming flight of an evil
spirit. It was not till broad daylight that Hans again
found the road. With the speediest trot into which he
could urge his steed, he approached the town, where he
found the physician sound asleep; the latter was awakened,
dressed himself slowly, and at last set out. Four and
twenty hours had been lost in deciding upon and effecting
this step.

Albert tried in vain to sleep. A burning anxiety and
the fearful noises of the storm kept him awake all night.
He dare not come down, fearing again to scandalize his
aunt, who had lectured him in the morning on the impro-
priety of his continual presence near the apartment of the
two young ladies. He left his door open, and heard frequent steps in the lower story. He ran to the staircase;
but seeing no one, and hearing nothing more, he tried to
take courage and to place to the account of the wind and
the rain, the deceitful noises which had terrified him.
Since Consuelo had requested it, he nursed his reason and
his moral health with patience and firmness. He repelled
his agitations and fears, and strove to raise himself above
his love by the strength of that love itself. But suddenly,

in the midst of the rattling of the thunder and the creaking of the old timbers of the château, which groaned
under the force of the hurricane, a long, heart-rending
cry ascended even to him, and pierced his bosom like
the stroke of a poniard. Albert, who had thrown
himself all dressed upon his bed with the resolution of
going to sleep, bounds up, rushes forward, clears the staircase with the speed of lightning, and knocks at Consuelo's
door. Silence once more reigned. No one came to open
it. Albert thought he had dreamed again ; but a second
cry, more dreadful, more piercing than the first, rent his
heart. He hesitates no longer, rushes down a dark corridor, reaches the door of Amelia's chamber, shakes it and
announces himself by name. He hears a bolt shot, and
Amelia's voice imperiously orders him to begone. Still
the cries and shrieks redouble. It is the voice of Consuelo,
who is suffering intolerable agony. He hears his own
name breathed with despair by those adored lips. He
pushes the door with rage, makes latch and lock fly, and
thrusting aside Amelia, who plays the part of outraged
modesty on being surprised in a damask dressing-gown and
lace cap, pushes her back upon her sofa, and rushes into
Consuelo's apartment, pale as a specter, his hair erect with
terror!

CHAPTER XLIX.

CONSUELO, a prey to violent delirium, was struggling in
the arms of two of the most vigorous maid-servants of the
house, who could hardly prevent her from throwing herself out of bed. Haunted, as happens in certain cases of
brain fever, by phantoms, the unhappy girl endeavored to
fly from the visions by which she was assailed, and imagined she saw, in the persons who endeavored to restrain
and relieve her, savage enemies or monsters bent upon her
destruction. The terrified chaplain, who every moment
feared to see her sink under her sufferings, was already repeating by her side the prayers for the departing, but she
took him for Zdenko chanting his mysterious psalms,
while he built up the wall which was to inclose her. The
trembling canoness, who joined her feeble efforts with
those of the other women to hold her in bed, seemed to

her the phantom of the two Wandas, the sister of Ziska and the mother of Albert, appearing by turns in the grotto of the recluse and reproaching her with usurping their rights and invading their domain. Her delirious exclamations, her shrieks, and her prayers, incomprehensible to those about her, had all a direct relation to the thoughts and objects which had so violently agitated and affected her the night before. She heard the roaring of the torrent, and imitated with her arms the motion of swimming. She shook her dark, disheveled tresses over her shoulders, and imagined she saw floods of foam falling about her. She continually saw Zdenko behind her, engaged in opening the sluice, or before her, making frantic efforts to close the path. She talked of nothing but water and rocks, with a continued throng of images which caused the chaplain to shake his head and say: "What a long and painful dream! I cannot conceive why her mind should have been so much occupied of late with that cistern; it was doubtless a commencement of fever, and you see that in her delirium she always recurs to it.

Just as Albert entered her room, aghast, Consuelo, exhausted by fatigue, was uttering only inarticulate sounds terminating at intervals in wild shrieks. The frightful adventures she had undergone, being no longer restrained by the power of her will, recurred to her mind with frightful intensity. In her delirium she called on Albert with a voice so full and so vibrating that it seemed to shake the whole house to its foundations; then her cries died away in long-drawn sobs which seemed to suffocate her, although her haggard eyes were dry and absolutely blazing with fever.

"I am here! I am here!" cried Albert, rushing toward the bed. Consuelo heard him, recovered all her energy, and imagining that he fled before her, disengaged herself from the hands that held her, with that rapidity of movement and muscular force which the delirium of fever gives to the weakest beings. She bounded into the middle of the room, her hair disheveled, her feet bare, her form wrapped in a thin white night-dress, which gave her the appearance of a specter escaped from the tomb; and just as they thought to seize her again, she leaped with the agility of a wild-cat upon the spinet which was before her, reached the window, which she took for the opening of the fatal cistern, placed one foot upon it, extended her arms, and again calling on the name of Albert, in accents which floated out on the dark and stormy night, was about to dash herself down, when Albert, even more strong and agile than she, encircled her in his arms, and carried her back to her bed. She did not recognize him, but she made no resistance, and ceased to utter his name. Albert lavished upon her in Spanish the tenderest names and the most fervent prayers. She heard him with her eyes fixed, and without seeing or answering him; but suddenly rising and throwing herself on her knees in the bed, she began to sing a stanza of Handel's *Te Deum*, which she had recently read and admired. Never had her voice possessed more expression and brilliancy; never had she been more beautiful than in that ecstatic attitude, her hair flowing, her cheeks lighted up with the fire of fever, and her eyes seeming to pierce the heavens opened for them alone. The canoness was so much moved that she knelt at the foot of the bed and burst into tears; and the chaplain, notwithstanding his want of sympathy, bent his head and felt penetrated with a sentiment of pious respect. Hardly had Consuelo finished the stanza, when she uttered a deep sigh, and a holy rapture shone in her countenance. "I am saved!" cried she, and she fell backward, pale and cold as marble, her eyes still open, but fixed and motionless, her lips blue and her arms rigid. A momentary silence and stupor succeeded to this scene. Amelia, who, erect and motionless at the door of her chamber, had witnessed the frightful spectacle without daring to move a step, fainted away with terror. The canoness and the two women ran to help her. Consuelo remained pale and motionless, resting upon Albert's arm, who had let his head fall upon the bosom of the dying girl, and appeared scarcely more alive than herself. The canoness had no sooner seen Amelia laid upon her bed, than she returned to the threshold of Consuelo's chamber. "Well, Mr. Chaplain?" said she, dejectedly.

"Madam, it is death!" replied the chaplain, in a hollow voice, letting fall Consuelo's arm, the pulse of which he had been examining attentively.

"No, it is not death! no! a thousand times no!" cried Albert, raising himself impetuously. "I have consulted her heart better than you have consulted her arm. It still

beats; she breathes—she lives. Oh! she will live! It is
not thus, it is not now, that her life is to end. Who is
bold and rash enough to believe that God had decreed her
death? Now is the time to apply the necessary remedies.
Chaplain, give me your box of medicines. I know what is
required, and you do not. Wretch that you are, obey me!
You have not assisted her; you might have prevented this
horrible crisis, you did not do it; you have concealed her
illness from me; you have all deceived me. Did you wish
to destroy her? Your cowardly prudence, your hideous
apathy, have tied your tongue and your hands! Give me
your box, I say, and let me act."

And as the chaplain hesitated to trust him with medicines, which in the hand of an excited and half frantic
man might become poisons, he wrested it from him
violently. Deaf to the observations of his aunt, he
selected and himself poured out doses of the most powerful and active medicines. Albert was more learned on
many subjects than they supposed, and had practiced upon
himself, at a period of his life when he had studied carefully the frequent disorders which affected his brain, and
he knew the effects of the most energetic stimulants.
Actuated by a prompt judgment, inspired by a courageous
and resolute zeal, he administered a dose which the chaplain would never have dared to recommend. He succeeded,
with incredible patience and gentleness, in unclosing the
teeth of the sufferer, and making her swallow some drops
of this powerful remedy. At the end of an hour, during
which he several times repeated the dose, Consuelo
breathed freely; her hands had recovered their warmth,
and her features their elasticity. She neither heard nor
felt any thing yet ; but her prostration seemed gradually
to partake more of the nature of sleep, and a slight color
returned to her lips. The physician arrived, and seeing
that the case was a serious one, declared that he had been
called very late, and that he would not be answerable for
the result. The patient ought to have been bled the day
before ; now the crisis was no longer favorable. Bleeding
would certainly bring back the paroxysm. That was
embarrassing.

"It will bring it back," said Albert; "and yet she
must be bled."

The German physician, a heavy, self-conceited personage,

accustomed, in his country practice, where he had no competitor, to be listened to as an oracle, scowlingly raised his heavy eyes toward the person who thus presumed to cut the question short.

"I tell you she must be bled," resumed Albert, firm, "With or without bleeding the crisis will return."

"Excuse me;" said Doctor Wetzelius; "that is not so certain as you seem to think." And he smiled in a disdainful and sarcastic manner.

"If the crisis do not return, all is lost," repeated Albert; "and you ought to know it. This stupor leads directly to suffusion of the brain, to paralysis and death. Your duty is to arrest the malady, to restore its intensity in order to combat it, and in the end to overcome it. If it be not so, why have you come here? Prayers and burials do not belong to you. Bleed her, or I will."

The doctor well knew that Albert reasoned justly, and he had from the first the intention of bleeding; but it was not expedient for a man of his importance to determine and execute so speedily. That would have led people to conclude that the case was a simple one and the treatment easy, and our German was therefore accustomed, on the pretense of serious difficulties and varying symptoms, to prolong his diagnosis, in order to secure in the end for his professional skill a fresh triumph as if by a sudden flash of genius, and to hear himself thus flattered, as he had been a thousand times before: "The malady was so far advanced, so dangerous, that Doctor Wetzelius himself did not know what to determine; no other than he would have seized the moment and divined the remedy. He is very prudent, very learned, very firm. He has not his equal, even in Vienna."

"If you are a physician, and have authority here," said he, when he saw himself contradicted and put to the wall by Albert's impatience, "I do not see why I should have been called in, and I shall therefore leave the room."

"If you do not wish to decide at the proper time, you may retire," said Albert.

Doctor Wetzelius, deeply wounded at having been associated with one of the fraternity who treated him with so little deference, rose and passed into Amelia's room to attend to the nerves of that young lady, who impatiently called him, and to take leave of the canoness; but the latter prevented his sudden retreat.

" Alas, my dear doctor," said she, " you cannot abandon us in such a situation. See what heavy responsibility weighs on us. My nephew has offended you, but you should not resent so seriously the hastiness of a young man who is so little master of himself."

" Was that Count Albert ?" asked the doctor, amazed. " I should never have recognized him. He is so much altered!"

" Without doubt, the ten years which have elapsed since you saw him have made a great change in him."

" I thought him completely cured," said the doctor, maliciously; " for I have not been sent for once since his return."

" Ah! my dear doctor, you are aware that Albert never willingly submitted to the decisions of science."

" And now he appears to be a physician himself!"

" He has a slight knowledge of all sciences, but carries into all his uncontrollable impatience. The frightful state is which he has just seen this young girl has agitated him terribly, otherwise you would have seen him more polite, more calm, and grateful to you for the care you bestowed on him in his infancy."

" I think he requires care more than ever," replied the doctor, who, in spite of his respect for the Rudolstadt family, preferred afflicting the canoness by this harsh observation, to stooping from his professional position, and giving up the petty revenge of treating Albert as a madman.

The canoness suffered the more from this cruelty, that the exasperation of the doctor might lead him to reveal the condition of her nephew, which she took such pains to conceal. She therefore laid aside her dignity for the moment to disarm his resentment, and deferentially inquired what he thought of the bleeding so much insisted on by Albert.

" I think it is absurd at present," said the doctor, who wished to maintain the initiative, and allow the decision to come perfectly free from his respected lips. " I shall wait an hour or two ; and if the right moment should arrive sooner than I expect, I shall act; but in the present crisis, the state of the pulse does not warrant me taking any decisive step."

" Then you will remain with us? Bless you, excellent doctor!"

"When I am now aware that my opponent is the young count," replied the doctor, smiling with a patronizing and compassionate air, "I shall not be astonished at any thing, and shall allow him to talk as he pleases."

And he was turning to re-enter Consuelo's apartment, the door of which the chaplain had closed to prevent Albert hearing this colloquy, when the chaplain himself, pale and bewildered, left the sick girl's couch, and came to seek the physician.

"In the name of Heaven! doctor," he exclaimed, "come and use your authority, for mine is despised, as the voice of God himself would be I believe, by Count Albert. He persists in bleeding the dying girl, contrary to your express prohibition. I know not by what force or stratagem we shall prevent him. He will maim her, if he do not kill her on the spot, by some untimely blunder."

"So, so," muttered the doctor, in a sulky tone, as he stalked leisurely toward the door, with the conceited and insulting air of a man devoid of natural feeling, "we shall see fine doings if I fail in diverting his attention in some way."

But when they approached the bed, they found Albert with his reddened lancet between his teeth; with one hand he supported Consuelo's arm, while with the other he held the basin. The vein was open, and dark-colored blood flowed in an abundant stream.

The chaplain began to murmur, to exclaim, and to take Heaven to witness. The doctor endeavored to jest a little to distract Albert's thoughts, conceiving he might take his own time to close the vein, were it only to open it a moment after, that his caprice and vanity might thus enjoy all the credit of success. But Albert kept them all at a distance by a mere glance; and as soon as he had drawn a sufficient quantity of blood, he applied the necessary bandages, with the dexterity of an experienced operator. He then gently replaced Consuelo's arm by her side, handing the canoness a vial to hold to her nostrils, and called the chaplain and the doctor into Amelia's chamber.

"Gentlemen," said he, "you can now be of no further use. Indecision and prejudice united paralyze your zeal and your knowledge. I here declare that I take all the responsibility on myself, and that I will not be either opposed or molested in so serious a task. I beg therefore that the chaplain may recite his prayers and the doctor administer his potions to my cousin. I shall suffer no prognostics, nor sentences of death around the bed of one who will soon regain her consciousness. Let this be settled. If in this instance I offend a learned man — if I am guilty of culpable conduct toward a friend — I shall ask pardon when I can once more think of myself."

After having thus spoken in a tone, the serious and studied politeness of which was in strong contrast with the coldness and formality of his words, Albert re-entered Consuelo's apartment, closed the door, put the key in his pocket, and said to the canoness : " No one shall either enter or leave this room without my permission."

CHAPTER L.

THE terrified canoness dared not venture a word in reply. There was something so resolute in Albert's air and demeanor that his good aunt quailed before it, and obeyed him with an alacrity quite surprising in her. The physician finding his authority despised, and not caring, as he afterward affirmed, to encounter a madman, wisely determined to withdraw. The chaplain betook himself to his prayers, and Albert, assisted by his aunt and two of the domestics, remained the whole day with his patient, without relaxing his attentions for an instant. After some hours of quiet, the paroxysm returned with an intensity almost greater than that of the preceding night. It was, however, of shorter duration, and when it yielded to the effect of powerful remedies, Albert desired the canoness to retire to rest, and to send him another female domestic to assist him while the two others took some repose.

" Will you not also take some rest?" asked Wenceslawa, trembling.

" No, my dear aunt," he replied, " I require none."

" Alas! my child," said she, " you will kill yourself, then," and she added as she left the room, emboldened by the abstraction of the count, " This stranger costs us dear."

He consented however to take some food, in order to keep up his strength. He eat standing in the corridor, his eye fixed upon the door, and as soon as he had finished his hasty repast, he threw down the napkin, and reentered the room. He had closed the communication between the chamber of Consuelo and that of Amelia, and only allowed the attendants to gain access by the gallery. Amelia wished to be admitted to tend her suffering companion; but she went so awkwardly about it, and, dreading the return of convulsions, displayed such terror at every feverish movement, that Albert became irritated, and begged her not to trouble herself further but retire to her own apartment.

"To my apartment!" exclaimed Amelia; "impossible! do you imagine I could sleep with these frightful cries of agony ringing in my ears?"

Albert shrugged his shoulders, and replied that there were many other apartments in the castle, of which she might select the best, until the invalid could be removed to one where her proximity should annoy no one.

Amelia, irritated and displeased, followed the advice. To witness the delicate care which Albert displayed toward her rival was more painful than all. "O, aunt!" she exclaimed, throwing herself into the arms of the canoness, when the latter had brought her to sleep in her own bedroom, where she had a bed prepared for her beside her own, "we did not know Albert. He now shows how he can love."

For many days Consuelo hovered between life and death; but Albert combated her malady with such perseverance and skill as finally to conquer it. He bore her through this rude trial in safety; and as soon as she was out of danger, he caused her to be removed to an apartment in a turret of the castle, where the sun shone for the longest time, and where the view was more extensive and varied than from any of the other windows. The chamber, furnished after an antique fashion, was more in unison with the serious tastes of Consuelo than the one they had first prepared for her, and she had long evinced a desire to occupy it. Here she was free from the importunities of her companion, and in spite of the continual presence of a nurse, who was engaged each morning and evening, she could enjoy the hours of convalescence agreeably with her preserver. They always conversed in Spanish, and the tender and delicate manifestation of Albert's love was so

much the sweeter to Consuelo in that language, which recalled her country, her childhood, and her mother. Im-
buéd with the liveliest gratitude, weakened by sufferings in
which Albert alone had effectively aided and consoled her,
she submitted to that gentle lassitude which is the result
of severe indisposition. Her recollections of the past returned by degrees, but not with equal distinctness. For
example, if she recalled with undisguised satisfaction the
support and devotion of Albert, during the principal events
of their acquaintance, she saw his mental estrangement,
and his somewhat gloomy passion, as through a thick cloud.
There were even hours, during the half consciousness of
sleep, or after composing draughts, when she imagined
that she had dreamed many of the things that could give
cause for distrust or fear of her generous friend. She was
so much accustomed to his presence and his attentions,
that if he absented himself at prayer or at meals, she felt
nervous and agitated until his return. She fancied that
her medicines, when prepared and administered by any
other hand than his, had an effect the contrary of that which
was intended. She would then observe with a tranquil
smile, so affecting on a lovely countenance half-veiled by
the shadow of death; "I now believe, Albert, that you are
an enchanter; for if you order but a single drop of water,
it produces in me the same salutary calmness and strength
which exist in yourself."

Albert was happy for the first time in his life; and as if
his soul was strong in joy as it had been in grief, he deemed
himself, at this period of intoxicating delight, the most
fortunate man on earth. This chamber where he constantly saw his beloved one had become his world. At
night, after he was supposed to have retired, and every one
was thought asleep in the house, he returned with stealthy
steps ; and while the nurse in charge slept soundly, he
glided behind the bed of his dear Consuelo, and watched
her sleeping, pale and drooping like a flower after the
storm. He settled himself in a large arm-chair, which he
took care to leave there when he went away, and thus
passed the night, sleeping so lightly that at the least movement of Consuelo, he awoke and bent toward her to catch
her faint words; or his ready hand received hers when, a
prey to some unhappy dream, she was restless and disquieted. If the nurse chanced to awake, Albert declared

he had just come in, and she rested satisfied that he merely visited his patient once or twice during the night, while in reality he did not waste half an hour in his own chamber. Consuelo shared his feeling, and although discovering the presence of her guardian much more frequently than that of the nurse, she was still so weak as to be easily deceived as to the number and duration of his visits. Often when, after midnight, she found him watching over her, and besought him to retire and take a few hours repose, he would evade her desire by saying that it was now near daybreak, and that he had just risen. These innocent deceptions excited no suspicion in the mind of Consuelo of the fatigue to which her lover was subjecting himself; and to them it was owing that she seldom suffered from the absence of Albert. This fatigue, strange as it may appear, was unperceived by the young count himself; so true is it that love imparts strength to the weakest. He possessed, however, a powerful organization; and he was animated, besides, by a love as ardent and devoted as ever fired a human breast.

When, during the first warm rays of the sun, Consuelo was able to bear removal to the half-open window, Albert seated himself behind her, and sought in the course of the clouds and in the purple tints of the sunbeams, to divine the thoughts with which the aspect of the skies inspired his silent friend. Sometimes he silently took a corner of the veil with which she covered her head, and which a warm wind floated over the back of the sofa, and bending forward his forehead as if to rest, pressed it to his lips. One day Consuelo, drawing it forward to cover her chest, was surprised to find it warm and moist; and turning more quickly than she had done since her illness, perceived some extraordinary emotion on the countenance of her friend. His cheeks were flushed, a feverish fire shone in his eyes, while his breast heaved with violent palpitations. Albert quickly recovered himself, but not before he had perceived terror depicted on the countenance of Consuelo. This deeply afflicted him. He would rather have witnessed there an emotion of contempt, or even of severity, than a lingering feeling of fear and distrust. He resolved to keep so careful a watch over himself that no trace of his aberration of mind should be visible to her who had cured him of it, almost at the price of her own life.

He succeeded, thanks to a superhuman power, and one which no ordinary man could have exercised. Accustomed to repress his emotions, and to enjoy the full scope of his desires, when not incapacitated by his mysterious disease, he restrained himself to an extent that he did not get credit for. His friends were ignorant of the frequency and force of the attack which he had every day to overcome, until, overwhelmed by despair, he fled to his secret cavern—a conqueror even in defeat, since he still maintained sufficient circumspection to hide from all eyes the spectacle of his fall. Albert's madness was of the most unhappy and yet elevated stamp. He knew his madness and felt its approach, until it had completely laid hold of and overpowered him. Yet he preserved in the midst of his attacks the vague and confused remembrance of an external world, in which he did not wish to reappear while he felt his relations with it not perfectly established. This memory of an actual and real life we all retain, when in the dreams of a painful sleep we are transported into another life—a life of fiction and indefinable visions. We occasionally struggle against these fantasies and terrors of the night, assuring ourselves that they are merely the effects of nightmare, and making efforts to awake; but on such occasions a hostile power appears to seize upon us at every effort, and to plunge us again into a horrible lethargy, where terrible spectacles, ever growing more gloomy, close around us, and where griefs the most poignant assail and torture us.

In alternations of being which bore a striking analogy to the state we have described, passed the miserable life of this powerful intellect, so totally misunderstood by all around him, and whom an active yet delicate and discriminating tenderness alone could have saved from his own distresses. This tenderness had at last been manifested. Consuelo was, of a truth, the pure and heavenly soul which seemed formed to find access to that somber and gloomy spirit, hitherto closed to all sympathy. There was something sweet and touching in the solicitude which a romantic enthusiasm had first aroused in the young girl, and in the respectful friendship which gratitude inspired in her since her illness, and which God doubtless knew to be peculiarly fitted for Albert's restoration. It is highly probable, that if Consuelo, forgetful of the past, had shared the ardor of his passion, transports so new to him, and joy so sudden, wouid have had the most fatal effects. The discreet and chastened friendship which she felt for him was calculated to have a slower but a more certain effect upon his health. It was a restraint as well as a benefit, and if there was a sort of intoxication in the renewed heart of the young count, there was mingled with it an idea of duty and of sacrifice, which gave other employment and another object to his will, than those which had hitherto consumed him. He therefore experienced, at the same time, the happiness of being loved as he had never been before, the grief of not being so with the ardor he himself felt, and the fear of losing his happiness if he did not appear contented with it. This threefold effect of his love soon filled his soul so completely as to leave no room for the reveries toward which his inaction and solitude had so long compelled him to turn. He was delivered from them as by the power of enchantment; for they faded from his memory and the image of her whom he loved kept his enemies at a distance, and seemed placed between them and himself like a celestial buckler.

That repose of spirit and calmness of feeling, which were so necessary to the re-establishment of the young patient, were hereafter therefore no more than very slightly and very rarely troubled by the secret agitations of her physician. Like the hero in the fable, Consuelo had descended into Tartarus to draw her friend thence, and had brought after her horror and frenzy. In his turn, he applied himself to deliver her from the inauspicious guests who had followed her, and he succeeded by means of delicate attentions and passionate respect. They began a new life together, resting on each other, not daring to look forward, and not feeling courage to plunge back in thought into the abyss they had passed through. The future was a new abyss, not less mysterious and terrible, which they did not venture to fathom. But they calmly enjoyed the present, like a season of grace which was granted them by Heaven.

CHAPTER LI.

THE other inhabitants of the castle were by no means so tranquil. Amelia was furious, and no longer deigned even to visit the invalid. She affected not to speak to Albert, never turned her eyes toward him, and never answered his morning and evening salutation. And the most provoking part of the affair was, that Albert did not seem to pay the least attention to her vexation.

The canoness, seeing the very evident, and, as it were, declared passion of her nephew for the *adventuress*, had not a moment's peace. She racked her brains to find some means of putting a stop to the danger and scandal, and to this end she had long conferences with the chaplain. But the latter did not very earnestly desire the termination of such a state of things. He had for a long time past been useless and unnoticed amid the cares of the family, but since these new and agitating occurrences, his post had recovered a kind of importance, and he could at least enjoy the pleasure of spying, revealing, warning, predicting, consulting—in a word, moving the domestic interests at his will, while he had the air of not interfering, and could hide himself from the indignation of the young count behind the old aunt's petticoats. Between them both they continually found new subjects of alarm, new motives for precaution, but no means of safety. Every day the good Wenceslawa approached her nephew with a decisive explanation on the tip of her tongue, and every day a mocking smile or a freezing look caused the words to miscarry. Every instant she watched for an opportunity of slipping secretly into Consuelo's chamber, in order to administer a skillful and firm reprimand, but every instant Albert, as if warned by a familiar spirit, came to place himself upon the threshold of the chamber; and, by a single frown, like the Olympian Jupiter, he disarmed the anger, and froze the courage of the divinities hostile to his beloved Ilion. Nevertheless, the canoness had several times engaged the invalid in conversation, and as the moments when she could enjoy a *tête-à-tête* were very rare, she had profited by these occasions to address some very absurd reflections to her, which she thought exceedingly significant. But Consuelo was so far removed

from the ambition attributed to her, that she understood
nothing of it. Her astonishment and her air of candor
and confidence immediately disarmed the good canoness,
who, in all her life, could never resist a frank manner or a
cordial caress. She hastened in confusion to confess her
defeat to the chaplain, and the rest of the day was passed
in planning measures for the morrow.

In the meantime, Albert, divining this management
very clearly, and seeing that Consuelo began to be astonished and uneasy, resolved to put a stop to it. One morning he watched Wenceslawa as she passed, and while she
thought to elude him by surprising Consuelo alone at that
early hour, he suddenly appeared just at the moment when
she was putting her hand to the key in order to enter the
invalid's chamber.

"My good aunt," said he, seizing her hand and carrying
it to his lips, "I must whisper in your ear something in
which you are very much interested. It is that the life
and health of the person who reposes within, are more
precious to me than my own life and my own happiness:
I know very well that your confessor has made it a point
of conscience with you to thwart my devotion toward her,
and to destroy the effect of my care. Without that, your
noble heart would never have conceived the idea of endangering, by bitter words and unjust reproaches, the recovery
of an invalid hardly yet out of danger. But since the
fanaticism or bitterness of a priest can perform such prodigies as to transform the most sincere piety and the purest
charity into blind cruelty, I shall oppose with all my
power the crime of which my poor aunt consents to be
made the instrument. I shall watch over my patient
night and day, and no longer leave her for a moment; and
if, notwithstanding my zeal, you succeed in carrying her
away from me, I swear by all that is most sacred to human
belief, that I will leave the house of my fathers never to
return. I trust that when you have communicated my
determination to the chaplain, he will cease tormenting
you, and combating the generous instincts of your affectionate heart."

The amazed canoness could only reply to this discourse
by melting into tears. Albert had led her to the end of
the gallery, so that the explanation could not be heard by
Consuelo. She complained of the threatening tone which

Albert employed, and endeavored to profit by the occasion, to show him the folly of his attachment toward a person of such low birth as Nina.

"Aunt," replied Albert, smiling, "you forget that if we are of the royal blood of the Podiebrads, our ancestors were kings only through favor of the peasants and revolted soldiery. A Podiebrad, therefore, should not pride himself on his noble origin, but rather regard it as an additional motive to attach him to the weak and the poor, since it is among them that his strength and power have planted their roots, and not so long ago that he can have forgotten it."

When Wenceslawa related this conference to the chaplain, he gave it as his opinion that it would not be prudent to exasperate the young count by remonstrances, nor drive him to extremity by annoying his protegée.

"It is to Count Christian himself that you must address your representations," said he. "Your excessive delicacy has too much emboldened the son. Let your wise remonstrances at length awaken the disquietude of his father, that he may take decisive measures with respect to this dangerous person."

"Do you suppose," replied the canoness, "that I have not already done so? But alas! my brother has grown fifteen years older during the fifteen days of Albert's last disappearance. His mind is so enfeebled that it is no longer possible to make him understand any suggestion. He appears to indulge in a sort of passive resistance to the idea of a new calamity of this description, and rejoices like a child at having found his son, and at hearing him reason and conduct himself as an intelligent man. He believes him cured of his malady, and does not perceive that poor Albert is a prey to a new kind of madness, more fatal than the first. My brother's security in this respect is so great, and he enjoys it so unaffectedly, that I have not yet found courage to open his eyes completely as to what is passing around him. It seems to me that this disclosure coming from you, and accompanied with your religious exhortations, would be listened to with more resignation, have a better effect, and be less painful to all parties."

"It is too delicate an affair," replied the chaplain, "to be undertaken by a poor priest like me. It will come much better from a sister, and your highness can soften the bitterness of the event, by expressions of tenderness which I could not venture upon toward the august head of the Rudolstadt family."

These two grave personages lost many days in deciding upon which should bell the cat. During this period of irresolution and apathy, in which habit also had its share, love made rapid progress in the heart of Albert. Consuelo's health was visibly restored, and nothing occurred to disturb the progress of an intimacy which the watchfulness of Argus could not have rendered more chaste and reserved than it was, simply through true modesty and sincere love.

Meantime the Baroness Amelia, unable to support her humiliation, earnestly entreated her father to take her back to Prague. Baron Frederick, who preferred a life in the forest to an abode in the city, promised every thing that she wished, but put off from day to day the announcement and preparations for departure. The baroness saw that it was necessary to urge matters on to suit her purpose, and devised one of those ingenious expedients in which her sex are never wanting. She had an understanding with her waiting-maid—a sharp-witted and active young Frenchwoman—and one morning, just as her father was about to set out for the chase, she begged him to accompany her in a carriage to the house of a lady of their acquaintance, to whom she had for a long time owed a visit. The baron had some difficulty in giving up his gun and his powder-horn to change his dress and the employment of the day, but he flattered himself that this condescension would render Amelia less exacting, and that the amusement of the drive would dissipate her ill-humor, and enable her to pass a few more days at the Castle of the Giants without murmuring. When the good man had obtained a respite of a week he fancied he had secured the independence of life ; his forethought extended no further. He therefore resigned himself to the necessity of sending Sapphire and Panther to the kennel, while Attila, the hawk, turned upon its perch with a discontented and mutinous air, which forced a heavy sigh from its master.

The baron at last seated himself in the carriage with his daughter, and in three revolutions of the wheel was fast asleep. The coachman then received orders from Amelia to drive to the nearest post-house. They arrived there after two hours of a rapid journey; and when the baron opened his eyes, he found post-horses in his carriage, and every thing ready to set out on the road to Prague.

"What means this?" exclaimed the baron; "where are we, and whither are we going? Amelia, my dear child, what folly is this? What is the meaning of this caprice, or rather this pleasantry with which you amuse yourself?"

To all her father's questions the young baroness only replied by repeated bursts of laughter, and by childish caresses. At length when she saw the postilion mounted, and the carriage roll lightly along the highway, she assumed a serious air, and in a very decided tone spoke as follows: "My dear papa, do not be uneasy; all our luggage is carefully packed. The carriage trunks are filled with all that is necessary for our journey. There is nothing left at the Castle of the Giants, except your dogs and guns, which will be of no use at Prague; and besides you can have them when you wish to send for them. A letter will be handed to Uncle Christian at breakfast, which is so expressed, as to make him see the necessity of our departure, without unnecessarily grieving him, or making him angry either with you or me. I must now humbly beg your pardon for having deceived you, but it is nearly a month since you consented to what I at this moment execute. I do not oppose your wishes therefore in returning to Prague; I merely chose a time when you did not contemplate it, and I would wager that, after all, you are delighted to be freed from the annoyance which the quickest preparations for departure entail. My position became intolerable, and you did not perceive it. Kiss me, dear papa, and do not frighten me with those angry looks of yours."

In thus speaking, Amelia, as well as her attendant, stifled a great inclination to laugh, for the baron never had an angry look for any one, much less for his cherished daughter. He only rolled his great bewildered eyes, a little stupified it must be confessed by surprise. If he experienced any annoyance at seeing himself fooled in such wise, and any real vexation at leaving his brother and sister without bidding them adieu, he was so astonished at the turn things had taken, that his uneasiness changed into admiration of his daughter's tact, and he could only exclaim:

"But how could you arrange every thing, so that I had

not the least suspicion? Faith, I little thought when I took off my boots, and sent my horse back to the stable, that I was off for Prague, and that I should not dine to-day with my brother. It is a strange adventure, and nobody will believe me when I tell it. But where have you put my traveling cap, Amelia? who could sleep in a carriage with this hat glued to one's ears?"

"Here it is, dear papa," said the merry girl, presenting him with his fur cap, which he instantly placed on his head with the utmost satisfaction.

"But my bottle? you have certainly forgotten it, you little wicked one."

"Oh! certainly not," she exclaimed, handing him a large crystal flask, covered with Russia leather and mounted with silver. "I filled it myself with the best Hungary wine from my aunt's cellar. But you had better taste it yourself; I know it is the description you prefer."

"And my pipe and pouch of Turkish tobacco?"

"Nothing is forgotten," said Amelia's maid; "his excellency the baron will find every thing packed in the carriage. Nothing has been omitted to enable him to pass the journey agreeably."

"Well done!" said the baron, filling his pipe, "but that does not clear you of all culpability in this matter, my dear Amelia. You will render your father ridiculous, and make him the laughing-stock of every one."

"Dear papa, it is I who seem ridiculous in the eyes of the world, when I apparently refuse to marry an amiable cousin, who does not even deign to look at me, and who, under my very eyes, pays assiduous court to my music mistress. I have suffered this humiliation long enough, and I do not think there are many girls of my rank, my age, and my appearance, who would not have resented it more seriously. Of one thing I am certain, that there are girls who would not have endured what I have done for the last eighteen months; but, on the contrary, would have put an end to the farce by running off with themselves, if they had failed in procuring a partner in their flight. For my part I am satisfied to run off with my father; it is a more novel as well as more proper step. What think you, dear papa?"

"Why, I think the devil's in you," replied the baron, kissing his daughter; and he passed the rest of his journey gaily, drinking, eating, and smoking by turns, without making any further complaint, or expressing any further astonishment.

This event did not produce the sensation in that family at the Castle of the Giants which the little baroness had flattered herself it would do. To begin with Count Albert, he might have passed a week without noticing the absence of the young baroness, and when the canoness informed him of it, he merely remarked: "This is the only clever thing which the clever Amelia has done since she set foot here. As to my good uncle, I hope he will soon return to us."

"For my part," said old Count Christian, "I regret the departure of my brother, because at my age one reckons by weeks and days. What is not long for you, Albert, is an eternity for me, and I am not so certain as you are of seeing my peaceful and easy-tempered Frederick again. Well, it is all Amelia's doings," added he, smiling as he threw aside the saucy yet cajoling letter of the young baroness. "Women's spite pardons not. You were not formed for each other, my children, and my pleasant dreams have vanished."

While thus speaking, the old count fixed his eyes upon the countenance of his son with a sort of melancholy satisfaction, as if anticipating some indication of regret; but he found none, and Albert, tenderly pressing his arm, made him understand that he thanked him for relinquishing a project so contrary to his inclination.

"God's will be done," ejaculated the old man, "and may your heart, my son, be free. You are now well, happy, and contented among us. I can now die in peace, and a father's love will comfort you after our final separation."

"Do not speak of separation, dear father," exclaimed the young count, his eyes suddenly filling with tears; "I cannot bear the idea."

The canoness, who began to be affected, received at this moment a significant glance from the chaplain, who immediately rose, and with feigned discretion left the room. This was the signal and the order. She thought, not without regret and apprehension, that the moment was at length come when she must speak, and closing her eyes like a person about to leap from the window of a house on fire, she thus began — stammering and becoming paler than usual:

"Certainly Albert loves his father tenderly, and would not willingly inflict on him a mortal blow."

Albert raised his head, and gazed at his aunt with such a keen and penetrating look that she could not utter another word. The old count appeared not to have heard this strange observation, and in the silence which followed, poor Wenceslawa remained trembling beneath her nephew's glance, like a partridge fascinated before the pointer.

But Count Christian, rousing from his reverie after a few minutes, replied to his sister as if she had continued to speak, or as if he had read in her mind the revelations she was about to make.

"Dear sister," said he, "if I may give you an advice, it is not to torment yourself with things which you do not understand. You have never known what it was to love, and the austere rules of a canoness are not those which befit a young man."

"Good God!" murmured the astonished canoness. "Either my brother does not understand me, or his reason and piety are about to desert him. Is it possible that in his weakness he would encourage or treat lightly——"

"How? aunt!" interrupted Albert, in a firm tone, and with a stern countenance. "Speak out, since you are forced to it. Explain yourself clearly; there must be an end to this constraint—we must understand each other."

"No, sister; you need not speak," replied the count; "you have nothing new to tell me. I understand perfectly well, without having seemed to do so, what has been going on for some time past. The period is not yet come to explain ourselves on that subject; when it does, I shall know how to act."

He began immediately to speak on other subjects, and left the canoness astonished, and Albert hesitating and troubled. When the chaplain was informed of the manner in which the head of the family received the counsel which he had indirectly given him, he was seized with terror. Count Christian, although seemingly irresolute and indolent, had never been a weak man, and sometimes surprised those who knew him, by suddenly arousing himself from a kind of somnolency, and acting with energy and wisdom.

The priest was afraid of having gone too far, and of being reprimanded. He commenced therefore to undo his work very quickly, and persuaded the canoness not to interfere further. A fortnight glided away in this manner without any thing suggesting to Consuelo that she was a subject of anxiety to the family. Albert continued his attentions, and announced the departure of Amelia as a short absence, but did not suffer her to suspect the cause. She began to leave her apartment ; and the first time she walked in the garden, the old Christian supported the tottering steps of the invalid on his weak and trembling arm.

CHAPTER LII.

It was indeed a happy day for Albert when he saw her whom he had restored to life, leaning on the arm of his father, and offer him her hand in the presence of his family, saying, with an ineffable smile, " This is he who saved me, and tended me as if I had been his sister."

But this day, which was the climax of his happiness, changed suddenly, and more than he could have anticipated, his relations with Consuelo. Henceforth, the formalities of the family circle precluded her being often alone with him. The old count, who appeared to have even a greater regard for her than before her illness, bestowed the utmost care upon her, with a kind of paternal gallantry which she felt deeply. The canoness observed a prudent silence, but nevertheless made it a point to watch over all her movements, and to form a third party in all her interviews with Albert. At length, as the latter gave no indication of returning mental alienation, they determined to have the pleasure of receiving, and even inviting, relations and neighbors long neglected. They exhibited a kind of simple and tender ostentation in showing how polite and sociable the young Count Rudolstadt had become, and Consuelo seemed to exact from him, by her looks and example, the fulfillment of the wishes of his relations, in exercising the duties of a hospitable host, and displaying the manners of a man of the world.

This sudden transformation cost him a good deal; he

submitted to it, however, to please her he loved, but he would have been better satisfied with longer conversations and a less interrupted intercourse with her. He patiently endured whole days of constraint and annoyance, in order to obtain in the evening a word of encouragement or gratitude. But when the canoness came, like an unwelcome specter, and placed herself between them, he felt his soul troubled and his strength abandon him. He passed nights of torment, and often approached the cistern, which remained clear and pellucid since the day he had ascended from it, bearing Consuelo in his arms. Plunged in mournful reverie, he almost cursed the oath which bound him never to return to his hermitage. He was terrified to feel himself thus unhappy, and not to have the power of burying his grief in his subterranean retreat.

The change in his features after his sleeplessness, and the transitory but gradually more frequent return of his gloomy and distracted air, could not fail to excite the observation of his relatives and his friend; but the latter found means to disperse these clouds and regain her empire over him whenever it was threatened. She commenced to sing, and immediately the young count, charmed or subdued, was consoled by tears, or animated with new enthusiasm. This was an infallible remedy; and when he was able to address a few words to her in private, "Consuelo," he exclaimed, "you know the paths to my soul; you possess the power refused to the common herd, and possess it more than any other being in this world. You speak in language divine; you know how to express the most sublime emotions, and communicate the impulses of your own inspired soul. Sing always when you see me downcast; the words of your songs have but little sense for me, they are but the theme, the imperfect indication on which the music turns and is developed. I hardly hear them; what alone I hear, and what penetrates into my very soul, is your voice, your accent, your inspiration. Music expresses all that the mind dreams and foresees of mystery and grandeur. It is the manifestation of a higher order of ideas and sentiments than any to which human speech can give expression. It is the revelation of the infinite; and when you sing, I only belong to humanity in so far as humanity has drunk in what is divine and eternal in the bosom of the Creator. All that your lips refuse of consolation and support in the ordinary routine of life—all that social tyranny forbids your heart to reveal—your songs convey to me a hundredfold. You then respond to me with your whole soul, and my soul replies to yours in hope and fear, in transports of enthusiasm and rapture."

Sometimes Albert spoke thus, in Spanish, to Consuelo in presence of his family; but the evident annoyance which the canoness experienced, as well as a sense of propriety, prevented the young girl from replying. At length one day when they were alone in the garden, and he again spoke of the pleasure he felt in hearing her sing:

"Since music is a language more complete and more persuasive than that of words," said she, "why do you not speak thus to me, you who understand it better than I do?"

"I do not understand you, Consuelo," said the young count, surprised; "I am only a musician in listening to you."

"Do not endeavor to deceive me," she replied; "I never but once heard sounds divinely human drawn from the violin, and it was by you, Albert, in the grotto of the Schreckenstein. I heard you that day before you saw me; I discovered your secret; but you must forgive me, and allow me again to hear that delightful air, of which I recollect a few bars, and which revealed to me beauties in music, to which I was previously a stranger."

Consuelo sang in a low tone a few phrases which she recollected indistinctly, but which Albert immediately recognized.

"It is a popular hymn," said he, "on some Hussite words. The words are by my ancester, Hyncko Podiebrad, the son of King George, and one of the poets of the country. We have an immense number of admirable poems by Streye, Simon Lomnicky, and many others, which are prohibited by the police. These religious and national songs, set to music by the unknown geniuses of Bohemia, are not all preserved in the memory of her inhabitants. The people retain some of them, however, and Zdenko, who has an extraordinary memory and an excellent taste for music, knows a great many, which I have collected and arranged. They are very beautiful, and you will have pleasure in learning them. But I can only let you hear them in my hermitage; my violin, with all my music, is there. I have there precious manuscripts, collections of ancient Catholic and Protestant authors. I will wager that you do not know either Josquin, many of whose themes Luther has transmitted to us in his choruses, nor the younger Claude, nor Arcadelt, nor George Rhaw, nor Benoit Ducis, nor John de Weiss. Would not this curious research induce you, dear Consuelo, to pay another visit to my grotto, from which I have been exiled so long a time, and to visit my church, which you have not yet seen?"

This proposal, although it excited the curiosity of the young artist, was tremblingly listened to. This frightful grotto recalled recollections which she could not think of without a shudder, and in spite of all the confidence she placed in him, the idea of returning there alone with Albert caused a painful emotion, which he quickly perceived.

"You dislike the idea of this pilgrimage," said he, "which nevertheless you promised to renew; let us speak of it no more. Faithful to my oath, I shall never undertake it without you."

"You remind me of mine, Albert," she replied, "and I shall fulfill it as soon as you ask it; but, my dear doctor, you forget that I have not yet the necessary strength. Would you not first permit me to see this curious music, and hear this admirable artist, who plays on the violin much better than I sing?"

"I know not if you jest, dear sister, but this I know, that you shall hear me nowhere but in my grotto. It was there I first tried to make my violin express the feelings of my heart; for, although I had for many years a brilliant and frivolous professor, largely paid by my father, I did not understand it. It was there I learned what true music is, and what a sacrilegious mockery is substituted for it by the greater portion of mankind. For my own part, I declare that I could not draw a sound from my violin if my spirit were not bowed before the divinity. Were I even to see you unmoved beside me, attentive merely to the composition of the pieces I play, and curious to scrutinize my talent, I doubt not that I would play so ill that you would soon weary of listening to me. I have never, since I knew how to use it, touched the instrument consecrated by me to the praise of God or to the expression of my ardent prayers, without feeling myself transported into an ideal world, and without obeying a sort of mysterious inspiration not always under my control."

"I am not unworthy," replied Consuelo, deeply impressed, and all attention, "to comprehend your feelings with regard to music. I hope soon to be able to join your prayer with a soul so fervent and collected that my presence shall not interfere with your inspiration. Ah, my dear Albert, why cannot my master Porpora hear what you say of the heavenly art? He would throw himself at your feet. Nevertheless, this great artist himself is less severe in his views on this subject than you are. He thinks the singer and the virtuoso should draw their inspiration from the sympathy and admiration of their auditory.

"It is perhaps because Porpora confounds, in music, religious sentiment with human thought, and that he looks upon sacred music with the eyes of a Catholic. If I were in his place I would reason as he does. If I were in a communion of faith and sympathy with a people professing the same worship as myself, I would seek in contact with these souls, animated with a like religious sentiment, the inspiration which heretofore I have been forced to court in solitude, and which consequently I have hitherto imperfectly realized. If ever I have the pleasure of mingling the tones of my violin with those of your divine voice, Consuelo, doubtless I would ascend higher than I have ever done, and my prayer would be more worthy of the Deity. But do not forget, dear child, that up to this day my opinions have been an abomination in the eyes of those who surrounded me, and that those whom they failed to shock, would have turned them into ridicule. This is why I have hidden, as a secret between God, poor Zdenko, and myself, the humble gift which I possess. My father likes music, and would have this instrument, which is sacred to me as the cymbals of the Elusinian mysteries, conduce to his amusement. What would become of me if they were to ask me to accompany a cavatina for Amelia? and what would be my father's feelings if I were to play one of those old Hussite airs which have sent so many Bohemians into the mines or to the scaffold? or a more modern hymn of our Lutheran ancestors, from whom he blushes to have descended? Alas! Consuelo, I know nothing more modern. There are, no doubt, admir-

able things of a later date. From what you tell me of
Handel and the other great masters from whose works you
have been instructed, their music would seem to me superior in many respects to that which I am about to teach
you. But to know and learn this music, it would be necessary to put myself in relation with another musical world,
and it is with you alone that I can resolve to do so—with
you alone I can seek the despised or neglected treasures
which you are about to bestow on me in overflowing
measure."

"And I," said Consuelo, smiling, "think I shall not
undertake the charge of this education. What I heard in
the grotto was so beautiful, so grand, so incomparable,
that I should fear, in doing so, only to muddy a spring of
crystal. Oh! Albert, I see plainly that you know more of
music than I do. And now what will you say to the profane music of which I am forced to be a professor? I fear
to discover in this case, as in the other, that I have hitherto
been beneath my mission, and guilty of equal ignorance
and frivolity."

"Far from thinking so, Consuelo, I look upon your profession as sacred ; and as it is the loftiest which a woman
can embrace, so is your soul the most worthy to fill such
an office."

"Stay!—stay!—dear count," replied Consuelo, smiling.
"From my often speaking to you of the convent where I
learned music, and the church where I sung the praises of
God, you conclude that I was destined to the service of
the altar, or the modest teachings of the cloister. But if
I should inform you that the zingarella, faithful to her
origin, was from infancy the sport of circumstances, and
that her education was at once a mixture of religious and
profane, to which her will was equally inclined, careless
whether it were in the monastery or the theater ——"

"Certain that God has placed his seal on your forehead
and devoted you to holiness from your mother's womb, I
should not trouble myself about these things, but retain
the conviction that you would be as pure in the theater
as in the cloister."

"What! would not your strict ideas of morality be
shocked at being brought in contact with an actress?"

"In the dawn of religion," said he, "the theater and
the temple were one and the same sanctuary. In the

purity of their primitive ideas, religious worship took the form of popular shows. The arts have their birth at the foot of the altar, the dance itself, that art now consecrated to ideas of impure voluptuousness, was the music of the senses in the festivals of the gods. Music and poetry were the highest expressions of faith, and a woman endowed with genius and beauty was at once a sibyl and priestess. To these severely grand forms of the past, absurd and culpable distinctions succeeded. Religion proscribed beauty from its festivals, and woman from its solemnities. Instead of ennobling and directing love, it banished and condemned it. Beauty, woman, love, cannot lose their empire. Men have raised for themselves other temples which they call theaters, and where no other god presides. Is it your fault, Consuelo, if they have become dens of corruption? Nature, who perfects her prodigies without troubling herself as to how men may receive them, has formed you to shine among your sex, and to shed over the world the treasures of your power and genius. The cloister and the tomb are synonymous; you cannot, without morally committing suicide, bury the gifts of Providence. You were obliged to wing your flight to a freer atmosphere. Energy is the condition of certain natures; an irresistible impulse impels them; and the decrees of the Deity in this respect are so decided, that he takes away the faculties which he has bestowed, so soon as they are neglected. The artist perishes and becomes extinct in obscurity, just as the thinker wanders and pines in solitude, and just as all human intellect is deteriorated, and weakened, and enervated, by inaction and isolation. Repair to the theater, Consuelo, if you please, and submit with resignation to the apparent degradation, as the representative for the moment of a soul destined to suffer, of a lofty mind which vainly seeks for sympathy in the world around us, but which is forced to abjure a melancholy that is not the element of its life, and out of which the breath of the Holy Spirit imperiously expels it."

Albert continued to speak in this strain for a considerable time with great animation, hurrying Consuelo on to the recesses of his retreat. He had little difficulty in communicating to her his own enthusiasm for art, or in making her forget her first feeling of repugnance to re-enter the grotto. When she saw that he anxiously desired it, she began to entertain a wish for this interview, in order to become better acquainted with the ideas which this ardent yet timid man dared to express before her so boldly. These ideas were new to Consuelo, and perhaps they were entirely so in the mouth of a person of noble rank of that time and country. They only struck her, however, as the bold and frank expression of sentiments which she herself had frequently experienced in all their force. Devout, and an actress, she every day heard the canoness and the chaplain unceasingly condemn her brethren of the stage. In seeing herself restored to her proper sphere by a serious and reflecting man, she felt her heart throb and her bosom swell with exultation, as if she had been carried up into a more elevated and more congenial life. Her eyes were moistened with tears and her cheeks glowed with a pure and holy emotion, when at the end of an avenue she perceived the canoness, who was seeking her.

"Ah! dear priestess," said Albert, pressing her arm again his breast, "will you not come to pray in my church?"

"Yes, certainly I shall go," she replied.

"And when?"

"Whenever you wish. Do you think I am able yet to undertake this new exploit?"

"Yes; because we shall go to the Schreckenstein in broad daylight and by a less dangerous route than the well. Do you feel sufficient courage to rise before the dawn and to escape through the gates as soon as they are opened? I shall be in this underwood which you see at the side of the hill there, by the stone cross, and shall serve as your guide."

"Very well, I promise," replied Consuelo, not without a slight palpitation of heart.

"It appears rather cool this evening for so long a walk—does it not?" asked the canoness, accosting them in her calm yet searching manner.

Albert made no reply. He could not dissemble. Consuelo, who did not experience equal emotion, passed her other arm within that of the canoness, and kissed her neck. Wenceslawa vainly pretended indifference, but in spite of herself she submitted to the ascendancy of this devout and affectionate spirit. She sighed, and on entering the castle proceeded to put up a prayer for her conversion.

CHAPTER LIII.

MANY days passed away however without Albert's wish being accomplished. It was in vain that Consuelo rose before the dawn and passed the drawbridge; she always found his aunt or the chaplain wandering on the esplanade, and from thence reconnoitering all the open country which she must traverse in order to gain the copsewood on the hill. She determined to walk alone within range of their observation, and give up the project of joining Albert, who, from his green and wooded retreat, recognized the enemy on the look-out, took a long walk in the forest glades, and re-entered the castle without being perceived.

" You have had an opportunity of enjoying an early walk, Signora Porporina," said the canoness at breakfast. " Were you not afraid that the dampness of the morning might be injurious to your health?"

" It was I, aunt, who advised the signora to breathe the freshness of the morning air; and I think these walks will be very useful to her."

" I should have thought that, for a person who devotes herself to the cultivation of the voice," said the canoness, with a little affectation, " our mornings are somewhat foggy. But if it is under your direction——"

" Have confidence in Albert," interrupted Count Christian, " he has proved himself as good a physician as he is a good son and a faithful friend."

The dissimulation to which Consuelo was forced to yield with blushes, was very painful to her. She complained gently to Albert when she had an opportunity of speaking to him in private, and begged him to renounce his project, at least until his aunt's vigilance should be foiled. Albert consented, but entreated her to continue her walks in the environs of the park, so that he might join her whenever an opportunity presented itself.

Consuelo would gladly have been excused, although she liked walking, and felt how necessary to her convalescence it was, to enjoy exercise for some time every day, free from the restraint of this enclosure of walls and moats, where her thoughts were stifled as if she had been a prisoner; yet it gave her pain thus to practice deception toward those whom she respected, and from whom she received hospitality. Love, however, removes many obstacles, but friendship reflects, and Consuelo reflected much. They were now enjoying the last fine days of summer; for several months had already passed since Consuelo had come to dwell in the Castle of the Giants. What a summer for Consuelo! The palest autumn of Italy was more light, and rich, and genial But this warm, moist air, this sky, often veiled by white and fleecy clouds, had also their charm and their peculiar beauty. She found an attraction in these solitary walks, which increased perhaps her disinclination to revisit the cavern. In spite of the resolution she had formed, she felt that Albert would have taken a load from her bosom in giving her back her promise; and when she found herself no longer under the spell of his supplicating looks and enthusiastic words, she secretly blessed his good aunt, who prevented her fulfilling her engagement by the obstacles she every day placed in the way.

One morning, as she wandered along the bank of the mountain streamlet, she observed Albert leaning on the balustrade of the parterre, far above her. Notwithstanding the distance which separated them, she felt as if incessantly under the disturbed and passionate gaze of this man, by whom she suffered herself in so great a degree to be governed. "My situation here is somewhat strange!" she exclaimed; "While this persevering friend observes me to see that I am faithful to the promise I have made, without doubt I am watched from some other part of the castle, to see that I maintain no relations with him that their customs and ideas of propriety would proscribe. I do not know what is passing in their minds. The Baroness Amelia does not return. The canoness appears to grow cold toward me, and to distrust me. Count Christian redoubles his attentions, and expresses his dread of the arrival of Porpora, which will probably be the signal for my departure. Albert appears to have forgotten that I forbade him to hope. As if he had a right to expect every thing from me, he asks nothing, and does not abjure a passion which seems, notwithstanding my inability to return it, to render him happy. In the meantime, here I am, as if I were engaged in attending every morning at an appointed place of meeting, to which I wish he may not come, exposing myself to the blame—nay, for aught I know, perhaps to the scorn—of a family who cannot understand either my friendship for him nor my position toward him; since indeed I do not comprehend them myself nor foresee their result. What a strange destiny is mine! Shall I then be condemned forever to devote myself to others, without being loved in return, or without being able to love those whom I esteem?"

In the midst of these reflections a profound melancholy seized her. She felt the necessity of belonging to herself —that sovereign and legitimate want, the necessary condition of progress and development of the true artist. The watchful care which she had promised to observe toward Count Albert, weighed upon her as an iron chain. The bitter recollections of Anzoleto and of Venice clung to her in the inaction and solitude of a life too monotonous and regular for her powerful organization.

She stopped near the rock which Albert had often shown her as being the place where he had first seen her, an infant, tied with thongs on her mother's shoulders like the pedlar's pack, and running over mountains and valleys, like the grasshopper of the fable, heedless of the morrow, and without a thought of advancing old age, and inexorable poverty. "O, my poor mother!" thought the young zingarella, "here am I, brought back by my incomprehensible fate to a spot which you once traversed only to retain a vague recollection of it and the pledge of a touching kindness. You were then young and handsome, and doubtless could have met many a place where love and hospitality would have awaited you—society which would have absolved and transformed you, and in the bosom of which your painful and wandering life would have at last tasted comfort and repose. But you felt, and always said, that this comfort, this repose, were mortal weariness to the artist's soul. You were right—I feel it; for behold me in this castle, where, as elsewhere, you would pause but one night. Here I am, with every comfort around me, pampered, caressed, and with a powerful lord at my feet ; and nevertheless I am weary, weary, and suffocated with restraint."

Consuelo, overpowered with an extraordinary emotion, seated herself on the rock. She looked at the sandy path, as if she thought to find there the prints of her mother's naked feet. The sheep in passing had left some locks of their fleece upon the thorns. This fleece, of a reddish brown, recalled the russet hue of her mother's coarse mantle— that mantle which had so long protected her against sun and cold, against dust and rain. She had seen it fall from her shoulders piece by piece. "And we, too," she said, "were wandering sheep; we, too, left fragments of our apparel on the wayside thorn, but we always bore with us the proud love and full enjoyment of our dear liberty."

While musing thus, Consuelo fixed her eyes upon the path of yellow sand which wound gracefully over the hill, and which, widening as it reached the valley, disappeared toward the north among the green pine-trees and the dark heath. "What is more beautiful than a road?" she thought. "It is the symbol and image of a life of activity and variety. What pleasing ideas are connected in my mind with the capricious turns of this! I do not recollect the country through which it winds, and yet I have formerly passed through it. But it should indeed be beautiful, were it only as a contrast to yonder dark castle, which sleeps eternally on its immovable rocks. How much pleasanter to the eye are these graveled paths, with their glowing hues and the golden broom which shadow them, than the straight alleys and stiff palings of the proud domain? With merely looking at the formal lines of a garden, I feel wearied and overcome. Why should my feet seek to reach that which my eyes and thoughts can at once embrace, while the free road, which turns aside and is half hidden in the woods, invites me to follow its windings, and penetrate its mysteries? And then it is the path for all human kind—it is the highway of the world. It belongs to no master, to close and open it at pleasure. It is not only the powerful and rich that are entitled to tread its flowery margins and to breathe its rich perfume. Every bird may build its nest amid its branches ; every wanderer may repose his head upon its stones—nor wall nor paling shuts out his horizon. Heaven does not close before him; so far as his eye can reach, the highway is a land of liberty. To the right, to the left, woods, fields—all have masters; but the road belongs to him to whom nothing else belongs, and how fondly therefore does he love it! The meanest beggar prefers it to asylums, which, were they rich as palaces, would be but prisons to him. His dream, his passion, his hope will ever be the highway. O, my mother, you knew it well, and often told me so! Why can I not reanimate your ashes which repose far from me, beneath the seaweed of the lagunes? Why canst thou not carry me on thy strong shoulders, and bear me far, far away, where the swallow skims onward to the blue and distant hills, and where the memory of the past and the longing after vanished happiness cannot follow the light-footed artist, who travels still faster than they do, and each day places a new horizon, a second world, between her and the enemies of liberty? My poor mother, why canst thou not still by turns cherish and oppress me, and lavish alternate kisses and blows, like the wind which sometimes caresses and sometimes lays prostrate the young corn upon the fields, to raise and cast it down again according to its fantasy? Thou hadst a firmer soul than mine, and thou wouldst have torn me, either willingly or by force, from the bonds which daily entangle me."

In the midst of this entrancing yet mournful reverie, Consuelo was struck by the tones of a voice that made her start as if a red-hot iron had been placed upon her heart. It was that of a man from the ravine below, humming in the Venetian dialect the song of the "*Echo*," one of the most original compositions of Chiozzetto.* The person who sung did not exert the full power of his voice, and his breathing seemed affected by walking. He warbled a few notes now and then, stopping from time to time to converse with another person, just as if he had wished to dissipate the weariness of his journey. He then resumed his song as before, as if by way of exercise, interrupted it again to speak to his companion, and in this manner approached the spot where Consuelo sat, motionless, and as if about to faint. She could not hear the conversation which took place, as the distance was too great; nor could she see the travelers in consequence of an intervening projection of the rock. But could she be for an instant deceived in that voice, in those accents, which she knew so well, and the fragrants of that song which she herself had taught, and so often made her graceless pupil repeat?

At length the two invisible travelers drew near, and she heard one whose voice was unknown to her say to the

---

* Jean Croce de Chioggio, sixteenth century.

other, in bad Italian, and with the patois of the country, "Ah, signor, do not go up there—the horses could not follow you, and you would lose sight of me; keep by the banks of the stream. See, the road lies before us, and the way you are taking is only a path for foot passengers."

The voice which Consuelo knew became more distant, and appeared to descend, and soon she heard him ask what fine castle that was on the other side.

"That is Riesenburg, which means the Castle of the Giants;" replied the guide, for he was one by profession, and Consuelo could now distinguish him at the bottom of the hill, on foot and leading two horses covered with sweat. The bad state of the roads, recently inundated by the torrent, had obliged the riders to dismount. The traveler followed at a little distance, and Consuelo could at length see him by leaning over the rock which protected her. His back was toward her, and he wore a traveling-dress, which so altered his appearance and even his walk, that had she not heard his voice she could not have recognized him. He stopped, however, to look at the castle, and taking off his broad-leafed hat, wiped his face with his handkerchief. Although only able to distinguish him imperfectly from the great height at which she was placed, she knew at once those golden and flowing locks, and recognized the movement he was accustomed to make in raising them from his forehead or neck when he was warm.

"This seems a very fine castle," said he. "If I had time I should like to ask the giants for some breakfast."

"Oh, do not attempt it," said the guide, shaking his head. "The Rudolstadts only receive beggars and relations."

"Are they not more hospitable than that? May the devil seize them then!"

"Listen—it is because they have something to conceal."

"A treasure or a crime?"

"Oh, nothing of that kind; it is their son, who is mad."

"Deuce take him too, then; it would do them a service."

The guide began to laugh; Anzoleto commenced to sing.

"Come," said the guide, "we are now over the worst of the road; if you wish to mount we may gallop as far as Tusta. The road is magnificent—nothing but sand.

Once there, you will find the highway to Prague, and excellent post-horses."

"In that case," said Anzoleto, adjusting his stirrups, "I may say the fiend seize thee too! for your jades, your mountain roads, and yourself, are all becoming very tiresome."

Thus speaking, he slowly mounted his nag, sunk the spurs in its side, and without troubling himself about the guide, who followed him with great difficulty, he darted off toward the north, raising great clouds of dust on that road which Consuelo had so long contemplated, and on which she had so little expected to see pass, like a fatal vision, the enemy of her life, the constant torture of her heart. She followed him with her eyes, in a state of stupor impossible to express. Struck with disgust and fear, so long as she was within hearing of his voice, she had remained hidden and trembling. But when he disappeared, when she thought she had lost sight of him perhaps forever, she experienced only violent despair. She threw herself over the rock to see him for a longer time ; the undying love which she cherished for him awoke again with fervor, and she would have recalled him, but her voice died on her lips. The hand of death seemed to press heavily on her bosom ; her eyes grew dim ; a dull noise, like the dashing of the sea, murmured in her ears ; and falling exhausted at the foot of the rock, she found herself in the arms of Albert, who had approached without being perceived, and who bore her, apparently dying, to a more shady and secluded part of the mountain.

CHAPTER LIV.

THE fear of betraying by her emotion a secret so long hidden in the depths of her soul, restored Consuelo to strength, and enabled her to control herself, so that Albert perceived nothing extraordinary in her situation. Just as the young count received her in his arms, pale and ready to swoon, Anzoleto and his guide disappeared among the distant pine-trees, and Albert might therefore attribute to his own presence the danger she had incurred of falling down the precipice. The idea of this danger, of which he supposed himself to be the cause in terrifying her by his sudden approach so distressed him, that he did not at first perceive Consuelo's confused replies. Consuelo, in whom he still inspired at times a kind of superstitious terror, feared that he might divine the mystery. But Albert, since love had made him live the life of other men, seemed to have lost the apparently supernatural faculties which he had formerly possessed. She soon conquered her agitation, and Albert's proposal to conduct her to his hermitage did not displease her at this moment as it would have done a few hours previously. It seemed as if the grave and serious character and gloomy abode of this man, who regarded her with such devoted affection, offered themselves as a refuge in which she could find strength to combat the memory of her unhappy passion. "It is Providence," thought she, "who has sent me this friend in the midst of my trials, and the dark sanctuary to which he would lead me, is an emblem of the tomb in which I should wish to be buried, rather than pursue the track of the evil genius who has just passed me. Oh! yes, my God, rather than follow his footsteps, let the earth open to receive me, and snatch me forever from the living world!"

"Dear Consolation," said Albert, "I came to tell you that my aunt, having to examine her accounts this morning, is not thinking of us, and we are at length at liberty to accomplish our pilgrimage. Nevertheless, if you still feel any repugnance to revisit places which recall so much suffering and terror——"

"No, my friend," replied Consuelo; "on the contrary, I have never felt better disposed to worship with you, and to soar aloft together on the wings of that sacred song which you promised to let me hear."

They took the way together toward the Schreckenstein, and as they buried themselves in the wood in an opposite direction to that taken by Anzoleto, Consuelo felt more at ease, as if each step tended to undo the charm of which she had felt the force. She walked on so eagerly, that, although grave and reserved, Count Albert might have ascribed her anxiety to a desire to please, if he had not felt that distrust of himself and of his destiny, which formed the principal feature of his character.

He conducted her to the foot of the Schreckenstein, and

stopped at the entrance of a grotto filled with stagnant water, and nearly hidden by the luxuriant vegetation. "This grotto, in which you may remark some traces of a vaulted construction," said he, "is called in the country 'The Monk's Cave.' Some think it was a cellar of a convent, at a period when, in place of these ruins, there stood here a fortified town; others relate that it was subsequently the retreat of a repentant criminal, who turned hermit. However this may be, no one dares to penetrate the recesses; and every one says that the water is deep, and is imbued with a mortal poison, owing to the veins of copper through which it runs in its passage. But this water is really neither deep nor dangerous; it sleeps upon a bed of rocks, and we can easily cross it, Consuelo, if you will once again confide in the strength of my arm and the purity of my love."

Thus saying, after having satisfied himself that no one had followed or observed them, he took her in his arms, and entering the water, which reached almost to his knee, he cleared a passage through the shrubs and matted ivy which concealed the bottom of the grotto. In a very short time he set her down upon a bank of fine dry sand, in a place completely dark. He immediately lighted the lantern with which he was furnished, and after some turns in subterranean galleries similar to those which Consuelo had already traversed, they found themselves at the door of a cell, opposite to that which she had opened the first time.

"This subterranean building," said he, "was originally destined to serve as a refuge in time of war, either for the principal inhabitants of the town which covered the hill, or for the lords of the Castle of the Giants, to whom this town belonged, who could enter it secretly by the passages with which you are already acquainted. If a hermit, as they assert, since inhabited the monk's cave, it is probable that he was aware of this retreat; because the gallery which we have just traversed, has been recently cleared out, while I have found those leading from the castle so filled up in many places with earth and gravel that I found difficulty in removing them. Besides, the relics I discovered here, the remnants of matting, the pitcher, the crucifix, the lamp, and above all the skeleton of a man lying on his back, his hands crossed on his breast, as if in a last prayer at the hour of his final sleep, proved to me that a hermit had here piously and peaceably ended his mysterious existence. Our peasants still believe that the hermit's spirit inhabits the depths of the mountain. They affirm that they have often seen him wander around it, or flit to the heights by the light of the moon; that they have heard him pray, sigh, sob, and that even a strange incomprehensible music has been wafted toward them, like a suppressed sigh, on the wings of the breeze. Even I myself, Consuelo, when despair peopled nature around me with phantoms and prodigies, have thought I saw the gloomy penitent prostrate under the Hussite. I have fancied that I heard his plaintive sobs and heartrending sighs ascend from the depths of the abyss. But since I discovered and inhabited this cell, I have never seen any hermit but myself—any specter but my own figure—nor have I heard any sobs save those which issued from my own breast."

Since Consuelo's first interview with Albert in the cavern, she had never heard him utter an irrational word. She did not venture, therefore, to allude to the manner in which he had addressed herself, nor to the illusions in the midst of which she had surprised him. But she was astonished to observe that they seemed absolutely forgotten, and not wishing to recall then, she merely asked if solitude had really delivered him from the disquietude of which he spoke.

"I cannot tell you precisely," he replied; "and, at least not until you exact it, can I urge my memory to the task. I must have been mad, and the efforts I made to conceal it, betrayed it yet more. When, thanks to one to whom tradition had handed down the secret of these caverns, I succeeded in escaping from the solicitude of my relatives and hiding my despair, my existence changed. I recovered a sort of empire over myself, and, secure of concealment from troublesome witnesses, I was able at length to appear tranquil and resigned in the bosom of my family."

Consuelo perceived that poor Albert was under an illusion in some respects, but this was not the time to enlighten him; and, pleased to hear him speak of the past with such unconcern, she began to examine the cell with more attention than she had bestowed on it the first time. There was no appearance of the care and neatness which she formerly observed. The dampness of the walls, the cold of the atmosphere, and the moldiness of the books, betrayed complete abandonment. "You see that I have kept my word," said Albert, who had just succeeded with great difficulty in lighting the stove. "I have never set foot here since the day you displayed your power over me by tearing me away."

Consuelo had a question on her lips, but restrained herself. She was about to ask if Zdenko, the friend, the faithful servant, the zealous guardian, had also abandoned and neglected the hermitage. But she recollected the profound sorrow which Albert always displayed when she hazarded a question as to what had become of him, and why she had never seen him since the terrible encounter in the cavern? Albert had always evaded these questions, either by pretending not to understand her, or by begging her to fear nothing for the *innocent.* She was at first persuaded that Zdenko had received and faithfully fulfilled the command of his master never to appear before his eyes. But when she resumed her solitary walks, Albert, in order to completely reassure her, had sworn, while a deadly paleness overspread his countenance, that she should not encounter Zdenko, who had set out on a long voyage. In fact no one had seen him since that time, and they thought he was dead in some corner, or that he had quitted the country.

Consuelo believed neither of these suppositions. She knew too well the passionate attachment of Zdenko to Albert to think a separation possible. As to his death, she thought of it with a terror she hardly admitted to herself, when she recollected Albert's dreadful oath to sacrifice the life of this unhappy being if necessary to the repose of her he loved. But she rejected this frightful suspicion on recalling the mildness and humanity which the whole of Albert's life displayed. Besides he had enjoyed perfect tranquility for many months, and no apparent demonstration on the part of Zdenko had reawakened the fury which the young count had for a moment manifested. He had forgotten that unhappy moment which Consuelo also struggled to forget; he only remembered what took place in the cavern while he was in possession of his reason. Consuelo therefore concluded that he had forbidden Zdenko to enter or approach the castle, and that the poor fellow, through grief or anger, had condemned himself to voluntary seclusion in the hermitage. She took it for granted that Zdenko would come out on the Schrecken-stein only by night for air, and to converse with Albert, who no doubt took care of, and watched over him who had for so long a time taken care of himself. On seeing the condition of the cell, Consuelo was driven to the conclusion that he was angry at his master, and had displayed it by neglecting his retreat. But as Albert had assured her when they entered the grotto, that there was contained in it no cause of alarm, she seized the opportunity when his attention was otherwise engaged, to open the rusty gate of what he called his church, and in this way to reach Zdenko's cell, where doubtless she would find traces of his recent presence. The door yielded as soon as she had turned the key, but the darkness was so great that she could see nothing. She waited till Albert had passed into the mysterious oratory which he had promised to show her, and which he was preparing for her reception, and she then took a light and returned cautiously to Zdenko's chamber, not without trembling at the idea of finding him there in person. But there was not the faintest evidence of his existence. The bed of leaves and the sheep-skins had been removed. The seat, the tools, the sandals of undressed hide—all had disappeared, and one would have said, to look at the dripping walls, that this vault had never sheltered a living being.

A feeling of sadness and terror took possession of her at this discovery. A mystery shrouded the fate of this unfortunate, and Consuelo accused herself of being perhaps the cause of a deplorable event. There were two natures in Albert: the one wise, the other mad ; the one polished, tender, merciful; the other strange, untamed, perhaps violent and implacable. His fancied identity with the fanatic John Ziska, his love for the recollections of Hussite Bohemia, and that mute and patient, but at the same time profound passion which he nourished for herself—all occurred at this moment to her mind, and seemed to confirm her most painful suspicions. Motionless and frozen with horror, she hardly ventured to glance at the cold and naked floor of the grotto, dreading to find on it tracks of blood.

She was still plunged in these reflections, when she heard Albert tune his violin, and soon she heard him playing on the admirable instrument the ancient psalm which

she so much wished to hear a second time. The music
was so original, and Albert performed it with such sweet
expression, that, forgetting her distress, and attracted and
as if charmed by magnetic power, she gently approached
the spot where he stood.

CHAPTER LV.

THE door of the church was open, and Consuelo stopped
upon the threshold to observe the inspired virtuoso and
the strange sanctuary. This so-called church was nothing
but an immense grotto, hewn, or rather cleft out of the
rock irregularly by the hand of nature, and hollowed out
by the subterranean force of the water. Scattered torches,
placed on gigantic blocks, shed a fantastic light on the
green sides of the cavern, and partially revealed dark recesses, in the depths of which the huge forms of tall stalactites loomed like specters alternately seeking and shunning
the light. The enormous sedimentary deposits on the
sides of the cavern assumed a thousand fantastic forms.
Sometimes they seemed devouring serpents, rolling over
and interlacing each other. Sometimes hanging from the
roof and shooting upward from the floor, they wore the
aspect of the collossal teeth of some monster, of which the
dark cave beyond might pass for the gaping jaws. Elsewhere they might have been taken for mis-shapen statues,
giant images of the demi gods of antiquity. A vegetation
appropriate to the grotto—huge lichens, rough as dragon's
scales; festoons of heavy-leaved scolopendra, tufts of young
cypresses recently planted in the middle of the inclosure
on little heaps of artificial soil, not unlike graves—gave the
place a terrific and somber aspect which deeply impressed
Consuelo. To her first feeling of terror, admiration however quickly succeeded. She approached and saw Albert
standing on the margin of the fountain which sprung up
in the midst of the cavern. This water, although gushing
up abundantly, was inclosed in so deep a basin that no
movement was visible on its surface. It was calm and
motionless as a block of dark sapphire, and the beautiful
aquatic plants with which Albert and Zdenko had
clothed its margin, were not agitated by the slightest mo-

tion. The spring was warm at its source, and the tepid exhalations with which it filled the cavern caused a mild and moist atmosphere favorable to vegetation. It gushed from its fountain in many ramifications, of which some lost themselves under the rocks with a dull noise, while others ran gently into limpid streams in the interior of the grotto and disappeared in the depths beyond.

When Count Albert, who until then had been only trying the strings of his violin, saw Consuelo advance toward him, he came forward to meet her, and assisted her to cross the channels, over which he had thrown, in the deepest spots, some trunks of trees, while in other places rocks, on a level with the water, offered an easy passage to those habituated to it. He offered his hand to assist her, and sometimes lifted her in his arms. But this time Consuelo was afraid, not of the torrent which flowed silently and darkly under her feet, but of the mysterious guide toward whom she was drawn by an irresistible sympathy, while an indefinable repulsion at the same time held her back. Having reached the bank she beheld a spectacle not much calculated to reassure her. It was a sort of quadrangular monument, formed of bones and human skulls, arranged as if in a catacomb.

"Do not be uneasy," said Albert, who felt her shudder. "These are the honored remains of the martyrs of my religion; and they form the altar before which I love to meditate and pray."

"What is your religion then, Albert?" said Consuelo, in a sweet and melancholy voice. "Are these bones Hussite or Catholic? Were not both the victims of impious fury, and martyrs of a faith equally sincere? Is it true that you prefer the Hussite doctrines to those of your relatives, and that the reforms subsequent to those of John Huss do not appear to you sufficiently radical and decisive? Speak, Albert—what am I to believe?"

"If they told you that I preferred the reform of the Hussites to that of the Lutherans, and the great Procopius to the vindictive Calvin, as much as I prefer the exploits of the Taborites to those of the soldiers of Wallenstein, they have told you the truth, Consuelo. But what signifies my creed to you, who seem instinctively aware of truth, and who know the Deity better than I do? God forbid that I should bring you here to trouble your poor soul and peaceful conscience with my tormenting reveries! Remain as you are, Consuelo; you were born pious and good; moreover, you were born poor and obscure, and nothing has changed in you the pure dictates of reason and the light of justice. We can pray together without disputing —you who know every thing although having learned nothing, and I who know very little after a long and tedious study. In whatever temple you raise your voice, the knowledge of the true God will be in your heart, and the feeling of the true faith will kindle your soul. It is not to instruct you, but in order that your revelation may be imparted to me, that I wished our voices and our spirits to unite before this altar, formed of the bones of my fathers."

"I was not mistaken, then, in thinking that these honored remains, as you call them, are those of Hussites, thrown into the fountain of the Schreckenstein during the bloody fury of the civil wars, in the time of your ancestor John Ziska, who, they say, made fearful reprisals? I have been told that, after burning the village, he destroyed the wells. I fancy I can discover in the obscurity of this vault, a circle of hewed stones above my head, which tells me that we are precisely under a spot where I have often sat when fatigued after searching for you in vain. Say, Count Albert, is this really the place that you have baptized as the Stone of Expiation?"

"Yes, it is here," replied Albert, "that torments and atrocious violence have consecrated the asylum of my prayers, and the sanctuary of my grief. You see enormous blocks suspended above our heads, and others scattered on the banks of the stream. The just hands of the Taborites flung them there by the orders of him whom they called the Terrible Blind Man ; but they only served to force back the waters toward those subterranean beds in which they succeeded in forcing a passage. The wells were destroyed, and I have covered their ruins with cypress, but it would have needed a mountain to fill this cavern. The blocks which were heaped up in the mouth of the well, were stopped by a winding stair, similar to that which you had the courage to descend in my garden at the castle. Since that time, the gradual pressure of the soil has thrust them closer together, and confines them better. If any portion of the mass escapes, it is during the winter frosts ; you have therefore nothing to fear from their fall."

"It was not that of which I was thinking, Albert," replied Consuelo, looking toward the gloomy altar on which he had placed his Stradivarius. "I asked myself why you render exclusive worship to the memory of these victims, as if there were no martyrs on the other side, and as if the crimes of the one were more pardonable than those of the other?"

Consuelo spoke thus in a severe tone, and looking distrustfully at Albert. She remembered Zdenko, and all her questions, had she dared so to utter them, assumed in her mind a tone of interrogation, such as would befit a judge toward a criminal.

The painful emotion which suddenly seized upon the count seemed the confession of remorse. He passed his hands over his forehead, then pressed them against his breast, as if it were being torn asunder. His countenance changed in a frightful manner, and Consuelo feared that he might have only too well understood her.

"You do not know what harm you do me," said he, leaning upon the heap of bones, and drooping his head toward the withered skulls, which seemed to gaze on him from their hollow orbits. "No, you cannot know it, Consuelo, and your cold remarks recall the memory of the dreary past. You do not know that you speak to a man who has lived through ages of grief, and who, after being the blind instrument of inflexible justice in the hands of God, has received his recompense and undergone his punishment. I have so suffered, so wept, so expiated my dreary destiny, so atoned for the horrors to which my fate subjected me, that I had at last flattered myself I could forget them. Forgetfulness! — yes, forgetfulness! — that was the craving which consumed my aching breast; that was my vow and my daily prayer; that was the token of my alliance with man and my reconciliation with God, which, during long years, I had implored, prostrate upon these moldering bones. When I first saw you, Consuelo, I began to hope; when you pitied me, I thought I was saved. See this wreath of withered flowers ready to fall into the dust, and which encircles the skull that surmounts the altar. You do not recognize it, though I have watered it with many a bitter yet soothing tear. It was you who gathered them, you who sent them to me by the companion of my sorrows, the faithful guardian of this sepulcher. Covering them with kisses and tears, I anxiously asked myself if you could ever feel any true and heartfelt regard for one like myself—a pitiless fanatic, an unfeeling tyrant ——"

"But what are the crimes you have committed?" said Consuelo firmly, distracted with a thousand varying emotions, and emboldened by the deep dejection of Albert. "If you have a confession to make, make it here to me, that I may know if I can absolve and love you."

"Yes, you may absolve me; for he whom you know, Albert of Rudolstadt, has been innocent as a child; but he whom you do not know, John Ziska of the Chalice, has been whirled by the wrath of Heaven into a career of iniquity."

Consuelo saw the imprudence of which she had been guilty, in rousing the slumbering flame and recalling to Albert's mind his former madness. This, however, was not the moment to combat it, and she was revolving in her mind some expedient to calm him, and had gradually sunk into a reverie, when suddenly she perceived that Albert no longer spoke, no longer held her hand—that he was not at her side, but standing a few paces off, before the monument, performing on his violin the singular airs with which she had been already so surprised and charmed.

CHAPTER LVI.

ALBERT at first played several of those ancient canticles whose authors are now either unknown or forgotten in Bohemia, but of which Zdenko had preserved the precious tradition, and the text of which the count had found by dint of study and meditation. He was so imbued with the spirit of these compositions, barbarous at the first glance, but profoundly touching and truly beautiful to an enlightened and serious taste, and had made himself so familiar with them, as to be able to improvise on them at length, mingling with them his own ideas, then resuming and developing the original idea, and again giving way to his own inspiration, all without changing the original austere and striking character of these ancient productions by his ingenious and learned interpretation. Consuelo had determined to listen to and retain those precious specimens of the popular genius of ancient Bohemia; but all her endeavors soon became impossible, as much from her musing mood as the vague impression which the music itself produced.

There is a species of music which may be termed natural, because it is not the production of science and reflection, but rather of an inspiration which escapes from the trammels of rules and conventions. Such is popular music, that of the peasants in particular. What glorious poetry appears, lives, and dies, as it were, among them, without ever having been correctly noted down, or appearing in any regular form! The unknown artist, who improvises his rustic ballad while he tends his flocks or drives the plow—and such exist even in the most prosaic countries— can rarely be induced to give a form to his fugitive ideas. He communicates it to others, children of nature like himself, and they chant it from hamlet to hamlet, from hut to hut, each one according to his taste. It is for this reason that these songs and pastoral romances, so lively and simple, or so tender in sentiment, are for the most part lost, and have never lasted more than one century. Educated musicians will not trouble themselves to collect them. The most part despise them, for want of an intelligence and sentiment sufficiently elevated to comprehend them; others are turned aside by the difficulties they encounter in their search for the true and real version, with which perhaps the author himself was unacquainted, and which certainly was not acknowledged as an invariable type by its numerous interpreters. Some have changed it through ignorance; others have developed, modified, or embellished it by their superior taste and intelligence, because cultivation has not taught them to repress their natural impulses. They do not know that they have transformed the primitive work, and their candid hearers are no more aware of it than themselves. The peasant neither examines nor compares. When Heaven has made him a musician, he sings after the fashion of the birds, the nightingale especially, whose improvisation is endless, though the elements of her song be the same. Moreover, the genius of the people is unbounded. It is needless to register its productions, which, like those of the earth they cultivate, are unceasing; it creates every hour, like nature, which inspires it.*

Consuelo had all the candor, poetry, and sensibility in her composition which are requisite to comprehend and 'ove popular music. In this she proved that she was a great artist, and that the learned theories which she studied had in no respect impaired the freshness and sweetness which are the treasures of inspiration and the youth of the soul. She had sometimes whispered to Anzoleto, so that Porpora could not hear, that she loved several of the barcaroles sung by the fishermen of the Adriatic, better than all the science of Padre Martini and Maestro Durante. Her mother's songs and boleros were a source of poetic life from which she never wearied in drawing inspiration. What impression then must the musical genius of the Bohemians—that pastoral, warlike, fanatic people, grave and mild in the midst of the most potent elements of activity—have produced upon her! Such characteristics were at once striking and new to her. Albert performed this music with rare perception of the national spirit, and of the pious and energetic feelings in which it originated. He combined in his improvisation the profound melancholy and heart-rending regret with which slavery had imbued his soul and that of his people ; and this mingling of sorrow and bravery, of exultation and depression, these hymns of gratitude united with cries of distress, pictured in the deepest and most lively colors the sorrows of Bohemia and of Albert.

It has been justly said, that the aim of music is to awaken feeling. No other art so reveals the sublime emotions of the human soul; no art so depicts the glories of nature, the delights of contemplation, the character of nations, the whirl of passion, and the cry of suffering. Hope, fear, regret, despair, devotion, enthusiasm, faith, doubt, glory, peace—all these, and more, music gives us, and takes away from us again, according to its genius and our own capacity. It presents things in an entirely new

---

*The author here enters, in a note, into some particulars relative to the hurdy-gurdy players in France. The principal instructors, it appears, are in Bourbonnais, in the woods. Their simple compositions, which they reckon by the hundreds, and are yearly renewed embrace only the simplest elements of music.

and original aspect, and without being guilty of the puerilities of mere sound, and the imitation of external noises, it suffers us to perceive, through a dreamy haze which enhances and ennobles them, the exterior objects to which it transports our imagination. Certain anthems will evoke the gigantic phantoms of ancient cathedrals, allow us to penetrate into the secret thoughts of their constructors, and of those who, kneeling within their holy precincts, utter their hymns of praise to God. Those who are able to express simply and powerfully the music of different nations, and know how to listen to it as it deserves, need not to make a tour of the world in order to behold different nations, to visit their monuments, to read their books, or to traverse their plains, their mountains, their gardens, and their wildernesses. A Jewish air at once transports us into the synagogue; a pibroch conveys us to the Highlands of Scotland; while all Spain is revealed to us by a melody of that fair land. Thus have I been many a time in Poland, Germany, Naples, Ireland, India; and thus have I come to be better acquainted with the inhabitants of these countries than if I had known them for years. It required but an instant to transport me there and make me a sharer in all their thoughts and emotions. I identified myself with every phase of their existence by studying their music and making it my own.

Consuelo gradually ceased to hear Albert's violin. Her soul was rapt, and her senses, closed against all outward objects, awoke in another world, to traverse unknown regions inhabited by a new race of beings. She beheld, amidst a strange chaos at once horrible and magnificent, the spectral form of the heroes of old Bohemia; she heard the mournful clang of bells, while the formidable Taborites descended from their fortified mounts, lean, half-clad, bloody and ferocious. Then she beheld the angels of death assembled in the clouds, the cup and sword in their hands. Hovering in a compact troop over the heads of the prevaricating pontiffs, she saw them pour out upon the accused earth the vial of divine wrath. She fancied she heard the rushing of their wings, and the dropping blood which extinguished the conflagration lighted by their fury. Sometimes it was a night of terror and gloom, wherein she heard the sobs and groans of the dying on the field of battle. Sometimes it was a glowing day, of which she could hardly bear the splendor, in which she saw the thundering chariot of the Terrible Blind Man, with his helmet and his rusty cuirass, and the gore-stained bandage which covered his eyes. Temples opened of themselves as he approached; monks fled into the bosom of the earth, carrying away their relics and their treasures in a corner of their robes. Then the conquerors brought feeble old men, mendicants covered with sores like Lazarus; madmen who ran singing and laughing like Zdenko; executioners stained with blood, little children with pure hands and angel looks, amazons carrying torches and bundles of pikes, and seated them round a table, while an angel radiant with beauty, like those which Albert Durer has introduced into his apocalyptic compositions, presented to their greedy lips the wooden cup, the chalice of forgiveness, of restoration, and of sacred equality. This angel re-appeared in all the visions that floated around Consuelo. She saw him, the beautiful one, the sorrowful, the immortal, proudest among the proud. He bore along with him his broken chains; and his torn pinions dragging on the ground betrayed tokens of violence and captivity. He smiled compassionately on the men of crime, and pressed the little children to his bosom.

Excited, fascinated, she darted toward him with open arms while her knees bent under her. Albert let fall his violin, which gave out a plaintive sound as it fell, and received the young girl in his arms while he uttered a cry of surprise and transport. It was he whom Consuelo had listened to and looked at, while dreaming of the rebellious angel—his form, his image which had attracted and subdued her—it was against his heart that she had come to rest her own, exclaiming in a choking voice—"Thine! thine! Angel of Grief, thine and God's forever!"

But hardly had Albert's lips touched hers, than a deadly chill and scorching pain ran through limb and brain. The illusion, so roughly dissipated, inflicted so violent a shock upon her system that she felt as if about to expire, and extricating herself from the arms of the count, she fell against the bones of the altar, which gave way with a frightful crash. Seeing herself covered with these dread remains, and in the arms of Albert, who gazed on her with surprise and alarm, she experienced such dreadful anguish and terror that, hiding her face in her disheveled hair, she exclaimed with sobs: "Away! away! in the name of Heaven—light! air! O God, rescue me from this sepulcher, and restore me to the light of the sun!"

Albert, seeing her pale and delirious, darted toward her, and would have lifted her in his arms to extricate her from the cavern. But in her consternation she understood him not, and, abruptly rising, she began to fly recklessly toward the recesses of the cavern, without giving any heed to the obstacles by which she was beset, and which in many places presented imminent danger.

"In the name of God," said Albert, "not that way! Death is in your path! Wait for me!"

But his cries only served to augment Consuelo's terror. She bounded twice over the brook with the lightness of a roe, and without knowing what she did. At last, in a gloomy recess planted with cypress, she dashed against a sort of mound, and fell with her hands before her on earth freshly turned up.

This shock made such an impression upon her that a kind of stupor succeeded to her terror. Suffocated, breathless, and not well comprehending what she felt, she suffered the count to approach. He had hastened after her, and had had the presence of mind in passing to seize one of the torches from the rocks, in order to light her along the windings of the stream in case he should not overtake her before she reached a spot which he knew to be deep, and toward which she appeared to direct her course. The poor young man was so overwhelmed by such sudden and contrary emotions, that he dared not speak to her, nor even offer her his hand. She was seated on the heap of earth which had caused her to stumble, and dared not utter a word, but confused, and with downcast eyes, she gazed mechanically upon the ground. Suddenly she perceived that this mound had the form and appearance of a tomb, and that she was really seated on a recently made grave, over which were strewed branches of cypress and withered flowers. She rose hastily, and with fresh terror which she could not conquer, exclaimed, "Oh, Albert, whom have you buried here?"

"I buried here what was dearest to me in the world before I knew you," replied Albert, with the most painful emotion. "If I have committed an act of sacrilege during my delirium, and under the idea of fulfilling a sacred duty,

God will, I trust, pardon me. I shall tell you another time what soul inhabited the body which rests here. At present you are too much agitated, and require the fresh air. Come, Consuelo, let us leave this place, where you made me in one moment the happiest and most miserable of men."

"Oh, yes!" she exclaimed, "let us go hence. I know not what vapors are rising from the earth, but I feel as if I were about to die, and as if my reason were deserting me."

They left the cavern together without uttering another word. Albert went first, stopping and holding down his torch before each stone, so that his companion might see and shun it. When he was about to open the door of the cell, a recollection occurred to Consuelo, doubtless in consequence of her artistic turn of thought, though otherwise seemingly out of place.

"Albert," said she, "you have forgotten your violin beside the spring. This admirable instrument, which caused me emotions hitherto unknown, I could not consent to abandon to certain destruction in this damp place."

Albert made a gesture indicating the little value he now attached to any thing beside Consuelo. But she insisted. "It has caused me much pain," said she, "nevertheless——"

"If it has caused you only pain, let it be destroyed," said he, with bitterness. "I never wish to touch it again during my life. Oh! I have been too late in destroying it."

"It would be false were I to say so," replied Consuelo, whose respect for the musical genius of the count began to revive. "I was too much agitated, that is all, and my delight changed into anguish. Seek it, my friend; I should wish to put it in its case until I have courage to place it in your hands and listen to it again."

Consuelo was affected by the look of satisfaction which the count gave her as he re-entered the grotto in order to obey her. She remained alone for a few moments, and reproached herself for her foolish fears and suspicions. She remembered, trembling and blushing as she did so, the delirium which had cast her into his arms; but she could not avoid admiring the respect and forbearance of this man, who adored her, and yet who did not take advantage of the opportunity to speak of his love. His sad and languid demeanor plainly indicted that he hoped nothing either from the present or from the future. She acknowledged his delicacy, and determined to soften by sweetest words their mutual farewell on leaving the cavern.

But the remembrance of Zdenko was fated to pursue her like a vengeful shadow, and force her to accuse Albert in spite of herself. On approaching the door, her eyes lighted on an inscription in Bohemian which she could easily decipher, since she knew it by heart. Some hand, which could be no other than Zdenko's, had traced it with chalk on the dark deep door: "May he whom they have wronged ——." The rest was unintelligible to Consuelo, but the alteration of the last word caused her great uneasiness. Albert returned, grasping his violin, but she had neither courage nor presence of mind to assist him as she had promised. She was impatient to quit the cavern. When he turned the key in the lock, she could not avoid placing her finger on the mysterious word, and looking interrogatively at her host.

"That means," said Albert, with an appearance of tranquility, "may the acknowledged angel, the friend of the unhappy——"

"Yes, I know that; and what more?"

"May he pardon thee!"

"And why pardon?" she replied, turning pale.

"If grief be pardonable," said the count, with a melancholy air, "I have a long prayer to make."

They entered the gallery, and did not break silence until they reached the Monk's Cave. But when the light of day shed its pale reflection through the foliage on the count's features, Consuelo observed the silent tears flow gently down his cheeks. She was affected, yet when he approached with a timid air to carry her to the entrance, she preferred wetting her feet rather than permit him to lift her in his arms. She alleged his fatigue and exhaustion as a pretext for refusing, and already her slippers were moistened, when Albert exclaimed, extinguishing his torch:

"Farewell, then, Consuelo! I see your aversion, and I must return to eternal night, like a specter evoked for a moment from the tomb, only to inspire you with fear."

"No! your life belongs to me," exclaimed Consuelo, turning and stopping him; "you made an oath never to enter this cavern without me, and you have no right to withdraw it."

"And why do you wish to impose the burthen of life on a phantom? A recluse is but the shadow of a man, and he who is not loved, is alone, everywhere and with every one."

"Albert! Albert! you rend my heart! Come, take me away. In the light of day I shall perhaps see more clearly into my own destiny."

CHAPTER LVII.

ALBERT obeyed, and when they began to descend from the base of the Schreckenstein to the valleys beneath, Consuelo became calmer.

" Pardon me," said she, leaning gently on his arm; "I have certainly been mad myself in the grotto."

"Why recall it, Consuelo? I should never have spoken of it; I knew that you would wish to efface it from your memory, as I must endeavor to blot it from mine."

"I do not wish to forget it, my friend, but to entreat your pardon for it. If I were to relate the strange vision which I had while listening to your Bohemian airs, you would find that I was out of my senses when I caused you such terror. You cannot believe that I would trifle with your reason or your repose. Heaven is my witness that I would lay down my life for you."

"I know that you set no great value on life, Consuelo; but I—I feel that I would covet it earnestly, if——"

" Well; if what?"

" If I were beloved even as I love."

"Albert, I love you as much as is allowable : "I would doubtless love you as you deserve to be loved, if——"

" It is your turn to speak."

"If insurmountable obstacles did not make it a crime."

" And what are these obstacles ? I vainly seek them around you; I only find them in your heart — doubtless in the memory of the past."

" Do not speak of the past; it is hateful to me. I would rather die than live over that past again. Your rank, your fortune, the opposition and anger of your relatives, where should I find courage to meet these, Albert? I possess nothing in this world but my pride and independence; what would remain were I to sacrifice them?"

" My love and yours, if you loved me. But I feel that this is not the case, and I only ask your pity. How could you be humiliated by giving me happiness as an alms? Which of us could then take precedence of the other? How would you be lowered by my fortune? Could we not quickly cast it to the poor if it oppressed you? Know you not that I have long resolved to employ it according to my convictions and my tastes, that is to say, to get rid of it, when my father's loss should add the trouble of his inheritance to that of separation? Are you afraid of being rich? I have vowed poverty. Are you afraid of my name rendering you illustrious? It is a false name; the true one is proscribed. True, I shall never resume it, lest I were to injure the memory of my father; but in my obscurity I swear to you no one shall be dazzled by it, and as to the opposition of my friends—oh, if there be no other obstacle but that—only tell me so, and you shall see!"

"It is the greatest of all; the only one which all my devotion, all my gratitude toward you, cannot remove."

" You do not speak the truth, Consuelo. You dare not swear it. It is not the only obstacle."

Consuelo hesitated. She had never told an untruth, yet she wished to repair the evil she had done her friend, who had saved her life, and who had watched over her for months with the tender solicitude of a mother. She wished to soften her refusal by pointing out obstacles which she really believed insurmountable. But Albert's questions troubled her, and her own heart was a labyrinth in which she lost herself, because she could not say with certainty whether she loved or hated this singular man, toward whom a mysterious and powerful sympathy had attracted her, while at the same time an invincible dread, and something even approaching dislike, made her tremble at the mere idea of an engagement with him.

It seemed to her at this moment as if she hated Anzoleto. Could it be otherwise when she compared his coarse selfishness, his low ambition, his baseness, his perfidy, with Albert's generous, humane, pure spirit, so deeply imbued with lofty virtue? The only stain which could sully the latter was this attempt on Zdenko's life, which she could not help believing. But this suspicion might be the offspring of her imagination, a nightmare which a moment's explanation could dispel. She pretended to be preoccupied, and not to have heard Albert's last question. "Heavens!" she exclaimed, stopping to look at a peasant who passed at some distance. "I thought I saw Zdenko!"

Albert shuddered, dropped Consuelo's arm, which he held within his own, took a few steps forward, then stopped and returned toward her, saying, "What an error is yours, Consuelo! this man has not the least resemblance to——" he could not say Zdenko; his features betrayed violent agitation.

"You thought it yourself, however, for a moment," said Consuelo, who looked at him attentively.

"I am near-sighted; and I ought to have recollected that this meeting was impossible."

"Impossible? Zdenko is then far away?"

"So far, that you need fear nothing from his madness."

"Can you explain his sudden hatred to me after his previous display of sympathy?"

"I told you that it arose from a dream which he had on the eve of your descent into the cavern. He saw you in a vision follow me to the altar, where you consented to pledge your faith to me; and there you sang our old Bohemian hymn with a clear and thrilling voice which made the whole church ring; and while you sang he saw me grow pale and sink into the floor, until at length I was dead and buried in the sepulcher of my fathers. Then he beheld you cast away your hymeneal crown, push the flat stone over my head, which covered me on the instant, and dance on it, singing incomprehensible words in an unknown language, with all the marks of unbounded joy. Enraged, he threw himself on you ; but you had already disappeared in a thick vapor, and he awoke, bathed in perspiration, and transported with anger. He awoke me also, for his cries and imprecations made the vault echo again. I found it difficult to induce him to narrate his dream, and still more to hinder him from looking upon it as the counterpart of my future destiny. I could not easily convince him, for I was myself laboring under morbid mental excitement, and had never tried previously to dissuade him when I saw him place implicit belief in his visions and dreams. Nevertheless, I hoped that he had ceased to think of it or attach any importance to it, for he never said a word on the subject ; and when I asked him to go and speak to you about me, he did not oppose it. It never entered into his conceptions that you should seek me here, and his frenzy was roused only when he saw you attempt the task. Nevertheless, he displayed no hatred against you till the moment we met him on our return from the subterranean galleries. He then informed me very laconically in Bohemian that he intended to deliver me from you—that was his expression—and to destroy you the first time he met you alone; for that you were the bane of my life, and had my death written in your eyes. Pardon these details, and say if I had not ground for apprehension. Let us speak no more about it, if you please, the subject is truly painful. I loved Zdenko as a second self. His mental wanderings were identified with my own to such an extent that we had the same dreams, the same thoughts, and even the same physical indispositions. But he was more cheerful, and to some extent of a more poetical turn than myself; the phantoms which appalled me were, to his more genial organization, simply melancholy, or, perchance, even gay. The greatest difference between us was that my attacks were irregular, whereas he was ever the same. While I was a prey to delirium or despair, he lived constantly in a kind of dream, in which all objects assumed a symbolical aspect; and this was even of so sweet and gentle a form, that in my lucid moments, certainly the most painful of all, I required the sight of his peaceful delusion to cheer and reconcile me to life."

"Oh, my friend!" said Consuelo, "you should hate me, as I hate myself, for having deprived you of so devoted and precious a friend! But his exile has lasted long enough; he is by this time surely recovered from his temporary attack."

"Probably," said Albert, with a strange and bitter smile.

"Well, then," replied Consuelo, whose mind revolted at the idea of Zdenko's death, "why not recall him? I should see him without fear, I assure you, and we should make him forget his prejudices."

"Do not speak of it, Consuelo," said Albert, sorrowfully; "he will never return. I have sacrificed my best friend, my companion, my servant, my stay—my provident, laborious mother—my dear, submissive, unconscious child; he who provided for all my wants, for my innocent yet melancholy pleasures: he who upheld me in moments of despair, and who resorted to force and cunning to prevent me from leaving my cell, when he saw me incapable of preserving my own dignity and existence in the world of living men. I have made this sacrifice without remorse, because I felt I ought; for since you have faced the dangers of the cavern and restored me to reason and a sense of duty, you are at once more sacred and precious to me than even Zdenko himself."

"This is an error—an outrage, Albert! A moment's courage is not to be compared to a whole life of devotion."

"Do not suppose that a wild and selfish love has induced me to act as I have done. I should have thrust it back into my bosom, and shut myself up in my cavern with Zdenko, rather than break the heart of the best of men. But the hand of Providence was in it. I had resisted the impulse which mastered me ; had fled from your sight so long as the dreams and presentiments which made me hope to find in you an angel of mercy, were unrealized. Up to the moment when a frightful vision deranged the gentle and pious Zdenko, he shared my aspirations, my hopes, my fears, and my religious desires. Poor soul ! he mistook you the very day you declared yourself. The light of his soul grew dim, and he was condemned to confusion and despair. It was my duty also to abandon him; for you appeared wrapped in rays of glory, your descent was a prodigy, and you cleared away the mists from my eyes, by words which your calm intellect and education as an artist did not permit you to study and prepare. Pity and charity alike inspired you, and under their wonder-working influence you told me what I ought to do in order to know and understand the life of man."

"What then did I say so wise and so good? Truly, Albert, I know not."

"Nor I either; but Heaven was in your voice and in the calm serenity of your looks. With you I learned in an instant that which I never should have learned alone. I knew that my previous life was an expiation, a martyrdom; and I sought the accomplishment of my destiny in darkness, solitude, and tears—in anger, study, penance, and macerations. You gave me another life, another martyrdom—one all patience, sweetness, toleration, and devotion. My duties, which you so simply traced out for me, beginning with those toward my family—I had forgotten them, and my family, through excess of kindness, overlooked my faults. Thanks to you, I have atoned for them; and from the first day I knew you, I have felt, from the calmness that I have experienced, that no more was required from me at present. I know, indeed, that this is not all, and I await the ulterior revelations of my destiny ; but I have confidence, because I have found an oracle that I can consult. You are that oracle, Consuelo. You have received power over me, and I shall not rebel against it. I therefore ought not to have hesitated a moment between the power which was to regenerate me, and the poor passive creature who had hitherto shared my distresses and borne with my outbreaks."

"Do you speak of Zdenko? But how do you know that I might not have cured him also ? You saw that I had already gained some power over him, since I could convince him by a word when he was about to kill me."

"Oh, Heavens! it is too true. I have been wanting in faith. I was afraid. I knew what the oaths of Zdenko were. He had sworn to live only for me, and he kept his oath in my absence as since my return. When he swore to *destroy* you I did not think it possible to change his resolution, and I determined to offend, banish, crush, *destroy* him."

"To *destroy* him! What do you mean, Albert? Where is Zdenko ?"

"You ask me, as God asked of Cain, 'Where is thy brother ?'"

"Oh, Heavens ! you have not killed him, Albert ?" And Consuelo, as she uttered the word clung to Albert's arm, and looked at him with a mixture of pity and terror. But she recoiled from the proud and cold expression of his pale countenance, where grief seemed to have fixed her abode.

"I have not *killed* him, yet I have taken his life assuredly. And if I have preferred regret and repentance to the fear of seeing you assassinated by a madman, have you so little pity in your heart that you always recall my sorrow, and reproach me with the greatest sacrifice I could make? You also are cruel ! Cruelty is never extinct in a human breast."

There was such solemnity in this reproach, the first that Albert had ever addressed to her, that Consuelo felt more than ever the fear which he inspired her. A sort of humiliation—weak, perhaps, but inherent in the female heart—replaced the pride with which she had listened to his passionate declaration. She felt herself humbled, no doubt misunderstood, because she did not wish to discover his secret, save with the intention, or at least the desire, of responding to his affection if he could justify himself. At the same time she perceived that she was guilty in the eyes of her lover, because if he had really killed Zdenko, the only person in the world who had no right to condemn him, was she whose life required the sacrifice of another life infinitely precious to Albert.

Consuelo could not reply; she endeavored to speak of something else, but tears choked her utterance. In seeing them flow Albert was distressed in his turn; but she begged him never to recur to so painful a subject, and promised on her part, with a feeling bordering on despair, never to mention a name which caused him such terrible emotion. They were constrained and unhappy during the remainder of the day, and vainly endeavored to converse on some other subject. Consuelo did not know either what she said or heard. This sad but deep tranquility, with such a load on his conscience, bordered on madness, and Consuelo could not justify her friend save in remembering that he was mad. If he had killed some bandit in fair fight in order to save her life, she would have felt gratitude and perhaps admiration for his strength and courage; but this mysterious murder, doubtless perpetrated in the darkness of the cavern—this sepulcher dug in the very sanctuary—this morose silence after such a deed — the stoical fanaticism with which he dared to lead her to the grotto, and there deliver himself up to the charms of music—all this was horrible, and Consuelo felt that love for such a man was a feeling which could not enter her heart. "When could he have committed the murder?" she asked herself. "I have not for months seen a trace of remorse on his brow. Was there not, perhaps, blood on his hands some day when I offered him mine? Dreadful! He must be made of stone or ice, or else he loves me to the verge of madness. And I who so wished to inspire a boundless love—I who so bitterly regretted being loved so coldly! Behold what heaven has reserved for me in answer to my wish!"

Then she once more endeavored to guess at what time Albert had accomplished his horrible sacrifice. She thought it must have been during her severe illness, when she was indifferent to all outward things; but when she remembered the tender and delicate care which Albert had lavished on her, she could not reconcile the two characters, so dissimilar to each other, and to those of mankind in general.

Lost in dreary reverie, she received with an absent air the flowers which Albert gathered for her on their way, and which he knew she loved. She never even thought of leaving him and entering the castle alone, so as to conceal their meeting; and whether it was that Albert thought no more about it, or that he deemed it unnecessary to dissemble any longer with his family, he did not suggest such a precaution, and they found themselves face to face with the canoness, at the entrance of the castle. For the first time, Consuelo — and, doubtless, Albert also — observed those features, which were rarely ugly in spite of their deformity, inflamed with anger.

"It is high time for you to return, signora," said she to the Porporina, in a voice trembling with indignation. "We were really uneasy about Count Albert. His father, who would not breakfast without him, wished to have a conference with him this morning, which you have thought proper to make him forget. And, as for yourself, there is a young fellow in the saloon who calls himself your brother, and who awaits your arrival with rather ill-bred impatience."

After having expressed herself in these extraordinary terms, the poor Wenceslawa, terrified at her own exploit, set off for her own apartment, where she coughed and wept for more than an hour.

CHAPTER LVIII.

"My aunt is in a strange mood," said Albert, as they ascended together the steps of the entrance. "I beg you will pardon her; and be assured that this very day she will alter her manner and language."

"My brother?" said Consuelo, stupified with the news which had just been announced, and not hearing what the young count said.

"I did not know you had a brother," said Albert, who was more struck by his aunt's ill-temper than by this occurrence. "You will doubtless be glad to see him, dear Consuelo, and I am rejoiced."

"Better not, signor count," replied Consuelo, a painful presentiment rapidly occurring to her mind; "some dreadful sorrow is perhaps in store for me, and——" She paused, trembling, for she was on the point of asking advice and protection; but she was afraid of drawing closer the bonds already existing between them; and, not daring either to receive or avoid the visitor who introduced himself to her under color of an untruth, she felt her knees fail her, and, turning pale, was obliged to support herself against the balustrade.

"Do you fear bad news from your family?" said Albert, who now began to grew uneasy.

"I have no family," replied Consuelo, endeavoring to move on. She was about to say that she had no brother, but some vague terror prevented her. In crossing the dining-hall, she heard the creaking of the traveler's boots pacing backward and forward impatiently. By an involuntary movement she approached the young count, and as she took his arm, pressed it against her own, as if to seek refuge in his affection from the sufferings which she anticipated.

Albert, struck by this movement, felt a deadly apprehension. "Do not go in," said he, in a low tone of voice, "without me; I feel, by a sort of presentiment which has never yet failed me, that this brother is your enemy and mine. I am chilled—I am afraid, as if I were about to be forced to hate some one!"

Consuelo withdrew her arm, which Albert had pressed close to his bosom; she trembled lest he should adopt one of those singular ideas—one of those implacable resolutions —of which Zdenko's presumptive death afforded a deplorable instance.

"Let us part here," she said in German, for their voices could now be heard in the adjoining apartment. "I have nothing to fear at present; but, if the future threaten, Albert, be assured I shall have recourse to you."

Albert yielded with extreme reluctance. Fearing to be found wanting in delicacy, he dared not disobey; but he could not resolve to leave the hall. Consuelo, who under·

stood his thoughts, closed the double doors of the saloon when she entered, in order that he might neither hear nor see what was about to occur. Anzoleto (for his effrontery left no doubt on her mind that it was indeed he) was prepared to salute her bodily, in the presence of witnesses, with a fraternal embrace; but when he saw her enter alone, pale, but cold and severe, he lost all his courage, and, stammering, threw himself at her feet. It was not necessary, indeed, for him to feign joy or tenderness; he experienced both these feelings in their full reality, at discovering her whom, notwithstanding his baseness, he had never ceased to love. He burst into tears, and as she would not let him take her hands, he covered the border of her garment with kisses and tears. Consuelo had not expected to find him thus. For months she had thought of him as he had appeared on the night of their separation—the most bitter, hateful, and detestable of men. That very morning she had seen him pass with an insolent and careless air. Now he was on his knees, repentant, prostrate, bathed in tears, as in the stormiest days of their once passionate reconciliations, and handsomer than ever; for his traveling costume, though common enough, became him to admiration, and his sunburnt complexion imparted a more manly expression to his classic features. Trembling like the dove in the grasp of the hawk, she was forced to seat herself and hide her face in her hands, to avoid the fascination of his gaze. This gesture, which Anzoleto took for shame, encouraged him, and the return of his evil thoughts soon destroyed the effect of his first warm and unaffected transports. Anzoleto, in flying from Venice, and the vexations inseparable from his faults, had no other aim but that of seeking his fortune; but he had always cherished the desire and expectation of once more finding out his dear Consuelo. Such talents as hers could not, in his opinion, remain long hidden, and by dint of chatting with innkeepers, guides, and travelers, he left no means untried of procuring information. At Vienna he had met persons of distinction from his native city, to whom he had confessed his folly and his flight. They advised him to wait in some place at a distance from Venice, until Count Zustiniani had forgotten or forgiven his escapade; and, while promising to intercede for him, they gave him letters of introduction to Prague, Dresden, and Berlin.

When passing by the Castle of the Giants, Anzoleto had never thought of questioning his guide ; but after about half an hour's rapid ride, having paused to breathe the horses, he had entered into conversation with him relative to the people and the surrounding country. Naturally enough, the guide spoke of the lords of Rudolstadt, their strange mode of life, and particularly of the eccentricities of Count Albert, which were no longer a secret to any body, especially since Doctor Wetzelius had declared open enmity toward him. The guide added to this the local gossip that the count had refused to marry his cousin, the beautiful Baroness Amelia de Rudolstadt, in order to take up with an adventuress, not so remarkable for her beauty as for her admirable singing, which enchanted every one.

This description was so applicable to Consuelo, that our traveler immediately asked the name of the adventuress, and learning that she was called the Porporina, instantly guessed the truth. He retraced his steps; and after having rapidly invented the pretext by which to introduce himself into so well-guarded a castle, he continued to question his guide still further. The man's gossip induced him to believe that Consuelo was the young count's betrothed, and was about to become his wife ; for the story was, that she had enchanted the whole family, and instead of turning her out of doors as she deserved, they paid her more respect and attention than they had ever done to the Baroness Amelia.

These details stimulated Anzoleto quite as much as, and perhaps even more, than his real attachment for Consuelo. He had indeed sighed for the return of that peaceful existence which he had led with her; he had truly felt that in losing her advice and direction, he had destroyed, or at least put in jeopardy, the success of his musical career; and, in short, he was strongly attracted to her by a love at once selfish, deep-seated, and unconquerable. But to all this was added the vainglorious wish of disputing the affections of Consuelo with a rich and noble lover, of snatching her from a brilliant marriage, and causing it to be said in the neighborhood and in the world, that this highly cherished girl had preferred to follow his fortunes rather than become countess and chatelaine. He amused himself, therefore, by making his guide repeat that the Porporina was lady paramount at Riesenburg ; and inwardly gloried in the childish idea that this same guide should relate to future travelers, that one day a gay young fellow rode up to the inhospitable Castle of the Giants, *came, saw,* and *conquered,* and a day or two afterward took his leave, carrying with him this pearl of singers, before the very eyes of the puissant lord of Rudolstadt.

At this idea he struck the rowels into his horse's sides, and laughed so loud and long, that the guide concluded that of the two certainly Count Albert was not the madder.

The canoness received Anzoleto with distrust, but did not like to dismiss him, as she hoped that he would perhaps take with him his pretended sister, He was out of temper when he learned that Consuelo was walking, and he questioned the domestics on the subject while they served breakfast. Only one of them understood a little Italian, and he replied, without any malicious intention, that he had seen the signora on the mountain with the young count. Anzoleto said to himself, that if Consuelo were the betrothed of the count, she would have the proud attitude of a person in her position ; but if it were otherwise, she would be less certain of her standing, and would tremble before an old friend who might thwart her projects.

Anzoleto was too acute not to perceive the ill-temper and uneasiness with which the canoness viewed this long walk of Porporina with her nephew. As he did not see Count Christian, he thought that the guide must have misinformed him, that the family were displeased with the count's affection for the young adventuress, and that the latter would be abashed before her first lover.

Interpreting in this manner the irresistible emotion she had felt on first seeing him, he thought, when he saw her sink in her chair, fainting and agitated, that he might go any lengths. He therefore gave full scope to his eloquence, reproached himself for the past, humbled himself hypocritically, wept, related his torments and despair, painting them somewhat more poetically than the truth warranted, and finally implored her pardon with all the persuasive eloquence of a Venetian and an accomplished actor.

Agitated by his voice, and fearing her own weakness more than his remaining influence, Consuelo, who also had had time for reflection during the last four months, was sufficiently self-possessed to detect in these professions, and in this passionate eloquence, what she had already heard a thousand times at Venice, in the latter days of their unhappy attachment. It mortified her to find that he used the same assurances, the same oaths, as if nothing had happened since those quarrels in which she was far from suspecting the infamous part Anzoleto had played. Indignant at such audacity and such flowery language, when tears and shame alone should have manifested themselves, she cut him short by rising and coldly replying. "It is enough, Anzoleto ; I have already pardoned you, and I wish to hear no more. Anger has given place to pity, and your misconduct and my sufferings are equally forgotten. There is nothing more to say. I thank you for the kindness which induced you to interrupt your journey with a view to a reconciliation ; but your pardon, as you see, was already granted. So now adieu!"

"I leave you?—I quit you?" exclaimed Anzoleto, now really terrified. "No! I would rather you would kill me at once. No! never should I be able to live without you. I could not do it, Consuelo—I have tried, and I know it is in vain. Where you are not, there is nothing for me. My hateful ambition, my miserable vanity, to which I wished, but in vain, to sacrifice my love, have been my torment, and have never yielded me a moment's pleasure. Your image follows me everywhere ; the memory of our happiness, so pure, so chaste, so delightful (and where could you yourself find any thing approaching to it?) is ever before my eyes ; I am disgusted with all around me. Oh! Consuelo, do you remember the lovely nights at Venice, our boat, the stars, our endless songs, and your gentle lessons? Did I not love you then? If I have acted ill toward others, oh, do not forget that at least I have been faultless toward you! You once professed to love me ; but how have you forgotten your pledge! I—thankless monster! wretch that I am!—have never once forgotten it ; and I do not wish to forget it, although you do so without effort or regret."

"It is possible," replied Consuelo, struck by the truth which these words seemed to display, "that you do indeed regret this lost happiness — lost, destroyed by your own misconduct. It is a punishment which you must endure, and which I ought not to prevent. Happiness corrupted you, Anzoleto, and you require suffering to purify you. Go, and remember me, if this affliction prove salutary ; if not, forget me, as I forget you — I, who have nothing either to expiate or atone."

" Ah! you have a heart of iron!" exclaimed Anzoleto, surprised and wounded by her tranquility ; " but do not expect thus to drive me away. It is possible that I annoy you, and that I am here somewhat in the way. You would sacrifice, I know, the memory of the past to rank and fortune. But it shall not be so. I will stay with you ; and if I lose you it shall not be without a struggle. I will recall the past, and that too before all your new friends, if you force me to it. I will repeat the oaths which you made at the bedside of your dying mother, and which you repeated a hundred times on her tomb and in the churches where we knelt side by side, listened to the music, and conversing in whispers. I will tell your new lover that of which he is not aware—for they know nothing of you, not even that you were an actress. Yes, I will tell them ; and we shall see if the noble Count Albert will dispute you with an actor, your friend, your equal, your betrothed, your lover. Ah! do not drive me to despair, Consuelo, or ——"

" What! threats?" said the angry maiden ; " at last I have found you out, Anzoleto. I rejoice at it, and I thank you for having raised the mask. Yes, thanks to Heaven! I shall regret and pity you no more. I see the venom which rankles within your heart ; I recognize your baseness and your hateful love. Go, wreak your vengeance— you will only do me a service ; but unless you are equally expert in calumny as in insult, you cannot say any thing to make me blush."

Thus saying, she retreated to the door, opened it, and was just leaving the room when she met Count Christian. Anzoleto, who had rushed forward to detain her by force or cunning, on seeing the venerable old man, who advanced with an affable and majestic air after having kissed Consuelo's hand, fell back intimidated and bereft of his audacity.

CHAPTER LIX.

" Dear signora," said the old count, "pardon me for not having more courteously received your brother. I had forbidden them to interrupt me, as I had some important business to transact this morning, and they obeyed my directions too faithfully in thus leaving me in ignorance of the arrival of a guest so welcome to me and all my family. Be assured, sir," added he, turning to Anzoleto, " that I am happy to see in my house so near a relative of our beloved Porporina. I trust, therefore, that you will remain here as long as may be agreeable to you. I presume that after so long a separation you must have much to say to each other, and I hope you will not hesitate to enjoy at leisure a happiness in which I sincerely sympathize."

Contrary to his usual custom, Count Christian spoke to a stranger with ease. His timidity had long since disappeared toward the gentle Consuelo, and on this day a vivid ray of joy seemed to illumine his countenance, like those which the sun sheds before sinking beneath the horizon. Anzoleto was confused in the presence of that majesty which rectitude and serenity of soul reflect upon the brow of an aged and venerable man. He was well skilled to bow low before the nobles of his native land, but in his inmost soul he hated and mocked them. He had found only too much to despise in them, and in the fashionable world in which he had for some time lived. He had never before seen dignity so lofty, and politeness so cordial, as those of the old chatelain of Riesenburg. He stammered forth his thanks, and almost repented having procured by an imposition, the kind and fatherly reception with which he was greeted. He feared above all lest Consuelo should unmask him, by declaring to the count that he was not her brother, and he felt that he could not at this moment repay her with impertinence, and study his revenge.

" I feel much gratified by your lordship's goodness," replied Consuelo, after an instant's reflection; " but my brother, who is deeply sensible of its value, cannot have the happiness of profiting by it. Pressing business calls him to Prague, and he has just this moment taken leave of me."

" Impossible ! you have hardly seen each other an instant," said the count.

" He has lost several hours in waiting for me," replied she, "and his moments are now counted. He knows very well," added she, looking at her pretended brother with a significant expression, "that he cannot remain here a minute longer."

This cold determination restored to Anzoleto all his hardihood and effrontery. " Let what will happen," said he, " I take the devil—I mean God," he added, recovering himself—" to witness, that I will not leave my dear sister so hastily as her reason and prudence require. I know of no business that is worth an instant of such happiness; and since my lord the count so generously permits me, I accept his invitation with gratitude. I shall remain, therefore, and my engagements at Prague must be fulfilled a little later, that is all."

" That is speaking like a thoughtless young man," returned Consuelo, offended. " There are some affairs in which honor calls more loudly than interest."

"It is speaking like a brother," replied Anzoleto, " but you always speak so like a queen, my good little sister."

" It is spoken like a good young man!" added the old count, holding out his hand to Anzoleto. " I know of no business which cannot be put off till the morrow. It is true that I have always been reproached for my indolence; but I have invariably found that more is lost by hastiness than by reflection. For example, my dear Porporina, it is now several days, I might say weeks, since I have had a request to make of you, and I have delayed it until now. I believe I have done well, and that the proper moment has arrived. Can you grant me to-day the hour's conversation I was just about to request when I was informed of your brother's arrival ? It seems to me that this happy circumstance has occurred quite *apropos,* and perhaps he would not be out place in the conference I propose."

" I am always, and at all hours, at your lordship's command," answered Consuelo. " As to my brother, he is yet a mere child, and I do not usually entrust him with my private affairs."

"I know that very well," returned Anzoleto, impudently; " but as my lord count authorizes me, I do not require any other permission than his to join in your conference."

" You will permit me to judge of what is proper for you and for myself," replied Consuelo, haughtily. " My lord count, I am ready to follow you to your apartment, and to listen to you with respect."

" You are very severe with this young man, who has so frank and cheerful an air," said the count, smiling; then turning toward Anzoleto: " Do not be impatient, my child," said he, " your turn will come. What I have to say to your sister cannot be concealed from you, and soon, I hope, she will permit me to confide it to you."

Anzoleto had the impertinence to reply to the unsuspecting gaiety of the old man, by retaining his hand in his own, as if he wished to attach himself to him, and discover the secret from which Consuelo excluded him. He had not the good taste to perceive that he ought at least to have left the saloon, in order to spare him the necessity of doing so. When he found himself alone, he stamped with anger, fearing lest this young girl, now so collected and self-possessed, should disconcert all his plans, and cause him to be dismissed in spite of his address. He longed to glide steathily through the house, and listen at all the doors. He left the saloon with this purpose, wandered in the gardens for a few moments, then ventured into the galleries, pretending, whenever he met a domestic, to be admiring the beautiful architecture of the château. But at three different times he saw passing, at some distance, a personage dressed in black, and singularly grave, whose attention he was not very desirous of attracting. It was Albert, who appeared not to remark him, and yet who never lost sight of him. Anzoleto, seeing that he was a full head taller than himself, and observing the serious beauty of his features, perceived plainly that he had not so despicable a rival as he had at first thought, in the person of the madman of Riesenburg. He therefore decided to return to the saloon, and commenced trying his fine voice in the lofty apartment, as he passed his fingers absently over the keys of the harpsichord.

" My daughter," said Count Christian to Consuelo, after having led her to his study, and placed a large arm-chair for her, covered with red velvet with gold fringes, while he seated himself on an easy chair by her side, " I have a favor to ask of you, and yet I know not by what right I can do so while you are yet in ignorance of my intentions.

May I flatter myself that my gray hairs, my tender esteem for you, and the friendship of the noble Porpora your adopted father, will inspire you with sufficient confidence in me to induce you to open your heart without reserve?"

Affected and yet somewhat terrified at this commencement, Consuelo raised the old man's hand to her lips, and frankly replied, "My lord count, I love and respect you as if I had the honor and happiness to be your daughter, and I can answer all your questions without fear and without evasion, in whatever concerns me personally."

"I will ask you nothing else, my dear daughter, and I thank you for this promise. Believe me, I am as incapable of abusing your confidence, as I believe you incapable of breaking your pledge."

"I do believe it, my lord. Be pleased to speak."

"Well, then, my child," said the old man, encouragingly, "what is your name?"

"I have none," replied Consuelo, frankly; "my mother was called Rosmunda. At my baptism they named me Maria of Consolation; I never knew my father."

"But you are acquainted with his name?"

"No, signor; I never heard him spoken of."

"Has Master Porpora adopted you? has he given you his name by any legal act?"

"No, signor; among artists these things are not thought of. My generous master possesses nothing, and has nothing to bequeath. As to his name, it was unimportant in my situation whether I adopted it from custom or otherwise. If my talents justify it, it will be well; if not, I shall be unworthy of the honor of bearing it."

The count was silent for some moments; then taking Consuelo's hand:

"Your noble candor," said he, "gives me a yet higher opinion of you. Do not think that I ask these particulars in order to esteem you more or less according to your condition and birth. I wished to ascertain if you had any disinclination to tell the truth, and I see you have none. I am infinitely indebted to you; you are more ennobled by your character than we are by our birth and titles."

Consuelo smiled at the simplicity of the old patrician, who wondered that she could, without blushing, make so plain a declaration. There was apparent in his conduct a remnant of aristocratic prejudice, all the more tenacious that Christian had nobly combated and evidently desired to vanquish it.

"Now," said he, "I must put a question yet more delicate, and I require all your indulgence to excuse me."

"Fear nothing, signor; I shall reply frankly."

"Well, then, my child, you are not married?"

"No, signor."

"And——you are not a widow—you have no children?"

"I am not a widow—I have no children," replied Consuelo, who had a great inclination to laugh, although not well knowing what the count's drift was.

"And you·are not engaged to any one ? you are perfectly free?"

"Pardon, signor ; I was engaged with the consent, even by the command, of my dying mother, to a young man whom I loved since childhood, and to whom I was betrothed up to the period of my quitting Venice."

"Then you are engaged?" said the count, with a singular mixture of vexation and satisfaction.

"No, signor, I am perfectly free," replied Consuelo. "He whom I loved, unworthily betrayed his faith, and I left him forever."

"Then you did love him?" said the count, after a pause.

"From my heart."

"And——perhaps you love him still?"

"No, signor, that is impossible."

"Then you have no wish to see him again?"

"It would be a torment to me. But since I am called upon to confess fully, as I do not wish to take any advantage of your esteem for me I shall inform you of every thing. We lived together as children, followed the same amusements, drank from the same cup, we were ever together, we loved each other, and we were to be married. I had sworn to my mother to be prudent; I have kept my word, if indeed it be prudent to believe in a man who wished to deceive me, and repose confidence, affection, esteem, where they were not deserved. When he proved himself to be faithless, I tore him from my heart. This man without honor may indeed tell a different tale, but that is of no great importance to one in my humble position. Provided I sing well, nothing more is required of me. While I can pray without remorse before the crucifix on which I have sworn to my mother, I need not trouble myself as to what is thought of me. There is no one to blush on my account; no brothers, no cousins, to fight for my sake."

"No brothers? but you have a brother?"

Consuelo was on the paint of confiding all to the old count, under the seal of secrecy; but she feared it would be base to seek any extrinsic defense against one who had so meanly threatened her. She thought that she herself should have the firmness to defend and deliver herself from the pursuit of Anzoleto. Besides, her generous soul recoiled at the idea of having the man expelled whom she had so faithfully loved. Whatever courtesy Count Christian might display in this case toward Anzoleto, however culpable the latter might be, she had not courage to subject him to such indignity. She replied therefore that she looked upon her brother as a person of little understanding, whom she was accustomed to treat as a child.

"But he is not surely an ill-conducted person?" said the count.

"Possibly," she replied; "I have little intercourse with him. Our characters and modes of thinking are quite different. Your highness might have observed that I was not anxious to detain him here."

"It shall be as you wish, my child; you have an excellent judgment; and now that you have confided every thing to me with such noble frankness——"

"Pardon me, signor," said Consuelo; "I have not told you every thing, because you have not asked me. I am ignorant of your motives in putting these questions to me, but I presume that some one has spoken unfavorably of me, and that you wish to know if I am a discredit to your household. Hitherto your inquiries have been of so general a nature that I should have felt myself wanting in propriety if I had spoken of my affairs without your permission. But since you wish to know me thoroughly, I must mention a circumstance that will perhaps injure me in your estimation. It is not only possible, as you have often suspected, though I had no wish for it myself, that I should have embraced a theatrical career, but it is asserted that I appeared last season at Venice, under the name of Consuelo. I was called the Zingarella, and all Venice was acquainted with my appearance and my voice."

" Ha!" exclaimed the count, astounded at this new reve-lation; "you are then the wonder that created so great a sensation at Venice last year, and whom the Italian papers so often and so highly eulogized? The finest voice, the most splended talents, that had appeared within the memory of man——"

" Upon the theater of San Samuel, my lord. Those eulogiums were without doubt exaggerated ; but it is an incontestible fact that I am that same Consuelo, that I sang in several operas—in one word, that I am an actress, or, to use a more polite term, a cantatrice. You can now judge if I deserve to retain your good opinion."

" This is very extraordinary ! what a strange destiny!" said the count, absorbed in thought. " Have you told this to—to any one besides me, my child?"

" I have told nearly all to the count your son, my lord, although I did not enter into the details you have just heard."

" So Albert knows your birth, your former love, your profession?"

" Yes, my lord."

" It is well, my dear signora. I cannot thank you warmly enough for the admirable straightforwardness of your conduct toward us, and I promise you that you will have no reason to repent it. Now, Consuelo—(yes, I remember that was the name Albert gave you on your first coming, when he talked Spanish to you)—permit me to collect my thoughts a little. I feel deeply agitated. We have still many things to say to each other, and you must forgive a little anxiety on my part in coming to so grave a decision. Have the goodness to wait here for me an instant."

He left the room, and Consuelo, following him with her eyes, saw him, through the glazed glass doors, enter his oratory and kneel down with fervor.

Herself greatly agitated, she was lost in conjectures as to the object of a conversation which was ushered in with so much solemnity. At first she thought that Anzoleto, while waiting for her, had out of spite already done what he had threatened; that he had been talking to the chaplain or Hans, and that the manner in which he had spoken of her, had excited grave suspicions in the minds of her hosts. But Count Christian could not dissemble, and hitherto his manner and his words had announced increased affection, rather than a feeling of mistrust. Besides, the frankness of her answers had affected him as unexpected revelations would have done ; the last especially had seemed to strike him like a flash of lightning. And now he was praying, he was asking God to enlighten and sustain him in the accomplishment of a great resolution. "Is he about to ask me to leave the house with my brother? Is he about to offer me money?" she asked herself. "Ah! may God preserve me from that insult! But no! this good old man is too highminded, too good, to dream of humiliating me. What did he mean to say at first, and what can he mean to say now? Most probably my long walk with his son may have given him uneasiness, and he is about to scold me. I have deserved it perhaps, and I will submit to his rebuke, since I cannot answer sincerely the questions which may be asked me respecting Albert. This is a trying day; my chest feels all on fire, and my throat is parched."

Count Christian soon returned. He was calm, and his pale countenance bore witness of a victory obtained over himself from a noble motive. "My daughter," said he to Consuelo, reseating himself beside her, and insisting on her retaining the sumptuous arm-chair which she had wished to yield to him, and on which she seemed enthroned, in spite of herself; "it is time that I should respond by my frankness to the openness and confidence which you have testified toward me. Consuelo, my son loves you."

Consuelo became pale and red by turns. She attempted to answer, but Christian interrupted her.

"It is not a question which I ask you," said he. "I should have no right to do so, and perhaps you would have none to answer me; for I know that you have not in any way encouraged Albert's hopes. He has told me all; and I believe him, for he has never told a falsehood, nor I either."

"Nor I either," said Consuelo, raising her eyes to heaven with an expression of mingled humility and pride. "Count Albert must have told you, my lord——"

"That you have repelled every idea of a union with him."

"It was my duty. I knew the usages and the ideas of the world ; I knew that I was not made to be Count Albert's wife, for the sole reason that I esteem myself inferior to no person under God, and that I would not receive grace or favor from any one on earth."

"I know your just pride, Consuelo. I should consider it exaggerated, if Albert had been alone in the world; but believing as you did that I would not approve of such a union, you were right to answer as you have done."

"And now, my lord," said Consuelo, rising, "I understand what you are about to add, and beseech you to spare me the humiliation I feared. I will leave your house, as I would before this have left it, if I had thought I could do so without endangering the reason and perhaps the life of Count Albert, over whom I have more influence than I could have wished. Since you know what it was not permitted me to reveal to you, you can watch over him, prevent the bad effects of this separation, and resume the exercise of a care which belongs to you rather than to me. If I arrogated it to myself indiscreetly, it is a fault which God will forgive me ; for He knows by what pure and disinterested feelings I was actuated."

"I know it," returned the count, "and God has spoken to my conscience, as Albert has spoken to my heart. Sit down therefore, Consuelo, and do not be hasty in condemning my intentions. It was not to order you to quit my house, but to beseech you from my inmost soul to remain in it all your life, that I asked you to listen to me."

"All my life?" replied Consuelo, falling back upon her chair, divided between the satisfaction she felt at this reparation made to her dignity, and the terror which such an offer caused her. "All my life ! your lordship cannot mean what you are kind enough to say."

"I have thought seriously on it, my daughter," replied the count, with a melancholy smile, "and I feel that I shall not repent it. My son loves you to distraction, and you have complete power over his soul. It is you who restored him to me, you who ventured to seek him in some mysterious place which he will not disclose to me, but into which he says no one but a mother or a saint would have dared to penetrate. It is you who risked your life to save him from the gloomy seclusion and delirium which consumed him, Thanks to you he has ceased to cause us horrible anxiety by his absences. It is you who have restored him to calmness, health—in a word, to reason. For it must not be dissembled that my poor boy was mad, and it is certain that he is so no longer. We have passed nearly the whole night together, and he has displayed to me a wisdom superior to mine. I knew that you were to walk with him this morning, and I therefore authorized him to ask of you that which you refused to hear. You were afraid of me, dear Consuelo; you thought that the old Rudolstadt, encased in his aristocratic prejudices, would be ashamed to owe his son to you. Well! you were mistaken. The old Rudolstadt has had pride and prejudices without doubt; perhaps he has them still—he will not conceal his faults before you—but he now abjures them, and in the transport of a boundless gratitude, he thanks you for having restored to him his last, his only child!" So saying, Count Christian took both of Consuelo's hands in his, and covered them with kisses and tears.

CHAPTER LX.

CONSUELO was deeply affected by an explanation which restored to her her self-respect, and tranquilized her conscience. Until this moment she had often feared that she had imprudently yielded to the dictates of her generosity and her courage, but now she received their sanction and recompense. Her joyful tears mingled with those of the old man, and they both remained for some time too deeply agitated to continue the conversation.

Nevertheless Consuelo did not yet understand the proposition which had been made to her, and the count, thinking that he had sufficiently explained himself, regarded her silence and her tears as signs of assent and gratitude. "I will go," said he at last, "and bring my son to your feet, in order that he may unite his blessings with mine on learning the extent of his happiness."

"Stop, my lord!" said Consuelo, astonished at this haste. "I do not understand what you require of me. You approve of the attachment which Count Albert has manifested for me, and my gratitude and devotion toward him. You have given me your confidence, you know that I will not betray it; but how can I engage to consecrate my whole life to a friendship of so delicate a nature? I see clearly that you depend on time and my reason to preserve you son's health of mind and to calm the enthusiasm of his attachment for me. But I do not know if I shall long have that power ; and even if such an intimacy were not dangerous for so excitable a nature as his, I am not free to devote my days to that glorious task. I am not my own mistress."

" O Heavens! what do you say, Consuelo ? Did you not understand me, then? Or did you deceive me in saying that you were free, that you had no attachment of the neart, no engagement, no family?"

" But, my lord," said Consuelo, stupified, " I have an object, a vocation, a calling; I belong to the art to which I have devoted myself since my childhood."

" Great Heavens! what do you say? Do you wish to return to the stage?"

" On that point I am not decided, and I spoke the truth in affirming that my inclination did not lead me thither. I have hitherto experienced only excruciating sufferings in that stormy career, but I feel nevertheless that I should be rash in resolving to renounce it. It has been my destiny, and perhaps I cannot withdraw myself from the future which has been traced out for me. Whether I again appear on the stage, or only give lessons and concerts, I am still—I must be—a singer. What should I be good for otherwise ? Where can I attain independence? In what pursuit can I occupy my mind, accustomed as it is to labor and nursed by sweet sounds?"

" O Consuelo, Consuelo!" cried Count Christian, sadly, " what you say is too true. But I thought you loved my son, and now I see that you do not love him!"

" And what if I should learn to love him with the passion which I must feel in order to sacrifice myself for him, my lord?" cried Consuelo, growing impatient in her turn. " Do you think it absolutely impossible for a woman to feel love for Count Albert that you ask me to remain always with him?"

" What! can I have explained myself so badly, or do you think me crazy, dear Consuelo? Have I not asked your heart and your hand for my son? Have I not placed at your feet a legitimate and certainly an honorable alliance? If you loved Albert, you would doubtless find in the happiness of sharing his life a sufficient recompense for the loss of your glory and your triumphs. But you do not love him, since you consider it impossible to renounce what you call your destiny!"

This explanation had been tardy, even without the good Christian being aware of it. It was not without a mixture of terror and of extreme repugnance that the old nobleman had sacrificed to the happiness of his son all the ideas which he had cherished through life, all the prejudices of his caste; and even when, after a long and painful struggle with Albert and with himself, he had completed the sacrifice, he could not without an effort pronounce the absolute ratification of so terrible an act.

Consuelo perceived or guessed this; for at the moment when Count Christian appeared to despair of obtaining her consent to this marriage, there certainly was upon the old man's countenance an expression of involuntary joy, mingled with strange consternation.

Consuelo understood her situation in an instant, and a feeling of pride, perhaps a little too personal, served to increase her repugnance for the match proposed to her.

" You wish that I should marry Count Albert?" said she, still stunned by so strange a proposal. " You consent to call me daughter, give me your name, present me to your relatives and friends? Ah, my lord, how very deeply you love your son, and how much should your son love you!"

" If you find so much generosity in that, Consuelo, it is because your heart cannot conceive an equal amount, or that the object does not appear to you worthy of it."

" My lord," replied Consuelo, endeavoring to collect her thoughts, and hiding her face in her hands, " I must be dreaming. My pride is roused despite of my efforts at the idea of the humiliation to which I would be exposed should I accept the sacrifice suggested by your paternal love."

" And who would dare to offer them, Consuelo, when father and son should unite in shielding you with their legitimate ægis of protection?"

" And the canoness, my lord? she who fills here the post of a mother, would she see all that unmoved?"

" She would join her prayers to ours, if you promise to allow yourself to be persuaded. Do not ask more than the weakness of human nature can grant. A lover, a father, can undergo the grief and humiliation of a refusal ; my sister could not. But with the certainty of success, we shall lead her to your arms."

"My lord," said Consuelo, trembling, "did Count Albert inform you that I loved him?"

"No," replied the count, suddenly recollecting himself; "Albert assured me the obstacle would be in your own heart; he has told me so a hundred times, but I could not believe him. Your reserve appeared to be founded on rectitude and delicacy, but I thought that in removing your scruples, I should obtain the avowal you refused to him."

"And what did he mention of our walk to-day?"

"A single word; ' Try, my father; it is the only way of ascertaining whether pride or estrangement closes her heart against me.' "

"Alas, my lord, what will you think when I say that I do not know myself ?"

"I must think that it is estrangement, my dear Consuelo. Oh, my son, what a destiny is thine! You cannot gain the love of the only woman on whom you could bestow your own. This last misfortune is all that was needed."

" Oh, Heavens ! you must hate me, my lord. You do not understand that my pride resists, when yours is overcome. Perhaps the pride of a person in my situation may appear to have slight foundation, and yet at this moment there is as violent a combat waging in my heart, as that in which you yourself have proved victorious."

"I know it. Do not think, signora, that I so lightly esteem modesty, rectitude,. and disinterestedness, as not to appreciate your lofty feelings. But what paternal love can overcome, I think woman's love may do also; you see, I speak without reserve. Well, suppose that Albert's whole life, yours, and mine, should prove a continual struggle against the prejudices of the world ; suppose we were to suffer long and much, would not our mutual tenderness, the approval of our conscience, and the fruits of our devotion render us stronger than this world united? Toils which seem heavy to you and to us, are lightened by devoted love. But this love you timidly seek in the depths of your soul, and do not find, Consuelo, because it is not there."

" Yes, that is indeed the question," said Consuelo,

pressing her hands upon her heart; "the rest is nothing.
I, too, had prejudices; your example proves that I ought
to overcome them and be great and heroic like you. Let
us then speak no more of my aversion, my false shame.
Let us not even speak of the future—of my profession,"
added she sighing deeply. "I could renounce all—if—if
I loved Albert. This is what I must find out. Listen to
me, my lord. I have asked myself this question a hundred times, but never so seriously as I now can with your
consent. How could I seriously interrogate myself when
even the question seemed a madness and a crime? Now I
think I may know and decide, but I ask a few days to
collect my thoughts, to discover whether this devotion
which I experience toward him, the unlimited esteem,
great good-will and respect which his virtues inspire, the
extraordinary sympathy and strange power which he
exercises over me, be love or admiration; for I experience
all this, and yet it is combated by an indefinable terror,
profound sadness, and—I shall tell you every thing, my
noble friend—by the memory of a love less enthusiastic,
but far more sweet and tender, and in nothing resembling
this."

"Strange and noble girl!" replied Christian with
emotion, "what wisdom and at the same time what
strange ideas, in your words and thoughts! You resemble
my poor Albert in many respects, and the agitation and
uncertainty of your feelings recall to me my wife—my
noble, my beautiful, my melancholy Wanda! O, Consuelo! you awaken in me a recollection at once tender and
bitter in the extreme. I was about to say to you: surmount these irresolutions, triumph over these dislikes,
love—from virtue, from greatness of soul, from compassion, from the effort of a noble and pious charity—this
poor man who adores you, and who, while perhaps making you unhappy, will owe his salvation to you, and will
entitle you to a heavenly recompense. But you have
recalled to my mind his mother—his mother, who gave
herself to me from duty and from friendship. She could
not feel for me, a simple, gentle, timid man, the enthusiasm with which her imagination burned. Still she was
faithful and generous to the last; but how she suffered !
Alas! her affection was at once my joy and my punishment; her constancy, my pride and my remorse. She

died in suffering, and my heart was broken forever. And now, if I am a useless being, worn out, dead before being buried, do not be too much astonished, Consuelo. I have suffered what no one has ever known, what I have never spoken to any one, and what I now confess to you with trembling. Ah! rather than induce you to make such a sacrifice, rather than advise Albert to accept it, may my eyes close in sadness and my son at once sink under his sad fate. I know too well the cost of endeavoring to force nature and combating the insatiable desires of the soul. Take time therefore to reflect, my daughter," added the old count, pressing Consuelo to his breast, which heaved with emotion, and kissing her noble brow with a father's love. "It will be much better so. If you must refuse, Albert, when prepared by anxious uncertainty, will not be so utterly prostrated as he would now be by the frightful news."

They separated with this understanding; and Consuelo, stealing through the galleries in fear of meeting Anzoleto, shut herself up in her chamber, overpowered with emotion and fatigue.

At first she endeavored to take a little rest, in order to attain the calmness which she felt to be necessary. She felt exhausted, and, throwing herself on her bed, she soon fell into a state of torpor, which was more painful than refreshing. She had wished to go to sleep while thinking of Albert, in order that in her dreams she might perhaps be visited with one of those mysterious revelations which sometimes serve to guide and mature our decisions. But the interrupted dreams which she had for several hours, constantly recalled Anzoleto, instead of Albert, to her thoughts. It was always Venice, always the Corte Minelli, always her first love, calm, smiling, and poetic!

Every time she awoke, the remembrance of Albert was connected with the gloomy grotto; or the sound of his violin, echoing ten-fold in the solitude, evoked the dead, and wailed over the freshly closed tomb of Zdenko. Fear and sorrow thus closed her heart against the impulses of affection. The future which was required of her, seemed filled with chill darkness and bloody visions, while the radiant and fruitful past occupied all her thoughts, and caused her heart to beat. It seemed then as if she heard her voice echoing in space, filling all nature, and mounting upward even to the immeasurable heavens; but when the sounds of the violin recurred to her memory, it seemed as if her voice became hoarse and hollow, and died away in mournful wailings in the depths of the earth.

These wandering visions fatigued her so much that she rose in order to dispel them; the first sound of the bell informed her that dinner would be served in half an hour, and she went to her toilet, her mind still full of the same ideas. But how strange!—for the first time in her life she was more attentive to the mirror, and the adjustment of her attire, than to the serious problems she would fain resolve. She made herself beautiful in spite of herself, and wished to be so. It was not to awaken jealousy in rival lovers that this coquettish whim had seized her, for she thought and could think only of one. Albert had never made an allusion to her appearance. In the enthusiasm of passion he perhaps deemed her more beautiful than she was; but his thoughts were so devoted and his love so great, that he would have considered it profanation to have looked at her with the intoxicated gaze of a lover or the satisfied scrutiny of an artist. To him she was always enveloped in a cloud which his gaze never dared to penetrate, and in his thoughts she was ever surrounded by a beaming halo. Whatever she was, he saw her always the same. He had seen her half dead, emaciated, prostrate, more like a specter than a woman. He had then sought in her features with anxiety and attention for the evidence of disease; but he never seemed to perceive moments of ugliness, or dream that she could be an object of terror or disgust. And now that she had recovered the splendor of youth and health, he had never inquired of himself whether she had lost or gained in beauty. She was all to him in life as in death, the ideal of youth, beauty, and sublimity. Therefore Consuelo had never thought of him while arranging her dress before the mirror.

But how different was it with Anzoleto! how carefully had he examined, judged, and compared, on the day that he sought to find if she were ugly. He had taken into account the slightest graces of her form, the least efforts she had made to please. How well was he acquainted with her hair, her arms, her feet, her walk, the colors which became her, even the least fold of her garment; and with what ardent vivacity had he praised her, with what voluptuous languor had he contemplated her! The innocent girl, indeed, had not then understood the emotions of her own heart; nor did she yet understand them, though she felt them not the less at the idea of appearing before him. She was angry with herself, blushed with shame and vexation, and tried to adorn herself for Albert alone, but nevertheless sought out the head-dress, the ribbon, and even the very look that pleased Anzoleto. " Alas! alas!" said she, tearing herself from the mirror when her toilet was completed : " it is true, then, that I can think only of him, and that past happiness exercises a greater power over me than present scorn and the promise of another love! I may look forward to the future, but without him it is but terror and despair. What would it be with him? Ah! well I know that the days of Venice can never return; that innocence can dwell with us no more ; that the soul of Anzoleto is utterly corrupt ; that his caresses would degrade me, and that our life would be hourly poisoned by shame, jealousy, regret, and fear."

Questioning herself on this point with sincerity, Consuelo saw that she was not deceived, and that she had not the remotest wish to please Anzoleto. She loved him indeed no longer in the present ; she almost hated and feared him as regarded the future, in which his faults could only become more aggravated ; but then she cherished his memory in the past to such a degree, that neither in heart nor mind could she sever herself from it. He was henceforward to her but as a picture which recalled the adored object of past happiness ; but, like one who hides herself from her new husband to look upon the image of the first, she felt that the memory of the past was better than the living present.

CHAPTER LXI.

Consuelo had too much judgment and elevation of character not to know that, of the two attachments which she inspired, the truest, the most noble, and most precious, was beyond all comparison that of Albert. Thus, when she again found herself between them, she thought she had triumphed over the enemy. The earnest

look of Albert, which seemed to penetrate her very soul—
the gentle yet firm pressure of his faithful hand—gave her
to understand that he knew the result of her conference
with Count Christian, and that he waited her decision with
submission and gratitude. In reality, Albert had obtained more than he hoped for ; and even this irresolution
was sweet after what he had feared, so much was he
astonished at Anzoleto's impertinent folly. The latter, on
the contrary, was armed with all his boldness. Divining
pretty nearly the state of matters around him, he was determined to battle foot by foot, should they even thrust
him neck and shoulders out of the house. His free and
easy attitude, and his forward jeering look, inspired Consuelo with the deepest disgust , and when he impudently
approached to offer his hand to conduct her to the table,
she turned her head, and took in preference that of
Albert.

As usual, the young count seated himself opposite Consuelo, and Count Christian placed her on his left, where
Amelia had formerly sat. The chaplain's usual place was
to the left of Consuelo, but the canoness invited the pretended brother to seat himself between them, and in this
way Anzoleto's sneers could be overheard by Consuelo, and
his irreverent sallies scandalize the old priest, as he had
intended.

Anzoleto's plan was exceedingly simple. He wished to
make himself intolerable to that part of the family whom
he presumed hostile to the projected marriage, so as to
give them the worst possible impression of the connections
and birth of Consuelo. "We shall see," said he, "if
they can swallow *the brother* that I will cook for them."

Anzoleto, although a poor singer and tragedian, was yet
an excellent comic performer. He had seen enough of
the world to enable him to imitate with ease the elegant
manners and language of good society ; but this part
might have only served to reconcile the canoness to the
low extraction of Consuelo, and he took the opposite one
with the more ease that it was natural to him. Being
well assured that Wenceslawa, notwithstanding her determination only to speak German — the language of the
Court and of all loyal subjects — did not lose a word of
what he said in Italian, he began to chatter right and left,
and to quaff the generous wine of Hungary, which, hard-

ened as he was to the most heady drinks, he did not fear, but the heady influence of which he affected to feel in order that he might assume the air of an inveterate drunkard.

He succeeded to admiration. Count Christian, who good humoredly laughed at his first sallies, soon only smiled with an effort, and required all his urbanity as a host, as well as his paternal affection, to refrain from reproving the disagreeable future brother-in-law of his noble son. The angry chaplain fidgeted on his seat, and murmured exclamations in German which sounded very like exorcisms, while his dinner and digestion were sadly deranged. The canoness listened to the insolent guest with suppressed contempt and somewhat malignant satisfaction. At every fresh outbreak, she raised her eyes toward her brother, as if taking him to witness; and the good Christian, drooping his head, endeavored to distract the attention of the auditors by some awkward enough reflection. Then the canoness looked at Albert; but Albert was immovable— he appeared neither to see nor hear the absurd and vainglorious visitor.

The most cruelly tormented of all was undoubtedly poor Consuelo. At first she thought that Anzoleto had contracted these habits in a life of debauchery, for she had never seen him thus before. She was so disgusted and annoyed that she was about to quit the table; but when she perceived that it was no better than a scheme, she regained the self-possession suited to her innocence and dignity. She had not mixed herself up with the secrets and affections of this family to instal herself among them by means of intrigue. Their rank had never flattered her ambition, and her conscience was secure from the secret charges of the canoness. She felt, she knew, that Albert's love and his father's confidence were superior to this miserable trial. The contempt which she felt for Anzoleto, cowardly and wicked in his vengeance, rendered her still more decided; once only her eyes met those of Albert, and they immediately understood each other. Consuelo said " *Yes!*" and Albert replied, " *In spite of all!*"

"It won't do," said Anzoleto, in a low tone, to Consuelo; for he had observed and passed his own comments on this interchange of looks.

" You have done me a great service," replied Consuelo; "and I thank you."

They spoke in the Venetian dialect, which seems composed only of vowels, and which the Romans and Florentines, when they first hear it, cannot always understand.

"I can imagine that you hate me," replied Anzoleto, "and that you think you will always hate me, but you shall not escape me for all that."

"You have unmasked yourself too soon," said Consuelo.

"But not too late," replied Anzoleto, "Come, *padre mio benedetto*," said he, addressing the chaplain, and giving him at the same time a jog, so as to spill half his wine, "drink more vigorously of this famous wine, which is equally good for body and soul. Signor Count," said he, extending his glass to Count Christian, "you keep there beside your heart a flask of yellow crystal which sparkles like the sun. I feel that if I were to swallow but a drop of that nectar, that I should be changed into a demigod."

"Take care, my child," said the count, placing his wasted and meager hand, covered with rings, on the cut neck of the flask; "the wine of old men sometimes closes the mouth of the young."

"Your anger has made you as handsome as a young witch," said Anzoleto to Consuelo, in good, clear Italian, so that every one could understand him. "You remind me of the *Diavolessa* of Galuppi, which you played so well last year at Venice. Ha! Signor Count, do you intend to keep my sister long in this gilt cage, lined with silk? She is a singing-bird, I must tell you, and a bird that loses its voice soon loses its feathers also. She is well off here, I admit; but the public, who ran crazy after her, want her back to them again. As to myself, were you to give me your name and your castle, all the wine in your cellar, and your chaplain into the bargain, I would not part with my footlights, my buskin, or my roulades."

"Then you are an actor also?" said the canoness, with an air of cold contempt.

"Comedian and jack-pudding, at your service, *illustrissima*," replied Anzoleto, without being at all disconcerted.

"Has he any talent?" asked old Christian, turning to Consuelo with a calm and benevolent air.

"None whatever," replied Consuelo, looking at her adversary with an air of pity.

"If that be true, it is you who are to blame," said Anzoleto; "for I am your pupil. I hope, however," continued he in Venetian, "that I have still enough to frustrate your plans."

"You will only harm yourself," replied Consuelo in the same dialect. "Base intentions contaminate the heart, and yours will suffer more than you could possibly cause me to do, in the opinion of others."

"I am delighted to see that you accept my challenge. To arms then, my fair amazon; it is of no use to lower the visor of your casque—I see uneasiness and fear painted in your eyes."

"Alas! you can only see there profound sorrow for your degradation. I hoped to have forgotten the contempt I owe you, and you force me to remember it."

"Contempt and love often go together."

"In mean souls."

"In the proudest. It has been and always will be so."

The same scene lasted during the whole of dinner. When they retired into the drawing-room, the canoness, who appeared determined to amuse herself with Anzoleto's impertinence, requested him to sing. He scarcely waited to be asked, and after vigorously preluding upon the old creaking harpsichord with his sinewy fingers, he thundered out one of those songs with which he had been in the habit of enlivening Zustiniani's select suppers. The words were rather free. The canoness did not understand them, but felt herself amused at the force with which he uttered them. Count Christian could not avoid being struck with the fine voice and wonderful execution of the singer. He abandoned himself with artless delight to the pleasure of hearing him, and, when the first air was concluded, asked for another. Albert, who was seated by the side of Consuelo, appeared deaf to all that passed, and said not a word. Anzoleto imagined that he was annoyed, and that he at last felt himself surpassed in something. His design had been to banish his auditors by his musical improprieties; but seeing that, whether from the innocence of his hosts, or from their ignorance of the language, it was labor lost, he gave himself up to the thirst for admiration, and sang for the pleasure of singing; and besides, he wished to let Consuelo see that he had improved. He had in fact made considerable progress in the species of talent he possessed. His voice had perhaps already lost its original freshness, but he had become more complete master of it, and more skillful in the art of overcoming the difficulties toward which his taste and genius continually led him. He sang well, and received warm eulogiums from Count Christian, from the canoness, and even from the chaplain, who liked display, and who considered Consuelo's manner too simple and too natural to be very learned.

"You told us he had no talent," said the count to the latter; "you are either too severe or too modest as regards your pupil. He has a great deal of talent, and, moreover, I recognize in him something of your style and genius."

The good Christian wished, by this little triumph of Anzoleto's, to efface the humiliation which his manner of conducting himself had caused his pretended sister. He therefore insisted much upon the merit of the singer, and the latter, who loved to shine too well not to be already tired of the low part he had played, returned to the harpsichord, after having remarked that Count Albert became more and more pensive. The canoness, who dozed a little at the long pieces of music, asked for another Venetian song; and this time Anzoleto chose one which was in better taste. He knew that the popular airs were those which he sang the best. Even Consuelo herself had not the piquant accent and dialect in such perfection as he, a child of the lagunes, and gifted by nature with high comic powers.

He counterfeited with so much ease and grace, now the rough and frank manner of the fishermen of Istria, now the free and careless nonchalance of the gondoliers of Venice, that it was impossible not to look at and listen to him with the liveliest interest. His handsome features, flexible and expressive, assumed at one moment the grave and bold aspect of the former, at another the caressing and jesting cheerfulness of the latter mentioned race. His somewhat *outré* and extravagant costume, which smacked strongly of Venice, added still more to the illusion, and on this occasion improved his personal advantages instead of injuring them. Consuelo, at first cold, was soon obliged to take refuge in indifference and preoccupation. Her emotion gained upon her more and more. She again saw all Venice in Anzoleto, and in that Venice the Anzoleto of former days, with his gaiety, his innocent love, and his childish pride. Her eyes filled with tears, and the merry strokes which made the others laugh, penetrated her heart with a feeling of deep and tender melancholy.

When the songs were ended, Count Christian asked for sacred music. "Oh, as for that," said Anzoleto, "I know every thing which is sung at Venice; but they are all arranged for two voices, and unless my sister, who knows them also, will consent to sing with me, I shall not be able to comply with your highness' commands."

They all entreated Consuelo to sing. She refused for a long time, although she felt tempted to do so. At length, yielding to the request of Count Christian, who wished to induce her to be on good terms with her brother by seeming so himself, she seated herself beside Anzoleto, and began in a trembling voice one of those long hymns in two parts, divided into strophes of three verses, which are heard at Venice during the festivals of the church, and all the night long before the images of the madonnas at every corner. The rhythm is rather lively than otherwise, but in the monotony of the burden and in the poetical turn of the words, in which there is somewhat of a pagan expression, there is a sweet melancholy that gains upon the hearer by degrees, and carries him away.

Consuelo sang in a soft and mellow voice, in imitation of the women of Venice, and Anzoleto in one somewhat rough and guttural, like the young men of the same locality. He improvised at the same time on the harpsichord, a low, uninterrupted, yet cheerful accompaniment, which reminded his companion of the murmuring waters of the lagunes, and the sighing of the winds among the reeds. She imagined herself in Venice during one of its lovely summer nights, kneeling before one of the little chapels, covered with vines, and lighted by the feeble rays of a lamp reflected from the rippled waters of the canal. Oh! what a difference between this vision of Venice, with its blue sky, its gentle melodies, its azure waves sparkling in the light of rapid flambeaus, or dotted with shining stars, and the harrowing emotions inspired by Albert's violin, on the margin of the dark, motionless, and haunted waters. Anzoleto had wakened up this magnificent vision, full of ideas of life and liberty; while the caverns and the wild and dreary hymns of old Bohemia, the heaps of bones on which flashed the light of torches, reflected on waters filled perhaps with the same sad relics, and in the midst of all these, the pale yet impassioned form of the ascetic Albert—the symbol of a hidden world—and the painful emotions arising from his incomprehensible fascination—were too much for the peaceful soul of the simple-minded Consuelo. Her southern origin, still more than her education, revolted at this initiation into a love so stern and forbidding. Albert seemed to her the genius of the north—deep, earnest, sublime, but ever sorrowful—like the frozen nightwinds or the subterranean voices of winter torrents. His was a dreamy inquiring soul that sought into every thing— the stormy nights, the course of meteors, the wild harmonies of the forests, and the half-obliterated inscriptions of ancient tombs. Anzoleto, on the contrary, hot and fiery, was the image of the sunny south, drawing its inspiration from its rapid and luxuriant growth, and its pride from the riches hidden in its bosom. His was a life of sensation and feeling, drinking in pleasure at all his pores, artistic, rejoicing, careless, fancy-free, ignorant and indifferent alike as to good or ill, easily amused, heedless of reflection—in a word, the enemy and the antipodes of thought.

Between these two men, so diametrically opposed to each other, Consuelo was lifeless and inactive as a soul without a body. She loved the beautiful, thirsted after the ideal. Albert taught and offered it to her; but, arrested in the development of his genius by disease, he had given himself up too much to a life of thought. He knew so little the necessities of actual life, that he almost forgot his own existence. He never supposed that the gloomy ideas and objects to which he had familiarized himself, could, under the influence of love and virtue, have inspired his betrothed with any other sentiments than the soft enthusiasm of faith and happiness. He had not foreseen nor understood, that like a plant of the tropics plunged into a polar twilight, he had dragged Consuelo into an atmosphere of death. In short, he was not aware of the violence to her feelings which it would have required, to identify her being with his own.

Anzoleto, on the contrary, although wounding the feelings and disgusting the mind of Consuelo at every point, had all the energy and warmth of character which the *Flower of Spain* (as he was wont to call her) required to make her happy. In hearing him, she once more recalled her unthinking and joyous existence, her bird-like love of song, her life of calm and varied enjoyment, of innocence undisturbed by labor, of uprightness without effort, of pity without thought. But is not an artist something of a bird, and must he not thus mingle in the pursuits and drink of the cup of life common to his fellow-man, in order to perfect his character and make it useful and instructive to those around him?

Consuelo sang with a voice every moment more sweet and touching, as she gave herself up, by a vague and dreamy instinct, to the reflections which I have just made, perhaps at too great length, in her place. I must, however, be pardoned. For otherwise how could the reader understand the fatal mobility of feeling by which this sincere and prudent young girl, who had such good reason, only fifteen minutes before, to hate the perfidious Anzoleto, so far forgot herself as to listen to his voice, and to mingle, with a sort of delight, her sweet breath with his. The saloon, as has been already said, was too large to be properly lighted, and the day besides was declining. The music-stand of the instrument, on which Anzoleto had left a large sheet of music, concealed them from those at a distance, and by degrees their heads approached closer and closer together. Anzoleto, still accompanying himself with one hand, passed his other arm round Consuelo's waist, and drew her insensibly toward him. Six months of indignation and grief vanished from her mind like a dream—she imagined herself in Venice— she was praying to the Madonna to bless her love for the dear betrothed her mother had given her, and who prayed with his hand locked in hers, his heart beating against her heart. At the end of a strophe she felt the burning lips of her first betrothed pressed against her own—she smothered a cry, and leaning on the harpsichord, burst into tears.

At this instant Count Albert returned, heard her sobs, and saw the insulting joy of Anzoleto. This interruption had not astonished the other spectators of this rapid scene, as no person had seen the kiss, and every one believed that the recollection of her infancy and the love her art had caused these tears. Count Christian was somewhat vexed at a sensitiveness that implied so much regret for pursuits of which he required the sacrifice. As for the canoness and the chaplain, they were rejoiced at it, hoping that the sacrifice could never take place. Albert had not yet even asked himself whether the Countess of Rudolstadt could once more become an artist or not. He would have accepted every thing, permitted every thing, even exacted every thing, so that she should be happy and free—in retirement, in the world, or in the theater—at her pleasure. His complete absence of prejudice or selfishness produced a total want of foresight, even regarding the most simple matters. It never occurred to him that Consuelo should think of submitting to sacrifices which he did not wish to impose. But although not perceiving this first step, he saw beyond, as he always saw; he penetrated to the heart of the tree and placed his hand upon the cankerworm. Anzoleto's true relation toward Consuelo, his real object, and the feeling which he inspired, were revealed to him in an instant. He looked attentively at this man, between whom and himself there existed a violent antipathy, and on whom he had not deigned till then to cast a glance, because he would not hate the brother of Consuelo. He saw in him a bold, a dangerous, and a persevering lover. The noble Albert never thought of himself—a whisper of jealousy never entered his heart—the danger was all for Consuelo: for with his profound and lucid, yet delicate, vision—that vision which could hardly bear the light, nor distinguish color and form—he read the soul, and penetrated by mysterious intuition into the most hidden thoughts of the wicked and abandoned. I shall not attempt to explain this strange gift by natural causes. Certain of his faculties appeared incomprehensible to those around him, as they appear to her who relates them, and who, at the end of a hundred years, is not a whit more advanced in their knowledge than the greatest intellects of her time. Albert, in laying bare the vain and selfish soul of his rival, did not say " Behold my enemy;" but he said " Behold the enemy of Consuelo." And without letting his discovery appear, he resolved to watch over and preserve her.

CHAPTER LXII.

As soon as Consuelo found a favorable opportunity, she left the saloon and hastened to the garden. The sun had set, and the first stars of evening shone bright and clear in the sky, still tinged with its setting rays. The young artist

sought calmness and quietude in the refreshing atmosphere
of one of the earliest evenings of autumn.   Her bosom was
oppressed with a languid delight; yet she felt a pang of remorse, and called to her aid all the powers of her soul. She
might well say to herself, " Do I not then know whether I
love or hate?" She trembled as if her courage were about
to fail her, and for the first time in her life she did not experience that rectitude of impulse, that sacred confidence
in her intentions, which had hitherto sustained her in all
her trials.   She had left the saloon to avoid Anzoleto's fascinating gaze, and yet she had experienced a vague desire
that he should follow her.   The leaves had begun to fall,
and when the hem of her garment rustled them behind
her, she imagined she heard footsteps following hers,
and, ready to fly, and yet not daring to return, she remained rooted to the spot, as if by some magic power.

Some one indeed had followed her, but without daring
and without wishing to show himself ; it was Albert. A
stranger alike to dissimulation and formality, the purity
and strength of his love rose above all false shame, and he
had left the saloon the instant after her, resolved to protect
her, unobserved, and to prevent her would-be lover from
rejoining her.   Anzoleto saw this movement, but it gave
him no concern.   He was too well aware of Consuelo's agitation not to look upon his victory as certain, and, thanks
to the conceited assurance which his previous easy conquests had inspired, he resolved not to hasten matters, not
to irritate his beloved, nor to outrage the family.   "It is
not at all necessary," said he, " that I should hurry myself;
anger might give her strength, while a look of pain and
dejection will dissipate the remains of her displeasure
against me.   Whether from fear or compassion, she has
not betrayed my real character ; and the old people, in
spite of all my folly, seem resolved to support me out of
affection for her.   I must change my tactics ; I have got
on better than I expected, and shall now call a halt."

Count Christian, the canoness, and the chaplain, were
therefore much surprised to see him assume all at once an
air of good manners, and a moderate, mild and considerate
demeanor. He had sufficient address to complain to the chaplain in a low voice of a severe headache, and to mention that,
being usually very temperate, the Hungarian wine, which he
had not distrusted at dinner, had confused his brain. This de-

claration was soon repeated to the canoness, and the count, who charitably accepted the excuse. Wenceslawa was at first less indulgent; but the pains which the actor took to please her, the respectful praise which he adroitly lavished on the nobility, and the admiration he expressed for the order which prevailed in the castle, quickly disarmed the benevolent and forgiving soul. She listened at first carelessly, and ended by chatting to him with pleasure, and agreeing with her brother that he was an excellent and charming young man. An hour elapsed before Consuelo returned from her walk, during which Anzoleto had not lost his time. He had so well established himself in the good graces of the family as to be able to remain at least for some days at the castle, until his designs should be accomplished. He did not understand what the count said to Consuelo in German, but he guessed from the looks turned toward him, and the surprise and embarrassment depicted on Consuelo's features, that Count Christian was praising him very highly, while he scolded Consuelo for the little interest she manifested in so amiable a relative.

"Come, signora," said the canoness, who, notwithstanding her anger against Consuelo, still wished her well, and besides thought she was doing a good action, "you were displeased with your brother at dinner, and it is true he then deserved it; but he is better than he appeared to be. He has just been speaking of you with the greatest affection and respect. Do not be more severe than we are. I am sure if he remembers how he behaved at dinner, he is sincerely sorry, especially on your account. Speak to him, and do not be so cold to one who is so nearly allied to you. For my part, although my brother Baron Frederick annoyed me many a time in his early days, I never could remain an hour without being reconciled to him."

Consuelo, neither daring to confirm nor correct the good lady's mistake, was confounded at this new trick of Anzoleto's, the nature of which she understood very well.

"You are not aware of what my sister says," said Christian to the young man; "I shall tell you in a couple of words. She is reproaching your sister with taking too many airs, while Consuelo, I am certain, is dying to make peace. Be friends, my children. Come," said he to Anzoleto, "make the first advance, and if you have ever done any thing toward her that you repent of, tell her so, that she may pardon you."

Anzoleto had not to be told a second time, and seizing the trembling hand of Consuelo, who dared not withdraw it, "Yes," he exclaimed, "I have been very guilty toward her ; I repent bitterly, and all my efforts to harden my conscience only crushed my heart more and more. She knows it well, and if she had not a soul of iron, at once proud and merciless, she would feel that I am sufficiently punished. Therefore, sister, grant me your affection and pardon, else I shall carry despair and weariness over the world. Everywhere a stranger, without support, advice, or love, I shall no longer believe in a Providence, and my excesses must fall on your head."

This homily greatly moved the count, and drew tears from the good canoness.

"You hear him, Porporina," she exclaimed; "what he says is as beautiful as it is true. Mr. Chaplain, you should exhort the signora, in the name of religion, to be reconciled to her brother."

The chaplain was about to interfere; but Anzoleto, without heeding him, seized Consuelo in his arms, and in spite of her terror and resistance, embraced her passionately, to the great edification of those around.

Consuelo, shocked at such insolent deceit, could bear it no longer. "Stop!" she exclaimed; "Signor Count, listen to me——." She was about to reveal every thing, when Albert appeared. On the instant, on the point of confessing all, the remembrance of Zdenko froze her soul. The implacable protector of Consuelo might resolve to free her, without noise or deliberation, from the enemy against whom she was about to invoke his aid. She turned pale, and looked at Anzoleto with an air of painful reproach, while the words died on her lips.

At seven o'clock the supper bell was rung. If the idea of these frequent repasts is calculated to injure the appetite of my delicate lady readers, I must tell them that the fashion of not eating had not yet been introduced into these countries. In fact, half the time was spent at Riesenburg in eating, slowly, as well as often and heartily. And I must confess that Consuelo, accustomed from her infancy, and for good reasons too, to confine herself to a few spoonfuls of rice boiled in water, found these Homeric repasts extremely tedious. For the first time she knew not whether the present one lasted an hour or a moment;

she was scarcely more alive than Albert in his cave. It seemed to her as if she were intoxicated, so much was she agitated by mingled feelings of love, terror, and shame. She eat nothing, saw nothing, heard nothing, around her. Like one who slides down the brink of a precipice, and who sees the slight twigs break by which he hoped to stay his fall, she gazed on the abyss, and delirium seized on her brain. Anzoleto was beside her—garment against garment, elbow against elbow, foot against foot; in his eagerness to serve her, his hands met hers, and he held them clasped an instant in his own. All the past came back in that burning pressure. He uttered words which suffocate, darted looks which devour. Quick as lightning he changed his glass for hers, and kissed the crystal which her lips had touched—to her he was all fire, though seeming ice to others. He was perfectly self-possessed, spoke with propriety, was most attentive to the canoness, treated the chaplain with respect, and offered him the best morsels within his reach. He saw that the good man was a glutton, but that his timidity imposed frequent privations on him; and the chaplain was so much gratified at this attention, that he would have been delighted to see the new carver pass the rest of his days at the Castle of the Giants.

Anzoleto drank nothing but water; and when the chaplain, in return for his attentions, offered him wine, he replied loud enough to be heard: "Many thanks; but I do not intend to be taken in again. I sought to stupify myself with your perfidious wine before, but now I am no longer in pain, and I return to water, my usual beverage and right trusty friend."

They remained longer at table than usual; Anzoleto sang, and this time he sang for Consuelo. He chose the favorite airs of her old author, which she had taught him herself, and repeated them with the care and delivery which she was wont to exact of him. It was to recall the dearest and most delightful recollections of her affections and of her art.

When they were on the point of rising, he seized a favorable moment to whisper to her: "Dear Consuelo, you must endeavor to meet me early to-morrow morning in the gardens of the castle, as I have much to say to you. I dare scarcely hope to regain your love; alas! I fear that another is happy in the possession of it, and that, if I

would not expire at your feet, I must fly far from this.
But will you not utter one word of pity and farewell? If
you do not consent, I shall set off at break of day, and my
death be upon your head."

"Do not say so, Anzoleto. Here we must part, here
bid each other an eternal farewell. I pardon you and I
wish you——"

"A pleasant journey," he ironically replied. "You are
pitiless, Consuelo. But you cannot be so cruel; I will be
there."

"No, no; do not come," said Consuelo, terrified.
"Count Albert's apartment overlooks the garden; perhaps
he has guessed every thing. Anzoleto, if you expose yourself, I cannot answer for your life. I speak seriously—my
blood freezes in my veins."

Consuelo at this moment perceived Albert's usually
vague glance become deep and clear, as he fixed it on Anzoleto. He could not hear, yet it would seem he understood with his eyes. She withdrew her hand, saying in
stifled accents:

"Ah! if you love me, do not brave that terrible man."

"Is it for yourself you fear?" said Anzoleto, quickly.

"No, but for all who approach and threaten me."

"And for all who adore you, doubtless? Well, be it so.
To die before your eyes—at your feet—I ask but that.
To-morrow, at break of day, I shall be there. Resist, and
you will but hasten my doom."

"You set out to-morrow, and yet take leave of no one!"
said Consuelo, observing that he saluted the count and
canoness, without mentioning his departure.

"No," he replied, "they would wish to detain me, and
in spite of myself, seeing every thing conspire to prolong
my agony, I would yield. You shall offer my excuses and
adieus. My guide has received orders to have the horses
in readiness at four in the morning."

This last assertion was more than true. The singular
looks of Albert for some hours had not escaped Anzoleto.
He was resolved to brave every thing, but, in case of mis-
chance, held himself prepared for flight. His horses were
saddled in the stable, and his guide had orders to watch.

When Consuelo had returned to her chamber she was
seized with real terror. She did not wish to meet Anzoleto, and yet she feared that he might take some desperate

step if she refused. She had never felt so unhappy, so unprotected, and so lonely upon the earth.

"Oh, my dear master, where are you," she exclaimed. "You alone know the perils which surround me — you alone could save me. You are rough, severe, distrustful, as a friend and father should be to drag me from the abyss into which I fear to fall. But have I not friends around me? Have I not a father in Count Christian?—would the canoness not be a mother, if I had but courage to brave her prejudices and open my heart? And is not Albert my protector, my brother, my husband, if I only consent to say a word? Ah! yes, it is he who should be my protector; yet I fear I repel him. I must go and seek all three," she added, rising and walking hurriedly about the chamber; "I must be one with them, cling to their protecting arms, and take shelter under the wings of these guarding angels. Repose, dignity, honor, dwell with them; misery and despair would await me with Anzoleto. Ah! yes, I must confess what has passed in my mind during this frightful day, that they may protect and defend me from myself. I shall bind myself to them with an oath, and say the terrible *yes*, which shall place an invincible barrier between myself and this scourge. I will go——"

But instead of going, she fell back exhausted on a chair, and bitterly wept her exhausted strength, her lost peace.

"But what?" said she, "shall I utter a fresh falsehood? Shall I consent to pledge my faith to a man I do not love? Alas! I feel that Anzoleto is still dearer to me than he. What shall I do? What is to become of me?"

While absorbed in these reflections, she saw through the window of her closet, which opened upon an inner courtyard, a light from the stables. She examined attentively a man who went in and out without waking the other servants, and who appeared to be preparing for his departure. She saw by his dress that it was Anzoleto's guide, and that he was getting ready the horses, conformably to his instructions. She also saw a light with the keeper of the drawbridge, and concluded that he had been informed by the guide of their approaching departure, the hour for which had not been exactly settled. Considering these matters in detail, a bold and somewhat strange project rushed across Consuelo's thoughts. But as it opened out to her between two extremes a fresh point of departure in the events of her life, it seemed to her little less than inspiration. She had no time to inquire into the means or the consequences. She trusted the one to Providence, while she thought she could obviate the others. She began to write as follows, in haste as may be supposed, for the castle clock had sounded eleven.

"Albert, I am compelled to depart. I esteem and admire you, as you know, from my very soul. But there are in my nature contradictions, sufferings, and oppositions which I cannot explain either to you or myself. Could I see you at this moment I should perhaps tell you that I confide in you, that I yield you up the care of my future life, that I consent to become your wife. Perhaps I should even say that I desire it. Nevertheless, I should be deceiving you, or at least make a rash vow, for my heart is not yet suff ently purified from its old love to belong to you witnout fear, or to merit yours without remorse. I fly, I hasten to Vienna, to meet or await Porpora, who is to be there in a few days, as his letter to your father has recently announced. I swear to you that I shall only endeavor to forget the past beside him, and cherish the hope of a future of which you are the cornerstone. Do not follow me; I forbid you in the name of this future which your impatience might compromise and perhaps destroy. Wait for me, and keep the oath, which you have sworn, not to return without me to——you will understand what I mean! Rely upon me; I enjoin it on you, for I go with the blessed hope of one day returning or asking you to come to me. At this moment I seem as if I labored under a frightful dream. I feel that when I am again alone I shall awaken worthy of you. I am determined that my brother shall not follow me. I mean to keep all my movements secret from him, and induce him to take a direction opposite to that which I shall follow myself. By all that you hold dear on earth I implore you not to oppose my project, and to believe that I am sincere. By so doing I shall see that you love me truly, and I shall then be able to sacrifice, without blushing, my poverty to your riches, my obscurity to your rank, and my ignorance to your lofty knowledge. Adieu, Albert, but only for a time! To prove to you that I do not go irrevocably, I charge you to render your good and excellent aunt favorable to our union, and to preserve for me the esteem of your father—that best and worthiest of men. Tell him the truth in all respects. I shall write to you from Vienna."

The hope of convincing and calming by such a letter a man so much in love as Albert was rash, no doubt, but not altogether unreasonable. Consuelo, even while she wrote, felt her energy and rectitude of principle return. She felt every thing she wrote, and every thing she said she meant to do. She was aware of Albert's wonderful penetration—his almost second sight—and she did not hope to deceive him; she was sure from his character that he would believe in her and obey her punctually. At this moment her judgment of the circumstances in which she was placed, and the conduct of Albert toward her, was as pure and lofty as his would have been in a similar position.

Having folded her letter without sealing it, she threw her traveling cloak over her shoulders, covered her head with a thick dark veil, put on very strong shoes, gathered together the little money she possessed, made up a small packet of linen and descending on tip-toe, with extreme precaution, she traversed the lower stories, arrived at Count Christian's apartment, and glided into the oratory, which she knew he regularly entered at six in the morning. She placed the letter on the cushion on which he usually opened his book before kneeling, then, descending still further to the court-yard without awaking any one, she proceeded straight to the stables.

The guide, who did not feel very comfortable at finding himself alone in the middle of the night in this great castle, where every one was fast asleep, was at first afraid of this figure in black, which glided toward him like a phantom. He retreated to the furthest corner of the stable, neither daring to cry out nor question her. This was just what Consuelo wished. As soon as she saw herself out of sight and hearing, for she knew that neither Albert's nor Anzoleto's windows opened on the court-yard, she said to the guide: "I am the sister of the young man you brought here this morning; he takes me with him. It has just been settled on. Put a side-saddle quickly on his horse; there are several here. Follow me to Tusta, without saying a single word, and without making a single movement which could betray me to the people of the castle. You shall have double pay. You appear surprised? Come, make haste; the moment we reach the town you must return with the same horses to bring my brother." The guide shook his head. "You shall be paid threefold." The guide nodded assent. "And you will bring him full gallop to Tusta, where I shall await you." The guide again shook his head. "You shall have four times as much for the latter stage as for the former." The guide obeyed, in an instant the horse was ready. "This is not all," said Consuelo, mounting even before the bridle was perfectly adjusted; "give me your hat, and throw your cloak over mine, only for an instant."

"I understand," said the man, "to deceive the porter, that is easy! Oh, it is not the first time I have carried off a young lady. Your lover will pay well, I suppose, although you *are* his sister," added he, with a grin.

"You will be well paid by me first. But be silent—are you ready?"

"I am mounted."

"Pass on then and have the bridge lowered."

They crossed it at a foot pace, made a circuit in order not to pass under the walls of the castle, and at the end of a quarter of an hour had gained the sandy road. Consuelo had never been on horseback before. Happily the animal though strong was tractable. His master encouraged him with his voice, and striking into a steady and rapid pace through woods and thickets, the lady arrived at her destination in a couple of hours.

Consuelo sprang down at the entrance of the town. "I do not wish that they should see me here," said she to the guide, at the same time placing in his hand the money agreed upon for herself and Anzoleto. "I shall proceed through the town on foot, and hire from some people here whom I know a carriage to convey me on the road to Prague. I shall travel quickly, in order to get to a distance from the places where I would be recognized, before the break of day. In the morning I shall stop and await my brother."

"But in what place?"

"I cannot say; but tell him that it will be at a posthouse. Let him not ask any questions until he shall be ten leagues from this. Then let him inquire for Madam Wolf; it is the first name that occurs to me; do not forget it, however. There is but one road to Prague?"

" Only one as far as———"

" It is well. Stop in the suburbs to refresh your horses. Do not let them see the side-saddle, throw your cloak over it; do not answer any question, and start off. Stay—another word—tell my brother not to hesitate, but to set off at once without being seen. His life is in danger in the castle."

" God be with you, my pretty maiden," said the guide, who had had time enough to count his money. " Even if my poor horses should be knocked up, I shall be glad to have served you. I am sorry, however," he said to himself when she had disappeared in the obscurity, " that I could not have a peep at her. I would like to know if she is handsome enough to run away with. She frightened me at first with her black veil and resolute step; besides they told me so many stories in the kitchen that I did not know what to think. How foolish and superstitious those people are with their ghosts and their man in black of the oak of the Schreckenstein! Pooh! I passed it a hundred times, and never saw any thing. I took good care to look aside when I passed the ravine at the foot of the mountain."

Thus reflecting, the guide, having fed his horses, and having taken a good dram by way of rousing himself, turned again toward Riesenburg, without hurrying himself in the least, as Consuelo had foreseen and hoped, though she had recommended him to use all speed. The honest fellow was lost in conjectures upon the romantic adventure in which he found himself involved. By degrees the vapors of the night, and perhaps also the strong drink, made things appear still more wonderful to him. " It would be curious," thought he, "if this dark woman in black were to turn out to be a man, and this man the ghost of the castle—the dark spirit of the Schreckenstein. They say that he plays all sorts of scurvy tricks on night travelers, and old Hans swore that he saw him often when he was feeding Baron Frederick's horses before daybreak. The devil! it would not be so pleasant to meet the like, as something bad is sure to come of it. If my poor hack has carried Satan this night he will die for certain. I fancy there is fire coming out of his nostrils already ; it is very well if he does not take the bit between his teeth. I wish I were at the castle, to see if, in place of the money which this she-devil has given me, I shall not find dried leaves in my pocket; and if they tell me that Signora Porporina is sleeping quietly in her bed, instead of being on the road to Prague, what the devil is to become of me? Truth to say she galloped like the wind, and vanished when she left me, as if she had sunk into the ground!"

CHAPTER LXIII.

ANZOLETO did not fail to rise at daybreak, seize his stiletto, and perform an elaborate toilet. But when he proceeded to open the door, which he had observed previously was easily enough unlocked, he was surprised beyond measure to find that he could not turn the key. He bruised his fingers and tired himself in the attempt, at the risk of awakening some one by his violent efforts. It was of no avail; there was no other outlet from his room, and the window looked down upon the garden from a height of fifty feet, so steep and dangerous that it made him giddy only to think of it. "This is not the work of chance," said Anzoleto, after giving the door a last push, "but whether it be Consuelo (and that would be a good omen), or whether it be the count, both will have to reckon with me for it."

He endeavored to go to sleep again, but vexation, and perhaps also a certain uneasiness allied to fear, prevented him. If Albert had been the author of this precaution, he alone of all the household had not been the dupe of his pretended relationship to Consuelo. The latter had appeared really frightened when she warned him to beware of *that terrible man.* It did not console Ansoleto to say, that being crazy, the young count had probably not much connection in his ideas, or that being of illustrious birth, he would not be willing, according to the prejudices of the day, to commit himself in an affair of honor with an actor. These suppositions did not reassure him. Albert had appeared to him a very quiet madman, and one who was quite master of his actions; and as to his prejudices, they could not be very deeply rooted, if they permitted him to entertain the idea of marrying an actress. Anzoleto therefore began seriously to fear having any difference with him before the accomplishment of his object, and thus getting into trouble without profit. This termination of his adventure appeared to him rather disgraceful than tragic. He had learned how to handle a sword, and flattered himself that he was a match for any nobleman whatsoever. Nevertheless he did not feel easy, and could not sleep.

Toward five o'clock he imagined he heard steps in the corridor, and shortly afterward his door was opened without noise and without difficulty. It was not yet broad daylight, and on seeing a man enter his chamber with so little ceremony, Anzoleto thought the decisive moment had arrived. He darted toward his stiletto with a desperate bound. But by the glimmer of the dawn he immediately recognized his guide, who made signs to him to speak low and to make no noise. "What do you mean by your grimaces, and what do you want with me, you stupid ass?" said Anzoleto, angrily. "How did you get in?"

"Get in? How should I get in but by the door, my good sir?"

"The door was locked."

"But you had left the key outside."

"Impossible! there it is on my table."

"That is strange! then there are two."

"And who can have played me the trick of locking me in thus? There was but one key yesterday. Was it you when you came for my valise?"

"I swear that it was not; I never saw the key."

"Then it must be the devil! But what do you want with me, with your busy and mysterious air? I did not send for you."

"You did not give me time to speak! However, you see me, and you must of course know very well what I want of you. The signora reached Tusta without accident, and according to her directions I am here with my horses to conduct you thither."

It was some minutes before Anzoleto could comprehend what was the matter, but when he did so, he joined in the deception quickly enough to prevent his guide, whose superstitious fears had completely vanished with the shades of night, from again falling into his perplexities about it being a trick of the devil. The knave had begun by examining and ringing Consuelo's money on the pavement of the stable, and felt himself well satisfied with his part of the bargain with Satan. Anzoleto understood in a moment what had occurred, and imagined that the fugitive on her side had been so closely watched as not to be able to inform him of her resolution, and that threatened, urged to extremity perhaps, by her jealous lover, she had seized a favorable moment to baffle his projects, escape, and seek the open country. "However that may be," said he to himself, "there is no room for doubt or hesitation. The direction which she has sent to me by this man, who has conducted her on the road to Prague, is clear and precise. Victory! that is, if I can get out of this house without being obliged to cross swords!"

He armed himself to the teeth; and while he was hastening to get ready, he sent his guide as a scout to see if the road was clear. Upon his bringing intelligence that all seemed to be still buried in sleep, except the bridge-keeper who had just opened the gate for him, Anzoleto descended without noise, remounted his horse, and met in the court-yard only a single stable-boy, whom he called to give him some money, in order that his departure might not bear the appearance of a flight. "By Saint Wenceslas!" said the servant to the guide, "how strange it is! your horses on coming out of the stable are covered with sweat, as if they had been traveling all night."

"It must have been that your black devil came and dosed them," replied the other.

"That must be the reason," returned the stable-boy, "why I heard such a horrible noise in this direction all night! I did not dare to come and see what was the matter; but I heard the portcullis creak and the drawbridge lowered, just as I see it now; I certainly thought you were going away, and I did not expect to see you this morning."

The warder at the drawbridge was also surprised. "Your lordship is double then?" asked the man, rubbing his eyes. "I saw you depart about midnight, and now I see you again."

"You must have been dreaming, my honest fellow," said Anzoleto, making him a present also. "I should not have gone without asking you to drink my health."

"Your lordship does me too much honor," said the porter, who spoke a little broken Italian. "But, for all that," said he to the guide in his own tongue, "I have seen two to-night."

"And take care that you do not see four to-morrow night," replied the guide, galloping over the bridge after Anzoleto. "The black devils always play such tricks with sleepers like you."

Anzoleto, who got full instructions from his guide, reached Tusta, or Tauss—for they are, I believe, the same town. He passed through it, after having discharged the man and taken post-horses, abstained from making any inquiries for ten leagues, and at the appointed place stopped to breakfast (for he was now nearly worn out), and asked for one Madam Wolf, who was to meet him there with a carriage. But no one could give him any news of her, and for a very good reason.

There was indeed a Madam Wolf in the village, but she had been established there fifty years, and kept a mercer's shop. Anzoleto, tired and exhausted, concluded that Consuelo had not thought it best to stop in this place. He inquired for a carriage to hire, but there was none. He was therefore obliged to mount on horseback again, and ride post once more. He thought every moment that he was certain to overtake the welcome carriage, into which he could throw himself, and be recompensed for his anxieties and his fatigues. But he met very few travelers, and in no carriage did he see Consuelo. At last, overcome by excess of fatigue, and finding no vehicle to be hired anywhere, he resolved to stop, although with much reluctance, and to wait in a little town on the roadside until Consuelo should join him, for he was certain he must have passed her. He had plenty of time during the rest of the day and the following night to curse the women, the inns, the roads, and all jealous lovers. The next day he found a public passenger coach, and continued to hurry toward Prague, but without being more successful. Let us leave him traveling toward the north, a prey to rage, impatience, and despair not unmixed with hope, and return for an instant to the château, in order to observe the effect of Consuelo's departure upon the inhabitants of that abode.

It may readily be conceived that Count Albert did not sleep, any more than the other two personages engaged in this hurried adventure. After having provided a second key to Anzoleto's chamber, he had locked him in from the outside, and was no longer anxious about his attempts, knowing well that unless Consuelo herself interfered, no one would go to deliver him. Respecting this possibility, the bare idea of which made him shudder, Albert had the extreme delicacy not to wish to make any imprudent discovery. "If she loves him so well," thought he, "I need struggle no more; let my destiny be accomplished; I shall know it soon enough; for she is sincere, and to-morrow she will openly refuse the offers I have made her to-day. If she is merely persecuted and threatened by this dangerous man, she is now sheltered from his pursuits for one night at least. In the meantime, no matter what passing noise I hear around me, I will not stir; I will not make myself odious, and inflict upon that unfortunate the punishment of shame, by presenting myself before her without being called. No! I will not play the part of a cowardly spy, of a suspicious and jealous lover, since hitherto her refusals and irresolution have given me no claim over her."

The courageous Albert religiously kept the resolution he had made, and although he imagined he heard Consuelo's footsteps in the lower story at the moment of her flight, and some other more inexplicable noises in the direction of the portcullis, he prayed and suffered in silence, and restrained with clasped hands the throbbings of his heart.

When the hour arrived at which Count Christian was accustomed to rise, Albert hastened to him, with the intention, not of informing him of what was passing, but of persuading him to enter into a fresh explanation with Consuelo. He was certain that she would speak the truth. He thought that she must even desire such an explanation, and he prepared to comfort her in her trouble, and to pretend a resignation which would qualify the bitterness of their farewell. Albert did not ask what would become of himself afterward. He felt that neither his reason nor his life could support such a shock, but he did not shrink from undergoing suffering beyond his strength.

He found his father at the moment when the latter was entering the oratory. The letter placed upon the cushion struck their eyes at the same instant. They seized and read it together. The old man was deeply dejected, thinking that his son could not endure the shock; but Albert, who was prepared for a much greater misfortune, was calm, resigned, and unshaken in his confidence.

"She is pure," said he; "and she wishes to love me. She feels that my love is true, and my faith immovable. God will protect her from danger. Let us accept this promise, my father, and remain tranquil. Fear not for me; I shall be stronger than my sorrow, and will subdue any anxiety that might disturb me."

"My son," said the old man, deeply affected, "we are here before the image of the God of your fathers. You have chosen another form of belief, and I have never reproached you for it, although, as you well know, my heart has suffered deeply. I am about to prostrate myself before that God in whose presence I promised you, the night before this, to do all that was in my power in order that your love might be heard, and sanctified by an honorable union. I have kept my promise, and I now renew it to you. I am again about to pray that the Almighty may fulfill your wishes; my own will not oppose them. Will you not unite with me in this solemn hour, which will perhaps decide in heaven the destiny of your love upon the earth? O my noble son! in whom the Eternal has preserved every virtue, notwithstanding the trials He has permitted your first faith to undergo—whom I have seen in your childhood kneeling by my side at the tomb of your mother, and praying like a young angel to that Sovereign Master whom you did not then doubt!—will you this day refuse to raise your voice toward Him, that mine may not be in vain?"

"Father," replied Albert, folding the old man in his arms, "if our faith differs, our souls are in unison as to the divine and eternal principle. You adore the God of wisdom and purity, the ideal of perfection, knowledge, justice, truth; I have never ceased to do so. O thou Crucified One!" he exclaimed, kneeling with his father before the sacred image, "Thou whom men have worshiped, and whom I too worship, as the purest and most noble manifestation of divine love—Thou who dwellest in God and in us, hear my prayer—bless just impulses and upright intentions, defeat triumphant wickedness, sustain oppressed innocence! Let the issue of my affection be as Heaven wills; but let Thy influence direct and animate those hearts who have no other strength or support than Thy sojourning and example upon earth!"

CHAPTER LXIV.

ANZOLETO pursued his way toward Prague to no purpose, for Consuelo, after having given the false instructions to the guide which she deemed necessary to the success of her enterprise, had taken a road to the left which she was acquainted with, from having twice accompanied the Baroness Amelia to a castle in the neighborhood of the little village of Tauss. This castle was the most distant journey which Consuelo had undertaken during her stay at Riesenburg. The aspect of the country, therefore, and the direction of the roads which traversed it, naturally occurred to her when she projected and executed her bold and hasty flight. She recollected also that, when walking on the terrace, the lady of the castle, in pointing out the vast extent of country which could be seen from it, had said: "That noble road bordered with trees which you see yonder, and which is lost in the distance, joins the great southern highway, and leads direct to Vienna." Consuelo, with this direction in her mind, was certain of not going astray. She reached the castle and grounds of Biela, which she skirted, and found without much difficulty, notwithstanding the darkness, the road bordered with trees; so that before daybreak she had accomplished a distance of three leagues as the bird flies. Young, active, and accustomed from childhood to long walks, and supported moreover by a resolute will, she saw the day dawn without experiencing much fatigue. The sky was clear, the roads were dry, sandy, and pleasant under foot. The rapid pace of the horse, to which she was not accustomed, had somewhat exhausted her; but in such cases it is better to go on than pause, for with energetic temperaments one species of fatigue is the best alleviation of another.

However by degrees as the stars grew pale, and the dawn brightened into day, she became frightened at being alone. She felt tranquil so long as it was dark, since, always on the watch, she was certain of being able to hide herself before she could be discovered; but during the day, obliged as she would be to cross extensive plains, she dared no longer follow the beaten track, the more so as she now began to perceive groups of persons in the distance, spreading like dark spots over the white line which marked the road on the yet obscure surface of the adjoining country. So near Riesenburg she might be recognized by the first person she met, and she therefore resolved to take a path which promised to shorten her journey by avoiding a circuit which she would otherwise be obliged to make round the hill. She proceeded in this direction for about an hour without meeting any one, and at last entered a thicket where she could easily conceal herself, if necessary. "If I could thus advance," thought she, "some eight or ten leagues unobserved, I would then proceed quietly along the high road, and at the first favorable opportunity hire a carriage and horses."

This reflection caused her to examine her purse, and see what was left for the remainder of her journey after her generous donation to the guide from Riesenburg. She had not yet had time for reflection; but had she reflected, and listened to the suggestions of prudence, would she have set out on such an expedition? But what were her surprise and consternation when she found that her purse contained a great deal less than she had supposed. In her haste she had only taken the half of the small sum which she possessed, or else she had given gold in place of silver to the guide; or perhaps, in opening her purse, she had dropped some of the money on the ground. However it might be, it was evident that she had no alternative but to proceed to Vienna on foot.

This discovery discouraged her a little, not so much on the score of the fatigue which it would occasion her, as the danger to which a young woman would be inevitably exposed in going on foot so long a journey. The fear which she had hitherto surmounted, under the impression that she could procure a conveyance, and thus avoid any risk of danger, overpowered her to such a degree, that, overcome by a sense of weakness and vague apprehension, she hurried forward, seeking the deepest shade, in order to conceal herself in case of attack.

To add to her disquietude, she saw that she had lost her way, and that she was wandering at random in the pathless forest. If the solitude reassured her in some respects, how could she be certain, on the other hand, that she might not take a direction the very opposite of what she wished, and so return to Riesenburg. Anzoleto might still be there, detained by suspicion, chance, or the hope of revenge; even Al'>crt himself might be dreaded in the first moment of his agitation and despair. Consuelo knew that he would submit to her decision; but suppose she were to present herself in the neighborhood of the castle, would he not hasten to assail her with supplications and tears? Ought she to expose this noble young man and his family, as well as to her own pride, to the scandal and ridicule of an enterprise abandoned as soon as undertaken? Anzoleto's return in the course of a few days might plunge every thing into fresh confusion, and so renew the danger which she had so generously and boldly obviated. Every thing must be hazarded rather than return to Riesenburg.

Resolved to seek carefully for the road leading to Vienna, and follow it at all risks, she paused in a shady and retired spot, where a spring gushed from between rocks sheltered by lofty trees. The ground around seemed marked by the footsteps of animals. Were they those of the neighboring flocks, or of beasts of prey who occasionally came to quench their thirst at this secluded fountain? Consuelo knelt down on the dripping stones, and satisfied both hunger and thirst with a draught of the cool and limpid water; then remaining in her kneeling posture, she reflected on her situation. "I am a weak and helpless creature," thought she, "if I cannot carry out what I have planned. What! shall it be said that my mother's child is no longer able to bear cold or hunger, fatigue or danger? I have dreamed to little purpose of freedom and poverty in the bosom of that plenty from which I always longed to free myself, if I am to be thus terrified. Was I not born to suffer and to dare? Or am I changed since the time when I used to journey on foot, sometimes before daybreak and often hungry, with my poor mother, and when all the nourishment we had was perhaps a draught at some roadside fountain? I am a worthy Zingara truly, who can only sing in a theater, sleep upon down, and travel in a coach! What dangers did I incur with my mother? Did she not say to me, when we met doubtful characters, 'Fear nothing; those who possess nothing have nothing to dread; the wretched do not prey upon each other,' She was young and handsome in those days, yet was she ever insulted by the passers-by? Even the worst men respect the defenseless. How do those poor mendicant girls do, who go about with nothing but the protection of God? Shall I be like those damsels who cannot move out of doors without thinking that the whole world, intoxicated with their charms, hastens in pursuit of them? Shall it be said that, because alone, and journeying on the broad and free highway, I must be degraded and dishonored, without some guardians to watch over me? My mother was as bold as a lion, and would have defended herself like one. Am not I also strong and courageous, with nought but good plebeian blood flowing in my veins? Besides, I am in a quiet country, with peaceful inhabitants; and were I even in some unknown land, I should be very unfortunate if in the hour of need I did not meet some of those upright, generous spirits, whom God has placed everywhere, as a sort of providence for the weak and helpless. But, courage! this day I have incurred no worse evil than hunger, I shall enter no cabin to purchase bread till toward the evening, when it becomes dark, and when I shall be far, far from this. I know what hunger is, and how to combat it, notwithstanding the constant feasting at Riesenberg. A day soon passes over. When it begins to get warm, and my limbs grow weary, I shall recall the saying which I heard so often in my infancy, 'He who sleeps dines.' I shall hide in some cave in the rocks, and you shall see, O my poor mother, who watchest over me, and journeyest at this hour invisible by my side, that I am able to repose without pillow or couch!"

While thus engaged in devising plans for her conduct, the poor girl forgot for a short time her distress. She had gained a victory over herself, and Anzoleto was already less dreaded. From the very moment when she had resisted his solicitations, she felt her soul partially relieved from her fatal attachment; and now, in putting into execution her romantic project, she experienced a sort of mournful gaiety, which made her repeat each instant to herself, "My body suffers, but it saves my soul. The bird which cannot defend itself by strength has wings to flee; and when it soars through the fields of air it laughs at nets and stratagems."

The recollection of Albert, and the picture she drew of his suffering and terror, presented themselves very differently to Consuelo; but she combated with all her might the tenderness which this thought was calculated to inspire. She determined to repel his image, until she should be beyond the reach of sudden repentance or imprudent emotion. "Dear Albert! noble friend!" said she, "I cannot help sighing deeply when I think of thee! But in Vienna alone shall I pause to sympathize with thee; here I shall only permit my heart to say how much it venerates and regrets thee."

"Forward!" continued Consuelo, endeavoring to rise, "I must proceed on my journey." But in vain she attempted, twice or thrice, to leave the wild and pretty fountain, whose pleasant murmur invited her to repose. Sleep, which she had purposed putting off till midday, weighed heavy on her eyelids, and hunger, which she was unable to resist so well as she had supposed, added to her exhaustion. She would gladly have deceived herself on this point, but in vain. She had been too much agitated to take any refreshment the evening before. A mist crept over her eyes, while languor and uneasiness took possession of her frame. She yielded to fatigue without being aware of it, and, firmly resolving to get up and proceed on her journey, she gradually sank on the grass, her head fell upon her little bundle, and she slept soundly. The sun, warm and glowing as it often is during the short summers of Bohemia, rose gaily in the sky, the fountain murmured over the pebbles, as if it had wished to lull the slumbers of the traveler, while the birds fluttered overhead, warbling their melodious carols.

CHAPTER LXV.

CONSUELO had slept thus about three hours, when she was aroused by another noise than that of the fountain and the warbling birds around her. She half opened her eyes, without having power to rise or well knowing where she was, and saw at two paces distant a figure leaning over the rocks, drinking like herself without much ceremony from the stream, by dipping his mouth into the water. Her first feeling was one of terror, but a further glance at the companion of her retreat restored her confidence; for whether he had had leisure to observe her features while she slept, or perhaps that he was not much interested in the matter, he appeared to take little notice of her; besides, he was rather a boy than a man. He appeared about fifteen or sixteen years of age at most, and was little, lean, sallow, and weather-beaten, while his countenance, which was neither handsome nor otherwise, expressed only calm indifference.

By an instinctive movement Consuelo drew down her veil, thinking that if the traveler troubled himself so little about her it would be better to appear to sleep than run the risk of provoking troublesome questions. Through her veil, however, she closely observed the unknown, expecting every moment that he would take up his knapsack and stick to continue his journey.

But she soon discovered that he was resolved to rest also, and even to breakfast, for he opened his bag and took out a huge lump of bread, which he gravely cut and began to eat, casting from time to time a timid glance toward the sleeper, and taking care to make no noise in opening and shutting his knife, as if he feared to awaken her suddenly. This mark of respect inspired Consuelo with perfect confidence, and the sight of the bread which he eat with such relish aroused the pangs of hunger. Being assured from the careless attire and dusty shoes of the youth, that he was a poor traveler and a stranger in the country, she believed that Providence had sent her unexpected aid by which she ought to profit. It was an immense hunch, and the boy, without stinting his appetite, could spare her a morsel. She rose, therefore, pretended to rub her eyes, as if she had just awakened, and looked boldly at the youth, in order if needful to keep him within bounds.

This precaution was unnecessary. As soon as the boy saw the sleeper standing up, he became uneasy, cast down his eyes, and at length, encouraged by the sweet and gentle expression of Consuelo's countenance, he ventured to look at her, and addressed her in a tone of voice so mild and harmonious, that she was immediately prepossessed in his favor.

" Well, mademoiselle," said he, smiling, " you are awake at last. You slept so soundly, that, only for the fear of being rude, I would have followed your example."

" If you are as kind as you are polite," replied Consuelo, assuming a maternal tone, " you can render me a slight service."

"Any thing you please," replied the young traveler, to whom Consuelo's voice seemed equally agreeable and penetrating.

"You must sell me some bread for breakfast then, if you can do so without inconvenience to yourself."

"Sell you some!" he exclaimed, surprised and blushing. "Oh! if I had a breakfast worth offering, I should not sell it. I am not an innkeeper, but I will give it to you with all my heart."

"You shall give it, then, on condition that you take in exchange something to buy a better breakfast."

"No, no," he replied; "by no means. Are you jesting? Are you too proud to accept a bit of bread? Alas! you see I have nothing else to offer you."

"Well, I accept it," said Consuelo, holding out her hand; "your kindness makes me blush for my pride."

"Here! here! my dear young lady," exclaimed the young man, joyously, "take the bread and cut for yourself. Do not hesitate, for I am not a great eater, and I have had sufficient already for the whole day."

"But will you have an opportunity of purchasing more?"

"Is not bread to be had everywhere? Eat, then, if you wish to oblige me."

Consuelo did not require to be asked again, and fearing that she might otherwise seem ungrateful to her host, she sat down beside him and began to eat with a relish which the most dainty food at the tables of the rich had never given her.

"What a good appetite you have!" said the boy. "Ah, I am so glad to have met you; it makes me quite happy to see you eat. Take it all. We shall soon come to some house or other, although the country here seems a desert."

"You are not acquainted with it, then?" said Consuelo, in a careless tone.

"It is the first time I have traveled it, although I know the way from Vienna to Pilsen, which is the road I have just come, and by which I am now about to return *yonder.*"

"Where? to Vienna?"

"Yes, Vienna; are you also going there?"

Consuelo, uncertain whether she should accept her companion as a fellow-traveler, pretended not to hear him, in order to gain time for a reply.

"Pshaw! what am I saying?" replied the young man. "A young lady like you would not be going alone to Vienna. However, you are on a journey, for you too have a parcel and are on foot like myself."

Consuelo determined to evade this question until she saw how far she might trust him, and hit upon the plan of replying to one question by asking another.

"You are from Pilsen, then?" she inquired.

"No," replied the boy, who had no motive for distrust, "I am from Rohran in Hungary. My father is a cartwright there."

"And why do you travel so far from home? You do not follow your father's trade, then?"

"I do, and I do not. My father is a cartwright—I am not. But he is also a musician, and I aspire to become one."

"A musician? That is a noble calling."

"It is perhaps yours also?"

"You are not going, however, to study music at Pilsen, which is merely a dull fortified town?"

"Oh no, I have been entrusted with a commission for that quarter, and I am now on my way back to Vienna, to endeavor to gain a livelihood while I continue my studies."

"Which have you embraced, vocal or instrumental music?"

"Both, up to the present time. I have a tolerable voice, and I have a poor little violin, by which I can make myself understood; but my ambition is great, and I would go yet further."

"Become composer, perhaps?"

"You have hit it. There is nothing in my head but this weary composition. I shall show you in my traveling bag a famous companion. It is a book which I have cut in pieces in order to be able to carry some portions of it with me over the country. When I am tired walking I sit down in some corner and read a little; that refreshes me."

"It is well done. I would wager that your book is the *Gradus ad Parnassum* of Fuchs."

"Precisely. Ah, I see you are acquainted with it, and I am now sure that you also are a musician. Just now, while you slept, I looked at you, and said to myself, that is not a German countenance, it is from the south —

Italian, perhaps—and what is more, it is the countenance of an artist. It was for that reason you made me so happy by asking me for bread. I now perceive that you have a foreign accent, although no one could speak better German."

"You might be deceived. You have not a German countenance, either. Your complexion is Italian, and yet——"

"Oh, you are very kind, mademoiselle. I know I have the complexion of an African, and my companions in the choir of St. Stephen used to call me the Moor. But to return to what I was saying; when I found you sleeping alone there in the middle of the wood I was a little surprised. Then a hundred ideas occurred to me respecting you. 'It is, perhaps,' thought I, 'my happy star which has led me hither to meet one who may be of use to me.' But shall I tell you every thing ?"

"Say on without fear."

"Observing that you were too well dressed and too fair for a poor wayfarer, but that you had a bundle with you, I imagined that you might be connected with some stranger—an artist, perhaps—oh, a great artist—she whom I seek and whose protection would be my glory and my happiness! Come, mademoiselle, tell me the truth ; you are from some neighboring castle, and you have been on business in the vicinity ? You must surely know the Castle of the Giants ?"

"You mean Riesenburg. And are you going there ?"

"At least I am trying; but I have so lost myself in this abominable wood, in spite of the directions which they gave me at Klatau, that I do not know whether I shall be able to find my way out of it. Happily you know Riesenburg, and you will have the goodness to inform me if I am still far from it."

"But what are you going to do at Riesenburg ?"

"I wish to see the Porporina."

"Indeed ?" And Consuelo, fearing to discover herself to a traveler who might speak of her at the Castle of the Giants, recovered herself sufficiently to ask with an indifferent air:

"And who is the Porporina ?"

"Do you not know ? Alas, you must be indeed a stranger in this country. But since you are a musician, and know the name of Fuchs, without doubt you are acquainted with that of Porpora."

" And do you know Porpora ?"

" Not yet; it is because I wish to know him that I seek to obtain the protection of his famous and beloved pupil, the Signora Porporina."

" Tell me how this idea came into your head. I might perhaps assist you to find her out."

"I shall relate my history. I am, as I have already told you, the son of a cartwright, and a native of a small town on the confines of Hungary. My father is sacristan and organist in the village. My mother, who had been cook to the lord of our district, has a fine voice, and my father, to refresh himself after his work, used to accompany her in the evenings on the harp. In this manner a love of music was instilled into me, and I recollect that my greatest pleasure when I was quite a child, was to join our family concerts with a bit of wood which I sawed with a lath, fancying all the while that I held a violin and bow in my hand and drew from it the most magnificent sounds. Oh, yes! it still seems to me, even yet, that my dear sticks were not dumb, but that a divine voice, unheard by others, floated around me and intoxicated me with celestial melody!

" Our cousin Franck, who was a schoolmaster at Haimburg, came to see us one day when I was playing on my imaginary violin, and was amused at the kind of ecstacy in which I was plunged. He assured my parents that it was the indication of extraordinary talent, and he brought me with him to Haimburg, where he gave me a very rude musical education, I assure you. What fine organ stops, with beats and flourishes, he executed with his conducting baton on my fingers and ears ! Nevertheless, I was not discouraged. I learned to read and write; I had a real violin, which I learned the use of, as well as the rudiments of singing and the Latin language. I made as rapid a progress as was possible with so impatient a master as my cousin Franck.

"I was about eight years old, when chance, or rather Providence, in which as a good Christian I have always believed, led me to the house of my cousin Reuter, chapel master of the cathedral at Vienna. I was presented to him as a little wonder, and when I had read with ease a piece at first sight, he took a fancy to me, brought me to Vienna, and took me into St. Stephen as one of the choir.

" There we had about two hours' work each day, and the rest of the time being at our own disposal, we could wander about as we pleased. But my passion for music stifled in me the idleness and playfulness of childhood. When sporting in the square with my companions, the moment I heard the sound of the organ I left them, to enter the church and delight myself by listening to the hymns and the music. I forgot myself in the streets beneath windows from which issued the sounds of a concert, or even those of an agreeable voice. I was at once curious and desirous to know and understand every thing which struck my ear. Above all, I wished to compose. When I was thirteen, I dared, without knowing any of the rules, to write a mass, which I showed to our master, Reuter. He laughed at me, and advised me to learn before attempt-ing to create. That was easily said, but I had no means of paying a master; my parents were too poor to advance the needful sums for my support and education. At last one day they gave me six florins, with which I bought the book which you see and that of Mattheson, which I began to study with ardent delight. My voice improved, and was considered the most beautiful in the choir. Amidst all this uncertainty and ignorance, I felt my mind enlarge and my ideas develop themselves within me. But I saw with terror the period approaching when, according to the rules of the chapel, I should be obliged to leave the estab-lishment ; and beholding myself without resources and without masters, I asked myself if these eight years of study were really to be my last, and if I must return to my parents to learn the trade of a cartwright. To add to my vexation, I saw that Master Reuter, in place of taking an interest in my welfare, treated me with increased severity, and only sought to hasten the period of my dis-missal. I know not why he disliked me, but I certainly did not deserve it. Some of my companions were silly enough to say that he was jealous of me because there was some degree of genius in my compositions, and that he was accustomed to hate and discourage young people who promised to surpass himself. I am far from having the vanity to accept this explanation as the true one, but doubtless he looked upon me as a brainless fool for having the presumption to show him my crude essays."

" And besides," said Consuelo, interrupting him, " old teachers do not like to see their pupils appear to understand faster than they do themselves. But tell me your name, my child."

" I am called Joseph."

" Joseph what?"

" Joseph Haydn."

" I will endeavor to recollect this name, so that, if one day you should turn out a distinguished man, I shall know what to think of the hatred of your master, and the interest with which you inspire me. But proceed, if you please."

Young Haydn resumed his narrative in the following words, while Consuelo, struck by the similarity of their artistic and poverty-stricken destiny, looked attentively at the countenance of the young chorister. His insignificant sallow countenance became singularly animated during his recital; his blue eyes sparkled with genial fire, and every thing he said and did bespoke no ordinary mind.

CHAPTER LXVI.

" WHATEVER may have been the cause of Master Reuter's antipathy, he displayed it toward me very harshly and for a very trifling cause. I happened to have a pair of new scissors, which, like a child as I was, I tried on every thing I could lay my hands on. One of my companions having turned his back toward me, and his long cue, of which he was very vain, dangling across the chalked notes on my slate, a fatal idea came on the instant into my head. Snip went the scissors, and lo! the cue lay on the ground! My master followed all my movements with the eye of a vulture, and before my poor comrade was aware of his loss, I was reprimanded, stamped with infamy, and sent about my business without further ceremony.

" I left the establishment in the month of November last year, at seven o'clock in the evening, and found myself in the streets without money or clothes, except the tattered garments on my back. I was in despair, and thought, in seeing myself thus dismissed, that I had been guilty of some dreadful crime. Thereupon I began to weep and cry, when my companion, whose head I had thus dishonored, passed me weeping likewise. Never were so many tears or so much remorse seen before or since for a Prussian cue. I could have thrown myself into his arms—at his feet; but I dared not, and hid my shame in the darkness. Yet perhaps the poor lad wept for my disgrace more than his own loss.

"I spent the night in the streets; and as I was sighing next morning when thinking of the impossibility of procuring a breakfast, I was met by Keller, the barber to the chapel. He had been just dressing Master Reuter, who, in his fury, had talked of nothing but the terrible loss of the cue. The facetious Keller, perceiving my distress, burst into a loud fit of laughter, and overwhelmed me with sarcasms. 'So, so,' cried he as far as he could see me; 'there goes the scourge of wigmakers, the enemy of all, who, like myself, profess to deal with hair! Ho! my little executioner of cues, my little ravager of love-locks! come hither till I trim your dark curls, as a set-off for all the cues that are destined to fall by your hands!' I was furious—desperate; I hid my face in my hands, and thinking I was the object of general indignation, was about to fly. The good Keller, however, stopped me, exclaiming with a gentle voice, 'My poor little fellow, where are you going?—with no food, no friends, no clothes, and such a crime on your conscience! Come, I shall have pity on you, especially on account of your sweet voice, which I have so often heard at the cathedral. I have but one apartment for myself and my children, on the fifth story, but then I have a garret higher up, which is not occupied, and which is at your service. You shall live with me till you get something to do, on the condition, however, that you spare my customers and do not try your fine scissors on my wigs.'

"I followed the generous Keller—my preserver and father. Besides board and lodging, he even gave me, poor as he was, a little money to enable me to pursue my studies. I hired an old worm-eaten harpsichord, and there, with my Fuchs and my Mattheson, I gave myself up without restraint to my ardor for composition. From this moment I considered myself the favorite of Providence. The six first sonatas of Emmanual Bach were my delight all that winter, and I think I learned and understood them thoroughly. At the same time Heaven rewarded my zeal and perseverance, permitting me to procure a little occupation, by which I managed to live and recompense my dear host. I played the organ every Sunday in the chapel of Count Haugwitz, after having taken, in the morning, the part of first violin in the church of the Merciful Brethren. Besides I found two protectors. One is an abbé, who writes Italian verses, very beautiful, they say, and approved of by her majesty, the empress. He is called Metastasio; and as he lives in the same house with Keller and myself, I give lessons to a young lady who is his niece. My other protector is his highness the Venetian ambassador."

" Signor Corner?" exclaimed Consuelo, hastily.

"Ah! you know him then," replied Hadyn; "it was Metastasio who introduced me into his house. My humble talents pleased him, and his excellency promised that I should have lessons from Master Porpora, who is at this moment at the baths of Manendorf with Madam Wilhelmina, his excellency's lady. This promise, that I should become the pupil of the first professor of singing in the universe, filled me with joy. To learn the pure and correct principles of Italian composition! I looked on myself as saved, and blessed my stars, as if I were already myself a maestro. But his excellency's good intentions were not so easily realized as I expected; and unless I obtain a more powerful recommendation, I fear I shall never be able even to approach Porpora. It is said that the illustrious master is strange, rough, unhappy in his temper; and while he is as attentive, generous, and devoted to some pupils, he is just as capricious to others. Reuter, it seems, is nothing in comparison to Porpora, and I tremble at the very idea of seeing him. He has refused all the proposals of the ambassador, saying that he will take no more pupils. But as I know that the Signor Corner will persist, I still venture to hope, as I am determined to put up with every rebuff, so that I succeed at last."

"Your resolution," said Consuelo, "is highly praiseworthy. The great master's rude and forbidding manners were not exaggerated; but you have reason to hope; for, with patience, submission, talent, and judgment, I promise you that after three or four lessons you will find him the mildest and most conscientious of masters. Perhaps even, if your heart and disposition correspond with your understanding, Porpora will prove himself a firm friend, a just and beneficent father."

"Oh! you fill me with joy. I see that you know him, and that you must also know his famous pupil, the new Countess of Rudolstadt—the Porporina——"

"But where have you heard this Porporina spoken of, and what do you expect from her?"

"I expect a letter from her to Porpora, and her recommendation to him when she comes to Venice; for she will doubtless proceed there after her marriage with the rich lord of Riesenburg."

"How did you hear of this marriage?"

"By the greatest chance in the world. I must tell you that, last month, my friend Keller heard that a relation of his at Pilsen had just died, and left him a little property. Keller had neither time nor means to undertake the journey, and did not venture to determine upon it, for fear that the inheritance should not pay the expense of his trip, and the loss of his time. I had just received some money for my labor, and I offered to go and attend to his interests. I have just been at Pilsen, and, during the week I passed there, I have had the satisfaction of seeing Keller's inheritance realized. It is little, no doubt, but that little is not to be despised by him; and I carry with me the titles of a small property, which he can sell or let out as he shall judge best. Returning from Pilsen I found myself yesterday evening in a place called Klatau, where I passed the night. It had been a market-day, and the inn was full of people. I was seated near a table where a large fat man was eating, whom they called Doctor Wetzelius, and who is the greatest gourmand and the greatest babbler I ever met with. 'Do you know the news?' said he to his neighbors; 'Count Albert of Rudolstadt — he who is mad, almost a complete maniac — is going to marry his cousin's music mistress, an adventuress, a beggar, who has been, they say, an actress in Italy.' The old buffoon went on to relate a variety of anecdotes concerning the Porporina, all of which tended to prove that she had imposed on and basely deceived her worthy hosts at Riesenburg."

"Oh! it is horrible; it is infamous!" cried Consuelo, almost beside herself. "It is a tissue of abominable calumnies and revolting absurdities."

" Do not believe that I gave credence to it for an instant," returned Joseph Haydn; " the face of the old doctor was as stupid as it was wicked, and before they had given him the lie, I was already convinced that he was retailing only slanders and falsehoods. But hardly had he ended his story when five or six young men who were near him, took the young lady's part, and it was thus that I learned the truth. Each praised the beauty, the grace, the modesty, the sense, and the incomparable talent of the Porporina. All approved of Count Albert's passion for her, envied his happiness, and admired the old count for having consented to the union. Doctor Wetzelius was treated as an insane dotard, and as they spoke of the high esteem which Master Porpora felt for a pupil to whom he had consented to give his name, the idea occurred to me of going to Riesenburg, throwing herself at the feet of the future or perhaps the present countess (for they said the marriage was already celebrated, but kept secret for fear of offending the court), relating my history to her and endeavoring to procure from her the favor of becoming the pupil of her illustrious master."

Consuelo remained some instants buried in thought; the last words of Joseph respecting the court had struck her. But quickly recovering herself: " My child," said she, "do not go to Riesenburg, you will not find the Porporina there. She is not married to the Count of Rudolstadt, and nothing is less certain than this marriage. It has been talked of, it is true, and I believe the betrothed were worthy of each other; but the Porporina, although she felt for Count Albert a sincere friendship, a high esteem, and a respect without bounds, thought she ought not to decide lightly upon so serious a matter. She weighed, on the one side, the injury she might inflict on that illustrious family, by causing them to lose the good graces and perhaps the protection of the empress, as well as the esteem of the other nobles and the consideration of the whole country; and on the other, the injury she would inflict on herself, by renouncing the practice of that divine art which she had passionately studied and embraced with courage. She said to herself that the sacrifice was great on both sides, and that, before deciding on it hastily, she ought to consult Porpora, and give the young count time to discover if his passion would resist the effects of absence.

Therefore she set out suddenly for Vienna on foot, without a guide, almost without money, but with the hope of thus restoring repose and reason to one who loves her, and of carrying away, of all the riches that were offered to her only the testimony of her conscience and the pride of her, profession as an artist."

"Oh! she is indeed a true artist! She has a powerful mind and a noble soul, if she has acted thus!" cried Joseph, fixing his sparkling eyes on Consuelo; "and if I am not deceived it is to her that I speak—it is before her that I kneel."

"It is she who holds out her hand to you, and who offers you her friendship, her advice and support with Porpora; for it appears to me we shall travel together; and if God protects us, as He has hitherto protected us both, as He protects all those who trust only in Him, we shall soon be at Vienna, and shall take our lessons from the same master."

"God be praised!" cried Haydn, weeping with joy, and raising his hands enthusiastically toward heaven; "something whispered to me when I saw you asleep, that you were no common being; and that my life—my destiny—were in your hands!"

CHAPTER LXVII.

WHEN the young people had made a more ample acquaintance, by discussing on each side in friendly chat the details of their situation, they thought of the precautions and arrangements necessary for their journey to Vienna. The first thing they did was to take out their purses and count their money. Consuelo was still the richer of the two; but their united funds would only furnish means sufficient to enable them to travel agreeably on foot, without suffering from hunger, or sleeping in the open air. They could not hope for any thing better, and Consuelo had already made up her mind to it. Still, notwithstanding the philosophical gaiety she manifested on this subject, Joseph was anxious and thoughtful.

"What is the matter with you?" said she; "perhaps you are afraid of my company proving an embarrassment to you, and yet I will wager that I can walk better than you."

"You ought to do every thing better than I," replied he; "it is not that which troubles me. But I am sorry and even frightened when I think how young and handsome you are, and how every one must admire you that sees you; while I am so mean and little, that though I were resolved to die for you a thousand times, my strength would not suffice for your protection."

"What are you thinking of, my poor child? Do you suppose that, even if I were handsome enough to attract the attention of the passers-by, a woman who respects herself does not know always how to repel ——"

"Ugly or handsome, faded or young, bold or modest, you would not be safe on these roads, covered as they are with disbanded soldiers and scoundrels of every description. Since the peace, the country swarms with soldiers returning to their garrisons, and especially with licensed volunteers, who in order to increase their means, pillage travelers, put whole districts under contribution, and treat the country as a conquered land. I am thinking seriously of changing our route; and in place of going by Piseck and Budweiss — fortified towns, and consequently frequented by all sorts of military stragglers and others not much better—of descending the course of the Moldau, and keeping in the gorges of the almost deserted mountains, where cupidity and rascality find nothing to attract them, proceed along the bank of the river as far as Reichenau, and enter Austria by Freistadt. Once there, we shall be under the protection of a better police than exists in Bohemia."

"You know this road, then?"

"I do not even know if there be one; but I have a small map in my pocket, for I took it into my head on leaving Pilsen to try and return by the mountains, so as to see a little of the country."

"It seems a good idea," said Consuelo, looking at the map; "there are footpaths every where, and cabins for the reception of those whose means are slender. I see here in fact a chain of mountains which extend to the source of the Moldau, and which border the river."

"It is the great Böhmer Wald, which contains the highest mountains in the range, and serves as a boundary between Bavaria and Bohemia. We can easily reach it; and by keeping on the heights, can always ascertain the valleys which lead down to the two provinces. Since— Heaven be thanked!—I have no longer to deal with this hidden Castle of the Giants, I am certain of guiding you aright, and not taking a longer route than is needful."

"Let us set out then," said Consuelo. "I feel perfectly refreshed; my sleep and your good bread have restored my strength, and I can accomplish at least ten miles to-day. Besides I am anxious to leave this neighborhood, where I expect every instant to meet some one who knows me."

"Stop!" said Joseph; "a strange idea occurs to me."

"What is it?"

"If you did not object to put on man's attire, you could then preserve your *incognito* perfect, and you would escape all the disagreeable consequences which might result from seeing a young girl traveling alone with a youth."

"It is not a bad idea, but you forget our scanty means. Besides, where could I find clothes that would fit me?"

"Listen; I should not have proposed this step if I had not had the means of putting it in execution. We are precisely the same height—which is more honorable to you than me—and I have in my bag an entire suit of clothes, perfectly new, which will disguise you completely. The reason I happened to have them is that they are a present from my good mother, who thought they would be useful to me when going to the embassy, and giving lessons to young ladies. They were made by the village tailor, and certainly the costume is sufficiently picturesque, and the materials well selected, as you may see. But imagine the sensation I would have produced at the embassy, and the wicked laughter of Metastasio's niece, if I had appeared in this rustic doublet and puffed-out pantaloons. I thanked my poor mother; but promised to myself that I would sell the dress to some peasant or strolling actor. This is how I happened to have the suit with me, but fortunately, as it has turned out, I was unable to get rid of it. The people here have an idea that it is some old Polish or Turkish fashion."

"Well, the opportunity of doing so has arrived at last," said Consuelo, laughing. "Your idea is an excellent one, and the traveling actress will be content with your Turkish dress, which is not very unlike a petticoat. I shall take it on credit, or rather on condition that you will take charge of our *strong box*, as Frederick of Prussia used to call it, and advance the needful funds until we reach Vienna."

"We shall see about that," said Joseph, putting the purse into his pocket, firmly resolved not to let her pay. "In the meantime we must see if the dress fits you. I shall take myself off to the wood, and you will find many a spacious secluded boudoir among these rocks."

"Enter upon the stage," replied Consuelo, pointing toward the forest, "while I retire behind the scenes."

She hastened behind the rocks and proceeded to transform herself, while her respectful companion removed to a distance. The fountain served her as a mirror, and it was not without pleasure that she saw herself converted into the prettiest little peasant that the Slavonic race ever produced. Her slender and agile figure was encircled by a large woollen belt, her ankles, slender as those of a roe, appeared below the heavy folds of her Turkish pantaloons, and her dark hair, in which she had never worn powder, had been cropped short during her illness, and curled naturally about her face. She ran her fingers through it, in order to give it the rustic negligence becoming a young shepherd. She wore her costume with theatrical grace, and assuming, thanks to her mimic talents, an air of rustic simplicity, she found herself so completely disguised, that on the instant a sense of courage and security returned, and as it happens to actors when they have donned their costume to appear on the stage, she identified herself with her part so thoroughly, as to experience all the careless freedom and innocent gaiety of a schoolboy playing truant in the woods.

She had to whistle three times before Hadyn, who had withdrawn further than was necessary into the wood, either to testify his respect, or to escape the temptation of turning his eyes toward the openings in the rocks, returned to her. He uttered a cry of surprise and admiration on seeing her, and although he had expected to find her completely disguised, could hardly believe his eyes. The transformation became Consuelo prodigiously, and at the same time gave an entirely different turn to the young man's imagination.

The kind of pleasure which the beauty of a woman produces on an adolescent is always mingled with fear, and the dress that makes her, even in the eyes of the most daring, a being so veiled and so mysterious, has much to do with this feeling of agitation and disquietude.

But the change of costume, which was so completely successful as to seem a real change of sex, suddenly changed also the disposition of the young man's mind. He no longer apparently felt any thing more than that warm and brotherly attachment which springs up between two travelers of kindred feelings and sentiments. The same desire to travel and see the country, the same security as to the dangers of the road, and the same sympathizing gaiety, which animated Consuelo at this instant, took possession of him also, and they began their journey through wood and meadow as gay and joyous as two birds of passage.

However, after proceeding a few steps, he forget that she was a boy, on seeing her carry over her shoulder, on the end of a stick, her little packet, now enlarged by the addition of her own dress. A dispute arose between them on this point. Consuelo affirmed that with his bag, his violin, and the music of the *Gradus ad Parnassum*, he was sufficiently burthened, while Joseph, on his side, declared that he would put Consuelo's packet in his bag, and that she should carry nothing. She had to yield the point, but in order that she might seem the character which she assumed, as well as to keep up an appearance of equality between them, he allowed her to carry the violin.

" You know," said Consuelo, in order to induce him to submit, " that I must be your servant, or at least your guide, because I am plainly a peasant while you are a citizen."

" What! a citizen?" replied Hadyn, laughing, " I dare say I have something the cut of Keller's apprentice." But the good youth felt a little mortified in not being able to appear before Consuelo in better trim than was possible from the state of his clothes, faded by the sun, and somewhat the worse of the wear.

" No," said Consuelo, in order to relieve his mind : "you are the prodigal son returning to the paternal home, with the gardener's boy, the companion of his rambles."

" I believe we had better assume the parts appropriate

to our situation," replied Joseph. "We can only pass for what we really are—poor wandering artists. We might even say, if we are questioned, that we have been making a professional tour. I can speak of the celebrated village of Rohran which nobody knows, and of the grand city of Haimburg about which nobody cares. As for you, your pretty accent will betray you, and you had better not deny that you are an Italian, and a singer by profession."

"By the bye, we must have suitable names; yours is quite new to me. I should, conformably to my Italian manners, call you Beppo; it is the contraction of Joseph."

"Call me what you will, I shall be equally unknown by one name as by another. It is quite different with you; you must positively have a name. What do you choose?"

"The first short Venetian name that occurs—Nello, Maso, Renzo, Zoto——oh! not that," she exclaimed, after having uttered involuntarily the childish abbreviation of Anzoleto.

"Why not?" replied Joseph, who observed her hasty exclamation.

"It would be an unlucky one; they say there are such names."

"Well, then, what shall we call you?"

"Bertoni. That is an Italian name, and a kind of diminutive of Albert."

"Il Signor Bertoni! that sounds well," said Joseph, trying to smile. But this indication of Consuelo's regard for her noble betrothed struck a dagger to his heart. He watched her as she bounded before him, as light and agile as a young fawn. "By the bye," said he to himself, by way of comfort, "I forgot he was a boy!"

CHAPTER LXVIII.

THEY soon found the boundary of the forest, and turned toward the southeast. Consuelo's head was uncovered, but Joseph, although observing the sun scorch her beautifully clear complexion, dared not express his regret. The hat which he himself wore not being new, he could not offer it to her; and feeling his anxiety useless, he did not wish to say any thing about it. But he placed his own hat under his arm with an abrupt movement which his companion remarked.

"Well, that is a strange idea," said she; "it would seem as if you found the air close and the plain shaded with trees. It reminds me that I have nothing on my own head; but as I have not always had every comfort within my reach, I know many ways of procuring them at little cost." So saying, she snatched a clustering vine-branch, and rolling it into a circle, she made of it a cap of verdure.

"Now she has something the air of a Muse," thought Joseph, "and the boy vanishes afresh!" They were now passing through a village, and Joseph seeing one of those shops where they sell every thing, rushed in suddenly ere she could prevent him, and immediately appeared again with a little straw hat with broad rims flapping over the ears, such as is worn by the peasants of the Danube.

"If you begin by luxuries," said she, trying on this new headdress, "we may want bread before our journey is over."

"Want bread?" exclaimed Joseph, eagerly; "I would rather beg by the way-side and tumble in the streets for pence! Oh, no! you shall want for nothing with me." Then seeing that Consuelo was surprised at his enthusiasm, he added somewhat more composedly: "Reflect, *Signor Bertoni*, that all my prospects depend on you, that you are as it were in my charge, and that I am bound to bring you safe and sound to Master Porpora."

The idea that her companion should fall in love with her never entered Consuelo's mind. Modest and single-minded women rarely entertain such ideas, which coquettes on the contrary are forever hatching. Besides even very young women usually esteem men of their own age as children, and Consuelo was two years older than Haydn, who was so small and meager that he seemed hardly fifteen. She knew very well that he was more, but she never could have supposed that love had dawned upon his imagination. It was evident, however, that Joseph experienced some extraordinary emotion, for once when she stopped to breathe a little and admire the lofty prospect, she detected him gazing at her with a sort of ecstasy.

"What is the matter with you, friend Beppo?" said she, artlessly, "methinks you are melancholy; I cannot get it out of my head that I am a burthen to you."

" Do not say that," said he, with much emotion ; " it were to refuse me that esteem and confidence for which I would gladly give my life."

" In that case do not look so sad unless you have some vexation at heart that you have not told me of."

Joseph fell into a gloomy silence, and they walked on for a long time before he was able to break it. But the longer the silence continued, the greater became his confusion and his fear of being found out. At last, unable to resume the conversation, he said abruptly:

" Do you know what I was thinking seriously of?"

" No; I cannot guess," replied Consuelo, who during all this time was lost in her own reflections, and did not observe his silence.

" I was thinking that if it would not tire you, you might teach me Italian as we went along. I began with books this winter, but having no one to guide me in the pronunciation, I dare not pronounce a word before you. Nevertheless I understand what I read, and if you would be so good as to cause me to surmount my false shame, and would teach me syllable by syllable, I think I have so correct an ear that you would not lose your trouble."

" Oh, with all my heart," replied Consuelo. " It would delight me if every one would thus employ their leisure moments in self-instruction; and as we learn by teaching others the exercise will serve to improve us both in the pronunciation of so musical a language. You think I am an Italian, but I am not, although my accent is tolerably pure. However, I pronounce perfectly only when I sing ; and, when I wish you to seize the harmony of Italian sounds, I shall sing the difficult words to you. I am persuaded that no one pronounces badly who does not hear badly. If your ear appreciates the shades of sound, it will be but an effort of memory to repeat them correctly."

" That would be at the same time an Italian and a singing lesson," exclaimed Joseph, "and a lesson which would last fifty leagues," thought he in his ecstacy. " Ah ! long live art, the least dangerous and ungrateful of all our passions."

The lesson began that instant, and Consuelo had at first some difficulty in not laughing outright at every word he uttered, but she was soon amazed at the facility and justness with which he corrected himself. However, the young musician, who was dying to hear the famous singer's voice, and who did not see an opportunity present itself quickly enough, succeeded by a little stratagem. He pretended to be greatly embarrassed in giving to the Italian *à* the proper force, and he sung a phrase from Leo, where the word *Felicitià* is several times repeated. Immediately Consuelo, without stopping or being more out of breath than if she were seated at the harpsichord, sang it several times. When he heard her glorious accents, so much superior to those of any other singer then existing, Joseph felt a thrill run through his whole frame, and he could not help clasping his hands in passionate admiration.

" It is now your turn to try," said Consuelo, without perceiving his transports.

Haydn tried and succeeded so well that the young professor clapped her hands.

" Extremely well," said she good-naturedly, " you learn quickly and you have a magnificent voice."

" You may say what you like of it," replied Joseph, " but I feel that I can never trust myself to speak of you."

" And wherefore?" said Consuelo. But turning toward him she saw that his eyes were filled with tears, and his hands were clasped in ecstasy.

" Let us sing no more," said she, " here are some horsemen coming toward us."

" Ah! yes," exclaimed Joseph, quite beside himself; "do not let them hear you, for they would instantly throw themselves on their knees at your feet."

" I do not fear these frantic lovers of song. See, they are only butchers' boys with their calves behind them."

" Ah, pull down your hat, turn your head away," said Joseph, with a jealous pang. " Do not let them see you, do not let them hear you! Let no one see or hear you but me."

The remainder of the day was passed in serious study or gay and animated conversation. In the midst of his intoxication, Joseph did not know whether he was a trembling adorer of beauty or a devoted admirer of art. At once a dazzling idol and a delightful companion, Consuelo filled all his thoughts and transported his whole being. Toward evening he perceived that she walked with difficulty, and that fatigue had quenched her gaiety. Indeed for several hours previously, notwithstanding their frequent halts in the shady parts of the road, she had felt very weary. But she wished it to be so, and even had it not been evident that she must soon leave that part of the country, she would have sought in motion and a sort of forced gaiety, for forgetfulness of her mental pain and suffering. The shades of evening, which now gave a melancholy aspect to the country, brought back to her mind the sad feelings which she had so courageously combated. She then imagined to herself the mournful evening which was about to commence at the Castle of the Giants, and the dreary night which Albert might spend. Overcome by this idea, she involuntarily stopped at the foot of a large wooden cross on the summit of a naked hill, which marked the scene of some miracle or traditional crime.

"Alas! you are more fatigued than you are willing to allow," said Joseph; "but a resting-place is at hand, for I see in the distance the light gleaming from the cottages of a hamlet. You think perhaps that I would not be strong enough to carry you, nevertheless if you will trust——"

"My child!" replied she, smiling, "you are very proud of your sex; but I beg of you not to despise mine, and to believe that I have more strength left than you have yourself. I am out of breath climbing this ascent, that is all; and if I pause it is because I wish to sing."

"Heaven he praised!" exclaimed Joseph. "Sing then at the foot of this cross; but it will only tire you still more."

"It will not take long," said Consuelo; "it is a fancy which seized me to sing a little Spanish hymn, which my mother made me repeat every morning and evening, wherever we met a chapel or a cross."

Consuelo's idea was even more romantic than she was willing to admit. In thinking of Albert she recollected his almost supernatural faculty of seeing and hearing at a distance. She fancied that at this very moment he thought of, and perhaps saw her; and thinking it might soothe his pain were she to sing to him, though night and distance separated them, she mounted the stones which supported the cross, and turning toward Riesenburg, she sung at the full pitch of her voice the Spanish hymn, commencing:

"*O Consuelo de mi alma,*"

"Oh Heavens!" exclaimed Hadyn, when she had finished, and speaking to himself, "I never heard singing before. I did not even know what singing was. Are there other human voices like this? I will never hear any thing similar to what has been revealed to me to-day. O, music —thrice sacred music! O, genius of art, thou dost consume me—thou dost terrify me!"

Consuelo came down from the stone, where, like another Madonna, her profile stood out in relief against the clear azure of the night. Inspired like Albert, she fancied she saw him through the intervening woods and mountains, seated on the stone of Schreckenstein, calm, resigned, and filled with holy expectation. "He has perhaps heard me," thought she, "recognized my voice and the hymn which he loves, and will soon return to the castle, embrace his father, and perhaps spend a tranquil night."

"All is going on well," said she to Joseph, without heeding his passionate admiration. Then returning once again, she kissed the rude wood-work of the cross. Perhaps at this very moment, by some strange sympathy, Albert felt an electric impulse thrill through his melancholy being, and flood his soul with divine rapture. It might be the very moment when he was sinking into his calm and refreshing slumber, in which his father would have the satisfaction of finding him on the returning dawn.

The hamlet whose light they had perceived was nothing else than a large farm-house, where they were hospitably received. The honest and industrious laborers were eating their evening meal before the door, on a table of rude structure, at which room was made for the travelers without bustle or constraint. The peasants did not ask them any questions, and scarcely looked at them. Fatigued with the toils of the scorching day, they enjoyed their simple but wholesome and nourishing fare with silent satisfaction. Consuelo found the supper excellent, and did every honor to it. Joseph forgot to eat; besides, he was gazing at Consuelo's pale and noble countenance, which formed such a striking contrast with the sunburned peasants, tranquil and indifferent as the oxen that grazed around them, who made but little more noise than they did as they slowly ruminated.

Each as he felt himself satisfied retired to rest, making

a sign of the cross, and leaving the more robust to enjoy the pleasures of the table as they thought fit. The serving women and the children took the vacant places. More animated and curious than their predecessors, they retained and questioned the young travelers. Joseph gave them an account which he had ready prepared to satisfy them, and did not deviate much from the truth in telling them that his companion and himself were poor wandering musicians.

"What a pity it is not Sunday," said one of the youngest girls, "for then we should have a dance." They cast inquiring glances on Consuelo, who appeared a pretty lad, and who, the better to sustain her part, looked boldly at them in return. For a moment she had sighed, when thinking of these delightful patriarchal manners, from which her wandering and artistic habits so widely severed her. But seeing these poor women standing up behind their husbands and cheerfully eating their leavings, some suckling their little ones, others slaves by instinct to their sons, and waiting upon them without minding their little girls or themselves, she perceived that they were no better than victims of hunger and necessity. The men chained to the soil, and servants to the cattle and the plow, the women chained to their masters, shut up in their houses in perpetual servitude, and condemned to unrelaxing labor, amidst all the sufferings and anxieties of maternity. The owner of the soil, on the one hand extorting the last penny of the husbandman's wretched gains, on the other hand, imparting avarice and fear to the tenant, who in his turn doomed those under him to the same sordid, remorseless necessity that he was subjected to himself. Their apparent cheerfulness now seemed to Consuelo nothing more than the callous indifference of misfortune, or the deadening effect of toil, and she felt that she would rather a thousand times be a wandering artist than lord or peasant, since the possession of the soil, or even of a grain of corn, seemed only to entail on the one side tyrannical exaction, and on the other meanness and sycophancy. "*Viva la liberta!*" said she to Joseph, speaking in Italian, while the women washed and laid aside the household utensils with huge clatter, and an aged crone plied her spinning-wheel with the regularity of a machine.

Joseph was surprised to find that some of these peasants

spoke German tolerably well. He learned that the head of the family, whom he had seen dressed in the costume of a peasant, like the rest, was of noble extraction, and had received some degree of fortune and education, but ruined by the wars of the succession, he had no other means of rearing his numerous family than that of becoming tenant to a neighboring abbey. This abbey ground him to the earth with their exactions, and he was further obliged to liquidate the imperial tax on religious houses, which was imposed upon every change of their superior. This exaction was always levied from the vassals of the church, in addition to their other obligations. As for the farm servants, they were serfs, and considered themselves no worse off than the individual who employed them. The person who farmed the tax was a Jew, and, sent by the abbey whom he harassed to the peasants whom he harassed still more, he had come that morning to collect a sum which exhausted the hard earnings of many years. So that between their Superiors and the Jewish extortioners, the poor agriculturist did not know which to hate or dread the most.

"Did I not say truly, Joseph," said Consuelo, "that we alone are rich in the world, who pay no tax on our voice, and only labor when we please?"

The hour for repose having now arrived, Consuelo felt so much fatigued that she had fallen asleep on a bench before the door. Joseph, meanwhile, inquired about beds from the farmer's wife.

"Beds, my child?" replied she, smiling; "if we can give you one it will be very well, and you must be content with it."

This reply made the blood rush into poor Joseph's face. He looked at Consuelo, and finding she did not hear a word of what passed, he suppressed his emotion.

"My companion is sadly tired," said he, "and if you could give him a little bed to himself we will pay you whatever you ask. As for myself, a corner in the barn or in the stable will do very well."

"Oh, if the boy is ill, we will on that account give him a bed in the common room; our three daughters can sleep together. But tell him to be very quiet and orderly, or else my husband or son-in-law, who sleep on the same floor, will soon bring him to reason."

"I can answer for the good conduct of my companion;

but perhaps he may still prefer sleeping in the hay to a chamber where there are so many people."

The good Joseph had now to awaken Signor Bertoni in order to acquaint him with this arrangement. Consuelo was not shocked as he expected. She thought as the three girls slept in the same room as the father and son-in-law, she would be safer there than elsewhere, and having wished Joseph a good night, she glided behind the four curtains of brown woolen which inclosed the bed, and, scarcely taking time to undress, she soon slept soundly.

CHAPTER LXIX.

AFTER a few hours of deep and dreamless repose, she was awakened by the continued noises around her. On one side the old grandmother, whose bed almost touched hers, coughed and wheezed distressingly; on the other was a young woman who suckled her infant, and sang lullabies to sooth it to sleep again; there were men who snored like horses, boys four in a bed quarreling with each other, women rising to quiet them and only adding to the uproar by their threats and chidings. This perpetual annoyance, the crying children, the dirt, the heavy odors and heated atmosphere, became so disagreeable to Consuelo, that she could not bear it any longer. She dressed herself quietly, and seizing a moment when every one was asleep, she left the house and sought a corner where she could repose till daybreak.

She thought she would rest better in the open air. Having walked all the preceding night, she did not feel the cold ; but, besides that she was now overwhelmed with fatigue and in a condition very different from the excitement consequent on her departure, the climate of this elevated region was keener than the neighborhood of Riesenburg. She shuddered, and a sense of severe indisposition made her fear she would be unable to support one day's journey after another, without resting at night, when the beginning proved so disagreeable. In vain she reproached herself with having turned into a *princess*, in consequence of her luxurious life at the castle. She would have given all the world for an hour's good sleep.

However, not venturing to re-enter the house lest she should awaken or displease her hosts, she sought the barn, and finding the door partly open, crept in. Every thing was silent. Thinking that the place was empty, she lay down on a heap of straw; the heat and the wholesome odor appeared delicious.

She was just falling asleep, when she felt on her face a warm moist breath, which was suddenly withdrawn with a snort and what seemed to her a stifled imprecation. Her first apprehension being allayed, she perceived in the twilight a huge head surmounted by two formidable horns, just above her. It was that of a fine cow which had thrust its head into the rack, and having breathed on her, drew back affrighted. Consuelo withdrew into the corner, so as not to disturb her, and fell fast asleep. Her ear soon grew accustomed to all the noises of the place, to the clank of chains, the bellowing of heifers, and the rubbing of their horns against the bars. She did not awake even when the milkmaids came in to drive out the beasts to be milked in the open air. The dark corner where Consuelo had taken refuge hindered her from being observed, and the sun was high in the heavens when she next opened her eyes. Buried in the straw, she enjoyed for a few moments the comfort of her situation, and was delighted at feeling herself refreshed and rested, and ready to resume her journey without effort or inquietude.

When she started up to look for Joseph, the first object she encountered was Joseph himself seated beside her.

" You have occasioned me great uneasiness, Signor Bertoni," said he. " When the young women informed me that you were not in the apartment, and that they did not know what had become of you, I sought you everywhere, and it was only in despair that I returned here where I passed the night, and where, to my great surprise, I have found you. I left the barn in the gray of the morning, and had little idea that you were then close by me, and under the very nose of this animal who might have hurt you. Really, signora, you are very rash, and you do not reflect on all the perils to which you expose yourself."

" You see, Joseph," replied Consuelo, " that in my imprudence Heaven does not abandon me, since it conducted me to you. It was Providence who caused me to meet you yesterday morning by the fountain, when you shared your good-will and your bread with me, and it was the same Providence which confided me this night to your brotherly care."

She then related to him, laughing, the disagreeable night she had passed in the common room, and how happy and tranquil she felt among the cows.

"Is it true then," said Joseph, "that the beasts have a more agreeable habitation and better manners than those who take care of them?"

"That is just what I was thinking of before I fell asleep in this manger. These animals caused me neither terror nor disgust, and I blamed myself for having contracted so aristocratic habits, that the society of my equals, and contact with their indigence, has become insupportable to me. How comes it so, Joseph? He who is born in poverty, should not experience, when he falls back into it, the disdainful repugnance to which I have yielded. When the heart is not perverted in the lap of luxury, why should one remain fastidious, as I have been to-night in shunning the nauseous warmth and noisy confusion of this poor swarming human hive?"

"It is because cleanliness, purity, and order are doubtless wants of all elevated minds," replied Joseph. "Whoever is born an artist has the feeling of the beautiful and the good, just as he feels aversion for the hateful and ugly. And poverty is ugly! I am myself a peasant; I was born in a cottage. But my parents were artists, and our house although small was neat and orderly. It is true that our poverty bordered on comfort, while excessive privation takes away even the sense of what is better."

"Poor people!" said Consuelo, "if I were rich I would forthwith build them a house; and were I a queen, I would put down these taxes, these Jews, and these monks who prey upon them."

"If you were rich you would never think of it; if you were a queen you would not do it. Thus runs the world."

"The world runs very badly then."

"Alas! yes; and without music, which transports the soul into an ideal world, we would be miserable when we think of what is going on here below."

"It is easy to talk of being miserable, Joseph, but what good does it do? it is better to grow rich, and remain happy."

"And how is that possible, unless all poor people were to turn artists?"

"That is not a bad idea, Joseph. If the poor had a love of art, it would ennoble their sufferings and lighten their misery. There would then exist no longer uncleanliness, discouragement, or neglect; and the rich would no longer harass and despise the poor. Artists, you know, are always somewhat respected."

"Ah! I never thought of that before," replied Hadyn. "Art then may have a serious aim, and one truly useful to mankind?"

"What! did you think it was no better than an amusement?"

"No, I held it to be a disease, a passion, a storm raging in the heart, a fever that communicated itself to others—in short if you know what it is, tell me."

"I will tell you when I find out myself, Joseph; but it is something very great; no doubt of that. Come, let us set out, and do not forget your violin—your only inheritance, friend Beppo, and the foundation of our future opulence."

They commenced by making preparations for breakfast, which they intended to eat upon the grass in some romantic spot; but when Joseph pulled out his purse and proposed to pay, the farmer's wife smiled and would not hear of it. Whatever Consuelo could say she would take nothing, and she even watched her young guests to see that they slipped nothing to the children. "Recollect," said she, with some little evidence of disdain, "that my husband is noble by birth, and that misfortune has not so far reduced him as to cause him to sell his hospitality."

"This pride seems to me rather superfluous," said Joseph to his companion when they had once more set out. "There is more pride than charity in the feeling which animates them."

"I see nothing in it," said Consuelo, "but what is charitable, and I am ashamed at heart and repent to think that I could not put up with a house that harbored a wanderer like myself. Ah! accursed refinement, foolish delicacy of the spoiled children of the world!—thou art a malady, since thou art health to some only at the expense of others!"

"For a great artist like you," said Joseph, "I think you are somewhat too sensitive to worldly matters. Methinks an artist should be rather more indifferent to what does not beseem his profession. They said in the inn at Klatau, where they talked about you and the Castle of the Giants, that Count Albert of Rudolstadt was a great philosopher with all his eccentricity. You knew very well, signora, that one could not be both artist and philosopher, therefore you took yourself off. Do not trouble yourself any more then with human misfortune, and let us resume yesterday's lesson."

"With all my heart, Beppo; but first learn that Count Albert is a greater artist than us both, philosopher as he is."

"Indeed?" said Joseph with a sigh, "he seems to want no quality then to make him beloved."

"Nothing in my eyes but that of being poor and of humble birth," answered Consuelo; and interested by the attention which Joseph paid to her remarks, and stimulated by his timid questions, she yielded to the pleasure she felt in speaking openly and fully respecting her betrothed. Each reply brought on a fresh explanation, until from one circumstance to another she came to relate minutely all the particulars of her preference for Albert. This confidence in a youth whom she had only known since the preceding morning, would, under any other circumstances, have been imprudent. Certainly these circumstances alone could justify it. However, Consuelo yielded to an irresistible impulse in recalling to her own mind and confiding to a friendly heart the virtues of her betrothed. And as she spoke she had the satisfaction of feeling that she loved Albert more than she could have supposed when promising to endeavor to love but him. Her imagination rose to a loftier height the greater the distance that intervened ; and all that was beautiful, and great, and excellent in his character, appeared in a more brilliant light when she felt herself no longer under the necessity of hastily coming to a positive decision. Her pride was soothed by the idea that she could no longer be accused of ambition, for in flying him she renounced in some measure the worldly advantages connected with the proposed union. She could therefore without shame or restraint yield to the impulses of her soul. Anzoleto's name never once passed her lips, and she felt with pleasure that she

had not once thought of mentioning him in the account of
her stay in Bohemia.

These disclosures, however rash or misplaced, brought
about the best results. They made Joseph understand
how much Consuelo's affections were pre-occupied ; and
the vague hopes which he had ventured to cherish, vanished like dreams, the very memory of which he hastened
to forget. After one or two hours' silence which succeeded
this animated conversation, he formed the firm resolution
to see in Consuelo neither a beautiful siren nor a dangerous companion, but a great artist and a noble-minded
woman, whose advice and friendship would exercise the
happiest influence on his life.

As much to regain her confidence as to raise up a barrier against rash desires, he opened his heart to her, and
told her how he also was in a manner engaged. The
romance of his affection was less poetical than that of Consuelo, but he who knows the issue of this romance in
Hadyn's after life, is aware that it was not less noble-
minded or less pure. He had evinced a preference for
the daughter of his generous host, Keller the barber, and
the latter seeing this innocent attachment, said to him :
" Joseph, I confide in thee ; thou dost appear to love my
daughter, and I see that she is not indifferent to thee. If
thou art as honest and successful as thou art grateful and
laborious, thou shalt be my son-in-law." In a moment of
exaggerated gratitude, Joseph had sworn—promised ; and
though his betrothed did not inspire him with the least
passion, he considered himself bound to her forever.

He related all this with a feeling of melancholy, suggested
by the difference between his actual position and his
intoxicating dreams with reference to Consuelo. Nevertheless, the latter looked upon it as evincing the warmth
of his attachment for Keller's daughter. He did not
venture to undeceive her, and consequently her esteem
and confidence in Beppo's good faith increased pro-
portionately.

Their progress therefore was not interrupted by any
of those symptoms of love, which might have been anticipated from a tête-à-tête journey of two amiable, intelligent,
and sympathetic young persons for fifteen days together,
although Joseph felt not the slightest love for Keller's
daughter. He allowed the fidelity of his conscience to be

taken for that of his heart, and though his bosom chafed, he knew so well how to subdue his feelings, that his unsuspecting companion never had the least suspicion of the truth. When Haydn in his old age read the first book of Rousseau's Confessions, he smiled through his tears as he recalled to mind his journey through the Böehmer Wald with Consuelo—trembling love and pious innocence their only guardians.

CHAPTER LXX.

HAYDN never had reason to regret his journey, nor the sufferings to which it had subjected him, for he made considerable progress in Italian, and acquired a more thorough knowledge of music than he ever had before. During their long halts in the shady recesses of the Böehmer Wald, the young artists revealed to each other all their genius and skill. Though Joseph Haydn sang well, and played agreeably on the violin and other instruments, he soon saw, when listening to Consuelo, that she was infinitely his superior, and that she could make him an excellent artist without Porpora's aid. But Haydn's ambition was not confined to singing merely, and Consuelo, seeing him so backward as to the practical part, while in theory he was so lofty and correct, said to him one day, smiling; "I am not sure that I am right to confine you to vocal music, for, if you once become attached to the profession of singer, you will perhaps sacrifice to it the still higher powers which you possess. Let me look at your composition. Notwithstanding my long and arduous study of counterpoint with so severe a master as Porpora, what I have learned only suffices to enable me to understand the creations of genius, and I have no longer time, even had I sufficient ability, to produce original works; whereas, if you indeed possess creative power, you should follow this path, and only look upon singing and instrumentation as materials."

Since Haydn had met Consuelo, he had, in fact, thought only of becoming a singer. To follow or live near her, to find her everywhere in his wandering life, had become his ardent dream during the last few days. He therefore hesitated to show her his first manuscript, although he had it with him, having written it out before going to Pilsen. He feared equally to appear deficient as to display talents that might induce him to combat his desire to be a singer. However he yielded at last, and half willingly and half reluctantly he allowed her to get possession of the mysterious manuscript. It was a little sonata for the harpsichord, which he intended for his pupils. Consuelo read it with her eyes, while Joseph marveled to see her comprehend it as easily as if she had heard him play it. She afterward made him try different passages on the violin, and sang those herself which were practicable for the voice. I know not if Consuelo divined from this trifle the future author of *The Creation,* and so many other remarkable works; but assuredly she foresaw in him an able master, and said, as she returned his manuscript:

"Courage, Beppo! thou art already a distinguished artist, and mayest be a distinguished composer, if thou wilt only study. Thou hast ideas, that is certain; with these and science much may be done. Acquire science, therefore, and let us triumph over Porpora's temper; for he is the master that you require. But think no longer of the stage; thy place is elsewhere, and thy baton of command is the pen. Thou must not obey, but rule. When you may become the animating soul, would you rank yourself among the machinery? Come then, thou maestro in the bud! study shakes and cadences no more: only study where you are to place them in your compositions, and not how they are to be executed. This concerns your very humble servant and subordinate, who requests from you the post of prima donna in the first mezzo-soprano part that you intend to write."

"Oh, *Consuelo de mi Alma!*" exclaimed Joseph, transported with joy and hope; "write for you?—be understood and expressed by you?—what glory! what ambition! But, no, it is madness—it is a dream! Teach me to sing. I would rather study to render according to your genius and feeling the ideas of others, than to sully your divine lips by placing in them accents unworthy of you."

"Come, come," said Consuelo, "a truce to ceremony. Improvise a little, sometimes on the violin, sometimes with your voice. It is thus that inspiration flows from the lips and from the points of one's fingers. I shall see if you have within you the divine impulse, or if you are merely an echo of the thoughts of others."

Haydn obeyed. She observed with pleasure that he was not learned, and that there was youth, freshness, and ability in his ideas. She encouraged him more and more, and henceforth would only teach him to sing in order as she said to point out to him in what manner the voice parts should be introduced.

They amused themselves afterward with little Italian duets, which she taught him, and which he learned by heart. "If we want money," said she, "before our journey is finished, we can very well sing a little by the way. Besides, the police may put us to the trial, in order to see that we are none of those wandering cut-purses (alas! too numerous) who dishonor the profession! Let us be prepared for every casuality. My voice, keeping in *contralto* passages, may very well pass for that of a boy before it is broken. You must also learn a few airs on the violin in order to accompany me. You will find that it is no bad study. These popular melodies are full of nerve and originality, and as to my old Spanish ballads, they are perfect gems of originality and genius. Turn them to account, my dear maestro; ideas beget ideas."

These were enchanting days for Haydn. It was then perhaps that he first conceived the idea of those infantile and delightful compositions which he afterward composed for the amusement of the young Princess Esterhazy. Consuelo introduced into her lessons such gaiety, grace, and animation, that the good Joseph, recalled once more to the happy and innocent petulance of youth, forgot his privations and his disquietude, and only longed that this wandering education might never cease.

We do not intend to describe accurately their route. As we are but slightly acquainted with the paths of the Böehmer Wald, we should only lead the reader astray were we to attempt to trace it from the confused record which has been transmitted to us. Suffice it to say, the first half of their journey was, upon the whole. more agreeable than otherwise, until an adventure befell them which we cannot pass over in silence.

They had followed the northern bank of the Moldau from its source, both because it was less frequented and seemed more picturesque. They had been descending therefore during one entire day the steep ravine which extended parallel with the Danube, but when they reached the heights of Schenau, and saw the mountain chain sinking to the level of the plain, they regretted that they had not followed the other bank of the river, and, consequently, the opposite chain, whose lofty peaks they saw in the distance taking the direction of Bavaria. These woody mountains offered them more natural shelter and romantic halting-places than the valleys of Bohemia. During their pauses by day in the forest, they amused themselves by snaring small birds, and when, their siesta being at an end, they found their snares filled with game, they cooked them in the open air, and found their repast sumptuous. They spared only the nightingales, as they professed to consider them as professional brethren.

The poor children therefore proceeded in search of a ford ; but the river was rapid, bordered by steep banks, and swollen by the rains. They came at length to a sort of pier, to which was moored a boat in charge of a child. They hesitated to approach it, as they saw several people before them bargaining for a passage. These men, after taking leave of each other, separated, three proceeding to the north, while two entered the boat. This determined Consuelo. "We must meet strangers," said she, "either on the right or left ; therefore it is just as well to cross at once."

Haydn hesitated a little, and was assuring her that these people looked ill, and were otherwise noisy and savage, when one of them, as if to contradict this unfavorable impression, stopped the boat and cried to Consuelo in German with an air of mingled gaiety and benevolence, "Come, my child, get in, the boat is not very heavy, and we can easily take you with us if you choose."

"Many thanks, sir," replied Haydn ; "we shall take advantage of your kind permission."

"Come, then," said the one who had spoken, and whom his companion called Herr Mayer, "jump in.'

Hardly had Joseph entered the boat when he remarked that the strangers gazed at Consuelo and himself with marked attention and curiosity. Herr Mayer's face, however, seemed animated only by gaiety and good nature. His voice was agreeable, his manners polished, and Consuelo felt assured by his gray hairs and paternal aspect.

" You are a musician, my lad ?" said he to the latter.

" At your service, worthy sir," replied Joseph.

" You also?" said Herr Mayer to Joseph, and then pointing to Consuelo, "this is doubtless your brother," added he.

" No, sir, he is a friend," replied Joseph ; " we are not even from the same country, and he understands very little German."

" To what country then does he belong?" continued Herr Mayer, still looking at Consuelo.

" To Italy; sir," replied Haydn.

" Venetian, Genoese, Roman, Neapolitan, or Calabrian?" said Herr Mayer, pronouncing each name in its peculiar dialect with admirable exactness.

" Oh, sir! I see that you can speak with all kinds of Italians," said Consuelo, at length, not wishing to make herself remarkable by remaining longer silent ; "I am from Venice."

" Ah, that is a lovely country!" replied Herr Mayer, immediately using the dialect so familiar to Consuelo. " Is it long since you left it?"

" Only six months."

" And you travel about the country playing the violin?"

" No ; *he* plays," said Consuelo, pointing to Joseph, " and I sing."

" And you play on no instrument — neither hautboy, flute, nor tambourine?"

" No ; it would be useless."

" But if you are a good musician you could easily learn ; is not that so?"

" Oh, certainly ; if it were necessary."

" But you would not care about it?"

" No; I would rather sing."

" And you are right; nevertheless, you will be forced to quit it or change your profession, at least for some time."

" Why so, sir?"

" Because your voice will soon break, if it have not already done so. How old are you—fourteen or fifteen at most?"

" Something like that."

" Well, then, before a year is past you will sing like a little frog, and it is not at all certain that you will once more become a nightingale. It is a trying period from childhood to youth. Sometimes the voice is lost with the approach of manhood. In your place, I would learn to play on the fife; you could always gain a living."

"I shall see to it, should it come to pass."

"And you, my fine fellow," said Herr Mayer, addressing Joseph in German; "do you play only the violin?"

"Excuse me, sir," replied Joseph, becoming confident in his turn on seeing that the good Mayer in no way embarrassed Consuelo; "I play a little on different instruments."

"Which, for instance?"

"The piano, the harp, the flute—in short, a little on every thing."

"With such talents, you are wrong to wander about thus: it is a rude calling. And I perceive that your companion, who is still younger and more delicate than yourself, limps already."

"Do you think so?" said Joseph, who in fact had only too plainly observed it, although Consuelo would not confess that her feet were swollen and painful.

"I saw that it was with difficulty he got into the boat," replied Mayer.

"What would you have, sir?" said Haydn, assuming a philosophical air; "we cannot have every thing, and when we suffer—why, we must suffer."

"But when you can live more happily and more respectably by remaining in one fixed place, is it not better? I do not like to see intelligent and gentle lads, as you appear, going about thus. Believe one who has children of his own, my young friends, and who probably will never see you again. It destroys both health and happiness to seek after adventures in this way; remember what I say."

"Thanks for your good advice," replied Consuelo, with an affectionate smile, "we shall perhaps avail ourselves of it."

"God preserve you, my little gondolier," said Mayer to Consuelo, who had mechanically taken an oar and commenced, according to her Venetian habits, to urge forward the boat.

The bark touched the shore at last, not however without having been swept down the river a considerable distance by the strength of the current. Herr Mayer bade them a friendly adieu, while his silent comrade paid the hire of the boat. After suitable thanks, Consuelo and Joseph struck into a path which led to the mountains, while their late companions kept along the level margin of the river.

"That Mayer seems an honest fellow," said Consuelo, looking back once more ere he disappeared from their sight; "I am sure he is a good father."

"He is both inquisitive and a babbler," replied Joseph, "and I am rejoiced you are freed from his cross-questions."

"Like all persons who have traveled much, he likes to converse. He is doubtless a cosmopolitan, as least if one may judge from his skill in languages. Of what country can he be?"

"He seems a native of Saxony, although he speaks the Austrian dialect uncommonly well. He is probably from the north of Germany; a Prussian perhaps."

"So much the worse; I do not like the Prussians, and King Frederick still less, after all I heard of him at the Castle of the Giants."

"In that case you will be pleased at Vienna, for there this philosophic and warlike king has no partisans."

Thus conversing they advanced into the forest by paths which sometimes were lost amid the pine-trees, and sometimes led along the scarp of the hills. Consuelo found these Carpathian mountains more agreeable than sublime; she had frequently crossed the Alps, and could not comprehend Joseph's transports, who had never seen such majestic peaks before. The latter's impressions, therefore, found vent in enthusiastic praises, while Consuelo was more disposed for reverie. Besides, Consuelo was dreadfully tired, and did her utmost to conceal her fatigue from Joseph, in order not to give him any fresh uneasiness.

They rested for some hours, and after a slight repast, enlivened by music, they set out once more at sunset. But soon Consuelo, although she had often bathed her delicate feet in the crystal stream, like the heroines of romance, felt her feet bruised against the stones, and was obliged perforce to declare that her strength would not suffice for the night's journey. Unhappily the country was quite deserted on that side; there was no monastery,

not so much as a cabin or a chalet to be seen on the slopes
of the Moldau. Joseph was in despair. The night was
too cold to permit them to sleep in the open air. At
length through an opening between two hills they perceived lights at the foot of an opposite declivity. The valley toward which they descended was Bavaria. But the
town which they discerned was further off than they
had at first imagined, and it appeared to the unhappy
Joseph that it receded in proportion as they advanced.
To crown their misfortunes, the weather changed, and a
small cold rain began to fall. In a few moments the air
became so thick that the lights disappeared, and our
travelers having arrived, not without danger and difficulties, at the foot of the mountain, knew not how to direct
their course. They were in a tolerably broad and level
road, however, and they continued to drag along their
weary limbs, still descending, when they heard the noise
of an approaching carriage. Joseph did not hesitate to
ask directions respecting the road, and the possibility of
finding an asylum for the night.

"Who goes there?" replied a loud voice; and, at the
same time, they heard the click of a pistol. "Be off, or
I will blow your brains out."

"We are not very dangerous opponents," said Joseph,
without being disconcerted. "We are only two poor
youths who ask our way."

"Ha!" cried another voice, which Consuelo recognized
as that of the good Herr Mayer, "if these are not my
little companions of the morning! I recognize the accent
of the eldest. Are you there, too, my little gondolier?"
he added in Venetian, addressing Consuelo.

"I am," she replied, in the same dialect. "We have
lost our way, and we wish to know where we can find a
stable or a palace where we might obtain shelter. Tell us
if you know."

"Oh, my poor children," replied Herr Mayer, "you are
ten long miles, at least, from any habitation. You will
not find even a dog-kennel all along these mountains. But
I pity you; get into my carriage, I can give you two
places without inconvenience. Come, no ceremony—get
in."

"Oh! sir, you are a great deal too good," said Consuelo,
touched by the good man's kindness; "but you are going
northward, and we toward Austria."

"No; I am going to the west. In an hour at most I shall set you down at Biberach. You can spend the night there, and to-morrow you may reach Austria. It will even shorten your journey. Come, decide; if you do not prefer the rain, and wish to keep us back."

"Courage, then!" said Consuelo, in an under-tone to Joseph; and they got into the carriage. They observed that there were three passengers; two before, one of whom drove; the other, who was Herr Mayer, sat behind. Consuelo took a corner; Joseph the middle. The spacious vehicle had room for six persons. The horse, who was a powerful brute, lashed by a vigorous hand darted forward, jingling the bells on his collar, and tossing his head with impatience.

CHAPTER LXXI.

"DID I not tell you it was a dreary calling," said Herr Mayer, resuming the conversation where he had left off in the morning. "When the sun shines all is well; but the sun does not always shine, and your destiny is mutable as the atmosphere."

"What destiny is not variable and uncertain?" replied Consuelo; "when the sky lowers, Heaven throws benevolent hearts in our way. It should be the last thing in our thoughts, then, to accuse Providence just now."

"You are witty, my young friend," said Mayer, "but you are from that beautiful land where all are so. Believe me, however, my young friend, that neither your wit nor your fine voice would preserve you from starving in these dreary Austrian provinces. Were I in your place, I would seek fortune and preferment under some great prince."

"And under whom?" said Consuelo, surprised at this remark.

"Faith I do not know; there are several."

"But is not the Queen of Hungary a great princess?" said Hadyn; "and is not one protected in her States?"

"Doubtless," replied Mayer, "but her Majesty Maria Theresa detests music, and you would be expelled from Vienna were you to appear there as wandering troubadours as you are."

Just then Consuelo saw at a little distance, in some low lying land, the lights which she had already perceived, and she pointed them out to Joseph, who forthwith professed a desire to get down, in order to pursue the nearest route to Biberach.

"Those lights," replied Herr Mayer, "are no other than 'Will-o'-the-Wisp,' and many a traveler have they engulphed in those dangerous morasses. Have you never seen them before?"

"Yes, often on the lagunes of Venice, as well as on the lakes of Bohemia."

Herr Mayer discoursed for a long time to the young people on the necessity of establishing themselves, and on the few resources they would meet with in Vienna, without however mentioning where he would advise them to go in preference. At first Joseph was struck with his perseverance, and feared he had discovered his companion's sex; but the apparent sincerity with which Herr Mayer addressed her as a youth, and even advised her to go into the army, restored his serenity, and he concluded that the good Mayer was one of these easy going souls who reflect all day long on whatever comes into their head first. Consuelo for her part took him for a schoolmaster, or Protestant clergyman, full of reform, education, and conversions.

After proceeding for about an hour they arrived at Biberach, but the night was so dark that they absolutely could not see. The carriage stopped before an inn, and Mayer was immediately addressed by two men, who took him aside. When they returned to the kitchen where Consuelo and Joseph were drying and warming themselves by the fire, Joseph recognized the two individuals from whom they had separated on the left bank of the Moldau. The first had but one eye; the second, although not deficient in this respect, was not a bit handsomer on that account. The man who had crossed the river with Herr Mayer, and who had returned with him in the carriage, now advanced; the fourth did not make his appearance.

They all chattered in a dialect which Consuelo, although acquainted with so many languages, could not make out. Mayer appeared to exercise authority over the others, for after an animated discussion in a low voice, at the end of which he gave them some direction, they disappeared; with the exception of the one whom Consuelo, in speaking of him to Joseph, called the *Silent,* and who never left Herr Mayer.

Haydn was preparing to serve their frugal supper, on the corner of the table in the kitchen, when Herr Mayer returning, invited them to share his repast, and pressed them so kindly, that they did not venture to refuse. Nevertheless, Consuelo partook with reserve of her host's good cheer, while the eager attention of the servants to his numerous wants, and the quantity of wine which he drank, obliged her to abate a little the elevated opinion she had formed of his apostolic virtues. She was particularly shocked at the eagerness which he manifested to make Joseph and herself drink more than they wished, and the vulgar and boisterous gaiety with which he prevented them from mixing their wine with water. She began to grow still more uneasy, however, when Joseph, taking rather more than he should, whether from fatigue or inattention, grew more communicative and animated than she could have wished. At last she grew displeased when he paid no attention to the warnings which she gave him with her elbow, and snatching away the glass, which Mayer was about to fill again :

" No, sir," said she, " we shall not imitate you, if you please; it is not fit that we should."

" You are stange musicians !" said Mayer, laughing, with his frank and careless air. " Musicians that do not drink ! You are the first of the kind that I have met with !"

" And you, sir ?" said Joseph. " Are you not a musician? I wager you are! Devil take me if I don't think you are chapel-master to some Saxon prince !"

" Perhaps I am," replied Mayer, smiling, " and hence the sympathy which I feel for you, my children."

" If you be a chapel-master, sir," replied Consuelo, " there is too great a distance between your powers and ours—poor wandering singers that we are—to interest you much."

" There is many a wandering singer who has more talent than one might imagine," said Mayer, " and there are very great masters—even the chapel-masters of the first sovereigns in the world — who have begun in this manner. What if I were to tell you that I heard this morning on the mountain's brow, on the left bank of the

Moldau, two charming voices, which performed a pretty Italian duet, accompanied with delightful and even scientific ritornellas on the violin? Well! this is what happened to me while I breakfasted this morning between nine and ten on a green slope with my friends. But when the musicians who thus delighted me descended the hill, what was my surprise to see two young people, one dressed as a peasant, the other plainer and simpler, and without much distinction in his appearance! Do not be ashamed or surprised then at the good-will which I have displayed toward you, but do me the favor to drink to the muses, our mutual and divine patronesses."

"Sir!—maestro!" exclaimed the happy Joseph, quite won over, "let me pledge you. Oh! you are a real musician, I am certain, since you have been delighted with the talent of Signor Bertoni, my companion."

"No, you shall drink no more," said Consuelo, impatiently snatching away his glass, "nor I either," added she, turning her own down also. "We have only our voices to trust to for our support, Herr Professor, and wine spoils the voice; you should encourage us to keep sober, instead of endeavoring to intoxicate us."

"You speak reasonably," said Mayer, replacing the decanter on the table. "Yes, let us take care of the voice. It was well said. You have more prudence than your age would lead one to expect, friend Bertoni; and I am delighted to have witnessed this proof of your self-denial. You will get on well, I see, not only from your prudence, but your talents. You will succeed triumphantly, and I shall have the honor and the pleasure of contributing to your success."

Hereupon the pretended professor, throwing himself back into his chair in an easy position, and speaking with an air of the utmost sincerity and good nature, offered to bring them to Dresden, where he would procure them lessons from the celebrated Hasse, and the protection of the Queen of Poland and the electoral Princess of Saxony.

This Princess, Maria Antoinette of Austria, daughter of the Emperor Joseph I and married to Augustus III, King of Poland, had been a pupil of Porpora's. There was a rivalry existing between his master and the Saxon (as Hasse was named), for the favors of the dilettante sovereign, which was the original cause of their deep enmity.

Even had Consuelo been inclined to seek preferment in the north of Germany, she certainly would not have chosen to appear at this court, where she would have been opposed to the school and the coterie which had triumphed over her master. She had heard enough from the latter in his moments of bitterness and resentment, to have little inclination in any case to follow the advice of Professor Mayer.

As to Joseph, his position was very different. Intoxicated by the good cheer, he imagined he had discovered in Herr Mayer a powerful protector and the promoter of his future fortune. He did not indeed for a moment dream of abandoning Consuelo to follow this new friend, but, excited as he was, he gave himself up to the hope of one day meeting him again. He trusted firmly in his benevolent intentions, and warmly thanked him. Then led away by his extravagant joy, he took his violin, and played completely at random. Herr Mayer, whether unwilling to annoy him by observing his false notes, or whether, as Consuelo thought, he was so indifferent a musician as not to observe them, only applauded him the more. Indeed his error with regard to her sex, though he had heard her sing, showed her clearly that he had not a very correct ear, since he had been as easily imposed upon as some village trumpeter or player on the trombone.

Herr Mayer still continued to press them to accompany him to Dresden! Joseph, though he refused, indeed appeared highly flattered at the offers, and promised so warmly to go there as soon as possible, that Consuelo was forced to undeceive Herr Mayer respecting the possibility of such an arrangement. " He cannot think of it at present," said she in a very decided tone. " You know, Joseph," she added, " that cannot be, as you have other designs in view." Herr Mayer repeated his seductive offers, and was surprised to find her unassailable, as well as Joseph, whose reason returned the moment Signor Bertoni opened his lips.

While this conversation was going on, the silent traveler, who had joined them but for a short time at supper, appeared at the door, and called Herr Mayer, who left the room with him; and Consuelo took advantage of his absence to scold Joseph for his easy credulity in listening, under the influence of wine, to the fine words of any chance companion.

"What! have I done any thing wrong, then?" said Joseph, frightened.

"No," replied she; "but it is wrong to be so intimate with strangers. By dint of staring at me they will soon perceive, or at least suspect, that I am not what I appear; although I rubbed my hands with crayons to darken them, and endeavored to keep them as much as possible under the table, it would have been easy to see how weak they were, if happily these two gentlemen had not been so absorbed, one by his bottle and the other by his talk. The most prudent thing we can now do, is to remove to some other inn, for I feel any thing but comfortable with these new acquaintances who seem to dog our steps."

"What!" said Joseph, "would you have us be so ungrateful as to leave this worthy man, and perhaps illustrious professor, without thanking or bidding him adieu? Who knows that it is not the great Hasse himself?"

"I will answer for it, he is no such thing; and if your wits had not been wool-gathering, you would have observed his miserable remarks on music. No master would thus express himself. He is at best some good-natured musician of the lowest ranks of the orchestra—a babbler, and a good deal of the sot to boot. It is plain from his countenance that he has never blown on anything but brass, and one would say from his look, that his eyes had never taken a higher flight than the footlights.

"*Corno* or *Clarino secondo!*" exclaimed Joseph, bursting into a laugh. "well, he is a pleasant fellow at any rate."

"It is more than you can say for yourself at any rate," replied Consuelo, a little out of temper. "Sober yourself, and bid good-by if you choose, but let us go."

"The rain is falling in torrents; do you hear how it dashes against the panes?"

"I hope you are not going to fall asleep on the table," said Consuelo, shaking him.

At this moment Herr Mayer returned.

"Here is a complete change in our plans," cried he, gaily. I expected to be able to sleep here, and set out in the morning for Chamb; but, behold! my friends will not permit me to proceed, alleging that my presence is necessary on some business of theirs at Passau. I must yield the point. By my faith, my children, if I might offer you a piece of advice, it is since I cannot have the pleasure of bringing you to Dresden, that you will take advantage of this opportunity. I have always two seats for you in my carriage, as these gentlemen have one of their own. To-morrow we shall be at Passau, about thirty miles from this, and then I shall bid you farewell; you will then be near the Austrian frontier, and you can descend the Danube in boats as far as Vienna, with little expense or difficulty."

Joseph thought it an admirable proposal, as it would rest poor Consuelo. It certainly seemed a favorable opportunity, and the navigation on the Danube was an expedient which had not occurred to them. Consuelo agreed, therefore, seeing plainly besides that Joseph was incapable for that evening of taking any precautions for the security of their quarters. Once in the carriage, she had nothing to fear from the observations of her traveling companions, and Herr Mayer declared that they would arrive at Passau before daybreak. Joseph was delighted with her determination; nevertheless Consuelo experienced an indefinable repugnance to the arrangement, and the appearance of Herr Mayer's friends dissatisfied her more and more. She asked him if they also were musicians.

" All more or less," he replied drily.

They found the carriages ready, the drivers on their seats, and the servants of the inn well pleased with Herr Mayer's liberality, bustling about to serve him till the last moment. During an interval of silence, in the midst of this confusion, Consuelo heard a groan which seemed to issue from the middle of the court. She turned toward Joseph, who heard nothing, and the groan being again repeated, she felt a shudder run through her frame. However, as no one appeared to observe it, she fancied it might be some dog pining on his chain. But whatever effort she made to distract her thoughts, the unpleasant impression remained. This stifled cry, proceeding, amid the darkness, wind, and rain, from among a group of animated and indifferent persons, without her being able to ascertain precisely whether it was an imaginary noise or a human voice, struck her with terror and sadness. Her thoughts instantly reverted to Albert, and, as if she could have shared in the mysterious power with which he seemed endowed, she trembled at the idea of some danger impending over Albert or to herself.

In the meantime the carriage was already in motion. A fresh horse, still stronger than the first, drew it quickly along, while the other carriage, moving on with equal rapidity, was sometimes before and sometimes behind. Joseph chattered afresh with Herr Mayer, and Consuelo endeavored to sleep, pretending indeed to be so already, in order to furnish a pretext for her silence.

Fatigue at last overcame her sadness and disquietude, and she fell into a profound sleep. When she awoke she found that Joseph had fallen asleep also, and that Mayer was at last silent. The rain had ceased, the sky was clear, and the day commenced to dawn. The country was quite strange to Consuelo, except that she saw from time to time the summit of a chain of mountains that resembled the Böehmer Wald.

As the heaviness of sleep wore off, Consuelo remarked with surprise the position of these mountains, which should have been on her left hand, whereas they were to the right. The stars had now disappeared, and the sun, which she expected to see rise in front of her, was not yet visible. She thought that the range which she saw must be another chain than that of the Böehmer Wald, but Herr Mayer was snoring, and she dared not address the driver, who was the only one awake at the time.

The horse now slackened his pace to mount a steep ascent, and the noise of the wheels died away in the moist sand of the road. It was then that Consuelo plainly perceived the same low groan that she had already heard in the inn at Biberach. The voice seemed to come from behind; she turned around mechanically, and saw nothing but the leathern cushion against which she leaned. She imagined herself the sport of some hallucination, and her thoughts always reverting to Albert, she was certain that he was dying, and that the sounds which she heard were his last sighs. This idea so seized upon her imagination that she was very nearly fainting, and, fearing to be suffocated, she asked the driver, who had stopped to breathe his horses, to allow her to walk up the rest of the hill. He nodded assent, and, getting down himself, walked whistling behind the horses.

This man was too well-dressed to be the driver of a vehicle by profession, and as he moved Consuelo thought she saw pistols in his belt. This precaution in so wild and uninhabited a country seemed perfectly natural, and besides, the form of the carriage, which Consuelo examined as she walked beside the wheel, denoted that it carried merchandise. It was wide enough to afford space to a coffer behind, such as is generally employed to hold dispatches or valuables. But the conveyance did not seem heavily laden, since it was drawn without difficulty by one horse. But what surprised Consuelo much more was to see her shadow project before her, and, turning round, she saw that the sun had risen, and in a part of the horizon opposite to that in which it ought to have been if the vehicle had been proceeding in the direction of Passau.

"Where are we going now?" said she hastily, "we are turning our backs on Austria."

"Yes, for half an hour," he quietly replied. "We are retracing our steps because the bridge over which we had to cross is broken, and we are obliged to make a detour of a few miles to find another."

Consuelo, somewhat reassured, got into the carriage, and exchanged a few unimportant observations with Mayer, who was awake, but who soon slept again. Joseph had not moved all the time. They soon gained the summit, and Consuelo now saw before her a long, winding, and somewhat steep road, and the river of which the driver had spoken at the bottom. But as far as the eye could reach she could see no bridge, and they were still going northward. Consuelo, surprised and disturbed, could sleep no more.

A second hill soon presented itself, which the horse seemed too tired to ascend. The travelers all got down except Consuelo, who still suffered from her feet. Again the sobs struck her ear, but now so distinctly and so often repeated that she could no longer ascribe them to any trick of her imagination. The noise undoubtedly came from the back division of the carriage. She examined it attentively, and saw in the corner where Herr Mayer always sat, a little opening of leather, in the form of a wicket, which communicated with this recess. She tried to push it open but did not succeed. It had a lock, of which the key was probably in the pocket of the pretended professor.

Consuelo, at once ardent and courageous in such adventures, drew from a pocket in her dress, a sharp and strong bladed knife, which she had procured on setting out, perhaps with some vague idea of defending herself against the dangers of the road. Embracing an opportunity when her fellow-travelers, and even the driver, whose horse was now in no danger of running off, were in advance, she opened a slit in the panel with a steady hand, so as to obtain a glance at the contents of this mysterious case. But what was her surprise and terror when she saw in the narrow cell, which only received air and light from above, a man of athletic proportions, gagged, bound hand and foot, lying covered with blood, and evidently in a state of dreadful suffering and constraint! His face was livid, and he seemed at the point of death.

CHAPTER LXXII.

HORROR-STRUCK, Consuelo jumped down, and, joining Joseph, pressed his arm without being observed, as a sign to draw apart from their companions. When the rest had gone on a little, she exclaimed in a low voice, "We are lost if we do not instantly fly. These people are robbers—murderers. The proof is at hand. Let us quicken our pace and make off through the fields, for they have good reasons for deceiving us as they do."

Joseph thought that some hideous dream had disturbed his companion's imagination. He scarcely understood what she said. For his own part, he felt oppressed by unusual languor, and the pains which he experienced in his stomach led him to believe that the wine he had drank must have been drugged. Assuredly he had not so far infringed on sobriety as to feel himself affected to such an extent.

"Dear signora," said he, "you have had the nightmare, and I almost imagine that I am suffering from it in listening to you. Were these honest fellows banditti, as you fancy, what could they hope to gain from seizing us?"

"I know not, but I feel terrified; and if you had seen a murdered man in yonder carriage, as I have done——"

Joseph could not help laughing, for this assertion of Consuelo's seemed like a dream.

"But don't you see," said she, earnestly, "that they are leading us to the north, while Passau and the Danube are to the south? Look where the sun is, and see what sort of a desert we are now in, in place of approaching a great city!"

The correctness of these remarks struck Joseph, and began to dissipate the dreamy security into which he had fallen.

"Well,"·said he, "let us go on, and if they attempt to detain us, we shall then see plainly their intentions."

"And if we cannot escape all at once, let us be cool, Joseph, do you hear? We must have our wits about us, so as to be always ready to escape in an instant."

Then she began to lean on his arm, pretending to limp worse than ever, but gaining ground notwithstanding.

But they had not advanced ten paces before they were called back by Herr Mayer, at first in mild terms, then in a sharper tone, and lastly, as they paid no attention, with oaths. Joseph looked back, and saw with terror a pistol leveled at their heads.

"They are going to kill us," said he to Consuelo, slackening his pace.

"Are we beyond pistol range?" said she coolly, pulling him on, and beginning to run.

"I do not know," said Joseph, trying to stop her. "Do not fly yet; the time is not yet come. They are going to fire.

"Halt, or you die!" exclaimed the driver, running faster than they did, and keeping them within his fire.

"Now for assurance," said Consuelo, stopping. "Do as I do, Joseph. By my faith!" she exclaimed, turning and laughing with all the self-possession of a finished actor, "if I were not so lame, you would not have had your joke for nothing."

And looking at Joseph, who was pale as death, she laughed loud and long, pointing him out to the travelers as they came up.

"He believed it all!" said she, with a gaiety perfectly acted. "Ah, my poor Beppo, I did not think you were such a coward! Do, Mr. Professor, look at Beppo ; you would think he had a ball through him already!"

Consuelo spoke in the Venetian dialect, and the man with the pistol, not knowing what she said, did not venture to take any step with regard to them. Herr Mayer pretended to laugh likewise, and turning to the driver:

"What do you mean," said he, with a wink that did

not escape Consuelo, "by such stupid jokes? Why did you terrify these poor children?"

"I wanted to see if they had courage," replied the man, replacing his pistol in his belt.

"Ah!" said Consuelo, "they will have a poor opinion of you, friend Beppo! For my part, I was not a bit afraid: I appeal to you, Mr. *Pistol.*"

"You are a brave fellow," replied Herr Mayer, "and would make a famous drummer at the head of a regiment, with grape shot whistling round you."

"As for that I do not know," said she; "I dare say I should have shown the white feather if I had thought he really meant to kill us. But we Venetians are too wide awake, and are not to be taken in so."

"No matter," replied Herr Mayer; "it was a scrry joke."

And addressing the driver, he appeared to scold him a little; but Consuelo was not their dupe, and she saw by the tone of their dialogue that they entered into an explanation, the result of which was that they thought they had been mistaken respecting her intention to fly.

Consuelo in the meantime had re-entered the carriage with the others. "Confess," said she to Herr Mayer, laughing, "that your driver with his pistols is a very strange fellow! I shall call him henceforth *Signor Pistola.* You must allow, however, Mr. Professor, that yonder joke had nothing new in it!"

"It is a piece of German humor," said Herr Mayer; "you have better wit than that at Venice, have you not?"

"Oh! do you know what Italians would have done in your place, if they had wished to play us a good trick? They would have driven the carriage into the first thicket on the roadside, and would have all hidden themselves. Then when we turned round, not seeing any thing and thinking that the devil had carried every body away, should we not have been well caught? I especially, who can hardly drag myself along, and Joseph also, who is as cowardly as any doe of the Böehmer Wald, and who would have believed himself abandoned in this desert."

Herr Mayer laughed at her childish drollery. which he translated as she proceeded to the *Signor Pistola,* who was not less amused than he at the simplicity of the *gondolier.*

"Oh! you are quite too sharp-sighted," replied Mayer;

"no person will try to lay a trap for you again!" And Consuelo, who at last saw the deep irony of his false good nature show itself through his jovial and fatherly air, continued on her side to play the part of a fool who considers himself witty—a well-known character in every melodrama.

Their adventure was certainly becoming very serious, and even while playing her part with skill, Consuelo felt that she was a prey to fever. Happily, fever only stimulates to action, while stupor, on the contrary, deadens and destroys every faculty.

Thenceforth she appeared as gay as she had been hitherto reserved, and Joseph, who had recovered all his faculties, seconded her well. Even while appearing not to doubt that they were approaching Passau, they pretended to lend a favorable ear to the proposition to go to Dresden, which Herr Mayer did not fail to recur to. By this means they gained his complete confidence, and he only waited for some favorable opportunity to confess frankly that he was carrying them there without their permission. The expedient was soon found. Herr Mayer was by no means a novice in such matters. There commenced a lively dialogue in the strange language between the three individuals, Herr Mayer, *Signor Pistola,* and the silent man. Then all at once they talked German, and appeared to continue the same subject:

" I tell you it is so!" cried Herr Mayer, " we have taken the wrong road, a proof of which is that their carriage does not come up. It is more than two hours since we left it behind, and though I looked back from the summit of the hill, I could see nothing."

" I cannot see it anywhere, said the driver, putting his head out of the carriage and drawing it in again with a disappointed air.

Consuelo herself had remarked, after passing the first hill, the disappearance of the carriage in company with which they had left Biberach.

" I was sure we had lost our way," observed Joseph, " but I did not wish to say so."

" And why the devil did you not say so ?" returned the silent man, affecting great displeasure at this discovery.

" Because it was so amusing!" said Joseph, inspired by Consuelo's innocent deceit; "it is so amusing to lose one's way in a carriage! I thought that happened only to foot travelers."

"Well! it amuses me too," said Consuelo. "I wish now we were on the road to Dresden!"

"If I knew where we were," returned Herr Mayer, "I would rejoice with you, my children; for I must confess to you that I did not like going to Passau for the good pleasure of those gentlemen, my friends, and I should be delighted if we had gone far enough astray to excuse our complying with their wishes."

"Faith, Mr. Professor," said Joseph, "arrange that as you like, it is your business. If we do not inconvenience you, and you still wish us to go to Dresden, we are ready to follow you to the end of the world. What say you, Bertoni?"

"I say as you do," replied Consuelo. "We will take our chance!"

"You are good children!" replied Mayer, concealing his joy under an air of pretended vexation; "still I should like greatly to know where we are."

"No matter where we are, we must stop," said the driver; "the horse is done up. He has eaten nothing since yesterday evening, and he has traveled all night. None of us would be at all the worse for some refreshment. Here is a little grove. We have some provisions left; and I say, halt!"

They entered the wood; the horse was unharnessed, Joseph and Consuelo earnestly offering their services, which were accepted without distrust. The chaise was let down upon its shafts; and in this movement the position of the invisible prisoner doubtless becoming more painful, Consuelo again heard him groan; Mayer heard it also, and looked steadily at Consuelo, to see if she remarked it. But notwithstanding the pity that rent her bosom, she succeeded in appearing deaf and impassible. Mayer went round the carriage, and Consuelo, who had withdrawn a little, saw him open on the outside a little door behind, cast a glance into the interior of the back division, again close it, and replace the key in his pocket.

"Is the merchandise damaged?" cried the silent man to Herr Mayer.

"All is well," replied he, with brutal indifference, and commenced to make preparations for their breakfast.

"Now," said Consuelo rapidly to Joseph as she passed, "do as I do, and follow all my movements." She assisted in spreading the provisions on the grass, and in uncorking the bottles. Joseph imitated her example, affecting great gaiety, and Herr Mayer saw with pleasure these voluntary servants devote themselves to his comfort. He loved his ease, and began to eat and drink as well as his companions, displaying manners even more gluttonous and gross than he had shown the night before. Every minute he reached out his glass to his two new pages, who immediately rose, reseated themselves, and were off again, running now on this side, now on that, watching for the moment of running once for all, but waiting until the wine and the digestion should render those dangerous guardians less clear-sighted. At last Herr Mayer stretched himself at full length upon the grass, and unbuttoning his vest exposed to the sun his broad chest, ornamented with pistols. The driver went to see if the horse was properly fed, and the silent man undertook to search for some place in the miry stream, beside which they had stopped, where the animal could drink. This was the moment for flight. Consuelo pretended to search likewise. Joseph entered the thicket with her, and as soon as they were hidden by the closeness of the foliage, they took to their heels through the wood like two hares. They had nothing to fear from bullets in that thick undergrowth, and when they heard themselves called, they concluded that they had got far enough in advance to pursue their course without danger.

"It is better to reply, however," said Consuelo, stopping, "that will avert suspicion and give us time for a fresh race." Joseph therefore called out:

"This way! there is water this way!"

"A spring! a spring!" cried Consuelo, and turning instantly to the right to confuse the enemy, they flew onward. Consuelo thought no longer about her swollen and painful feet; and as for Joseph, he had quite recovered from the effects of the narcotic which Herr Mayer had administered to him the night before. Fear gave them wings.

They ran on this way for about ten minutes, in an opposite direction from that which they had taken at first, without pausing to listen to the voices which called them from different sides, when they found the margin of the wood, and before them a steep and turfy slope which descended to the beaten road, bordered with thickets and clumps of trees.

"Let us not leave the wood," said Joseph. "They will come this way; and from this elevation they can see us in whatever direction we go."

Consuelo paused a moment, explored the country with a rapid eye, and said:

"The wood behind us is too small to conceal us for any length of time; before us there is the road and the chance of meeting some one."

"Ah!" exclaimed Joseph, "it is the very same road that we were traveling just now; see, it turns to the right toward the spot we left. If one of our pursuers get upon horseback, he will overtake us before we reach the level ground."

"That is what we must see," said Consuelo; "we shall run quickly down the hill. I see something below there on the road, which comes this way. We must reach it before we are overtaken. Come, follow me!"

There was no time to lose in deliberation. Joseph trusted implicitly in Consuelo; the hill was passed in an instant, and they had gained the first clump of trees, when they heard the voices of the enemy in the wood. This time they took care not to reply, and ran till they came to a sunk brook which the trees had hidden from their observation. A long plank served as a bridge, and, after crossing, they threw it into the water. When they had gained the other side they continued to descend, always under cover of the dense foliage, and, hearing themselves no longer called, they concluded that their enemies had lost their track, or else were feigning in order to take them by surprise. Here the underwood disappeared, and they paused, fearing to be observed. Joseph thrust his head out cautiously and saw one of the brigands, probably the swift-footed Signor Pistola, at the foot of the hill, not far from the river. While Joseph kept watch, Consuelo had been surveying the road and all at once returned to him.

"It is a carriage which is coming toward us," said she; "we are saved! We must get up to it before our pursuers think of crossing the river."

They ran straight in the direction of the road, in spite of the exposed nature of the ground; the carriage in the meantime approached rapidly.

"Oh, Heavens!" cried Joseph, "if it were the other conveyance, that of the accomplices."

"No," said Consuelo, "it is a barouche with six horses, two postilions, and two outriders. Courage! we are saved, I tell you."

It was indeed time for them to reach the road; Pistola had found the print of their feet on the sand of the brook. He had the strength and rapidity of a wild boar. He soon found out where they had crossed, and the props that had sustained the plank. He perceived the trick, swam across the river, found their footsteps on the other side, and, following them, came likewise to the outlet. He saw the fugitives traverse the thicket, but he also saw the carriage, understood their design, and, unable to prevent it, he re-entered the thicket and kept on the watch.

At the cries of the young people, who they supposed were mendicants, the barouche did not at first stop. The travelers threw them some pieces of money, and the couriers seeing that in place of picking them up, they ran alongside of the carriage, still exclaiming, quickened their pace to a gallop, in order to free their masters from their importunity. Consuelo, out of breath, and losing her strength, as often happens, just at the moment of success, continued her pursuit, clasping her hands, with a supplicating gesture, while Joseph, clinging to the steps at the risk of losing his hold and being crushed under the wheels, cried out with a panting voice.

"Help! help! robbers! assassins! we are pursued!"

One of the travelers by degrees understood their broken accents, and signed to the couriers to stop their horses. Consuelo then, dropping the bridle to which she had clung, although the horse had reined upright and the man had·threatened her with the whip, joined Joseph. Her animated countenance struck the travelers, who entered into conversation with them.

"What does all this mean?" said one of them; "is this some new way of asking alms? You have got alms; what do you want more? Can't you speak?"

Consuelo felt as if she should expire, and Joseph, breathless, could only gasp out.

"Save us! save us!"

And they pointed to the wood and the hill without being able to utter a word.

"They look like two foxes hard pressed in the chase,"

said the other traveler; "let us wait till they recover breath," and the two gentlemen, who were magnificently attired, smiled with a coolness which contrasted strongly with the agitation of the poor fugitives.

At length Joseph succeeded in uttering the words, "Robbers! assassins!" The nobleman forthwith opened the door, and stepping out, looked around on all sides, astonished to see nothing that could justify such an appeal; for the scoundrels had concealed themselves, and the country appeared silent and deserted. At length Consuelo, recovering herself, spoke as follows, stopping at each word to regain breath:

"We are two poor wandering musicians; we have been carried off by some men whom we do not know, and who, under a pretext of doing us a service, made us enter their carriage and travel all night. At daybreak we found out that they were deceiving us, and carrying us northward instead of following the road to Vienna. We endeavored to fly, but they threatened us, pistol in hand. At last they stopped in that wood, and we escaped and ran toward your carriage. If you abandon us here, we are lost; they are only a few paces from the road—one in the thicket, and the others in the wood."

"How many are there then?" asked one of the couriers.

"My good fellow," said one of the travelers, in French —he to whom Consuelo had addressed herself because he was nearest to her on the foot-board—"learn that this does not concern you. How many are there, indeed! a fine question, truly! Your duty is to fight if I command you, and I shall give you no orders to count the enemy."

"Do you really wish to amuse yourself with a little sword practice?" returned the other nobleman in French; "remember, baron, that will take time."

"It will not take long, and the exercise will warm us. Will you be of the party, count?"

"Certainly, if it amuses you." And the count, with majestic indifference, took his sword in one hand, and in the other two pistols, the handles of which were ornamented with precious stones.

"Oh! you do well, gentlemen," cried Consuelo, whose impetuosity made her forget for an instant her humble part, and pressing the count's arm with both her hands.

The count, surprised at so much familiarity on the part

of a little vagabond of that class, looked down at his sleeve with an air of comic disgust, shook it, and raised his eyes with contemptuous deliberation toward Consuelo, who could not help smiling, when remembering with what ardor Count Zustiniani and so many other illustrious Venetians had requested in former times the favor of kissing one of those hands whose insolence now appeared so shocking. Whether there was in her countenance at that instant a ray of calm and gentle dignity which contradicted the poverty of her appearance, or the ease with which she spoke the language then fashionable in Germany led him to suspect she was some young nobleman in disguise, or whether, lastly, the charm of her sex made itself felt instinctively, the count suddenly changed his expression, and instead of his former smile of disdain, he looked at her with a kind and benevolent air. The count was still young and handsome, and his appearance would have dazzled the spectator, if the baron had not surpassed him in youth, in regularity of features, and in nobleness of form. They were the two handsomest men of their age, to use the common phrase, applied to them as well as probably to many others.

Consuelo, seeing the expressive looks of the young baron also fixed upon her with an appearance of uncertainty, surprise, and interest, turned their attention from her person by saying:

" Go! gentlemen, or rather come! for we will act as your guides. Those bandits have in their carriage an unfortunate man hidden in a concealed partition, and shut up as in a dungeon. He is confined there, with his hands and feet tied, all covered with blood, and closely gagged. Hasten to deliver him; such a task belongs to noble hearts like yours!"

" By Jove, a fine boy!" cried the baron, " and I see, my dear count, that we have not lost our time in listening to him. Perhaps it is some brave gentleman whom we shall rescue from the hands of the bandits."

" You say they are there?" said the count, pointing to the wood.

" Yes, but they are now scattered," said Joseph; " and if your excellencies would listen to my humble advice, you will divide your attack. You will advance along the highway in your carriage as quickly as possible, and having skirted the hill, you will find just at the entrance of the wood, on the opposite side, the carriage with the prisoner, while I conduct those on horseback directly across. There are only three of them, although well armed, but the rascals, seeing themselves between two fires, will offer no resistance."

"It is good advice," said the baron. "Do you, count, remain in the carriage and let your servant accompany you. I will mount his horse. One of these young people will serve you as guide and show you where to stop; I will take the other along with my chasseur. Let us be quick; for if the banditti, as it is probable, have taken the alarm, they will be beforehand with us."

"The carriage cannot escape," observed Consuelo; "for their horse is tired out."

The baron mounted one of the servant's horses, while the servant got up behind the carriage.

"Jump in!" said the count to Consuelo, making her enter first, without being himself aware of the deference he paid her.

Nevertheless he took the back seat, she the front; then leaning over the door, as the postilions galloped forward, his eye followed his companion, who rode across the brook followed by his escort, behind whom was seated Joseph. Consuelo was not without some anxiety for her poor comrade, thus exposed to the first fire ; yet she felt esteem and approbation for his conduct on seeing him bravely face the danger. She saw him ascend the hill, followed by the horsemen, who spurred their horses vigorously and disappeared in the wood. Two shots were heard, then a third. The barouche turned the hill, and Consuelo, unable to distinguish any thing further, prayed fervently, while the count, anxious for his noble companion, shouted to the postilion with an oath :

"Galop, you scoundrel! spare neither whip nor spur!"

CHAPTER LXXIII.

SIGNOR PISTOLA, to whom we can give no other name than that bestowed on him by Consuelo, for we are not sufficiently interested in him to institute any inquiries as to his real one, had seen from his place of concealment the carriage stop at the cries of the fugitives. The Silent One, to use the cognomen given him also by Consuelo, had made a similar observation from the hill. He forthwith ran to rejoin Mayer, and both consulted on the means of saving themselves. Before the baron had crossed the stream, Pistola had gained the road and concealed himself in the wood. He allowed them to cross, and then fired both his pistols, one ball of which pierced the baron's hat, while the other slightly wounded his attendant's horse. The baron turned sharply round, saw him, and riding up stretched him on the earth with a pistol bullet. He then left him kicking and swearing among the brambles, and followed Joseph, who reached the carriage of Herr Mayer almost at the same moment as the count. The latter had already sprung out. Mayer and the Silent One had disappeared with the horse, without taking time to conceal the carriage. The first care of the victors was to force the lock of the recess where the prisoner was confined. Consuelo joyfully assisted to cut the bonds of this unfortunate man, who no sooner found himself at liberty than he threw himself prostrate on the ground before his liberators; thanking God ; but the moment he beheld the baron, it seemed as if he had fallen from Charybdis into Scylla.

"Ah! your excellency, Baron Trenck," he exclaimed, "do not destroy me — do not give me up. Mercy for a poor deserter, the father of a family! I am no more a Prussian than you are, sir ; I am like yourself an Austrian subject, and I beg of you not to have me arrested. Oh! show mercy!"

"Oh! pardon him, your highness!" exclaimed Consuelo, without knowing to whom she spoke, nor what it was about.

"I pardon you," replied the baron, "but on one condition—that you engage by the most solemn oaths never to tell who gave you life and liberty."

Thus saying, the baron tied a handkerchief over his own face, leaving only one eye exposed.

"Are you wounded?" asked the count.

"No," he replied, pulling his hat over his brows ; "but if we meet these pretended robbers I do not wish to be recognized. I do not stand very well already in my sovereign's graces, and there only needs such an affair as this to finish me!"

"I understand," replied the count ; "but do not fear, I will take all the responsibility upon myself."

"That may save this deserter from stripes and the gallows, but will not ward off disgrace from me. But whatever comes of it, one should serve one's fellow-creatures at every risk. Let us see, my poor fellow, can you stand up? Not well, I fancy. Are you wounded?"

"I have received some hard blows, but I do not feel them now."

"Have you strength sufficient to fly?"

"Oh! yes, Mr. Aide-de-camp."

"Do not call me by that name, you scoundrel! Be off; and count, let us do the same; I long to get out of these woods. I have given one of these fellows his quietus; if the king knew it I should be a gone man. But, after all, I care not a jot for his anger," he added, shrugging his shoulders.

"Alas!" said Consuelo, while Joseph gave the sufferer a drink, "if we leave him here he will soon be seized again. His feet are swollen, and he can hardly lift his hands. See how pale he is!"

"Do not let us forsake him," said the count, whose eyes were fixed on Consuelo. "Franz, get down," said he to his servant, and then turning to the deserter he added, "mount this horse, I give him to you; and this also," tossing him his purse. "Will you be able to reach Austria?"

"Oh, yes! my lord."

"Do you wish to go to Vienna?"

"Yes, my lord."

"Are you willing to serve again?"

"Yes, my lord, except in the Prussian army."

"Go then and seek her majesty, the Empress Queen. She grants audiences to all who wish it, once a week. Tell her that Count Hoditz presents her with a handsome grenadier drilled in the Prussian fashion."

"I hasten, my lord."

"And never mention the baron's name, or I will get you seized and sent to Prussia."

"I would rather die at once. Oh! if the rascals had only left me the use of my hands, I would have killed myself rather than be taken."

"Be off!"

"Yes, my lord."

He took another drink of the contents of the gourd, returned the vessel to Joseph, thanked him without being aware of the far more important service he owed him, and, prostrating himself before the count and the impatient baron, he crossed himself, kissed the ground, and mounted with the help of the servants, for he was totally unable to set his feet to the ground; but scarcely was he in the saddle than, regaining vigor and courage, he put spurs to his horse and darted off toward the south like the wind.

"If they ever find out what I have done," said the baron, "my destruction is certain. No matter," added he, bursting into a fit of laughter; "it is a rare idea to present Maria Theresa with one of Frederick's grenadiers. This fellow, whose balls have whistled by the soldiers of the empress, will now return the compliment to those of the King of Prussia. Most faithful subjects and well-selected troops!"

"The sovereigns are none the worse served for that. And now what are we going to do with these young creatures?"

"We may say, like the grenadier," replied Consuelo, "that if you forsake us we are lost."

"Methinks," replied the count, who affected a chivalrous style in all his sayings and doings, "you have had little reason hitherto to doubt our humanity. We will bring you where you will be free from all danger. My servant will mount the box"—then addressing the baron, he added in a low voice, "Would you not prefer these young people inside to a valet, before whom we would be obliged to practice more reserve!"

"Without any doubt," replied the baron; "artists, however poor, are fit society for any one. Who knows if in yonder lad we have not picked up a Tartini in embryo? Look with what rapture he seizes on his fiddle again. Come, troubadour," said he to Joseph, who had just succeeded in regaining possession of his bag, his violin, and his music — "come with us, you shall sing this glorious combat in which we could find nobody to kill."

"You may jest at my expense as much as you please," replied the count, reclining at the back of the carriage (the young people being seated in front), as they rapidly rolled along toward Austria — "you have brought down one gallows bird at any rate."

"Perhaps he is not killed outright, and may, some day

or other, meet me at King Frederick's door. I will give you the honor of the exploit, therefore, with all my heart."

"As for me who never even saw the enemy," replied the count, "I quite envy you; I was in, however, for the adventure, and could have been glad to punish these fellows as they deserve. To seize deserters and carry off recruits on the very borders of Bavaria, the faithful ally of Maria Theresa!—it is insolence beyond all bounds!"

"It would be an excellent pretext for going to war if they were not both tired fighting, and if peace at this moment were not much more convenient. I shall therefore feel thankful, Sir Count, if you will be silent on the subject of this adventure, as well on account of my sovereign as on the score of my mission to your empress. I should find her but ill disposed to receive me after such an impertinent demonstration on the part of my government."

"Fear nothing," replied the count. "You know that I am not a zealous subject, because I am not an ambitious courtier."

"And what scope for ambition could you have, dear count, crowned as you are at once by love and fortune ? Whereas I—ah ! how unlike are our respective destinies, analogous as they may at first sight seem !" Thus saying the baron drew from his bosom a portrait set in diamonds, and began to gaze at it with moistened eyes and deep-drawn sighs. Consuelo felt very much inclined to laugh ; she thought so open a display of attachment was not in the best taste, and inwardly ridiculed the person who could be guilty of it.

"Dear baron," replied the count, lowering his voice, while Consuelo did her utmost not to hear him, "I entreat you to make no one your confidant but myself, nor ever to display this portrait again. Put it back in its case, and reflect that this child knows French as well as you or I do."

"By the way,' said the baron, putting back his portrait, which Consuelo took care not to glance at, "what the devil were they going to do with these little fellows? What did they say to induce you to follow them?"

"I never thought of that," said the count, "nor can I even now understand what they, who seek only to enlist giants, wished to do with a couple of children."

Joseph related that Mayer represented himself as a musician, and talked continually about Dresden and an engagement in the electoral chapel.

"Now I have it!" replied the baron; "and this Mayer, I wager I know him. It must be one N——, formerly a drum-major, and now recruiting for the Prussian regimental bands. Our people have no ear or taste, and his majesty, who even excels his father in the justness of his musical perceptions, is obliged to procure his trumpeters and fifers from Bohemia and Hungary. The professor of Rubadub thought to secure in those little musicians a fine present for his master, in addition to the deserter; and it was not a bad idea to promise Dresden and the court to these intelligent young performers. But you would never have seen Dresden, my children, and, with your leave or without your leave, a regiment of infantry would have been your destination for the rest of your days."

"Now I know what to think of the fate which awaited us," replied Consuelo. "I have heard of the abominations of this dull, heavy régime, and of their bad faith and cruelty toward recruits. I see from the way they treated the poor grenadier what was in store for us. Oh, the Great Frederick!"

"Know, my young friend," said the baron, somewhat ironically, "that his majesty is ignorant of the means; he is only aware of the results."

"Of which he unconcernedly takes advantage," replied Consuelo, with irrepressible indignation. "O, my lord baron! kings are never wrong, and are ignorant of all the evil which is practiced to gratify them."

"The rogue is witty!" exclaimed the count, smiling. "But be prudent, my pretty drummer, and do not forget that you speak before the commander of the regiment in which you were perhaps about to enter."

"Knowing how to be silent myself, Signor Count, I never doubt the discretion of others."

"You hear, baron; he promises the silence which was not even asked of him! Come! he is a fine fellow!"

"I confide in him with all my heart. Count, you must enroll him, and offer him as page to her highness."

"I agree," said the count, smiling, "if he consent to the arrangement. Will you accept this arrangement, my child? you will find it much more agreeable than the Prussian service. You will neither have to blow a trumpet nor to call the reveillé before break of day, nor eat powdered brick in place of bread, but simply to bear the train and carry the fan of a gracious lady, live in a fairy palace, preside at sports, and take your part in concerts, quite as good as those of the Great Frederick. Are you tempted? You do not take me for another Mayer?"

" And who is this highness, so gracious and magnificent?" asked Consuelo, smiling.

" It is the Dowager Margravine of Bareith, Princess of Culmbach, and my illustrious spouse," replied Count Hoditz, " who is now residing at her ancestral castle of Roswald, in Moravia."

Consuelo had often heard the canoness relate the history and alliances of all the aristocracy, great and small, of Germany, and among others that of Count Hoditz-Roswald, a rich Moravian nobleman, banished by his father (justly irritated at his conduct), an adventurer in all the courts of Europe, and latterly grand equerry and lover of the Dowager Margravine of Bareith, whom he had secretly married, carried off, and conducted to Vienna, and thence to Moravia, where, having received his paternal inheritance, he had placed her at the head of a brilliant establishment. The canoness had often recurred to this history, at which she was excessively shocked, because the Margravine was a reigning princess and the count a simple nobleman, and she therefore made it her continual text for inveighing against all *mésalliances* and love matches. Consuelo, on her part, was well pleased to make herself acquainted with aristocratic prejudices, and did not forget these revelations. The first time the name of Count Hoditz was mentioned before her, she had been struck by a sort of vague recollection, but now she remembered clearly all the particulars of the life and romantic marriage of this celebrated adventurer. As to Baron Trenck, who was then at the outset of his remarkable career, and who little foresaw his frightful downfall, she had never heard of him. The count now proceeded to dilate with some degree of vanity on his recent opulence. Ridiculed and looked down upon by the little courts of Germany, Hoditz had long blushed to be regarded as a poor wretch enriched by his wife; but having succeeded to vast possessions, he maintained from thenceforth regal state in his Moravian domain, and displayed his titles and his consequence before the eyes of petty princes much poorer than himself. Delicately attentive to the Margravine, he thought himself no otherwise bound to a woman so much older than himself; and whether she shut her eyes through complaisance or good taste, or believed that her husband could never be sensible of the decline of her beauty, she never ventured to thwart his fancies.

After proceeding a few leagues, the noble travelers found a fresh relay of horses ready harnessed for them. Joseph and Consuelo would have here taken leave of their friends, but they kindly dissuaded them, alleging the possibility of new enterprises on the part of the recruiters, who were spread everywhere over the country.

"You do not know," said Trenck, "how skillful and how much to be feared this race of men are. In whatever part of Europe you may happen to set foot, if you are poor and in difficulties and are possessed of any talent, you are exposed to their machinations or violence. They know all the passages of the frontiers, all the mountain paths, every place of ill-fame, and all the rascals from whom they may expect assistance or support in case of need. They speak all languages, all dialects, for they have traveled in every country, and have practiced every profession and trade. They can manage a horse to perfection; run, jump, swim, dive, cross valleys and precipices, like regular banditti. They are almost all brave, inured to fatigue, liars, dexterous, supple, subtle, cruel. It is from the refuse of the human race that the administration of his late Majesty, the great William, has selected the able purveyors of his forces and the props of his military discipline. They would lay hold of a deserter were he in the depths of Siberia, and would seek him in the midst of the enemy's balls, for the sole pleasure of bringing him back to Prussia, and hanging him for an example to others. They have before now torn a priest from the altar, because he was six feet high; they stole a physician from the electoral princess; they have ten times reduced the old Margrave of Bareith to a state of despair, by running off with his army of twenty men without his daring to seek redress openly; they made a soldier of a French gentleman, who went to see his wife and children in the neighborhood of Strasbourg; they have taken Russians from the Czarina Elizabeth, Hulons from Mar-

shal Saxe, Pandours from Maria Theresa, Hungarian magnates, Polish noblemen, Italian singers, women of all
nations—Sabines married by force to their soldiers.
Nothing comes amiss to them; and besides all the cost and
charges of their journeys, they have so much a head
—what do I say?—so much an inch, so much a line !"

" Yes," said Consuelo, " they furnish human flesh by the
pound! Ah, your great king is nothing but an ogre! But
do not be uneasy, Signor Baron; you have done a good deed
in restoring liberty to the poor deserter. I would rather
undergo all the punishments that were designed for him,
than utter a word to your prejudice."

Trenck, whose fiery character had little regard for prudence, and whose mind was already embittered by the singular severity and incomprehensible injustice of Frederick
toward him, experienced a savage satisfaction in revealing
to Count Hoditz the misdeeds of a system, of which he had
been the witness and the accomplice in prosperous times,
when his reflections had not always been so equitable and
so severe. Now secretly persecuted, though apparently
confided in so far as to be intrusted with an important
diplomatic mission to the court of Maria Theresa, he began
to hate his master, and to display his sentiments much too
openly. He related to the count the slavery, the sufferings,
and the despair of this numerous Prussian army, precious
in war, but dangerous in peace, and whose power was ma-
tured by unexampled severity. He then mentioned the
suicidal epidemic which had spread in the army, and the
crimes which soldiers, otherwise honest and devout, had
committed in order to be condemned to death, and thus
escape from the dreadful life they led.

" You may suppose," said he, " that the ranks *under
inspection* are those which are most sought after? You
must know that these are composed of foreign recruits, men
carried off by force, and young Prussians utterly disgusted
and wearied with a military career in which they are
doomed to end their days. They are divided into ranks,
in which they are forced to march, whether in peace or
war, before a line of men more submissive and determined,
to whom orders are given to fire on those before them, if
the latter display the least appearance of flying or resist-
ing. If the ranks charged with this duty neglect it, those
placed still further back—who are among the most insensi-

ble and ferocious of the hardened and rascally veterans of the army—are bound to fire on the two first, and so on, if the third flinch in their duty. Thus every rank in battle has the enemy before his face and the enemy behind his back; friends, brethren, fellow-creatures—nowhere! Nothing save violence, death, and terror! Thus does the Great Frederick form his invincible soldiers! Well! a place among these first ranks is envied and sought after by the Prussian soldier, and as soon as he obtains it, he throws down his arms, without the least hope of safety, in order to draw on him the balls of his comrades. This despair saves many, who, venturing all on the die, and braving unheard-of dangers, succeed in escaping to the enemy. The king is not unaware of the horror which his iron yoke inspires, and you probably know his remark to his nephew the Duke of Brunswick, who was present at one of his grand reviews, and could not help admiring the fine appearance and superb maneuvers of the troops.

" ' An assemblage of so many handsome fellows surprises you ?' said Frederick. ' Well, there is one thing that surprises me still more!'

" ' What is that?' said the young duke.

" ' It is, how it happens that you and I are safe in the midst of them,' replied the king."

" Dear baron," exclaimed Count Hoditz, " that is the reverse of the medal. Nothing can be accomplished with men except by natural means. How could Frederick become the first captain of his time if he were as mild as a dove? Hold! Say no more. You will force me, his natural enemy, to take his part against you, his aide-de-camp and favorite."

" From the capricious manner in which he treats his favorites, one may judge how he acts with his slaves. Let us speak no more of him—you are right, because when I think of it I am seized with a diabolical desire to return to the woods and strangle, with my own hands, his zealous purveyors of human flesh, whom I have through a stupid and cowardly prudence allowed to escape."

The generous enthusiasm of the baron pleased Consuelo; she listened with interest to his animated pictures of military life in Prussia, and not being aware that personal malice mingled somewhat with his courageous indignation, she only saw in it the evidence of a noble character.

There was, nevertheless, real greatness in the soul of Trenck. This proud and handsome young man was not born to creep. There was a great difference in this respect between him and his impromptu traveling friend, Count Hoditz. The latter, having been during infancy the terror and despair of his preceptors, had been left to himself; and although he had passed the age of sowing his wild oats, there was something boyish in his manners and demeanor which contrasted strangely with his Herculean stature and handsome features, somewhat worn indeed by forty years of dissipation and excess. The superficial information which he sometimes displayed was picked up in romances, popular philosophy, and the theater. He pretended to be an artist, though he was as deficient in discernment and depth in that as in every thing else. Nevertheless his grand air, and his exquisite condescension, soon impressed the young Hadyn, who preferred him to the baron, perhaps on account of the preference which Consuelo displayed for the latter.

The baron on the contrary was well-informed; and if the atmosphere of courts and the effervescence of youth had sometimes led him astray, he had nevertheless preserved those independent sentiments and just and noble principles which are developed by a good education, followed by serious study. His lofty character may indeed have been impaired by the caresses and flatteries of power; but his ardent and impetuous temperament had never stooped so low but that on the least injustice it bounded up fiery and brilliant as ever. Frederick's handsome page had tasted of the poisoned cup ; but love, however rash, had animated and exalted his courage and his perseverance. Pierced to the heart, he had not the less raised his head, and braved to his face the tyrant who would have humbled him.

At the period of our story he appeared to be about five-and-twenty years of age. His dark brown hair, which he would not sacrifice to the childish discipline of Frederick, clustered in thick curls around his lofty brow. His figure was superb, his eyes sparkling, his mustachios black as jet, his hand white as alabaster, although of Herculean strength, and his voice fresh and masculine, as were his countenance, his ideas, and the hopes of his love. Consuelo reflected upon this mysterious attachment which he had every moment on his lips, and which she no longer thought absurd, when she observed by degrees, in his outbursts and in his reserve, the mixture of natural impetuosity and well-founded distrust which made him continually at war with his destiny and with himself. She experienced in spite of herself a lively desire to know the queen of this fine young man's affections, and offered deep and romantic vows for the happiness of the lovers. She did not find the journey in the least tedious, though she expected it would prove so face to face with two strangers of a rank so different from her own. She had contracted at Venice the idea, and at Riesenburg the habits, of refined life—those polite and quiet manners, and those choice expressions, which constituted the better part of what was then called good society. Keeping herself in the background, and not speaking unless when spoken to, she felt herself much at her ease, as she reflected on all she heard. Neither the count nor baron appeared to have seen through her disguise, and, as for the latter, he paid no attention either to her or Joseph. If he occasionally addressed them, it was while speaking to the count; and being carried away by the subject, he at last was conscious of nothing but his own thoughts.

As to the count, he was by turns grave as a monarch and gay as a French marchioness. He drew his tablets from his pocket, and took notes with the serious air of a philosopher or a diplomatist; then he read them over in a humming voice, and Consuelo saw that they were little verses, written in a gallant and pleasing French. Sometimes he recited them to the baron, who declared them admirable without having listened to them. Sometimes he consulted Consuelo with a good-natured air, and asked her with false modesty, " What do you think of that, my little friend? You understand French, do you not?"

Consuelo, impatient of this pretended condescension, which appeared to seek to dazzle her, could not resist the temptation of mentioning two or three faults which she found in a quatrain " *To Beauty*." Her mother had taught her to pronounce and enunciate well those languages which she herself sang easily and with a certain elegance, and Consuelo, studious, and seeking in all things harmony, measure, and the neatness which her musical organization rendered easy to her, had found in books the key and rules of these various languages. She had examined prosody especially with care, exercising herself in translating lyric poetry, and in adjusting foreign words to national airs, in order to become mistress of the rhythm and accent. She had also succeeded in comprehending the rules of versification in several languages, and it was not difficult for her to detect the errors of the Moravian poet.

Astonished at her learning, but not able to resolve upon doubting his own, Hoditz consulted the baron, who confidently gave judgment in favor of the little musician. From this moment the count occupied himself exclusively with her, but without appearing to suspect her real age or sex. He only asked where *he* had been educated, that he knew the laws of Parnassus so well.

"At the charity school of the singing academy at Venice," replied she, laconically.

"It would appear that the studies of that country are more severe than those of Germany. And your comrade, where did he study?"

"At the cathedral of Vienna," replied Joseph.

"My children," resumed the count, "you have both much intelligence and quickness. At our first resting-place I wish to examine you upon music, and if your proficiency corresponds with the promise given by your faces and manners, I will engage you for the orchestra of my theater at Roswald. I wish, at any rate, to present you to the princess my spouse. What do you say? Ha! it would be a fortune for children like you."

Consuelo had been seized with a strong desire to laugh on hearing the count propose to examine Haydn and herself in music, and she could only make a respectful inclination, while she used all her efforts to preserve a serious countenance. Joseph, feeling more forcibly the advantageous consequences of a new protection for himself, thanked him, and did not refuse. The count resumed his tablets, and read to Consuelo half of a little Italian opera, singularly detestable and full of barbarisms, which he intended to set to music himself, and to have represented on his wife's fête-day, by the actors of the theater belonging to his château, or rather his *residence;* for, considering himself a prince in the right of his margravine, he never used any other phrase.

Consuelo pushed Joseph's elbow from time to time, to make him remark the count's blunders, and, overcome by *ennui*, thought to herself that to be seduced by such madrigals, the famous beauty of the hereditary margraviate of Bareith, with the appanage of Culmbach, must be a very stupid person, notwithstanding her titles, her beauty, and her years.

While reading and declaiming, the count kept crunching little comfits to moisten his throat, and incessantly offered them to the young travelers, who, having eaten nothing since the day before and dying of hunger, accepted, for want of a better, this aliment, fitted rather to deceive than to satisfy their appetite, saying to themselves that the count's sugar-plums and his rhymes were very insipid nourishment.

Toward evening the spires and clock-towers of the city of Passau, which Consuelo in the morning thought she would never reach, were visible. This prospect, after so many dangers and disquietudes, was almost as delightful to her as that of Venice had formerly been, and when she had crossed the Danube, she could not help grasping Joseph's hand with pleasure.

"Is he your brother?" said the count.

"Yes, my lord," replied Consuelo, answering at random in order to rid herself of his curiosity.

"Yet you are not in the least like each other," said the count.

"Oh, there are many children who do not resemble their father," said Joseph, gaily.

"But you were not brought up together?"

"No, my lord. In our unsettled profession we are educated how and where we can."

"Yet I cannot help thinking," said the count to Consuelo, lowering his voice, "that you are of gentle birth; every thing in your manner bespeaks a natural elevation."

"I do not know how I was born," she answered, laughing; "I must be descended from a long line of musicians, since I love nothing on earth but music."

"Why are you in the dress of a Moravian peasant?"

"Because, my clothes being worn out, I purchased this suit in one of the fairs."

"You have been in Moravia, then? at Roswald, perhaps?"

"I have seen it at a distance," replied Consuelo, slily, "but without daring to approach your proud domain, youɪ statues, your cascades, your gardens, your mountains, your fairy palace!"

"You saw it all then?" exclaimed the count, astonished, forgetting that Consuelo had heard him describe the beauties of his residence in detail for the last two hours; "oh, you would be delighted to see it again, I assure you!"

"I am dying to see it once more, since I have had the pleasure of knowing you," said Consuelo, who felt an irresistible desire to revenge herself for the infliction of his opera.

She bounded lightly from the bark in which they had crossed the river, exclaiming in a German accent:

"I salute thee, O Passau!"

The barouche conducted them to the dwelling of a rich nobleman, a friend of the count's, then absent, but whose house was placed at his disposal. The household was expecting them, and supper being ready, it was immediately served up. The count, who was delighted at the conversation of his little musician, for so he called Consuelo, would have wished to invite them to the table, but the fear of annoying the baron by this breach of etiquette prevented him. Consuelo and Joseph were well satisfied to sup in the servants' hall, and made no objection to sit down along with the valets. Haydn, indeed, had never held a higher place in the fêtes of the nobility to which he had been invited; and although a sense of the dignity of his art gave him sufficient elevation of character to understand the outrage inflicted on him, he recollected, without any feeling of shame, that his mother had been cook to Count Harrach, the lord of his village. In fact, at a later period, when arrived at the very zenith of his genius, Haydn was no better appreciated by his patrons as a man, although his fame as an artist was spread all over Europe. He lived for five-and-twenty years in the service of Prince Esterhazy; and when we say service, we do not mean merely as a musician, for Paër saw him, a napkin on his arm, and a sword by his side, standing behind his master's chair and performing the duties of major-domo, or principal domestic.

Consuelo had not eaten a meal in company with domestics since her travels in childhood with her mother the

Zingara. She was greatly amused, therefore, with the borrowed airs and graces of these aristocratic lackeys, who felt aggrieved at the company of two wandering musicians, and who did not hesitate to thrust them to the foot of the table, and help them to the worse morsels— which, however, thanks to their youth and good appetite, they did not the less enjoy. Their contented air having disarmed their haughty entertainers, the latter proceeded to ask for a little music by way of desert. Joseph revenged himself by playing the violin very willingly; and Consuelo, now completely recovered from her agitation of the morning, was about to sing, when intelligence was brought that the count and baron desired a little music for themselves.

It was impossible to refuse, after the generous aid they had received from the two noblemen. Consuelo would have considered any want of complaisance, or any excuse either of fatigue or hoarseness, as the basest ingratitude, since, in fact, her voice had already reached the gentlemen's ears.

She followed Joseph, who was already prepared to take every thing which happened in good part, and when they had entered the saloon, where, lighted by a score of wax tapers, the two noblemen were engaged in finishing their last bottle of Tokay, they stood near the door, and began to sing the little Italian duets which they had rehearsed on the mountains.

"Attention!" said Consuelo, slily, to Joseph. "Consider that his excellency the count is about to examine us as to our proficiency in music. Let us acquit ourselves to his satisfaction."

The count was much flattered by this observation. As for the baron, he had placed the portrait of his mysterious Dulchinea on the reverse of his plate, and was gazing at it, without heeding what was going on.

Consuelo took care not to display the full powers of her voice. Her pretended sex hardly agreed with her liquid and flute-like accents, and her apparent age did not warrant the expectation of any decided talent. She assumed the hoarse and somewhat worn voice of a young lad who has prematurely injured his tone by singing in the open air. It was an amusement for her to counterfeit in this manner the awkward attempts and rude flourishes which she had so often heard the street singers of Venice practice, but though the parody was excellent, still she could not hide her superior taste, and the duet was sung with such force and originality, that the baron, himself an excellent musician and artist, replaced his portrait in his bosom, raised his head, and ended by applauding vociferously, exclaiming that it was the sweetest music he had ever heard. As for Count Hoditz, who was full of Fuchs and Rameau, and other classic authors, he had less relish for this kind of performance. In his eyes the baron was a sort of barbarian, and the two young people intelligent indeed, but requiring his efforts to raise them from the depths of their ignorance. His ruling idea was to form his own artists, and he said in a sententious manner, shaking his head the while:

"It is not so bad, but there is a great deal to mend. Come, come, we will correct all that."

He looked upon Joseph and Consuelo, in imagination, as his already, and as forming part of his choir. He then asked Haydn to play the violin; and as the latter had no reason to conceal his abilities, he executed a piece of his own composition to admiration. This time the count was highly satisfied.

"Your position is fixed," said he. "You shall be first violin; but you must also practice on the viola and the *viole d'amour.* I will teach you the manner of execution."

"Is his highness the baron also satisfied with my comrade?" said Consuelo to Trenck, who had relapsed into his reverie.

"So much so," replied he, "that if I make any stay at Vienna, I will have no other master."

"I will teach you the *viole d'amour,*" replied the count, "and I expect that you will give me the preference."

"I prefer the violin, and this professor." replied the baron, with perfect frankness.

He took the violin, and played from memory, with great purity of tone and expression, several passages from the piece which Joseph had just performed.

"I wish to show you," said he, with great modesty, "that I am only fit to be your pupil, but that, with attention and docility, I might learn."

Consuelo requested him to continue, and he complied without affectation. He had talent, taste, and skill. Hoditz praised his performance beyond measure.

"It is but a poor thing," replied Trenck, "for it is my own. I like it, however, inasmuch as it pleased the princess."

The count made a hideous grimace, to warn him of his imprudence. Trenck paid no attention, but, lost in thought, ran the bow over the strings absently ; then, throwing the instrument on the table, he rose, and strode up and down the apartment, pressing his hand on his forehead. At last he returned toward the table, and said:

"Good-evening, my dear count. I am obliged to set out ere daybreak; the carriage which I have ordered is to call for me at three. Most probably I shall not see you again till we meet in Vienna. I shall be happy to see you there, to thank you for the pleasure I have received in your company, which I never can forget."

They pressed each other's hands repeatedly, and as the baron left the apartment, he slipped some pieces of gold into Joseph's hand, saying:

"This is on occount of my future lessons in Vienna. You will find me at the Prussian embassy."

He nodded to Consuelo as he passed, while he whispered in her ear:

"Should I ever find you as drummer or trumpeter in my regiment, we will desert together. Dost understand?"

Then saluting the count once more, he left the apartment.

CHAPTER LXXIV.

As soon as Count Hoditz was alone with his musicians, he felt more at ease, and became quite communicative. His mania was to set up for a chapel-master, and to play the *impresario*. He resolved, therefore, to commence Consuelo's education at once.

"Come here," said he, "and sit beside me. We are alone ; and need not sit so far apart. And do you also be seated," exclaimed he, turning to Joseph, "and profit by my instructions. You have no notion of a shake," continued he, turning to the great *cantatrice;* "listen, while I show you."

Here he ventured on a commonplace passage, in which he introduced that ornament several times after a very vulgar fashion. Consuelo amused herself by repeating the passage with the shake reversed.

"That is not it," roared the count with a voice of a stentor, as he struck the table. "Why did you not listen to me?"

He began again, and Consuelo cut it short this time still worse than before, preserving her gravity, however, and pretending to be all attention and docility. As for Joseph, he was on the point of suffocating, and pretended to cough in order to avoid a convulsion of laughter.

"La, la, la, trala, trala, tra, la," sang the count, imitating his awkward pupil, bounding on his chair with all the symptoms of extreme irritation, which he was far from feeling, but which he thought it right to assume, as being in keeping with his position.

Consuelo teased him this way for a good quarter of an hour, and wound up by singing the passage with faultless precision.

"Bravo! bravissimo!" exclaimed the count, falling back in his chair. "It is perfect at last! I knew I should make something of you! Give me but a peasant, and I should do more with him in a day than others in a year! Now, sing this once more, and see that you execute the notes trippingly. Better still! why, nothing could surpass that! We shall make something of you at last!"

Here the count wiped his forehead, though there was not a single drop of perspiration on it.

"Now," continued he, "let us have a falling cadence, and from the chest."

Here he set her an example, with that hackneyed facility with which the most inferior choristers ape the efforts of superior performers, fancying themselves equally skillful, because they succeed in imitating them. Again Consuelo amused herself with putting the count into one of his cool-blooded passions, when all at once she changed her manner, and finished with a cadence so perfect and so prolonged, that he was obliged to cry out:

"Enough! enough! now you have it! I was sure I should set you right. Let us go now to the roulade. You learn with wonderful facility, and I wish I had always pupils like you."

Consuelo, who began to feel overpowered by sleep and fatigue, abridged the lesson of the roulade considerably.

She executed with docility all that the opulent pedagogue prescribed to her, however faulty in taste it might be; and even allowed her exquisite voice to assume its natural tone, no longer fearing to betray herself, since the count was resolved to attribute to himself all the sudden splendor and celestial purity which it every moment displayed in a greater degree.

"How much clearer his voice becomes in proportion as I show him how to open his mouth and bring out his tone!" said he, turning to Joseph with an air of triumph. "Clearness in teaching, perseverance, and example, are the three requisites with which to form, in a brief period, finished singers and declaimers. We shall take another lesson to-morrow; for you must have ten lessons, at the end of which you will know how to sing. We have the *coulé*, the *flatté*, the *port de voix tenu*, and the *port de voix achevé*, the *chute*, the *inflexion tendre*, the *martellement gai*, the *cadence feinte*, etc., etc. Now go and repose yourselves; I have had apartments prepared for you in the palace. I shall stop here on some business until noon. You will breakfast here, and follow me to Vienna. Consider yourselves from this moment as in my service. To begin, do you, Joseph, go and tell my valet to come and light me to my apartment. Do you," said he to Consuelo, "remain and go over the last roulade again which I showed you; I am not perfectly satisfied with it."

Hardly had Joseph left the room, when the count, taking both Consuelo's hands in his, endeavored to draw her to him. Interrupted in her roulade, Consuelo looked at him with much astonishment; but she quickly drew away her hands and recoiled to the other end of the table, on seeing his inflamed eyes and his libertine smile. "Come, come! do you wish to play the prude?" said the count, resuming his easy and superb air. "So, so! my sweet one, we have a little lover, eh? he is very ugly, poor fellow, and I hope that you will renounce him from this day forward. Your fortune is made if you do not hesitate, for I do not like delays. You are a charming girl, full of sweetness and intelligence; you please me greatly, and from the first glance I cast upon you I saw that you were not made to tramp about with that little vagabond. Nevertheless, I will take charge of him also; I will send him to Roswald and establish him there. As for you, you shall remain at Vienna. I will lodge you properly, and if you are prudent and modest, even bring you forward in the world. When you have learned music, you shall be the prima donna of my theater, and you shall see your little chance friend when I carry you to my residence. Is it agreed?"

"Yes, my lord count," replied Consuelo with much gravity, and making a low bow, " it is perfectly agreed."

Joseph returned at that moment with the valet-de-chambre, who carried two candles, and the count retired, giving a little tap on the cheek to Joseph and addressing a smile of intelligence to Consuelo.

" He is perfectly ridiculous," said Joseph to his companion as he was left alone with her.

" More so than you think," replied she, thoughtfully.

" No matter, he is the best man in the world, and will be very useful to me at Vienna."

" Yes, at Vienna, as much as you please, Beppo; but at Passau not in the least, I assure you. Where are our bundles, Joseph?"

" In the kitchen. I will go and carry them to our apartments, which, from what they tell me, must be charming. You will get some rest at last."

" My good Joseph!" said Consuelo, shrugging her shoulders, " go, get your bundle quickly, and give up your pretty chamber in which you expected to sleep well. We leave this house on the instant—do you understand me? Be quick, for they will certainly lock the doors."

Haydn thought she must be dreaming. " What !" cried he, " is it possible? Are these great lords kidnappers too?"

" I fear Hoditz even more than Mayer," replied Consuelo, impatiently. "Come, run ! do not hesitate, or I shall leave you and go alone."

There was so much resolution and energy in Consuelo's tone and features, that Haydn, surprised and distracted, obeyed her hurriedly. He returned in a few minutes with the bag which contained their music and clothes ; and three minutes afterward they had left the place, without having been remarked by any one, and reached the suburb at the extremity of the city.

They entered a small inn and hired two apartments, which they paid for in advance, in order to be able to leave as early as they wished without being detained,

" Will you not at least tell me the occasion of this fresh alarm ?" asked Haydn, as he bade Consuelo good-night on the threshold of her chamber.

" Sleep in peace," replied she, "and know in two words that we have not much to fear now. His lordship the count divined with his eagle eye that I am not of his sex, and did me the honor to make me a declaration which has singularly flattered my self-love. Good-night, friend Beppo ; we must be off before daylight ; I will knock at your door to rouse you."

On the next day the rising sun saluted our young travelers as they were floating on the bosom of the Danube, and descending its rapid stream with a satisfaction as pure and hearts as light as the waves of that lovely river. They had paid for their passage in the bark of an old boatman who was carrying merchandise to Lintz. He was an honest man, with whom they were well satisfied, and who did not interfere in their conversation. He did not understand a word of Italian, and, his boat being sufficiently loaded, he took no other passengers, which gave them at last that security and repose of body and mind which they required in order to enjoy, in its full extent, the magnificent spectacle presented to their eyes every moment of their voyage. The weather was lovely. There was a remarkably clean little cabin in the boat, into which Consuelo could retire to rest her eyes from the glare of the water; but she had become so accustomed during the preceding days to the open air and beaming sun, that she preferred to pass almost the whole time lying upon the bales, delightfully occupied in watching the rocks and trees on the bank as they seemed to glide away behind her. She practiced music at her leisure with Haydn, and the droll recollection of the music-mad Hoditz, whom Joseph called the *maestro-maniac*, mingled much gaiety with their warblings. Joseph mimicked him to the life, and felt a malicious joy at the idea of his disappointment. Their laughter and their songs cheered and charmed the old mariner, who, like every German peasant, was passionately fond of music. He sang to them in his turn some airs which possessed a sort of aquatic character, and which Consuelo learned from him with the words. They completely gained his heart by feasting him as well as they could at the first landing-place, where they laid in their own provisions for the day

—the most peaceful and the most agreeable they had yet spent since the commencement of their journey.

"Excellent Baron de Trenck!" said Joseph, changing for silver one of the shining pieces of gold which that nobleman had given him; "it is to him that I owe the power of at last relieving the divine Porporina from fatigue, from famine, from danger, from all the ills which misery brings in its train. Yet I did not like him at first, that noble and benevolent baron!"

"Yes," said Consuelo, "you preferred the count. I am glad now that the latter confined himself to promises, and did not soil our hands with his gifts."

"After all, we owe him nothing," resumed Joseph. "Who first entertained the thought of fighting the recruiter?—it was the baron; the count did not care, and only followed his companion through complaisance and for fashion's sake. Who ran all the risk and received a ball through his hat, very close to the skull?—again the baron! Who wounded and perhaps killed that infamous Pistola? the baron. Who saved the deserter, at his own expense perhaps, by exposing himself to the anger of a terrible master? Lastly, who respected you, and did not appear to recognize your sex? Who comprehended the beauty of your Italian airs and the good taste of your style?"

"And the genius of Master Joseph Haydn?" added Consuelo, smiling; "the baron—always the baron!"

"Doubtless," returned Haydn, retorting the roguish insinuation; "and it is perhaps very fortunate for a certain noble and dearly-beloved absent one, of whom I have heard mention, that the declaration of love to the divine Porporina proceeded from the ridiculous count instead of the brave and fascinating baron."

"Beppo!" replied Consuelo, with a melancholy smile, "the absent never suffer wrong except in mean and ungrateful hearts. That is why the baron, who is generous and sincere, and who loves a mysterious beauty, could not think of paying court to me. I ask you yourself, would you so easily sacrifice the love of your betrothed and the fidelity of your heart to the first chance caprice?"

Beppo sighed deeply. "You cannot be the *first chance caprice* for any one," said he, "and the baron would have been very excusable had he forgotten all his loves, past and present, at the sight of you."

" You grow gallant and complimentary, Beppo! I see that you have profited by the society of his lordship the count; but may you never wed a Margravine, nor learn how love is treated when one marries for money !"

They reached Lintz in the evening, and slept at last without terror and without care for the morrow. As soon as Joseph awoke, he hastened to buy shoes, linen, and many little niceties of musculine attire for himself, and especially for Consuelo, who could thus make herself look like a smart and *handsome* young man, as she jestingly said, in order to walk about the city and vicinity. The old boatman had told them that if he could find a freight for Moelk he would take them on board the following day, and would carry them twenty leagues further down the Danube. They spent that day therefore at Lintz, amusing themselves by climbing the hill, and examining the fortification below and that above, from which latter they could contemplate the majestic windings of the river through the fertile plains of Austria. Thence they also saw a spectacle which makes them very merry; this was Count Hoditz's berlin, which entered the city in triumph. They recognized the carriage and the livery, and being too far off to be perceived by him, amused themselves with making low salutations down to the very ground. At last, toward evening, on returning to the river's edge, they found their boat laden with merchandise for Moelk, and joyfully made a fresh bargain with their old pilot. They embarked before daybreak, and saw the stars shining above their heads, while their reflection glistened in long lines of silver upon the rippled surface of the stream. This day passed no less agreeably than the preceding. Joseph had but one source of grief, which was the thought that he approached Vienna, and that this journey, of which he forgot all the sufferings and the dangers to recall its delightful moments, would soon be brought to a close.

At Moelk they were obliged to leave their honest pilot, which they did not do without regret. They could not find in the vessels which offered for a continuation of their voyage the same conditions of privacy and security. Consuelo, who now felt herself rested, refreshed, and strengthened against all accidents, proposed to Joseph to resume their journey on foot until some more favorable opportunity. They had still twenty leagues to travel, and this manner of journeying was not very expeditious. The truth is, that Consuelo, even while persuading herself that she was impatient to resume the dress of her sex and the proprieties of her position, was, it must be confessed, at the bottom of her heart as little desirous as Joseph to arrive at the end of their expedition. She was too much of an artist in every fiber of her organization not to love the liberty, the danger, the deeds of courage and address, the constant and varied aspect of that nature which the pedestrian alone enjoys in its full extent—in short, all the romantic activity of wandering and solitary life.

I call it solitary, dear reader, in order to express a secret and mysterious charm, which you can more easily comprehend than I define. It is a state of mind, I think, which has no name in our language, but which you must have experienced if you have ever traveled on foot to any distance, either alone or with another self, or, like Consuelo, with an accommodating companion, at once cheerful, obliging, and sympathizing. In such moments, if you were free from all immediate anxiety, from all disturbing thoughts, you have, I doubt not, felt a kind of strange delight, a little selfish perhaps, as you said to yourself, "At this instant, no person is troubled about me, and no person troubles me ; no one knows where I am. Those who rule over my life would search for me in vain ; they cannot discover me in this situation—unknown to all, new even to myself — in which I have taken refuge. Those over whom I exercise an influence no longer feel the agitating effects of my presence, and I, in my turn, feel relieved at ceasing to impose it. I belong solely to myself, both as master and as slave." For there is not one of us, O reader! who is not, with regard to a certain group of individuals, at the same time somewhat of a slave and somewhat of a master, independently of his own will, and often even without his own knowledge.

No one knows where I am! That is indeed a thought of loneliness which has its charm — an inexpressible charm, rude and repulsive at first sight, but in reality gentle and legitimate. We are created for a life of reciprocity. The road of duty is long, rough, and bounded by no horizon but death, which is perhaps only the repose of a single night. Let us march onward then boldly, and without sparing our feet! But if, by a rare and happy chance which may render repose and solitude blameless, some green and flowery by-path opens before us, let us profit by it to wander apart for a season from our fellow-men, and give ourselves up to silence and contemplation. These calm and peaceful moments are indispensable for the active and energetic man to recover his strength ; and just in proportion as you are a zealous worshiper in the Temple of God, and, consequently, a lover of your fellow-man, will you feel the sanctifying effects of these periods of reflection and self-examination. The selfish man is alone always and everywhere. His soul is never fatigued by loving, suffering, and persevering ; it is inert and cold, and has no more need of sleep and silence than a corpse. He who loves is rarely alone, and even when he is so, he is happy. His soul then enjoys a suspension of activity, which is as a deep sleep to a vigorous body, That sleep is an evidence of past fatigues, and the precursor of the new labors for which he is preparing. I can scarcely believe in the real grief of those who do not seek a refuge from their thoughts, nor in the absolute devotedness of those who have no need of rest. In the one case their grief is a sort of torpor which reveals that their spirit is broken and dead within them, and possesses no longer the power of loving ; in the other, their devotedness, knowing no cessation or pause, generally conceals some low and unworthy motive.

These observations, though perhaps a little too long, are not out of place in a history of the life of Consuelo, an active and devoted spirit, if ever there was one, but who, notwithstanding, might otherwise have been accused of selfishness and frivolity by those who were unable to understand her.

CHAPTER LXXV.

On the first day of their new journey, as our young travelers were crossing a small river by means of a wooden bridge, they saw a poor beggar-woman, who held a little girl in her arms, seated upon the parapet and extending her hand to the passers-by for alms. The child was pale and ill, the woman wan and shaking with fever. Consuelo was seized with a deep feeling of sympathy and pity for those unfortunates, who recalled to her mind her mother and her own childhood. "That is the condition we were in sometimes," said she to Joseph, who immediately understood her, and stopped with her to look at and question the beggar woman.

"Alas!" said the latter, "only a few days ago I was very happy. I am a peasant from the neighborhood of Harmanitz in Bohemia. I was married five years since to a tall and handsome cousin of mine, who was the most industrious of workmen and the best of husbands. About a year after our marriage, my poor Karl, who had gone to cut wood on the mountain, disappeared suddenly, without any one knowing what had become of him. I sank into poverty and grief. I thought that my husband had fallen from some precipice, or that the wolves had devoured him. Although I had an opportunity of being married again, the uncertainty of his fate and the affection I felt for him prevented my thinking of it. Ah! I was well rewarded, my children. Last year, some person knocked at my door one evening; I opened it and fell on my knees on seeing my husband before me. But in what a condition, good God! He looked like a specter. He was withered up, sallow, his eyes haggard, his hair stiffened with ice, his feet all bleeding — his poor feet which had traveled I know not how many hundreds of miles over the most horrible roads, and in the most severe weather! But he was so happy at once more finding his wife and his poor little daughter, that he soon recovered his courage, his health, his strength, and his good looks. He told me that he had been kidnapped by banditti, who had carried him far, very far away, even to the sea, and had sold him to the King of Prussia for a soldier. He had lived for three years in that most gloomy of all countries, suffering severe hardships and receiving blows from morning to night. At last he succeeded in escaping—deserting, my good children. In fighting desperately against those who pursued him, he had killed one and put out the eye of another with a stone; then, traveling day and night, hiding in the swamps and in the woods like a wild beast, he had crossed Saxony and Bohemia—he was saved, he was restored to me! Ah! how happy we were during the whole winter, in spite of our poverty and the rigor of the season. We had but one anxiety, that of again seeing in our neighborhood those birds of prey who had caused all our sufferings. We formed the project of going to Vienna, presenting ourselves to the empress, and relating our misfortunes to her, in order to obtain her protection, military service for my husband, and some subsistence for myself and child. But I fell ill in consequence of the shock I had experienced at again seeing my poor Karl, and we were obliged to pass the whole winter and all the summer in our mountains, always waiting for the moment when I could undertake the journey, always on our guard and sleeping with watchful eyes. At last this happy moment arrived: I felt myself strong enough to walk, and our little girl, who was also suffering, was to make the journey in her father's arms. But an evil destiny awaited us on leaving the mountains. We were walking tranquilly and leisurely by the side of a much-frequented road, without paying attention to a carriage which, for a quarter of an hour, had been slowly ascending in the same direction with ourselves. Suddenly the carriage stopped, and three men got out. 'Is that he?' cried one. 'Yes,' replied another, who was blind of an eye, 'that is he! quick! quick!' My husband turned at these words. 'Ah!' said he, 'those are Prussians; that is the man whose eye I put out; I recognize him!' 'Run! run!' said I, 'save yourself!' He commenced to fly, when one of those abominable men rushed upon me, threw me down, and presented one pistol at my head and another at my child's. But for that diabolical idea, my husband would have been saved, for he ran better than the ruffians and had the start of them. But at the shriek which escaped me on seeing my child under the muzzle of the pistol, Karl turned, uttered loud cries to prevent him from firing, and retraced his steps. When the villain who had his foot on my body saw Karl within reach, 'Yield,' cried he, 'or I kill them. Make but an attempt to fly and it is done!'

"'I yield, I yield! here I am!' replied my poor man, running toward them with greater speed than he had fled, notwithstanding the prayers and signs I made that he should let us die. When the tigers had him in their grasp, they overwhelmed him with blows and left him covered with blood. I endeavored to defend him; they maltreated me also. On seeing him bound before my eyes, I shrieked, I filled the air with my cries. They told me they would kill my little one if I did not keep still, and they had already torn her from my arms, when Karl said to me, ' Silence! wife, I command you; think of our child!' I obeyed, but the effort was so violent that I fell as if dead upon the road. When I opened my eyes it was night; my poor child was lying upon me, and was sobbing so bitterly that it nearly broke my heart. There was no trace of what had occurred but my husband's blood on the road and the mark of the wheels which had carried him away. I remained there an hour or two more, trying to console and warm Maria, who was benumbed and half dead with fear. At last when my senses returned, I thought that the best plan was not to run after the kidnappers whom I could not overtake, but to go and make my declaration to the officers of Wiesenbach, the nearest city. I did so, and then I resolved to continue my journey to Vienna, throw myself at the feet of the empress, and beseech her to prevent the King of Prussia from having the sentence of death executed upon my husband. Her majesty could claim him as her subject, in case the recruiters should not be overtaken. Aided by some alms which had been given me in the territory of the Bishop of Passau, where I related my disaster, I succeeded in reaching the Danube, and thence I descended in a boat to the city of Moelk. People to whom I tell my story are not willing to believe me, and suspecting me to be an impostor give me so little that I must continue my journey on foot—happy if I can arrive in five or six days without dying of fatigue, for illness and despair have exhausted me. Now, my dear children, if you have the means of giving me some little assistance, do so immediately, for I cannot remain here any longer ; I must travel on and on, like the wandering Jew, until I have obtained justice."

"Oh, my good woman, my poor woman!" cried Consuelo, clasping the poor creature in her arms, and weeping with joy and compassion; "courage! courage! Take hope and comfort! Your husband is delivered. He is galloping toward Vienna on a good horse, with a well-lined purse in his pocket."

"What do you say?" cried the deserter's wife, her eyes becoming red as blood, and her lips trembling with a convulsive movement. "Are you certain you have seen him? Oh, my God! Oh God of goodness!"

"If you should inspire her with false hopes? If the deserter whom we assisted to save, should be another than her husband? Alas! what have you done?" said Joseph to Consuelo.

"It is himself, Joseph! I tell you it is he. Remember the man with the one eye; remember Pistola's style of proceeding. Remember that the deserter said he was the father of a family and an Austrian subject. Besides, we can easily ascertain exactly. What sort of a man is your husband?"

"Red haired, with gray eyes, a large face, six feet and an inch high; his nose a little flattened, his forehead low. A superb man!"

"That is he," said Consuelo, smiling, "and his dress?"

"A green frock, much worn, brown breeches, and gray stockings."

"That is he again; and the recruiters? Did you remark them?"

"Do you ask me if I remarked them? Holy Virgin! their horrible faces will never leave my memory." The poor woman then gave with much exactness a description of Pistola, the One-eyed, and the Silent Man. "There was also a fourth," continued she, "who remained by the horse, and took no part in the deed. He had a great un-meaning face, which seemed to me even more cruel than the others; for, while I was weeping, and they were beating my husband, and tying him with cord like an assassin, that brute sang and made a noise with his mouth, as if he were sounding a charge on the trumpet: broum, broum, broum, broum. Ah! he had a heart of iron!"

"Ha! that must have been Mayer," said Consuelo to Joseph. "Do you still doubt? Has he not that trick of singing and playing the trumpet with his mouth every moment?"

"It is true," said Joseph. "Then it was Karl whom we saw delivered? Thank Heaven."

"Oh! yes, thanks to the good God before all!" said the poor woman, throwing herself upon her knees. "Maria," said she to her little girl, "kiss the earth with me to thank the guardian angels and the Holy Virgin. Your father is found, and we shall soon see him again."

"Tell me, my good woman," observed Consuelo, "has Karl also the custom of kissing the ground when he is well pleased?"

"Yes, my child, he never fails to do so. When he re-

turned after having deserted, he would not pass the door ol
our house until he had kissed the threshold."

"Is that the custom of your country?"

"No; it is a manner of his own, which he taught us, and
which has always brought us luck."

"Then it was certainly he whom we saw," returned
Consuelo; "for we saw him kiss the earth to thank those
who had delivered him. You remember that, Beppo?"

"Perfectly! It was he; there is no longer any doubt of
it."

"Oh? let me press you to my heart," cried the wife of
Karl, "angels of paradise! who bring me such good news.
But tell me all about it."

Joseph related all that had happened; and when the poor
woman had breathed forth all her transports of joy and
gratitude toward Heaven, and thanked Joseph and Consuelo over and over again, whom she rightly considered as
the primary cause of her husband's deliverance, she asked
them what she must do to find him again.

"I think," said Consuelo, "that the best thing you can
do is to continue your journey. You will find him at
Vienna, if you do not meet him on the road. His first care
will be to make his declaration to his sovereign, and to request of the offices of the administration that you may be
informed in whatever place you happen to be. He will not
fail to make the same declaration in every important town
through which he passes, and obtain information of the
route you have taken. If you reach Vienna before him,
do not fail to communicate to the administration the
place where you lodge, that notice may be given to Karl
as soon as he presents himself."

"But what offices? what administration? I know nothing
of these customs. And such a great city! I shall lose
myself, I, a poor peasant!"

"Oh!" said Joseph, "we have never had an opportunity
of knowing any more than yourself, but ask the first person
you meet to show you the Prussian embassy. Ask for his
lordship, the Baron——"

"Take care what you are about to say, Beppo!" said
Consuelo in a low voice to Joseph, as a hint that he must
not compromise the baron in this adventure.

"Well, Count Hoditz?" returned Joseph.

Yes, the count; he will do from vanity that which the

other would have done from charity. Ask for the dwelling of the Margravine Princess of Bareith, and present to her husband the note I am going to give you."

Consuelo tore a blank leaf out of Joseph's memorandum book, and wrote the following words on it with a pencil:

" Consuelo Porporina, prima donna of the San Samuel Theater at Venice, ex-Signor Bertoni, and wandering singer at Passau, recommends to the noble heart of the Count Hoditz-Roswald the wife of Karl the deserter, whom his lordship rescued from the hands of the recruiters and covered with benefits. The Porporina promises to thank his lordship the count for his protection in presence of madame the margravine, if his lordship will permit her the honor of singing in the private apartments of her highness." Consuelo wrote the address with care, and then looked at Joseph, who understood her, and drew out his purse. Without any further consultation and by a spontaneous movement, they gave the poor woman the two gold pieces which remained of Trenck's present, in order that she might pursue her journey in some vehicle, and they then conducted her to the neighboring village, where they assisted her to make a bargain with an honest vetturino. After they had made her eat something and bought her some clothes, an expense which was defrayed from the remainder of their little fortune, they sent off the poor creature whom they had just restored to life. Consuelo then asked, laughingly, how much remained at the bottom of their purse. Joseph took his violin, shook it at his ear, and replied, "Nothing but sound."

Consuelo tried her voice in the open air with a brilliant roulade and cried, "There is still a good deal of sound remaining!" Then she joyously stretched out her hand to her companion, and clasped his heartily, saying, "You are a brave lad, Beppo!"

"And you also!" replied Joseph, wiping away a tear, and bursting into a loud shout of laughter.

CHAPTER LXXVI.

It is not a very alarming predicament to find one's self without money when near the end of a journey, but even though our young artists had still been very far from their destination, they would not have felt less gay than they were on finding themselves entirely penniless. One must thus be without resources in an unknown country (Joseph was almost as much a stranger at this distance from Vienna as Consuelo) to know what a marvelous sense of security, what an inventive and enterprising genius, is revealed as if by magic in the artist who has just spent his last farthing. Until then, it is a species of agony, a constant fear of want, a gloomy apprehension of sufferings, embarrassments, and humiliations, which disappear as soon as you have heard the ring of your last piece of money. Then, for romantic spirits, a new world begins—a holy confidence in the charity of others, and numberless charming illusions; but also an aptitude for labor and a feeling of complacency which soon enabled them to triumph over the first obstacles. Consuelo, who experienced a feeling of romantic pleasure in this return to the indigence of her earlier days, and who felt happy at having done good by the exercise of self-denial, immediately found an expedient to ensure their supper and night's lodging. "This is Sunday," said she to Joseph; "you shall play some dancing tunes in passing through the first village we come to; we shall find people who want to dance before we have gone through two streets, and we shall be the minstrels. Do you know how to make an oaten pipe? I can soon learn to use it, and if I can draw some sounds from it, it will serve very well as an accompaniment to you."

"Do I know how to make a pipe?" replied Joseph; "you shall see!"

They soon found a fine reed growing at the river's side, and having pierced it carefully, it sounded wonderfully well. A perfect unison was obtained, the rehearsal followed, and then our young people marched off very tranquilly until they reached a small hamlet three miles off, into which they made their entrance to the sound of their instruments, and crying before each door, "Who wishes to

dance? Who wishes to dance? Here is the music, the
ball is going to begin."

They reached a little square planted with lofty trees,
escorted by a troop of children, who followed them, march-
ing, shouting, and clapping their hands. In a short time
some joyous couples came to raise the first dust by opening
the dance; and before the soil was well trodden, the whole
population assembled and made a circle around a rustic
ball, got up impromptu, without preparation or delay,
After the first waltzes, Joseph put his violin under his
arm, and Consuelo, mounting upon her chair, made a
speech to the company to prove to them that fasting artists
had weak fingers and short breath. Five minutes afterward they had as much as they wished of bread and cheese,
beer and cakes. As to the salary, that was soon agreed
upon; a collection was to be made, and each was to give
what he chose.

After having eaten, they mounted upon a hogshead
which had been rolled triumphantly into the middle of the
square, and the dance began afresh; but, after the lapse of
two hours, they were interrupted by a piece of news
which made every body anxious, and passed from mouth to
mouth until it reached the minstrels. The shoemaker
of the place, while hurriedly finishing a pair of shoes for
an impatient customer, had just stuck his awl into his
thumb.

" It is a serious matter, a great misfortune," said an old
man, who was leaning against the hogshead which served
them as a pedestal. " Gottlieb, the shoemaker, is the organist of our village, and to-morrow is the fête-day of our
patron saint. Oh, what a grand fête! what a beautiful fête!
There is nothing like it for ten leagues round. Our mass
especially is a wonder, and people come a great distance
to hear it. Gottlieb is a real chapel-master; he plays the
organ, he makes the children sing, he sings himself;
there is nothing he does not do, especially on that day.
He is the soul of every thing; without him all is lost.
And what will the canon say, the canon of St. Stephen's,
who comes himself to officiate at the mass, and who is always so well pleased with our music? For he is music-
mad, the good canon, and it is a great honor for us to see
him at our altar, he who hardly ever leaves his benefice,
and does not put himself out of his way for a trifle."

"Well!" said Consuelo, "there is one means of arrang
ing all this ; either my comrade or myself will take charge
of the organ, of the direction — in a word, of the mass ;
and if the canon is not satisfied, you shall give us nothing
for our pains."

"Oh, ho!" said the old man, "you talk very much at
your ease, young man ; our mass cannot be played with a
violin and a flute. Oh no! it is a serious matter, and you
do not understand our scores."

"We will understand them this very evening," said
Joseph, affecting an air of disdainful superiority which
imposed upon the audience grouped around him."

"Come," said Consuelo, "conduct us to the church ;
let some one blow the organ, and if you are not satisfied
with our style of playing, you shall be at liberty to refuse
our aid."

"But the score? Gottlieb's master-piece of arrangement?"

"We will go and see Gottlieb, and if he does not declare
himself satisfied with us, we renounce our pretensions.
Besides, a wound in his finger will not prevent Gottlieb
from directing the choir and singing his part."

The elders of the village, who were assembled around
them, took counsel together and determined to make the
trial. The ball was abandoned ; the canon's mass was
quite a different amusement, quite another affair from
dancing!

Haydn and Consuelo, after playing the organ alternately
and singing together and separately, were pronounced to
be very passable musicians for want of better. Some
mechanics even dared to hint that their playing was preferable to Gottlieb's, and that the fragments of Scarlatti, of
Pergolese, and of Bach, which they produced, were at
least as fine as the music of Holzbaüer, which Gottlieb always stuck to. The curate, who hastened to listen to
them, went so far as to say that the canon would much
prefer these airs to those with which they usually regaled
him. The sacristan, who was by no means pleased with this
opinion, shook his head sorrowfully ; and not to make his
parishioners discontented, the curate consented that the
two virtuosi sent by Heaven should come to an understanding if possible with Gottlieb to accompany the mass.

They proceeded in a body to the shoemaker's house ; he

was obliged to display his inflamed hand to every one in order that they might see plainly he could not fill his post of organist. The impossibility was only too apparent. Gottlieb had a certain amount of musical capacity, and played the organ passably ; but spoiled by the praises of his fellow-citizens, and the somewhat mocking flatteries of the canon, he displayed an inconceivable amount of conceit in his execution and management. He lost temper when they proposed to replace him by two birds of passage ; he would have preferred that there had been no fête at all, and that the canon had gone without music, rather than share the honors and triumph. Nevertheless he had to yield the point ; he pretended for a long time to search for the different parts, and it was only when the curate threatened to give up the entire choice of the music to the two young artists that he at last found them. Consuelo and Joseph had to prove their acquirements by reading at sight the most difficult passages in that one of the twenty-six masses of Holzbaüer which was to be performed next day. This music, although devoid of genius and originality, was at least well written and easy to comprehend, especially for Consuelo, who had surmounted much more difficult trials. The auditors were enraptured, and Gottlieb, who grew more and more out of sorts, declared he had caught fever, and that he was going to bed, delighted that every body was content.

As soon as the voices and instruments were assembled in the church, our two little chapel-masters directed the rehearsal. All went on well. The brewer, the weaver, the school-master, and the baker of the village, played the four violins. The children, with their parents, all good-natured, attentive, and phlegmatic artisans and peasants, made up the choir. Joseph had already heard Holzbaüer's music at Vienna, where it was in vogue. They set to work, and Consuelo, taking up the air alternately in the different parts, led the choristers so well that they surpassed themselves. There were two solos, which the son and niece of Gottlieb, his favorite pupils, and the first singers in the parish, were to perform ; but the neophytes did not appear, alleging as a reason that they were already sure of their parts.

Joseph and Consuelo went to sup at the parsonage, where an apartment had been prepared for them. The

good curate was delighted from his heart, and it was clear
that he set great store by the beauty of his mass, in the
hopes of thereby pleasing his reverend superior.

Next day all the village was astir. The bells were
chiming, and the roads were covered with the faithful
from the surrounding country, flocking in to be present at
the solemnity. The canon's carriage approached at a slow
and majestic pace. The church was decked out in its
richest ornaments, and Consuelo was much amused with
the self-importance of every one around her. It almost
put her in mind of the vanities and rivalries of the theater,
only here matters were conducted with more openness,
and there was more to occasion laughter than arouse indignation. Half-an-hour before the mass commenced, the
sacristan came in a dreadful state of consternation to disclose a plot of the jealous and perfidious Gottlieb. Having
learned that the rehearsal had been excellent, and that the
parish was quite enraptured with the new-comers, he had
pretended to be very ill, and forbid his son and niece, the
two principal performers, to leave his bedside for a moment; so that they must want Gottlieb's presence to set
things a-going, as well as the solos, which were the most
beautiful *morceaux* in the mass. The assistants were so
discouraged, that the precise and bustling sacristan had
great difficulty to get them to meet in the church in order
to hold a council of war.

Joseph and Consuelo ran to find them, made them repeat over the more intricate passages, sustained the flag-
ging, and gave confidence and courage to all. As for the
solos, they quickly arranged to perform them themselves.
Consuelo consulted her memory, and recollected a religious
solo by Porpora, suitable to the air and words of the part.
She wrote it out on her knee, and rehearsed it hastily with
Joseph, so as to enable him to accompany her. She also
turned to account a fragment of Sebastian Bach which
he knew, and which they arranged as they best could to
suit the occasion.

The bell tolled for mass while they were yet rehearsing,
and almost drowned their voices with its din. When the
canon, clothed in all his robes of state, appeared at the
altar, the choir had already commenced, and was getting
through a German fugue in very good style. Consuelo
was delighted in listening to these good German peasants

with their grave faces, their voices in perfect tune, their accurate time, and their earnestness, well sustained because always kept within proper bounds.

" See!" said she to Joseph during a pause, "those are the people to perform this music. If they had the fire which the composer was deficient in, all would go wrong; but they have it not, and his forced and mechanical ideas are repeated as if by mechanism. How does it happen that the illustrious Count Hoditz-Roswald is not here to conduct these machines? He would have taken a world of trouble, been of no use whatever, and remained the best satisfied person in the world."

The male solo was awaited with much anxiety and some uneasiness. Joseph got well through his part, but when it came to Consuelo's turn, her Italian manner first astonished the audience, then shocked them a little, and at last ended by delighting them. The cantatrice sung in her best style, and her magnificent voice transported Joseph to the seventh heaven.

" I cannot imagine," said he, "that you ever sang better than at this poor village mass to-day—at least with more enthusiasm and delight. This sort of audience sympathizes more than that of a theater. In the meantime, let me see if the canon be satisfied. Ah! the good man seems in a state of placid rapture, and from the way in which every one looks to his countenance for approbation and reward, it is easy to perceive that heaven is the last thing thought of by any present, except yourself, Consuelo! Faith and divine love could alone inspire excellence like yours."

When the two virtuosi left the church after mass was over, the people could scarcely be dissuaded from bearing them off in triumph. The curate presented them to the canon, who was profuse in his eulogiums upon them, and requested to hear Porpora's solo again. But Consuelo, who was surprised, and with good reason, that no one had discovered her female voice, and who feared the canon's eye, excused herself on the plea that the rehearsal and the different parts she sang in the choir had fatigued her. The excuse was overruled, and they found themselves obliged to accept the curate's invitation to breakfast with the canon.

The canon was a man about fifty years of age, with a benevolent expression and handsome features, and re-

markably well-made, although somewhat inclined to cor-
pulence. His manners were distinguished, even noble,
and he told every one in confidence that he had royal blood
in his veins, being one of the numerous illegitimate de-
scendents of Augustus II, Elector of Saxony and King of
of Poland.

He was gracious and affable, as a man of the world and
a dignified ecclesiastic should be. Joseph observed along
with him a layman whom he appeared to treat at once with
consideration and familiarity. Joseph thought he had
seen this person at Vienna, but he could not recollect his
name.

" Well, my children," said the canon, " you refuse me
a second hearing of Porpora's composition. Here is one
of my friends, a hundred times a better musician and
judge than I am, who was equally struck with your execution of the piece. Since you are tired," added he, addressing Joseph, "I shall not torment you further, but
have the goodness to inform me what is your name, and
where you have studied music?"

Joseph perceived that he got the credit of Consuelo's
performance, and he saw at a glance that he was not to
correct the canon's mistake.

" My name is Joseph," replied he, briefly, " and I
studied at the free school of St. Stephen's."

" And I also," replied the stranger; " I studied with the
elder Reuter, as you probably with the younger."

" Yes, sir."

" But you have had other lessons? You have studied in
Italy?"

" No, sir."

" It was you who played the organ?"

" Sometimes I played it, and sometimes my companion?"

" But who sang?"

" We both sang."

" Yes; but I mean Porpora's theme; was it not you?"
said the unknown, glancing at Consuelo.

" Bah! it was that child!" said the canon, also looking
at Consuelo; " he is too young to be able to sing in that
style."

" True, sir; it was not I, but he," she replied quickly,
looking at Joseph. She was anxious to get rid of these
questions, and turned impatiently toward the door.

"Why do you tell fibs, my child?" said the curate. "I saw and heard you sing yesterday, and I at once recognized your companion's voice in Bach's solo."

"Come, you are deceived, Mr. Curate," continued the stranger, with a knowing smile, "or else this young man is unusually modest. However it may be, you are both entitled to high praise."

Then drawing the curate aside, he said, "You have an accurate ear, but your eyes are far from being equally so; it speaks well for the purity of your thoughts. But I must not the less inform you that this little Hungarian peasant is a most able Italian *prima donna.*"

"A woman in disguise!" cried the curate, endeavoring to repress an exclamation of surprise.

He looked attentively at Consuelo, while she stood ready to reply to the canon's questions, and whether from pleasure or indignation, the good curate reddened from his skull-cap to his hands.

"The fact is as I have informed you," replied the unknown. "I cannot imagine who she is, and as to her disguise and precarious situation, I can only ascribe them to madness or to some love affair. But such things concern us not, Mr. Curate."

"A love affair?" exclaimed the excited curate. "A runaway match—an intrigue with this youth? Oh! it is shocking to be so taken in! I who received them in my abode! Fortunately, however, from the precautions which I took, no scandal can occur here. But what an adventure! How the free-thinkers of my parish—and I know several, sir—would laugh at my expense if they knew the truth!"

"If your parishioners have not recognized her woman's voice, neither have they, it is probable, detected her features or her form. But what pretty hands, what silken hair, and what little feet, in spite of the clumsy shoes which disfigure them!"

"Do not speak of them," exclaimed the curate, losing all command of himself; "it is an abomination to dress in man's attire. There is a verse in the Holy Scriptures which condemns every man and woman to death who quits the apparel of their sex — you understand me, sir — to death. That indicates what a heinous sin it is. And yet she dared to enter the church and to sing the praises of the Lord sullied with such a crime!"

"Yes, and sang divinely! Tears flowed from my eyes, never did I hear any thing like it. Strange mystery! Who can she be? Those whom I should be inclined to guess are all much older."

"But she is a mere child, quite a young girl," replied the curate, who could not help looking at Consuelo with a heartfelt interest which his severe principles combated. "What a little serpent! See with what a sweet and modest air she replies to the canon! Ah! I am a lost man if any one finds it out. I shall have to fly the country."

"What! have neither you nor any of your parishioners detected a woman's voice? Why, you must be very simple."

"What would you have? We thought there was certainly something strange in it; but Gottlieb said it was an Italian voice, one from the Sistine chapel, and that he had often heard the like! I do not know what he meant by that; I know no music except what is contained in my ritual, and I never suspected. What am I to do, sir?— what am I to do?"

"If nobody suspects, I would have you say nothing about it. Get rid of them as soon as you can. I will take charge of them if you choose."

"Oh, yes! you will do me a great service! Stay! Here is money—how much shall I give them?"

"Oh! that is not my business. Besides, you know we pay artists liberally. Your parish is not rich, and the church is not bound to act like the theater."

"I will act handsomely—I will give them six florins! I will go at once. But what will the canon say? He seems to suspect nothing. Look at him speaking to her in so fatherly a manner! What a pious man he is!"

"Frankly, do you think he would be much scandalized?"

"How should he be otherwise? But I am more afraid of his raillery than of his reproaches. Oh! you do not know how dearly he loves a joke—he is so witty! Oh! how he would ridicule my simplicity!"

"But if he shares your error, as he seems to do, he will not be able to ridicule you. Come, appear to know nothing, and seize a favorable moment to withdraw your musicians."

They left the recess of the window where they had been conversing, and the curate gliding up to Joseph, who appeared to occupy the canon's attention much less than Signor Bertoni, slipped the six florins into his hands. As soon as he received this modest sum, Joseph signed to Consuelo to disengage herself and follow him out; but the canon called Joseph back, still believing, after his answers in the affirmative, that it was he who had the female voice.

"Tell me then," said he, "why did you choose this piece of Porpora's in preference to Holzbaüer's solo ?"

"We were not acquainted with it," said Joseph. "I sang the only thing which I remembered perfectly."

The curate hastened to relate Gottlieb's ill-natured trick, whose pedantic jealousy made the canon laugh heartily.

"Well," said the unknown, "your good shoemaker has rendered us an essential service. Instead of a poor solo, we have had a masterpiece by a great composer. You have displayed your taste," said he, addressing Consuelo.

"I do not think," replied Joseph, "that Holzbaüer's solo was bad; what we sang of his was not without merit."

"Merit is not genius," said the unknown, sighing ; then seemingly anxious to address Consuelo, he added, "What do you think, my little friend ? Do you think they are the same?"

"No, sir; I do not," she answered briefly and coldly; for this man's look irritated and annoyed her more and more.

"But nevertheless you found pleasure in singing this mass of Holzbaüer's?" resumed the canon. "It is well written, is it not?"

"I neither felt pleasure nor the reverse," said Consuelo, whose increasing impatience rendered her incapable of concealing her real sentiments.

"That is to say that it is neither good nor bad," replied the unknown, laughing. "It is well answered, and I am quite of your opinion."

The canon burst out laughing, the curate seemed very much embarrassed, and Consuelo, following Joseph, disappeared without heeding in the least this musical discussion.

"Well, Mr. Canon," said the unknown, maliciously, "how do you like these young people?"

"They are charming! admirable! Excuse me for saying

so after the rebuff which the little one dealt you just now."

"Excuse you? Why, I was lost in admiration of the lad. What precious talents! It is truly wonderful! How powerful and how early developed are these Italian natures!"

"I cannot speak of the talent of one more than the other," replied the canon, with a very natural air, "for I could not distinguish your young friend's voice in the choruses. It is his companion who is the wonder, and he is of our own country—no offense to your *Italianomania.*"

"Oh!" said the unknown, winking at the curate, "then it is the eldest who sang from Porpora?"

"I think so," replied the curate, quite agitated at the falsehood into which he was led.

"I am sure of it," replied the canon; "he told me so himself."

"And the other solo," said the unknown, "was that by one of your parishioners?"

"Probably," replied the curate, attempting to sustain the imposture.

Both looked at the canon to see whether he was their dupe or whether he was mocking them. He did not appear even to dream of such a thing. His tranquility reassured the curate. They began to talk of something else, but at the end of a quarter of an hour the canon returned to the subject of music, and requested to see Joseph and Consuelo, in order to bring them to his country-seat and hear them at his leisure. The terrified curate stammered out some unintelligible objections, while the canon asked him, laughing, if he had popped his little musicians in the stew-pan to add to the magnificence of the breakfast, which seemed sufficiently splendid without that. The curate was on the tenter-hooks, when the unknown came to his assistance.

"I shall find them for you," said he to the canon; and he left the room, signing to the good curate to trust his discovering some expedient. But there was no occasion to employ his inventive powers. He learned from the domestic that the young people had set off through the fields, after generously handing over to him one of the florins they had just received.

"How! set out?" exclaimed the canon, with the utmost

mortification; "you must run after them. I positively must hear them and see them again."

They pretended to obey, but took care not to follow them. They had, besides, flown like birds, anxious to escape the curiosity which threatened them. The canon evinced great regret, and even some degree of ill-temper.

"Heaven be praised! he suspects nothing," said the curate to the unknown.

"Mr. Curate," replied the latter, "do you recollect the story of the bishop who, inadvertently eating meat one Friday, was informed of it by his vicar-general. "The wretch!" exclaimed the bishop, 'could he not have held his tongue till after dinner!' We should perhaps have let the canon undeceive himself at his leisure."

CHAPTER LXXVII.

THE evening was calm and serene, the moon shone full in the heavens, and nine o'clock had just sounded with a clear, deep tone from the clock of an ancient priory, when Joseph and Consuelo, having sought in vain for a bell at the gate of the inclosure, made the circuit of the silent habitation, in the hope of being heard by some hospitable inmate. But in vain, all the gates were locked; not the barking of a dog was heard, nor could the least light be seen at the windows of the gloomy edifice.

"This is the palace of silence," said Haydn, laughing, "and if that clock had not twice repeated, with its slow and solemn voice, the four quarters in *ut* and in *si*, and the nine strokes of the hour in *sol* below, I should think the place abandoned to owls and ghosts."

The surrounding country was a desert. Consuelo felt much fatigued, and moreover this mysterious priory had an attraction for her poetic imagination. "Even if we have to sleep in some chapel," said she to Beppo, "I long to pass the night here. Let us endeavor to get in at any rate, even if we are obliged to scale the wall, which does not seem a very difficult task."

"Come," said Joseph, "I will make a short ladder for you, and when you are on the top, I will pass quickly to the other side to serve you as steps in descending."

No sooner said than done. The wall was extremely low, and two minutes afterward our young sacrilegious adventurers were walking calmly within the sacred precints. It was a beautiful kitchen garden cultivated with the nicest care. The fruit trees, trained along the wall in a fan-like shape, opened to all comers their long arms loaded with rosy apples and golden pears. From the graceful trellises of vines hung, like so many chandeliers, enormous bunches of juicy grapes. The large square beds of vegetables had likewise their peculiar beauty. The asparagus, with its graceful stalks and silky foliage, brilliant with the evening dew, resembled forests of lilliputian furs covered with a silvery gauze. The peas, spread in light garlands upon their branches, formed long alleys and narrow and mysterious lanes, in which the little birds, hardly yet asleep, murmured with low quavering voices. The sunflowers, huge leviathans of this sea of verdure, displayed great masses of orange on their broad and dark green leaves. The little artichokes, like tributary crowned heads, grouped themselves round their chief which grew from the central stem ; and the melons, like lazy Chinese mandarins in their palanquins, hid coyly beneath their shades, each of whose crystal domes, reflected in the light of the moon's rays, seemed an enormous sapphire against which the dazzled beetles dashed their heads with a low and prolonged hum.

A hedge of roses separated the kitchen garden from the parterre, and surrounded the building as with a girdle of flowers. This inner enclosure was a species of elysium. Rare and magnificent shrubs shaded exotic plants of exquisite perfume; the flowers were so close together as to completely hide the soil, and each plot resembled an immense vase.

How singular the influence of outward objects on the mind and body! Consuelo had no sooner breathed the perfumed air, and cast a glance upon this sweet and tranquil spot, than she felt herself refreshed as if she had already slept the sound and dreamless sleep of the monks.

"Well, is it not wonderful, Beppo?" said she ; "in looking at this garden I have already forgotten the stony road and my tired and swollen feet! It seems to me that I am refreshed through the medium of my eyes. I have always hated well-kept, orderly gardens, and every place

surrounded with walls; and yet after so much dust and so
long a march upon the parched and withered soil, this appears to me a paradise. I was dying with thirst just now,
but by looking upon these sweet plants, open to the dew of
night, it seems as if I drank along with them, and my
thirst is already quenched. Look, Joseph, is it not charming to see these flowers display their beauties beneath the
light of the moon? Ah, look at them, but smile not at
those great white stars, nestling in the velvet grass. I am
not quite sure of their name—sweet-by-night, I think it
is. Oh! they are well named. They are, indeed,
bright and beautiful as the stars of heaven! They nod
their graceful heads with the slightest breath, and seem as
if they laughed and sported, like a crown of young girls
all clad in white. They recall to my mind my companions
of the *scuola*, when on Sundays, dressed in the costume of
novices, they tripped past the long walls of the church.
Now see how they pause, motionless, and turn toward the
moon! It would almost seem as if they were looking at
and admiring her. And the moon too seems to look at
them, and hover over them like some huge bird of the
night. Do you think, Beppo, that these creatures are insensible? I cannot think that a beautiful flower should
stupidly vegetate without experiencing some delightful
feelings. I do not speak of those poor little thistles which
one sees along the hedge-rows, dusty, sickly-looking,
browsed upon by all the herds that pass! They seem like
poor beggars sighing for a drop of water, which never
comes to them; for the parched and thirsty soil drinks all
up without heeding their supplicating looks. But these
garden-flowers, so cared for, so tended—they are proud
and happy as queens! They pass their time coquettishly
waving on their stems, and when the moon, their sweet
friend, visits them, then they are already half asleep and
rocked by gentle dreams. Perhaps they ask if there be
flowers in the moon, as we ourselves ask whether there be
men. Come now, Joseph, you are mocking me, and yet
the pleasure which these snow-white flowers impart is no
illusion. There is, in the air which they purify and refresh, a sovereign balm, and I feel as if there were an intimate relation between my life and that of all which
breathes around me.

"How! mock you?" replied Joseph, sighing; "your

words pass into my soul and vibrate in my heart, as on the strings of some instrument. But behold this dwelling, Consuelo, and explain to me, if you can, the sweet yet deep-seated melancholy with which it inspires me."

Consuelo looked at the priory; it was a little building dating from the twelfth century, formerly fortified with battlements, which had given place to pointed roofs of gray slate. The machiolated turrets which had been left as an ornament resembled large baskets. Luxuriant masses of ivy gracefully relieved the monotony of the walls; and upon the uncovered portions of the façade, now lighted by the moon, the breath of night cast the slender and uncertain shadow of the young poplars. Huge festoons of vine and jessamine encircled the doors and twined themselves around the windows.

" The dwelling is calm and melancholy," said Consuelo; " but it does not inspire me with the same sympathy as the garden. Plants are made to vegetate—men to move and stir about. If I were a flower I should wish to grow here, for here a flower were happy ; but being a woman, I should not wish to live in a cell and be cased in stone. Would you be a monk, then, Beppo?"

" Heaven forbid ! but I should love to work without having to look after either dwelling or food. I should like to lead a peaceful retired life, tolerably comfortable, without the cares of poverty; in short, an easy existence, were it even dependent, provided always my mind were free, with no other duty, no other care, than to study and compose."

" Well, my dear comrade, you would compose calm and tranquil music by dint of being calm and tranquil yourself."

" And why not ? What is more delightful than tranquility? The heavens are calm, the moon is calm ; these flowers also, whose peaceful habits you admire, I like their immobility, because it succeeds the undulations which the breeze gives them. The serenity of the heavens strikes us because we so often see them clouded by the storm. The moon is never so sublime as when she shines amid the dark clouds that sweep across her. Can repose be sweet without fatigue? In that case it is no longer repose, but only a species of immobility; it is nonentity—it is death."

" Ah, if you had lived with me for months together in

the Castle of the Giants, you would have seen that tranquility is not life."

" But what would you call tranquil music?"

" Music too correct and too cold. Avoid such, if you would avoid the pains and fatigue of this world. "

Thus conversing they approached close to the priory. A fountain of the purest water gushed from a globe of marble, surmounted by a golden cross, and fell from basin to basin till it reached a granite reservoir, hollowed into a shell, where a number of those little gold and silver fish with which children amuse themselves frisked about. Consuelo and Beppo, who were still children, entertained themselves by casting in grains of sand to deceive their gluttony, and to enable them to admire their rapid movements, when all at once there advanced toward them a tall figure dressed in white and carrying a pitcher. As she approached the fountain, she bore no bad resemblance to one of the *midnight washers* who have formed part of the fanciful superstitions of most countries. The absence of mind or indifference with which she filled her vessel, without testifying either terror or surprise on seeing them, had in truth something strange and solemn in it; but the shriek which she uttered, as she let her pitcher fall to the bottom of the water, soon showed that there was nothing supernatural in her character. The good woman's sight was simply dim with years, and as soon as she perceived them she fled toward the house, invoking the Virgin Mary and all the saints.

" What is the matter now, Dame Bridget?" exclaimed a man's voice from the interior ; "have you seen an evil spirit?"

" Two devils, or rather two robbers, are there beside the fountain!" replied Dame Bridget, joining her interlocutor, who stood for some moments uncertain and incredulous on the threshold.

" It must be one of your panic terrors, dame! Would robbers, think you, come at this hour?"

" I swear by my salvation, that there are two dark motionless figures there; don't you see them from this?"

" I do see something," said the man, affecting to raise his voice; " but I will ring for the gardener and his boys, and will soon bring these rascals to reason; they must have come over the wall, for I closed the doors."

" Meanwhile, let us close this one also," said the old lady, " and then we shall sound the alarm-bell."

The door was closed, and the wanderers remained standing outside, not knowing well what to do. To fly were to confirm this bad opinion of them; to remain were to expose them to an attack. While they consulted together they saw a ray of light stream through the shutters of a window on the first story. The light increased, and a curtain of crimson damask, behind which shone a lamp, was gently raised, and a hand, to which the light of the full moon imparted a white and plump appearance, was visible on the border of the curtain, the fringes of which it carefully grasped, while a hidden eye probably examined objects outside.

" Sing," said Consuelo to her companion, " that is what we had better do. Follow me—let me lead. But no, take your violin and play me a ritornella—the first key you happen on."

Joseph having obeyed, Consuelo began to sing with a clear full voice; improvising, between music and prose, the following species of recitative in German:

" We are two poor children of fifteen, no larger and yet no worse than the nightingales, whose gentle strains we copy.

(" Come, Joseph," said she in a low tone, " something to sustain the recitative.") Then she went on:

" Worn with fatigue, and woe-begone in the dreary night, we saw this house afar off, which seemed a solitude, and we ventured over the wall. (A chord in *la* minor, Joseph.)

" We have reached the enchanted garden, filled with fruits worthy of the promised land. We die of hunger, we die of thirst; yet if one apple be wanting from the espalier, if one grape be missing from the vine, let us be expelled, undeserving as we should then prove. (A modulation to return to *ut* major, Joseph.)

" But they suspect, they threaten us, and yet we would not flee. We do not seek to hide ourselves, because we have done no harm, unless indeed it be wrong to enter the house of God over walls, though, were it to scale a paradise, all roads are surely good."

Consuelo finished her recitative by one of those pretty hymns in mock Latin, called at Venice *Latino di pati,* and which people sing at eve before the Madonna. Hardly had she finished when the two white hands, at first scarcely visible, applauded with transport, and a voice not altogether strange, sounded in her ears:

"Disciples of the muses, you are welcome! Enter quickly, hospitality invites and awaits you."

The minstrels approached, and in an instant after, a domestic in red and violet livery courteously threw open the door.

"We took you for robbers; a thousand pardons, my dear young friends," he laughingly said; "it is your own fault —why did you not sing sooner? With such a passport you would never fail of a welcome from my master. But enter, it appears he knows you already."

Thus saying, the civil domestic preceded them a dozen steps up an easy stair covered with a beautiful Turkey carpet. Before Joseph had time to inquire his master's name, he had opened a folding door, which fell back of its own accord without noise, and after having crossed a comfortable ante-chamber, he introduced them to an apartment where the gracious patron of this happy abode, seated before a roast pheasant flanked by two flasks of mellow wine, began his first course, keeping a majestic and anxious eye at the same time on the second. On returning from his morning's excursion he had caused his valet to arrange his toilet, and had reclined for some time in order to restore his looks. His gray locks curled softly under the sweetly smelling hair-powder of orris root, while his white hands rested on his black satin breeches secured by silver buckles. His well-turned leg, of which he was somewhat vain, and over which a violet-colored stocking was tightly stretched, reposed on a velvet cushion, while his corpulent frame, attired in a puce-colored silk dressing gown, was luxuriously buried in a huge tapestried chair, so stuffed and rounded that the elbow never incurred the risk of meeting an angle. Seated beside the hearth, where the fire glowed and sparkled before her master's chair, Dame Bridget, the old housekeeper, prepared the coffee with deep care and anxiety, and a second valet, not less urbane in his manner and appearance than the first, carved the wing of the fowl which the holy man waited for without either impatience or disquietude. Joseph and Consuelo bowed on recognizing in their benevolent host the canon major of the cathedral chapter of St. Stephen, before whom they had sung that very morning.

CHAPTER LXXVIII.

THE canon was perhaps one of the most comfortable men in the world. When he was seven years old, he had (thanks to royal patronage) been pronounced of age, conformably to the laws of the church, which admit the very liberal principle that, though at that early period of life a man may not be exactly a sage, he at least possesses all the wisdom requisite to receive and consume the fruits of a benefice. In virtue of this decision, the tonsured child, although the illegitimate offspring of a prince, had been created a canon—still, however, strictly in accordance with the rules of the church, which tolerantly take for granted the legitimacy of such juvenile churchmen as owe their benefices to the patronage of sovereigns, although under other circumstances these same rules require that every aspirant to ecclesiastical distinction should be the offspring of lawful marriage, failing in proof of which, he might be declared "disqualified"—nay, even "unworthy" and "infamous," if necessary. There are indeed many ways of managing these affairs. It was provided for by the canonical laws that a foundling might be considered legitimate, for the cogent reason that in cases of mysterious parentage we should charitably suppose good rather than evil. The little canon came into possession of a rich prebendary, under the title of canon major; and toward the age of fifty, after forty years' service in the chapter, he was recognized as an extra or retired canon, free to reside where he pleased, and required to perform no duty in return for the immunities, revenues, and privileges of his benefice. It is true, indeed, that the worthy canon had, from the earliest years of his clerical life, rendered considerable service to the chapter. He was declared *absent*, which, according to the laws of the church includes permission to reside away from the chapter, under pretexts more or less specious, without subjecting the non-resident placeman to the loss of the emoluments attached

to the discharge of ministerial duties. The breaking out
of plague, for example, in a priest's dwelling, is an admis-
sible plea for *absence.* Delicate health also affords a convenient excuse. But the best founded and best received
of the various reasons for the "absence" of a
canon from his benefice, is that furnished by
study. For instance, some important work is undertaken and announced on a case of conscience on
the fathers, the sacraments, or, better still, the constitution
and foundation of the chapter, the honorary and actual
advantages connected with it, its superiority over other
chapters, the grounds of a lawsuit with some rival community about an estate or a right of patronage—these and
similar subtleties being much more interesting to ecclesiastical bodies than commentaries on creed or doctrine; so
that, if it should appear requisite for a distinguished member of the chapter to institute researches, collate deeds,
register acts and protests, or enter libels against rich
adversaries, the lucrative and agreeable option of resuming
a private life, and spending his income, whether in
traveling about or at his own fireside, is readily conceded.
Thus did our cannon.

A wit, a fluent speaker, and an elegant writer, he had
long promised, and would probably continue to promise
all his life, to write a book on the laws, privileges, and immunities of his chapter. Surrounded by dusty quartos
which he had never opened, he had not as yet produced
his own, and it was obvious never would do so. His two
secretaries, whom he had engaged at the expense of the
chapter, had only to perfume his person and prepare his
meals. They talked a great deal about this famous book ;
they expected it, and based upon its powerful arguments a
thousand dreams of revenge, glory, and profit. This book,
which had no existence, had procured for its author a
reputation for learning, perseverance, and eloquence, of
which he was in no haste to produce proofs; not that he
was by any means incapable of justifying the good opinion
of his brethren, but merely because life was short, meals
were long, the toilet indispensable, and the *far niente*
delicious. And then our canon indulged in two passions,
innocent indeed, but insatiable: he loved horticulture, and
he doated on music. With so much to do, how could he
have found leisure to write a book? Then it is so pleasant

for a man to talk of a book that he has not written, and so disagreeable, on the contrary, to speak of one that he has!

The benefice of this saintly personage consisted of a tract of productive soil, attached to the secular priory where he resided for some eight or nine months of the year, absorbed in the culture of his flowers and his appetite. His mansion was spacious and romantic, and he had made it comfortable, and even luxurious. Adandoning to gradual decay those portions which had in former times been inhabited by the old monks, he preserved with care and adorned with taste those suited to his own tastes and habits. Alterations and improvements had transformed the ancient monastery into a snug château, where the canon lived as became a gentleman. He was a good-natured son of the church; tolerant, liberal on occasion, orthodox with those of his own calling; cheerful, full of anecdote, and accessible to men of the world; affable, cordial, and generous toward artists. His domestics, sharing his good cheer, aided him with all their power. His housekeeper indeed would now and then cross him a little ; but then she made such delicious pastry, and was so excellent a hand at preserves, that he bore her ill-humor calmly, saying that a man might put up with the faults of others, but that it would not be so easy a matter to do without a nice dessert and good coffee.

Our young artists were accordingly most graciously received.

" Ah!" said he, " you are dear creatures, full of wit and cleverness, and I love you with all my heart. Besides, you possess infinite talent; and there is one of you, I don't know which, who has the sweetest, the most touching, the most thrilling voice I have ever heard. That gift is a prodigy—a treasure; and I was quite melancholy this evening after you left the curate's, fearing that I should perhaps never see you, never hear you again. I assure you I quite lost my appetite on your departure, and I was out of sorts all the rest of the evening. That sweet music and sweeter voice would not leave my mind or my ears. But Providence, and perhaps also your good hearts, my children, have sent you to me; for you must have known that I comprehended and appreciated you."

" We are forced to admit, reverend canon," replied Joseph, "that chance alone brought us here, and that we were far from reckoning on this good fortune."

"The good fortune is mine," said the amiable canon, "for you are going to sing for me. But, no; it would be selfish in me to press you. You are tired—hungry, perhaps. You shall first sup, next have a good night's rest, and then to-morrow for music! And, then, such music! We shall have it all day long! André, you will conduct these young people to the housekeeper's room, and pay them every attention. But, no—let them remain and sup with me. Lay two covers at the foot of the table."

André zealously obeyed, and even evinced the utmost satisfaction; but Dame Bridget displayed quite an opposite feeling. She shook her head, shrugged her shoulders, and deprecatingly muttered between her teeth.

"Pretty people to eat at your table!—strange companions truly for a man of your rank!"

"Hold your peace, Bridget!" replied the canon, calmly; "you are never satisfied with any one, and when you see others enjoying a little pleasure you become quite violent."

"You are at a loss how to pass your time," said she, without heeding his reproaches. "By flattering you and tickling your ears you are as easily led as a child."

"Be silent!" repeated the canon, raising his voice a little, but without losing his good humor. "You are cross as a weasel, and if you go on scolding you will lose your wits and spoil the coffee."

"Great pleasure and great honor, forsooth; to make coffee for such guests!"

"Oh! you must have great people, must you? You love grandeur, it would seem; nothing short of princes, and bishops, and canonesses, with sixteen quarterings in their coats of arms, will serve your turn! To me all that sort of nonsense is not worth a song well sung."

Consuelo was astonished to hear so exalted a personage disputing, with a kind of childish pleasure, with his housekeeper, and during the whole evening she was surprised at the puerile nature of his pursuits. He incessantly uttered silly remarks upon every subject, just to pass the time, and to keep himself in good humor. He kept calling to the servants continually—now seriously discussing with them the merits of a fish sauce, anon the arrangement of a piece of furniture! He gave contradictory orders, entering into the most trifling details with a gravity worthy of

more serious affairs; listening to one, reproving another,
holding his ground against the unruly Bridget, yet never
without a pleasant word for question or reply.   One would
have thought, that, reduced by his secluded and simple
habits of life to the society of his domestics, he tried to
keep his wit alive, and to promote his digestion, by a moderate exercise of thought.

The supper was exquisite, and the profusion of the
viands unparalleled.   Between the removes the cook was
summoned, praised for some of his dishes, and gently reprimanded and learnedly instructed with respect to others.
The travelers felt as if they had fallen from the clouds,
and looked at each other as though all they saw around
them were an amusing dream, so incomprehensible did such
refinements appear.

" Come, come; it is not so bad," said the good canon,
dismissing the culinary artist; " I see I shall make something of you, if you only show a desire to please and
attend to your duty."

" One would fancy," thought Consuelo, " that all this
was paternal advice or religious exhortation."

At the dessert, after the canon had given the housekeeper her share of praise and admonition, he at length
turned from these grave matters and began to talk of
music.   His young guests then saw him in a more favorable
point of view.   On this subject he was well-informed ; his
studies were solid, his ideas just, and his taste was refined.
He was a good organist, and having seated himself at the
harpsichord after the removal of the cloth, played for
them fragments from the old German masters, which he
executed with purity and precision of style.   Consuelo
listened with interest ; and having found upon the harpsichord a collection of this ancient music, she began to turn
over the leaves, and forgetting the lateness of the hour,
she requested the canon to play in his own free and peculiar style several pieces which had arrested her attention.
The canon felt extremely flattered by this compliment to
his performance.   The music with which he was acquainted being long out of fashion, he rarely found an
audience to his mind. He therefore took an extraordinary
liking to Consuelo in particular ; for Joseph, tired out,
had fallen asleep in a huge arm-chair, which, deliciously
alluring, invited to repose.

"Truly," exclaimed the canon in a moment of enthusiasm, "you are a most wonderful child, and your precocious genius promises a brilliant career. For the first time in my life I now regret the celibacy which my profession imposes on me."

This compliment made Consuelo blush and tremble lest her sex should have been discovered, but she quickly regained her self-possession when the canon naïvely added :

"Yes, I regret that I have no children, for Heaven might perhaps have given me a son like you, who would have been the happiness of my life — even if Bridget had been his mother. But tell me, my friend, what do you think of that Sebastian Bach, with whose compositions our professors are so much enraptured nowadays? Do you also think him a wonderful genius? I have a large book of his works which I collected and had bound, because, you know, one is expected to have every thing of that kind. They may be beautiful for aught I know ; but there is great difficulty in reading them, and I confess to you that the first attempt having repelled me, I have been so lazy as not to renew it ; moreover, I have so little time to spare. I can only indulge in music at rare intervals, snatched from more serious avocations. You have seen me much occupied with the management of my household, but you must not conclude from that that I am free and happy. On the contrary, I am enslaved by an enormous, a frightful task, which I have imposed upon myself. I am writing a book on which I have been at work for thirty years, and which another would not have completed in sixty — a book which requires incredible study, midnight watchings, indomitable patience, and profound reflection. I think it is a book that will make some noise in the world."

"But is it nearly finished?" asked Consuelo.

"Why, not exactly," replied the canon, desirous to conceal from himself the fact that he had not commenced it. "But we were observing just now that the music of Bach is terribly difficult, and that, for my own part, I consider it peculiar."

"If you could overcome your repugnance I think you would perceive that his is a genius which embraces, unites, and animates all the science of the past and the present."

"Well," returned the canon, "if it be so, we three will

to-morrow endeavor to decipher something of it. It is now time for you to take some rest and for me to betake myself to my studies. But to-morrow you will pass the day with me ; that is the understanding, is it not?"

"The whole day? that is asking too much, sir—we must hasten to reach Vienna ; but for the morning we are at your service."

The canon protested—nay, insisted — and Consuelo pretended to yield, promising herself that she would hurry the adagios of the great Bach a little, and leave the priory about eleven o'clock, or by noon at furthest. When they intimated a wish to retire, an earnest discussion arose on the staircase between Dame Bridget and the principal valet-de-chambre. The zealous Joseph, desirous of pleasing his master, had prepared for the young musicians two pretty cells situated in the newly-restored building occupied by the canon and his suite. Bridget, on the contrary, insisted on sending them to sleep in the desolate and forsaken rooms of the old priory, because that part of the mansion was separated from the new one by good doors and solid bolts. "What !" said she, elevating her shrill voice on the echoing staircase, "do you mean to lodge these vagabonds next door to us? Do you not see from their looks, their manners, and their profession, that they are gypsies, adventurers, wicked little rogues, who will make off before morning with our knives and forks. Who knows but they may even cut our throats?"

"Cut our throats? those children!" returned Joseph, laughing ; "you are a fool, Bridget ; old and feeble as you are, you would yourself put them to flight, merely by showing your teeth."

"Old and worn out indeed! Keep such language for yourself!" cried the old woman in a fury. "I tell you they shall not sleep here ; I will not have them. Sleep, indeed? I should not close my eyes the whole night!"

"Don't be so silly. I am sure that those children have no more intention than I have to disturb your respectable slumbers. Come, let us have an end of this nonsense. My master ordered me to treat his guests well, and I am not going to shut them up in that old ruin, swarming with rats and open to every breeze. Would you have them sleep in the court-yard?"

"I would have had the gardener make up two good beds

of straw for them there; do you imagine that those bare-footed urchins are accustomed to beds of down?"

"They shall have them to-night at least, since it is my master's desire; I obey no orders but his, Dame Bridget. Let me go about my business; and recollect that it is your duty as well as mine to obey, and not to command."

"Well said! Joseph," exclaimed the canon, who, from the half-open door of the ante-chamber, had, much to his amusement, heard the whole dispute. "Go get my slippers, Bridget, and have mercy on our ears. Good-night, my little friends. Follow Joseph. Pleasant dreams to you both! Long live music, and hey for to-morrow!"

Long, however, after our travelers had taken possession of their snug bed-rooms, they heard the scolding of the housekeeper, shrill as the whistling of the wintry wind, along the corridors. When the movement which announced the ceremony of the canon's retiring to bed had ceased, Dame Bridget stole on tip-toe to the doors of his young guests, and, quickly turning the key in each lock, shut them in. Joseph, buried to the ears in the most luxurious bed he had ever met with in his life, had already fallen asleep, and Consuelo followed his example, after having laughed heartily to herself at Bridget's terrors. She who had trembled almost every night during her journey, now made others tremble in their turn! She might have applied to herself the fable of the hare and the frogs, but I cannot positively assert that Consuelo was acquainted with La Fontaine's fables. Their merit was disputed at that epoch by the most noted wits of the universe; Voltaire laughed at them, and the Great Frederick, to ape his philosopher, despised them profoundly.

CHAPTER LXXIX.

At break of day, Consuelo, seeing the sun shining, and feeling invited to a walk by the joyous warblings of a thousand birds, which were already making good cheer in the garden, endeavored to leave her chamber. But the embargo was not yet raised, and Dame Bridget still held her prisoners under lock and key. Consuelo at first thought that it was perhaps an ingenious idea of the canon's, who wished to secure the musical enjoyment of the day and had thought it prudent in the first place to make certain of the persons of the musicians. The young girl, rendered hardy and agile by her masculine costume, examined the window, and saw that the descent was rendered easy by a large vine supported by a massive trellis which covered the whole wall. Descending slowly and carefully, so as not to injure the magnificent grapes of the priory, she reached the ground and buried herself in the recesses of the garden, laughing inwardly at Bridget's surprise and disappointment when she should find her precautions frustrated.

Consuelo now saw the superb flowers and magnificent fruits which she had admired by moonlight under another aspect. The breath of morning and the oblique rays of the rosy and smiling sun invested these beautiful productions of the earth with a new poetry. A robe of velvet-like satin enveloped the fruits, the dew hung in pearls of crystal from every branch, and the turf, frosted with silver, exhaled that light vapor which seems the breath of earth aspiring once more to ascend to heaven, and unite itself with the blue and cloudless firmament.

But nothing could exceed the freshness and beauty of the flowers, still loaded as they were with the moisture of the night, at this mysterious and shadowy hour of dawn, when they open as if to display those treasures of purity, and to shed those sweetest perfumes, which the earliest and purest of the sun's rays are alone worthy to behold and to possess for an instant. The canon's garden was in truth a paradise for a lover of horticulture. To Consuelo's eyes, indeed, it seemed somewhat too symmetrical and too carefully tended; but the fifty species of roses which adorned its parterres, the rare and charming hibiscus, the purple sage, the geraniums varied almost to infinity, the perfumed daturas, with their deep opal cups, impregnated with nectar worthy of the gods, the graceful asclepiades, in whose subtle poison the insect finds a voluptuous death, the splendid cactuses, displaying their scarlet effulgence on their strangely rugged stems—a thousand curious and superb plants which Consuelo had never seen, and of whose names and origin she was alike ignorant, long riveted her attention.

Examining their various attitudes and the sentiments which their several peculiarities seemed to convey, she endeavored to seize and define the analogy existing between music and flowers, and sought to explain their joint influence on the temperament of her host. The harmony of sounds had long appeared to her related in some way to the harmony of colors; but the harmony of both these harmonies seemed to her *perfume.* Plunged at this instant in a soft and dreamy reverie, she fancied she heard a voice issue from each of these painted chalices, and tell her their poetic mysteries in a language hitherto unknown. The rose spoke of her burning loves, the lily of her chaste delight; the superb magnolia told of pure enjoyments and lofty pride, and the lovely little hepatica related all the pleasures of a simple and retired existence. Some flowers spoke with strong and powerful voices, which proclaimed in accents trumpet-tongued, "I am beautiful and I rule." Others murmured in tones scarcely audible, but exquisitely soft and sweet, "I am little and I am beloved." And they all waved gracefully together in the breath of morning, and united their voices in an aërial choir which died away gently amid the listening herbs and beneath the foliage that drank in with greedy ears its mystic meaning.

All at once amid these ideal harmonies and ecstatic reveries, Consuelo heard piercing cries proceed from behind the trees which hid the wall. To these cries, which died away in the silence of the surrounding country, succeeded the rolling of carriage wheels; then the carriage appeared to stop, and blows were heard on the iron railing which inclosed the garden on that side. But whether it was that all the household was still asleep, or that no person cared to reply, they knocked in vain, and the shrill exclamation of a female voice, joined to the oaths of a man calling for help, fell upon the walls of the priory without awaking in the senseless stones any more echo than in the hearts of those whom they sheltered. All the windows which looked out on this side of the building were so firmly closed in order to protect the canon's repose, that no noise could penetrate the oaken window-shutters garnished with leather and stuffed with hair. The servants, busied in the green behind the house, did not hear the application for admittance, and there were no dogs in the priory, as the canon had no fancy for those importunate guardians, who, under the pretext of keeping thieves at a distance, ruffle the repose of their masters. Consuelo endeavored to obtain an entrance into the house, in order to acquaint the inmates that there were travelers in distress, but every door was carefully shut; so, yielding to the impulse of the moment, she ran to the wicket whence the noise proceeded. A traveling carriage, loaded with packages and covered with dust from the journey, had drawn up at the principal entrance of the garden. The postilions had alighted and vainly tried to shake the inhospitable gate, while groans and cries issued from the carriage. "Open!" cried they to Consuelo, "if you are Christians! There is a lady dying here."

"Open!" cried a woman, leaning out of the door, whose features were unknown to Consuelo, but whose Venetian accents impressed her vividly, "My mistress will die if you do not immediately grant her hospitality. Open if you are men."

Consuelo, without reflecting on the consequences of her first impulse, endeavored to open the gate; but it was closed by an enormous padlock, the key of which was probably in Dame Bridget's pocket. The bell was also fastened by a secret spring. In that quiet and honest country such precautions had not been taken against evil doers, but merely against the noise and inconvenience of unseasonable visitors. It was impossible for Consuelo to gratify her kind wishes on the poor woman's behalf, and she listened in melancholy silence to the reproaches of the maid, who, speaking Venetian to her mistress, cried with impatience, "The stupid creature! the awkward little fellow! he does not know how to open a gate." The German postilions, more patient and phlegmatic, were endeavoring to assist Consuelo, but without success, when the suffering lady, appearing in her turn at the window of the carriage, cried with a commanding voice in bad German, "Go this minute, you miserable little wretch, and find some person to open the gate!"

This energetic apostrophe reassured Consuelo respecting the imminent danger of the lady. "If she be near dying," thought she, "it is at least by a violent death;" and addressing herself in Venetian to the traveler, whose accent was as plainly marked as the maid's:

"I do not belong to this house," said she; "I was merely received as a guest here last night; I will go and try to awaken the inmates, which will be neither a quick nor an easy matter. Are you in such danger, madam, that you cannot wait here a little while without disparing?"

"I expect my confinement immediately, you stupid creature!" cried the traveler; "I have not a moment to wait; run, shout, break every thing, bring somebody and procure me admittance—you shall be well paid for your trouble."

She again commenced to utter loud cries. Consuelo felt her knees tremble—that face, that voice were not unknown to her! "What is the name of your mistress?" cried she to the maid.

"What concern is it of yours?" replied the agitated soubrette. "Run, you miserable being! If you lose any time, I warn you you will not get a farthing."

"I want nothing from you," replied Consuelo, warmly; "but I wish to know who you are. If your mistress be a musician, she will be received at once, and if I am not mistaken, she is a celebrated singer."

"Run, my little fellow," said the lady, who between her attacks regained all her coolness and energy; "you are not mistaken. Tell the inhabitants of this house that the celebrated Corilla is at the point of death, if some Christian soul do not take pity on her situation. I shall pay them—say that I shall pay them handsomely. Alas! Sophia," said she to her maid, "lay me upon the ground; I shall suffer less than in this infernal conveyance."

Consuelo hurried toward the priory, determined to rouse every one in the house, and at all hazards to reach the canon. She had already forgotten the strange concurrence of circumstances which had led her rival and the cause of all her sufferings to this spot; she only thought of lending her every assistance. But she had no need to make a noise. On her way she met Bridget, who, at length aroused by the cries, had left the house escorted by the gardener and the canon's valet.

"A fine story!" she replied harshly, when Consuelo had explained the case. "Don't go a step further, André; don't stir from this spot, gardener! Don't you see that it is a scheme got up by banditti to rob and murder us? I expected no less. A surprise — a pretense — a band of robbers prowling about the house, while those to whom we have given shelter endeavor to gain them admission on some false pretext! Run for your muskets, my lads, and be ready to shoot this pretended lady who is on the point of being confined. Marry come up! a nice story! But were it even so, I wonder does she take this house for an hospital? I know nothing about such matters myself, and the canon does not like to hear such screaming sounding in his ears. How could any lady undertake a journey under such circumstances? If she have done so, who is to blame? Can we prevent her from suffering? Let her stay in her carriage; she will be just as well off as here where there is no provision for such an occurrence."

This tirade, commenced for Consuelo's edification, and growled out along the whole length of the alley, was finished at the gate for the benefit of Corilla's maid. While the travelers, having pleaded in vain, exchanged reproaches, exclamations, and even abuse, with the intractable housekeeper, Consuelo, hoping something from the canon's good nature and passionate love of art, had regained the house. In vain she sought his suite of apartments—she only lost herself in the intricacies of the vast dwelling. At last she met Haydn, who was in search of her, and who told her he had just seen the canon enter his conservatory. They repaired there together, and met their worthy host advancing to meet them under an arch of jessamine, with a countenance fresh and smiling as the morning, which was one of the sweetest and loveliest of autumn. Looking at the good man, as, folded in his soft quilted dressing-gown, he daintily picked his steps along the freshly raked and sanded paths, where not the smallest pebble appeared to hurt his delicate foot, Consuelo never doubted but that a being so happy, so serene, and agreeable, would be delighted to do a good action. She was commencing to prefer a plea for the poor suffering Corilla, when Bridget, suddenly appearing, cut her short in the following words:

"There is a stroller yonder at your gate, a singer of the theater, who says she is a celebrated performer, and who has the voice and manner of a profligate! She says she is momentarily expecting her confinement, screams and swears like thirty demons, and requests permission to await her recovery here. Would that suit your convenience?"

The canon made a gesture expressive of refusal and disgust.

"Reverend sir," said Consuelo, "whatever this woman may be, she is suffering. Her life, as well as that of the innocent creature whom God calls into existence, and whom religion requires you to foster, is endangered. You will not abandon this unhappy being—you will not suffer her to groan and languish at your doors?"

"Is she married?" inquired the canon coldly, after a moment's reflection.

"I am not aware; probably she is. But what matters it? Has not God granted her the happiness of being a mother? He alone has the right to judge her."

"She mentioned her name," interrupted Bridget, violently, "and you must be acquainted with it as you know all the play-actors of Vienna. She is called Corilla."

"Corilla!" exclaimed the canon. "She has already been in Vienna once before—I have heard much of her. It is said she has a fine voice."

"For the sake of her sweet voice, then, open your doors to her," said Consuelo; "she lies stretched on the dusty road."

"But she is an ill-conducted person," replied the canon. "She scandalized all Vienna some two years ago."

"There are many who are jealous of your benefice, reverend sir—you understand me"—screamed Dame Bridget. "A woman of irregular life awaiting her confinement in your house—that would scarcely seem a matter of chance, and still less a work of charity. You know that the canon Herbert has pretensions to your succession, and that he has already unseated a brother, under pretext that he neglected his duty and led an irregular life. A benefice like yours is more easily lost than gained."

These words made a sudden and decisive impression upon the canon. He prudently noted them in his secret thoughts, though he did not appear even to have heard them.

"There is an inn some two hundred paces from this," said he, "let the lady be conducted there; she will receive the needful attentions, and be more fitly accommodated than with me. Go and tell her so, Bridget; but civilly—mark me—civilly! Point out the inn to the postilions. Come, my children," said he Consuelo and Joseph, "let us try a fugue of Bach's while breakfast is being served up."

"Reverend canon," said Consuelo, agitated, "will you abandon——"

"Ah!" said the canon with a terrified air, "there is my most beautiful volkameria withered! I often told the gardener that he did not water it! A plant the rarest and most wonderful of all my garden! But it was fated, Bridget, you see! Call the gardener till I scold him soundly."

"I must first chase the celebrated Corilla from your gate," replied Bridget, moving off.

"And you consent? you order it, sir?" exclaimed the indignant Consuelo.

"It is impossible to do otherwise," replied he, in a calm but inflexible tone of voice. "I request that I may not be spoken to further on the subject. Come, begin; I await you."

"There is no more music for us here," exclaimed Consuelo with energy. "You would not be capable of understanding Bach, you who are without pity or compassion! Ah, perish your fruits and flowers! May frost destroy the bloom of your jasamines and blight the promise of your most precious trees! May this fruitful soil, which yields its bounties in such profusion, produce only thorns and thistles! For you have no heart. You rob Heaven of its gifts, in refusing to share them with your suffering neighbor."

So saying, Consuelo left the astounded canon, who gazed vacantly around him, as if he feared this withering malediction had already fallen on his precious volkamerias and cherished anemones. She ran to the wicket, which was still closed, and promptly climbed it, in order to follow Corilla's conveyance toward the wretched wayside cabaret which the canon had dignified with the title of an inn.

CHAPTER LXXX.

HAYDN, by this time accustomed to obey implicitly the sudden resolutions of his friend, but endowed with a more calm and thoughtful temperament, rejoined her after having secured his traveling bag, his music, and, above all, his precious violin—his bread-winner, and the delight and comfort of his travels. Corilla was laid on one of those wretched German beds, which are so short that the occupier must project outside either his feet or his head. Unluckily there was not a woman on the spot, the mistress having set out on a pilgrimage to a shrine six leagues off, and the female servant having gone to drive the cow to the pasture. An old man and a child looked after the house meanwhile; and, more frightened than satisfied at having to lodge their distinguished guest, they allowed their household gods to be invaded, without thinking how they should turn it to account. The old man was deaf, and the child proceeded to seek the village midwife, who lived at least three miles off. The postilions were much more uneasy about their horses, who had nothing to eat, than about their charge, and the latter, left without any assistance but that of her femme-de-chambre, who was completely bewildered, and made almost as much noise as her mistress, filled the air with her shrieks and lamentations.

Consuelo, seized with terror and pity, resolved not to abandon the unhappy creature.

"Joseph," said she to her companion, "return to the priory, even if you were to be badly received; we must not be proud when we are asking for others. Tell the canon to send linen, soup, some good wine, a mattress, a coverlet— in short, every thing necessary for a sick person. Speak mildly, but firmly; promise, if necessary, that we will return and perform, provided he sends succor to this unfortunate woman."

Joseph set out, and poor Consuelo, half-hidden in the background, watched with pitying gaze this wretched woman without faith or feeling, who suffered with imprecations and outcries the sacred martyrdom of maternity. The chaste and pious girl shuddered on beholding tortures which nothing could allay, since in place of joy and hope, anger and displeasure consumed Corilla's heart. She never left off cursing her hard fate, her journey, the canon and his housekeeper, and even the child unborn. She heaped volumes of abuse on her servant, and rendered her incapable of doing any thing. "Leave my sight!" cried she, "you only irritate and annoy me!"

Sophia, angry and wretched, left the house weeping, and Consuelo, left alone with the unfortunate creature, tried to comfort and soothe her,

In a short time Sophia returned, and a quarter of an hour afterward the child saw the light. The maid snatched from a trunk the first garment that came to hand, which happened to be a theatrical mantle of faded satin, adorned with tinsel, and wrapping the infant in this strange swaddling-cloth, placed it in Consuelo's arms.

"Come, madam, be consoled," said the poor waiting-woman, with an accent of simple and heartfelt kindness; "you are happily delivered, and you have a lovely little girl."

"Girl or boy, I no longer suffer," replied Corilla, raising herself on her elbow; "give me a glass of wine."

Joseph had just brought some from the priory, and it was of the best. The canon had behaved generously, and the patient soon had a plenteous supply of all that her situation required. Corilla raised with a firm hand the silver goblet which was presented to her, and emptied it with the steadiness of a toper; then, throwing herself back upon the canon's comfortable cushions, she immediately fell asleep with that carelessness which is the result of an iron frame and an unfeeling heart. During her slumber the child was properly clothed, and Consuelo went to the neighboring field for a ewe, which served as its first nurse. When the mother woke she caused herself to be raised by Sophia, and having swallowed another glass of wine she seemed collecting her strength for some effort. Consuelo held the child toward her, expecting some expression of maternal tenderness, but Corilla had a very different idea in her thoughts. She pitched her voice in *ut* major, and gravely went through a gamut of two octaves. Then she clapped her hands and cried, "*Brava*, Corilla! you have not lost a note of your voice!" And bursting into a shout of laughter, she embraced Sophia, and put upon her finger a diamond which she took from her own, saying, "That is to console you for the insults I heaped upon you. Where is my little monkey? Ah, Heavens!" cried she, looking at her child, "it is fair, it resembles him! So much the worse! Do not unpack so many trunks, Sophia. What are you thinking of? Do you imagine I wish to stay here all my life? Come, come, you are foolish; you do not yet know what life is. To-morrow I mean to be on the road again. Ah! my little Zingara, you hold the baby just as if you were a woman. How much do you want for your care and your trouble? Do you know, Sophia, that I never was better nursed and tended ? So you are from Venice, my little friend? Did you ever hear me sing?"

Consuelo made no reply to these questions, and indeed her answers would not have been listened to. Corilla horrified her. She committed the child to the care of the servant, who had just entered, and who appeared a good creature; then calling Joseph, she returned with him to the priory.

"I did not promise to the canon to bring you back," said he, as they walked along. "He appeared ashamed of his conduct, though he affected much ease and cheerfulness of manner. Notwithstanding his selfishness, he is not an ill-disposed man. He appeared really happy in sending Corilla all that could be useful to her."

"There are some minds so frightfully hard and unfeeling," replied Consuelo, "that weak ones ought to cause us more pity than horror. I wish to make amends for my anger against the poor canon, and since Corilla is not dead—since, to use the common phrase, both mother and child are as well as can be expected —since our canon has contributed to that result as much as he could without risking the possession of his dear benefice— I wish to thank him. Besides, I have reasons for remaining at the priory until after Corilla's departure. To-morrow I will tell you what they are."

Bridget had gone to pay a visit to a neighboring farmhouse, and Consuelo, who had expected to confront that griffin, was agreeably disappointed at being received by the gentle and prepossessing André.

"Come along, my little friends," cried he, leading the way to his master's apartments ; "the canon is dreadfully melancholy ; he hardly eat any thing at breakfast, and his noonday siesta was repeatedly interrupted. He has met with two great misfortunes to-day ; he has lost his most splendid volkameria, as well as the hope of hearing some good music. Happily you are returned, and one at least of his sufferings will be allayed."

"Does he mock his master or us?" said Consuelo to Joseph.

"Both," replied Haydn. "In case the canon be not in a pouting mood, we shall have some rare sport."

Far from finding fault, the canon received them with

open arms. Consuelo made him admire and understand the admirable preludes of Bach ; and to complete his satisfaction, she sang her most beautiful songs, without trying to disguise her voice, and without troubling herself much whether he discovered her age and sex or not. The canon was determined to discover nothing, and to enjoy to the uttermost what he heard, He was passionately fond of music, and his transports seemed so sincere and heartfelt that Consuelo could not help being touched.

"Ah! my dear, good, noble child?" cried the worthy man, with tears in his eyes, "this is the happiest day of my life! But what is henceforth to become of me? No! I can never bear the loss of such an enjoyment. I shall be eaten up with weariness ; I can no longer take pleasure in music of my own performance. My soul is filled with an ideal which I never can attain, and which I shall regret forever. I shall no longer love any thing, not even my flowers."

"You are very wrong to say so," said Consuelo, "for your flowers sing better than I do."

"What say you ? — my flowers sing! I never heard them."

"That is because you never listened ; but I heard them this morning. I heard their mystic melodies, and understood their meaning."

"You are a strange child — a true child of genius!" exclaimed the canon, stroking Consuelo's brown locks with fatherly regard. "You wear the livery of poverty, while you should be borne aloft in triumph. But who are you, tell me? Where have you learned what you know?"

"Nature—chance—were my teachers."

"Ah! you deceive me," said the canon, laughing good-humoredly ; "you are some relation of Farinelli or Cafarelli. But listen, my children," he added, with a serious yet cheerful air ; "you must leave me no more. I shall take charge of you—remain with me. I have some means — they shall be yours. I shall be to you what Gravina was to Metastasio. It shall be my honor and my glory. Stay with me ; it will only be necessary for you to enter into secondary orders. You shall have a handsome benefice, and after my death you will inherit some pretty little savings, which I do not intend to leave to that harpy, Bridget."

As the canon spoke thus, the harpy herself entered suddenly, and heard his last words.

Choking with rage and tears, she exclaimed : "And I, for my part, I do not intend to serve you any longer? It is a pretty thing to sacrifice my youth and my reputation to an ungrateful master!"

"Your reputation? — your youth?" replied the canon, mockingly. "Ah! you flatter yourself, my poor old woman! What you are pleased to term the one, protects the other."

"Yes, yes," said she ; "jest on, but prepare to see me no more. I leave a house where I can no longer preserve order or decency. I would prevent you from making a fool of yourself, from squandering your means, and degrading your office ; but I perceive that it is all in vain. Your feeble character and your declining star impel you on to your ruin, and the first mountebanks that fall in your way, so turn your head that you are ready to sacrifice every thing to them. Well, well, the Canon Herbert has long wished me to enter his service, and offers me a better salary than you can afford. I am weary of all I see here. Pay me my wages — I will not pass another night under your roof."

"Oh! is that the way?" said the canon, calmly. "Well, then, Bridget, you do me a great favor, and I hope most fervently you will keep to your word. I have never dismissed any one from my service, and I think, if the devil himself were in my employment, I would not put him out, such is my easy temper ; but if he left me of his own accord, I would wish him a good journey, and sing a *magnificat* at his departure. Make up your packages, Bridget ; and as to your wages, take them yourself—whatever you wish—all that I possess, if you will—so that you rid me of your presence quickly."

"Ah! reverend canon," said Haydn, moved at this domestic scene, "you will regret an old domestic who seems warmly attached to you."

"She is attached to my benefice," replied the canon, "and I only regret her coffee."

"You will accustom yourself to do without good coffee," said the austere Consuelo, firmly, "and you will do well. Hold your tongue, Joseph, and do not intercede for her. I mean to speak openly before ner, because it is the truth.

She is ill-natured, and she is hurtful to her master. He is good; nature has made him noble and generous; but this woman renders him selfish. She stifles all the good impulses of his soul, and if he keeps her in his service he will become at last as hard and inhuman as herself. Pardon me, reverend canon, for thus addressing you. You have made me sing so much, and have so intoxicated me in displaying your own enthusiasm and delight, that I am hardly myself. If this be so, you are to blame ; but be assured that truth reigns supreme in such moments of enthusiasm, because they are noble in their nature and develop in us the loftiest qualities of our being. It is then that our heart is on our lips, and it is my heart which now speaks to you. When I am calm, I shall be more respectful, but not more sincere. Believe me, I do not want your fortune. I have no desire for it, and no need. Did I wish for fortune, I might have more than you, and the life of an artist is subjected to so many risks, that you may possibly survive me. It would then be for me to inscribe your name in my will, in grateful recollection of what you have wished to do for me. To-morrow we shall leave this, most probably never to meet again ; but we shall leave you with hearts overflowing with joy, respect, and gratitude, if you get rid of this Madame Bridget, whose pardon I sincerely ask for thus thinking of her."

Consuelo spoke with so much fire, and the frankness of her disposition depicted itself so strongly on her features, that her words made an electric impression on the canon.

" Begone! Bridget," said he, with a firm and dignified air, to his housekeeper. " Truth speaks by the mouth of children, and this youth has a great soul. Begone! for you have this day made me do a base action, and you would make me do others, because I am weak and at times timid. Begone! because you make my life unhappy, and that is not necessary to your salvation. Begone!" he added, smiling, " because you begin to scorch the coffee and sour the cream."

This last reproach touched Bridget more than all the rest, and her pride, wounded in the most sensitive point, closed her mouth completely. She rose, cast a look of pity—almost of scorn—on the canon, and left the apartment with a theatrical air. Two hours afterward, this dethroned queen left the priory, which she did not fail to pillage a little. The canon took no notice of it, and from the happiness that shone on his countenance, Haydn saw that Consuelo had rendered him a real service. After dinner, the latter, to prevent him from feeling any regret, made coffee for him after the Venetian fashion, which is by far the best in the world. André took lessons under her directions, and the canon declared that he had never tasted better coffee in his life. They had more music in the evening, first, however, sending to inquire for Corilla, who, the messenger brought word, was already seated in the arm-chair which the canon had sent her. In the evening, which was one of the loveliest of the season, they took a long stroll through the garden by moonlight, during which the canon, leaning on Consuelo's arm, continually entreated her to enter into secondary orders, and to be to him as his adopted son.

"Take care," said Joseph, when they were about to retire to their several apartments; "this good canon is wonderfully taken with you."

"Nothing ought to put one out when traveling," replied she. "But do not be afraid, I shall not be an abbé any more than a trumpeter. Herr Mayer, Count Hoditz, and the canon, have all reckoned without their host."

CHAPTER LXXXI.

NEVERTHELESS Consuelo bade good-evening to Joseph, and retired to her apartment, without giving him, as he expected, the signal for departure next morning at daybreak. She had her own reasons for not hastening, and Joseph waited patiently until she should disclose them— enchanted meanwhile to spend a few hours with her in this lovely abode, and to lead for a short time longer this canonical and comfortable life, which by no means displeased him. Consuelo slept until late next morning, and did not make her appearance till the canon's second breakfast. The worthy ecclesiastic's usual practice was to rise early, take a light pleasant repast, and stroll through his garden and inclosures (breviary in hand), to examine his plants, and afterward to take a second sleep pending the preparation of a more substantial breakfast.

"Our neighbor is getting on well this morning," said he

to his young guests the moment they appeared. "I have sent André to prepare her breakfast. She expresses much gratitude for your attentions, and as she proposes (very imprudently, I admit) to set out to-day for Vienna, she wishes to see you before she leaves, in order to recompense you in some measure for the kind and zealous assistance you gave her. Therefore breakfast quickly, my children, and go to her; doubtless she has some handsome present for you."

"We shall breakfast as slowly as you choose, sir," replied Consuelo, "and we shall not go to see the sick woman. She has no longer occasion for our services, and we shall never accept her presents."

"Strange child!" said the astonished canon· "your romantic disinterestedness, your enthusiastic generosity, gain my heart so completely that never—no never—shall I be able to part with you!"

Consuelo smiled, and they sat down to table. The repast was exquisite, and lasted fully two hours; but the desert was different from what the canon expected.

"Reverend sir," said André, appearing at the door, "here is Bertha from the cabaret, bringing you a basket from the lady."

"It is the silver things which I lent her," said the canon; "take them from her André, that is your business. The lady is positively going, then?"

"Reverend sir, she is gone."

"Already! she is mad! she will kill herself outright!"

"No, sir," said Consuelo; "she will not kill herself, and she does not wish to kill herself."

"Well, André, why do you stand there with such an air of ceremony?" said the canon to his valet.

"Reverend sir, Mother Bertha refuses to give me the basket; she says she will only give it to you, and that she has something to say to you."

"Nonsense! It is some scruple of the old woman's about trusting you with the plate; however, let her come in and let us have done with it."

The old woman was introduced, and after many courtesies laid a large covered basket on the table. Consuelo immediately glanced at the contents while the canon's head was turned toward Bertha, and then replacing the covering, she said in a low tone to Joseph:

"It is what I expected; and this is why I remained. Oh! yes, I was sure that Corilla would act thus."

Joseph, who had not had time to examine the contents of the basket, looked at his companion with astonishment.

"Well, Mother Bertha," said the canon, "so you return the little things which I lent you? Ah! very good. It is quite unnecessary to examine them—I am sure they are all correct."

"Reverend sir," replied the old woman, "my servant has brought back everything; I gave them to your officers. Nothing is wanting, and I am quite easy on that score. But this basket the lady made me swear that I would give into your own hands; the contents you know as well as I do."

"May I be hanged if I do!" said the canon, advancing his hand carelessly toward the basket.

But his hand was paralyzed as if with catalepsy, and his mouth remained half opened with surprise, when the covering, moving apparently of itself, fell aside, and disclosed to view a rosy little hand, which seemed as if endeavoring to seize the canon's finger.

"Yes, reverend sir," replied the old woman, with a confident and satisfied smile; "there it is, safe and sound, the little darling; wide awake, and likely to do well."

The amazed canon could not utter a word; the old woman continued:

"You know you requested its mother to allow you to adopt and bring it up. The poor lady indeed found it somewhat hard to part with it; but we told her her baby could not be in better hands, and she recommended it to Providence in giving it to us to bring to you. 'Tell this worthy canon—this holy man,' she exclaimed, as she got into her carriage, 'that I shall not long take advantage of his charitable zeal. I shall soon return for my daughter, and pay whatever expenses he may incur. Since he is absolutely determined to procure a good nurse, be kind enough to hand him this purse, which I request he may divide between the nurse, and the little musician, if he be still there, who took such good care of me yesterday.' As for myself, reverend sir, she has paid me well; I am quite content."

"Ah! you are content, are you?" exclaimed the canon, with a tragi-comic air. "I am delighted to hear it!

But be kind enough to take this purse and this infant away with you. Spend the money—rear the child—it is no concern of mine."

"Rear the child? Oh, by no means, reverend sir! I am too old to take charge of a new-born babe; it would cry all night long, and my poor old man, although he be deaf, would not put up with that very well."

"It seems that I must put up with it, then? Many thanks. Do you imagine that is likely?"

"Since your reverence asked it from its mother!"

"*I* beg? Who the deuce told you so?"

"Why, since your reverence wrote this morning——"

"*I* write? Where is my letter, if you please? Who was the bearer of it?"

"Oh! faith, I did not see it, and even if I had, I could not have read it; but Mr. André came to her on the part of your reverence, and she told us that he had brought a letter from you. We are honest, unsuspecting people, and we believed it. Who would not?"

"It is an abominable lie! some gipsy trick. You are concerned in the plot. Come, take this infant away—give it back to its mother—keep it—arrange it as you please—I wash my hands of the transaction! If you want money, you shall have it. I never refuse charity, even to scoundrels and impostors; it is the only way to get rid of them. But to take a baby into my house—many thanks! Be off out of my sight!"

"As to taking the child," replied the old woman, in a decided tone, "I positively will not—no offense to your reverence. I did not take charge of the child on my own account. I know how all these matters end. They dazzle you with a little gold at first, and promise you marvels for the future; and then you hear no more of it—the child remains with you for good and all. But such creatures never turn out well; they are idle and proud by nature. One does not know what to do with them. If boys, they turn out robbers; if girls, it is still worse. By my faith, no; neither the old man nor myself will have any thing to do with the child. We were told your reverence wanted it, and we believed it—that is all. There is the money; and now we are quits. As to being in the plot, we know nothing of those sorts of tricks; and I ask pardon of your reverence, but you must be jesting with us when you speak of such a thing. I must now return home. We have some pilgrims stopping with us, who are returning from their *vow*, and thirsty souls they are! Your reverence's humble servant."

And the old woman made many curtseys and retired; then coming back:

"I forgot one thing," said she; "the child is to be called Angela, in Italian. Ah! by my faith, I forget the word."

"Angiolina, Anzoleta?" said Consuelo.

"That's it, precisely," said the old woman, and, again saluting the canon, she calmly retired.

"Well, what do you think of this trick?" said the stupified canon, turning toward his guests.

"I think it worthy of her who imagined it," replied Consuelo, taking the child, who began to be uneasy, from the basket, and gently making it swallow some spoonfuls of the milk which was left from breakfast, and which was still smoking in the canon's china ewer.

"This Corilla must be a heartless wretch, then!" resumed the canon; "do you know her?"

"Only by reputation; but now I know her thoroughly, and so do you, reverend sir."

"It is an acquaintance I could very well have dispensed with. But what shall we do with this poor little deserted one?" added he, casting a look of pity on the child.

"I will carry it," replied Consuelo, "to your gardener's wife, whom I saw yesterday nursing a fine boy five or six months old."

"Do so, then," said the canon, "or rather ring and let her be sent for to come here and receive it. She will be able to tell us of a nurse in some neighboring farm-house —not too near though—for God knows the injury that might be done to a man of the church, by the least mark of interest shown toward a child fallen thus from the clouds as it were into his house."

"In your place, sir, I would raise myself above such paltry considerations. I would neither anticipate nor fear the absurd and malicious efforts of slander—I would disregard such foolish reports as if they did not exist. I would always act as if it were impossible they could affect or harm me. Of what use would be a life of innocence and dignity, if it did not secure us calmness of conscience and the liberty of doing good? See! this child is confided to you, reverend sir. If it suffers for want of care, far from your sight—if it languishes and dies—you will reproach yourself forever."

"What do you say? this infant confided to me? Have I accepted the trust, and can the caprice or craftiness of another impose such duties upon us? You are excited, my child, and you reason falsely."

"No, my dear and reverend sir," returned Consuelo, becoming more and more animated; "I do not reason falsely. The wicked mother who abandons her infant here, has no right and has no power to impose any duties upon you. But He who has the right to command you— He who decrees the destinies of the new-born babe—He to whom you will be eternally responsible—is GOD. Yes, it is God who has had especial views of mercy toward this innocent little creature, in inspiring its mother with the bold idea of intrusting it to you. It is He who by a strange concurrence of circumstances brings it into your house, and casts it into your arms in spite of your prudence. Ah! sir, remember the example of St. Vincent de Paul, who went about collecting poor distressed orphans from the door-steps of houses, and do not reject this little one which Providence brings to your bosom. I do indeed believe that were you to do so, it would bring you misfortune; and the world, which has a kind of instinct of justice even in its wickedness, would say, with some appearance of truth, that you had good reasons for removing it from you. Instead of which, if you keep it, no motives can be supposed other than the true ones—viz. your pity and your charity."

"You do not know," said the canon—a good deal shaken, and undecided how to act—" what the world is. You are a child, severe in rectitude and virtue. You do not know, especially, what the clergy are, and Bridget—the wicked Bridget—knew well what she said yesterday, when she asserted that certain people were jealous of my position and were striving to ruin me. I hold my benefices by the protection of the late Emperor Charles, who befriended me and was the means of my obtaining them. The Empress Maria Theresa has also protected me, and permitted me to pass as jubilary before the usual age. Well! what we imagine we hold from the Church is never positively assured to us. Above us, as well as above the sovereigns who favor us, we have always a master—the Church. As she declares us *capable* when she pleases, even when we are not so, she also declares us *incapable* when it suits her, even when we have rendered her the greatest services. The *ordinary*, that is to say, the diocesan bishop and his council, if they are unfriendly or irritated against us, can accuse us, bring us to their bar, judge us, and deprive us of our benefices—under pretext of misconduct, of irregularity of morals or scandalous examples—in order to confer upon their new creatures the gifts which they had formerly granted us. Heaven is my witness that my life has been as pure as that of this child, born yesterday! Well! without extreme prudence in all my proceedings, my virtue would not have been sufficient to defend me from evil interpretations. I am not much of a courtier toward the prelates; my indolence, and perhaps a little pride of birth, have always prevented me. There are those in the chapter who envy me and——"

"But you have on your side Maria Theresa, who is a high-souled monarch, a noble woman, and tender mother," returned Consuelo. "If she were then to judge you, and you should say to her with that accent which truth alone possesses, 'Gracious queen, I hesitated an instant between the fear of placing weapons against me in the hands of my enemies, and the necessity of practicing the first virtue of my calling, charity—I saw on one side calumnies and intrigues, under which I might fall; on the other, a poor creature abandoned by Heaven and by men, who had no refuge but in my pity, no protection but in my care—and I chose to risk my reputation, my repose, and my fortune, to do the works of faith and mercy!' Ah! I do not doubt if you spoke thus to Maria Theresa, that mighty princess, who is all-powerful, instead of a priory would give you a palace—instead of a canon would create you a bishop. Has she not overwhelmed the Abbé Metastasio with honors and riches for having made rhymes? What would she not do for virtue, if she thus rewards talent? Come, dear and reverend sir, you will keep this poor Angiolina in your house; your gardener's wife will nurse her, and afterward you will educate her in religion and virtue. Her mother would have made her a fallen spirit fit for punishment, you will make her an angel for heaven!"

"You do with me as you please," said the canon, deeply touched, and allowing his favorite to place the child on his knees. "Well, we will baptize Angela to-morrow, and you shall be godfather. If Bridget were still here, she would be godmother with you, and her rage at being selected for the office would amuse us. Ring and let the nurse be sent for, and may God's will be done! As to the purse which Corilla left us—(ha! fifty Venetian sequins, I see!)—we will have nothing to do with it. I take upon myself the present expenses of the infant, and her future lot, if she be not claimed. Take this gold, therefore; it is indeed your due for the singular virtue and the noble spirit you have manifested in the whole affair!"

"Gold to pay for my virtue and the goodness of my heart?" cried Consuelo, rejecting the purse with disgust. "And the gold of Corilla! the price of falsehood! Ah! sir, it sullies even the sight! Distribute it among the poor; that will bring good fortune to our poor Angela."

CHAPTER LXXXII.

FOR the first time in his life, perhaps, the canon that night scarcely closed his eyes. He left agitated by a strange emotion. His brain was flooded with chords, melodies, and modulations, which a light slumber interrupted every instant, and which, in every interval of awakening, he strove, in spite of himself and even with a kind of vexation, to recall and connect, without being able to succeed. He had retained by heart the most striking passages of the pieces which Consuelo had sung to him; he heard them still resounding in his brain—in his heart; and then suddenly the thread of the musical idea was broken in his memory at the most beautiful place, and he recommenced it mentally a hundred times in succession, without being able to proceed a single note further. In vain, fatigued by these imaginary melodies, did he try to drive them away; they returned always to haunt his ear, and it seemed to him that even the light of his fire danced, in time to the music, upon his curtains of crimson satin. The faint hissings which issued from the burning wood seemed also to be singing those cursed airs, the termination of which remained ever an impenetrable secret to the canon's fatigued imagination. If he could have only completed one, it seemed to him that he would have been delivered from this plague of faithless reminiscences. But the musical memory is so constituted, that it torments and persecutes us, until we have satisfied it with that for which it thirsted.

Never had music made such an impression upon the canon, although he had been a distinguished dilettante all his life. Never had human voice so completely taken possession of his heart as that of Consuelo. Never had features and expression, never had language and manners, exercised upon his soul a fascination in the least to be compared with that which Consuelo's had exercised upon him during the last thirty-six hours! Did the canon guess, or did he not, the sex of the pretended Bertoni? Yes and no. How shall I explain this to you? You must know that at fifty the canon's thoughts and habits were as pure and blameless as those of a child. His independent position had allowed him to cultivate friendship, tolerance, and the arts; but love was forbidden him, and he had banished love from his heart, as the most dangerous enemy of his repose and his fortune. Still, as love is of a divine origin, and immortal in its nature, when we believe we have annihilated it, we have done nothing more than bury it alive in our hearts. It may sleep there silently for long years, until the day when it is destined to be reanimated. Consuelo appeared in the autumn of the canon's life, and his long apathy of soul was changed at once into a tender languor, more profound and tenacious than could have been foreseen. That apathetic heart knew not how to bound and palpitate for a beloved object ; but it could melt as ice before the sun, give itself up to the abandonment of self, to patient submission, and that kind of passive self-denial which one is sometimes surprised to find in the most selfish, when love has taken possession of their hearts.

He loved then, this poor canon; at fifty, he loved for the first time, and he loved one who could never respond to his love. He was only too sensible of this, and this was why he wished to persuade himself, in spite of all probability, that it was not love which he experienced, since it was not a woman who inspired it.

In this respect he deceived himself completely, and in all the simplicity of his heart he took Consuelo for a boy. While performing canonical duties at the cathedral of Vienna, he had seen many young and handsome boys at the foundation; he had heard voices clear, silvery, and almost female in their purity and flexibility. True, Bertoni's was purer and more flexible a thousand times, but it was an Italian voice, he thought, and then Bertoni was an exception to the usual routine of nature—one of those precocious children whose faculties, genius, and aptitude proclaim them prodigies. And, proud and enthusiastic at having discovered this treasure on the highway, the canon, giving way to the transports of a fatherly affection and benevolent pride, already dreamed of making him known to the world, of bringing him forward, and of contributing to his fortune and his future fame.

No one would have imagined the existence of such simple-minded and romantic ideas in a man of the canon's character—satirical, jocular, and well acquainted with the usages of society, and the springs of human character. There was nevertheless a whole world of ideas, instincts, and feelings, formerly unknown, now thronging his breast. He had fallen asleep in the joy of his heart, planning a thousand projects for his young protegé, promising himself that he would pass his life in the midst of a perfect atmosphere of delicious music, and feeling his heart moved at the idea of cultivating, while he tempered them a little, the virtues which shone in that generous and ardent soul ; but awakened every hour of the night by a singular emotion, pursued by the image of that wonderful child — now affrighted at the idea of seeing him escape from his already jealous tenderness, now impatient for the morrow to reiterate seriously the offers, promises, and prayers which Bertoni had appeared to take in jest—the canon, astonished at what passed in his mind, lost himself in a thousand fanciful conjectures. "Was I then destined by nature to have children, and to love them passionately?" asked he with an honest simplicity, "since the mere thought of adopting one throws me now into such a state of agitation ? Yet it is the first time in my life that this feeling has been revealed to my heart, and now, in a single day, admiration attaches me to one, sympathy to another, pity to a third ! Bertoni, Beppo, Angiolina! Here have I a family all of a sudden—I who pitied the trouble of parents, and who thanked God for being destined by my calling to solitude and repose. Can it be the quantity and excellence of the music I have heard to-day which so excites my ideas? It is rather that delicious Venetian coffee, of which I took two cups instead of one, out of pure gluttony! My brain has been so excited all day, that I have hardly once thought of my volkameria, withered from the effects of Peter's carelessness!

' Il mio cor si divide——'

"Ah! there again that cursed phrase recurs to me! plague take my memory!—What shall I do in order to sleep?—Four o'clock in the morning—it is unheard of!—I shall make myself ill!"

A bright idea came at last to the rescue of the good canon; he rose, took his writing-desk, and resolved to set to work on that famous book, so long since undertaken, but not yet begun. He was obliged, however, to consult the dictionary of canonical law, in order to refresh his memory on the subject, but he had not read two pages before his ideas became confused, his eyes closed, the book slid gently down from the eider-down cushion to the floor, the taper was extinguished by a sleepy sigh, and the worthy canon at last slept the sleep of the just until ten o'clock next morning.

Alas! how bitter was his awakening, when with a nerveless and careless hand he opened the following note, deposited by André upon the taper-stand along with his cup of chocolate!

"We depart, reverend and dear sir; an, imperious duty calls us to Vienna, and we feared lest we might not be able to resist your generous entreaties. We fly as if we were ungrateful; but we are not so, and never shall we lose the recollection of your hospitality toward us, and of your noble and Christian charity for the deserted infant. We shall come back to thank you for it. Before a week you will see us again; please defer till then the baptism of Angela, and depend upon the respectful and tender affection of your humble protegés,
"BERTONI, BEPPO."

The canon turned pale, sighed, and rang his bell. "Then they have gone?" said he to André.

"Before daybreak, your reverence."

"And what did they say on departing? I hope they

breakfasted, at least? Did they mention the day on which they would return?"

"Nobody saw them go, sir. They went as they came, over the wall. When I awoke, I found their chambers empty; the note which you hold in your hand was on their table, and all the doors of the house and inclosure were locked as I left them last night. They have not taken the value of a pin, they have not plucked even an apple, poor children!"

"I can readily believe it!" cried the canon, his eyes filling with tears. To dissipate his melancholy, André tried to induce him to consult the bill of fare and order dinner. "Give me what you please, André!" replied the canon in a heartrending voice, and fell back moaning on the pillow.

On the evening of the same day Consuelo and Joseph entered Vienna under cover of the darkness. The honest hairdresser, Keller, was admitted to their confidence, received them with open arms, and lodged his distinguished guest as well as his circumstances would permit. Consuelo was all amiability toward Joseph's betrothed, although secretly disappointed at finding her neither graceful nor handsome. On the morrow, Keller braided Consuelo's flowing tresses, and his daughter assisted her to resume the garments of her sex, and served her as a guide to Porpora's dwelling.

CHAPTER LXXXIII.

To THE joy which Consuelo experienced on once more pressing in her arms her master and benefactor, succeeded a painful feeling which she had some difficulty in concealing. A year had scarcely elapsed since she left Porpora, and yet that year of uncertainty, vexation, and sorrow, had imprinted on the gloomy brow of the maestro deep traces of suffering and old age. He had acquired that unhealthy *embonpoint* which inaction and languor of mind produce on a failing frame. His look had lost the fire which formerly animated it, and a certain bloated coloring of his features betrayed the fatal attempt to seek in wine the forgetfulness of his misfortunes, or the renewal of his inspiration, chilled by age and discouragement. The unfortunate composer had flattered himself that he should find at Vienna fresh chances of success and fortune; but he was received there with cold esteem, and he found his happier rivals in possession of the imperial favor and the admiration of the public. Metastasio had written dramas and oratorios for Caldara, for Predieri, for Fuchs, for Reuter, and for Hasse ; Metastasio, the court poet (*poeto Cesareo*), the fashionable author, the *new Albano*, the favorite of the muses and the ladies, the charming, the incomparable, the harmonious, the flowing, the divine Metastasio—in a word, he, of all the dramatic cooks, whose dishes had the most agreeable flavor and easiest digestion —had not written any thing for Porpora, and had refused to promise him any thing. The maestro had still ideas perhaps; he had at least his science, his admirable knowledge of the voice, his sound Neapolitan traditions, his severe taste, his broad style, and his bold and masculine recitatives, the grandeur and beauty of which had never been equaled. But he had no public, and he asked in vain for a poem. He was neither a flatterer nor an intriguer; his rough frankness created him enemies, and his ill-humor repulsed every body. He displayed this feeling even in the warm and affectionate welcome which he gave Consuelo.

"And wherefore did you leave Bohemia so soon?" said he, after having embraced her with paternal emotion. "What are you going to do here, unhappy girl? There are no ears to listen, no hearts to comprehend you ; this is no place for you, my child. Your old master has fallen into disgrace, and if you wish to succeed, you would do well to follow the example of those who feign to despise or not to know him, while they owe to him their skill, their fortune, and their glory."

"What! do you suspect me too?" said Consuelo, whose eyes filled with tears. "Would you deny my affection and devotion, and visit upon me the suspicion and contempt with which others have inspired you? Oh ! my dear master, you will find that I do not deserve this cruel reproach; it is all I can say."

Porpora knit his brow, turned away, and walked up and down the apartment. Then returning to Consuelo, and seeing that she wept, but not finding any thing mild or gentle to say to her, he took the handkerchief from her hands, and drying her eyes somewhat roughly, said :

"Come! come! now." Consuelo observed that he was pale, and that deep sighs burst from his ample chest; but he suppressed his emotion, and drawing his chair beside her:

"Come!" said he, "tell me about your sojourn in Bohemia, and wherefore you have returned so quickly. Speak!" he added, somewhat impatiently; "have you not a thousand things to say to me? Were you weary there, or did the Rudolstadts not act well by you? Yes, they also are capable of having wounded and tormented you! God knows they were the only people in the world whom I still trusted. God also knows that all men are capable of every wickedness!"

"Do not say so, my friend," said Consuelo; "the Rudolstadts are angels, and I ought never to speak of them but on my knees. But I thought it right to leave them, and to fly without even giving them warning or bidding them adieu."

"What does all this mean? Have you aught to reproach yourself with? Must I blush for you, and reproach myself for having sent you to these excellent people?"

"Ah! no; Heaven be praised, my dear master! I have no reason to blame myself, nor you to blush for me."

"In that case, what is it?"

Consuelo, who knew how necessary it was to give brief and prompt replies to Porpora when he was anxious to learn a fact or an idea, informed him in a few words that Count Albert had wished to marry her, but that she could not give him a decided answer before consulting her adoptive father.

Porpora made an angry and sarcastic grimace.

"Count Albert!" he exclaimed, "the heir of the Rudolstadts, the descendant of the kings of Bohemia, the future lord of Riesenburg? He wants to marry you, you little gipsy! You, the ugly pupil of the *scuola,* the friendless orphan, the penniless actress! You who, barefoot, have begged your bread in the thoroughfares of Venice?"

"Yes, even me, your pupil, your adopted daughter—yes, me, the Porporina!" replied Consuelo, with gentle pride.

"An honorable distinction and most brilliant condition!" said the maestro, bitterly. "Yes, I had forgotten those in the catalogue! The last and only pupil of a master without a school! The heiress of his rags and of his shame! The preserver of a name already blotted out from the memory of men. Yes, this is indeed something to be proud of—something to fascinate and bewilder the scions of the most illustrious families!"

"Apparently, my dear master," said Consuelo, with a melancholy and caressing smile, "we have not fallen so low in the estimation of the world as it pleases you to imagine, since it is certain that the count wished to marry me, and that I came here to ask your consent to the marriage, or your assistance and advice to enable me to avoid it."

"Consuelo," replied Porpora, in a cold and severe tone, "I like not such folly. You ought to be aware that I hate the romances of school-girls or the adventures of coquettes. I should never have believed you capable of entertaining such absurd ideas, and I am really ashamed to hear you speak of them. It is possible that the young Count of Rudolstadt may have take a fancy to you, and that wearied by the tedium of solitude, or carried away by his enthusiasm for music, he may have paid you some trifling attention. But how could you be so presumptuous as to take the affair seriously, and give yourself on the strength of it the airs of a heroine of romance? I can feel only pity for such conduct, and still more so, if the old count, the canoness, or the Baroness Amelia should be informed of your pretensions! I tell you again that I blush for you!"

Consuelo knew that it would be of no avail to contradict or interrupt Porpora when he had launched out into one of his splenetic tirades. She therefore allowed him full scope to vent his indignation; and when he had said every thing that he could think was most calculated to vex and annoy her, she related to him word for word, with the most scrupulous exactness, all that had taken place at the Castle of the Giants between herself, Count Albert, Count Christian, the canoness, Amelia, and Anzoleto. Porpora, who, after having vented all his spleen, knew also how to listen and to understand, lent the most serious attention to her narrative, and when she had finished, put several questions to her respecting details, so as to enter completely into the private life and the sentiments of the family. "In that case," said he at last, "you have acted well,

Consuelo. You have been prudent, straightforward, courageous, as I would have expected you to be. It is well; Heaven has protected you, and will recompense you by delivering you once for all from this infamous Anzoleto. As for the young count, you must not think of him; I positively forbid you. Such a union does not suit you. Never would Count Christian, be assured, permit you to become an artist again. I know better than you the unconquerable pride of the nobles. Unless you absurdly and childishly deceive yourself, you cannot hesitate for an instant between the career of the great and that of art. What think you? Speak! *Corpo di Bacco!* one would think you did not hear me!"

"I hear you very well, my dear master; but I see that you do not in the least understand what I have said to you."

"How? Not understand? Then I am no longer capable of understanding any thing, I suppose? Is that what you mean?" And the little jet-black eyes of the master sparkled with anger. Consuelo, who knew him thoroughly, saw that she must put a bold face on the matter, if she wished to be heard at all.

"Sir, you do not understand me," she replied firmly; "for you ascribe to me an ambition very different from that which I entertain. Be assured I do not envy the position of the great, and do not imagine, dear master, that any such considerations weighed with me for a moment. I despise those worldly advantages which are not the result of merit. These are the principles which you have instilled into me, and I shall never belie them. But there is in life something besides vanity and gold, and this something will always suffice to counterbalance the intoxication of glory and joys of public applause. It is the affection of such a man as Albert—it is domestic happiness—it is family joys! The public is a capricious, tyrannical, and ungrateful master, but a good husband is a friend, a support, a second self. If ever I love Albert as he loves me, I should think of fame no more, and probably should be much happier."

"What sort of babble is this?" exclaimed the maestro; "are you mad? or have you merely been initiated into the mysteries of German sentimentalism? Good Heavens! how much you have come to despise art of late, my lady countess! You tell me that your Albert, as you permit yourself to call him, inspires you with more fear that love; that you feel ready to expire with cold and terror at his side, and a thousand other things which—no offense to you—I did not pay much attention to; and now, free from his solicitations and completely at liberty—the only happiness, the only condition necessary to the development of the artist—you ask me if you must not again tie the stone about your neck and throw yourself into the well which your visionary lover inhabits! Go, in Heaven's name! if it seems good to you. I shall have nothing more to do with you; nothing more to say in the matter. I shall not lose my time talking to a person who does not know what she says, nor whom she wants. You have not common sense. I am your obedient humble servant."

Thus saying, Porpora proceeded to the harpsichord, and with a firm yet cold hand improvised several elaborate modulations, during which Consuelo, despairing of bringing him to examine the matter more closely, reflected on the best means of restoring his equanimity. She accomplished her purpose in singing some ancient national airs which she had learned in Bohemia, and which from their originality and genius delighted the old maestro. She then induced him to show her his recent compositions, and she sang them at sight with such perfection that he instantly regained all his enthusiasm and all his tenderness for her. The unhappy man having no longer an able pupil beside him, and distrusting all who approached him, had long ceased to enjoy the pleasure of hearing his ideas rendered by a fine voice, and understood by a lofty intellect. He was so moved by hearing himself thus rendered by his own docile Porporina, that he shed tears of joy, and pressing her to his bosom, he exclaimed:

"Ah! you are the first singer in the world! Your voice has doubled in volume and extent, and you have made as much progress as if I had given you lessons every day for a year. Repeat this theme once more, my daughter. This is the first moment of happiness I have enjoyed for months!"

They dined together, poorly enough, at a little table near the window. Porpora was badly lodged, his gloomy and neglected chamber looking out upon the angle of a narrow and deserted street. Consuelo seeing him in a good temper ventured to speak of Joseph Haydn. The only thing she had concealed from him was the long pedestrian excursion with this youth, and the strange occurrences which had created so close an intimacy between them. She knew that her master would according to custom rebel at praises given to any aspirant after fame. She therefore related with an air of indifference, that she had met on her way to Vienna with a poor little fellow who had spoken with such respect and enthusiasm of the school of Porpora, that she had promised to intercede in his behalf with the maestro herself.

"Well, what is he, this young man?" asked the maestro, "and what is his aim in life? To become an artist, without doubt, since he is a poor devil! Oh! I thank him for his patronage! I mean to teach singing henceforth only to young noblemen. They pay, learn nothing, and are proud of our lessons, because they flatter themselves they know something on leaving our hands. But artists? all mean, all ungrateful, all traitors and liars! Do not speak to me of them. I never wish to see one pass the threshold of this apartment. If one of them should show his face here, look you, I would throw him from the window that very instant!"

Consuelo endeavored to overcome his prejudices, but she found him so obstinate that she gave up the attempt, and leaning from the window, at a moment when her master had his back turned, she made one sign with her fingers, and afterwards a second, to Joseph, who was prowling about the street awaiting this previously arranged signal, and who understood from the first movement of the fingers that he must renounce all hope of being admitted by Porpora as a pupil, while the second gave him notice not to appear for half an hour.

Consuelo talked of something else to make Porpora forget what she had just said, and when the half-hour had elapsed, Joseph knocked at the door. Consuelo hastened to open it, pretended not to know him, and returned to announce to the maestro that it was a domestic who wished to enter his service.

"Let me see your face!" cried Porpora to the trembling young man; "approach! who told you that I wanted a servant? I do not want one."

"If you have no need of a servant," answered Joseph,

a little confused, but keeping a good countenance as Consuelo had recommended, "it is very unfortunate for me, sir, for I have great need of a master."

"One would imagine that nobody but I could give you the means of earning your livelihood," replied Porpora. "Here! look at my apartment and my furniture ; do you think I require a lackey to arrange all that?"

"Oh! certainly, sir, you must require one," returned Haydn, affecting a confiding simplicity ; "for it is in very bad order."

Saying so, he went immediately to work, and began to arrange the chamber with a diligence and business-like coolness which highly amused Porpora. Joseph staked all upon the hazard ; for if his zeal had not diverted the maestro, he ran the risk of being recompensed for his services by a few blows of his cane. "This is a droll rascal, who wishes to serve me in spite of myself," said Porpora, as he watched his proceedings. "I tell you, idiot, I have no means of paying a servant. Why will you continue to be so zealous?"

"No matter for that, sir ; provided you give me your old clothes and a bit of bread every day, I shall be satisfied. I am so poor that I should consider myself fortunate not to be obliged to beg my bread."

"But why do you not enter some rich person's service?"

"Impossible, sir ; they consider me too little and too ugly. Besides, I know nothing of music ; and you are aware that all the great lords nowadays wish their domestics to know a little of the violin or the flute, in order to take a part in chamber concerts. But, for my part, I have never been able to beat a note of music into my head."

"Ah! you know nothing of music? Well, you are the very man to suit me. If you are satisfied with your food and my old clothes, I will take you ; for, now I think of it, here is my daughter who will require a faithful lad to run her errands. Let us see! What can you do? Brush clothes, black shoes, sweep the house, open and shut the door?"

"Yes, sir, I know how to do all that."

"Well, begin. Brush that coat which you see lying on my bed yonder, for I am going in an hour to the ambassador's. You will accompany me, Consuelo. I wish to present you to Signor Corner, whom you know already, and who has just arrived from the Baths of Ems with the signora. There is a little apartment below which shall be yours; go and arrange your dress a little, while I also make some preparations."

Consuelo obeyed, crossed the ante-chamber, and entering the little gloomy cabinet which was to be her apartment, dressed herself in her eternal black gown and her faithful white neckerchief, which had made the journey on Joseph's shoulder. "This is not a very magnificent toilette for the ambassador's," thought she; "but they saw me make my début thus at Venice, and it did not prevent my singing well, and being listened to with pleasure.

When she was ready, she again passed into the ante-chamber, and there found Haydn gravely curling Porpora's wig, which he had hung upon a stick. On looking at each other, they both stifled a burst of laughter. "Ha! how do you manage to arrange that beautiful wig?" said she to him in a low voice, so as not to be heard by Porpora, who was dressing in the next chamber.

"Bah!" replied Joseph, "it is easy enough. I have often seen Keller at work! And besides, he gave me a lesson this morning, and will give me more, so that in time I may reach the perfection of the *lisse* and the *crepe.*"

"Take courage! my poor lad," said Consuelo, clasping his hand; "the maestro will at last be disarmed. The paths of art are strewed with thorns, but from among them you may pluck the fairest flowers!"

"Thanks for the metaphor, dear sister Consuelo. Be sure that I shall not be discouraged; and if, in passing me on the stairs or in the kitchen, you will say a word or two of encouragement and friendship to me from time to time, I shall bear all with pleasure."

"And I will assist you to fulfill your duties," replied Consuelo, smiling. "Do you imagine that I also did not commence like you? When I was little, I was often Porpora's servant. I have more than once run his errands, made his chocolate, and ironed his bands. Here now to begin, I will show you how to brush this coat, for you know nothing about it; you break the buttons and spoil the facing." And she took the brush from his hands, and set him an example with address and dexterity; but, hearing Porpora approach, she hastily handed the brush to him, and resumed a grave air as she said, "Come, come! my little fellow, make haste!"

CHAPTER LXXXIV.

It was not to the embassy of Venice, but to the ambassador's private residence, that Porpora conducted Consuelo. Wilhelmina, who did the honors of the mansion, was a beautiful creature, infatuated with music, and whose whole pleasure and ambition was to assemble at her house those artists and dilettanti whom she could attract there, without compromising by too much ostentation the diplomatic dignity of Signor Corner. At the appearance of Consuelo, there was at first a moment of surprise and doubt, then a cry of joy and cordiality, as soon as the company ascertained that it was indeed the zingarella who had made such a sensation the preceding year at San Samuel. Wilhelmina, who had seen her, when quite a child, trotting to her house behind Porpora, carrying his music and following him like a little dog, had cooled considerably toward her on seeing her afterward receive so much applause and homage in the saloons of the nobility, and so many wreaths upon the stage. It was not that this handsome creature was ill-natured, or that she deigned to be jealous of a girl so long considered frightfully ugly. But Wilhelmina liked to play the great lady, as all those do who are not so. She had sung grand pieces with Porpora (who, treating her as an amateur, had let her try every thing), while poor Consuelo was still studying that famous little manuscript in which the master had concentrated all his method, and to which he kept his real pupils for five or six years. Wilhelmina did not imagine therefore that she could feel for the zingarella any other sentiment than that of a charitable interest. But because she had formerly given her some sugar-plums, or put into her hands a picture-book to prevent her being wearied when waiting in her ante-chamber, she concluded that she had been one of the most efficient patronesses of the youthful songstress. She had therefore considered it very extraordinary and improper that Consuelo, having reached at one bound the highest pinnacle of triumph, had not shown herself humble, zealous, and grateful toward her. She had expected that whenever she happened to have a select and *récherché* party, Consuelo would graciously and gratuitously provide the entertainment of the evening, by singing for her, and with her, as often and as long as she desired, and that she could present her to her friends with all the *prestige* of having been mainly instrumental to her success, and having almost formed her taste for music. Matters had happened otherwise. Porpora, who had much more at heart the raising of his pupil Consuelo to the rank which belonged to her in the hierarchy of art, than that of pleasing his protectress Wilhelmina, laughed in his sleeve at the pretensions of the latter, and forbade Consuelo to accept the invitations—at first rather too familiar, afterward rather too imperious—of madam the ambassadress *of the left hand.* He found a thousand pretexts to excuse himself from taking her there; and Wilhelmina had thereupon taken a strange dislike to the débutante, even going so far as to say that she was not handsome enough ever to have undisputed success; that her voice, agreeable indeed in a saloon, wanted power and effect in the theater; that she did not fulfil upon the stage all the promise of her childhood; and a thousand other malicious remarks of the same kind, known in every age and country. But the enthusiastic clamor of the public soon smothered these little insinuations, and Wilhelmina, who piqued herself on being a good judge, a scientific pupil of Porpora, and a generous soul, did not venture to pursue this underhand war against the maestro's most brilliant pupil and the idol of the public. She joined her voice to those of the true dilettanti to exalt Consuelo, and if she still slandered her a little for the pride and ambition she had shown in not placing her voice at the disposal of *madam the ambassadress,* it was in a very low voice, and only to a very few particular friends that she thus blamed her.

On this occasion, when she saw Consuelo appear in her modest toilet of former days, and when Porpora presented her officially, which he had never done before, Wilhelmina, vain and frivolous as she was, forgave all, and took credit to herself for acting a great and generous part, as she kissed the zingarella on both cheeks. "She is ruined," thought she; "she has committed some folly, or lost her voice perhaps; for we have heard nothing of her for a long while. She returns to us unconditionally. Now is the proper moment to pity her, to protect her, and to put her talents to the proof, or to use them for my own profit."

Consuelo had so gentle and conciliating an air, that Wilhelmina, not finding in her that tone of haughty prosperity which she supposed her to have assumed at Venice, felt herself quite at ease with her, and paid her marked attention. Some Italians, friends of the ambassador, who were present, united with her in overwhelming Consuelo with praises and questions, which she succeeded in eluding with address and cheerfulness. But suddenly her countenance became grave, and even displayed symptoms of emotion, when, in the midst of a group of Germans who were gazing curiously at her from the extremity of the saloon, she recognized a face which had already troubled her elsewhere—that of the unknown friend of the canon, who had so minutely examined and questioned her, three days before, at the curate's of the village in which she had sung the mass with Joseph Haydn. This unknown person again examined her with extreme curiosity, and it was easy to see that he was questioning his neighbors respecting her. Wilhelmina remarked Consuelo's absence of mind. "You are looking at Mr. Holzbaüer?" said she. "Do you know him?"

"I do not know him," replied Consuelo, "and I am ignorant if it be he whom I am looking at."

"He is the first to the right of the mantelpiece," returned the ambassadress. "He is at present the director of the court theater, where his wife is prima donna. He abuses his position," added she, in a low voice, "in order to favor the court and city with his operas, which, between ourselves, are good for nothing. Do you wish me to introduce you to him? He is a very agreeable man."

"A thousand thanks, signora," replied Consuelo; "I am of too little consequence here to be presented to such a personage, and I am certain beforehand that he will not engage me for his theater."

"And why so, sweet one? Can that beautiful voice, which had not its equal in all Italy, have suffered by your residence in Bohemia? For you have lived all this time in Bohemia, they say—the coldest and dullest country in the world! Such a climate must be very hurtful to the voice and I am not astonished that you have experienced its bad effects. But that is nothing; you will soon recover your voice in our lovely Venetian clime."

Consuelo, seeing that Wilhelmina was determined to consider her voice as deteriorated, abstained from contradicting this opinion, especially as her companion furnished both question and answer. She was not agitated at this charitable supposition, but at the antipathy she had a right to expect from Holzbaüer, in consequence of the somewhat rude and rather too sincere answer respecting his music, which had escaped her at the breakfast in the presbytery. The court maestro would not fail to revenge himself by relating in what costume and in what company he had met her on the road; and Consuelo feared that if this adventure should reach Porpora's ears, it might prejudice him against her, and especially against poor Joseph.

It happened otherwise. Holzbaüer said not a word of the adventure, for reasons which will be known hereafter; and far from showing the least animosity toward Consuelo, he approached her with a good humored, though arch and meaning smile. She pretended not to understand it. She feared even to seem to request his secrecy in the matter, and whatever might be the consequences of this meeting she was too proud not to brave them firmly. Her attention was distracted from this incident by the countenance of an old man, who had a hard and haughty expression, but who nevertheless evinced a strong desire to engage in conversation with Porpora; but the latter, faithful to his crusty humor, hardly answered him, and every moment made an effort, or sought a pretext to get rid of him. "That," said Wilhelmina, who was not displeased to point out to Consuelo the celebrities who adorned her saloon, "is an illustrious composer, Buononcini. He has just arrived from Paris, where he himself played the violoncello in an anthem of his own composition before the king. You know that it is he who excited such enthusiasm in London, and who, after an obstinate contest of theater and theater with Handel, ended by vanquishing the latter in the opera."

"Do not say so, signora," said Porpora, who had just disengaged himself from Buononcini, and approaching the two ladies, had heard Wilhelmina's last words; "oh! do not utter such a slander! No one has surpassed Handel—

no one ever will surpass him. I know Handel; you do not yet know him. He is the first among us, and I confess it frankly, although I was foolish enough to struggle against him in my youth; I was crushed as I ought to have been, and it was right. Buononcini, more fortunate, but not more modest or skillful than myself, triumphed in the eyes and ears of fools and barbarians. Do not believe those who tell you of this triumph; it will be the eternal disgrace of my associate Buononcini, and England will one day blush for having preferred his works to those of a genius—what do I say?—of a giant, such as Handel. The mode—the *fashion,* as they say there—bad taste, the skillful arrangement of the theater, a clique, intrigues, and, more than all, the wonderful talent of the singers whom Buononcini brought to his aid, apparently gained the day. But Handel has had his revenge in sacred music. As to Buononcini himself, I do not place great store by him. I am not fond of jugglers; and Buononcini has juggled in the opera just as much as in the cantata."

Porpora alluded to a shameful theft which had put all the musical world in commotion; Buononcini having taken to himself in England the credit of a piece which Lotti had composed thirty years before, and which the latter had succeeded in triumphantly proving his own, after a long dispute with the audacious maestro. Wilhelmina endeavored to defend Buononcini, and this contradiction excited Porpora's spleen still more.

"I tell you, and I will maintain it," he exclaimed, without caring whether Buononcina heard him or not, "that Handel is superior, even in the opera, to all composers past or present. I shall prove it to you directly. Consuelo, seat yourself at the harpsichord, and sing the air I shall point out."

"I am dying to hear the wonderful Porporina," exclaimed Wilhelmina; "but I entreat that she may not make her début here in presence of Buononcini and Holzbaüer, by singing any thing of Handel's. They would not be flattered by such a selection."

"I believe it well," said Porpora. "It is their condemnation, their death-warrant."

"Well, in that case," replied she, "let her sing something of your own, maestro."

"You are aware, doubtless, that that would excite no

one's jealousy; but for my part, I wish that she should sing from Handel. I will have it so!"

"Do not ask me to sing to-day, master," said Consuelo; "I have just arrived from a long journey."

"Certainly it would be imposing on her good nature," said Wilhelmina, "and for my part I do not press her to sing. In presence of the judges who are here, and Holzbaüer in particular, who has the direction of the imperial theater, you must not compromise your pupil. Look you to it!"

"Compromise her? What are you dreaming of?" said Porpora, bluntly, shrugging his shoulders; "I heard her this morning, and I know whether she runs any risk before you Germans."

This contention was happily interrupted by the arrival of a new personage. Every one hastened to receive him, and Consuelo, who had seen and heard in her childhood at Venice this lean, effeminate-looking man, with his assuming manners and bravado air, although he was now old, faded, ugly, ridiculously frizzled, and dressed out with the bad taste of a superannuated Celadon, recognized on the instant, so well had she remembered him, the incomparable, the inimitable soprano, Caffarelli, or as he was more generally called Caffariello.

It would have been impossible to find a more impertinent self-conceited fool than this good Caffariello. The women had spoiled him with their flatteries, and the applause of the public had turned his brain. He had been so handsome, or rather so pretty in his youth, that he had made his début in Italy in female parts, but now when he was bordering on fifty, he appeared much older than he really was, as sopranos generally do, and one could not imagine him acting Dido or Galatea, without a great inclination to laugh. To make the matter worse, he affected the bravo, and at every turn raised his sweet, clear voice, without being able to change its expression. There was, nevertheless, something good under all this vanity and affectation. Caffariello felt his superiority too much to be amiable, but he was also too well aware of the dignity of the artist to be a servile flatterer. He held his own, however absurdly, with the highest personages, even with sovereigns, and therefore he was not liked by those whose flattery his own impertinence too severely criticised. The true lovers of art pardoned every thing on the score of his genius, and notwithstanding the baseness which was imputed to him in his private life, they were forced to admit that he displayed courage and generosity as an artist.

It was not voluntarily or deliberately that he had seemed ungrateful and neglectful toward Porpora. He recollected having studied eight years with him, and having learned from him all that he knew; but he remembered still better the day on which his master had said to him :

"I can now teach you nothing more ; *va, figlio mio, tu sei il primo musico del mondo.*"*

And from this day, Caffariello, who, after Farinelli, was really the finest singer in the world, ceased to trouble himself about any thing except himself.

"Since I am the greatest," said he to himself, "apparently I am the only one. The world has been made for me; Heaven has bestowed genius on poets and composers to enable Caffariello to sing. Porpora was thought the first master of singing extant, only because he was destined to form Caffariello. Now Porpora's work is ended, his mission is accomplished, and it is sufficient for his glory, his happiness, his fame, that Caffariello lives and sings."

Caffariello had lived and sung; he was rich and prosperous, Porpora was poor and neglected; but Caffariello was very easy on that head, and said to himself that he had amassed so much gold and so much fame, that his master should consider himself fully recompensed in having ushered such a prodigy into the world.

CHAPTER LXXXV.

CAFFARIELLO, on entering, saluted the company very distantly, but kissed Wilhelmina's hand tenderly and respectfully; after which he accosted his director, Holzbaüer, with an affable and patronizing air, and shook Porpora's hand with careless familiarity. Porpora, divided between his indignation at his pupil's ingratitude and the necessity of being civil—for, if Caffariello asked him to write an opera for the theater, and would take the first part, it would com-

---

* "Go, my son, thou art the first singer in the world."

pletely re-establish his affairs—began to compliment and question him somewhat maliciously on his recent triumphs in France, but in a tone of irony so guarded that Caffariello was not aware of his drift.

"France?" replied Caffariello; "do not speak to me of France! It is the country of paltry music, paltry musicians, paltry amateurs, and a paltry aristocracy. Only imagine a scoundrel like Louis XV, after having heard me in half-a-dozen admirable concerts, sending me by one of his lords—guess what? a miserable snuff-box!"

"But of gold, and ornamented with valuable diamonds, doubtless?" said Porpora, ostentatiously taking out his own box, which was of the commonest description.

"Oh, of course!" replied the soprano; "but mark the impertinence! no portrait! A mere snuff-box, as if I required one to use in that manner. Fie! What royal vulgarity! I was so indignant!"

"I hope," said Porpora, taking a pinch to refresh his malicious old nose, "that you gave the little king a lesson."

"Faith, I did not fail. I said to the gentleman who brought it—opening a drawer at the same time before his dazzled gaze—'There are thirty snuff-boxes, of which the meanest is thirty-fold more valuable than that which you offer me; and you perceive, besides, that other sovereigns have not disdained to honor me with their miniatures. Tell your master that Caffariello is not in want of snuff-boxes, Heaven be praised!"

"*Per Bacco!* you must have put the paltry monarch to the blush," replied Porpora.

"Wait! that is not all! The gentleman had the insolence to reply, that as regarded foreigners, his majesty gave his portrait only to ambassadors!"

"What a clown! And what did you say?"

"'Harkye, sir!' said I; 'learn that all the ambassadors in the world put together would not make one Caffariello!'"

"A most excellent reply! Ah! how well I recognize my Caffariello in such an answer! And you would not take the box?"

"No, by Jupiter!" replied Caffariello, drawing from his pocket, in an absent manner, a snuff-box set with brilliants.

"It was not that one, perchance, was it?" said Porpora, with a careless air. "But tell me, did you see our young Princess of Saxony there, her whom I placed at the harpsichord for the first time, when her mother the Queen of Poland honored me with her patronage? She was an amiable little princess."

"Maria Josephine?"

"Yes, the Grand Dauphiness of France."

"Did I see her? Oh, very frequently. She is an excellent creature—a perfect angel! On my honor, we are the best friends in the world. Stay! she gave me this!"

And he displayed an enormous diamond ring on his finger.

"But they say that she laughed immoderately at your reply to the king respecting his present."

"Undoubtedly! she thought I answered very well, and that the king her father-in-law had acted toward me like a pedant."

"She told you so? indeed?"

"She gave me to understand so, and sent me a passport which she had made the king sign with his own hand."

All who heard this dialogue turned aside to laugh in their sleeve. Buononcini, when speaking of Caffariello's braggadocio doings in France, had related, only an hour before, that the dauphiness, on sending him the passport dignified with the royal signature, had remarked to him that it was available only for ten days—a clear indication that he was to leave the kingdom with the least possible delay.

Caffariello, fearing perhaps lest he should be questioned respecting this circumstance, changed the conversation. "Well, my dear master," said he to Porpora, "have you brought out many pupils at Venice in these latter times? Have you produced any who promise well?"

"Do not speak to me of them!" replied Porpora. "Since yourself, Heaven has been avaricious and my school sterile. Since Porpora made Caffariello, he has crossed his arms, and has given himself up to weariness and disgust."

"My kind master!" returned Caffariello, charmed by this compliment, which he took entirely in earnest, "you are too indulgent to my imperfections. But nevertheless you had some pupils of promise when I saw you at the

Scuola dei Mendicanti. You had already formed there the little Corilla, who was approved of by the public! by my faith, a beautiful creature!"

"A beautiful creature, nothing more."

"Nothing more? are you serious?" asked Herr Holzbaüer, who listened with open ears.

"Nothing more, I assure you," replied Porpora, authoritatively.

"I am obliged to you for the hint," said Holzbaüer, in his ear. "She arrived here yesterday evening, very ill as I am told, and yet this very morning I received a proposal from her to enter the court treater."

"She is not what you want," returned Porpora. "Your wife sings ten times—better than she does!" He had almost said "less badly," but he corrected himself in time.

"Many thanks for your information," replied the manager.

"What! no other pupil than the plump Corilla?" resumed Caffariello. "Is Venice barren? I have a great mind to go there next spring with Madame Tesi."

"Why not?"

"But the Tesi is infatuated with Dresden. Can I not find some kitten to mew at Venice? I am not very difficult to please, nor is the public, when it has a *primo uomo* of my quality *to bear the weight* of the whole opera. A tolerable voice, docile and intelligent, would satisfy me for the duets. Ah! by the bye, master, what have you done with a little Moorish-looking girl I saw with you?"

"I have taught many Moorish-looking girls."

"Oh! but this one had a prodigious voice, and I remember I said to you when I heard her, 'There is a little fright who will make some noise in the world!' I even amused myself by singing something to her. Poor child! she shed tears of admiration and delight."

"Ah! ha!" said Porpora, looking at Consuelo, who turned as red as the maestro's rubicund nose.

"What the devil was she called?" resumed Caffariello. "A strange name—come; you must recollect her, maestro; she was ugly as sin."

"It was I," replied Consuelo, who, overcoming her embarrassment with frankness and cheerfulness, advanced and saluted Caffariello gaily, but at the same time respectfully.

Caffariello was not to be disconcerted by such a trifle.

"You?" said he quickly, taking her hand. "You are jesting; for you are a very handsome girl, and she of whom I speak——"

"Oh! it was I, indeed!" returned Consuelo, "Look at me well! You will easily recognize me. It is indeed the same Consuelo."

"Consuelo! yes, that was her devil of a name. But I do not recognize you in the least, and I fear much that they have changed you. But, my child, if, in acquiring beauty, you have lost the voice and talent you gave promise of, you would have done much better to have remained ugly."

"I want you to hear her!" said Porpora, who burned with impatience to display his pupil's talents before Holzbaüer. And he pushed Consuelo to the harpsichord, a little against her will, for it was a long time since she had encountered a learned audience, and she was by no means prepared to sing that evening.

"You are mystifying me," said Caffariello. "This is not the same person whom I saw at Venice."

"You shall judge," replied Porpora.

"Indeed, my dear master, it is cruel to make me sing, when I have still the dust of a long and fatiguing journey in my throat," said Consuelo, timidly.

"No matter—sing!" replied the maestro.

"Be not afraid of me, my child," said Caffariello, "I know what indulgence you require, and to encourage you, I will sing along with you, if you wish."

"On that condition I consent," replied she; "and the happiness I shall have in hearing you will prevent my thinking of myself."

"What can we sing together?" asked Caffariello of Porpora. "Do you choose a duet."

"Choose one yourself. There is nothing she cannot sing with you."

"Well, then, something in your style. I wish to gratify you to-day, my dear maestro, and besides, I know that the Signora Wilhelmina has all your music here, bound and gilded with oriental luxury."

"Ah!" grumbled Porpora between his teeth, "my works are more richly clad than I."

Caffariello took the books, turned over the leaves, and

chose a duet from the *Eumene*, an opera which the maestro
had written at Rome for Farinelli.   He sang the first solo
with that grandeur, that perfection, that *maestria*, which
made his hearers forget in an instant all his ridiculous
vanity, and left room in their minds only for admiration
and enthusiasm.   Consuelo felt herself animated and inspired with all the power of that extraordinary man, and
sang in her turn the soprano solo better perhaps than she
had ever sung before in her life.

Caffariello did not wait till she had finished, but interrupted her with rapturous applause. "Ah! *cara*," cried he
several times, " now I recognize you !   It is indeed the
wonderful child I remarked at Venice; but now, *figlia mia*,
you are a prodigy! it is Caffariello who tells it to you."

Wilhelmina was somewhat surprised and a little disconcerted to find Consuelo's success even greater than at
Venice.   In spite of the pleasure she felt at having such a
prodigy to produce in her saloons at Vienna, she saw herself, not without some degree of annoyance, silenced, and
unable, after such a virtuoso, to display her own feebler
powers to her guests.   She affected great admiration, however.   Holzbaüer, secretly gratified, but at the same time
fearing there would not be money enough in his coffers to
requite such abilities, preserved amid his praises a diplomatic reserve. Buononcini declared that Consuelo surpassed
even Hasse and Cuzzoni. The ambassador gave way to such
transports that Wilhelmina was terrified, especially when
she saw him take a large sapphire off his finger
and give it to Consuelo, who dared neither accept nor
refuse it.   The duet was rapturously encored, but at that
moment the door opened, and a lackey announced with respectful solemnity: " The Count Hoditz!"   Every one rose
with the instinctive deference which the world ever displays, not for the worthiest, not for the most illustrious,
but for the richest.

" It is very unfortunate," thought Consuelo, " that I
should meet here together, without any preparation, two
persons who have seen me on the road with Joseph, and
who doubtless have formed a false idea of my morals and
conduct.   No matter, I shall never deny, in heart or word,
whatever it may cost me, the friendship I feel for the excellent Joseph."

Count Hoditz, glittering with gold and embroidery, advanced toward Wilhelmina and kissed her hand. Consuelo saw at a glance, from his manner toward her, the difference between a lady of her description and the proud patrician dames of Venice. There was more gallantry and gaiety with Wilhelmina; but the conversation was louder, the company more noisy, nor did the guests refrain from crossing their legs, and standing with their backs to the fire. The company seemed to enjoy themselves the more from this want of formality; but there was something insulting in it, which Consuelo instantly felt and appreciated, although this something, concealed as it was by the habits of high life, and the respect due to the ambassador, was almost imperceptible.

Count Hoditz was remarkable for this delicate shade of manner, which, far from offending Wilhelmina, seemed to please her. Consuelo felt for this poor woman, whose gratified vanity only made her seem more an object of pity. As to herself, she was in nowise annoyed. A zingarella, she laid claim to no distinction, and it was of small importance to her whether a bow were deep or otherwise.

"I came here," thought she, "in my professional capacity, and so that I give my employers satisfaction, I am content to sit quiet in my corner; but this woman, who mingles love—if indeed there be love in the matter—with vanity, how she would blush could she witness the secret disdain and irony concealed under the ostentatious politeness and gallantry!"

Again she sang, and was applauded to the skies, literally sharing with Caffariello the honors of the evening. Every instant she expected to be saluted by Count Hoditz, and to be made the butt of some malicious pleasantry. But, strange to say, Count Hoditz never approached the instrument, toward which she had kept her face turned so that he could not see her features, and when he inquired her name and age, he seemed as if he had never heard of her before. The fact was, he had never received the imprudent note which Consuelo had so boldly addressed him by the deserter's wife. He was, moreover, short-sighted, and as it was not then usual to employ eye-glasses in private company, he discerned very imperfectly the pale features of the cantatrice. It may appear strange that, lover of the drama as he was, he had no curiosity to see more closely so remarkable a performer, but the reader must bear in mind that he loved only his own music, his own method, and his own singers. Great talents inspired him with no interest and no sympathy, and he rather loved to humble them and their pretensions. When he was told that Faustina Bordoni had made two thousand guineas a year in London, and Farinelli six thousand, he merely shrugged his shoulders, and said, "that for some twenty pounds a year he had singers in his theater at Roswald in Moravia, that were worth Farinelli, Caffariello, and Faustina put together."

Caffariello's pretensions and airs were particularly revolting and disagreeable to him, just because in his own sphere Count Hoditz had precisely the same defects. If boasters displease modest and retiring persons, they inspire other boasters with still more aversion and disgust. The vain detest the vain. While listening to Caffariello's singing, no person thought of Count Hoditz and his pretensions; and while Caffariello retailed his gossip, Count Hoditz had unhappily no scope for his. No saloon was sufficiently vast, no audience sufficiently attentive, to satisfy two men so devoured, to use the phrenological term of the day, with such a *love of approbation.*

A third reason prevented the Count Hoditz from recognizing the Bertoni of Passau, and that was that he had hardly looked at her at Passau, and even if he had, he would have had some difficulty in remembering her in her present change of costume. He had seen a tolerably handsome little girl, he had heard an agreeable and flexible voice, he had surmised an understanding susceptible of cultivation, but he felt nothing more, and he required nothing more for his theater at Roswald. Extravagantly rich, he was accustomed to buy without much examination every thing he took a fancy for. He had wished to purchase Consuelo's services, as we have seen, just as one would buy knives at Chatellerault or glassware at Venice. The bargain had not succeeded, and he thought nothing more of the matter, and experienced no regret. His serenity indeed had been a little ruffled on awaking at Passau and finding his pupils gone, but people who have so very high an opinion of themselves are not long dejected. They forget quickly, for is not the world their own, especially when they are rich? "One chance is lost," thought he, "but a hundred others remain." He whispered with Wilhelmina during the last piece which Consuelo sang, and seeing that Porpora darted looks of fiery indignation at him, he soon took his leave, having found little pleasure among these pedantic and ill-instructed musicians.

CHAPTER LXXXVI.

THE first impulse of Consuelo, on returning to her apartment, was to write Albert; but this was more easily said than done. In her first rough copy she had commenced to relate to him all the occurrences of her journey, when suddenly it occurred to her that she might affect him too violently by depicting the perils and fatigue which she had undergone. She remembered the sort of delirious frenzy which had taken possession of him when she recounted in the subterraneous grotto the terrors she had braved in order to reach him. She destroyed this letter therefore, thinking that so earnest and impressionable a being required the manifestation of some ruling and prominent idea, and resolved to omit the moving detail in order to express, were it only in a few words, the fidelity and affection which she had promised him. But these few words, if not precise and clear, would only arouse fresh apprehension, nor could she say that she experienced that deep-seated love and immovable resolve which would enable Albert to hope on with patience. Consuelo was all sincerity and honor, and could not stoop to utter an equivocation. She took her heart and conscience to task, and found, from the calmness which she experienced, that she had gained a complete victory over the remembrance of Anzoleto. She found also in her heart the most complete indifference toward every other man but Albert; but the sort of love and enthusiasm which she now experienced for him, was just the same that she had felt when beside him. It was not sufficient that the memory of Anzoleto should be banished, in order that Count Albert should become the object of a violent passion in her heart. Was she to be blamed for recalling poor Albert's malady, the dreary solemnity of the Castle of the Giants, the aristocratic prejudices of the canoness, the murder of Zdenko, the dreary cavern of the Schreckenstein — in short, all that strange and somber existence which, after having breathed the free air of the Böehmer Wald and enjoyed the melodies of Porpora, recurred to her memory as a frightful dream? Although she had opposed the maestro's cruel maxims as to an artist's career, she found herself in a mode of life so appropriate to her education, her intellectual faculties, and habits, that she no longer conceived it possible for her ever to become the Lady of Riesenburg.

What could she say then to Albert? What new promise or statement could she make? Was she not in the same state of irresolution, a prey to the same fear, as when she left the château? If she had come to take refuge at Vienna rather than elsewhere, it was because she was there under the safeguard of the only legitimate protection that had ever been vouchsafed to her. Porpora was her benefactor, her father, her support, her master, in the most religious acceptation of the word. Near him, she no longer felt herself an orphan, or recognized the right of disposing of herself according to the sole inspiration of her heart or her judgment. But Porpora blamed, ridiculed, and repelled with energy the idea of a marriage which he considered as the grave of her genius, as the immolation of a splendid career on the altar of romantic and childish affection. At Riesenburg, also, there was a generous, noble, and affectionate old man, who offered himself as a father to Consuelo, but can we change fathers according to the necessities of our position? And when Porpora said *no*, could Consuelo accept Count Christian's *yes?*

That neither could nor ought to be, and she felt she must wait for the decision of Porpora, when he had better examined the facts of the case and the feelings of the different parties concerned. But while waiting for this confirmation or reversal of his judgment, what could she say to the unhappy Albert — how give him sufficient hope to enable him to wait her decision with patience? To acquaint him with the first storm of Porpora's dissatisfaction, would be to overthrow all his security ; to conceal it was to deceive him, and Consuelo could not bring herself to practice the least dissimulation toward him. Had the noble young man's life depended on a falsehood, Consuelo would not have spoken that falsehood, There are some beings whom we respect too much to deceive, even in saving them.

She began again, therefore, and destroyed twenty letters when scarcely commenced, without being able to decide on continuing a single one. In whatever manner she made the attempt, at the third word she always fell into a rash assertion or a doubt which might produce evil effects. She went to bed, overpowered by fatigue, sorrow, and anxiety, and lay long awake, shivering with cold, without being able to come to any resolution, or to trace out any fixed plan for her future career. At last she fell asleep, and remained in bed so late that Porpora, who was an early riser, had already departed on his rounds. She found Haydn busy as on the previous day brushing the clothes and arranging the furniture of his new master. "Welcome, fair sleeper," cried he on seeing his friend appear at last, "I die of ennui, of sadness, and especially of fear, when I do not see you appear, like a guardian angel, between that terrible professor and me. It seems as if he were always about to penetrate my intentions, to discover the plot, and shut me up in his old harpsichord to perish there of harmonic suffocation. He makes my hair stand on end, your Porpora; and I cannot persuade myself that he is not an old Italian demon, the evil spirits of that country being known to be much more wicked and crafty than our own."

"Be reassured, my friend," replied Consuelo; "our master is only unhappy, he is not ill-natured. Let us begin by bestowing our utmost care to procure him a little happiness, and we shall soon see him soften and return to his true character. In my childhood I have seen him cordial and cheerful; he was even noted for the wit and gaiety of his repartees. But at that period he was successful; he had friends and hope. If you had known him at the time when his *Polyphemus* was sung at the St. Moses theater, when he took me on the stage with him and placed me in the wing, from which I could see the back scenes and the head of the giant! How beautiful and yet how terrible all that seemed to me from my little corner! Crouching behind a rock of pasteboard, or clambering upon a lamp-ladder, I hardly breathed, and involuntarily I imitated with my head and my little arms all the gestures and motions which I saw the actors make. And

when the maestro was recalled .seven times before the curtain, I imagined that he was a god! He was grand, he
was majestic, in such moments! Alas! he is not yet very
old, and yet so changed, so cast down! Come, Beppo, let
us to work, that on his return he may find his poor lodging a little more agreeable than when he left it. In the
first place I will make an inspection of his clothes to see
what he wants."

"What he wants will make rather a long catalogue, and
what he has a very short one," replied Joseph, "for I
don't know that my wardrobe is in a much worse condition."

"Well! I shall take care to furnish yours also; for I am
your debtor, Joseph; you fed and clothed me during our
entire journey. But let us first think of Porpora. Open
that press. What! only one suit? that which he wore
yesterday at the ambassador's?"

"Alas! yes, a maroon suit with cut steel buttons, and
that not very new either! The other suit, which is old
and miserably ragged, he put on to go out; and as to his
dressing-gown, I don't know if he ever had one; at all
events I have hunted an hour for it in vain."

Consuelo and Joseph having searched in every corner,
ascertained that Porpora's dressing-gown was a chimera of
their imagination, as well as his overcoat and muff. Taking an inventory of the shirts, they found there were but
three, in tatters, the ruffles all in rags, and so of all the
rest. "Joseph," said Consuelo, "here is a beautiful ring
which was given me yesterday evening in payment for my
songs; I do not wish to sell it, that would draw attention
to me, and perhaps prejudice the doners against what they
would consider my avarice, but I can pawn it, and borrow
on its security the money which is necessary for us.
Keller is honest and intelligent; he will know the value of
this jewel, and must certainly be acquainted with some
broker who will advance me a good sum on the deposit.
Go, and return quickly."

"It will not take long," replied Joseph. "There is a
sort of Israelitish jeweler who lives in Keller's house, and
as he is well accustomed to transact such matters for some
of our court ladies, he will have the money with you in
half an hour; but I want nothing for myself, you understand, Consuelo! You, however, whose equipment made

the whole journey on my shoulder, have great need of a new toilet, and you will be expected to appear to-morrow, perhaps this very evening, in a dress a little less rumpled than this is."

"We shall settle our accounts by and bye, and as I please, Beppo. As I did not refuse your services, I have a right to demand that you do not refuse mine. Now run to Keller's."

In less than an hour Haydn returned with Keller and fifteen hundred florins. Consuelo having explained her intentions, Keller disappeared again and soon came back with one of his friends, a skillful and expeditious tailor, who, having taken the measure of Porpora's coat and other parts of his dress, engaged to bring in a few days two other complete suits, a good wadded dressing-gown, as well as linen and other articles necessary for the toilet, which he promised to order from work-women whom he could recommend.

"In the meantime," said Consuelo to Keller, when the tailor had gone, "I wish to have the greatest secrecy observed respecting all this. My master is as proud as he is poor, and he would certainly throw my poor gifts out of the window if he ever suspected that they came from me."

"How will you manage, then, signora," observed Joseph, "to make him put on his new clothes and abandon his old ones without remarking the change ?"

"Oh, I understand his ways, and I promise you that he will not perceive it. I know how to manage him."

"And now, signora," resumed Joseph, who, except when tête-à-tête, had the good taste to address his friend very ceremoniously, in order not to give a false opinion of the nature of their friendship, "will you not think of yourself also? You brought scarcely any thing with you from Bohemia, and your dresses, moreover, are not fashionable in this country."

"I had almost forgotten that important affair. Good Mr. Keller must be my counselor and guide."

"Oh !" returned Keller, "I understand; and if I do not procure you a most tasteful wardrobe, I shall give you leave to call me ignorant and presumptuous."

"I will trust to you, my good Keller, and will only observe in general, that my taste is simple, and that very gay dresses and decided colors do not agree with my habitual paleness of complexion and quiet manners."

"You do me injustice, signora, in supposing that I require such a warning. Am I not obliged from my calling to know what colors correspond to particular complexions and style of features, and do I not see from yours what will suit you. Rest easy; you shall be satisfied with me, and in a short time you can appear at the court if you please without ceasing to be as modest and simple as you now are. To adorn the person, and not to change it, is the art of the hairdresser and of the milliner."

"Another word, dear Mr. Keller," said Consuelo, drawing the hairdresser aside. "You will also have Master Haydn dressed anew from head to foot, and with the rest of the money you will offer to your daughter, from me, a beautiful silk dress for the day of her wedding with him. I hope it will not be long delayed; for if I am successful here, I can be useful to our friend, and help him to make himself known. He has talent, great talent, be assured of that."

"Has he really, signora, I am happy to hear you say so. I have always thought so. What do I say?—I was sure of it from the first day I remarked him, quite a little boy, in the choir of the cathedral."

"He is a noble youth," returned Consuelo, "and you will reap an ample reward in his gratitude and loyalty for all that you have done for him, for you also, Keller, as I know, are a worthy man and possess a noble heart. In the meantime," added she, approaching Joseph along with Keller, "tell us if you have already done what we agreed upon respecting Joseph's protectors. The idea came from you; have you put it in execution?"

"Have I done so, signora?" replied Keller; "to say and to do are one and the same thing with your humble servant. On going to dress my customers this morning, I first informed his excellency the Venetian ambassador (I have not the honor to dress his own hair, but I curl his secretary), then the Abbé Metastasio, whom I shave every morning, and Mademoiselle Marianna Martinez, his ward, whose head is also intrusted to my care. She lives, as he does, in my house—that is to say, I live in their house—but no matter! Lastly, I saw two or three other persons who likewise know Joseph's face, and whom he is exposed to meet at Master Porpora's. Those who were not my customers, I visited under some pretext or other, such as the following: 'I have been informed that Madame the Baroness has sent to some of my neighbors for genuine bear's grease for the hair, and I have hastened to bring her some which I can warrant. I offer it gratis to distinguished personages as a sample, and only ask their custom for the article if they are pleased with it,' or else: 'Here is a prayer-book which was found at St. Stephen's last Sunday, and as I dress the hair of the cathedral (that is to say, of the scholars), I have been requested to ask your excellency if this book does not belong to you.' This book was an old worm-eaten concern of gilt and blazoned leather, which I had taken from the stall of some canon or other, knowing that no one would claim it. In fine, when I had succeeded in making myself heard under one pretext or another, I commenced to chat with that ease and spirit which is tolerated in persons of my profession. I said, for example: 'I have often heard your lordship spoken of by one of my friends who is a skillful musician, Joseph Haydn. It was this that emboldened me to present myself in your lordship's honorable mansion.' 'What!' they said to me, 'little Joseph? a charming performer, a young man of great promise.' 'Ah! truly!' replied I, enchanted to come to the point, 'your lordship will be amused by the singular and advantageous position in which he is at this moment placed.' 'What has happened to him then? I have heard nothing of it.' 'Oh! there can be nothing more comical and at the same time more interesting! He has become a valet-de-chambre!' 'How? a valet? Fie! what a degradation, what a misfortune, with so much talent as he possesses! Then he is very poor? I will certainly assist him.' 'It is not on that account, your lordship,' replied I; 'it is the love of art which has made him adopt this singular resolution. He was most anxious at any sacrifice to procure the lessons of the illustrious master Porpora.' 'Ah! yes, I know that, and Porpora refused to hear him and admit him. He is a very fanciful and most morose man of genius.' 'He is a great man, a great heart,' replied I, according to the instructions of the Signora Consuelo, who in all this does not wish her master to be blamed or ridiculed. 'Be assured,' added I, 'that he will soon recognize little Haydn's genius, and will bestow on him all his care ; but, not to irritate his gloomy temper, and to obtain admittance to his house without exciting his anger, Joseph has hit upon nothing more ingenious than to enter his service as valet, and to pretend the most complete ignorance of music.' 'The idea is touching, charming,' replied they, quite moved; 'it is the heroism of a real artist; but he must hasten to obtain the good grace of Porpora before he is recognized and mentioned to the latter as an already well-known artist; for young Haydn is liked and protected by some persons who frequently visit at Porpora's house.' 'But those persons,' said I then, with an insinuating air, 'are too generous, too high-minded, not to keep Joseph's little secret for him, and even to dissemble a little with Porpora in order to preserve his confidence in him.' 'Oh,' cried they, 'I certainly will not be the one to betray the good and learned Joseph, and I shall forbid my people to drop an imprudent word which might find its way to the maestro's ears.' Then they sent me away with a trifling present, or an order for bear's grease, and as for the gentleman secretary of the embassy, he was greatly interested in the adventure, and promised to entertain Signor Corner with it at breakfast, in order that he, who is a particular admirer of Joseph's, may be the earliest on his guard with Porpora. Thus my diplomatic mission has been fulfilled. Are you satisfied, signora?"

"If I were a queen, I would appoint you my ambassador on the spot," replied Consuelo. "But I see the maestro returning. Fly, dear Keller, do not let him see you!"

"And why should I fly, signora? I will begin to dress your hair, and it will be supposed you sent your valet Joseph for the nearest hairdresser."

"He has more wit a hundred times than we," said Consuelo to Joseph; and she abandoned her ebon tresses to the skillful hands of Keller, while Joseph resumed his duster and apron, as Porpora heavily ascended the staircase humming an air of his forthcoming opera.

CHAPTER LXXXVII.

As HE was naturally very absent, Porpora, on kissing the forehead of his adopted daughter, did not even remark Keller, who had possession of her hair, and began to search in his music for the written fragment of the air which was running through his brain. On seeing his papers, usually scattered upon the harpsichord in indescribable disorder, ranged in symmetrical piles, he roused himself from his reverie and exclaimed:

"Wretch that he is! He has had the impertinence to touch my manuscripts! These valets are all alike! They think they arrange when they heap up! I had great need, by my faith, to take a valet. This is the commencement of my punishment."

"Forgive him, master," replied Consuelo; "your music was in a perfect chaos——"

"I knew my way in that chaos! I could get up at night and find any passage in my opera by feeling in the dark; now I know nothing about it; I am lost, it will cost me a month's hard work to put it to rights again."

"No, master, you will find your way at once. Besides, it was I who committed the fault, and although the pages were not numbered, I believe I have put every sheet in its place. Look! I am sure you will be able to read more easily in the book I have made, than in all those loose sheets which a gust of wind might carry out of the window."

"A gust of wind! Do you take my chamber for the lagunes of Fusina?"

"If not a gust of wind, at least a stroke of the duster, or a sweep of the broom."

"But what need was there to sweep and dust my chamber? I have now lived here a fortnight and have never let any one enter it."

"That was plain enough, indeed," thought Joseph.

"Well, master, you must allow me to change that habit. It is unhealthy to sleep in a chamber which is not aired and cleaned every day. I will undertake myself to arrange your papers every day in the exact order in which they were before Beppo commenced to sweep."

"Beppo? Beppo? who is Beppo? I know no Beppo."

"There is Beppo," said Consuelo, pointing to Joseph. "He has a name so difficult to pronounce that you would have been shocked by it every instant. I have given him the first Venetian name I thought of. Beppo is a good name; it is short, and can be sung."

"As you will!" replied Porpora, who began to soften on turning over the leaves of his opera and finding it arranged with exactness, and stitched in a single book.

"Confess, master," said Consuelo, seeing him smile, "that it is more convenient so."

"Ah! you wish to be always in the right," returned the maestro. "You will be obstinate all your days."

"But, master, have you breakfasted?" resumed Consuelo, whom Keller had now restored to liberty.

"Have you breakfasted yourself?" replied Porpora, with a mixture of impatience and solicitude.

"Oh! yes. And you, master?"

"And this boy, this—Beppo, has he eaten any thing!"

"He has breakfasted. And you, master?"

"Then you found something here? I did not remember that I had any provisions."

"We have breakfasted very well. And you, master?"

"And you, master! And you, master! Go to the devil with your questions. What is it to you?"

"You have not breakfasted, my dear master," replied Consuelo, who sometimes permitted herself to treat Porpora with Venetian familiarity.

"Ah! I see plainly that some wicked spirit has entered my house. She will not let me be quiet! Come here now, and sing this air for me. Attention, I beseech you."

Consuelo seated herself at the harpsichord and sung the air, while Keller, who was a decided dilettante, remained at the other end of the chamber, with comb in hand and mouth half open. The maestro, who was not satisfied with his air, made her repeat it thirty times in succession, sometimes making her lay the emphasis upon certain notes, sometimes upon certain others, seeking for the shade he dreamed of, with an obstinacy that could only be equaled by Consuelo's patience and docility.

In the meanwhile, Joseph, upon a signal from the latter, had gone to get the chocolate which she herself had prepared during Keller's absence. He brought it, and guessing the intentions of his friend, placed it softly upon the music-desk without attracting the notice of the master, who, an instant afterward, took it mechanically, poured it into the cup, and swallowed it with great appetite. A second cup was brought and swallowed in the same manner with a supply of bread and butter; and Consuelo, who was a little mischievous, said to him, on seeing him eat with pleasure:

"I knew, master, that you had not breakfasted."

"It is true," replied he, without evincing any anger; "I think I must have forgotten it. That often happens to me when I am composing, and I do not recollect it till later in the day, when I have gnawings at my stomach and spasms."

"And then you drink brandy, master?"

"Who told you so, you little fool?"

"I found the bottle."

"Well! what is that to you? You are not going to forbid me brandy?"

"Yes, I shall. You were temperate at Venice and you always enjoyed good health."

"That is the truth," said Porpora, sadly. "It seemed to me that every thing went badly there, and that here it would be better. Nevertheless every thing goes on from bad to worse with me. Fortune, health, ideas—every thing!" And he dropped his head on his hands.

"Shall I tell you why you find a difficulty in working here?" returned Consuelo, who wished to distract his thoughts, by matters of detail, from the desponding humors that weighed him down. "It is because you have not your good Venetian coffee, which gives so much strength and spirits. You excite yourself after the manner of the Germans with beer and liquors; that does not agree with you."

"Ah! that is also the truth. My good Venetian coffee! It was an inexhaustible source of witty phrases and great ideas. It was genius, it was wit, which flowed through my veins with gentle warmth. Every thing that I drink here makes me sad or crazy."

"Well, master, return to your coffee!"

"Coffee? here? I won't have it. It gives too much trouble. You need a fire, a maid-servant, a coffee-pot which has to be washed and moved about, and gets broken, making a most discordant noise in the midst of a harmonious combination! No, no! My bottle on the floor, between my legs; that is more convenient and sooner done."

"That is sometimes broken too. I broke it this morning, when I was going to put it into the wardrobe."

"You have broken my bottle! I don't know what hinders me, you little fright, from breaking my cane over your shoulders."

"Pshaw! you've been saying that to me for fifteen years, and yet you have never given me a single slap. I am not at all afraid."

"Chatterbox! will you sing? will you get me out of this cursed air? I would wager you do not know it yet, you are so absent this morning,"

"You shall see," said Consuelo, quickly shutting the book. And she sang the air as she conceived it, that is to say, differently from Porpora. Knowing his temper, although she had seen plainly from the first attempt that he had become confused in his ideas, and that he had consequently given it a labored and unnatural turn, she had not permitted herself to give him any advice. He would have rejected it from the spirit of contradiction, but by singing the air in' her own manner, while pretending all the while to make a mistake of memory, she was very sure he would be struck by it. Hardly had he heard it, than he bounded from his chair, clapping his hands and exclaiming:

"That is it! that is it! that is what I wanted, and what I could not find. How the deuce did it come to you?"

"Is it not what you have written? or can I by chance —— But no, that is certainly your phrase."

"No, it is yours, you cheat!" cried Porpora, who was candor itself, and who, notwithstanding his diseased and immoderate love of glory, would never have appropriated anything from vanity; "it was you who found it! Repeat it to me. It is good and I will profit by it."

Consuelo recommenced several times, and Porpora wrote from her dictation; then he pressed his pupil to his heart, saying, "You are a fairy! I always thought you were a fairy!"

"A good fairy, believe me, master," replied Consuelo, smiling.

Porpora, delighted at having found out what he wanted,

after a whole morning of fruitless disturbance and musical torment, sought mechanically on the floor beside him for the neck of the bottle, but not finding it, he felt about upon the desk and swallowed what he happened to find there. It was delicious coffee which Consuelo had skillfully and patiently prepared at the same time as the chocolate, and which Joseph had just brought in piping hot, at a fresh signal from his friend.

"Oh! nectar of the gods!—Oh! tutelary genius of musicians!" exclaimed Porpora as he sipped it; "what angel, what fairy brought thee from Venice under his wing?"

"It was some sprite," replied Consuelo.

"Thou art at once angel and fairy, my child," said Porpora, mildly, returning to his desk. "I see that you love me, care for me, and would make me happy. Even this poor youth feels an interest in me," he added as he perceived Joseph standing at the threshold of the outer chamber, and looking at him with moistened eyes. "Ah! poor children, you wish to cheer my unhappy life! Foolish creatures, you know not what you do. I am fated to be solitary and miserable, and a few brief days' sympathy and happiness will only make me feel more sensibly my wretched fate when they are fled."

"I shall never leave you—I will be always your daughter and servant," said Consuelo, throwing her arms round his neck. Porpora bent his aged head over the paper before him, and burst into tears. Consuelo and Joseph wept also; and Keller, whose passion for music had kept him spell-bound, and who, to give a color to his delay, had busied herself in arranging the master's periwig, seeing, through the half-open door, this affecting picture of grief, Consuelo's filial piety, and Joseph's enthusiasm, let fall his comb, and in his agitation mistaking Porpora's wig for a handkerchief, rubbed his eyes with it in a distracted manner.

Consuelo was confined to the house for some days by a cold. During her long and adventurous journey she had braved every vicissitude of weather, and all the changes of the autumn—sometimes burning, sometimes wet and cold, according to the regions which she traversed. Lightly clothed, a straw hat upon her head, and having neither cloak nor coat to change when her garments were wet, she had never sustained the least injury; but hardly was she shut up in Porpora's dark, damp, and badly aired abode, than she felt cold, and indisposition paralyzed her energy and her voice. Porpora was out of sorts at this untimely occurrence. He knew that to obtain an engagement for his pupil at the theater, he must lose no time, for Tesi, who had wished to go to Dresden, afterward hesitated, owing to the intreaties of Caffariello, and the brilliant promises of Holzbaüer, who were desirous to secure so celebrated a singer for themselves. On the other hand, Corilla, still confined to bed, was intriguing with the directors through such of her friends as she found at Vienna, and declared she would be able to appear in eight days should they require her services. Porpora devoutly wished that Consuelo should be engaged, as well for her own sake, as for that of his forthcoming opera.

Consuelo on her part did not know what to resolve. To accept an engagement was to protract the possibility of her union with Albert, was to carry terror and consternation into the family of the Rudolstadts, who certainly did not expect she would resume the career of the stage; it would be to renounce the honor of the connection, and make known to the young count that she preferred glory and liberty to him. On the other hand, by refusing this engagement she would destroy the last hopes of Porpora, and evince in her turn the ingratitude which had been the despair and misery of his life: it would be a dagger-stroke to his happiness. Consuelo, terrified at this dilemma, and seeing that whatever part she took she would inflict a mortal blow, fell into a deep melancholy. Her vigorous constitution preserved her indeed from serious illness; but during this fit of anguish and terror, preyed on by alternate chill and fever, crouching over a miserable fire, or dragging herself from chamber to chamber, to attend to domestic duties, she secretly wished and hoped that some serious malady might free her for a time from the duties and difficulties of her situation.

Porpora's temper, which had been softened for a moment, became once more gloomy, querulous, and inquiet when he saw Consuelo, his hope and stay, become sorrow-stricken and irresolute; instead of supporting and animating her with enthusiasm and tenderness, he manifested a morbid impatience which completed her dismay. Alternately weak and violent, the tender and irritable old man, devoured with that spleen which was in a short time to inflict a fatal blow on Jean Jacques Rousseau, saw on all sides enemies, persecutors, and ingrates, without being aware that his suspicions, his anger, and his false accusations furnished a pretext for the evil intentions and misconduct which he ascribed to them. The first impulse of those whom he thus mortified was to look upon him as mad; the second to believe him ill-natured and malicious ; the third to have nothing to say to him, or to study revenge. Between cowardly submission and savage misanthropy there is a happy medium which Porpora never dreamed of, and which he certainly never realized.

Consuelo, after making several vain efforts, seeing that he was less disposed than ever to hear of love or marriage, resolved no longer to provoke explanations which merely served to sour her unfortunate master more and more. She never mentioned Albert's name, and held herself ready to sign any engagement that might be proposed by Porpora. It was only when she was alone with Joseph that she experienced some solace in opening her heart to him.

" What a strange destiny is mine!" she said to him frequently. " Heaven has gifted me with talents, a soul for art, a love of liberty, and of a proud and lofty independence; but, at the same time, instead of that fierce selfishness which imparts the necessary firmness to meet the unavoidable difficulties and seductions of life, the same celestial power has implanted in my breast a tender and sensitive heart, which beats only with affectionate emotion. Thus divided between two opposing impulses, my existence is annihilated, and my prospects destroyed. If I am born for devotion, may the Almighty blot out from my soul that love for art, for poetry, and that desire for liberty, which is an agony and a torment; but if I am born for art and for liberty, let Him then take away that pity, that devotion, that anxiety, and fear of giving offense, which will ever poison my triumphs and embarrass my career."

" If I had any advice to give you, my poor Consuelo," said Haydn, " it would be to listen to the voice of genius, and to stifle the impulses of your heart ; but now I know your position, and I know that you are unable to act thus."

" No, Joseph, I am not able; it seems to me that I never shall be able. But see my misfortune! consider my strange and unhappy lot! My heart is torn in opposite directions, and

I cannot go whither it would impel me, without, on the right hand or the left, breaking a heart that leans upon me for support. If I give myself up to the one, I abandon and destroy the other. I am betrothed to one whose wife I cannot be without killing my adopted father; and if I fulfill my duties as a daughter I abandon those of a wife. The wife, it has been written, shall leave father and mother to cleave to her husband; but in reality, I am neither wife nor daughter. The law has not pronounced its authoritive dictum. Society has not concerned itself with my lot. To my heart must be left the choice. I am not influenced by human passion, and in the dilemma in which I stand, duty and devotion throw no light upon my path. Albert and Porpora are equally unfortunate, equally threatened with the loss of reason or of life. I am necessary to them both, yet I must sacrifice one or other."

"And wherefore? If you were to marry the count, would not Porpora go and reside with you? You would thus rescue him from poverty; you would revive him by your care and solicitude, and thus accomplish your twofold aim."

"Ah! were it thus, Joseph, I swear to you I should renounce both art and freedom. But you do not know Porpora: it is glory, not happiness, which he desires. He is destitute, and yet he does not know it; he suffers, without knowing whence arises his pain ; besides, ever dreaming of triumph and admiration, he knows not how to stoop to accept pity. Be assured that his distress is mainly the result of his carelessness and his pride. Were he but to say the word, he has friends who would hasten to his assistance; but besides that he never looks whether his pocket be full or empty, and you are aware that he is little better informed as to his stomach ; he would rather die of hunger in his solitary chamber than seek a dinner from his best friend. It would be to degrade music in his estimation were any one to suspect that Porpora needed aught but his genius, his harpsichord, and his pen. Thus the ambassador and his lady, who cherish and respect him, never suspect his destitution. Were they to see him in a confined and mean abode, they would ascribe it to his habits of seclusion and carelessness. Does he not say himself he could not compose otherwise? I, who know better, have seen him clamber upon the roofs of Venice, to drink in inspiration from the music of the waves, and the stars of heaven. And when they receive them in his soiled attire, his rusty wig, and tattered shoes, do they not think they are gratifying his whim? He likes to be dirty and ragged, they say; it is the failing of artists and old men; he could not walk in new shoes. He also says so; but I remember the time when he was neat, clean, shaven, perfumed, with his lace ruffles sweeping the keys of the organ or pianoforte, just because he could be so without being obliged to any one. Never would Porpora consent to live an indolent and obscure life, in the recesses of Bohemia, and at the expense of his friends. He would not be there three months without abusing every one, and asserting that all around him had conspired with his enemies to prevent the production and publication of his works. Some fine morning, therefore, he would shake the dust from off his feet, and return to his garret, his rat-gnawed harpsichord, his fatal bottle, and darling manuscripts."

"And do you not think it possible to bring your count to Vienna, Dresden, Prague, or some other musical town? With your resources you could establish yourselves anywhere, cultivate art, surround yourselves with musicians, and give a free course to Porpora's ambition, without ceasing to watch over him."

"After what I have told you of Albert's character and state of health, how can you ask me such a question? He who could not bear a strange face, how could he face the crowd of evil-minded and foolish wretches which we call the world? And what ridicule, what aversion, what contempt, would not the world shower upon a man so rigidly pious, who would understand nothing of its laws, its customs, or its manners! All that were as hazardous to attempt with Albert, as what I now try in order to make him forget me."

"Be assured, nevertheless, that all these evils would seem lighter than your absence. If he truly love he will bear every thing; and if he does not love you sufficiently to put up with every thing, he will forget you."

"Therefore I pause, and decide upon nothing. Inspire me with courage, Beppo, and stay beside me, that I may at least have one heart unto which I can pour my sorrows, and from which I can seek a common hope."

"Oh, my sister, trust in me!" exclaimed Joseph; "if I

am so happy as to afford you this slight consolation, I shall cheerfully put up with Porpora's tirades. Were he even to beat me, I would bear it, if that would turn him aside from tormenting and afflicting you."

In planning thus with Joseph, Consuelo labored incessantly in preparing their common repast, or mending Porpora's worn-out garments. She introduced by degrees into the sitting apartment some necessary articles of furniture. A large, easy arm-chair, well stuffed, replaced the straw one in which he was wont to rest his old limbs, weakened by age. And after having enjoyed a comfortable nap in it, he was surprised, and asked with beetling brows where this good seat had come from.

" The mistress of the house sent it up," replied Consuelo; " it was in her way, and I allowed it a corner till she should ask for it again."

Porpora's mattress was changed, and he made no other remark on the goodness of his bed, save that for some nights past he had slept better. Consuelo replied, " that he might attribute this improvement to his coffee, and to his refraining from brandy." One morning, Porpora having put on an excellent dressing-gown, asked, with an anxious air, where it had been found. Joseph, who had received his lesson, replied that in settling an old trunk he had found it stuffed in a corner of it.

" I did not think I had brought it with me here," said Porpora. " It is, nevertheless, the one I had at Venice; at least it is the same color."

" And what other could it be?" replied Consuelo, who had taken care to match the worn-out garment carefully.

" Why, the fact is, I thought it was more worn," said the maestro, looking at his elbows.

" You are right," she replied, " I put in new sleeves."

" And with what?"

" With a part of the lining."

" Ah, you women are wonderful creatures, for making every thing of use."

And when the new coat had been worn a couple of days, although it was the same color as the old one, he was surprised to see it so fresh, and the buttons especially, which were very pretty, set him thinking:

" This coat is not mine," said he, in a grumbling tone.

" I desired Beppo to get it scoured," replied Consuelo,

"as it was much soiled. They have refreshed it, that is all."

"I tell you it is not mine," said the maestro, enraged; "they have changed it. Your Beppo is a fool."

"That could not be, for I marked it."

"And these buttons? Do you think to make me swallow them?"

"I changed the trimming, and sewed them on myself; the old were entirely worn out."

"You are pleased to say so; but it was still very decent. How stupid! am I a Celadon, to deck myself out in this fashion, and pay twelve sequins at least for a trimming?"

"It does not cost twelve florins," replied Consuelo, "it was picked up by chance."

His garments were gradually renewed with the help of such dexterous fibs, which gave Consuelo and Joseph many a hearty laugh. Some things passed unobserved, thanks to Porpora's absence of mind, the lace and linen found their way by degrees into his drawers, and when he looked attentively at them Consuelo took credit to herself for having renovated them so well. To give a semblance of truth to what she said, she mended some of his things before his eyes, and placed them with the rest.

"That will do," said Porpora, one day tearing a ruffle out of her hands; "what nonsense! an artist must not be a drudge, and I will not have you bent double all day with a needle in your fingers. Put it past, or I shall throw it into the fire; nor will I suffer you to go on cooking, and swallowing the fumes of charcoal. Do you wish to lose your voice? Would you be a scullion? Would you make me miserable?"

"Far from it," replied Consuelo; "your things are now in good order, and my voice is quite recovered."

"Good!" exclaimed the maestro, "in that case you shall sing to-morrow at the palace of the Countess Hoditz, dowager Margravine of Bareith."

CHAPTER LXXXVIII.

THE dowager Margravine of Bareith, widow of the Margrave George William, by birth Princess of Saxe Weisenfeld, and subsequently Countess Hoditz, had, "it was said, been beautiful as an angel. But she was so changed that hardly a trace of her charms remained. She was tall, and appeared to have had a fine figure, but time, that great destroyer, had made sad ravages upon it. Her face was long, as well as her nose, which latter feature disfigured her greatly, being red and frostbitten. Her eyes, accustomed to give law to those with whom she associated, were large, brown, and well set, but so dim that their vivacity was much impaired. She had false eyebrows, very thick and black as ink; her mouth, though large, was well formed and full of expression; her teeth regular and white as ivory; her complexion, though clear, was sallow, and leaden-colored; and her air and carriage were dignified but somewhat affected. She was the Lais of her time, and could have only pleased by her looks, for as to mind she had none."

If you find this portrait rather severe do not ascribe it to me, dear reader. It is word for word from the hands of a princess remarkable for her misfortunes, her domestic virtues, her petulance, and her pride — the Princess Wilhelmina, of Prussia, sister of Frederick the Great, married to the Hereditary Prince of Bareith, nephew of the Countess Hoditz. She had the most caustic tongue, perhaps, that royal blood ever produced. But her portraits, it must be confessed, are masterly, and it is difficult in reading them not to believe they are correct.

When Consuelo, her hair arranged by Keller, and dressed, thanks to his care and zeal with elegant simplicity, was introduced by Porpora into the margravine's saloon, she seated herself with him behind the harpsichord, which had been placed in a corner so as not to incommode the company. No one had yet arrived, so punctual was Porpora, and the valets had just finished lighting the candles. The maestro commenced to try the instrument, and had hardly sounded a few notes when a fair and exquisitely graceful young woman entered and approached him with graceful affability. As Porpora saluted her with the greatest respect, and called her princess, Consuelo took her for the margravine, and according to the usual custom, kissed her hand. That cold and colorless hand pressed the young girl's with a cordiality which is rarely found among the great, and which immediately gained Consuelo's heart. The princess appeared to be about thirty years of age; her form was elegant without being faultless; indeed there might be remarked in it certain deviations which seemed the result of great physical sufferings. Her features were remarkably noble and regular, but frightfully pale, and it seemed as if some concealed sorrow had imparted to them a worn and anxious expression. Her toilet was exquisite, but simple and decent even to severity. An air of melancholy sweetness and timid modesty was diffused over all her actions, and the sound of her voice had something humble and affecting which touched Consuelo to the heart. Before the latter had time to comprehend that this was not the margravine, the true margravine appeared. She was then more than fifty, and if the portrait which has been given at the beginning of this chapter, and which was drawn ten years before, was at that period a little overcharged, it certainly was no longer so at the present moment. It even required a great stretch of good nature to imagine that the Countess Hoditz had been one of the beauties of Germany, although she was painted and adorned with the skill of a finished coquette. The embonpoint of riper years had destroyed the shape which the margravine still persisted in imagining had still retained all its pristine beauty, for her neck and shoulders braved the eye of a spectator with all the proud confidence of an antique statue. She wore flowers, diamonds, and feathers in her hair, like a young lady, and her dress rustled with precious stones.

"Mamma," said the princess who had caused Consuelo's error, "this is the young person whom Master Porpora informed us of, and who will afford us the pleasure of hearing some of the fine music of his new opera."

"That is no reason," replied the margravine, measuring Consuelo from head to foot, "why you should hold her by the hand in that manner. Go and seat yourself at the harpsichord, mademoiselle. I am delighted to see you, you will sing when the company has assembled. Master Porpora, I salute you. Will you excuse my not attending to you; I perceive that something is amiss in my toilet. My daughter, converse a little with Master Porpora. He is a man of talent whom *I* esteem."

Having thus spoken, in a rough and masculine voice, the portly margravine turned heavily on her heel, and re-entered her apartment.

Hardly had she disappeared, when the princess, her daughter, approaching Consuelo, once more took her hand with a delicate and touching kindness, as if to make it apparent that she protested against her mother's impertinence. She then engaged in conversation with her and Porpora, and testified a graceful and unaffected interest in them. Consuelo was still more sensible of this kind proceeding when, several persons having been introduced, she remarked in the habitual manners of the princess a coldness and reserve at once proud and timid, which she evidently laid aside when addressing the maestro and herself.

When the saloon was almost filled, Count Hoditz, who had dined from home, entered in full dress, and, as if he had been a stranger in his own house, proceeded respectfully to kiss the hand and inquire after the health of his noble spouse. The margravine pretended to be of a very delicate constitution; she reclined upon a couch, inhaling every instant the perfume of a smelling-bottle, and receiving the homage of her guests with an air which she thought languishing, but which was only disdainful, and in short, she was so completely ridiculous, that Consuelo, although at first irritated and indignant at her insolence, ended by being highly amused, and promised herself a hearty laugh in drawing her portrait to her friend Beppo.

The princess had once more approached the harpsichord, and did not lose an opportunity of addressing either a word or a smile to Consuelo when her mother was not observing her. This situation allowed Consuelo to overhear a little family scene, which disclosed the state of matters in the household. Count Hoditz approached his daughter-in-law, took her hand, carried it to his lips, and kept it there for some instants with a very expressive look. The princess withdrew her hand, and addressed a few words to him in a cold and deferential manner. The count did not listen to them, and continuing to gaze upon her: "What! my beautiful angel," said he, "always sad, always severe, always muffled to the chin? One would imagine that you wished to become a nun."

"It is quite possible I shall come to that," replied the princess in a low voice. "The world has not treated me in such a manner as to inspire me with much attachment for its pleasures."

"The world would adore you, and would throw itself at

your feet, if you did not affect to keep it at a distance by your severity; and as to the cloister, could you endure its horrors at your age, and with your charms?"

"In more joyous days, and when far more beautiful than I am at present," replied she, "I endured the horrors of a more rigorous captivity; can you have forgotten it? But do not talk to me any longer, my lord; mamma is looking at you."

Immediately the count, as if moved by some piece of mechanism, quitted his daughter-in-law and approached Consuelo, whom he saluted very gravely; then, having addressed some words to her as an amateur respecting music in general, he opened the book which Porpora had placed upon the harpsichord, and pretending to be in search of something which he wished her to explain to him, he leaned upon the stand, and spoke thus to her in a low voice: "I saw the deserter yesterday morning, and his wife gave me a note. I request the beautiful Consuelo to forget a certain meeting, and in return for her silence I will forget a certain Joseph whom I just now saw in my ante-chamber."

"That certain Joseph," replied Consuelo, whom the discovery of the conjugal jealousy and constraint to which the count was subjected had made quite easy respecting the consequences of the adventure at Passau, "is an artist of talent who will not long remain in antechambers. He is my brother, my comrade, and my friend. I have no reason to blush for my sentiments toward him; I have nothing to conceal in that respect, and I have nothing to request from your lordship's generosity but a little indulgence for my voice, and a little protection for Joseph in the outset of his musical career."

"My interest is pledged for the said Joseph, as my admiration is already so for your beautiful voice; but I flatter myself that a certain jest on my part was never taken as serious."

"I was not so stupid, my lord; and besides, I know that a woman has never any reason to boast of having been made the subject of a jest of that nature."

"It is enough, signora," said the count, from whom the dowager never removed her eyes, and who was in a hurry to change his position in order not to excite her suspicion; "the celebrated Consuelo must know how to make allow-

ances for the gaiety and abandonment of a journey, and
she may depend in future upon the respect and devotion of
Count Hoditz."

He replaced the book upon the harpsichord, and hastened to receive most obsequiously a personage who had
just been announced with much pomp. It was a little
man, who might have been taken for a woman in disguise,
so rosy was he, so curled, trinketted, delicate, genteel, and
perfumed; it was he of whom Maria Theresa had said that
she wished she could have set him in a ring; it was he also
whom she said she had made a diplomatist, because she
could make nothing better of him. It was the Austrian
plenipotentiary, the prime minister, the favorite, some
even said the lover of the empress; it was no less a personage, in short, than the celebrated Kaunitz, that statesman
who held in his white hand, ornamented with rings of
a thousand colors, all the tangled strings of European
diplomacy.

He appeared to listen with a grave air to the would-be
grave personages who were supposed to converse with him
on serious and important subjects. But suddenly he interrupted himself to ask Count Hoditz, " Who is that young
person I see there at the harpsichord? Is that the little
girl I have heard of, Porpora's protegée? That Porpora is
an unfortunate wretch! I wish I could do something for
him ; but he is so exacting and so fanciful, that all the
other artists fear or hate him. When I speak to them of
him, it is as if I showed them a Medusa's head. He tells
one that he sings false, another that his music is good for
nothing, and a third that he owes his success to intrigue.
And he expects, with these savage and cutting remarks,
that people will listen to him and do him justice! What
the devil! We don't live in the woods. Frankness is no
longer in fashion, and we cannot lead men by truth. That
little one is not amiss; I rather like her face. She is very
young, is she not? They say she had great success at
Venice. Porpora must bring her to me to-morrow."

" He wishes," said the princess, "that you would procure her the honor of singing before the empress, and I
hope that you will not refuse him this favor. I ask it of
you on my own account."

" There is nothing so easy as to procure her an audience
of the empress, and it is sufficient that your highness de-

sires it, to induce me to exert myself to forward the matter. But there is a personage more powerful at the theater than even the empress. It is Madam Tesi; and even if her majesty should take this girl under her prctection, I doubt if the engagement would be signed without the approval of the all-powerful Tesi."

" They say it is you who spoil those ladies, my lord, and that without your indulgence they would not exert so much influence."

" What can I do, princess? Every one is master in his own house. Her majesty understands very clearly that if she were to interfere by an imperial decree in the affairs of the opera, the opera would go all astray. Now her majesty wishes that the opera should go on well, and that people should be amused there. But how could that be, if the prima donna takes cold on the very day she is to make her début? or if the tenor, in the very middle of a scene of reconciliation, instead of throwing himself into the arms of the bass, gives him a smart cuff on the ear? We have quite enough to do to satisfy the caprices of M. Caffariello. We have enjoyed some tranquility since Madame Tesi and Madame Holzbaüer have come to a good understanding with each other; but if you throw an apple of discord upon the stage, our cards will be in a worse confusion than ever."

" But a third woman is absolutely necessary," said the Venetian ambassador, who warmly protected Porpora and his pupil, " and here is an admirable one who offers her services."

" If she be admirable, so much the worse for her. She would excite the jealousy of Madame Tesi, who is also admirable, and wishes to be so alone; she would enrage Madame Holzbaüer, who wishes to be admirable also——"

" And who is not so?" retorted the ambassador.

" She is very well born; she is a person of good family," replied M. de Kaunitz, diplomatically.

" But she cannot sing two parts at a time. She must needs let the mezzo-soprano take her proper part in the operas."

" There is a lady called Corilla who offers herself, and who is certainly one of the most beautiful creatures I have seen."

" Your excellency has already seen her, then?"

"The very day she arrived. But I have not heard her yet. She is ill."

"You will hear this candidate, and you cannot hesitate to give her the preference."

"It is possible. I even confess to you that her face, although less beautiful than that of the other, seems to me more agreeable. She has a gentle and modest manner. But my preference will do her no good, poor child! She must please Madame Tesi, without displeasing Madame Holzbaüer; and hitherto, notwithstanding the close friendship that unites those two ladies, every thing that has been approved of by the one, has always had the misfortune to be strongly disapproved of by the other."

"A very trying crisis, indeed!" said the princess, with a slight expression of irony, on seeing the importance which these two statemen attributed to green-room dissensions. "Here is our poor little protegée weighed in the balance with Madame Corilla, and it is M. Caffariello, I wager, who will throw his sword into one of the scales."

When Consuelo had sung, every one was unanimous in declaring that, since Madame Hasse, they had heard nothing like it; and M. de Kaunitz, approaching her, said with a solemn air, "Young lady; you sing better than Madame Tesi; but let this be in strict confidence, for if such a judgment get abroad, you are lost, and will not appear this season at Vienna. Be prudent, therefore, very prudent," added he, lowering his voice, and seating himself beside her. "You have to struggle against great obstacles, and you cannot triumph except by address." Thereupon the great Kaunitz entered into the thousand windings of treatrical intrigue, and acquainted her minutely with all the little passions of the company, giving her in short a complete treatise on diplomatic science with reference to the stage.

Consuelo listened to him, her eyes wide open with astonishment, and when he had finished, as he had repeated twenty times in his harangue the words, "My last opera, the opera which I had played last month," she imagined that she had been mistaken on hearing him announced, and that this personage, who was so well versed in all the mysteries of the dramatic career, could only be a director of the opera, or a fashionable composer. She therefore felt quite at ease with him, and talked to him as she would have done to a person of her own profession. This freedom from constraint rendered her more gay and unreserved than the respect due to the all-powerful prime minister would have permitted her to be, and M. de Kaunitz found her charming. For a whole hour he attended to no one else. The margravine was highly offended at such a breach of propriety. She hated the liberty of great courts, accustomed as she was to the solemn formalties of little ones. But she could no longer act the margravine, as she was no longer one. She was tolerated and passably well treated by the empress, because she had abjured the Lutheran faith to become a Catholic. This act of hypocrisy was sufficient to excuse every sort of mis-alliance, even of crime, at the court of Austria; and Maria Theresa in acting thus only followed the example which her father and mother had given her, of welcoming whomsoever wished to escape from the rebuffs and disdain of Protestant Germany, by taking refuge within the pale of the Romish church. But princess and Catholic though she was, the margravin was nothing at Vienna, and M. de Kaunitz was every thing.

CHAPTER LXXXIX.

As SOON as Consuelo had sung her third air, Porpora, who knew the usual custom, made her a signal, rolled up his music, and retired with her through a little side door, without inconveniencing by his exit those noble persons who had been pleased to open their ears to her divine accents.

"All goes well," said he to her, rubbing his hands, as soon as they were in the street, where Joseph stood ready to escort them with a lighted torch. "Kaunitz is an old fool who understands how the land lies, and will push you on."

"And who is Kaunitz? I did not see him," said Consuelo.

"You did not see him, you stupid girl! He talked with you for more than an hour."

"But it cannot be that little gentleman in a rose and silver vest, who retailed so much gossip to me that I took him for an old box-opener?"

"The very same. What is there surprising about that?"

"It is very surprising to me," replied Consuelo, "and such was not the idea I had formed of a statesman."

"That is because you do not know how kingdoms are governed. If you did, you would consider it very surprising that statesmen should be any thing else than old gossips. However, let us keep silence on that head, and play our part in the masquerade of this world."

"Alas! my dear master," said the young girl, who had gradually become pensive while crossing the vast esplanade of the rampart, in order to reach the suburb in which their modest dwelling was situated, "I was asking myself just now, what our profession will become in the midst of such a cold and deceitful world."

"And what do you wish it should become?" returned Porpora, in his rough and abrupt manner; "it has not to become this or that. Happy or unhappy, triumphant or despised, it will ever remain the most fascinating as well as the noblest vocation on the earth."

"Oh, yes!" said Consuelo, taking the maestro's arm and causing him to moderate his rapid strides, "I understand that the grandeur and dignity of our art cannot be raised or lowered by the frivolous caprice or bad taste which governs the world. But why should we allow our persons to be debased? Why should we expose ourselves to the contempt, sometimes even to the more humiliating encouragements, of the profane? If art be sacred, are not we also sacred, we who are her priests and her Levites? Why do we not live retired in our garrets, happy in feeling and comprehending the beauty of music, and what business have we in those saloons where they whisper together during our performance, applaud us absently and unmeaningly, and would blush to retain us a moment, and treat us like fellow-creatures, after we have done exhibiting like actors?"

"Ha!" growled Porpora, stopping abruptly and striking his cane on the pavement, "what foolish vanities and what false ideas are coursing through your brain to-day? What are we, and what need we be but actors? They call us so in contempt! And what matters it if we be actors by taste, by vocation, or by the choice of Heaven, as they are great lords by chance, by constraint, or by the suffrages of fools? Ha! ha! actors? All cannot be so who wish it. Let them try to be actors, and we shall see what a figure they make, those minions who think themselves so fine! Let the dowager Margravine of Bareith put on the tragic mantle, case her huge mis-shapen leg in the buskin, and make three steps across the stage, and we shall see a strange princess! And what do you think she did at her little court of Erlangen, when she thought she reigned there? She tried to dress herself like a queen, and moved heaven and earth to play a part above her powers. Nature intended her for a sutler, and destiny, by a strange mistake, has made her a highness. Therefore she deserved a thousand hisses when she preposterously undertook the part. And you, foolish child that you are, God made you a queen; he has placed upon your brow a diadem of beauty, intelligence, and power! Carry you into the midst of a free, intelligent, and sensible people (supposing that such exist) and you would be at once a queen, because you have only to show yourself and sing, in order to prove that you are queen by divine right. Well! it is not so—the world is constituted otherwise. But being as it is, what do you wish to do with it? Chance, caprice, error, and folly govern it. What change can we make in it? Its rulers are for the most part counterfeit, slovenly, foolish, and ignorant. Thus are we placed; we must either die or accommodate ourselves to its ways; and as we cannot be monarchs, we are artists and have a kingdom of our own. We sing a heavenly language which is forbidden to vulgar mortals, we dress ourselves as kings and great men, we ascend the stage, we seat ourselves upon a fictitious throne, we play a farce, we are actors! Corpo Santo! The world sees us, but understands us not! It does not see that we are the true powers of the earth, and that our reign is the only true one, while their reign, their power their activity, their majesty, is a parody at which the angels weep, and which the people hate and curse. And the greatest princes of the earth come to look at us, and take lessons in our school; and admiring us in their own hearts as models of true greatness, they strive to resemble us when they exhibit themselves before their subjects. Go to, the world is turned topsy-turvey, and they know it well, they who govern it; and although they themselves may not be aware of it, although they may not confess it openly, it is easy to see, from the contempt they

display for our persons and our vocation, that they feel an
instinctive jealousy of our real superiority. Oh! it is only
when I am at the theater that I see clearly our true relations to society. The spirit of music unseals my eyes, and
I see behind the footlights a true court, real heroes, lofty
inspirations; while the miserable idiots who flaunt in the
boxes upon velvet couches are the real actors. In truth,
the world is a comedy, and that is the reason I said to you
just now, my noble daughter, to play our parts in it with
gravity and decorum, although conscious of the hollow
pageant which surrounds us on every side—— Plague take
the blockhead!" cried the maestro, pushing Joseph from him,
who, greedy to hear his glowing words, had insensibly approached, so as at last even to elbow him ; "he treads on
my toes, and covers me with pitch from his torch. Would
not you imagine that he understood what we are talking
about, and wishes to honor us with his approbation?"

"Cross over to my right, Beppo," said the young girl,
making a signal of intelligence; "you annoy the maestro
with your awkwardness." Then addressing Porpora: "All
that you have said, my dear friend," resumed she, "though
noble and inspiring, is shadowy and unreal ; moreover, it
does not answer what I have urged, for the intoxication of
gratified pride cannot afford a balm to the wounded heart.
Little matters it to me that I am born a queen, and yet do
not reign. The more I see of the great, the more does their
lot inspire me with compassion——"

"Well, is not that what I said?"

"Yes; but that is not what I asked you. They are
greedy of show and power. That is at once their folly and
misery. But we, if we be greater, and better, and wiser
than they, why do we strive with them—pride against
pride, royalty against royalty? If we possess more solid advantages, if we enjoy more precious and desirable treasures, what means this petty struggle in which we engage
with them, and which, subjecting our worth and our
strength to the mercy of their caprices, reduces us to their
own level?"

"The dignity, the holiness of art require it," cried the
maestro. "They have made the world a battle-ground,
and our life a martyrdom. We must fight, we must shed
our blood at every pore, to prove to them, even when dying
of misery, even when sinking under their hisses and con-

tempt, that we are as demigods compared with them—that we are legitimate sovereigns, while they are vile mortals, mean and shameless usurpers!"

"Oh! my master," replied Consuelo, shuddering with surprise and terror; "how you hate them! And yet you bend low before them, you flatter them, you speak them fair, and you take your leave by a side door, after having served up to them two or three courses of your genius."

"Yes, yes!" replied the maestro, rubbing his hands with a sardonic smile; "I mock them, I pay my court to their diamonds and crosses, overwhelm them with a few airs after my fashion, and turn my back upon them, well pleased to effect my escape, and rid myself of their foolish faces."

"Then," replied Consuelo, "art is a combat?"

"It is even so; honor to the brave!"

"It is a sarcasm on fools?"

"Yes, it is a sarcasm; honor to him who can make it deep and withering!"

"It is a perpetual war—a war to the knife?"

"Yes, it is a war; honor to the man whose arm is not weary, and whose anger pardons not!"

"And it is nothing more?"

"It is nothing more in this life. The glory and the crown are for another world."

"It is nothing more in this life, maestro—are you very sure?"

"Have I not told you?"

"In that case, it is indeed little," replied Consuelo, sighing, and raising her eyes to the serene and starlit heavens.

"Do you call that little? Do you dare to say so, you weak and fainting heart?" exclaimed Porpora, stopping afresh, and angrily shaking his pupil's arm, while the terrified Joseph let fall his torch.

"Yes, I repeat it, it is a paltry and worthless aim," she replied, calmly and firmly; "and I told you so once before at Venice, on that melancholy and fatal occasion which has tinged my whole after life with its somber hue. I have not changed my opinion; my heart is not made for such a struggle, and it cannot support the double weight of hatred and anger. There is not a corner in my bosom where rancor and vengeance can find a resting-place. Far from me all evil passions! far from me all feverish excitement! If, as the sole condition of my possessing genius and glory, I must yield up my bosom to you, adieu, genius and glory— forever adieu! Crown other brows with laurels, melt other hearts with your wondrous magic, you shall never extort a sigh of regret from me!"

Joseph expected to see Porpora burst into one of those terrific yet ludicrous fits of anger, which prolonged contradiction was apt to awaken in him, and he had already seized Consuelo's arm, in order to snatch her from the maestro's side, and protect her from those furious gestures with which he often threatened her, but which led to no other result than a smile or a tear. And thus it was on the present occasion; Porpora stamped on the ground, growled hoarsely like a caged lion, clasped her hand, and raised it vehemently toward heaven. But immediately afterward he let his arms fall by his side, uttered a deep sigh, and preserved an obstinate silence until they reached home. Consuelo's generous and unshaken mildness, energy, and uprightness, had inspired him with involuntary respect. Possibly he reproached himself bitterly in secret, but if so, he did not allow it to appear; for he was too old, too hardened and bitter, to amend. Nevertheless, when Consuelo approached to bid him good-night, he looked at her with a melancholy air, and said, in a subdued voice:

"And is it indeed so? You are no longer an artist, because the margravine is an old coquette, and Kaunitz an old gossip?"

"No, my dear master, I did not say so," replied Consuelo, gaily; "I did not say so. I can submit cheerfully to the folly and impertinence of the world. I do not require either hatred or anger to induce me to do so, but only a good conscience and good-humor. I am still an artist and shall always be an artist. But I conceive a different aim, I shadow out a different destiny for art, than the rivalries of pride, and the vengeance of humiliation. I have another spring of action and it will sustain me."

"What spring? what motive?" exclaimed Porpora, placing the light which Joseph had brought, on the table of the ante-chamber.

"I would make art loved and understood, without making the artist himself either feared or hated."

Porpora shrugged his shoulders.

"Dreams of youth!" said he; "I had the same dreams once myself."

"Well, if they be dreams," replied Consuelo, "the triumphs of pride are dreams also. Dream for dream, I like mine best. Then I have another motive, my dear master —the desire of pleasing and obeying you."

"I do not believe it—I do not believe a word of it!" exclaimed Porpora, snatching up the light and turning toward the door. But ere he had seized the handle, he returned to embrace Consuelo, who waited with smiles this reaction of feeling.

From the kitchen, which adjoined Consuelo's chamber, there ascended a little stair which led to a sort of terrace some six feet square on the roof. It was here that she dried Porpora's bands and ruffles when she had done them up; it was here that she sometimes climbed to have a chat with Beppo, when the maestro retired to rest too soon, or earlier than she felt any inclination to sleep. Unable to remain in her own room, which was too low and narrow to admit a table, and fearing to rouse her old friend by occupying the ante-chamber, she mounted to the terrace, sometimes to indulge in lonely reverie and gaze upon the heavens, sometimes to relate to her devoted companion the little incidents of the day. This evening they had a thousand things to say to each other. Consuelo wrapped herself in a pelisse, the hood of which she pulled over her head in order to avoid taking cold, and hastened to rejoin Beppo, who awaited her with impatience. These nocturnal conversations reminded her of her meetings with Anzoleto when both were children, but it was no longer the full and cloudless moon of Venice which looked down upon them with her serene smile, no longer its fantastic and picturesque roofs which called up such a throng of images, nor its nights glowing with love and hope. It was the cold and shadowy night of a German land, the dim and vapor-shrouded moon of a northern clime, and the sweet and healthful pleasure of friendship without the dangerous intoxication of passion.

When Consuelo had mentioned all that had amused, annoyed, or interested her at the margravine's, it was Joseph's turn to speak.

"You have seen the secrets of the court," said he; "the envelopes and armorial bearing, as it were; but as lackeys are accustomed to read their master's letters, it is in the ante-chamber that I have learned the hidden life of the great. I shall not tell you half the remarks of which the margravine was the subject. Oh! if great people only knew how their valets speak of them—if in these gorgeous saloons, where they parade themselves with so much dignity, they could hear what was said on the other side of the wall of their manners and characters! While Porpora just now on the rampart set forth his theory of strife and hatred against the lords of the earth, his was not the true standard of dignity. His bitterness perverted his judgment. Ah! you were in the right when you said that he reduced himself to their level, in seeking to crush them with his contempt. Had he heard the conversation of the valets in the ante-chamber, he would have seen that pride and contempt of others are the characteristics of base and perverse minds. Thus Porpora evinced grandeur, originality, and power of mind just now, when he struck the pavement with his cane and uttered as his war-cry, 'Courage, strife, bitter irony, eternal vengeance!' But your wisdom was lovelier than his phrenzy, and I was the more struck with it that I had just seen the tribe of domestics—timid victims, demoralized slaves—who also whispered in my ears with accents not loud yet deep, 'Trickery! perfidy! eternal vengeance and hate, toward our masters, who believe themselves our superiors and whose baseness we betray!' I have never been a lackey, Consuelo, but since I have become one in the same manner as you became a boy during our journey, I have reflected, as you may see, on the duties of my present situation."

"You have done well, Beppo," replied Porporina; "life is a great enigma, and we ought not to overlook the slightest fact without commenting and reflecting upon it. It is always so much discovered. But tell me, did you learn any thing from the household about this princess, the daughter of the margravine, who, of all those starched, painted, and frivolous puppets, seemed to me alone natural, amiable, and serious?"

"Oh! yes; not merely this evening, but often, from Keller, who waits upon her governess, and is well acquainted with the facts. What I am going to tell you, therefore, is not a story of the ante-chambers, a lackey's tale; it is a true story of public notoriety.

"The Princess of Culmbach was educated at Dresden by the Queen of Poland, her aunt, and it was there that

Porpora knew her, and gave her, as well as the Grand Dauphiness of France, her cousin, some lessons in music. The young Princess of Culmbach was as beautiful as she was prudent. Brought up by a severe and exacting queen, far from a depraved mother, she seemed destined to be honored and happy through life. But the dowager margravine, the present Countess Hoditz, would not have it so. She brought her home, and kept her with her, under pretense of marrying her, now to one of her relatives, also a margrave of Bareith, now to another, also prince of Culmbach ; for the principality of Bareith-Culmbach reckons more princes and margraves than it has villages and castles to belong to them. The beauty and modesty of the princess aroused in her mother's breast a violent feeling of jealousy ; she burned to disgrace her, and for this purpose fabricated the most atrocious slanders against her, and by her representations to the other members of the family, caused her to be imprisoned in the fortress of Plasenbourg, where passed several years in the most rigorous captivity. She would have been there still, had she not been induced by the promise of the Empress Amelia's protection to abjure the Lutheran faith. She yielded, however, solely from her ardent wish to recover her liberty, and the first use she made of it was to return to the religion of her ancestors. The young Margravine of Bareith, Wilhelmina of Prussia, received her with kindness in her little court. She was beloved and respected there for her virtues, her mildness, and the correctness of her demeanor. If broken-hearted, she is still an admirable creature, and although she is not in favor at the court of Vienna, on account of her Lutheranism, no one ventures to insult her ; no one, not even the lackeys, dares to utter the least slander against her. She is here on some business at present, but she usually resides at Bareith."

" That is the reason," replied Consuelo, "why she spoke so much of that country, and wished me to go there. Oh! what a history, Joseph, and what a woman that Countess Hoditz is! Never—no, never shall Porpora drag me to her house again — never shall I sing for her more!"

" Nevertheless, you would meet there the best and most estimable women at court. Such, they say, is the world.

Rank and wealth cloak every vice; and provided you go to church, every thing else is tolerated."

"This court of Vienna would seem somewhat hypocritical," said Consuelo.

"I fear, between ourselves," replied Joseph, lowering his voice, "that the great Maria Theresa is somewhat of a hypocrite herself."

CHAPTER XC.

A FEW days afterward, Porpora having busied himself and intrigued in the affair in his own way—that is to say, in threatening, scolding, and railing right and left—Consuelo was introduced to the imperial chapel by Reuter (Haydn's old enemy), and sang before Maria Theresa the part of Judith in the oratorio, *Bertulia Liberata*, a poem of Metastasio's, set to music by the aforesaid Reuter. Consuelo was magnificent, and Maria Theresa deigned to be pleased. When the sacred concert was over, Consuelo was invited, with the other singers (Caffariello among the number), to partake of a collation in the palace, at which Reuter was to preside. Hardly had she taken her seat between Reuter and Porpora, than a murmur, at once hurried and reverential, from an adjoining gallery, caused all the guests to start except Consuelo and Caffariello, who were busied in discussing a chorus, which the one would have in quick, the other in slow time. "There is no one who can settle the question but the maestro himself," said Consuelo, turning toward Reuter; but she no longer found Reuter on her right side nor Porpora on her left—all the company had risen from the table, and had ranged themselves in a row with an air of deep respect. It was then that Consuelo found herself standing face to face with a woman of about thirty years of age, beaming with health and energy, dressed in black (the usual costume for chapel), and followed by seven children, one of whom she held by the hand. This was the heir apparent, the young Cæsar Joseph II; and this handsome woman, so gracious and affable, was no other than Maria Theresa, the empress queen.

"*Ecco La Guiditta?*" inquired the empress, turning to

Reuter. " I am highly pleased with you, my child," added she, surveying Consuelo from head to foot ; "you have afforded me real pleasure, and never have I felt so deeply the sublime verses of our admirable poet as when uttered by your harmonious voice. You pronounce perfectly, a thing to which I attach great importance. What age may you be, madamoiselle? You are a Venetian, I believe — a pupil of the celebrated Porpora, whom I am pleased to see present? You wish to enter the court theater? You are formed to shine there ; and Herr Kaunitz takes an interest in your welfare."

Having thus interrogated Consuelo without waiting for her replies, Maria Theresa, looking alternately at Metastasio and Kaunitz, who accompanied her, beckoned to one of her chamberlains, who presented the songstress with a rich bracelet. Before the latter had time to utter her thanks, the empress had already left the saloon, and the splendor of royalty had vanished from her sight. The empress retired slowly, followed by her train of princesses and archduchesses, addressing a kind word to each of the musicians as she passed them, and leaving behind her as it were a luminous track, which dazzled the eyes of the spectators with her glory and her power. Caffariello was the only one who pretended to preserve his equanimity. He resumed the discussion just at the point where he had left off, and Consuelo, thrusting the bracelet in her pocket without so much as looking at it, met him with the same objections, to the astonishment and scandal of the other musicians, who, bewildered by the fascination of the imperial presence, could think of nothing else for the rest of the day. We need hardly add that Porpora, both from habit and from principle, was an exception to this general prostration. He knew how to conduct himself respectfully toward the sovereign, but in his heart he hated and despised slaves. Reuter, now appealed to by Caffariello on the subject of the debated chorus, screwed up his lips in a hypocritical style, and it was only on being repeatedly questioned by Caffariello that he at last replied, with marked coldness:

"I confess, sir, that I did not follow your conversation. When Maria Theresa is present I forget the whole world; and even long after she has disappeared I remain under the influence of an emotion which does not suffer me to think of myself."

"Mademoiselle does not appear at all dazzled by the honor she has procured us," said Holzbaüer, who was present, and whose veneration for royalty evinced more acuteness and reserve than that of Reuter. "It would seem an every-day matter with you, signora, to converse with crowned heads; one would think you had done nothing else all your life."

"I never spoke to a crowned head in my life," replied Consuelo, quietly, and without seeming to perceive the ill-nature of Holzbaüer's insinuations, "and her majesty did not procure me this felicity, for her mode of questioning denied me the honor as well as the trouble of replying."

"You would perhaps have wished to chat a little with the empress," said Porpora, in a reproving tone.

"No indeed," replied Consuelo, "I never thought of such a thing."

"Mademoiselle is more careless than ambitious," observed Reuter, with cold disdain.

"Master Reuter," said Consuelo, with frank confidence, "are you dissatisfied with the manner in which I rendered your music?"

Reuter confessed that no person had ever sung it better, even under the reign of the august and ever-to-be-lamented Charles VI.

"In that case," said Consuelo, "do not reproach me with indifference. I am ambitious to satisfy my masters, to perform my part well; what other ambition could I have? What other would not be absurd and ridiculous for me to entertain?"

"Oh! you are too modest, mademoiselle," said Holzbaüer; "there is no ambition too lofty for talents such as yours."

"I accept that as a polite compliment," replied Consuelo; "but I shall not believe I have satisfied you till the day when you invite me to sing in the court theater."

Holzbaüer, caught in his own trap, pretended to cough, in order to avoid the necessity of replying, and got out of the scrape by a courteous and respectful bow; then bringing back the conversation to the point at which it had commenced:

"Your calmness and disinterestedness," said he, "are truly unexampled; you do not seem even to have examined her majesty's beautiful present."

"Ah! it is true," said Consuelo, drawing it from her pocket, and handing it round for the inspection of her neighbors, who were eager to estimate its value.

"It will serve to buy wood for my dear master's stove," thought Consuelo, "if I have no engagement this winter. A little additional comfort in lodging will stand us in better stead than toys and trinkets."

"What a celestial beauty is her majesty!" said Reuter, with a touching sigh, as he glanced a hard and sidelong look at Consuelo.

"Yes, she seems very beautiful," replied Consuelo, not understanding and not heeding Porpora's nudges with his elbow.

"*Seems?*" replied Reuter; "you are hard to please!"

"I scarcely saw her, she passed so rapidly."

"But then her dazzling intellect—the genius which is revealed at every word she utters!"

"I had scarcely time to hear her, she spoke so little."

"You must be made of brass or adamant, mademoiselle; I do not know what would touch your feelings!"

"I felt deeply touched when singing your Judith," replied Consuelo, who could give a tolerably cutting retort when occasion required it, and who began to comprehend the unfriendly feelings of the Viennese composers toward her.

"This girl has wit and spirit, with all her simplicity," whispered Holzbaüer to Master Reuter.

"Yes, she is of Porpora's school," replied the other; "nothing but disdain and mockery."

"If we do not take care, the old recitatives and such antiquated stuff will flood us worse than ever," replied Holzbaüer; "but do not fear, I know how to prevent this minion of Porpora's from ever raising her voice in my theater."

When they rose from table, Caffariello whispered in Consuelo's ear:

"Look you, my child ; these fellows are all a set of paltry scoundrels. You will have great difficulty in making your way here. They are all against you. They would oppose me too if they dared."

"And what have we done to annoy them ?" said the astonished Consuelo.

"We were both educated by the greatest professor of

singing on earth. They and their creatures are our natural
enemies. They will prejudice Maria Theresa against you,
and all you have said here will be repeated with malicious
commentaries and additions. They will tell her that you
did not think her beautiful, and that you despised her gift
as mean and unworthy of you. I know their tricks. Take
courage, nevertheless — the opinion of Caffariello as regards music is well worth that of Maria Theresa."

"Between the ill-nature of the one party and the folly
of the others, I am fairly meshed," thought Consuelo to
herself. "O! Porpora !" exclaimed she in her heart, "I
will do all that I can to return to the stage ; but, O
Albert ! Heaven grant that I may be unsuccessful in my
attempts !"

The following day Master Porpora, having business in
the city which would occupy him during the whole day,
and finding Consuelo rather pale, requested her to take a
walk outside the town to the *Spinnerin am Kreutz* with
Keller's wife, who had offered to accompany her whenever
she wished. As soon as the maestro had gone out :

"Beppo," said the young girl, "go quickly and hire a
carriage, and we will both take a drive to see Angela and
thank the canon. We promised to do so earlier, but my
cold must be our excuse."

"And in what dress will you present yourself to the
worthy man ?" said Beppo.

"In the one I have on," replied she. "The canon
must know and receive me under my real character."

"The excellent canon ! I shall sincerely rejoice to see
him again."

"And I, too."

"The poor canon! it vexes me to think——"

"What ?"

"That his head will be completely turned."

"And why so? Am I a goddess? I did not flatter myself so far."

"Consuelo, remember he was almost crazy when we
left him !"

"And I tell you that it is only necessary for him to
know that I am a woman, and to see me as I really am, to
recover all his self-possession, and again become what God
made him—a reasonable man."

"It is true that the dress does something. Therefore,

when I saw you again transformed into a young lady, after having been accustomed for a fortnight to treat you as a boy, I experienced a vague sense of terror and constraint for which I cannot account; and it is certain that during our journey if you had permitted me to fall in love with you—— But I am talking nonsense."

"Certainly, Joseph, it is nonsense, and besides, you lose time while you are chatting. It is ten leagues to the priory and back. It is now eight o'clock, and we must be back here again by seven in the evening, in time for the maestro's supper."

Three hours afterward Beppo and his companion alighted at the gate of the priory. The day was lovely, and the canon was contemplating his flowers with a melancholy air. When he saw Joseph, he uttered a cry of joy and advanced hastily to meet him, but he remained speechless on recognizing his dear Bertoni in a woman's dress. "Bertoni! my well-beloved child!" cried the simple and venerable old man, "what means this masquerade, and why do you appear disguised in this manner? We are not now in the carnival."

"My respected and revered friend," replied Consuelo, kissing his hand, "you must forgive me for having deceived you. I never was a boy; Bertoni never existed, and when I had the happiness of becoming acquainted with you, I was really disguised."

"We thought," said Joseph, who feared to behold the canon's consternation change to dissatisfaction, "that your reverence was not the dupe of our innocent artifice. That disguise was not assumed to deceive you; it was a necessity imposed upon us by circumstances, and we have always thought that your reverence had the generosity and the delicacy to overlook it."

"You thought so?" resumed the canon, astonished and terrified; "and you, Bertoni—I should say, mademoiselle —did you think so too?"

"No, reverend sir," replied Consuelo, "I did not think so for an instant. I saw plainly that your reverence had not the least suspicion of the truth."

"And you only did me justice," said the canon, in a tone of severity tempered with regret, "I cannot tamper with my good faith, and if I had guessed your sex, I should never have thought of insisting, as I did, on your remaining with me. There has indeed been circulated in the neighboring village, and even among my own flock, a vague report, a suspicion which made me smile, so determined was I to deceive myself respecting you. It was said that one of the two little musicians who sang the mass on the day of our patron saint's fête, was a woman in disguise. And then it was asserted that this report was only a malicious falsehood circulated by the shoemaker Gottlieb to annoy and vex the curate. I myself contradicted it stoutly. You see that I was completely your dupe, and that no one could be more sincerely mistaken.

"There has been a great mistake, sir," replied Consuelo with modest dignity; "but their has been no dupe. I do not think I departed for a single instant from the respect due to you, nor from the proprieties which sincerity and self respect impose. I was overtaken by night on the road, without shelter, overcome by thirst and fatigue, after a long journey on foot. You would not have refused hospitality to a beggar woman under such circumstances. You granted it to me from your love of music, and I paid my scot in kind. If I did not depart the next day, in spite of your persuasions, it was owing to unforeseen circumstances which imperatively demanded of me a paramount duty. My enemy, my rival, my persecutor, fell as it were from the clouds at your gate, and, deprived of the care and assistance of others, had a right to my assistance and my care. Your reverence must well remember the rest; you know that if I took advantage of your benevolence, it was not on my own account. You know also that I departed as soon as my duty was accomplished, and if I return to-day to thank you in person for the kindness you have shown me, the reason is, that sincerity and good faith made it incumbent on me to be myself the means of undeceiving you and giving you the explanations which were necessary to your dignity as well as my own."

"In all this," said the canon, half convinced, "there is something very mysterious and extraordinary. You say that the unfortunate woman, whose child I have adopted, was your enemy, your rival. Who are you then yourself, Bertoni?—Forgive me if that name continually recurs to my lips, and tell me how I must call you from henceforth."

"I am called the Porporina," replied Consuelo; "I am the pupil of Porpora; I am a singer. I belong to the stage."

"Ah! yes;" said the canon with a deep sigh. "I ought to have guessed so from the manner in which you performed your part; and as to your prodigious talent for music, I am no longer astonished at it; you have been educated in a good school. May I ask if my friend Beppo is your brother or—your husband?"

"Neither the one nor the other. He is my brother by affection. No closer tie binds us, reverend sir; and if my soul had not felt itself as chaste as your own, I should not have stained by my presence the sanctity of your dwelling."

Consuelo's manner was in truth irresistible, and the canon yielded to its power, as pure and upright minds always do to the words of sincerity. He felt as if an enormous weight had been taken from his breast, and, while walking slowly between his two young protegés, he questioned Consuelo with a returning gentleness and affectionate sympathy against which he had gradually ceased to struggle. She related to him rapidly, and without mentioning any names, the principal occurrences of her life; her betrothal at the death-bed of her mother to Anzoleto, the latter's infidelity, the hatred of Corilla, Zustiniani's outrageous designs, Porpora's advice, her departure from Venice, the attachment which Albert had conceived for her, the offers of the Rudolstadt family, her own hesitations and scruples, her flight from the Castle of the Giants, her meeting with Joseph Haydn, her journey, her terror and compassion at Corilla's bed of suffering, her gratitude for the protection granted by the canon to Anzoleto's child, and lastly her arrival at Vienna, and even her interview with Maria Theresa the day before. Joseph had not until then known all Consuelo's history, she had never spoken to him of Anzoleto, and the few words she had just said of her past affection for that wretched man did not strike him forcibly; but her generosity toward Corilla, and her solicitude for the child, made such a deep impression on him, that he turned away to hide his tears. The canon did not attempt to restrain his. Consuelo's narrative, concise, energetic, and sincere, produced the same effect upon him as if he had read a stirring romance; but this was a style of reading which the canon had never ventured on, and this was the first time in his life that he had been thus initiated into the feelings and emotions of others, as evinced in their lives and actions. He seated himself upon a bench in order to listen better; and when the young girl had finished all, he exclaimed, " If all you have said is true, as I believe and feel in my heart it is, you are truly a sweet and angelic creature! You are St. Cecilia come once more to visit the earth! I confess to you frankly," added he, after an instant of silence and reflection, " that I never had any prejudice against the stage, and you prove to me that one's salvation can be secured there as well as elsewhere. Certainly if you continue to be as pure and generous as you have been hitherto, you will have deserved your reward in Heaven, my dear Bertoni!—I speak with perfect sincerity, my dear Porporina!"

" And now, sir," said Consuelo, rising, " give me some news of Angela before I take leave of your reverence."

" Angela is very well, and thrives wonderfully," replied the canon. " My gardener's wife takes the greatest care of her, and I see her constantly, as the good woman carries her about in my garden. A flower herself, she will shoot up in the midst of flowers, under my eye, and when the time to make her a Christian shall have come, I will not spare either time or pains on her education. Trust me for that care, my children. What I have promised in the face of Heaven I will religiously perform. It seems as if her mother did not intend to dispute this care with me, for though she is at Vienna, she has not once sent to ask tidings of her daughter."

" She may have done so indirectly, and without your knowledge," replied Consuelo ; " I do not believe that a mother can be so completely indifferent about her offspring. But Corilla is soliciting an engagement at the court theater. She knows that her majesty is very severe, and does not grant her protection to persons of a blemished reputation. She has an interest in concealing her faults, at least until her engagement is signed. Let us keep her secret, therefore."

" And yet she is opposing you!" cried Joseph; " and they say that she will succeed by her intrigues—that she has already spread unfounded and scandalous reports concerning you in the city. The matter was spoken of at the embassy; so Keller told me. Your friends were indignant at it, but they feared lest she should persuade Herr Kaunitz, who willingly listens to such stories, and who cannot say enough in praise of Corilla's beauty."

"Did she act so?" said Consuelo, reddening with indignation. Then she added calmly: "To be sure, I might have expected it."

"But there needs only one word to counteract her calumnies," returned Joseph, "and that word I will say myself! I will say that——"

"You will say nothing, Beppo; it would be mean and cruel. You will not speak it either, reverend sir, and if I nourished a desire to say it, you would prevent me, would you not?"

"Upright and pious girl!" cried the canon. "But reflect that this secret cannot be one long. There are servants and country people enough, who have known and can report the fact, to inform the world of the real state of the case."

"Before that time Corilla or myself will be engaged. I should not wish to succeed in the contest by an act of vengeance. Until then, Beppo, keep silence, or I withdraw from you my esteem and my friendship. And now, sir, farewell. Tell me that you forgive me, grant me once more the pleasure of pressing that kind and fatherly hand, and allow me to depart before your people have seen me in this dress."

"My people may say what they please, and my benefice may resort to my successor, if so it please Heaven! I have just received an inheritance which gives me courage to brave the thunders of the *Ordinary*. So, do not take me for a saint, my children; I am tired of constantly obeying and living under restraint; I wish to live honestly, and without childish and unmanly terrors. Since I am no longer under Bridget's sway, and especially since I see myself the possessor of an independent fortune, I feel as brave as a lion. So now then come and breakfast with me; we will baptize Angela afterward, and then have some music until dinner."

He led the way to the priory. "Here, André! Joseph!" cried he to his servants on entering; "come and see the Signor Bertoni metamorphosed into a lady. You did not expect that? well, nor I either! But make haste to recover from your surprise, and prepare breakfast quickly,"

The repast was exquisite, and our young people saw that if serious changes had taken place in the canon's mind, they had not operated against his habits of good cheer.

After breakfast the child was carried to the chapel of the priory. The canon put off his quilted dressing-gown, arrayed himself in cassock and surplice, and performed the ceremony. Joseph and Consuelo assumed the office of godfather and godmother, and the name of Angela was finally bestowed on the little girl. The rest of the after-noon was consecrated to music, and then followed the leave-takings. The canon regretted that he could not detain his friends for dinner, but he yielded to their reasons, and consoled himself with the idea of seeing them again at Vienna, whither he intended to proceed in a short time to spend a part of the winter. While their carriage was getting ready, he conducted them to his green-house, that they might admire several new plants with which he had enriched his collection. It was already twilight, but the canon, whose sense of smell was exquisite, had no sooner taken a few steps under the glass roof of his transparent palace than he cried out: " I perceive an extraordinary perfume here! Can the *glaïeul vanilla* have flowered? But no, that is not the odor of my glaïeul. The strelitza is not fragrant—the cyclamens have a less pure and less penetrating aroma, What can have happened here? If my volkameria, alas! were not dead, I should think it was its fragrance that I inhaled! My poor plant! But I will not think of it again."

But suddenly the canon uttered a cry of surprise and admiration on beholding in a box, before him, the most magnificent volkameria he had ever seen in his life, all covered with its clusters of small white roses tinged with rose color, the sweet perfume of which filled the green-house and overpowered all the vulgar scents around. " Is this a miracle? From what celestial garden has this lovely flower descended?" cried he, in a fit of poetic rapture.

" We brought it in our carriage with the utmost care," replied Consuelo; " and allow us to offer it to you as some reparation for a most unfriendly wish respecting its predecessor, which fell from my lips on a certain occasion, and which I shall repent all my life."

" Oh, my dear daughter! what a gift, and with what delicacy is it offered!" said the canon, much affected. " Oh my dear volkameria! like all my especial favorites you shall have a particular name, and I shall call you Bertoni, in memory of one who is no longer in being, and whom I loved with all the affection of a father."

"My dearest father," said Consuelo, clasping his hand, "you must learn to love your daughters as well as your sons. Angela is not a boy——"

"And Porporina is my daughter also!" said the canon; "yes, my daughter; yes, yes, my dear daughter!" repeated he, looking alternately at Consuelo and the Volkameria Bertoni, with eyes swimming in tears.

By six o'clock, Joseph and Consuelo were once more in their lodging. The carriage had dropped them at the entrance of the suburb, and nothing betrayed their innocent escapade. Porpora, however, was a little astonished that Consuelo had not a better appetite after her walk in the lovely meadows which surrounded the capital of the empire. The canon's breakfast had probably make Consuelo rather dainty that day. But the free air and exercise procured her an excellent sleep, and on the morrow she felt herself in better voice and spirits than she had been since her arrival at Vienna.

CHAPTER XCI.

In the uncertainty under which she labored respecting her future fate, Consuelo, hoping perhaps by such a step to find some comfort or assistance, at last decided to write to Count Christian of Rudolstadt, and inform him of her position with respect to Porpora, of the efforts which the latter was making to bring her again upon the stage, and of the hope she cherished of seeing them fail. She spoke to him with perfect sincerity, expatiated upon the gratitude, devotedness, and submission which she owed to her old master, and, confiding to him the fears she entertained respecting Albert, requested him to dictate to her immediately the letter she ought to write to the latter, in order to calm his mind and inspire him with confidence toward her. She concluded with these words: "I requested time from your lordship to examine my heart and to decide. I am resolved to keep my word, and I can safely affirm that I feel sufficient strength in myself to close my heart and mind to all conflicting fancies, as well as to all new affections. And yet, if I once more return to the stage, I take a step which is in appearance an infraction of my promises, a formal renunciation of the hope of keeping them. I wish your lordship to judge of my conduct, or rather of the circumstances in which I am unfortunately placed. I see no means of escaping from them without being guilty of a dereliction of duty. I anxiously await your advice, which is so superior to any judgment I could myself form, but which I cannot think will contradict the dictates of my conscience."

When this letter was sealed and intrusted to Joseph to despatch, Consuelo felt more tranquil, as generally happens when, in a difficult crisis, we have found some means of gaining time, and putting off the decisive moment. She therefore prepared to accompany Porpora on a visit, in his opinion important and decisive, to the celebrated and highly praised imperial poet, the Abbé Metastasio.

This illustrious personage was about fifty years of age, and possessed a good figure and captivating manners. He conversed admirably, and Consuelo would have been much prepossessed in his favor if, on her way to the mansion which Keller and the poet inhabited jointly, though at different altitudes, she had not had the following conversation with Porpora:

"Consuelo" (it is Porpora who is speaking), "you are going to see a handsome, keen looking man, with a fresh color and a constant smile upon his lips, and who, nevertheless, would have you believe that he is the prey of a cruel and dangerous disease ; a man who eats, drinks, sleeps, grows fat like his neighbors, and who, nevertheless, imagines that he is sleepless, starving, the victim of exhaustion and decline. Do not be so awkward, when he laments his maladies, as to tell him that he has no appearance of ill health, that his complexion is good, or any other similar remark; for he must be sympathized with and bewailed beforehand. Neither must you speak to him of death or the dead; for he is a coward, and fears to die. And yet do not be so silly as to say on leaving him that you hope his precious health will soon be restored ; for he wishes it to be imagined that he is dying, and if he could succeed in making others believe that he is at the point of death, he would be quite satisfied, so that he does not think so himself."

" What a silly idea!" replied Consuelo, "and how unworthy of a great man! But what am I to say to him, if I am neither to speak of death nor recovery?"

"Oh! you must talk to him about his illness, ask him a thousand questions, listen to the detail of all his sufferings, and wind up with telling him that he does not take sufficient care of himself, that he does not attend to his health, and that he works too hard. In this manner he may be rendered favorable to us."

"But are we not going to ask him for a poem, which you may set to music, and which I may sing? How can we advise him then not to write, and at the same time urge him to write as fast as possible?"

"All that can be easily managed in the course of conversation; it is only necessary to bring things into a proper train."

The maestro wished his pupil to make herself agreeable to the poet, but his sarcastic habits would not suffer him to conceal the foibles of others, and he committed the error of awakening Consuelo's clear-sighted judgment, and inducing her to regard him with that sort of inward contempt which was not likely to render her amiable or sympathizing toward him. Incapable of adulation or deceit, it pained her to see Porpora hypocritically bewail the sorrows of the poet, and ridicule him unmercifully under the seeming garb of sympathy for his imaginary ills. She blushed repeatedly, and could not help remaining silent, notwithstanding the signs which the master gave her to speak.

Consuelo's reputation had begun to spread through Vienna, she had sung in several saloons, and her admission to the Italian theater was a subject of discussion in the musical world. Metastasio was all-powerful; and should Consuelo secure his sympathy by adroitly flattering his self-love, he might confide to Porpora the care of setting to music his *Attileo Regolo*, which he had kept in his portfolio for several years. It was necessary for this purpose that the pupil should plead for her master, for the maestro was far from a favorite with the imperial poet. Matastasio was not an Italian for nothing, and Italians are not readily deceived respecting each other. He was well aware Porpora had no great admiration for his dramatic genius, and that, right or wrong, he had censured oftener than once his timidity, his selfishness, and false sensibility. Consuelo's icy reserve, and the slight interest she seemed to take in his disease, did not appear to him what they really were, the result of a feeling of respectful pity. It seemed no better than an insult, and if he had not been a slave to propriety and politeness, he would have refused plumply to hear her sing. He consented, however, after some little affectation, alleging as his excuse the state of his nerves, and the risk he ran of being excited. He had heard Consuelo sing his oratorio of *Judith*, but it was necessary he should form some idea of her dramatic powers, and Porpora insisted much.

"But what am I to do, and how am I to sing," whispered Consuelo, "if he is not to be excited?"

"On the contrary, he must be excited," replied the maestro; "he loves dearly to be roused from his torpor; for when he is so, he feels in a better vein for writing."

Consuelo sung an air from *Achillo in Sciro*, Metastasio's best opera, which had been set to music by Caldara in 1736, and performed at the marriage festival of Maria Theresa. Metastasio was as much struck with her voice and manner as on the first occasion, but he was resolved to maintain the same cold and rigid silence that she had displayed during the recital of his symptoms. But he could not succeed; for the worthy man was an artist in spite of every thing, and when the accents of a poet's muse and the remembrance of his triumphs are nobly interpreted, a cord is touched which thrills through his whole being, and rancor cannot hold its ground.

The abbé tried to defend himself against this potent charm. He coughed repeatedly, fidgetted on his chair like a man in the extremity of suffering, then all at once, carried away by his emotion, he hid his face in his handkerchief and sobbed aloud. Porpora, concealed behind the arm-chair, motioned to Consuelo not to spare him, and rubbed his hands with malicious glee.

These tears, which flowed so abundantly and so earnestly, immediately reconciled Consuelo to the pusillanimous abbé. As soon as she had finished, she approached and kissed his hand, saying with evident emotion:

"Alas! sir, I should be proud and happy to have produced an impression on your feeling, did it not inspire me with remorse. The dread of injuring your health poisons my joy."

"Ah! my dear child," replied the abbé, completely won over, "you do not—you cannot, know the mingled pleasure and suffering that you inflict upon me. I never till this moment heard a voice which reminded me of my dear Marianna; and you have so recalled her manner and expression, that I imagined I was listening to herself. Ah! you have pierced my heart!" And he began to sob afresh.

" His lordship speaks of a celebrated person whom you ought certainly to place before you as a model," said Porpora to his pupil, " the illustrious and incomparable Marianna Bulgarini."

" What! the Romanina?" exclaimed Consuelo. "Ah! I heard her in my childhood at Venice; she is the first who made a great impression on me, and I shall never forget her!"

" I see that you have indeed heard her, and that she has deeply impressed you," replied Metastasio. "Ah! young girl, imitate her in every thing, in her acting as in her singing, in her goodness of mind as in her greatness of character, in her power as in her tenderness! Ah! she was beautiful, when she represented the divine Venus in my first opera at Rome! I owe to her my earliest triumphs."

"And it is to your lordship that her most brilliant success was due," said Porpora.

" True, we assisted each other. But nothing could repay the obligation I feel toward her. Never was there such affection, such heroic perseverance and delicate attention, before in human breast. Angel of my soul! I shall lament thee forever, and my only hope is to meet thee again!"

Here the abbé wept afresh. Consuelo was deeply affected. Porpora pretended to be so ; but in spite of himself his countenance remained ironical and disdainful. Consuelo observed it, and resolved that she would reproach him for his coldness and distrust. As to Metastasio, he only observed what indeed he wished to observe, the tenderness and admiration displayed by the good Consuelo. He was possessed of the true distinguishing peculiarity of poets, for his tears flowed more readily before spectators than in the privacy of his chamber, and never did he feel his affections and his griefs so deeply as when he eloquently detailed them to an admiring audience. Carried away by his emotion, he related to Consuelo the history of that portion of his youth in which Romanina had borne so large a part, the services which this gentle creature had rendered him, her filial devotion to his old parents, the sacrifice to which she submitted in separating from him that he might be at liberty to seek advancement in Vienna; and when he came to the parting scene—when he told in the choicest and most tender terms, how his dear Marianna, with a broken heart and a bosom torn with sobs, had exhorted him to leave her—to think only of himself—he exclaimed:

"Oh! if she had foreseen what awaited me when far from her—if she could have known the grief, the fears, the anguish, the apprehensions, the sinking of the heart, and lastly, my terrible disease—she would have spared herself and me! Alas, I was far from thinking that our farewell was an eternal one—that we should never meet again on earth!"

"How? you never met again?" said Consuelo, whose eyes were bathed with tears, for Metastasio's manner was touching in the extreme. "She never came to Vienna?"

"No, she never came," replied the abbé in a heart-rending tone.

"After such devotion she had not courage to meet you again?" resumed Consuelo, to whom Porpora was making in vain the most hideous grimaces.

Metastasio did not reply; he seemed lost in thought.

"But she may yet come?" continued the kind-hearted Consuelo. "Ah! she will surely come, and this happy event will make you well again."

The abbé grew pale, and made a gesture indicative of terror. The maestro coughed with all his might, and Consuelo, suddenly recollecting that Romanina had been dead upward of ten years, became aware of the awkwardness of which she had been guilty in reminding Metastasio of the death of his well-beloved, whom he only desired to meet beyond the grave. She bit her lips with vexation, and soon after took her leave with Porpora, who only obtained vague promises and forced civilities as usual.

"What have you done, numskull?" exclaimed he to Consuelo, as soon as they were outside.

"Yes, I see I was very foolish. I forgot that Romanina was no longer alive. But do you really think, my dear master, that this tender-hearted and unhappy man is so attached to life as you are pleased to say? I fancy his want of sleep is the principal cause of his disease, and that if some superstitious terror makes him dread his last moments, he is not the less sincerely and painfully wearied of life."

"Child!" said Porpora; "people are never tired of life when they are rich, honored, paid court to, and in good health; when they have no other cares, no other passions than these, it is but a lying farce for them to rave at existence."

"Do not say he has had no others. He loved his Marianna, and I can very well imagine why he gave this cherished name to his grandchild, and to his niece, Marianna Martinez." Consuelo had almost said Joseph's pupil, but she suddenly checked herself.

"Go on," said Porpora, "his grandchild, his niece, or his daughter."

"So it is said, but it is of no moment to me."

"It would prove at least that the dear abbé quickly consoled himself for the absence of his beloved. When you asked him—plague take your stupidity—why his dear Marianna did not rejoin him, he did not answer you, but I shall answer in his place. Romanina had indeed rendered him the greatest services which a man could accept at the hands of a woman. She had supported him, lodged, clothed, succored, assisted him on all occasions, and had got him appointed *poeta cesareo.* She aided, befriended, nursed, and lavished every care upon his aged parents. All that is perfectly true. For Marianna had a great soul; I knew her well. But it is also perfectly true that she wished to join him again by procuring an engagement at the court theater, and still more, it is equally true that the abbé paid no attention to her wishes, and never acceded to them. There certainly was the tenderest correspondence in the world carried on between them. I have no doubt that his letters were masterpieces. He knew very well they would be printed. But although he wrote to his *dilettissima amica* that he sighed for the day when they should meet again, and that it was his constant effort to bring about that happy time, the cunning fox managed things so that the unhappy songstress should not disturb his illustrious and lucrative attachment to a third Marianna—for this name was fated to be a fortunate one with him—the noble and puissant Countess of Athan, the favorite of the last Cesar. Report says that there was a secret marriage; and I think therefore it is rather bad taste to tear his hair for poor Romanina, who died of a broken heart while in the meantime he wrote madrigals in honor of the charms of the court beauties."

"You criticise and judge his conduct very severely," replied Consuelo, mournfully.

"I only repeat what the world says—I invent nothing. I am merely the echo of public opinion. Come, there are more actors than those who walk the stage; it is an old saying."

"The public voice is not always the most enlightened, and never the most charitable. Ah! my dear master, I cannot believe that a man of such talent and renown should be no better than a mere actor. I saw him weep bitter and heartfelt tears, and even if he has cause to reproach himself for having too quickly forgotten his Marianna, his remorse would only add to his present grief. In all this I would rather consider him as weak than base. They made him an abbé, and loaded him with favors, the court was strict, and an attachment to an actress would have compromised his reputation. He did not deliberately intend to betray and deceive Bulgarini—he was afraid, he hesitated, he thought to gain time, and in the meantime she died."

"And he returned thanks to Heaven for the happy event," added the implacable maestro. "And now the empress sends him boxes and rings with her initials set in brilliants, pens of lapis lazuli with diamond laurels, gold boxes filled with Spanish tobacco, seals made out of a single diamond; and all these glitter so, that the poet's eyes are constantly watering."

"And will all that console him for having broken Romanina's heart?"

"Perhaps not; but his longing after these things induced him to do it. Paltry, yet fatal ambition! For my part I could hardly help laughing when he showed us his gold chandelier, with the ingenious motto suggested by the empress:

'Perche possa risparmiare i suoi occhi!'

"It is certainly very pretty, and made him exclaim

aloud—'*Affettuosa espressiona valutabile piu assai dell'oro!*' Poor man!"

"Unfortunate man," exclaimed Consuelo, sighing, as she returned home sorrowfully, for she could not help sadly comparing Metastasio's position with respect to Marianna, and her own in relation to Albert. "To wait and die! is this then the fate of those who love with passion? And is it the destiny of those who pursue the vain chimera, glory, to make others wait and die?"

"What are you dreaming of?" said the maestro. "It seems to me that all goes well, and that in spite of your awkwardness, you have won over Metastasio."

"It is a poor conquest, that of a weak mind," she replied; "and I do not believe that he who wanted courage to admit Marianna to the imperial theater, will exert himself any more to serve me."

"Metastasio, in matters of art, henceforth governs the court of the empress."

"Metastasio in matters of art will never advise the empress to do any thing she does not wish; and whatever may be said of her favorites and counselors, I have observed her countenance, and I tell you, master, that Maria-Theresa is too politic to have favorites — too absolute to have friends."

"Well, then," said Porpora, somewhat anxiously, "we must win over the empress herself. You must sing some morning in her apartments, and give her an opportunity of speaking to you and conversing with you. People say that she likes only well-conducted girls. If she have the eagle eye which is imputed to her, she will judge you and prefer you. It shall now be my endeavor to bring about such an interview."

CHAPTER XCII.

ONE morning Joseph, occupied in sweeping Porpora's ante-chamber, and forgetting that the partition was thin, and the maestro's slumbers light, amused himself by humming mechanically whatever came uppermost, and beating time with his brush upon the boards. Porpora, dissatisfied at being so early awakened, fidgetted about in his bed and tried to sleep again, but the sweet fresh voice, which sang with great taste and correctness a very agreeable air, still reaching his ear, he threw on his dressing-gown and peeped through the key-hole, partly pleased with what he heard, partly angry with the artist who had so unceremoniously rouse him. But what is his surprise!—it is no other than Bepp, whose fertile imagination pursues his theme while mechanically busied with household cares!

" What is that you are singing?" exclaimed the maestro in a voice of thunder, as he abruptly opened the door.

Joseph, bewildered like a man startled from his sleep, was on the point of pitching aside broom and feathers, and taking to his heels But if he no longer entertained the hope of becoming a pupil of Porpora, he still considered himself most fortunate in being able to hear Consuelo, and to receive lessons from this generous friend when the master turned his back! On no consideration, therefore, would he have been turned out of doors, so he ventured on a fib, in order to disarm suspicion.

" What was I singing?" said he, quite out of countenance. " Alas! master, I know not."

" Do people sing what they do not know? liar that you are!"

" I assure, you master, I know not what I sung. You have so frightened me that I already forget what it was. I know that it is wrong to sing so near your room, but I quite forgot myself ; I dreamed I was alone and far from this. I said to myself, ' Now you may sing ; there is no composer here to say, be silent, you sing false. Be silent, you ignoramus ; what do you know of music?'"

" Who told you that you sung false."

" Every body."

" And I tell you," exclaimed the maestro, in a severe tone, " that you do not sing false. Who taught you?"

" Why—Master Reuter, whom my friend Keller shaves ; he drove me from the class, saying I would never be anything but an ass."

Joseph knew enough of the master's prejudices to be aware that he held Reuter in the utmost contempt ; he had even reckoned upon the latter's advancing him in the good graces of Porpora, on the first occasion he might attempt to disparage him to the maestro. But Reuter, in his few visits to Porpora, had never so much as deigned to recognize his old pupil.

" Master Reuter is an ass himself," muttered Porpora to himself ; " but that is not the question," resumed he aloud. " I want to know where you learned that turn," and here he sang that which Joseph had repeated some ten times in succession, without being aware of it.

" Oh! is it that?" said Haydn, who began to draw a better augury of the maestro's disposition, but who did not venture to trust him yet ; " that is something I heard the signora sing."

" Consuelo? My daughter? I did not know that. Ah! you listen at the doors then?"

" Oh, no, sir! but music penetrates from room to room, even to the kitchen, and I hear in spite of myself."

" I do not like to be served by people who have so good a memory, and can sing my unpublished ideas in the street. You may pack off this very day. Seek a place elsewhere."

This announcement fell like a thunderbolt on poor Joseph ; he retired to weep in the kitchen, where Consuelo soon joined him, to listen to the recital of his mishap and to comfort him by promising to arrange matters.

" How is this, master ?" said she to Porpora, when she presented him his coffee. " You would drive away this laborious, faithful youth, because, for the first time in his life, he happened to sing well."

" I tell you that he is a deceiver and a hardened liar ; he has been sent by some enemy who wishes to discover the secrets of my compositions, and appropriate them to himself before they have seen the light. I will engage that this fellow knows my new opera by heart, and copies my manuscripts when my back is turned. How often have I been thus betrayed! How many of my ideas have I not found in those pretty operas which were all the rage in Venice, while they yawned at mine, saying: ' This crazy old Porpora gives us as new, these airs which are sung about all the thoroughfares of Venice !' Hold! the ass has betrayed himself ; he sang this morning a phrase which I am certain is by no other than Meinherr Hasse, and which I perfectly recollect. I shall note it down, and to revenge myself I shall put it in my new opera, to pay him back a trick which he has often practiced on me."

" Take care, master, it may be already published. You do not know by heart all existing productions."

" But I have heard them, and tell you this is too remarkable not to have struck me."

" Very well, master, a thousand thanks! I am proud of the compliment, for the air is mine,"

Consuelo here unfortunately told a fib. The phrase in question had only that morning seen the light in Joseph's brain; but she had taken the hint, and had already learned it by heart in order not to be taken at fault if questioned by the suspicious maestro. Porpora did not fail to ask her for it. She sang it immediately, and alleged that the evening before, in order to please the Abbé Metastasio, she had tried to set to music the first verses of his charming pastoral, commencing:

> " *Già reide la primavera,*
> *Col suo fiorito aspetto ;*
> *Già il grato zeffiretto*
> *Scherza fra l'erbe e i fiori.*
> *Tornan le frondi agli alberi*
> *L'erbette al prato tornano ;*
> *Sol non ritorna a me*
> *La pace del mio cor.*" *

" I had repeated the first phrase several times," she added, " when I heard Master Beppo in the ante-chamber who was warbling it like a canary — that is to say all astray. I grew impatient, and begged him to hold his tongue; but at the end of an hour he again repeated it so awkwardly on the stairs that I had no wish to go on with it."

" And how comes it that he sings so well to-day? What has happened to him while asleep ?"

" I shall explain it to you, my dear master. I observed that this boy had a fine and even a correct voice, but that he sang falsely from want of ear, judgment, and memory. I amused myself by making him repeat the notes, and sing the scale according to your method, to see if it would succeed even with an inferior organization."

" It must succeed with all organizations !" exclaimed

---

* Now, with its flowery face, the beauteous spring returns.
Among the grass and flowers the zephyrs sport with glee.
The leaves adorn the trees, the waving grass the fields
But my heart's peace returns not yet to me.

Porpora; " there is no such thing as a false voice, and never was there an ear properly exercised which——"

" That is exactly what I said to myself," replied Consuelo, anxious to end the discussion, " and the result proved that I was correct. In the first lesson according to your system, I succeeded in making him understand what Reuter and all the Germans in the world would never have instilled into him. After that I sang the air, and for the first time he understood it correctly. He immediately sung it, and he was so astonished, so wonder-stricken; that he could not sleep—it was like a new revelation to him. ' Oh! mademoiselle !' said he, ' if I had been taught thus I should have learned something like the other pupils. But I do assure you I never could understand what they taught at St. Stephens.' "

" And was he really taught there ?"

" Yes, and was shamefully expelled from the school. You have only to mention his name to Master Reuter ; he will tell you that he is a sad fellow, and a most impracticable scholar."

" Come hither !" cried Porpora to Beppo, who was in tears behind the door; " sit by me, till I see if you understand yesterday's lesson."

The malicious maestro then began to teach the rudiments of music to Joseph, but in the roundabout, confused, pedantic fashion which he ascribed to the Germans. If Joseph had allowed his intelligence to appear, purposely confused as Porpora's instructions were, he had been lost without retrieve. But he was too knowing to be so easily entrapped, and he displayed such determined stupidity throughout the long lesson that the maestro was satisfied.

" I see you know very little indeed," said he, rising and persisting in a feint with which the others were not in the least duped. " Go back to your broom and let us have no more singing if you wish to remain with me."

But at the end of two hours, unable to restrain himself, and stimulated by the love of a neglected calling which he had exercised for so long a period without a rival, Porpora once more became the professor of singing, and recalled Joseph to set him to work again. He explained the same principles indeed, but with that lucidness and logical precision which arranges and classifies all knowledge—in a word, with that incredible simplicity which characterizes men of genius.

Haydn now perceived that he might venture to understand a little, and Porpora was delighted at his success. Although the maestro taught him things which he had already long studied, and which he knew as well as possible, the lesson was interesting and useful to him. He learned to teach; and since, during those hours when Porpora did not employ him, he continued to give lessons through the city in order not to lose his few pupils, he determined to turn what he had learned to account without loss of time.

"Ah! most respected professor," said he to Porpora, pretending to play the simpleton to the end of the chapter, "I prefer this music to the other, and I think I could make some progress in it. But as to this morning's work I had rather go back to St. Stephen's than have any thing to say to it."

"And yet it is the same you learned there. Can there be two sorts of music, dolt? There is but one music, and can be but one."

"Oh! I ask your pardon, sir; there is Master Reuter's music which wearies me, and there is yours which does not weary me at all."

"You flatter me highly, Signor Beppo," said Porpora, laughing; but the compliment was far from being displeasing to him.

From that day Haydn received Porpora's instructions, and in a short time they began to study Italian song, and the fundamental ideas of lyrical composition. This was what the noble youth had so ardently wished, and so courageously pursued. His progress was so rapid that the maestro was at once charmed, surprised, and even terrified. When Consuelo saw his former distrust ready to spring up, she pointed out to her young friend the conduct he ought to pursue. A little obstinacy, a feigned abstraction, were necessary to rouse Porpora's peculiar genius and passion for teaching, just as some little drawback and difficulty always render the exercise of the higher powers more energetic and powerful. It frequently happened therefore that Joseph was obliged to feign languor and indifference in order to procure those precious lessons, the least of which he would have trembled to lose. The pleasure of opposition, and the desire of conquering, urged on the pugnacious soul of the old professor, and never did Beppo receive clearer conceptions than those which were drawn forth, warm and eloquent, from the satirical and excited master.

CHAPTER XCIII.

WHILE Porpora's abode was the theater of these apparently unimportant proceedings, the results of which might yet have so great an influence on the history of art, inasmuch as the genius of one of the most original, imaginative, and celebrated composers of the last century received from them its greatest development—events exercising a more immediate influence on Consuelo's existence took place out of doors. Corilla, much more active and able in the promotion of her own interests, gained ground every day, and, now perfectly recovered, negotiated the conditions of her engagement at the court theater. A vigorous actress, but an indifferent musician, she pleased the director and his wife much more than Consuelo. It was very evident that the learned Porporina looked down from too great a height, were it only in thought, on the operas of Master Holzbaüer and the talents of his lady. They were well aware that great artists, poorly aided, reduced to express second-rate ideas, and as it were oppressed by the violence thus offered to their taste and conceptions, do not always preserve the beaten track, or retain the self-command which bold mediocrity introduces into the most wretched productions, and amid the dreary jingle of works badly studied and ill understood.

When, thanks to their wonderful resolution and power, they succeed in triumphing over the difficulties of their position, the envious atmosphere around them utters nothing but discord. The composer is well aware of their discomfort, and fears lest this forced inspiration should suddenly cool, and impair his success. Even the public, surprised and disconcerted without well knowing why, find out at last that genius, held enslaved by vulgar prejudice, is struggling within its narrow limits, and it is almost with a sigh that they applaud her strenuous efforts. Holzbaüer perfectly recollected the little relish that Consuelo displayed for his music. She was so unfortunate

as to evince this one day, when, disguised and thinking
she had only to deal with a person such as one meets when
traveling for the first and last time, she had spoken her
sentiments openly, never suspecting that her position as
an artist could ever be at the mercy of the unknown
friend of the canon. Holzbaüer, however, had not forgotten it, and under his calm and courteous demeanor
was deeply hurt, and had sworn to throw every obstacle in
the way of her success. But as he was unwilling that
Porpora and his pupil, and what he called their clique,
should have it in their power to accuse him of un-
fairness, he had mentioned to no one except his wife his
meeting with Consuelo, and the adventure of the breakfast. This adventure therefore seemed to have made no
impression on the director; he appeared to have entirely
forgotten the little Bertoni, and not in the least to suspect
that the wandering singer and Porporina were one and
the same individual. Consuelo was lost in conjectures
respecting the conduct of Holzbaüer toward her.

"I must have been completely disguised then," said
she in confidence to Beppo, "and the arrangement of my
hair must have greatly changed my features, since this
man, who looked at me there so keenly, does not recognize me here at all."

"Neither did Count Hoditz know you the first time he
saw you at the ambassador's," replied Joseph, "and perhaps had he not received your note, he might never have
recognized you."

"Yes, but Count Hoditz has so proud and nonchalant a
manner of looking at people, that in reality he scarcely
sees them. I am sure he would not have divined my sex
at Passau if Baron Trenck had not given him a hint; while
Holzbaüer, as soon as he saw me, and, indeed, every time
he meets me, looks at me with the same attentive and prying eyes that he fixed on me at the curate's. Why is he so
generously silent on an adventure that might be misinter-
preted, and which might even embroil me with my master,
since he thinks I traveled to Vienna in the usual manner,
without experiencing any distress, or meeting even with the
shadow of an adventure? And all the while this same Holzbaüer depreciates, in an underhand manner, my voice and
method, and in short, exerts himself to the utmost against
me, in order not to be obliged to give me an engagement.

He hates and repels me, and as his weapons are stronger than mine, I must succumb. I am lost."

The solution of the enigma was soon apparent to Consuelo; but in order to understand her position, the reader must remember that a numerous and powerful coterie was working hard against her, that Corilla was handsome and not over scrupulous, that the minister, Kaunitz, who loved to dazzle in the gossip of the green-room, saw her often, and that Maria Theresa, to relieve her mind from the cares of state, amused herself by listening to his chatterings on these topics, ridiculing him inwardly for his littleness of mind. She took a sort of pleasure in this gossip, which afforded her, though on a smaller scale, and with more open effrontery, a spectacle somewhat similar to that which was then taking place in the three most important courts of Europe — governed as they were by female intrigues—to wit, her own, that of the Czarina, and that of Madame de Pompadour.

Maria Theresa, as is well known, gave audiences once a week to all who wished to speak to her—a hypocritical and hereditary custom, which her son, Joseph II, religiously observed, and which still exists at the court of Austria. Besides this, Maria Theresa gave individual audiences to those who wished to enter her service, and no sovereign was ever more easy of access.

Porpora at length obtained this musical audience, in which he hoped that the empress, having an opportunity of seeing more closely the pleasing countenance of Consuelo, might perhaps be favorably disposed toward her. He knew the requirements of her majesty with regard to propriety of demeanor and correct conduct, and he felt assured that she would be struck with the candor and modesty which characterized his pupil's whole appearance. They were introduced into one of the smaller saloons of the palace, where a harpsichord had been brought, and where the empress herself arrived after an interval of half an hour. She had just been giving audience to some persons of distinction, and she still wore the same costume, just as it is represented on the gold sequins of the period, viz.: a robe of brocade, a mantle, a crown on her head, and a small Hungarian saber by her side. She was truly beautiful, not with that ideal grandeur which her courtiers affected to attribute to her, but lively, animated, with a happy, open countenance, and a self-possessed and enterprising look. It was indeed the *king* Maria Theresa, whom the Hungarian magnates, during a day of enthusiasm, had proclaimed, saber in hand; but at first sight it was a good rather than a great king. She displayed no coquetry, and her familiar manners evinced a calm and equable mind, devoid of female cunning. When she was closely observed, and more especially when she questioned perseveringly, a keen and even cold-blooded cunning was evident in this otherwise affable and smiling countenance. But if so, it was masculine, or, to choose a better word, imperial cunning.

"You will let me hear your pupil by and bye," said she to Porpora. "I already know that she is deeply skilled in the science of music, and has a magnificent voice; and I have not forgotten the pleasure she afforded me in the oratorio of *Betulia Liberata*. But I should like in the first place to speak to her for a short time in private. I have many questions to ask, and as I reckon upon her sincerity, I hope to be able to grant her the protection which she requests."

Porpora hastened to retire, reading in her majesty's eyes that she wished to be quite alone with Consuelo. He repaired to a neighboring gallery, which he found very cold; for the court, ruined by the outlay of the last war, was governed with strict economy, and Maria Theresa's character rendered this conformity to the necessity of her position easy to her.

Although thus left alone with the daughter and the mother of Cesars, the heroine of Germany and the greatest woman at that period in Europe, Consuelo was nevertheless neither agitated nor frightened. Whether it was that her aritstic temperament made her indifferent to this warlike display which glittered around Maria Theresa, extending even to her costume, or that her frank and noble soul was raised above such considerations, she awaited calmly and with perfect composure her majesty's inquiries.

The empress seated herself upon a sofa, adjusted her jeweled baldric, which somewhat fretted her fair round shoulders, and thus began: "I repeat to you, my child, that I think highly of your talents. I do not doubt your excellent education and artistic faculties, but you must be aware that I hold talent and genius as nothing in comparison with a pious upright heart and irreproachable conduct."

Consuelo, standing, listened respectfully to this exordium, but it did not occur to her that it afforded any grounds for praising herself; and as, besides, she felt an utter repugnance to boasting of virtues which she unostentatiously exercised, she waited for the empress to question her more directly on her principles and intentions. This would have been the time, however, to address the sovereign with a well-turned madrigal on her angelic piety, her sublime virtue, and on the impossibility of going astray with such an example before one's eyes; but poor Consuelo never even dreamed of profiting by the occasion. Refined minds fear to insult a noble character by offering vulgar praise, but monarchs, if they are not the dupes of flattery, are at least so much in the habit of breathing its intoxicating incense, that they demand it as a simple act of submission and etiquette. Maria Theresa was astonished at the young girl's silence, and assuming a somewhat harsher and less encouraging tone, she continued:

"I know, my young friend, that your conduct has not been over scrupulous, and that, although not married, you lead a life of somewhat unwarrantable intimacy with a young man of your own profession, whose name I do not now recollect."

"I can at least assure your imperial majesty of one thing." said Consuelo, provoked by the injustice of this sharp accusation, "that I have never committed a single fault, the recollection of which prevents me from sustaining your majesty's look with pride and satisfaction."

Maria Theresa was struck with the noble and lofty expression which Consuelo's countenance assumed at that instant. At an earlier period of her life she would doubtless have remarked it with pleasure and sympathy; but Maria Theresa was already a queen to the heart's core, and the exercise of absolute power had produced that species of mental intoxication which would subject every thing and every person to its own will. Maria Theresa wished to be the only powerful mind, whether a woman or sovereign, in all her realms. She was astounded, therefore, at the unshrinking look and proud smile of this young girl, whom she esteemed but as a worm before her, and with whom she would have amused herself for the instant as with a slave whom one questions out of curiosity.

"I asked you, mademoiselle," resumed she with an icy

tone, "who is the young man who lives with you in Porpora's house? you have not yet told me."

"His name is Joseph Haydn," replied Consuelo, composedly.

"Well! he has entered Porpora's service as valet-dechambre, through love of you; and Master Porpora is ignorant of this young man's real motives, while you are aware of them and encourage them."

"They have calumniated me to your majesty. This youth never had any preference for me" (here Consuelo thought she spoke the truth); "and I even know positively that his affections are engaged elsewhere; and if there has been a little deceit employed toward my excellent master, the motives for it are innocent, perhaps praiseworthy. The love of art alone has induced Joseph Haydn to enter the service of Porpora, and since your majesty deigns to weigh and examine the conduct of the meanest of your subjects, and since nothing can escape your clear-sighted scrutiny, I feel assured your majesty will give me credit for sincerity if you will but look into the particulars of my case."

Maria Theresa was too clear-sighted not to recognize at once the accents of truth. She had not yet lost the heroism of youth, although she had begun to descend that fatal declivity of absolute power, which so certainly extinguishes little by little faith and confidence even in the most generous minds.

"Young girl," said she, "I believe that you speak the truth, and that you are strictly well conducted; but I discern in you great pride and mistrust of my maternal goodness, symptoms which make me fear I can do nothing for you."

"If I am to appeal to the maternal goodness of Maria Theresa," replied Consuelo, softened by language of which the poor soul, alas! was far from suspecting the empty and meaningless nature, "I am ready to bend before her and implore it; but if it be——"

"Go on, my child," said Maria Theresa, who, without being able to explain her own feelings, would have been rejoiced to bring this singular person to her knees; "Speak freely."

"But if, on the other hand, it be to your majesty's imperial justice I am to appeal, as I have nothing to confess, inasmuch as a pure breath does not taint the air which even the gods breathe, I feel sufficient pride to esteem myself worthy of your protection."

"Porporina," said the empress, "you are an intelligent girl, and your originality, which might perhaps offend another, does you no discredit with me. I have told you that I believe you sincere, yet I know that you have something to confess. Why do you hesitate? You love this Haydn; your attachment, I have no doubt, is pure, but still you love him, since, for the pleasure of seeing him more frequently (let us even suppose that it is out of anxiety for his progress in music with Porpora), you fearlessly expose your reputation, which to us women is, of all things, one of the most sacred and important. But you fear, perhaps, that your master and your adopted father will never consent to your union with a poor and obscure artist. Perhaps, also, for I wish to believe all your assertions, the young man's affections are placed elsewhere; and you, proud as I see you are, conceal your preference, and generously sacrifice your good fame without receiving any equivalent. Were I in your place, my dear girl, and had the opportunity you have now, and may never have again, I should open my heart to my sovereign and should say: 'To you who can do every thing I confide my destiny; remove all obstacles. With a word you can change the feelings of my master and my lover. You can make me happy, reestablish me in public esteem, and place me in a position so honorable that I may hope to enter the service of the court.' Such is the confidence you should have in the maternal kindness of Maria Theresa, and I am sorry that you have not already made the discovery."

"I perceive very well," thought Consuelo, "that actuated by the despotic capriciousness of a spoiled child, you are desirous, great queen, to see the zingarella prostrate herself at your feet, because it seems to you that her knees are stiff and will not bend before you, and this to you is an unheard-of phenomenon. Well! you shall not have this amusement unless you prove clearly that you deserve the homage!"

These and other reflections passed quickly through her mind while Maria Theresa lectured her. She reflected that Porpora's fortune hung on the cast of a die, upon a whim of the empress, and that her master's prospects were well deserving the price of a little humiliation. But she would not incur the humiliation in vain. She would not act a part with a crowned head who certainly was as well skilled as she was on this point. She waited till Maria Theresa should prove herself truly great in her eyes, in order that in prostrating herself before her she might be sincere.

When the empress had finished her homily, Consuelo replied:

"I shall reply to all your majesty has deigned to say to me, if your majesty will please to order me."

"Yes, speak—speak!" said the empress, annoyed at her inflexible countenance.

"In the first place then your majesty will permit me to say, that for the first time in my life I learn from your imperial lips, that my reputation is at stake owing to the presence of Joseph Haydn in my master's house. I confess I thought that I was of too little importance to call forth an expression of public opinion, and if I had been told when I entered the imperial palace that the empress herself had weighed and condemned my conduct, I should have thought it was a dream."

Maria Theresa interrupted her. She thought this reflection of Consuelo's was somewhat ironical.

"You must not be astonished," said she, in an emphatic tone, "that I should busy myself in the most minute concerns of a being for whom I am responsible to God."

"We may be permitted to wonder where we admire," replied Consuelo, adroitly, "and if great deeds be the most simple, they are at least sufficiently unusual to surprise at first sight."

"You must understand, moreover," said the empress, "that I attend particularly to the artists with whom I love to adorn my court. The theater in every country is a school of scandal—a pit of perdition. I entertain the hope, laudable at least, if not practicable, of raising in the eyes of men and of purifying before God, the class of actors—a class exposed to the contempt of men, and even to the anathemas of the church in several countries, and despised and proscribed by most nations. While in France the church shuts her doors upon them, I for my part would have the church open them wide to receive them. I have never admitted either into my Italian, my French, or my national theater, any except persons of irreproachable morality, or at least those who are firmly resolved to reform their conduct. You must know that I insist on their marriage, and that I even hold their children at the baptismal font, resolved as I am to encourage legitimate births and nuptial fidelity."

"If we had known that," thought Consuelo, "we should have asked her majesty to be the godmother of Angela in my place. Your majesty sows only to reap abundantly," replied she aloud; "and if I had a fault on my conscience, I should be happy to confide it to so merciful and just a confessor; but——"

"Continue what you were just about to observe," said Maria Theresa, haughtily.

"I was about to say," replied Consuelo, "that being ignorant of the blame cast on me with respect to Joseph Haydn's abode in the same house, I did not make any severe sacrifice for his sake in exposing myself to it."

"I understand," said the empress; "you deny every thing!"

"How should I plead guilty to a falsehood?" replied Consuelo; "I have no preference for my master's pupil, much less the slightest desire to marry him; and even were it otherwise," thought she, "I should hardly accept his heart in virtue of an imperial fiat."

"So you intend to remain unmarried?" said the empress, rising. "Very well; I must say that it is a position which in point of character does not yield me sufficient security. Besides it is unseemly that a young person should appear in certain parts, and represent certain passions, when she has not the sanction of marriage and the protection of her husband. It only depended upon yourself to distance your competitor, Madame Corilla, respecting whom I have received a very good character, but who does not pronounce Italian nearly so well as you do. But then Madame Corilla is married, and the mother of a family, which places her in a more favorable position than that which you have chosen to occupy."

"Married!" murmured poor Consuelo, astonished to hear who the virtuous personage was whom the thrice virtuous and clear-sighted empress preferred to her.

"Yes, married," replied the empress in a decided tone, already dissatisfied with the doubts expressed relative to her protegée. "She lately gave birth to an infant, whom she has placed in the hands of a worthy and respectable clergyman, the canon of——, in order that he may impart to it a Christian education; and doubtless this excellent personage would not have taken such a charge upon him, if he had not held the mother deserving of his esteem."

"Neither do I doubt it," replied the young girl, consoled amid her indignation, to find that the canon was approved of in place of being censured, for a step which she herself had induced him to take.

"Thus it is that history is written!" said she to herself, as the empress sailed out of the apartment, giving her as congé merely a slight inclination of the head; "and thus it is that kings are enlightened. Well! after all, even the greatest misfortunes have their bright side, and the errors of men are often instrumental in bringing about good. The good canon will not be deprived of his priory; Angela will not lose her kind guardian; Corilla will be converted if the empress thinks fit; and I have not been compelled to kneel before a woman not a whit better than myself."

"Well?" exclaimed Porpora with a smothered voice, when she met him in the gallery where he was waiting, clasping and unclasping his hands with mingled hope and anxiety. "I trust we have won the day!"

"On the contrary, dear master, we have lost it."

"How calmly you say it—the fiend take you!"

"You must not say that, my dear master; his majesty is exceedingly unwelcome at court! When we are outside the gate I shall tell you all."

"Well—what is it?" resumed Porpora impatiently, when they were on the ramparts.

"Do you recollect, dear master," replied Consuelo, "what we said of the great minister Kaunitz on leaving the margravine's?"

"We said he was an old gossip. Has he done us any ill turn then?"

"Without doubt he has; and in the meantime I may tell you that her majesty, the empress, Queen of Hungary, is a good deal of the gossip also."

CHAPTER XCIV.

CONSUELO mentioned nothing to Porpora of Maria Theresa's motives for thus disgracing or at least slighting her, except what it was necessary for him to know ; any thing else would have only served to annoy and vex the maestro, and perhaps irritate him against Haydn to no purpose. Consuelo said nothing either to her young friend of what she had been silent upon to Porpora. She justly despised the false accusations which she knew had been concocted and furnished to the empress by two or three unfriendly individuals, and as yet at least had obtained no circulation with the public. The Ambassador Corner, to whom she thought it right to confide every thing, confirmed her in this opinion ; and to prevent ill-natured persons from laying hold of these calumnies and turning them to her disadvantage, he arranged matters wisely and generously. He settled that Porpora should remain in his lodging with Consuelo, and that Haydn should become an attaché to the embassy, and be admitted to the table of the private secretaries. In this way the old maestro would escape some of the cares of poverty, and Joseph could still pay him a few personal attentions, which would give him an opportunity of coming frequently to the house and taking his lessons, while Consuelo would be protected against malignant imputations. In spite of these precautions Corilla was engaged in place of Consuelo at the imperial theater. Consuelo had been unable to give satisfaction to Maria Theresa. This great queen, while she amused herself with the intrigues behind the scenes, which Kaunitz and Metastasio only told her of by halves and always in a piquant and amusing fashion, wished to perform nothing less than the part of a special providence toward creatures who on their part acted to the life repentant sinners or converted demons. It may well be supposed that among these hypocrites who received pensions and gratuities for their assumed piety, neither Caffariello, nor Farinelli, nor Tesi, nor Madame Hasse, nor any of those great and celebrated virtuosi who occasionally came to display their talents at Vienna, were included. But the common herd were bribed by persons determined on flattering her majesty's devout and moralizing fantasies, and her majesty, who introduced her spirit of diplomatic intrigue into every thing, made the marriages and conversions of her actors an affair of state. One may read in the Memoirs of Favart, that entertaining romance of realities, the difficulties he experienced in sending proper actresses and singers, whom he had got a commission to furnish, to Vienna.

Thus Maria Theresa wished to give to her amusement an edifying pretext worthy of her beneficent character. Monarchs are always acting a part, and great monarchs probably more so than others. Porpora constantly said so, and he was not mistaken. The great empress, a zealous Catholic and mother of an exemplary family, conversed without repugnance with women of easy virtue, catechised them, and solicited strange confessions, in order to have the honor and glory of leading a repentant Magdalene to the foot of the cross. The empress' private purse, placed between vice and contrition, rendered these miracles of grace at once numerous and infallible. Thus Corilla, weeping and prostrate, if not in person—for her stubborn nature would have hardly bent to the humiliating act—at least through Kaunitz as her proxy, who went security for her conduct, must inevitably take precedence of a decided, proud, and fiery temperament, like that of Consuelo. Maria Theresa loved in her protegés of the drama only those virtues of which she could boast herself the author; those which had been self-created or self-maintained did not interest her very much ; she did not believe in them, as her own virtue should have made her believe. Then Consuelo's proud attitude had provoked her ; she found her logical and self-possessed. It was rather too much for a little Bohemian to wish to be wise and estimable without an empress interfering to bring it about, and when Herr Kaunitz, who pretended to be very impartial, while all the time he did his utmost to assist one and injure the other, asked her majesty if she had granted the *little one's* prayer, she replied :

" I was not satisfied with her principles; do not mention her name to me again."

And all was said. The voice, the features, and even the name of Porporina were thenceforth completely forgotten.

It was necessary to explain briefly to Porpora the meaning of this exclusion. Consuelo told him, that her being unmarried seemed to the empress an unsurmountable objection to her engagement.

" And Corilla?" exclaimed Porpora, on learning the admission of her rival; " has her majesty married her?"

" So far as I have been able to learn from her majesty's words, Corilla passes with her for a widow."

" A widow?" said Porpora with a bitter smile; "but what will they say when they know what she is, and when they see her conduct? And this child they tell me about, that she has left near Vienna with some canon?"

" She will turn the whole affair into ridicule with her companions, and she will laugh in private at the clever trick she has played the empress."

" But what if the empress learn the truth?"

" She will never learn it. Sovereigns are surrounded with ears which serve as barriers to exclude it. Many things apparently are never told, and nothing finds admission into the imperial sanctuary but what these guardians choose to give admission to."

" Besides," replied Porpora, " Corilla will always have confession as a last resource, and Herr Kaunitz can enjoin a proper penance."

The poor maestro endeavored to vent his spleen in these bitter sarcasms, but he was not the less deeply vexed. He lost all hope of seeing his opera performed, the more so as the libretto was not by Metastasio the court poet. He had some suspicion that Consuelo had not taken the proper means to secure the good graces of the sovereign, and he could not help evincing his ill-humor to her. To make matters worse, the Venetian ambassador, one day when he saw Porpora overjoyed at Haydn's rapid musical progress, was imprudent enough to tell him the whole truth, and to show him some of the young man's graceful compositions, which had begun to circulate and be admired among amateurs. The maestro exclaimed that he was imposed on, and became frightfully enraged. Happily he did not suspect Consuelo as an accomplice in the deceit, and Corner hastened to assuage the storm by a good-natured palliation. But he could not hinder Joseph from being banished for several days from Porpora's presence, and it required all the ambassador's influence to prevail upon the maestro to receive him again. Porpora, however, bore him a grudge for a long time, and it was even said

that he made him purchase his lessons by painful and unnecessary humiliations, since the servants of the embassy
were always at his disposal. But Haydn was not to be repulsed, and by dint of sweetness of temper, patience, and
docility, aided by the advice and assistance of the good
Consuelo, ever studious and attentive, he disarmed the
rough professor, and obtained all that it was in the power
of the one to impart or the other to receive.

But Haydn's genius dreamed of a different path from
that which he had hitherto pursued, and the future father
of the symphony confided to Consuelo his ideas respecting
instrumentation on a gigantic scale. These gigantic proportions which appear so simple and obvious to us at the
present day, might well seem to our ancestors a hundred
years ago rather the utopian dream of a madman than a
revelation of genius. Joseph distrusted himself, and confessed to Consuelo the ambition which tormented him.
Consuelo was at first a little terrified also. Hitherto the
orchestral accompaniment had been merely a secondary
consideration, and when it was severed from the human
voice, its resources were bald and simple in the extreme.
Nevertheless her young fellow-pupil evinced so much
calmness and perseverance, and displayed in all his conduct and opinions so much real modesty and conscientious
regard for truth, that Consuelo, unable to esteem him presumptuous, decided on considering him wise and encouraged him in his projects. It was at this period that
Haydn composed a serenade for three instruments, which,
accompanied by two of his friends, he proceeded to perform under the windows of those *ditettanti* whose attention
he wished to draw to his works. He began with Porpora,
who, without knowing the names of the performers,
listened with pleasure from his window and applauded
without reserve. The ambassador, who was also a listener,
took care this time not to betray the secret; for Porpora
would not have suffered the young composer to turn his
attention from vocal music to any other pursuit.

" About this time Porpora received a letter from his
pupil, the excellent contralto singer, Hubert, surnamed
Porporino, who had entered into the service of Frederick
the Great. This famous artist was not, like the other
pupils of the professor, so infatuated with his own merits
as to forget to whom he owed them. Porporino had been

imbued by him with a species of talent which he never sought to modify, and which had always been successful, viz. to sing in a chaste and severe style without unnecessary ornaments and without departing from the sound doctrines of his master. He was particularly admirable in the *adagio.* On this account Porpora entertained a preference for him which he had some difficulty in concealing in presence of the fanatical admirers of Farinelli and Caffariello. He readily conceded that the ability, brilliancy, and pliability of voice of these great performers were more captivating and better calculated to charm an audience greedy of difficulties; but he repeated mentally that Porporino would never make such sacrifice to bad taste, and that his audience would never tire of hearing him, although he always sung in the same manner. It appeared, in fact, that Prussia did not tire of him, for he shone there during his whole musical career, and died at a very advanced age, after a lengthened sojourn of more than forty years.

Hubert's letter informed Porpora that the latter's music was much liked at Berlin, and that if he would join him there, he would do his utmost to have his new compositions performed. He urged him to leave Vienna, where artists were continually at the mercy of intrigues, and to *recruit* for the Prussian court a distinguished cantatrice who could sing with him the operas of the maestro. He highly eulogized the enlightened taste of the king, and his honorable conduct toward musicians. "If this project meets with your approbation," said he at the close of the letter, "reply quickly and state your terms, and three months hence I promise to procure such as will secure you in your old days a comfortable support. As to glory, my dear master, it is sufficient for that purpose that you write and that we sing so as to do you justice, and I trust your fame will extend even to Dresden."

This last expression made Porpora prick his ears like a veteran war-horse. It was an allusion to the triumphs which Hasse and his singers had obtained at the court of Saxony. The idea of counterbalancing the fame of his rival in the north of Germany, so tickled the maestro, and he felt at this moment so much dislike for Vienna and the Viennese and their court, that he replied without hesitation to Porporino, authorizing him to make proposals for him at Berlin. He mentioned what he would expect, making a moderate demand in order to avoid disappointment. He spoke of Porporina in the highest terms, telling him that she was his sister in education, genius, and affection, as well as in name, and desiring him to arrange for her engagement on the most advantageous terms possible. In this he acted without so much as consulting Consuelo, who was only informed of this fresh resolve after the letter had been dispatched.

Poor Consuelo was terrified at the very name of Prussia, and that of the Great Frederick made her shudder. Since the adventure with the deserter she no longer looked upon this so much-vaunted monarch as any thing but an ogre or a vampire. Porpora scolded her a good deal for testifying so little joy at this new engagement, and as she could not relate to him the history of Karl and the promises of Mayer, she drooped her head, and submitted quietly to his tutoring.

On reflection, however, she found some comfort in the project. It served to delay her return to the stage, since the affair might not go on, and since Porporino under any circumstances required three months to conclude it. Until then she was at liberty to dream of Albert's love, and endeavor within herself to respond to it. Whether she finally admitted the possibility of a union or the contrary, she could still at least honorably keep her promise to think of it without force or constraint.

She determined to wait for Count Christian's reply to her first letter before announcing this intelligence to the family at Riesenburg; but this reply did not arrive, and Consuelo was beginning to think that Count Christian had renounced the idea of this mesalliance, and was endeavoring to make Albert renounce it also, when she received rom Keller a communication to the following purport:

"You promised to write to me; you have done so indirectly in acquainting my father with your present embarrassing position. I see that you are placed under a yoke from which I should think it criminal to withdraw you. My father is terrified at the consequences which your submission to Porpora may have upon me; but as for myself, Consuelo, I am not yet alarmed at any thing which has taken place, because you express regret and repugnance at what is imposed on you—a sufficient proof that you will not lightly decide upon the question of my eternal unhappiness. No, you will not break your promise! you will try to love me? What matters it to me where you are or what you do, or the rank which glory or prejudice may give you among men, or the lapse of time, or the obstacles which prevent us meeting —if I can hope, and if you tell me to hope? I doubtless suffer much, but I can suffer still more without sinking, so long as one solitary gleam of hope remains unextinguished.

"I wait! I can wait! Do not think to alarm me by taking time to reply; do not write under the influence of fear or pity, to which I would not wish to owe any thing. Weigh my destiny in your heart, my soul in yours, and when the time has come, when you feel sure of your decision, whether you be in the cell of a nun or on the boards of a theater, tell me never to trouble you more, or to come and rejoin you. I shall either be at your feet or forever dumb, as you may decide."

"Oh, noble Albert !" exclaimed Consuelo, pressing the letter to her lips, "I feel that I love you! It would be impossible not to love you, and I will not hesitate to tell you so; I long to reward you by my promise for your love and constancy."

She immediately began to write; but Porpora's voice made her quickly conceal Albert's letter as well as her reply. Throughout the day she had not a moment's leisure or security. It seemed as if the cynical old man had divined her desire to be alone, and had resolved to prevent it. When night came Consuelo was more tranquil, and could reflect that so important a determination required a longer trial of her own feelings. It would be wrong to subject Albert to the hazard of any change in her feelings toward him.

She read and re-read a hundred times the young count's letter, and perceived that he feared equally the pain of a refusal and the danger of a hasty promise. She determined to take some days to consider her reply, a step which Albert himself seemed to desire.

The life which Consuelo now led at the embassy was quiet and regular in the extreme. To give no grounds for scandal, Corner was considerate enough not to visit Consuelo in her own suit of apartments, and never invite her, even in company with Porpora, to his. He only saw her in the presence of Wilhelmina, where they could converse together with perfect propriety and enjoy a little music. Joseph also was admitted to these musical parties, where Caffariello came often, Count Hoditz sometimes, and the Abbé Metastasio rarely. All three regretted Consuelo's failure, but not one of them had the courage or perseverance to make any attempt in her favor. Porpora was indignant, and had much difficulty in concealing it. Con-

suelo endeavored to calm him, and persuade him to take
men as he found them, with all their faults and weaknesses.
She induced him to exert himself, and, thanks to her, he
was occasionally visited by gleams of hope and enthusiasm.
She encouraged him only in his dislike to bring her before
the public. Happy at being forgotten by those great
people whom she had looked upon with terror and repugnance, she addicted herself to serious study and delightful
reveries, cultivated the friendship of the good Haydn, and
each day said to herself, while she lavished every care and
attention on her old master, that if nature had not intended
her for a life free from emotion and bustle, still less had
it intended her for the pursuits of vanity and ambition. She
had dreamed, and still dreamed in spite of herself, of a
more animated existence, of deeper and more heartfelt
joys, of the pleasures of a boundless and ever expanding
intellect; but the world of art which she had imagined so
noble and so pure, had shown itself on a nearer view under
so ugly and forbidding an aspect, that she chose in preference a life of obscurity and retirement, gentle affections,
and a solitude sweetened by labor.

Consuelo had no further reflections to make relative to
the offer of the Rudolstadts. She could not entertain a
doubt of their generosity, of the unalterable love of the
son, and the indulgent tenderness of the father. It was
no longer her reason and her conscience that she felt it
necessary to interrogate: both spoke for Albert. She had
triumphed on this occasion without any effort to banish
the remembrance of Anzoleto. A victory over love gives
strength for every subsequent struggle. She no longer
feared his attractions, and she felt herself beyond the risk
of fascination; and yet, with all this, love did not plead
with passion in her heart for Albert. She had still to
question that heart whose mysterious calmness ever welcomed the idea of a full and perfect love. Seated at her
window, the gentle girl often gazed at the passers-by;
rough students, noble lords, melancholy artists, proud
cavaliers, all were in turns the object of a serious and
innocent inquiry.

" Alas!" said she, " is my heart frivolous or capricious?
Am I capable of loving, deeply loving, at first sight, as my
companions of the *Scuola* have so often confessed and even
boasted to each other before me. Is love a magic flame,

which overwhelms our whole being, and turns us irresistibly from our sacred and peaceful affections? Is there among those who sometimes raise their eyes to my window one whose look troubles and fascinates me? Is this one with his lordly walk and noble figure more beautiful than Albert? Or is that one with his curling and perfumed locks and elegant attire calculated to displace the image of my betrothed? Or would I be the decked-out lady whom I see rolling past in yonder carriage with her haughty and handsome cavalier, who holds her fan and presents her gloves? Is there aught in all that which makes me tremble or blush, or which causes my heart to palpitate? No; no, in truth. Speak, my heart, for now I will question you and submit to your decrees. Alas! I hardly know you, for since my birth we have been almost strangers. I have never contradicted you; I gave you up the empire of my life without examining or bridling your impulses. You have been crushed, poor heart, and, now that conscience rules you, you can no longer live, know no longer what to say. Speak, then; rouse yourself and choose! Well, you are tranquil, and would have nothing that you see there?"

"No."

"You would not have Anzoleto?"

Again "No."

"Then it is Albert whom you call? It seems to me that you whispered yes."

And Consuelo retired each day from her window with a joyous smile on her lips, and a gentler radiance in her eyes.

At the end of a month she replied to Albert calmly, with perfect self-possession, and her pulse beating as gently as an infant's:

"I love none but you, and I am almost certain that I love you. In the meantime, leave me to dream of the possibility of our union. Let it be ever present to your thoughts, and let us together find some expedient to avoid vexing either your father or my master, lest we become selfish in becoming happy."

She added to this note a short letter to Count Christian, in which she described the quiet life she led, and announced the respite which the new projects of Porpora had granted her. She begged that they would endeavor to find some means of disarming Porpora's resentment, and of breaking the intelligence to him in the course of the month. A month still remained to prepare the maestro for the announcement before the Berlin affair should be settled.

Consuelo, having sealed these two letters, placed them on the table and fell asleep. A delicious calm had descended upon her soul, and she had not for a long time enjoyed such deep and undisturbed repose. She awoke late, and rose hastily in order to see Keller, who had promised to return for her letter at eight. It was now nine, and, while hastening to dress, Consuelo saw with terror that the letter was no longer where she had placed it. She sought it everywhere, but in vain. She left the room to see if Keller might not be waiting in the antechamber, but neither Keller nor Joseph was to be found; and as she re-entered her apartment to search a second time for her letter, she saw Porpora there, who seemed to await her approach, and who fixed upon her a stern and threatening look.

" What do you seek?" said he.

" I have mislaid a sheet of music."

" You do not speak the truth ; it is a letter that you seek."

" Master——"

" Be silent, Consuelo; you are yet but a novice in deceit, do not now commence to study it."

" Master, what have you done with the letter?"

" I gave it to Keller."

" And wherefore did you give it to him?"

" Because he came for it, as you told him yesterday. You know not how to feign, or rather I have quicker ears than you think."

" But in one word," said Consuelo, firmly, " what have you done with my letter?"

" I have told you, why do you ask again? I did not think it right that a well-conducted girl, such as you are, and always will be, should give letters in confidence to her hairdresser. To prevent people having an ill opinion of you, I myself gave the letter quietly to Keller, and commissioned him from you to dispatch it. He will not think at least that you hide a secret from your father."

" Master, you have done well. Pardon me!"

" I pardon you. Let us say no more."

" And you have read my letter?" said Consuelo, with a timid and deprecating tone.

"For whom do you take me?" replied Porpora, with a terrible look.

"Pardon me for what I have done," said Consuelo, bending her knee before him, and endeavoring to take his hand; "let me open my heart to you, and——"

"Not another word," replied the maestro, repulsing her.

And he entered his own room, and shut the door violently behind him.

Consuelo hoped that this outburst once over, she might be able to appease his anger, and at the same time explain matters to him. She felt assured that she would have courage to open her whole mind to him, and hoped by so doing to hasten the issue of her wishes; but he refused all explanation, and evinced the utmost displeasure whenever the subject was mentioned. In other respects he was as friendly toward her as ever, and even appeared more contented and cheerful than he had been for a long time. Consuelo looked upon this as a good augury, and calmly awaited a reply from Riesenburg.

In one respect Porpora had not told an untruth, for he had burned Consuelo's letters without reading them, but he had kept the envelope, and substituted in place of the original letter, one from himself to Count Christian. He hoped by this bold step at once to save his pupil, and spare Count Christian a sacrifice beyond his strength. He believed that in so doing he was acting toward him as a faithful friend, and toward Consuelo as a wise and energetic father. He did not foresee that he might thus inflict a fatal blow upon Count Albert. Hardly knowing the young nobleman, he believed that Consuelo had been guilty of exaggeration with regard to him, and that he was neither so ill nor so attached to her as she had imagined. Moreover he held, like all old men, that love sooner or later comes to an end, and that disappointed affection kills nobody.

CHAPTER XCV.

AWAITING a reply which she could not receive, since Porpora had burned her letter, Consuelo persevered in the calm and studious course of life which she had adopted. Her presence attracted to Madame Wilhelmina's apartment many distinguished persons whom she had pleasure in meeting, and among others, Baron Frederick Trenck, for whom she felt a lively sympathy. He had the delicacy not to address her as an old acquaintance at their first meeting, but to have himself presented, after she had sung, as a profound admirer and as deeply affected by her performance. On seeing again this handsome and brave young man, who had so courageously saved her from Mayer and his band, Consuelo's first impulse was to hold out her hand. The baron, who would not suffer her to commit any imprudence in testifying her gratitude to him, hastened to take her hand as if to lead her to her chair, pressing it gently by way of thanks. She afterward learned from Joseph, from whom the baron took instructions in music, that he never failed to inquire kindly for her, and to speak of her with admiration, but from a feeling of almost romantic delicacy, forbore to question him as to the motives of their disguise, their adventurous voyage, and the sentiments which they might have had, or might still have, for each other.

"I do not know what he thinks of it," added Joseph; "but I can assure you that there is no woman of whom he speaks with so much esteem and respect."

"In that case, friend Beppo," said Consuelo, "I authorize you to tell him all our story, and my own as well, without, however, mentioning the family of Rudolstadt. I must have the unreserved esteem of a man to whom we owe our life, and who has conducted himself so nobly toward me in every respect."

Some weeks afterward, Baron Trenck, although having scarcely fulfilled his mission to Vienna, was abruptly recalled by Frederick, and came one morning to the embassy to bid a hasty adieu to Signor Corner. Consuelo, on descending the staircase to go out, met him under the portal, and as they were alone he approached and kissed her hand tenderly.

"Allow me," said he, "to express, for the first and perhaps the last time in my life, the sentiments I entertain toward you. There was no occasion for Beppo to tell your story to arouse my admiration. There are some countenances which never deceive, and it needed no more than a glance to assure me that yours was the index of a lofty intellect and a noble heart. Had I known at Passau that our dear Joseph was so little on his guard, I would have protected you against Count Hoditz's folly, which I foresaw only too plainly, although I did all that I could to make him aware that he was mistaken in your character, and would assuredly render himself ridiculous. However, the good-natured Hoditz told me himself how you had mocked him, and expressed himself infinitely obliged to you for having kept the secret. As to myself, I shall never forget the romantic adventure which procured me the pleasure of your acquaintance, and even were the loss of my fortune and my prospects to be the penalty, I should still look back to it as one of the happiest days of my life."

"Do you think then, baron," said Consuelo, "that such results could possibly ensue?"

"I hope not; nevertheless every thing is possible at the court of the King of Prussia."

"You make me greatly afraid of Prussia. Do you know, baron, it is possible I may have the pleasure of meeting you there soon, since there is some talk of an engagement at Berlin."

"Indeed?" exclaimed Trenck, his countenance beaming with sudden joy; "Heaven grant it! I may be of service to you at Berlin, and you may rely on me as a brother. Yes, Consuelo, I feel toward you the affection of a brother; and had I been free, I might perhaps have been unable to forbid myself a more endearing emotion. But you yourself are not free; and sacred, eternal bonds do not permit me to envy the fortunate nobleman who asks your hand. Whoever he may be, madam, he will find in me, if he wishes, a friend on whom he can reply, and, if needful, a champion against the prejudices of the world. Alas! Consuelo, there is also in my case a dreadful barrier existing between me and my loved one. He who loves you is a man and may break down the barrier, but she whom I love is of higher rank than mine, and has neither power, nor right, nor strength, nor liberty, to cast it down."

"I can do nothing then for you or her?" exclaimed Consuelo. "For the first time in my life I regret my poor and helpless position."

"Who knows?" exclaimed the baron, gaily, "you may do more than you think, if not indeed to insure our union, at least to soften the rigors of our separation. Do you feel sufficient courage to incur a little danger for us?"

"Yes! with the same readiness and joy that you exposed your life to save me."

"Well, I shall rely upon you. You will recollect your promise, and it may be that, one day or other, I shall require its fulfillment."

"Whatever be the day or hour, I shall never forget it," she replied, holding out her hand.

"Well then," said he, "give me a sign; some slight token which I can send to you when the time arrives. For I foresee great struggles, and circumstances may occur when my signature or even my seal might endanger both *her* and you."

"Will you have this roll of music, which I was carrying to one of my master Porpora's friends? I can get another, and shall mark this one, so as to know it again."

"Why not? A roll of music is one of those things which can be best sent without exciting suspicion. But I will separate the sheets, that I may make use of them several times. Make a mark on each page."

Consuelo, resting upon the balustrade of the staircase, wrote the name of Bertoni upon each sheet of the music. The baron rolled it up and carried it away, after having sworn eternal friendship to our heroine.

At this period Madame Tesi fell ill, and the performances at the imperial theater threatened to be suspended, as she performed the most important parts. Corilla could, if necessary, replace her. She had great success both at the court and in the city. Her beauty and her saucy coquetry turned the heads of the good German noblemen, and they did not dream of criticizing her voice, which was somewhat worn, or her rather forced and unnatural acting. All was thought beautiful coming from so beautiful a creature. Her snowy shoulders gave forth admirable sounds, her round and voluptuous arms always sang just, and her superb attitudes carried her through the most hazardous passages without opposition. Notwithstanding the musical taste on which they prided themselves, the Viennese, as well as the Venetians, surrendered to the fascination of a languishing look, and Corilla, by her exquisite beauty, prepared many to be rapt and intoxicated by her performances.

She therefore boldly presented herself to sing, in the meantime, the parts of Madame Tesi; but the difficulty was how to replace herself, in those she had sung. Madame Holzbaüer's flute-like voice did not permit her to be thought of. It was therefore necessary to admit Consuelo, or to be satisfied with inferior performers. Porpora worked like a demon; Metastasio, horribly dissatisfied with Corilla's Lombard pronunciation, and indignant at the attempts she made to drown the other parts (contrary to the spirit of the poem and in spite of the situation), no longer concealed his antipathy to her, nor his sympathy for the conscientious and intelligent Porporina.

Madame Tesi already detested Corilla cordially for endeavoring to rival her and dispute with her the palm of beauty, and Caffariello, who paid his court to Tesi, spoke loudly in favor of the admission of Consuelo. Holzbaüer, anxious to sustain the character of his management, but terrified at the ascendancy which Porpora would acquire if once admitted behind the scenes, knew not which way to turn. Consuelo's prudent and dignified conduct had won her so many friends that it would be difficult to misrepresent her to the empress much longer. On all these accounts Consuelo received proposals ; but they were purposely made humiliating in hopes of their meeting with a refusal. Porpora, however, accepted them at once, and as usual without consulting her. One fine morning Consuelo found herself engaged for six representations, and, without power to escape or being able to understand why, after waiting six weeks, she had not heard from the Rudolstadts, she was dragged by Porpora to a rehearsal of the *Antigone* of Metastasio, written for the music of Hasse.

Consuelo had already studied the part with Porpora. Without doubt it was a source of severe suffering for the latter to be obliged to teach her the music of his rival— the most ungrateful of his pupils, and the enemy which from henceforth he most bitterly hated — but besides that this was a necessary step to pave the way for his own compositions, Porpora was too conscientious an artist not to apply all his zeal and attention to the task. Consuelo aided him so generously, that he was at once ravished and in despair. In spite of herself, the poor girl found Hasse magnificent ; her heart responded more warmly to the tender and passionate accents of the Saxon, than to the somewhat cold and naked grandeur of her own master. Accustomed while studying the other great masters with him to give full vent to her enthusiasm, she was forced on this occasion to restrain herself on seeing the melancholy which was imprinted on his brow, and the gloomy reverie into which he sunk when the lesson was over. When she entered on the stage to rehearse with Caffariello and Corilla, although she was well acquainted with the part, she felt so agitated that she could hardly commence the scene between Ismenio and Berenice, which begins thus :

> " No; tutto, o Berenice,
> Tu non apri il tuo cor," etc. *

To which Corilla replied:

> " E ti par poco,
> Quel che sai de' miei casi?" †

Here Corilla was interrupted by a loud burst of laughter from Caffariello. Turning to him with eyes sparkling with anger she exclaimed :

" What do you find so amusing in that?"

" You have spoken well, plumpest of Berenices!" replied Caffariello, laughing still more loudly ; "no one could speak with more sincerity."

" Then it is the words which amuse you?" said Holzbaüer, who would not have been sorry to repeat to Metastasio the sarcasms of the soprano on his verses.

" The words are beautiful," replied Caffariello, drily, who knew his design ; " but their application just now is so happy, that I could not help laughing."

And he held his sides as he repeated to Porpora:

> " E ti par poco,
> Quel che sai di *tanti* casi?"

---

* " No, Berenice, thou dost not here fully open thy heart."
† " What thou knowest of my adventures seems to thee, then, a trifling matter?"

Corilla, now perceiving the bitter allusion to her habits, and trembling at once with hate, rage, and apprehension, was ready to fly at Consuelo, and sink her nails in her face ; but the countenance of the latter was so calm and gentle that she dare not venture. Besides, the feeble light which penetrated into the theater, falling on her rival's face, suggested vague recollections and strange terrors. She had never seen her closely or by daylight at Venice. Amidst the pains of her confinement, she had a confused remembrance of the little gypsy Bertoni hovering around her, but she could not understand the motives for his attentions. She now endeavored to recall the different occurrences which had taken place, but not succeeding, she remained discomfited and uneasy during the whole rehearsal. The Porporina's style of singing only added to her ill humor, and the presence of her former master, who like a severe judge listened silently and almost contemptuously, became gradually an insupportable torment. Holzbaüer was hardly less mortified when the maestro told him that his directions were altogether erroneous ; and he was perforce obliged to believe him, for Porpora had been present at the rehearsal which Hasse himself conducted at Dresden on the first bringing out of his opera.

The necessity of obtaining good advice dispelled ill-will, and imposed silence on the discontented. Porpora conducted the entire rehearsal, pointed out to each his duty, and even reproved Caffariello, who affected to listen to his advice with respect in order to give it more weight with the others. Caffariello's sole aim was to annoy the impertinent rival of Madame Tesi, and he spared no pains, not even an act of submission and modesty, to obtain that pleasure. It is thus among artists as among diplomatists, on the stage as in the cabinet, that the noblest as well as the meanest affairs have their hidden causes, often infinitely petty and frivolous.

On returning from the rehearsal, Consuelo found Joseph filled with some hidden joy. When they had an opportunity of speaking, he informed her that the good canon had arrived in Vienna, and that his first care had been to inquire for his dear Beppo, and make him partake of an excellent breakfast, asking him all the while a thousand affectionate questions about his dear Bertoni. They had already discussed the means of becoming acquainted with Porpora, so as to meet together without reserve or mystery. The very next day the canon presented himself as a protector of Joseph Haydn, and a warm admirer of the maestro, whom he thanked for the lessons he had been good enough to give his young friend. Consuelo saluted him as if she had seen him for the first time, and in the evening the maestro and his two pupils partook of a friendly dinner with the canon. Unless Porpora had affected a greater degree of stoicism than the musicians of that period, even the most celebrated, piqued themselves upon, it would have been difficult for him to avoid liking this excellent canon, whose table was so good, and whose admiration for his works was so great. They had some music after dinner, and from thenceforth saw each other every day.

This was a further relief to the anxiety which Consuelo felt at Albert's silence. The canon was of an unaffected, lively temperament, gay, yet observing the strictest propriety, and possessing an exquisite taste and a just and enlightened judgment. In short he was a most valuable friend, and a winning and amiable companion. His society animated and strengthened the maestro, softened the ascerbities of his temper, and in the same proportion relieved and gratified Consuelo.

One day that there was no rehearsal—it was the secon before the representation of *Antigone*—Porpora having gone to the country with an associate, the canon proposed to his young friends to make a descent on the priory in order to surprise his people whom he had left behind, and see if the gardener's wife took good care of Angela, and the gardener did not neglect the volkameria. The invitation was accepted. The carriage was loaded with pastry and bottles, to satisfy the appetite which a journey of four leagues is certain to create, and they arrived safely at the canon's residence, after making a slight détour and leaving the carriage at some distance, in order to create the greater surprise.

The volkameria was in splendid condition. Its bloom was over on account of the cold, but its beautiful leaves fell gracefully around its lofty stem. The hot-house was in the nicest order; the blue chrysanthemums had braved the winter stoutly, and seemed to laugh from behind the glass.

Angela, hanging by the nurse's breast, began to smile also when incited by her playful gestures, but the canon judiciously ordered that she should not be made to laugh too often, since with creatures so young, such a course might put the nervous system in disorder.

They were all three chatting pleasantly in the gardener's little abode, the canon, wrapped in his furred cloak, was warming his legs before a famous fire of dried roots and fircones, Joseph was playing with the pretty children of the gardener's handsome wife, while Consuelo, seated in the middle of the apartment, held Angela in her arms and looked at her with a mixture of pain and tenderness, when the door suddenly opened and Corilla stood before her, like a phantom summoned up by her melancholy musings.

For the first time since the birth of her child, Corilla had felt an impulse of maternal love, and had set out to see her child secretly. She was aware that the canon was residing in Vienna; and having arrived about half an hour after him, and not seeing the traces of his carriage-wheels in the vicinity of the priory, she had entered the garden, and proceeded straight to the house where she knew that Angela was at nurse, for she had taken care to procure information on this subject. She had laughed not a little at the embarrassment and Christian resignation of the canon, but she was wholly ignorant of the part which Consuelo had taken in the transaction. It was with a mixture of surprise and consternation therefore that she thus encountered her rival, and not knowing nor daring to guess what infant it was she rocked in her arms, she was about to turn on her heel and fly. But Consuelo, who had instinctively clasped the infant to her bosom, as the partridge hides her young at the approach of the hawk—Consuelo, who next day might present Corilla's secret in a very different point of view from that which was generally believed—Consuelo, who gazed at her with a mixture of terror and indignation, held her rooted as if by fascination to the spot. Corilla, however, had been too long accustomed to the stage to lose her presence of mind. Her tactics were to anticipate any humiliating remarks by offering her rival an insult, and to gain time she commenced the following bitter apostrophe in the Venetian dialect.

" Oh! ho! my poor zingarella, is this a foundling hospital

you have here? Are you come to seek or to leave? for I perceive our fortune has been much the same? Doubtless this infant is the handsome Anzoleto's, who I was sorry to hear did not hasten to rejoin you when he left us so suddenly in the midst of his engagement last season."

"Madam," replied Consuelo, pale but calm, "if I had had the misfortune to be as intimate with Anzoleto as you have been, and had the happiness of being a mother, for it is always a happiness to one who has a feeling heart, my child would not be here."

"Ah!" replied the other, with a gloomy fire in her eyes, "it would have been brought up at the Villa Zustiniani. But as you have not been, as you allege, unfortunate with Anzoleto, Joseph Haydn, your master's pupil, it seems, consoles you for the mishap, and doubtless the infant which you nurse——"

"Is your own, mademoiselle," exclaimed Joseph, who had learned the Venetian dialect, and who now interposed between Consuelo and Corilla with a look which made the latter recoil. "It is Joseph Haydn who will certify it, for he was present when you gave it birth."

Joseph's face, which Corilla had not seen since that unhappy day, brought back the circumstances which she had vainly endeavored to recall, and in the zingari Bertoni she at once recognized the features of the zingarella Consuelo. A cry of surprise escaped her, and for some minutes anger and shame struggled for supremacy in her bosom; but her sarcastic disposition soon resumed its sway.

"In truth, my young friends," she exclaimed, with a malignant yet fawning air, "I did not recollect you. You looked remarkably well when I met you seeking your fortune, and Consuelo, I must confess, was a pretty youth in her disguise. It was in this sacred house, then, that she piously spent the year and a half which has elapsed since she left Venice. Come, zingarella, my child, do not be uneasy. We are in possession of each other's secrets, and the empress, who wishes to know every thing, shall learn nothing about either of us."

"Even suppose I had a secret," replied Consuelo, calmly, "you have discovered it only to-day; while I was in possession of yours on the day when I had the interview with the empress, and three days before your engagement was signed, Corilla!"

"And you spoke ill of me to her?" exclaimed Corilla, reddening with anger.

"Had I told her what I know of you, you would not have been engaged. That you are so, proves sufficiently that I did not take advantage of the opportunity."

"And why did you not? You must be a great fool!" replied Corilla, with a candor and perversity truly wonderful.

Consuelo and Joseph could not avoid smiling as they looked at each other; but Joseph's smile was full of contempt, while that of Consuelo displayed only angelic goodness.

"Yes, madam," she replied, with unconquerable sweetness, "I am as you say, and I am happy that I am so."

"Not so happy, my poor girl, since I have been engaged, and you are not so," replied Corilla, a little shaken in her confidence, and becoming by degrees more thoughtful. "They said at Venice that you had no sense, and could not manage your affairs. It is the only true thing that Anzoleto told me of you. But what is to be done? It is not my fault if it be so. Had I been in your place, I would have said what I knew of Corilla; I would have represented myself as a vestal, a saint. The empress would have believed it, for she is not hard to persuade, and I would have supplanted all my rivals. But you have not done so! It is very strange, and I pity you sincerely for having so badly steered your bark."

For once, contempt got the better of their indignation, and Consuelo and Joseph burst into a laugh, while Corilla, whose bitterness had gradually evaporated on witnessing what she called her rival's impotence, ceased to act on the offensive, and assuming an easy air, drew her chair to the fire, in order to continue the conversation quietly, and thus learn better both the weak and strong side of her opponents. At this instant she found herself face to face with the canon, whom she had not hitherto perceived, since the latter, prompted by his professional prudence, had signed to the gardener's buxom wife and two children to stand before him, until he should find out what was going on.

CHAPTER XCVI.

AFTER the insinuation which she had so recently hazarded respecting Consuelo, the sight of the good canon produced upon Corilla the effect of a Medusa's head. She took courage, however, on reflecting that she had spoken in Venetian, and she saluted him with that mixture of effrontery and embarrassment which characterizes women of Corilla's description. The canon, usually so polished and graceful a host, neither rose nor even returned her salute. Corilla, who had made particular inquiries respecting him at Vienna, was informed by every one that he was a man of exquisite breeding, a great amateur in music, and incapable of lecturing any woman, and least of all a celebrated singer. She had therefore planned to go to see him, and as it were fascinate him into silence. But if she had more cleverness in invention and intrigue than Consuelo, she had also the careless, disorderly habits, the indolence, and even the slatterliness—for all these qualities are generally found united — characteristic of low and groveling minds. Bodily and mental slothfulness neutralize the efforts of intrigue ; and Corilla, though capable of any perfidy, had rarely sufficient energy to turn it to good account. She had therefore put off from day to day her visit to the canon, and when she found him so cold and severe, she began to be visibly disconcerted.

Then seeking to recover herself by a bold stroke, she said to Consuelo, who held Angela in her arms:

"Well, why don't you let me embrace my daughter and lay her at his reverence the canon's feet, that——"

"*Dame Corilla,*" said the canon, in the same dry and coldly satirical tone in which he had formerly said *Dame Bridget,* "have the goodness to let that child alone."

Then expressing himself in Italian with much elegance, although rather too slowly, he thus continued, without removing his cap from his head—"During the fifteen minutes I have been listening to you, although I am not very familiar with your patois, I have understood enough to warrant me in telling you that you are by far the most shameless creature I ever met with in my life. Nevertheless I believe you more stupid than wicked, more base and cowardly than dangerous. You comprehend nothing of the beauty of virtue, and it would be only a waste of time to attempt to make you comprehend it. I have merely one thing to say to you: that young girl, that spotless virgin, that saint, as you called her just now in mockery—you pollute by speaking to her; therefore speak not to her again. As to this child which was born of you, you would disgrace it by your touch; therefore touch it not. An infant is a holy being; Consuelo has said it, and I felt the truth of her words. It was from the intercession, the persuasion of Consuelo, that I ventured to take charge of your daughter, without a fear that the perverse instincts she might have inherited from you would one day make me repent it. We said to each other that divine goodness gives to every creature the power of knowing and practicing what is good, and we resolved to teach her what is good and to make the path of virtue pleasant and easy to her. With you it would be far otherwise. From this day, therefore, you will no longer consider this child as yours. You have abandoned it, ceded it, given it away; it no longer belongs to you. You remitted a sum of money to pay for its education——" Here he made a sign to the gardener's wife, who took from the wardrobe a purse tied and sealed, the same which Corilla had sent to the canon with her daughter, and which had not been opened. He took it and threw it at Corilla's feet, adding: "We will have nothing to do with it and do not want it. In the meantime I request you to leave my house, and never to set foot in it again under any pretext whatever. On these conditions, and provided you never utter a word respecting the circumstances which have forced us into a connection with you, we promise to observe the most absolute silence respecting all that concerns you. But if you act otherwise, I warn you that I have means which you know not of, of letting her imperial majesty hear the truth, and you may suddenly exchange your theatrical crown and the applause of your admirers, for a residence of some years in a Magdalene asylum."

Having thus spoken, the canon rose, signed to the nurse to take the child, and motioned to Consuelo to retire with Joseph to the other end of the apartment; he then pointed with his finger to the door, and Corilla, pale, trembling, terrified, tottered out, hardly knowing where she went or what she did.

The canon during this outburst had been inspired with
a feeling of honest and manly indignation which had rendered him unusually forcible. Consuelo and Joseph had
never before seen him so powerful. The authoritative
habits which never abandon a priest, and also the attitude
of royal command which is to some extent hereditary, and
which in this instance proclaimed him the son of Augustus
II, invested the canon, possibly without his being aware of
it, with a sort of irresistible majesty. Corilla, who, for
the first time in her life, heard herself addressed in the
calm and severe accents of truth, felt more terror and
affright than all her furious lovers in their revengeful outbursts had ever inspired her with. An Italian and superstitious, she felt a vivid terror of the ecclesiastic and his
curse, and fled in a distracted manner across the garden,
while the canon, exhausted by an effort so unusual to his
calm and benevolent character, fell back in his chair pale
and almost fainting.

While hastening to his assistance, Consuelo involuntarily
cast a glance at the uncertain and tottering steps of the
unfortunate Corilla. Whether it was that the wretched
woman missed her footing in her agitation, or that her
strength became exhausted, she saw her stumble at the end
of a walk, and fall prostrate upon the ground. The lesson
was a severer one than Consuelo's kind heart would have
been able to inflict, and leaving the canon to the care of
Joseph, she ran to aid her rival, whom she found struggling in a violent fit of hysterics. Unable to calm her,
and not daring to bring her to the priory, she was
obliged to limit her endeavors to preventing her from rolling
on the walk, or tearing her hands with the gravel. Corilla
was almost deranged for some moments; but when she saw
who was assisting and trying to console her, she became
calm and deadly pale. She kept her livid lips closed in a
gloomy silence, and her eyes immovably fixed upon the
ground. She suffered Consuelo, however, to lead her to
the carriage which waited at the gate, and, supported by
her rival, she entered it without uttering a word.

"You are very ill," said Consuelo, frightened at the expression of her countenance; "permit me to accompany
you a part of the way; I can return on foot."

Corilla's only reply was to thrust her back, while she
looked at her with an indefinable expression. Then sobbing

aloud, she hid her face with one of her hands, while with the other she signed to the coachman to proceed, at the same time pulling down the blind between herself and her generous enemy.

Next day being the last rehearsal of *Antigone*, Consuelo was at her post at the appointed hour, and they only awaited the arrival of Corilla to commence. The latter sent her servant to say that she would be there in half an hour. Caffariello consigned her to the infernal regions, affirming with an oath that he would not submit to the caprice of any such person, and that he was determined not to wait a moment longer. Madame Tesi, although pale and suffering, had determined to be present at the rehearsal, in order to amuse herself at Corilla's expense; and for this purpose she had dragged herself to the theater, and now lay reclining at full length on a sofa, which she had caused to be placed at one of the side-scenes. She calmed her friend, and persisted in awaiting Corilla's arrival, thinking that it was from fear of being controlled by her that she hesitated to appear. At last Corilla arrived, paler and more languishing than Tesi herself, who, on her side, regained her color and strength on seeing her rival in such a plight. In place of throwing off her hat and mantle in her usual saucy fashion, she seated herself on a gilt throne which had been forgotten on the stage, and thus addressed Holzbaüer:

"Mr. Director, I beg to tell you that I am exceedingly unwell, that my voice is completely gone, and that I have passed a frightful night."

Tesi languidly interchanged a malicious glance with Caffariello.

"And that, for all these reasons, it is impossible for me either to rehearse to-day or sing to-morrow, unless I resume the part of Ismenia, and you give that of Berenice to another."

"Is this really your intention, madam?" exclaimed the thunderstruck Holzbaüer. "Is it on the eve of representation, and when the court has fixed the hour, that you would allege indisposition? It is impossible! I can by no means consent to it."

"You must, however," replied she, resuming her natural tone of voice, which was any thing but gentle. "I am only engaged for second-rate parts, and nothing in my engagement obliges me to take the first. It was a feeling of civility on my part which induced me to accept them, in order to oblige Signora Tesi, and not to interrupt the pleasures of the court. I am too ill to keep my promise, and you cannot oblige me to sing against my will."

" My dear friend, they will make you sing by command," said Caffariello; " and you will sing badly; we were perfectly prepared for it. It is but a trifling misfortune in addition to those which you have so often confronted, but it is too late to draw back. You should have thought about it sooner. You have presumed too much upon your abilities. You will break down, but that is of little importance to us. I will sing in such a way that the audience will forget that there is even such a part as Berenice. Porporina also, in her little part of Ismenia, will compensate the public, and every one will be satisfied except yourself. It will be a lesson which you will profit by, or rather which you will not profit by, another time."

" You much deceive yourself as to the motives of my refusal," replied Corilla, boldly. " Were I not unwell, I should perhaps perform my part as well as *another*; but, as I cannot sing, there is one present who will sing the part better than it was ever sung at Vienna, and that no later than to-morrow. So the opera will not be put off, and I shall resume with pleasure the part of Ismenia, which will not fatigue me."

" What!" said Holzbaüer, affecting surprise; " do you suppose that Madame Tesi will be well enough to-morrow to resume her part?"

" I know very well that Madame Tesi cannot sing for a long time," said Corilla aloud, so that Tesi could hear her from her sofa, which was not ten paces distant. " See how changed she is! her face would frighten one. But I told you that you had a Berenice—a perfect, incomparable Berenice, superior to us all; and there she is," added she, rising, and taking Consuelo by the hand, and leading her into the midst of the turbulent group which had collected around her.

" I?" exclaimed Consuelo, as if waking from a dream.

" You," replied Corilla, pushing her upon the throne, almost with a convulsive effort. " You are now our queen, Porporina; your place is in the first rank. It is I who give it you; for I owe it to you. Never forget it!"

Holzbaüer, in the midst of his distress, and seeing himself on the point of failing in his duty, and perhaps being obliged to send in his resignation, was unable to refuse this unexpected aid. It was obvious enough to him from Consuelo's performance of Ismenia, that if she undertook the part of Berenice, she would perform it in a superior manner. In spite therefore of his repugnance toward Porpora and toward her, his only fear was that she would refuse the part.

She did, in fact, refuse it very earnestly, and cordially pressing Corilla's hands, she warmly entreated her, in a low tone, not to incur for her sake a sacrifice which would not gratify her, while to her rival it would afford the greatest triumph, and would seem an act of the most humble submission that could be tendered. But Corilla was immovable in her determination. Tesi, frightened at a junction which threatened such serious consequences to her, would have willingly attempted to resume her part should she even expire the moment after, for she was seriously indisposed; but she dared not do so. They were not suffered at the court theater to manifest those caprices to which the good-natured public of our day so patiently submits. The court expected something new in the part of Berenice; this had been announced, and the empress reckoned on it.

"Come," said Caffariello to Porporina, "you must decide. This is the first trait of common sense that Corilla has ever shown in her life; let us take advantage of it."

"But I do not know the part," said Consuelo. "I have not studied it; I cannot have it prepared for tomorrow."

"You have heard it; therefore you know it, and you can sing it to-morrow," thundered Porpora. "Come, no faces; let there be an end of the matter; we are only losing time, Mr. Director, you will instruct the orchestra to begin. And then, Berenice, to your place! Come, lay down that music! when the piece has been rehearsed three times, every one ought to know it by heart. I tell you you know it."

"*No, tutto, O Berenice,*" sang Corilla, becoming Ismenia again.

"*Tu non apri il tuo cor.*"

"And now," thought Corilla, who judged of Consuelo by herself, "*all that she knows of my adventures will appear nothing in her eyes.*"

Consuolo, with whose wonderful powers Porpora was well acquainted, sang her part, both music and words, without hesitation. Madame Tesi was so struck with her performance, that she found herself much worse, and had herself conveyed home after the rehearsal of the first act. Next day Consuelo had prepared her costume, gone over her striking positions, as well as repeated the whole, by five o'clock in the evening. Her success was so complete, that the empress said, on leaving the theatre: "That is really an admirable girl: I must positively marry her: I will see about it."

Next day the *Zenobia* of Metastasio, the music by Predieri, was put in rehearsal. Corilla still persisted in handing over the part of prima donna to Consuelo. Madame Holzbaüer took the second part, and, as she was a better musician than Corilla, the opera went off much better than the other. Metastasio was delighted to find his music, which had been somewhat neglected during the wars, once more regain favor and become the rage in Vienna. He no longer thought of his sufferings; and, urged both by the kindness of Maria Theresa, and the duties of his place, to write new lyric dramas, he prepared himself by the perusal of the Greek and Latin classics, to produce one of those master-pieces which the Italians of Vienna and the Germans of Italy unhesitatingly preferred to the works of Corneille, Shakespeare, Racine, or Calderon.

It is not here, amid these perhaps tedious details, that we shall weary the reader's patience by giving him our opinion of Metastasio. It matters little to him what that opinion may be. We shall merely repeat what Consuelo said privately to Joseph on the subject.

"My poor Beppo, you cannot imagine the difficulty I have in performing those parts which they tell us are so sublime and pathetic. The words to be sure are well arranged, and present themselves readily in singing; but when I think of the personage who utters them, I do not know where to find, not inspiration, but even gravity sufficient to pronounce them. How strange a mistake it is to ascribe the notions of the present day to antiquity, and to describe passions, intrigues, and morals, very apropos perhaps in the memoirs of a Margrave of Bareith, a Baron Trenck, or a Princess of Culmbach, but meaningless and absurd with such characters as Rhadamistus, Berenice, or Arsinoe. When I was a convalescent at the Castle of the Giants, Count Albert often read to me to put me to sleep, but so far from sleeping, I listened most attentively. He read the tragedies of Sophocles, Eschylus, or Euripides, translating them into Spanish without hesitation or obscurity, although it was a Greek text which was before him. He was so conversant with all the different languages, both ancient and modern, that you would have said he read from an excellent translation. He piqued himself on rendering the shades of meaning exactly, that I might become acquainted with the genius of the Greeks. Heavens! what grandeur! what images! what sobriety, and yet what poetry of thought! what energetic, as well as pure and lofty characters! what striking situations, what deep sorrows, what terrible and harrowing pictures, he displayed before my wrapt and wondering eyes! Still weak and nervous from my severe illness, I imagined while listening to him that I was by turns Antigone, Clytemnestra, Medea, and Alectra—not on the stage by the light of foot-lamps, but in frightful solitudes, on the threshold of yawning caverns, amid the columns of ancient temples, or beside dreary watch-fires where they wept the dead and conspired against the living. I heard the wailing of the Trojan women, the cries of the captives of Dardania! The Eumenides danced around me, but to what wild and fantastic music, and infernal cries! Even yet I cannot think of it without a thrill of mingled pain and pleasure which makes me shudder. Never in the theater or in the waking realities of life, shall I experience the same emotions, the same power as then sounded like the mutterings of the distant thunderstorm through my heart and brain. It was then that I first felt myself a tragedian, then first that I conceived types of excellence of which no artist had furnished me with a model. It was then that I comprehended the tragic drama, the poetry of the theater, and as Albert read I composed a strain of music which seemed to express and utter all that I heard. Sometimes I assumed the attitude and expression of the heroines of his drama, and he would then pause,

terrified, thinking he saw Andromache or Ariadne before
him.   Oh! I learned more from those readings in a month,
than I should all my life repeating the dramas of Metastasio; and if there were not more sense and feeling in the
music than in the words, I should break down under the
disgust which I feel, in making the Archduchess Zenobia
converse with the Landgrave Eglé, and in hearing the
Field-marshal Rhadamistus dispute with Zopyrus the Cor-
net. of Pandors.   Oh! it is false, Beppo; false as the light
periwig of Caffariello Tiridates, as the Pompadour des-
habille of Madame Holzbaüer the shepherdess of Armenia,
as the pink calves of Prince Demetrius, or as yonder
scenic decorations, which from this distance bear about as
strong a resemblance to Asia as the Abbé Metastasio does
to old Homer!"

"What you have just said," replied Haydn, "enables
me to understand why I feel so much more hope and inspiration when I think of composing oratorios than in
writing operas for the theater.   In the former, where scenic
artifice does not contradict the truth of the sentiment, and
where, in an atmosphere all music, soul speaks to soul by
the ear and not by the eye, the composer methinks is able
to develop all his inspiration, and to carry the imaginations of his auditors into the loftiest regions of thought."

Thus conversing, Joseph and Consuelo, while waiting
for the rehearsal, walked side by side along an enormous
sheet of canvas, which was that evening to be the River
Araxes, but which by the indistinct daylight of the theater,
presented only the appearance of an enormous stripe of
indigo running between huge stains of ochre, intended to
represent the mountains of Caucasus.   These scenes, as
every one knows, are placed one behind the other so as to be
rolled up on cylinders whenever the locality of the drama
changes.   During the day the actors walk up and down in
the space between them, repeating their parts, or conversing on their private affairs, and sometimes spying out the
little confidential communications or deep-laid machinations of their fellow-actors, who are perhaps separated
from them by an arm of the sea or some public building;
while the scene-shifters, sitting or crouching in the dust
under the dripping oil, nod lazily on their posts or exchange pinches of snuff with each other.

Happily, Metastasio was not on the opposite banks of

the Araxes, while the unsuspecting Consuelo thus vented her artistic indignation to Haydn. The rehearsal commenced. It was the second of *Zenobia,* and all went on so well that the musicians, according to custom, applauded by tapping the violins with the end of their bows. Predieri's music was charming, and Porpora directed it with more enthusiasm than he was able to command for that of Hasse. The part of Tiradates was one of Caffariello's triumphs, and would have been well conceived if he had not been equipped as a Parthian warrior while the composer made him warble like Celadon, or chatter like Clytander. Consuelo, although finding her part poor and mean when placed in the mouth of a heroine of antiquity, was at least pleased with the agreeable feminine cast of the character. It even seemed to suggest a sort of similarity to her own situation between Albert and Anzoleto; and forgetting the localities, and thinking only of the human sentiments expressed, she felt raised to a pitch of sublimity in this air, whose force and meaning had so often been present to her heart:

> "Voi leggete in ogni core ;
> Voi sapete, O! giusti Dei,
> Se non puri, voti miei,
> Se innocente è la pietà."

She possessed at this instant the consciousness of true emotion and well-deserved triumph. She did not need Caffariello's look (uninfluenced that day by Tesi's presence), to confirm what she already felt ; namely, her capacity to produce an irresistible effect on any audience, and under all circumstances, by so exquisite a union of melody and execution. She immediately became reconciled to her part, to the opera, to her associates, to herself—in a word to the theater, and notwithstanding all the sarcasms which she had so recently lavished on her calling, she could not help experiencing one of those deep-seated, hidden, and powerful emotions which it is impossible for any one but an artist to comprehend, and which compensate in an instant for whole years of toil, suffering, and disappointment.

CHAPTER XCVII.

HALF as pupil, half as attendant on Porpora, Haydn, who was most anxious to hear the music, and study the arrangement of operas in all their parts, obtained permission to glide behind the scenes when Consuelo sang. For a couple of days past he remarked that Porpora, at first unwilling to admit him to the theater, had good-humoredly invited him to be present, even before he requested it. The reason was, that events had contributed to change the intentions of the maestro. Maria Theresa, while chattering on the subject of music with the Venetian ambassador, had returned as usual to her *matrimomania* (as Consuelo termed it), and had expressed to him her wish that this great cantatrice should fix herself permanently at Vienna by marrying the maestro's young pupil. She had made inquiries about Haydn from the ambassador himself, and the latter having assured her that he evinced very great genius, and moreover that he was a good Catholic, her majesty had commissioned him to arrange the marriage, promising at the same time to provide handsomely for the young couple. Corner was delighted with the idea, for he had a strong affection for Joseph, and gave him a small allowance monthly to enable him to pursue his studies. He mentioned the subject in warm terms to Porpora, and the latter fearing that Consuelo would leave the stage in order to marry some nobleman, suffered himself after much opposition (for he would have much preferred his pupil's remaining unmarried), to be persuaded. To strike the blow more securely, the ambassador determined to show him Haydn's compositions, and to inform him that the serenade with which he had been so pleased was his own production. Porpora confessed that they displayed strong evidences of talent, and that with his instructions and assistance he might come to write for the voice ; and in short that the marriage of a cantatrice to a composer might be very suitable and advantageous to both parties. The youth of the young couple, and their slender resources, would impose on them the necessity of unremitting labor, and Consuelo would be thus chained to the theater. The maestro surrendered. He had received no reply from Riesenburg any more than Consuelo, and this silence made him dread some opposition to his views, or some frantic project on the part of the young count.

"If I could marry, or at least engage Consuelo to another," thought he, "I should have nothing more to apprehend from that quarter."

The difficulty was to bring Consuelo to this determination. To exhort her to it would only have tended to arouse the idea of resistance. With his Neapolitan acuteness, he said to himself, that the force of circumstances must bring about a change in the sentiments of the young girl. She had already a friendship for Beppo, and Beppo, although he had conquered love in his heart, yet displayed so much zeal, admiration, and devotion toward her, that Porpora might very well imagine that he was violently in love. He thought that by not putting any restraint on his intercourse with her, he would furnish him with opportunities for making himself heard, and that by informing him in proper time and place of the empress' designs and his own, he would impart to him the courage of eloquence and the force of persuasion necessary to his success. He consequently ceased to ill-treat and look down upon him, and gave a free course to their affections, flattering himself that the less he interfered the better affairs would proceed.

Porpora, in thus never doubting of success, committed a great error. He laid Consuelo open to misrepresentation and slander, for no sooner was Joseph seen twice with her behind the scenes than the whole dramatic staff proclaimed her attachment to this young man, and poor Consuelo, innocent and confiding like all upright minds, never dreamed of the danger she was in, nor took any means to avoid it. So from the day on which the last rehearsal of *Zenobia* took place, all eyes were on the watch, all tongues in motion. In every corner, behind every decoration, the actors, the choristers, and the underlings of all kinds, passed their good-natured or severe, their kind or malignant remarks, on the scandal of this budding intrigue, or on the happiness of the betrothed pair.

Consuelo, wholly absorbed in her part and in her feelings as an artist, saw or heard nothing of all this and suspected no danger. As for the thoughful Joseph, he was so completely taken up with the opera in course of performance, or that which he purposed composing himself, that he heard indeed some passing equivocal remarks, but did not in the least understand them, so far was he from flattering himself with vain hopes. At such times he would raise his head and look around as if to seek who they were leveled at, but not succeeding in his search, and completely indifferent to every thing of the kind, he relapsed into his meditations.

Between each act of the opera there was frequently performed a little buffa piece, and this day it happened to be the *Impressario delle Canarie,* a gay and comic production of Metastasio's. Corilla, who filled the part of an imperious, exacting, fantastic *prima donna* was nature itself, and her success in this little trifle consoled her in some degree for the loss of her grand part of Zenobia. While they were performing the last part of the interlude, and before the third act of the opera commenced, Consuelo, who felt somewhat oppressed by the emotion excited by her part, retreated behind the curtain, between the *horrible valley* bristling with *mountains* and *precipices,* which formed the first decoration, and the good river Araxes bordered by *pleasant mountains,* which was to appear in the third scene to recreate the eyes of the *feeling* spectator. She was walking rapidly up and down in the passage, when Joseph brought her her fan, which she had left in the prompter's box and which she used with much satisfaction. The promptings of his heart, and Porpora's voluntary inattention, had induced Joseph mechanically to rejoin his friend, and a feeling of confidence and sympathy always inclined Consuelo to receive him joyously. But from this mutual regard, at which the angels of heaven need not have blushed, fatal consequences were destined to ensue. Our lady readers, as we are well aware, always anxious to know the event, would ask no better than to be acquainted with the result at once, but we must entreat them to have a little patience.

"Well! my dear friend," said Joseph, smiling as he extended his hand, "you are no longer it would seem so dissatisfied with the dramas of our illustrious abbé; and you have found in the music of your prayer, a window by which the genius that possesses you can wing its upward flight."

"I have sung well, then?"

"Do you not perceive that my eyes are red?"

"Ah! yes, you have wept. So much the better; I am happy to have made you weep!"

"As if it were for the first time! But you are rapidly becoming the artist that Porpora wishes you to be, my good Consuelo. The fire of success is lighted up within you. When you sung in the leafy bowers of the Böehmer Wald you saw me weep heartily, and you wept yourself, melted by the beauty of your song. Now it is otherwise; you smile with pleasure and thrill with pride on beholding the tears you cause others to shed. Courage, my Consuelo, you are now a *prima donna* in the fullest sense of the term!"

"Say not so, my friend; I shall never be like yonder one," and she nodded toward Corilla, who was singing on the stage on the other side of the curtain.

"Do not take what I have said amiss," replied Joseph; "I merely meant to say that your inspiration has proved victorious. In vain does your calm reason, your austere philosophy, and the memory of Riesenburg, strive against the influences of the Python. His divine breath fills your bosom even to overflowing. Confess that your whole frame thrills with delight. I feel your arm tremble against mine; your countenance glows with animation; never have I seen you so lovely and majestic. No, you were not more agitated, not more inspired, when Count Albert read to you the tragedies of Greece!"

"Ah! how you pain me by that word," exclaimed Consuelo, turning pale, and withdrawing her arm from Joseph's. "Why do you utter that name here? it is a name too sacred to be mentioned in this temple of folly. It is a name which, like a peal of thunder, thrusts back into dim night the empty phantoms of these golden dreams."

"Well, then, Consuelo, since I am forced to tell you so," resumed Haydn, after a moment's silence, "never will you be able to decide on marrying that man."

"Hush! hush! Joseph; I have promised."

"Well, then, keep your promise; but you will never be happy with him. Quit the theater? Renounce your career as an artist? It is now too late. You have tasted a pleasure the remembrance of which would torment your whole after life."

"You terrify me, Beppo! Why do say such things to me to-day?"

"I know not; I say them in despite of myself. Your fever has passed into my veins, and I feel as if when I went home, I should write something sublime. It may probably be something very trivial after all; but no matter, for the moment I feel as if inspired."

"How gay and tranquil you are! While I, in place of the pride and joy of which you speak, feel nothing but a sentiment of grief, and could weep and smile in the same breath."

"I feel well assured that you suffer, for you ought to suffer; at the moment when you feel your power developed within you to its full extent, a pang seizes and overcomes you."

"Yes, it is true; what means it?"

"It means that you are an artist, and that you do violence both to nature and conscience in renouncing your profession."

"Yesterday it seemed as if this was not the case; to-day it seems as if it were. My nerves are shaken; the agitation I feel is frightful; on no other grounds can I account for my indecision. Hitherto I denied the influence of these feelings and their power. I always entered on the stage with calmness and a modest determination to fulfil my part conscientiously. But I am no longer my former self, and should I make my appearance on the stage at this moment, I feel as if I should commit the wildest extravagances; all prudence, all self-command would leave me. To-morrow I hope it will not be so, for this emotion borders on madness."

"My poor friend! I fear, or rather I hope, it will ever be so. Without true and deep emotion, where would be your power? I have often endeavored to impress upon the musicians and actors I have met, that without this agitation, this delirium, they could do nothing, and that, in place of calming down with years and experience, they would become more impressionable at each fresh attempt."

"It is a great mystery," said Consuelo, sighing. "Neither vanity, nor jealousy, nor the paltry wish of triumphing, could have exerted such overwhelming power over me. No! I assure you that in singing this prayer of Zenobia's and this duet with Tiradates, in which I am borne away as in a whirlwind by Caffariello's vigor and passion, I thought neither of the public nor of my rivals, nor of myself. I was Zenobia, and believed in the gods of Olympus with truly Christian fervor, and I burned with love for the worthy Caffariello, whom, the performance once over, I could not look at without a smile.

" All this is strange, and I begin to think that, dramatic art being a perpetual falsehood, Heaven inflicts upon us the punishment of making us believe as real the illusions we practice on the spectator. No! it is not permitted to man to turn the passions and emotions of actual life into a jest! We must keep our souls holy and pure for true affections and useful deeds; and when we pervert God's purposes and aims, he chastises us for our folly by inflicting on us mental blindness."

" Ay, there lies the mystery, Consuelo! Who can penetrate his designs? Would he impart these instincts to us from our very cradle—would he implant in us this craving desire for art which we can never suppress—if he entirely prescribed their application? Why, even from infancy, have I never loved the plays of my companions? Why, since I have been my own master, have I labored at music with an assiduity which would have killed any other at my age? Repose revives me, labor gives me life and strength. It was the same with yourself; you have told me so a hundred times; and when we related the history of our lives, we each thought the other's story was our own. Ah! the hand of God is in every thing, and every power, every impulse (even when we fail to understand it), is from Him. You are born an artist—it must be so; and whoever places a barrier in your way, inflicts death or worse than death upon you."

"Oh! Beppo,"exclaimed Consuelo, agitated and confused, " you terrify me; I know not what to do! Alas! if I could expire to-morrow when the curtain falls, after having tasted for the first and last time the joy and inspiration of a true artist, it would save me perhaps from a long career of pain and suffering."

" Ah!" said Joseph, with forced gaiety, " I would much rather that your Count Albert or your humble servant should expire first."

At this moment Consuelo raised her eyes in a melancholy reverie toward the wing which opened before her. The interior of a great theater, seen by day, is so different from what it appears to us from the front of the stage when bril-

liantly lighted, that it is impossible to form an idea of it
when one has not seen it thus. Nothing can present a more
gloomy or frightful appearance than the immense expanse,
lined with tier above tier of boxes and buried in darkness,
solitude and silence. If a human face were to appear in those boxes closed like tombs, it would seem
like a specter, and would make the boldest actor
recoil with fear. The dim and fitful light, which is
admitted from several windows in the roof at the extremity of the stage, glances obliquely over scaffoldings, torn
scenes, and dusty boards. Upon the stage, the eye, deprived of the illusion of perspective, is astonished at that
narrow and confined space where so many persons and passions are to play their part, representing majestic movements, imposing masses, ungovernable emotions, which
will seem such to the spectator, and which are studied,
nay measured to a line, in order to avoid embarassment,
confusion, or even coming in contact with the scenes.
But if the stage look small and mean, the height above it,
intended to receive so many decorations and to afford
space for so much machinery, appears on the other
hand immense, freed from all those scenes of fes-
tooned clouds, architectural cornices, or verdant boughs
which divide it in certain proportions to the eye
of the spectator. In its real disproportion this elevation
has in it something lofty and severe; and if on looking
upon the stage, you might imagine yourself in a dungeon,
on casting your eyes upward, you would think yourself in
a Gothic church, but a ruined or unfinished one, for every
thing there is dim, unformed, strange and incoherent.
Shapeless ladders for the use of the mechanist, placed as if
by chance and thrown without apparent motive against
other ladders, dimly seen in the confusion of these indistinct details, piles of oddly shaped boards, scenes upside
down, whose design presents no meaning to the mind,
ropes interlaced like hieroglyphics, nameless fragments,
pulleys and wheels which seem prepared for unknown tortures—all these recall to us those dreams we have when
about to awake in which we see strange and unheard of
things, while we make vain efforts to ascertain where we
are.

Every thing is vague, shadowy, unsubstantial. Aloft
you see a man at work, supported as it were by spiders'

webs. To your uncertain gaze he might be either a mariner clinging to the cordage of a vessel, or an enormous rat gnawing the worm-eaten carpentry. You hear sounds and words proceeding from you know not where. They are uttered some eight feet above your head, and the bewildering echoes which slumber amid the recesses of the fantastic dome, convey them to your ear either distinct or confused, according as you may happen to change your position. A fearful noise shakes the scaffolds, and is repeated in prolonged rattlings! Is the frail structure about to crumble, or are those trembling balconies about to fall and bury the poor workmen beneath the ruins. No, it is a fireman sneezing, or some cat pursuing its prey amid the mazes of the aerial labyrinth. Ere you are unaccustomed to those sounds and objects, you feel a sensation of terror. You are ignorant of what is going on, and know not what unheard-of apparitions may put all your philosophy and courage to the proof. You understand nothing of what surrounds you, and whatever is not clearly distinguished either by the bodily or mental vision—whatever is uncertain and incomprehensible, always alarms the logic of the senses. What seems the most reasonable supposition when entering on such a chaos, is that you are about to witness the fiendish revels of some wizard alchemist and his attendant demons in their magic laboratory.

Consuelo allowed her eyes to wander carelessly over the singular edifice, and the poetry of this disorder struck her for the first time. At each end of the alley formed by the two back scenes, was a long dark wing, across which shadow-like figures flitted from time to time. Suddenly one of these figures paused as if awaiting her, and she even fancied that it beckoned her to approach.

" Is it Porpora?" said she to Joseph.

" No," replied he, " but it is doubtless some one who has been sent to tell you that they are about to commence the third act."

Consuelo quickened her pace, and hastened in the direction of the person, whose features she could not distinguish as he had retreated back to the wall. But when she was within three paces of him, and on the point of questioning him, he glided rapidly through the adjacent wing, gained the back of the theater, and disappeared in the depths beyond.

"That person seems as if he had been playing the spy upon us." said Joseph.

"And as if he was now evading our pursuit," added Consuelo, struck with the man's anxiety to escape; "I cannot tell why, but I feel afraid of him."

She returned to the stage and rehearsed the last act, at the close of which she again experienced the enthusiastic impulse which had before inspired her. When she was about to put on her mantle before leaving the theater, and was looking around for it, she was dazzled by a sudden glare. They had opened a window in the roof, and the rays of the setting sun streamed through and fell obliquely before her. The contrast of the sudden light with the previous gloom caused her to take a random step or two, when all at once she found herself opposite the person in the dark cloak by whom she had been startled behind the scenes. She saw his figure indistinctly, and yet she thought she recognized him, but he had already disappeared, and she looked around for him in vain.

"What is the matter with you?" said Joseph, holding out her mantle: "have you hurt yourself against some of the decorations?"

"No," said she; "but I have seen Count Albert."

"Count Albert here! Are you sure—is it possible?"

"It is possible—it is certain," said Consuelo, drawing him along with her, and commencing to search behind the scenes in every direction. Joseph assisted her in her scrutiny, although convinced that she was mistaken, while Porpora summoned her impatiently to accompany him home. Consuelo could see no one who bore the least resemblance to Albert; and when, obliged to leave the theater with her master, she passed in review all those who had been on the stage along with her, she observed several cloaks similar to that which had already attracted her attention.

"No matter," she whispered to Joseph, who watched her anxious gaze, "I have seen him—he was there!"

"It must have been a deception of your senses," replied Joseph; "had it been Count Albert would he not have spoken to you, and yet you say he fled at your approach?"

"I do not say that it was really he, but I saw his features and I now think with you that it must have been a vision. Some misfortune must have happened to him!

I long to set out at once and hasten to Bohemia. I am sure that he is danger—that he calls me—that he expects me!"

" I see, among other bad offices, that he has infected you with his madness, my poor Consuelo; the excitement you felt in singing has disposed you to entertain these wild ideas. Be yourself again, I beseech you, and be assured that if Count Albert be in Vienna you will see him flying to you before the day be over."

This hope revived Consuelo's courage. She hastened forward with Beppo, leaving the old maestro, who on this occasion was not displeased at being forgotten, far behind. But Consuelo thought neither of Joseph nor Porpora. She hurried onward, arrived all breathless at the house, rushed up to her apartment, but found no one there. Joseph made inquiries from the domestics, but no one had called in their absence. Consuelo waited all day, but in vain. The whole evening, and even till far on in the night, she gazed anxiously from the window at every one who passed in the stréet. Every moment she was certain that the approaching comer was about to stop, but he always passed on, at one time with the light step of some youthful gallant humming a popular air, at another with the faltering gait and dry sharp cough of an aged invalid.

Consuelo, now convinced that she must have been dreaming, retired to rest, and next day when the impression had worn off, she admitted to Joseph that she had not clearly distinguished any of the features of the unknown. A sort of vague resemblance in his general appearance to Albert — a resemblance strengthened by his dress, his pale complexion, and his jet-black beard, or what seemed such by the fantastic light of the theater—had sufficed to convert a sudden impression into certainty.

" If a man such as you have often described to me," said Joseph, " had been behind the scenes, his neglected air, long beard, and dark hair would surely have attracted comment. Now I have asked every one belonging to the theater, even to the porters, who permit no one whom they do not know to enter without a proper authority, and they all agree in saying that they saw no stranger in the theater that day."

" My senses must have played me false, then. I was agitated, I scarcely knew what I did ; I was thinking of

Albert, his image was in my soul, some one passed me, and I took him for the person who occupied my thoughts. My mind must surely be much weakened. The cry which I uttered issued from my very heart; something strange and wonderful took place within me."

"Think no more of such chimeras," said Joseph, "study your part, and let your thoughts dwell only on this evening."

CHAPTER XCVIII.

In the course of the day Consuelo saw a strange group defile past her window and proceed toward the public square. They were robust, weatherbeaten men, with long mustachios, naked legs, and leather sandals secured like the buskins of the ancients with thongs ; they wore a sort of pointed caps, had their belts garnished with numerous pistols, and each held in his hand a long Albanian musket, while over their uncovered neck and arms was thrown a red cloak, which completed their costume.

" Is this a masquerade?" exclaimed Consuelo to the canon who had called to pay her a visit. " We are not now in the carnival that I know of."

" Look well those men," replied the canon; "it will be long ere we see the like again, if it please God to protect the reign of Maria Theresa. See how the people look at them, with a curiosity mingled with terror and disgust. Vienna saw them hasten to her assistance in her hour of anguish, and she received them more joyfully then than she does to-day, ashamed and terror-stricken as she is to have been indebted to them for her safety."

" Are these the Slavonian bandits of whom I heard so much in Bohemia, and who committed so many outrages there?" said Consuelo.

" They are no other," replied the canon; "they are the residue of those hordes of Croatian serfs and robbers whom the celebrated Baron Francis Trenck, cousin to your friend Baron Frederick Trenck, manumitted with incredible ability and daring, in order to enter them as regular troops in the service of the empress. Behold him! this redoubtable hero—this Trenck with the burned throat, as the soldiers call him—this famous partisan chief—the most cunning, intrepid, and necessary during the sad and bloody years gone by; the greatest romancer, the greatest robber certainly of his age, but at the same time one of the bravest, most vigorous, most active, and incredibly daring men of modern times. Behold him, Trenck, the Pandour, with his famished wolves, a savage and bloody herd, of which he is the savage shepherd!"

Baron Francis Trenck was even taller than his cousin of Prussia, and was nearly six feet six inches in height. His scarlet mantle, which was secured round his neck by a ruby clasp, was open at the breast, and displayed to view a whole museum of Turkish weapons, studded with precious stones, disposed around his person. Pistols, curved scimitars, and cutlasses—nothing was wanting to give him the appearance of the most determined and expeditious of man-slayers. His cap was adorned, instead of a plume of feathers, with a miniature scythe, with four blades falling in front. His face was frightful. Having descended into a cellar, during the pillage of a Bohemian town, in search of a quantity of concealed treasure, he incautiously approached the candle too near some barrels he thought contained the promised gold, but instead of gold the barrels contained powder, and the consequence of his mistake was an explosion which destroyed a portion of the vault and buried him in the ruins. When he was at last dug out he was almost expiring. His body was severely scorched, and his face seamed with deep and indelible wounds. "No person," say the annals of the time, "could look on him without shuddering."

"This is then that monster, that enemy of the human race!" exclaimed the horror-stricken Consuelo, turning away her eyes. "Bohemia will long remember his passage; cities burned and plundered—children and old men cut to pieces—women outraged—the country pillaged — the harvest rooted up—flocks destroyed, when they could not be carried away — everywhere ruin, murder, desolation and flames! Alas! unhappy Bohemia, the theater of so many sufferings, the scene of such dreadful tragedies!"

"Yes, unfortunate Bohemia!" replied the canon. "Ever the victim of man's fury — ever the arena of his strife! Francis Trenck renewed in that unhappy kingdom all the frightful excesses of John Ziska. Like him

unconquered, he never gave quarter, and the terror of his
name was so great that his outposts have taken cities even
when far in advance, and while the main body were struggling with other enemies. It might be said of him, as it
was of Attila, that the grass never grew where his horse
had left its footmarks. The conquered will curse him to
the fourth generation."

Baron Francis Trenck gradually disappeared in the distance, but Consuelo and the canon could long distinguish
his richly caparisoned horses led by gigantic Croatian
hussars.

"What you see," said the canon, "is but an insignificant sample of his riches. Mules and chariots, laden with
arms, pictures, precious stones, and ingots of gold and
silver, cover the roads which lead to his Slavonian estates.
It is there that he buries treasures which might serve to
ransom kings. He is served on gold plate which he took
from the King of Prussia at Soraw, where the King of
Prussia himself narrowly escaped being taken prisoner by
him. Some say he only got off by fifteen minutes; others
say that he was actually in Trenck's hands, and that he
purchased his liberty dearly. But, patience! the Pandour,
perhaps, will not long enjoy such glory and riches. It is
said that he is threatened with a criminal charge, and
that the most frightful accusations are impending over
him; that the empress is terribly afraid of him, and that
such of his Croatians as have not, according to their usual
practice, taken French leave, are about to be incorporated
with the regular troops, and disciplined in the Prussian
fashion. As for himself, I augur badly of the compliments and recompenses that await him at court."

"But general report attributes to them the honor of
having saved the Austrian throne."

"And doubtless they have. From the frontiers of
Turkey to those of France, they have spread terror everywhere around, and have taken places the most strongly
fortified and won battles at every odds. Always in the
van of the army, and ever first at the escalade or in the
breach, they have extorted admiration from our greatest
generals. The French fled before them in every direction,
and the great Frederick himself, it is said, grew pale like
any other mortal when he heard their war-cry. Neither
rapid torrents, nor pathless forests, nor treacherous

morasses, nor steep and shelving rocks, nor showering balls, nor crackling flames, arrested their progress by night or day, in winter or in summer. Yes, most certainly they have saved Maria Theresa's throne more effectually than all the antiquated military tactics of our generals, or all the schemes of our most accomplished diplomatists."

"In that case, their crimes will be unpunished, their thefts glorified."

"Perhaps, on the contrary, they will be too severely punished."

"But a monarch would not thus requite men who had rendered such services?"

"Pardon me," exclaimed the canon, with caustic irony ; "when the monarch has no more need of them ——"

"But were they not suffered to commit these excesses, which they practiced in the territories of the empire, or on those of the allies?"

"Doubtless, every thing was permitted to them, because they were indispensable."

"And now?"

"And now, as they are so no longer, they are reproached with the very misdeeds which were formerly winked at."

"And the high-minded Maria Theresa?"

"Oh! they have profaned churches!"

"I understand. Trenck is lost, reverend canon."

"Hush! Speak low," replied he.

"Have you seen the Pandours?" exclaimed Joseph, running in, quite out of breath.

"With very little satisfaction," replied Consuelo.

"And did you not recollect them?"

"I see them now for the first time."

"No, it is not the first time. We met those men in the Böehmer Wald."

"Thank God, not that I recollect."

"Do you not remember a chalet where we passed the night, and where our slumbers were disturbed by some strange, fierce-looking men demanding admittance."

Consuelo did in fact remember the circumstance, but as she was very drowsy, she had not paid much attention to the men, whom both she and Joseph had taken for contrabandists.

"Well," said he, "these pretended contrabandists, who did not observe our presence, and who left the chalet before daylight, carrying bags and heavy packages, were no other than Pandours. It was the arms, the faces, the mustaches, and the cloaks, which I have just seen pass, and Providence spared us, without our knowing it, from the worst encounter we could possibly have met with."

"Without any doubt," observed the canon, to whom Joseph had often related all the details of their journey, "these worthy fellows had disbanded themselves of their own free will, as they usually do when their pockets are lined, and they were regaining their homes by a long circuit, rather than carry their booty through the heart of the empire where they might have been subjected to a reckoning. But be assured they would not reach home without molestation. They rob and assassinate each other by the way, and it is only the strongest who regain their forests and their caverns, loaded with the booty of their slaughtered companions."

The hour for the performance, which was now approaching, distracted Consuelo's attention from Trenck and his cruel Pandours, and she hastened to the theater. Here she had no dressing-room. Madame Tesi had hitherto lent her hers; but on this occasion, enraged at her success and now her sworn enemy, she had carried off the key, and the prima donna of the evening was totally at a loss how to act. These pretty treacheries are usual at theaters; they serve to annoy and harass a rival whose power is feared. She loses time in looking for an apartment; she fears she will not succeed in finding one. The hour approaches; her companions say to her in passing: "What! not dressed yet? They are going to begin!" At last, after much running to and fro, and many angry threats, she obtains an apartment where nothing she requires is at hand. The dress-makers have been bribed, and the costume is not ready, or does not fit. The tire-women are at the service of any one but the unfortunate victim. The bell rings, and the call-boy (*butta fuori*) bawls along the corridors: "*Signore e signori, si va cominciar,*" terrible words which the débutante hears with affright, for she is not ready. In her haste she tears her sleeves, breaks her laces, puts on her mantle outside in, while her diadem totters and threatens to fall with the first step she makes upon the stage. Nervous, palpitating, indignant, her eyes full of tears, she must appear with a celestial smile upon her lips; her voice must be pure and fresh, when her throat is choking and her bosom ready to burst. Oh! all those crowns of flowers which rain upon the stage at the moment of her triumph are mingled with countless thorns!

Happily for Consuelo, she met Corilla, who said, taking her hand:

"Come to my room. Tesi flattered herself she could play you the same trick she practiced on me when I made my first appearance. But I will come to your assistance, were it only to enrage her! it is a Roland for her Oliver! At the rate you are getting on in public estimation, Porporina, I dread to see you outstrip me wherever I am so unfortunate as to be brought into contact with you. Then you will no doubt forget my conduct toward you here, and remember only the injury I have done you."

"The injury you have done me, Corilla?" said Consuelo, entering her rival's dressing-room and commencing her toilet behind a screen, while the German dressing-maids divided their attention between the two ladies, who could converse together in Venetian without being understood. "Really, I do not know what injury you have done me; I cannot recollect any."

"The proof that you bear a grudge against me is, that you speak to me as if you were a duchess, and look down upon me with contempt."

"Indeed," replied Consuelo, in a gentle voice, and endeavoring to overcome her repugnance to speak familiarly to a woman with whom she had so little in common. "I really cannot remember to what you allude."

"Is that true?" rejoined the other. "Have you so completely forgotten poor Zoto?"

"I was at liberty to forget him, and I did so," replied Consuelo, as she fastened her buskin with that courage and vivacity which a trying situation sometimes confers, and she warbled a brilliant roulade, to keep herself in voice.

Corilla replied by a similar one for the same purpose; then interrupting herself to address her soubrette: "What the plague! mademoiselle," said she; "you squeeze too tight. Do you take me for a Nuremburg doll? These Germans," continued she, in Venetian, "do not know what shoulders are. They would make us as square as their own dowagers, if we would suffer them. Porporina, do not let them muffle you up to the ears as they did the last time; it was ridiculous."

"As to that, my dear, it is the imperial order. These ladies are aware of it, and I do not care about such a trifle."

"A trifle! Our shoulders a trifle——"

"I do not say that with reference to you, whose shape is faultless; but as for myself——"

"Hypocrite!" said Corilla, sighing, "your are ten years younger than I am, and my shoulders will soon have nothing to recommend them but their former reputation."

"It is you who are the hypocrite," replied Consuelo, excessively wearied and annoyed with this species of conversation, and to put a stop to it she began, while arranging her hair, to repeat scales and exercises for the voice.

"Be silent!" exclaimed Corilla, suddenly, who listened in spite of herself; "you plunge a thousand daggers in my heart. Ah! I would gladly give you up all my admirers; I would be sure to find others; but your voice and manner, those I cannot compete with. Be silent, I say; I am half inclined to strangle you."

Consuelo, who saw that Corilla was but half in jest, and that this mocking flattery concealed real suffering, took it as it was intended. But after an instant's pause the latter resumed:

"How do you execute that ornament?"

"Would you like to have it? I will give it up to you," replied Consuelo, with admirable good nature. "Come, I will teach it to you; put it into your part this evening, and I shall find another."

"Yes, one still better, and I shall gain nothing by it."

"Very well, I shall not sing it at all. Porpora does not care about such things, and it will be one reproach less. Hold! here it is." And she drew from her pocket a line of music written on a scrap of folded paper, and handed it over the screen to Corilla. The latter hastened to study it, and with Consuelo's assistance succeeded in learning it, the toilet going on as before.

Before Consuelo had put on her robe, Corilla thrust aside the screen, and impatiently advanced to embrace her in gratitude for her gift. It was not gratitude alone however which prompted this demonstration; mingled with it was a treacherous wish to see if she could not detect some fault in her rival's figure. But Consuelo's waist was slender as a reed, and her chaste and noble outline needed no assistance from art. She guessed Corilla's intention, and smiled: "You may examine my person, and search my heart," thought she, "and find out nothing false in either of them."

"Zingarella," exclaimed Corilla, resuming, in spite of herself, her hostile air and sharp voice; "do you love this Anzoleto any longer?"

"No longer," replied Consuelo smiling.

"And he—did he not love you well?"

"He did not," continued Consuelo, with the same firmness and sincerity.

"Ah! then it was just as he told me," cried Corilla, fixing her clear, blue eyes on her rival's countenance, as if she hoped to detect there some hidden pang.

Consuelo was ignorant of finesse, but she had that openness and candor, which are far more powerful weapons when used to combat with trickery and cunning. She felt the blow, and calmly resisted it. She no longer loved Anzoleto, and felt no pang of wounded self-love. She therefore yielded this triumph to Corilla's vanity.

"He told you the truth," she replied; "he loves me not."

"But did you never love him?" replied the other, more astonished than pleased at this confession. Consuelo felt that here there could be no concealment. She determined that Corilla should be satisfied.

"Yes," said she, "I loved him dearly."

"And are you not ashamed to own it? Have you no pride, my poor girl?"

"Yes, enough to cure myself."

"That is to say you were philosopher enough to console yourself by encouraging another admirer. Tell me now, Porporina, who it was. It could not be that little Haydn, who is both friendless and penniless."

"That would be no reason for my not loving him. But I have consoled myself with no one in the manner you are pleased to imagine."

"Ah! I know you have pretensions. But say nothing about them here, my dear, if you would not be ridiculous."

"Therefore I shall not mention them unless I am questioned, and I do not allow every one to take that liberty; if I have suffered you to do so, Corilla, do not, unless you be an enemy, abuse the privilege."

"You are a mask!" exclaimed Corilla. "You have both wit and talent, although you pretend to be so frank. Ah! you are clever, zingarella. You will make the men believe what you please."

"I shall make them believe nothing, nor shall I suffer them to interfere in my affairs so far as to question me."

"It is the better way. They always abuse our confidence, and only extort it to load us with reproach. Ah! I admire you, zingarella. You so young, to triumph over love—the passion, of all others, the most fatal to our repose, our beauty, and our fortune. It fills me with respect! I know it by dear-bought experience; if I could have been cold, I should not have suffered so much. But look you, I am a poor creature; I was born unhappy. Ever, in the midst of my highest success, I have been guilty of some folly that spoiled every thing; I have fallen in love with some poor devil, and then adieu fortune! I might have married Zustiniani once. He adorned me, but I could not bear him. This miserable Anzoleto pleased me, and for him I sacrificed every thing. Come, you will give me your advice—will you not? You will be my friend? You will preserve me from the weaknesses, both of my heart and head. And to make a beginning, I must confess that latterly I have a feeling of preference for a man on whom fortune lowers, and who may soon prove more dangerous than useful at court. One who has millions, but who may be ruined in a twinkling. Yes, I must throw him off before he drags me down the precipice. Ah! speak of the devil—here he is! I hear him, and I feel a pang of jealousy shoot to my heart. Close your screen, Porporina, and do not stir; I would not have him know you are here."

Consuelo did as she was told: she had no wish to be seen by Corilla's admirers. A masculine voice echoed along the corridor, there was a knock, as a matter of form, and then the door was opened without the visitor waiting for a reply.

"Dreadful profession!" thought Consuelo; "no, the intoxication of the stage shall never seduce me; all behind it is too impure."

And she concealed herself in a corner, horrified at the company in which she found herself, indignant and even terrified at the manner in which Corilla had addressed her, and, for the first time in her life, brought in contact with scenes of which she could previously have formed no idea.

CHAPTER XCIX.

WHILE hurriedly completing her toilet, for fear of a surprise, she heard the following dialogue in Italian:

" Why do you come here? I told you not to enter my apartment. The empress has forbidden us, under the severest penalties, to receive the visits of any but our fellow-actors, and even then there must be some urgent necessity respecting the business of the theater. See to what you expose me! I did not think the police of the theater was so negligent."

" There is no police for those who pay well, my angel. Only fools meet with resistance or delay in their progress. Come, give me a little kinder reception, or, *mort du Diable!* I will not return in a hurry."

" You could not give me a greater pleasure. Come, be off! Well, why don't you go ?"

" You seem to desire it so earnestly, that I shall remain to provoke you."

" I warn you that I shall send for the manager to rid me of your presence."

" Let him come if he is tired of his life ! I am ready."

" But are you crazy? I tell you that you compromise me; that you make me break a rule recently introduced by her majesty; that you expose me to a heavy fine, perhaps to a dismissal."

" I shall take upon myself to pay the fine to your director with a few blows of my cane. As to your dismissal, I ask nothing better. I will carry you to my estates, where we will lead a jovial life together."

" I follow such a brute as you? never! Come, let us leave this together, since you are determined not to leave me here alone."

" Alone, say you, my charmer? That is what I mean to satisfy myself of before leaving you. There is a screen there which seems to me to occupy too much space in this little room. If I kicked it to one side 1 think it would be doing you a good service."

"Stop, sir; stop! a lady is dressing there. Would you injure a woman, bandit that you are?"

"A woman? oh! that is another affair; but I must see if this woman has not a sword by her side."

The screen began to yield, and Consuelo, now full attired, threw on her mantle, and while they opened the first fold of the screen, she endeavored to push the last so as to make her escape by the door, which was not two paces from her. But Corilla, who saw her intention, stopped her, saying: "Remain there, Porporina; if he did not find you he would say it was a man, and might perhaps kill me." Consuelo, frightened, was about to show herself; but Corilla, who had stationed herself between her lover and Porporina, again prevented her. She hoped, perhaps, by exciting his jealousy, to make him overlook the grace and beauty of her rival.

"If it be a lady," said he, smiling, "let her reply. Madam, are you attired? may I offer my respects to you?"

"Sir," replied Consuelo, on a sign from Corilla, "please reserve them for some other occasion; I am not to be seen."

"That is to say, that this is a good time to look at you," said Corilla's lover, again threatening to push aside the screen.

"Take care what you do," said Corilla, with a forced laugh "perhaps in place of a handsome shepherdess you may find a respectable duenna."

"By jove, it is not possible! Her voice hardly betokens twenty. If she had not been young and handsome, you would have shown her to me long ago."

The screen was very lofty, and, notwithstanding his height, the stranger could not see over it unless by throwing down all the articles of Corilla's dress which were scattered over the chairs; besides, as he had no longer feared the presence of a man, the sport amused him.

"Madam," cried he, "if you are old and ugly, do not speak, and I shall respect your asylum. But if on the other hand you are young and handsome, say but a word, were it only to refute Corilla's calumnies."

Consuelo did not reply.

"Ah! by my faith I am not going to be duped in that way! If you were old or ugly you would not acknowledge it so readily; you are doubtless angelic, and therefore mock my doubts. In any case I must see you, for either you are a prodigy of beauty, fit to bear the palm from the fair Corilla herself, or else you have wit enough to admit your ugliness, and I should be glad to see for the first time in my life an ugly woman who makes no pretentions to beauty."

He seized Corilla's arm with two of his fingers, and bent it in his grasp, as if it had been a straw. She uttered a shrill cry, and pretended to be bruised and hurt; but heedless of her plaint he thrust aside the screen and revealed to Consuelo's gaze the horrible countenance of Baron Francis Trench. A rich and fashionable dress had replaced his savage war costume, but his gigantic proportions and the reddish black scars which disfigured his weatherbeaten countenance, at once betrayed the bold and pitiless leader of the Pandours.

Consuelo could not repress a cry of terror, and suddenly turning pale she sank back into her chair.

"Do not be afraid of me, madam," said the baron, sinking on one knee before her, "and pardon the boldness which I now feel I cannot sufficiently expiate. But suffer me to believe that it was out of pity toward me, seeing that to see is to adore you, that you refused to show yourself. Do not grieve me so far as to make me believe I terrify you. I confess I am ugly enough; but if the wars have converted a tolerably handsome fellow into a sort of monster, they have not rendered him less good-natured on that account.

"Less good-natured? no, that would be impossible," replied Consuelo, turning her back on him.

"Come, come," replied the baron, "you are a somewhat wayward child, and your nurse has doubtless told you frightful stories about me, as the old women of this country do not fail to do. But the young ones do me more justice; they know that if I am a little rough with the enemies of my country, they can easily tame me if they will only take the trouble."

And he leaned toward the mirror in which Consuelo pretended to look, fixing on her at the same time the bold and ardent gaze which had fascinated and subdued Corilla.

Consuelo saw that she could not get rid of him, unless by affronting him.

"Sir," said she, "you do not inspire me with fear, but

with disgust and aversion; you delight in butchery, and though I do not fear death, I detest sanguinary minds such as yours. I am just come from Bohemia, where I have seen the bloody traces of your footprints."

The baron changed countenance, and shrugging his shoulders, said, turning to Corilla:

"What mad sybil have you got here? The baroness Lestocq, who once fired a pistol point blank at me, was not more frantic. Is it possible that I can have crushed her lover without knowing it in galloping over some bush? Come, my fair one, I was only jesting with you. If you are of so savage a turn, I ask your pardon; but I deserve to be served so for having for a moment forgotten the divine Corilla."

"The divine Corilla," replied the latter," "cares nothing about you, and only wishes to get rid of you. The director will be here presently, and if you do not disappear——"

"Well, I'm off," said the baron; "as I do not wish to vex you, and injure your voice in the estimation of the public, by making you shed a few pearly drops. My carriage will be waiting for you when the performance is over. Is it agreed?"

Here he saluted her, in spite of a pretended resistence before Consuelo, and retired.

Corilla forthwith embraced her companion, and thanked her for having so well repulsed the baron's advances. Consuelo turned her head away, for Corilla and her lover were at this moment equally disgusting in her eyes.

"How can you be jealous of a being so repulsive?" she said.

"Zingarella, you know nothing about it," replied Corilla, smiling. "The baron pleases women in a more lofty position than I am. His figure is superb, and his face, though somewhat scarred, has attractions which you could not withstand if he was determined to please you."

"Ah! Corilla, his face is not the worst; his soul is more hideous still. Do you not know that his heart is the heart of a tiger?"

"And do you not see that this is what has turned my head?" replied Corilla, warmly. "How tiresome is all the stupid stuff that those effeminate creatures say to us! But to chain a tiger, to tame a lion, and hold him in leading strings—to make one whose very glance has put armies to flight, one whose saber can chop off an ox's head as easily as a poppy—sigh and tremble—ah! that is indeed something! Anzoleto was a little savage also, and I liked him for it; but the baron is worse. Anzoleto might have beaten me, but the baron is capable of killing me. Oh! it is delightful!"

"Poor Corilla!" said Consuelo, casting on her a look of deep pity.

"You pity me for my love, and you are right; but you should also envy me. I would rather, however, that you should pity me for it than dispute it with me."

"Do not be uneasy," said Consuelo.

"*Signora si va cominciar!*" exclaimed the call-boy at the door.

"Begin!" shouted a stentorian voice from the quarter occupied by the chorus-singers.

"Begin!" repeated a hollow voice from the foot of the stairs which ascended from the back of the theater; and the last syllables echoed from scene to scene, becoming every moment fainter, until, almost expiring, it reached the prompter, who announced it to the leader by three blows upon the floor. The latter struck his bow twice upon the desk before him, and a momentary pause ensued before the overture commenced, during which each member of the orchestra collected his energies, and fixed his eye upon the conductor, after which, the first notes of the symphony enforced silence alike upon the boxes and the pit.

From the very first act of *Zenobia,* Consuelo produced the complete and irresistible effect which Haydn had predicted. The greatest actors are not always uniformly successful on she stage; and even supposing that no temporary weakness takes possession of their powers, every situation and every part is not equally adapted to their development. It was the first time that Consuelo filled a part in which she could be herself—in which she could manifest, in their full force, all her purity, strength, and tenderness, without, by an artificial effort, identifying herself with an uncongenial character. She was able to forget her painful task, abandon herself up to the inspiration of the moment, and drink in the deep and pathetic emotions which she had no time to study, but which were revealed to her, as it were, by the magnetic influence of a sympathizing audience. This was to her an unspeakable pleasure, and just as she had experienced in a less degree during the rehearsal, and as she had expressed herself to Joseph, it was not her public and overwhelming success which so intoxicated her with joy, but the happiness she felt at putting her powers to the test, and the glorious certainty of having realized for a moment the ideal perfection of which she had dreamed. Hitherto she had ever asked herself whether she could not have done better, but now she felt that she had revealed all her power, and almost heedless of the thunders of acclamation, she applauded herself in her secret soul.

After the first act she remained behind the scenes to listen to and applaud Corilla, who acquitted herself charmingly; but after the second act she felt the necessity of an instant's repose, and returned to her private apartment. Porpora, who was otherwise engaged, did not follow her, and Joseph, who, in consequence of the imperial patronage had obtained the privilege of being admitted to the orchestra, remained, as may be supposed, in his place.

Consuelo entered Corilla's room, of which she had procured the key, swallowed a glass of water, and threw herself for an instant on the sofa; but suddenly the recollection of the Pandour Trenck made her shudder, and she hastened to bolt the door. There was no probability, however, that he would make his appearance. He had been in the body of the theater from the raising of the curtain, and Consuelo had distinguished him in a balcony among the most enthusiastic of her admirers. He was passionately fond of music. Born and bred in Italy, he spoke the language with all the purity and grace of a native, he sang agreeably, and acted so well that it was said, had he not been born with other resources, he might have made his fortune on the stage.

But what was Consuelo's terror when, on retiring to her sofa, she saw the fatal screen pushed aside, and the hateful Pandour appear before her!

She darted to the door, but Trenck was there before her, and placed his back against it.

"Calm yourself, my charmer," said he, with a frightful smile. "Since you share Corilla's dressing-room, you must accustom yourself betimes to see her lover, and you could not be unaware that she had a duplicate key in her pocket. You have come to cast yourself into the lion's den—Oh, do not attempt to cry out! Nobody will come. Trenck's presence of mind is well known, as well as the vigor of his arm, and the little value he places on the lives of fools. If he is admitted here, in spite of all the empress' orders, it is because, to all appearance, there is not among all your knights-errant a single one bold enough to look him in the face. Come, why are you so pale? why do you tremble so? Have you so little self-reliance that you cannot listen to three words without becoming confused? Do you think I am a person to treat you rudely? These are old wives' stories, my child, which they have told you. Trenck is not so bad as they say. It is to convince you of that that he wishes to have a moment's conversation with you."

" Sir, I shall not listen to a word you utter till you have opened that door. On this condition I shall consent to hear what you have to say; but, if you persist in shutting me up, I shall think that this redoubted hero, as he proclaims himself, wants courage to meet my companions the knights-errant."

"Ah! you are right," said Trenck, opening the door wide. "If you do not fear getting cold, I would rather have it so than breathe the confounded musk with which Corilla has scented this little chamber."

Thus saying, he seized hold of both Consuelo's hands, and forced her to be seated, while he went on his knees, without relinquishing his grasp which she could not force him to loose unless by a childish and unbecoming struggle. Consuelo, therefore, resigned herself to what she was unable to prevent, but a tear which she could not restrain trickled slowly down her pale and anxious cheek. This, in place of softening and disarming the baron, merely served to elicit a gleam of satisfaction from under his bloody and puckered eyelids.

"You are unjust," said he, in a voice whose assumed mildness only served to betray his hypocritical satisfaction. "You hate without knowing me. I cannot submit without a murmur to your dislike. Once, indeed, I should not have cared; but since I have heard the divine Porporina, I feel that I adore her, and must live for her or die by her hand."

" Spare me this wretched farce," said Consuelo, roused to indignation.

" Farce?" exclaimed the baron. " Hold!" continued he, drawing from his pocket a loaded pistol, which he cocked and handed to her. " You shall keep this in one of your beautiful hands, and if I offend you—were it ever so little— if I continue to be hateful to you, kill me at your pleasure. As to this other hand, I am resolved to hold it so long as you do not give me permission to kiss it. But I wish to owe this favor only to your good nature, and you shall see me ask and await it patiently, under the muzzle of the deadly weapon which can rid you of me when you please."

Here Trenck placed the pistol in Consuelo's right hand, and holding her left, remained with incomparable self-conceit on his knees before her. Consuelo now felt herself completely reassured, and, holding the pistol so that she could make use of it if necessary, said to him with a forced smile:

" Now speak, if you please—I shall listen to you."

As she said this, she imagined she heard footsteps in the corridor, and saw a shadow projected on the door. The shadow, however, whether it was that the person had retreated, or that Consuelo's terror was imaginary, immediately disappeared. In the situation in which she was placed, having no longer any thing to dread but ill-natured remarks, the approach of an indifferent, or even friendly person, caused her rather fear than pleasure. If she kept silence, the baron on his knees before her, and with the door open, must seem to any passer-by in the insolent enjoyment of his position as a favored lover; if she called out, he would instantly destroy the first person who approached. Fifty such instances had already marked his career. In such a frightful alternative, Consuelo desired nothing so much as instant explanation, and hoped by her self-possession to bring Trenck to reason before any one should witness, and interpret after his own fashion, this extraordinary scene.

He understood her in part and proceeded to push the door to, but without closing it. "Surely, madam," said he, turning toward her, " it would be absurd to expose yourself to the misconstruction of passers-by; this matter must be settled between ourselves. Listen to me; I see your apprehensions and I understand your scruples with regard to

Corilla. Your honor and reputation are yet dearer to me
than the precious moments I can look upon you unobserved. I know very well that this fury, with whom I was
for a moment taken, will charge you with treachery if she
sees me at your feet. She will not have that pleasure; the
moments are counted. She has still ten minutes to amuse
the public with her sufferings, and I have time therefore
to tell you that if I have loved her for a brief period, I
have already forgotten it; do not hesitate, therefore, to
appropriate a heart no longer hers and from which nothing
can efface your image. You alone, madam, rule over me,
you alone are sovereign of my existence. Why do you
hesitate? You are guarded by a jealous, gloomy old tutor;
I will carry you off before his beard. You are beset in the
theater by a thousand intrigues; the public adores you,
but the public is ungrateful and would abandon you on the
first failure of your voice. I am immensely rich and I can
make you a princess, almost a queen, in my own wild
country, where I could build you, in the twinkling of
an eye, theaters and palaces larger and more sumptuous
than anything that Vienna can produce. I am not handsome it is true, but the scars on my face are more honorable than the paint which covers the sallow faces of your
fellow-actors. I am severe to my slaves, and implacable
to my enemies; but if so, I am kind to my faithful servants, and those I love breathe an atmosphere of glory and
opulence. Lastly, I am violent at times; in that you have
been correctly informed. People, who like me are strong
and brave, love to use their power when vengeance demands its exercise; but a woman, pure, timid, gentle, and
charming as you are, can quell my strength, tame my will,
and place me at her feet as she would a child. Only try
me, confide in me, were it but for a time, and when you
know me better, you will not hesitate to trust me and follow me to my native Slavonia. You smile—that name
you think betokens slavery; nay, heavenly Porporina, it
is I who will be your slave. Look at me, and accustom
yourself to deformity which you alone can embellish. Say
but the word and you shall see the red eyes of Trenck the
Austrian shed tears of tenderness and joy, as pure and
heartfelt as the beautiful eyes of Trenck the Prussian—
that dear cousin whom I love so well, though we fought on
different sides, and to whom it is said you were not indif-

ferent. But this Trenck is a child, while he who addresses you has passed his four-and-thirtieth year, though
the thunder of war which has furrowed his cheek makes
him seem sixty; he is beyond the age of caprice and will
assure you of long years of devotion. Speak—speak—say
yes—and you shall see the scarred and disfigured Trenck
transformed into a glowing Jupiter! You do not reply—a
touching modesty keeps you silent. Well, you need say
nothing, suffer me but to kiss your hand, and I will leave
you full of confidence and happiness. Judge now if I am
the tiger which I have been described; I ask you but this
little favor, I implore it on my knees."

Consuelo looked with surprise at this frightful man to
whom so many women had listened with pleasure, and she
could not help pondering on this fascination which might
have been irresistible in spite of his ugliness, had he been
but a good man and animated by an upright passion.

"Have you said all, sir?" she asked tranquilly; but all at
once she grew alternately red and pale, as the Slavonian
despot cast into her lap a whole handful of large diamonds,
enormous pearls, and rubies of price. She rose so suddenly that the precious stones rolled upon the ground for
the after-profit of Corilla. "Trenck," said she, with all
the force with which contempt and indignation could inspire her, "notwithstanding all your boasting, you are the
meanest of cowards. You have never fought but with
lambs and fawns, and you have slain them without pity.
If a man worthy of the name had turned against you, you
would have fled like a savage and cowardly hound as you are.
I know very well where your glorious scars were received
—in a cellar where you searched for the gold of the conquered, amid the bodies of the dead. Your palaces and
your little kingdom are cemented with the blood of a noble
people, on whom a cruel despotism imposes such a ruler as
you. You have torn from the orphan his bread, from the
widow her mite; your gold is the price of treason, your
riches the pillage of churches. where you pretended to
prostrate yourself in prayer, for you add hypocrisy to your
other noble qualities. Your cousin Trenck the Prussian,
whom you so tenderly love, you betrayed and would have
assassinated; the women whose happiness and glory you
boasted to have formed, have been torn from their husbands and fathers, and your present tenderness for me is

but the caprice of a dissipated libertine. The chivalrous
submission which has made you venture your life in my
hands, is but the act of a fool, who thinks himself irresistible, and the trifling favor you ask of me would be a stain
which death alone could wash away. This is my last word,
cut-throat Pandour! Fly from my presence—fly—for if
you do not let go my hand, which, for the last quarter of
an hour you have held palsied in your grip, I shall rid the
earth of a scoundrel who dishonors and disgraces it!"

"And is this your last word, daughter of Satan!" exclaimed Trenck; "well woe be to you! The pistol which
I deigned to place in your trembling hand is only loaded
with powder, and a little burn more or less is nothing to
one who is fire-proof. Fire this pistol—make a noise—it
is all that I desire! I shall be glad to have witnesses, before whose faces and in spite of whose beards I shall carry
you off to my Slavonic castle, which you just now despised,
but to which a short residence will soon reconcile you."

Thus saying, Trenck seized Consuelo in his arms; but
at the same instant the door opened, and a man whose
face was hidden by crape knotted behind his head, laid
hold of the Pandour, shook him to and fro like a reed,
beaten by the wind, and dashed him roughly to the floor.
This was but the work of a few seconds. The astonished
Trenck rose, and, with savage eyes and foaming mouth,
darted sword in hand after his enemy, who had passed the
door and appeared to fly. Consuelo also rushed toward
the doorway, thinking she recognized in this disguised individual the lofty figure and powerful arm of Count
Albert. She saw him retreat to the end of the corridor
where a steep and winding stair led in the direction of the
street. There he paused, awaited Trenck, stooped rapidly
while the baron struck his sword against the wall, and
seizing him by the body heaved him over his shoulders
headlong down the stairs. Consuelo heard the giant
thunder down the descent, and ran toward her liberator,
calling Albert, but ere she could advance three steps he
was gone. A frightful silence reigned upon the staircase.

"*Signora, cinque minuti,*" said the crier with a fatherly
air, as he issued from the theater stairs which terminated
on the same landing. "How does this door happen to be
open?" continued he, looking at the door of the staircase
down which Trenck had been hurled "Truly, signora,

you run great risk of getting cold in this corridor." He then pulled the door to and locked it, while Consuelo, more dead than alive, re-entered her apartment, threw the pistols out of the window, and thrusting aside with her foot Trenck's jewels as they lay strewn on the carpet, returned to the theater, where she found Corilla heated and breathless with her triumph in the intervening scene.

CHAPTER C.

In spite of the excessive agitation which Consuelo had undergone, she if possible surpassed herself in the third act. She neither expected nor calculated upon it. She had entered on the stage with the desperate resolution of submitting to an honorable failure, since she was convinced that her voice and strength would entirely desert her the moment she was called on to exercise them. She was not afraid; a thousand hisses would have been as nothing compared with the shame and danger she had just escaped by a sort of miraculous intervention. Another miracle followed the first. Consuelo's good genius seemed to watch over her; her voice far surpassed what it had ever been before, she sang with more *maestria*, and acted with more energy and passion than she had hitherto displayed. Her highest powers were called forth, and it seemed to her as if every moment she was about to give way like a cord too highly strung : but this feverish excitement merely served to translate her into another sphere. She acted as if in a dream, and was astonished to find there the energies and powers of life.

And then a ray of happiness came to cheer her when sinking under the dread of failure. Albert doubtless was there. He must have been in Vienna at least from the evening before. He observed and watched over all her movements ; for to whom else could she ascribe the unforseen succor which she had received, and the almost supernatural strength which it required to overthrow a man like Francis Trenck, the Slavonic Hercules. And if, from one of those eccentricities, of which his character offered but too many examples, he had refused to speak to her and had avoided her looks, it was evident that he still loved her passionately since he showed himself so anxious for her safety, so courageous in her defense.

"Well," thought Consuelo, "since Heaven permits my strength to remain unimpaired, I should wish him to see me look well in my part, and that from the corner of the box whence he now doubtless observes me, he should enjoy a triumph which I owe neither to charlatanism nor cabals."

While still preserving the spirit of her part, she sought him everywhere with her eyes, but could nowhere discover him, and when she retired behind the scenes she continued to seek him, but with the same want of success. "Where could he be? Where had he taken refuge? Had he killed the Pandour on the instant by his fall? Was he forced to evade pursuit? Would he seek an asylum with Porpora, or should she find him this time on returning to the embassy?" All these perplexities however vanished when she again entered on the stage, where she forgot as if by some magic power all the details of her actual life, only to experience a vague sense of expectation mingled with enthusiasm, terror, gratitude, and hope. All this was in her part, and was expressed in accents admirable for their tenderness and truth.

She was called for at the end of the performance, and the empress was the first to throw her from her box a bouquet to which was attached a handsome present. The court and city followed the example of the sovereign, and showered on her a perfect storm of flowers. Amid these perfumed gifts, Consuelo saw a green branch fall at her feet, on which her eyes were involuntarily fixed. When the curtain was lowered for the last time, she picked it up —it was a branch of cypress! Then all her triumphant laurels vanished from her thoughts, leaving as their sole occupant this funeral emblem, a symbol of grief and despair, and perhaps the token of a last adieu. A death-like chill succeeded to this feverish emotion, an insurmountable terror caused a cloud to pass before her eyes, her limbs refused to support her, and those around bore her fainting into the carriage of the Venetian ambassador, where Porpora vainly endeavored to extract a word from her. Her lips were icy cold, and her lifeless hand still grasped beneath her mantle the cypress branch, which seemed to have been thrown by the hand of death.

On descending the staircase of the theater she had not

seen the traces of blood, and, in the confusion attendant on leaving the theater, few people had observed them. But while she returned to the embassy, absorbed in her gloomy reverie, a painful scene took place with closed doors in the green-room of the theater. Shortly before the end of the performance, some supernumeraries had discovered Trenck lying in a fainting state at the foot of the stairs, and bathed in his own blood. He was carried into one of the rooms reserved for the performers, and, in order to avoid noise and confusion, the director, a medical attendant, and the police, had been secretly informed, in order that they might attend and certify the fact. The public and the great body of performers left the room, therefore, without knowing anything about the matter, while the professional gentlemen, the imperial functionaries, and some compassionate witnesses, exerted themselves to assist the Pandour, and draw from him the cause of the accident. Corilla, who had been waiting for his carriage to arrive, and who had despatched her waiting-maid several times to obtain some tidings of him, was so vexed and annoyed by the delay, that she descended by herself, at the risk of having to go home on foot. She met Holzbaüer, who, knowing her intimacy with Trenck, brought her to the green-room, where she saw the Pandour with his head cut and bleeding, and his body so covered with contusions that he could not move. She filled the air with her shrieks and lamentations. Holzbaüer dismissed the curious spectators, and closed the doors. The cantatrice could throw no light on the affair, but Trenck, having now somewhat recovered, declared that having penetrated into the interior of the theater without permission, in order to see the dancers a little more nearly, he had wished to leave the house before the end of the performance, and that, unacquainted with the intricacies of the building, he had missed his footing, and rolled down the cursed stairs to the bottom. They were satisfied with this explanation, and carried him home, where Corilla hastened to nurse him with such zeal as to lose the favor of Kaunitz and the good will of her majesty; but she boldly made the sacrifice, and Trenck, whose frame had already resisted worse assaults, escaped with eight days' lameness and an additional scar on his head.

He mentioned to no one his want of success, but secretly resolved to make Consuelo pay dearly for it. He would doubtless have fearfully redeemed this promise if an imperial mandate had not suddenly torn him from Corilla, to cast him, still suffering from the fever of his wound and hardly recovered from his fall, into the military prison. That which public rumor had vaguely informed the canon of was already in course of being realized. The Pandour's wealth had excited a burning, inextinguishable thirst in the breasts of several influential and adroit followers of the court, and to this lust for riches he fell a victim. Accused of all the crimes he had committed, as well as of all those which could possibly be imagined by persons interested in his ruin, he began to experience the delays, the vexations, the impudent prevarications, and refined injustice of a long and scandalous trial. Avaricious in spite of his ostentation, proud notwithstanding his vices, he was not willing to recompense the zeal of his protectors, or to bribe the conscience of his judges. We shall leave him confined, until fresh orders, in his prison, where, having been guilty of some violence, he had the mortification and shame to see himself chained by the foot. Shame and infamy! it was precisely the foot which had been shattered by the explosion of a bomb-shell in one of his most brilliant military actions. He had undergone the scarification of the ulcerated bone, and although hardly recovered, had remounted his horse and resumed his service with heroic firmness. An iron ring, to which was attached a heavy chain, was rivetted upon this horrible scar. The wound reopened, and he endured fresh tortures, no longer in the service of Maria Theresa, but as a reward for having served her too well.* The Great Queen—who had not been displeased at seeing him ravage and destroy unfortunate Bohemia, which afforded a rather uncertain rampart against the enemy, in consequence of the ancient national hatred—*the king* Maria Theresa, who, having no longer need of the crimes of Trenck and the excess of his pandours to strengthen her upon the throne, began to look upon them as monstrous and unpardonable—was supposed to be ig-

* Historical truth requires us to say also by what bravados Trenck provoked this inhuman treatment. From the first day of his arrival at Vienna he had been put under arrest in his own house by the imperial order. He had, nevertheless, shown himself at the opera that very evening, and in an interlude had tried to throw Count Gossaw into the pit.

norant of this barbarous treatment, in the same way that
the great Frederick was supposed ignorant of the ferocious
refinements of cruelty, the tortures of inanition, and the
sixty-eight pounds of iron, under which sank, a little later,
that other Baron Trenck, his handsome page, his brilliant
artillery officer, the rescuer and the friend of our Consuelo.
All those flatterers who have flippantly transmitted to us
the recital of these abominable deeds, have attributed the
odium of them to subaltern officers or to obscure deputies,
in order to clear the memory of their sovereigns. But those
sovereigns, so ill-informed respecting the abuses of their
jails, knew so well, on the contrary, what was passing there,
that Frederick the Great himself furnished the design for
the irons which Trenck the Prussian wore for nine years
in his sepulcher at Magdeburg; and if Maria Theresa
did not exactly order Trenck the Austrian, her valorous
pandour, to be chained by the mutilated foot, she was
always deaf to his complaints, always inaccessible to his pe-
titions. Besides, in the shameful havoc which her people
made of the riches of the vanquished, she knew very well
how to carry off the lion's share and refuse justice to his
heirs.

Let us return to Consuelo, for it is our duty as a roman-
cist to pass lightly over historical details. Still we know
not how to treat of the adventures of our heroine totally
apart from the facts which occurred in her time and under
her eyes. On learning the pandour's misfortune she remembered no longer the outrages with which he had
threatened her, and deeply revolted at the iniquity of his
treatment; she assisted Corilla in sending him money at a
time when all means of softening the rigor of his captivity
were refused him. Corilla, better skilled in spending
money than in acquiring it, found herself penniless exactly
on the day when a secret emissary of her lover came to
claim the necessary sum. Consuelo was the only person to
whom this girl, prompted by the instinct of confidence and
esteem, dared to have recourse. Consuelo immediately
sold the present which the empress had thrown upon the
stage at the conclusion of *Zenobia,* and handed the proceeds to her comrade, expressing at the same time her approval of her conduct in not abandoning the unfortunate
Trenck in his distress.

Corilla's zeal and courage, which went every length in

assisting the sufferer, induced Consuelo to regard with a sort of esteem a creature who although corrupted still had intervals of disinterested generosity. "Let us prostrate ourselves before the work of God's hand," said she to Joseph, who sometimes reproached her with being too intimate with this Corilla. "The human soul always preserves something great and good in its wanderings to which we owe respect, and in which we acknowledge with joy the impress of the divine hand. Where there is much to complain of there is also much to pardon, and where there is cause for pardon, good Joseph, be assured there is also cause to love! I confess to you that the part of a sister of charity seems to suit me better than a more secluded and gentler life, more glorious and agreeable resolves, the tranquillity of happy, respected, immaculate beings. My heart is made like the paradise of the gentle Jesus, where there is more joy over one repentant sinner than over ninety-and-nine just persons. I feel myself inclined to compassionate, sympathize, succor, and console. It seems to me as if the name my mother gave me at my birth, subjected me to this duty and this destiny. It is my only name, Beppo! Society has given me no family name to uphold, and if the world were to say that I lowered myself in seeking a few particles of pure gold from amid the dross of the misconduct of others, I owe the world no account. I am Consuelo, and nothing more! and this is enough for the daughter of Rosmunda, for Rosmunda was one on whom the world looked with coldness and contempt; yet such as she was, I was bound to love her, and I did love her. She was not respected as Maria Theresa is, yet she would not have chained Trenck by the foot, and left him to die in torture in order to obtain posession of his wealth. Corilla herself would not have done it; in place of seeking her own advantage she supports this Trenck who often treated her most cruelly. Joseph—Joseph! God is a greater emperor than ours, and since Mary Magdalene is seated in his presence, Corilla may perhaps one day take precedence even of the imperial queen. As for myself, I feel that if I had abandoned the culpable or the unhappy to seat myself at the banquet of the just, I should not have been on the highway of my salvation. The noble Albert, I feel assured, would join in this sentiment and would be the last to blame me for showing kindness to Corilla."

When Consuelo uttered these words to her friend Beppo,
fifteen days had elapsed since the representation of *Zenobia*
and the adventure of Baron Trenck. The six representations for which she had been engaged were completed, and
Tesi had resumed her place in the theater. The empress
busied herself privately through the ambassador Corner
with Consuelo's proposed marriage with Haydn, promising,
on that condition alone, an engagement for the latter in
the imperial theater. Joseph was ignorant of all this, and
Consuelo foresaw nothing. She thought only of Albert,
who did not reappear, and from whom she received no
intelligence. A thousand conjectures and contradictory
conclusions passed through her mind, which, together with
the shock she had experienced, tended to undermine her
health. She had remained confined to her apartment
since her engagement had expired, and continually gazed
at the cypress branch which seemed to have been plucked
from some tomb in the grotto of the Schreckenstein.

Beppo, the only friend to whom she could open her
heart, endeavored at first to dissuade her from the idea
that Albert had arrived in Vienna. But when he saw the
cypress branch, he pondered deeply on the mystery, and
ended by believing in the part the young count had taken
in Trenck's adventure. "Listen," said he; "I think I
know how it has all happened. Albert has been in
Vienna, he has seen you, heard you, observed what you
did, and followed your steps. The day that we conversed
together behind the scenes, he might have been on the
other side of the decoration and have heard the regret
which I expressed on seeing you snatched from the theater
when in the climax of your glory. You yourself made use
of some vague expressions which might have led him to
suppose that you preferred the splendor of your present
career to his somewhat gloomy love. Next day he saw you
enter Corilla's chamber, where, since he was always on the
watch, he probably saw the Pandour precede you. The
time which elapsed before he came to your assistance, almost proves that he believed you there of your own accord;
and it was only after yielding to the temptation of listening at the door, that he could be aware of the necessity of
his interference."

"Even if your supposition be correct," replied Consuelo, "why use this mystery? why assume this masked
countenance?"

" You know the suspicious nature of the Austrian police. Perhaps he does not stand well at the court; perhaps he may have political reasons for concealing himself, or perhaps again his countenance is not unknown to Trenck. Who knows whether he may not have encountered him during the wars in Bohemia? Whether he may not have threatened him, dared him, or perhaps forced him to let go his hold of some poor innocent? Count Albert may have secretly performed deeds of exalted courage and humanity when he was supposed to be asleep in his grotto at Schreckenstein, and if he had done such he certainly would be the last to relate them, since by your admission he is the most humble and modest of men. He acted wisely therefore in not openly chastising the Pandour; for if the empress punish the Pandour to-day for having devastated her dear Bohemia, she will not on that account be the more disposed to overlook any past act of resistance to his authority on the part of a Bohemian.

"All that you say is very just, Joseph, and gives room for deep thought. A thousand anxieties beset me. Albert may have been recognized and arrested, and that too without the public knowing any more about it than about the fall of Trenck down the stairs. Alas! perhaps even now he is in the prisons of the arsenal beside Trenck's dungeon, and it is on my account he incurs this misfortune!"

"Comfort yourself, Consuelo, I cannot believe that that is the case. Count Albert has left Vienna, and you will shortly receive a letter from him dated from Riesenburg."

"Do you think so, Joseph?"

"I do. But if I must tell you all, I believe that the tenor of this letter will be very different from what you expect. I am convinced that far from exacting from your generous friendship the sacrifice of your artistic career, that he has already renounced the idea of this marriage, and is about to restore you your liberty. If he be intelligent, noble, and just, as you say he is, he would hesitate to tear you from the theater which you love so passionately. Nay, never deny it! I have seen it, and he also must have seen and felt it, in witnessing *Zenobia*. He will therefore reject a sacrifice which is beyond your strength, and I should esteem him but little were he not to do so."

"But read his last letter! See, here it is, Joseph! Does

he not say he would love me as dearly in the theater as in the world or in a convent? Does he not propose in marrying me to leave me free?"

"Saying and doing, thinking and being, are two different things. In the dream of passion all seems possible, but when realities strike our vision we return with terror to our former ideas. Never will I believe that a man of rank could bear to see his wife exposed to the caprices and outrages of the audience of a theater. In venturing behind the scenes for the first time certainly in his life, the count must have witnessed in Trenck's conduct toward you a melancholy specimen of the miseries and dangers of a theatrical career. He has fled in despair it is true, but at the same time cured of his passion, and freed from his chimeras. Pardon me that I thus address you, my dear sister Consuelo, but I feel constrained to do so; for it were well for you that you never saw Count Albert more. You will one day feel the truth of this, though your eyes now swim with tears. Be just toward your betrothed instead of feeling humiliated at his change of sentiment. When he said he was not averse to the theater, he had formed an ideal picture of it which the first inspection completely dissipated. He then became aware that he should cause you misery in taking you from it, or consummate his own in following you."

"You are right, Joseph. I feel that you are; but suffer me to weep. It is not the humiliation of being forsaken and disdained that oppresses my heart: it is my regret for the image of ideal love and its power which I had formed just as Albert had done with respect to my theatrical career. He has now seen that I can no longer be worthy of him (in the opinion of men at least), in following such a profession, and I, on my part, am forced to admit that love is not strong enough to overcome all prejudices."

"Be just, Consuelo, and do not ask more than you have been able to grant. You did not love well enough to give up your art without hesitation or regret; do not therefore take it ill if Count Albert be unable to break with the world without some degree of terror or aversion."

"But whatever might have been my secret pain (and I may confess it), I was resolved for his sake to sacrifice every thing; while he——"

"Reflect that the passion was on his side, not on yours.

He asked with ardor—you consented with effort. He must have been aware that you were about to sacrifice yourself for him; and he felt that he was not only at liberty to free you from a love which you had not sought or desired, but that he was conscientiously bound to do so."

This reasoning convinced Consuelo of Albert's wisdom and generosity. She feared in giving herself up to grief to yield to the suggestions of wounded pride, and, accepting Joseph's hypothesis as correct, she succeeded in calming herself. But by a well-known contradiction of the human heart, she no sooner saw herself at liberty to follow her inclination for the theater without hindrance or remorse, than she felt terrified at her solitary position in the midst of such corruption, and at the prospect of the toils and struggles which lay before her. The theater is a feverish arena, in comparison with which all the emotions of life appear tame and lifeless; but when the actor retires from its precincts, broken down with fatigue, he feels a sensation of terror at having undergone such a fiery trial, and his longing to return is checked by fear. The rope-dancer, I imagine, is no bad type of this perilous and intoxicating life. He experiences a terrible pleasure on those lines and cords where he performs feats apparently beyond human power; but when he was descended, he shudders at the idea of again mounting the giddy height and facing at once death and triumph—that two-faced specter that ever hovers above his head.

It was then that the Castle of the Giants, and even the Stone of Terror, that nightmare of her dreams, appeared to the exiled Consuelo as a sort of lost Paradise, the abode of peace and the revered asylum of piety and virtue. She fastened the cypress branch—that last message from the grotto—to her mother's crucifix, and, thus mingling these emblems of catholicism and heresy, her heart rose to the conception of one only eternal and unalloyed religion. It was then that she found comfort for her personal sufferings, and faith in the providence of God toward Albert, and toward all that crowd of mortals, good and bad, whom henceforth she must encounter alone and unaided.

CHAPTER CI.

ONE morning Porpora summoned her earlier than usual into his apartment. He had a joyous air, and held an enormous letter in one hand and his spectacles in the other. Consuelo shook and trembled through her whole frame, thinking it was at last the answer from Riesenburg. But she was soon undeceived; it was a letter from Hubert, the Porporino. This celebrated singer announced to his master that all the proposed conditions for Consuelo's engagement had been accepted, and he sent the contract, signed by Baron Poëlnitz director of the theater royal at Berlin, and only requiring Consuelo's signature and his own to complete it. To this was added a kind and even respectful letter from the baron himself, who engaged Porpora to take the direction of the King of Prussia's chapel, with the permission at the same time to bring out as many new operas and fugues as he pleased. Porporino expressed his joy at the prospect of being so soon able to sing along with a *sister in Porpora*, and warmly invited the maestro to quit Vienna for *Sans Souci*, the delightful abode of Frederick the Great.

This letter was a source of joy and at the same time of perplexity to Porpora. Fortune it would seem was about to smile upon him at last, and kingly favor, then so necessary for the success of artists, awaited him alike at Berlin, whither Frederick invited him, and at Vienna, where Maria Theresa made him such brilliant promises. In either case Consuelo must be the instrument of his victory —at Berlin in impressing the public with a favorable idea of his productions, at Vienna in marrying Joseph Haydn.

The moment was now come to place his fate in the hands of his adopted child. He gave her the option of marriage or departure, but at the same time was much less urgent in pressing on her acceptance the hand and heart of Beppo than he had been the evening before. He was somewhat tired of Vienna, and the idea of being appreciated and feasted by the enemy seemed to him a sort of vengeance, the effect of which he highly exaggerated it is true upon Austria. In short, Consuelo having said nothing about Albert, and having apparently renounced the idea of a union with him, he much preferred that she should not marry at all. Consuelo soon put an end to his uncertainty on the score of Joseph Haydn, by telling him that for many reasons she could never marry him. In the first place he had never asked her, being engaged to his benefactor's daughter, Anna Keller.

"In that case," said Porpora, "we need no longer hesitate. Here is your engagement for Berlin drawn out. Sign it, and let us set out; for there are no longer any hopes here, unless you submit to the empress' mania for matrimony. This is the price of her protection, and any refusal would sink us to the lowest point in her esteem."

"My dear master," replied Consuelo, with more firmness than she had hitherto shown toward Porpora, "I am ready to obey you as soon as I can satisfy my conscience on one important point. Certain relations of affection and esteem, not lightly to be broken, connect me with the lord of Rudolstadt. I shall not conceal from you, that, notwithstanding your incredulity, your raillery, and your reproaches, I have kept myself, during the three months I have been here, free from every engagement opposed to this marriage. But, after a decisive letter which I wrote six weeks ago, and which went through your hands, certain events have taken place which lead me to believe that the family of Rudolstadt have given me up. Each day that passes adds to my conviction that I am freed from my engagement, and at liberty to devote myself to you. You see that I accept this destiny without hesitation or regret; nevertheless, after what I have written, I could not feel satisfied without a reply. I expect it every day; it cannot be long now. Permit me, therefore, to defer the Berlin engagement until after I receive——"

"Ah! my poor child," said Porpora, who, at his pupil's first words had leveled his batteries, which were already prepared, "you will have long to wait! The reply that you expect I have received a month ago."

"And you have never shown it to me?" exclaimed Consuelo. "You have left me in this state of uncertainty? Master, you are very strange! How can I confide in you, if you deceive me thus?"

"In what have I deceived you? The letter was addressed to me, and I was enjoined not to show it to you until after I saw you cured of your foolish love, and disposed to listen to the voice of reason and the dictates of propriety."

" Are those the terms that were made use of?" exclaimed
Consuelo, reddening; " it is impossible that Count Albert
or Count Christian could thus have designated a friendship
so calm, reserved, and proud as mine!"

" Terms are nothing," said Porpora; "people of the
world always speak in polite language; but the purport of
it was that the old count was not at all anxious to have a
daughter-in-law picked up behind the scenes, and that
when he knew that you had appeared here on the stage,
he forced his son to give up the idea of such a degrading
connection. The good Albert listened to reason, and set
you at liberty. I see with pleasure that you are not annoyed. Then everything is for the best, and hey for
Prussia!"

"Master, show me the letter," said Consuelo, "and I
shall sign the contract immediately after."

"The letter? the letter?—why do you wish to see it? It
would only vex you. There are certain follies which we
must forgive in others as well as in ourselves. Forget all
that!"

"We cannot forget by a mere act of the will," replied
Consuelo; "reflection assists us, and points out motives.
If I am repelled by the Rudolstadts with disdain, I shall
easily be consoled. If I am restored to liberty with expressions of esteem and affection, I shall still be consoled, but
in another manner and at less cost. Show me the letter
then. What can you be afraid of, since, in either case, I
shall obey you?"

"Well, I will show it to you," said the malicious professor
opening his secretary, and pretending to search in it for
the letter. He opened all his drawers, shook out all his
papers, but this letter, which had never existed, was
nowhere to be found. He feigned impatience, while Consuelo really felt it. She began herself to rummage, and
he allowed her to do so. Porpora then endeavored to
recollect the wording of it, and improvised on the instant
a polite and decided version. Consuelo could not suspect
her master of such systematic and prolonged dissimulation.
We must state, for the honor of the old professor, that he
dissembled very badly; but the candid and unsuspecting
Consuelo was easily persuaded; she at last concluded that
in a moment of abstraction Porpora had lighted his pipe
with the letter; and, after having returned to her chamber

to utter a short but fervent prayer, and vow eternal friendship on the cypress to Count Albert, even if his conduct toward her had been such as the letter stated, she returned tranquilly to sign an engagement for two months at Berlin, to commence from the end of the current month. This was more than sufficient time to arrange for their departure. When Porpora saw the freshly-written signature upon the paper, he embraced his pupil, and saluted her solemnly as an artist.

"To-day is your confirmation," said he, "and were it in my power to make you utter vows, I should dictate an eternal renunciation of love and marriage; for now you are priestess of harmony, and she who devotes herself to Apollo should remain, like the muses themselves, a vestal virgin."

"I feel that I ought not to vow celibacy," said Consuelo, "though at this moment it seems to me that nothing would be easier than to make such vow and keep it; but I might change my mind, and then I should regret a promise which I would be unable to break."

"You are the slave of your word, then? Yes, you differ in that respect from the rest of mankind; and I believe, did you make a solemn promise, you would religiously hold by it."

"I believe I have already given proof of that, my dear master; for, since the day of my birth, I have always been under the dominion of some vow. My mother taught me, both by precept and example, that kind of religion which she carried even to fanaticism. When we were traveling together, she was accustomed to say to me as we approached the large cities: 'My little Consuelo, if I am successful here, I take you to witness that I make a vow to go with bare feet and pray for two hours at the chapel which has the greatest reputation for the sanctity in the country.' And when she had been what she called successful, poor soul! that is to say, when she had earned a few crowns by her songs, we never failed to accomplish our pilgrimage, whatever might be the weather, and at whatever distance was the chapel in repute. That species of devotion was not indeed very enlightened nor very sublime, but nevertheless I look upon those vows as sacred; and when my mother, on her death-bed, made me swear to follow her injunctions, she knew well she could die tranquil, in the full confidence that I should keep my oath. At a later period I promised Count Albert not to think of any other but him, and to employ all my strength to love him as he wished. I have not failed in my promise, and if he did not now himself free me, I should have remained faithful to him all my life."

"Leave your Count Albert alone if you please, you must think no more of him ; and since it appears that you must be under the dominion of some vow, tell me by what one you are going to bind yourself to me."

"Oh ! master, trust to my reason, to my character, to my devotion toward you ! do not ask me for oaths, for they are a frightful yoke to impose upon one's self. The fear of breaking them takes away the pleasure one has in thinking and acting well."

"I shall not be content with such excuses," returned Porpora, with a half severe, half jesting tone ; "I see that you have made oaths to everybody except me. And since from mere good nature, without any feeling of love, you bound yourself by such weighty promises to Count Albert of Rudolstadt, who was a perfect stranger to you, I shall think it very strange if, on a day like this—a happy and memorable day, in which you are restored to liberty and wedded to your noble profession—you refuse to make the smallest vow for your old teacher and your best friend."

"Oh, yes ! my best friend, my benefactor, my support, and my father !" cried Consuelo with emotion, throwing herself into Porpora's arms—Porpora, who was so chary in showing tenderness, that only twice or thrice in his whole life had he displayed his fatherly affection without concealment or reserve. "Yes, I can truly make, without terror or hesitation, the vow to devote myself to your happiness and your glory, while I breathe the breath of life."

"My happiness is your glory, Consuelo, as you well know," said Porpora, pressing her to his heart. "I cannot conceive of any other. I am not one of those old German burghers, who dream of no other felicity than that of having their little girl by their side to fill their pipe or knead their cake. I am not an invalid, I require neither slippers nor potion, thank God, and when I am reduced to that state I will not consent that you devote your days to me, as you even now do with too much zeal. No, it is not devotion which I ask of you, that you know well ; what I demand is, that you shall be with heart and soul an artist. Do you promise me that you will be one, that you will combat that languor, that irresolution, that sort of disgust which you experienced at the commencement of your career?"

"I promise solemnly; and be assured also, my dear master, that you shall never have cause to charge me with the crime of ingratitude."

"Oh! as to that, I do not ask so much," replied he, bitterly; "it is more than belongs to human nature. When you are a prima donna, celebrated in every nation of Europe, you will have promptings of vanity and ambition —vices of the heart from which no great artist has ever been able to defend himself. You will long for success, no matter how purchased. You will not resign yourself to obtain it by patient perseverance, or to risk it for the sake of remaining faithful either to friendship or to the worship of beauty in its highest and purest forms. You will yield, as they all do, to the yoke of fashion; in each city you will sing the music that is in favor there, without troubling yourself about the bad taste of the public or the court. In fine, you will make your way and will be great notwithstanding, since there are no other means of seeming so in the eyes of the multitude. Provided that you do not forget to choose your subject with care, and sing well when you have to undergo the judgment of a little coterie of old heads like myself, and that, in the presence of the great Handel and Bach, you do honor to Porpora's method and credit to yourself, it is all that I ask—all that I hope! You see that I am not a selfish father, as some of your flatterers no doubt accuse me of being. I ask nothing from you which will not be for your own happiness and glory."

"And I care for nothing that relates to my personal advantage," replied Consuelo, touched by her old master's words. "I may allow myself to be carried away in the midst of success by an involuntary feeling of intoxication, but I cannot coolly think of planning a whole life of triumph in order to crown myself therein with my own hands. I wish to procure glory for your sake, my dear master; I wish to show you, spite of your incredulity, that it is for you alone that Consuelo labors and travels, and, in order to prove to you at once that you have calumniated

her, since you believe in her oaths I swear to you to prove
what I assert."

" And by what do you swear that?" said Porpora, with
a smile of tenderness which was still mingled with a shade
of distrust.

" By the white hairs on the sacred head of Porpora,"
replied Consuelo, drawing the old man's silvered head to
her breast with all a daughter's affection, and kissing it on
the brow with fervor.

They were interrupted at this moment by Count Hoditz,
who was announced by a gigantic heyduc. This man,
while requesting permission for his master to present his
respects to Porpora and his pupil, looked at the latter with
an air of attention, uncertainty, and embarrassment which
surprised Consuelo, who was unable to remember where
she had seen that good-natured though somewhat odd
face. The count was admitted and presented his request
in the most courteous terms. He was about to depart for
his manor of Roswald in Moravia, and, wishing to render
that residence agreeable to the margravine his spouse,
was preparing a magnificent festival to surprise her on her
arrival. In consequence he proposed to Consuelo to go
and sing for three consecutive evenings at Roswald, and
he requested that Porpora would be pleased to accompany
her in order to assist in directing the concerts, performances, and serenades, with which he intended to regale the
margravine.

Porpora alleged as an excuse the engagement he had just
signed, and the necessity he was under of being in Berlin
on a certain day. The count requested to see the engagement, and as Porpora had always found him civil and
obliging, he gratified him, admitting him into the secret
and allowing him the pleasure of commenting and giving
advice upon it; after which Hoditz persisted in his
demand, representing that they had more than sufficient
time to make all the necessary arrangements without failing in the time fixed. " You can settle every thing in
three days," said he, " and travel to Berlin by way of
Moravia." It was not the direct road, indeed ; but instead of proceeding slowly by way of Bohemia, through a
country badly supplied with post-horses and lately devastated
by war, Porpora and his pupil would thus arrive quickly
and easily at Roswald, in one of the count's carriages and

with his relays—in short, at his trouble and expense. He promised, also, to conduct them from Roswald to Pardubitz, if they chose to descend the Elbe to Dresden; or to Chrudim, if they decided to go by way of Prague. The facilities of traveling which he offered them would so far tend to shorten their journey, and the considerable sum which they were to receive would enable them to pursue the remainder of it with more comfort. Porpora therefore agreed to the proposal, notwithstanding Consuelo seemed somewhat disinclined to it. The terms were arranged and the time of departure was settled for the end of the week.

When Hoditz, after respectfully kissing Consuelo's hand, had left her alone with her master, she reproached the latter with having so easily yielded. Although she had no longer any thing to apprehend from the count's impertinence, she could not help feeling some degree of resentment against him, and never went to his house with pleasure. She did not like to tell Porpora of the adventure at Passau, but she reminded him of his sarcasms upon Count Hoditz's musical discoveries.

"Do you not see," said she, "that I shall be condemned to sing his music, and that you will have to direct his cantatas, and perhaps even his operas? Is this the fidelity which you would have me display for the culture of the beautiful?"

"Come, come!" said Porpora, smiling, "it will not be so bad as you think; I expect to be famously amused, without the patrician maestro suspecting it in the least. To perform these things in public before a respectable audience would be a shame and a disgrace; but it is allowable to the artist to amuse himself, and he would be much to be pitied if he was not sometimes permitted to laugh in his sleeve at those by whom he gains his bread. Besides you will see the princess of Culmbach there, whom you like, and who is truly charming; she will laugh with us, though she seldom laughs at all at her step-father's music."

There was nothing for it but to give up the point, make her arrangements, and say farewell. Joseph was in despair. Nevertheless a stroke of good fortune, a real gratification for an artist, helped to compensate him, or at least to turn his attention from the pain of separation. While performing a serenade beneath the window of the excellent comic actor Bernardoni, the famous harlequin of the theater of the Corinthian gate, his performance struck this amiable and excellent artist with admiration and surprise. He made him come in, and asked who was the author of the original and agreeable trio. On learning the truth, he was astonished at the young composer's youth and talent, and at once confided to him the music of a ballet which he was writing, and which was entitled *The Devil on Two Sticks.* Haydn worked indefatigably at the tempest incidental to the piece, which cost him much labor, and the remembrance of which made the good old man smile even when eighty years of age. Consuelo sought to amuse him and dissipate his melancholy by always talking to him about his tempest, which Bernardoni wished to be terrible, and which Beppo, never having beheld the sea, did not know how to describe. Consuelo pictured to him the Adriatic in a storm, and sang the mournful plaint of the waves, not without laughing with him at those imitative harmonies which require to be aided by blue cloths, shaken from scene to scene by vigorous arms.

"Listen," said Porpora to him one day, in order to put an end to his uncertainty; "you might labor a hundred years with the best instruments in the world, and the most intimate knowledge of winds and waters, without being able to translate the divine harmonies of nature. This is not the province of music. It is merely guilty of folly and conceit when it runs after noisy effects and endeavors to imitate the war of the elements. Its nature is much higher. Its domain is that of the emotions. Its aim is to inspire them, as its origin is from their inspiration. Think then of a man abandoned to the fury of the waves, and a prey to the deepest terror; imagine a scene at once frightful, magnificent, terrible; the danger imminent, and then, musician—or I should rather say, human voice, human wailing, living and thrilling soul — place yourself in the midst of this distress, this disorder, this confusion and despair; give expression to your anguish, and your hearers, intelligent or not, will share it. They will imagine that they behold the sea, that they hear the groaning of the riven timbers, the shouts of the mariners, the despair of the hapless passengers! What would you say of a poet, who in order to depict a battle, should tell you in verse that the cannon uttered *boom, boom,* and the drums *dub, dub?* It would be a better imitation than any image, but it would not be poetry. Painting itself, that descriptive art *par excellence,* does not consist in servile imitation. The artist would trace in vain the dull green sea, the dark and stormy heaven, the shattered ship. If his feelings do not enable him to render the terrible and poetical whole, his picture will make as little impression as any ale-house sign. Therefore, young man, inspire your whole being with the idea of some great disaster ; it is thus you will render it moving to the feelings of others."

He continued to repeat these paternal exhortations, while the carriage, now ready to start, was being packed with the travelers' luggage. Joseph listened attentively to his lessons, drinking them in as it were from the fountain-head, but when Consuelo, muffled in a cloak and fur cap, came to throw herself on his neck, he turned pale, stifled a cry, and not able to witness her departure, he fled, and hastened to hide his grief in the depths of Keller's back-shop. Metastasio by degrees conceived a friendship for him, perfected him in Italian, and compensated him, in some degree, by his good advice and generous services for Porpora's absence; but Joseph long continued to sigh with bitter regret for the loss of his tried friend and sister, Consuelo.

She on her side, although sincerely lamenting her separation from her faithful and amiable fellow-pupil, and feeling at first considerably dejected, found her spirits and courage gradually revive, and her poetic aspirations once more spring to life as she penetrated into the mountains of Moravia. A new and brighter horizon seemed opening before her. Freed and unfettered from all unfriendly ties, she saw herself at liberty to pursue her cherished art, and she inwardly resolved to devote herself heart and soul to its elevating and refining culture. Porpora, restored to the hope and the cheerfulness of his youth, thrilled her by his eloquent declamations ; and the noble girl, without ceasing to love Albert and Joseph as two brothers whom she humbly hoped to meet once more in the mansions of the blessed, felt her bosom bound lightly as the lark which soars aloft with swelling note to salute the rising day.

CHAPTER CII.

FROM the second relay Consuelo had recognized in the domestic who was seated before her upon the box of the carriage, and who paid the guides and scolded the postilions for their tardy pace, the same heyduc who had announced Count Hoditz on the day when he came to propose to her their pleasure excursion to Roswald. This tall showy looking man, who continually looked at her as if by stealth, and who seemed divided between his wish to speak to her and the fear of giving offense, at last fixed her attention, and one morning, when she was breakfasting in a solitary inn at the foot of the mountains—Porpora having gone to walk in pursuit of some musical theme, while waiting for the horses to be baited—she turned toward the man at the moment when he was handing her coffee, and looked at him somewhat angrily. But he assumed such a piteous expression that she could not help laughing. The April sun was reflected in dazzling rays from the snow which still crowned the mountain summits, and our young traveler found herself as if by sympathy in a gay and joyous frame of mind.

"Alas!" said the heyduc, "your highness does not deign to remember me then? But I should never forget you, were you disguised as a Turk or a Prussian corporal; yet I only saw you for an instant, but what an instant in my life!"

Thus saying, he placed the salver on the table, and coming close up to her, he gravely made the sign of the cross, kneeled on the ground, and kissed the floor at her feet.

"Ha!" exclaimed Consuelo, "Karl the deserter, is it not?"

"Yes, signora," replied Karl, kissing the hand which she held out to him; "at least they tell me I must address you so, though I could never tell exactly whether you were a lady or a gentleman."

"Indeed? And whence comes your uncertainty?"

"Because I saw you first as a boy, and since then, although I recollected you very well, you were as like a young girl as you were before otherwise. But that is nothing; whatever you are, you conferred favors on me which I shall never forget; and were you to command me to cast myself from the top of yonder peak, I would do so at your bidding without a moment's hesitation."

"I ask nothing from you, my brave Karl, but to be happy and free; for you are now at liberty, and I hope enjoy your life!"

"At liberty? yes," said Karl, shaking his head; "but happy—alas! I have lost my poor wife!"

Consuelo's eyes filled with tears as she saw Karl's manly features working with emotion.

"Ah!" said he, wiping away a tear, "poor soul, she had gone through too much! The vexation of seeing me taken prisoner by the Prussians a second time, the fatigue of a long journey on foot when she was very weak and ill, and then the joy of seeing me once more, gave her such a shock that she died in eight days after reaching Vienna, where, thanks to your note and Count Hoditz's assistance, she found me again. This generous gentleman sent his own doctor and gave every assistance, but nothing was of any use; she was weary of life, look you, and she has gone to rest in the heaven of the merciful."

"And your daughter?" continued Consuelo, who hoped by these questions to prevent his thoughts from dwelling on his loss.

"My daughter?" said he, gloomily, and seeming hardly conscious of what he said; "the King of Prussia has killed her too."

"How! killed? What do you mean?"

"Was it not the King of Prussia who killed the mother in bringing all this evil upon her? Well, the child followed her mother. Since the evening when, after seeing me bleeding, gagged, and torn off by the recruiters, they remained lying half dead upon the road, the little one took a raging fever, and fatigue and want did the rest. When you saw them on the bridge of some Austrian village, they had not eaten any thing for two days. You gave them money; you told them I was saved; you did every thing in your power to comfort and cure them; they told me all that, but it was too late. They continued to sink from the moment we again met; and just when we might indeed have been happy, they both went down to the grave. The earth was scarcely heaped over my poor wife's body when it had to be removed to make room for my child; and now, thanks to the King of Prussia, Karl is alone."

"No, my poor Karl, you are not alone; you have friends who will always take an interest in your welfare, on account of your good heart."

"I know it. Yes, there are good people, and you are one of them. But what do I want now? I have no wife, no child, no country! I would never be safe at home again, for my mountain is too well known to the robbers who sought me out twice before. One of the first questions I asked myself when I saw myself alone in the world, was, if we were at war, or if we should soon be so, for I had a notion of serving against Prussia, so as to kill as many of these Prussians as I could. St. Wenceslas, the patron saint of Bohemia, would have strengthened my arm, and not a ball would have left my gun in vain. Perhaps Providence would have suffered me to meet the King of Prussia himself in some defile, and then— were he armed like the Archangel Michael—should I have to follow him as a dog follows a wolf—but I learned that peace was settled, and then having no longer any taste for soldiering, I waited on Count Hoditz to ask him not to present me to the empress, as he had intended. I would have killed myself, but he was so kind to me, and the Princess of Culmbach his daughter, to whom he related my history, told me such fine things of the duties of a Christian that I consented to enter their service, where indeed I am too well fed and too well treated for all I have to do."

"But, in the meantime, tell me, my good Karl," said Consuelo, drying her eyes, "how you knew me again?"

"Did you not come one evening to sing at the house of the margravine, my new mistress? You then passed by me dressed all in white, and I knew you at once, although you had become a young lady. Why, you see, I may forget many places through which I pass, as well as the names of people I have met, but as to faces I never forget them. I began to cross myself when I saw a young man who followed you, and whom I recognized at once as Joseph; but in place of being your master (for he was better dressed in those days than you), he had become your servant, and remained in the antechamber. He did not know me; and as the count had forbidden me to mention a word to any body of what had happened (I never asked nor knew why), I did not speak to the good Joseph, though I was well inclined to give him a hug. He almost immediately retired to another apartment; and I had orders not to quit the one I was in, and a good servant you know holds by his orders. But when every one was gone, Henri, my lord's valet, who is in his confidence, came to me and said—'Karl, you said nothing to Porpora's little attendant although you knew him, and you did well. The count will be pleased with you. As to the young lady who sang this evening——' 'Oh! I knew her also!' I exclaimed, 'but I said nothing.' 'Very well,' he added, 'you did well, for the count wishes no one to know that she traveled with him as far as Passau.' 'That is nothing to me,' said I; 'but I wish to know how she delivered me out of the hands of the Prussians.' Henri told me all about it, for he was there; how you had run after the carriage, and how when you had nothing to fear on your own account you made them come back to free me. You told something of it to my poor wife, and she told me. She died blessing you; 'for,' said she, 'they are poor young things almost as ill off as ourselves; and for all that, they gave us what they had got, and wept as if they had belonged to us.' So when I saw Joseph in your employment, having been directed to bring him some money for playing on the violin for my master, I slipped a few ducats (the first I had earned) into the paper, and he never knew any thing about it. When we return to Vienna, I shall take care that he never wants, so long as I have a farthing."

"Joseph is no longer in my employment, my good Karl; he is my friend. He is no longer embarrassed; he is a musician, and earns his bread easily. Do not strip yourself, therefore, on his account."

"As to you, signora," said Karl, "I cannot do any thing for you, because you are a great actress, they say; but if you ever want a servant, do you see? and cannot pay him, send to Karl—that is all. He will wait upon you for nothing, and be glad to do it."

"Your gratitude, my friend, is sufficient recompense. I ask no further."

"Stay! Here is Master Porpora returning. Remember, signora, that I have not the honor to know you otherwise than as a servant placed at your command by my master."

The next day our travelers having risen very early, arrived not without difficulty about mid-day at the château of Roswald. It was situated in an elevated region, on the slope of one of the most magnificent mountains in Moravia, and so well protected from cold winds, that the spring was already felt there while at half a league round the winter still prevailed. Although the season was exceedingly early and the weather lovely, the roads were hardly passable. But Count Hoditz, who doubted of nothing and for whom the impossible was a jest, had already arrived, and had a hundred pioneers at work smoothing the road over which the majestic equipage of his noble spouse was to roll the next day. It would, perhaps, have been a more conjugal plan, as well as one more likely to be of assistance to the fair traveler, to have journeyed along with her, but it was not of so much consequence, it seemed, to hinder her from breaking her arms and legs on the road, as to give her a fête; and dead or alive, she must needs have a splendid entertainment on taking possession of Roswald.

The count hardly allowed our travelers time to change their dress until he forced them to sit down to a splendid entertainment, served in a mossy and rocky grotto, which an enormous stove, skillfully masked by false rocks, warmed to an agreeable temperature. At first sight this place seemed enchanting to Consuelo. The view which opened from the entrance of the grotto was really magnificent. Nature had done every thing for Roswald. Precipitous and picturesque hills, forests of evergreens, abundant springs of water, lovely and extensive prospects, immense prairies, surrounded it on every side. It seemed that with a comfortable habitation all this was enough to constitute a perfect paradise. But Consuelo soon perceived the strange contrivances by which the count had succeeded in spoiling the sublimity of nature. The grotto would have been charming without the windows, which made it merely an unseasonable dining-room. As the honeysuckles and climbing plants were only beginning to bud, the frames of the doors and the windows had been masked with artificial leaves and flowers, which only served to make the whole seem ridiculous. The shells and stalactites, somewhat damaged by the winter, disclosed to view the plaster and mastic which fastened them to the walls, and the heat of the stove, melting the remains of the frost which had been concentrated in the vaulted ceiling, brought down upon the heads of the guests a blackish and unhealthy rain, which the count was determined not to observe. Porpora was exceedingly annoyed, and two or three times put his hand to his hat, but without daring to clap it on his head, as he was dying to do. He feared above all that Consuelo might take cold, and he ate very fast, pretending a great impatience to see the music which was to be executed the next day.

"What is the matter with you, dear maestro?" said the count, who was a great eater, and loved to dilate on the pieces of plate of which his dinner service was composed; "able and accomplished musicians such as you are need but little time for study. The music is simple and natural. I am not one of those pedantic composers who seek to astonish by strange and elaborate combinations of harmony. In the country, we require simple pastoral music, and like the margravine, my spouse, I admire only unambitious and easy airs. You will see that everything will get on well. Besides we do not lose any time; while we breakfast my major-domo is giving the necessary directions, and we shall find the choruses ready and the musicians at their post."

As the lord of the mansion said these words he was informed that two strangers, traveling through the country, requested permission to pay their respects to the count, and to visit the palace and gardens of Roswald.

The count was accustomed to visits of this sort, and nothing afforded him greater pleasure than to be the *cicerone* of those who desired to inspect the splendors of his abode.

"Show them in, they are welcome!" he exclaimed; "and place seats for them at the table."

A few seconds after, two officers were introduced dressed in the Prussian uniform. He who walked first, and behind whom his companion seemed determined to conceal himself, was little and had rather a disagreeable countenance. His long, thick, and vulgar nose made his gaping mouth and retreating or rather absent chin seem more repulsive than they would otherwise have been. His shoulders were of a round and ungainly shape, and together with the ugly military costume invented by Frederick, gave him a sort of antiquated and even decrepit air. Yet this man was at the farthest about thirty years of age;

his step was firm; and when he took off the hideous hat which concealed the upper portion of his face, he displayed the only redeeming features it possessed—a decided, intelligent, reflecting forehead, expressive eyebrows, and eyes of extraordinary animation and brilliancy. His glance produced the same startling change in his appearance as the sun's rays which animate and embellish the most dreary and unpoetical landscape. He seemed a whole head taller when his eyes lighted up his pale, restless, and mean-looking countenance.

Count Hoditz received them with more cordiality than ceremony, and without losing time in compliments, he made them sit down at table, and helped them from the best dishes with true patriarchal hospitality; for Hoditz was one of the kindest of men, and his vanity, far from corrupting his heart, only increased his confidence and generosity. Slavery still reigned over his domain, and all the wonders of Roswald were created at little cost by his numerous vassals, whose chains, however, he decked with flowers. He made them forget what was necessary, in loading them with superfluities; and, convinced that pleasure was happiness, he amused them so well that they never thought of freedom.

The Prussian officer—for in reality there was only one, the other being little better than his shadow—appeared at first somewhat astonished, not to say affronted at the count's bluntness, and affected a degree of polite reserve, when the count said to him : "I entreat you, Captain, to put yourself at your ease, and act just as if you were in your own house. I know that you are accustomed to the strict and admirable regularity of the armies of the great Frederick; but here you are in the country, and if we do not amuse ourselves in the country, why do we visit it? I perceive that you are well-educated, polite persons, and you certainly are not officers of the king of Prussia without having given proofs of military science and unflinching bravery. I consider that you do honor to my poor dwelling, and I trust you will dispose of it at your pleasure, and prolong your stay so long as it shall be agreeable to you."

The officer immediately responded to this invitation like a man of tact and good sense. After having thanked his host he began to try the champagne, without however its producing the slightest effect on his coolness and self-possession, and vigorously attacked a pasty, on the cookery of which he made such profound and scientific remarks as were not calculated to raise him in the esteem of the abstemious Consuelo. She was nevertheless struck with his piercing glance; but although it astonished it did not charm her, as it seemed to express something haughty, prying, and suspicious, which was not calculated to inspire affection.

While eating, the officer informed the count that he was called the Baron de Kreutz, that he was originally from Silesia, where he had been sent to procure horses for the cavalry, and that finding himself at Neisse, he could not resist the desire of visiting the celebrated palace and gardens of Roswald. That in consequence he had that morning crossed the frontier with his lieutenant, and had purchased some cattle by the way, in order to turn the opportunity to good account. He even offered to visit the count's stables, if he had any horses to dispose of. He traveled on horseback and intended to return the same evening.

"I will not hear of it," said the count; besides, I have none to spare at present—indeed I have too few to carry out all my improvements here. But if you have no objection I will employ the time much better in enjoying your society, as long as you can make it convenient to remain."

"But we learned on our way hither that you were in momentary expectation of the Countess Hoditz's arrival, and as we should be most unwilling to put you to inconvenience, we shall take our leave the moment she arrives."

"I do not expect the countess till to-morrow," replied the count; "she will be accompanied by her daughter, the Princess Culmbach. For you are not unaware perhaps, gentlemen, that I have had the honor to contract a lofty alliance——"

"With the Dowager Margravine of Bareith," replied the baron rather abruptly, who did not appear so much dazzled with this title as the count had expected.

"She is the King of Prussia's aunt," resumed the latter with emphasis.

"Yes, yes, I know that," said the Prussian officer, taking a huge pinch of snuff.

"And as she is a most affable and condescending lady," continued the count, "I have no doubt she will feel in

finite pleasure in receiving and entertaining the brave
servants of his majesty, her illustrious nephew."

"We are truly sensible of the honor," said the baron,
smiling; "but we have not leisure to avail ourselves of it.
Our duties call us imperatively hence, and we must take
leave of your highness this evening; meanwhile we shall
be happy to admire this delightful residence with which
the king our master has nothing that can be compared."

This compliment completely restored all the Moravian
count's good humor toward his Prussian guest. They rose
from table. Porpora, who cared much less for the promenade than the rehearsal, wished to excuse himself.

"By no means," said the count; "you shall see, my
dear maestro, that we can manage both at the same time."

He offered his arm to Consuelo, and preceded the rest.
"Excuse me, gentlemen," said he, "if I offer my arm to the
only lady present; it is my right as host. Have the goodness to follow me; I shall serve as your guide."

"Permit me to ask, sir," said the Baron de Kreutz,
addressing Porpora for the first time, "who this amiable
lady is?"

"Sir," replied Porpora, who was not in the best of tem-
pers, "I am an Italian; I understand German indifferently, and French still worse."

The baron who had hitherto conversed with his host in
French, according to the fashion of the time, repeated his
question in Italian.

"This amiable lady, who has not spoken one word before
you," replied Porpora, dryly, "is neither margravine, nor
princess, nor baroness, nor countess; she is an Italian
singer not wholly devoid of talent."

"On that account I should wish so much the more to
know her name," said the baron, smiling at the maestro's
bluntness.

"It is my pupil, the Porporina," replied Porpora.

"I am informed that she is very clever," observed the
other, "and that she is impatiently expected at Berlin.
And since she is your pupil, I perceive that I address the
illustrious Master Porpora."

"At your service," replied Porpora, hastily, and clapping on his hat, which he had taken off in reply to a low
bow from the Baron Kreutz. The latter, seeing him so
little disposed to be communicative, dropped behind and

rejoined his lieutenant. Porpora, who might almost be said to have eyes in the back of his head, observed that they were laughing together and speaking about him in their own language. This conduct did not advance them in his opinion, and he did not so much as even look at them during the rest of the promenade.

CHAPTER CIII.

THEY descended a steep little slope, at the bottom of which they found a river in miniature, which had been formerly a pretty, limpid, and gurgling streamlet; but as it was necessary to make it navigable, its bed had been smoothed, its fall diminished, its banks pared and trimmed regularly, and its beautiful waters muddied by recent labors. The workmen were still busied in clearing away some rocks which obstructed its progess, and gave it some appearance of nature. A gondola was in waiting to receive the party, a real gondola which the count had brought from Venice, and which made Consuelo's heart beat with a thousand pleasant and painful reminiscences. The party embarked. The gondoliers were also real Venetians, speaking their native dialect; they had been brought along with the bark, as, in the present day, the negro-keepers are with the giraffe when they exhibit. Count Hoditz, who traveled a good deal, imagined that he could speak every language, but though he had a great deal of confidence, and gave his orders to the gondoliers in a loud voice and marked accent, the latter would have understood him with difficulty had not Consuelo served as interpreter. They were directed to sing some verses of Tasso, but these poor wretches, chilled by the icy coldness of the north, banished from their native clime, and bewildered by the strange scenes around them, gave the Prussians a very poor specimen of their style. Consuelo was obliged to prompt them at every stanza, and promise to hear them rehearse the portions they were to sing before the margravine the next day.

When they had rowed about a quarter of an hour in a space which might have been passed in three minutes, but in which the poor stream, thwarted in its course, had been tortured into a thousand intricate windings, they reached the open sea. This was a tolerably large basin which opened to their view from between clumps of cypresses and firs, and the unexpected *coup d'œil* of which was really pleasing. But they had no time to admire it. They were obliged to embark on board of a pocket man-of-war, in which every mast, sail, and rope was critically correct, and which presented a complete model of a ship with all her rigging. It was rather inconveniently crowded, however, with sailors and passengers, and ran the utmost risk of foundering. Porpora was shivering with cold, the carpets were quite damp, and I even believe that, in spite of the particular examination which the count, who had arrived the day before, had already made of every portion of her, the vessel leaked badly. No one was at ease excepting the count—who, thanks to his character of entertainer, never cared for the little discomforts connected with his pleasures —and Consuelo, who began to be much amused by the follies of her host. A fleet proportioned to the flag-ship came to place itself under her orders, and executed maneuvers which the count himself gravely directed, armed with a speaking-trumpet, and standing erect upon the poop, getting quite annoyed when matters did not go to his liking, and making them recommence the rehearsal. Afterward they advanced in squadron to the villainous music of a brass band, which completed Porpora's exasperation. "It is well enough to freeze us and make us catch cold," said he, between his teeth; "but to flay our ears in this style—it is too much!"

"Make all sail for the Peloponnesus!" roared the count through his trumpet, and the squadron floated toward a bank crowned with miniature buildings in imitation of Greek temples and antique tombs. They steered toward a little bay masked by rocks, from which, when about ten paces distant, they were received by a discharge of masketry. Two men fell dead upon the deck, and an active cabin-boy, who had his station in the rigging, uttered a loud cry, descended, or rather let himself slide down adroitly, and rolled into the very midst of the company, screaming that he was wounded and holding his head, which he said had been fractured by a ball.

"Come this way," said the count to Consuelo, "I want you for a little rehearsal I intend having on board my ship. Have the goodness to represent the margravine for a moment, and order this dying youth and these dead men, who, by the way, died very awkwardly, to rise, be cured, and defend her highness against the insolent pirates entrenched in yonder ambuscade." Consuelo hastened to assume her part, and filled it with far more natural grace and dignity than the countess would have done. The dead and dying rose on their knees and kissed her hand. The count however informed them that they were not really to touch her highness' fingers with their lips, but to kiss their own hands while they pretended to salute hers. Then dead and dying rose to arms with the utmost enthusiasm, while the little tumbler who acted the cabin-boy ran up the mast like a cat and discharged a light carbine at the pirates of the bay. The fleet ranged up close round this new Cleopatra and discharged their miniature broadsides with a fearful rattle.

Consuelo, warned by the count who did not wish to alarm her, was not taken by surprise at this rather strange comedy, but the Prussian officers, toward whom the same precaution had not been observed, seeing two men fall at the first fire, drew closer to each other and grew very pale. He who said least appeared terrified for his captain, and the visible uneasiness of the latter did not escape Consuelo's close and observing glance. It was not fear, however, that was depicted on his countenance so much as a sort of haughty indignation, as if his dignity as a Prussian soldier had been outraged. Hoditz paid no attention to him, and when the combat was at its height, the captain and his lieutenant laughed with the loudest, took the joke in good part, and soon waved their swords in the air, to add to the effect of the scene.

The pirates, who were embarked in light skiffs, and were dressed in Grecian costume, and armed with pistols and blunderbusses charged with powder, boarded the vessels, bold as lions. They were however repulsed with great slaughter, so as to give the good margravine an opportunity of bringing them to life. The only cruelty practiced was that of tumbling some of them into the sea. The water was very cold, and Consuelo felt very sorry for them, until she saw that they liked it, and took a pleasure in showing their companions how well they could swim.

When Cleopatra and her attendant fleet had thus borne off the victory and taken the pirate flotilla, they proceeded, to the sounds of triumphal strains—enough, according to Porpora, to raise the devil—to explore the isles of Greece. They soon approached an unknown island, on which were seen rude wigwams peeping forth from strange and exotic plants, real or imitated, one could not say which, so much was the real and the false everywhere confounded together. To the shores of this island were fastened canoes into which the natives of the country threw themselves, and with savage cries came out to meet the fleet, bringing with them fruits and flowers recently culled from the hot-houses of the establishment. The savages were frizzled, bristling, tattooed, and more like demons than men. The costumes were rather indifferently in keeping, some being crowned with feathers like Peruvians, others furred like Esquimaux, but they were not subjected to too close a scrutiny; provided they were ugly enough, they passed for cannibals at the very least. These creatures made abundant grimaces, and the giant who seemed their chief, and who had a false beard flowing down to his waist, delivered a discourse which Count Hoditz had composed in the supposed dialect of the country. This was a species of gibberish arranged at random to represent a language at once barbarous and grotesque. The man having finished his harangue to the count's satisfaction, the latter undertook to translate this fine speech to Consuelo, who still continued to play for the time the part of the absent countess.

"This discourse," said he, imitating the savage's gestures, "signifies, madam, that this cannibal people, whose wont it is to devour every stranger, suddenly touched and subdued by your charms, wish to lay at your feet their ferocity, and to offer you the sovereignty of these unknown lands. Deign to visit them, and although they now appear sterile and uncultivated the wonders of civilization will spring up under your feet."

They landed on the isle amid the dances and songs of the young female natives. Strange beasts and stuffed figures which knelt by means of a spring, saluted Consuelo on her approach. Then by means of ropes the freshly planted trees and shrubs fell down, the pasteboard rocks crumbled to pieces, and disclosed pretty cottages, decorated with leaves and flowers. Shepherdesses leading real flocks, village girls dressed after the latest fashion of the opera—although a little coarse it must be confessed when seen

near at hand — even tame fawns and kids came to offer
their homage to their new sovereign.

"It is here," said the count to Consuelo, "that you
will have to play your part to-morrow before her highness.
They will procure you the costume of a pagan divinity all
covered with flowers and ribbons, you will be in this
grotto, the margravine will enter, you will sing the cantata which I have in my pocket, and yield up your rights
to her, seeing that there can be only one goddess where
she deigns to appear."

"Permit me to see the cantata," said Consuelo, taking
the manuscript from Hoditz. It required little trouble to
read and sing this trifle at first sight ; the music and
words were each worthy of the other. It was only necessary to learn it off by heart. Two violins, a harp, and a
flute, concealed from view in the depths of the cave, and
observing neither time nor measure, constituted the accompaniment. Porpora made them begin again, and, at the
end of a quarter of an hour all went well. It was not the
only part Consuelo had to perform in the fête, nor the
only cantata Hoditz had in his pocket ; happily they were
short, for it was not desirable to fatigue her highness with
too much music.

Leaving the island, they set sail and landed on the
shores of China. Porcelain towers, gaudy kiosks, stunted
gardens and miniature bridges, bamboo thickets and tea
plantations — nothing was wanting. Men of letters and
mandarins in Chinese costume, uttered discourses in their
native language ; and Consuelo, who had taken an opportunity below to attire herself as a lady mandarin, had to
try a few couplets to a Chinese air, arranged in Count
Hoditz's usual style :

> "Ping, pang, tiong,
> Hi, hang, hong."

Such was the chorus, which signified, thanks to the
brevity of this wonderful language :

"Beautiful margravine, mighty princess, queen of
hearts, reign forever over your happy husband, and your
joyous empire of Roswald in Moravia.

Leaving China, they proceeded in rich palanquins,
borne on the shoulders of poor Chinese serfs, to the summit of a little mountain, where they found the city of

Lilliput, forests, lakes, mountains, houses with their fur
niture and utensils — all on the same miniature scale.
Puppets danced in the market-place to the accompaniment of hurdy-gurdys and kettle-drums. The persons
who moved the strings, and who produced this beautiful
music, were hidden in caves constructed for the purpose.

Descending the mountains of Lilliput, they came to a
desert some hundred paces in extent, filled with enormous
rocks and vigorous trees in all the wild luxuriance of
nature. It was the only spot which the count had not
spoiled or mutilated; he had left it just as he found it.

"What to do with this steep defile long puzzled me,"
said he to his guests. "I did not know what use to make
of these huge rocks, nor what shape to fashion these lofty
trees, when the idea occurred to me to baptize this desert
spot the 'Chaos.' The contrast I thought would not be
unpleasing, especially when after leaving these frightful
scenes, the visitor gains admission to scrupulously neat
parterres and smoothly-shaven lawns. You are about to
see a happy invention I have introduced here."

Thus saying, the count turned round a huge rock which
obstructed the path, for in the desert a smoothly-graveled
walk was indispensable, and Consuelo found herself at the
entrance of a hermitage hollowed out of the rock, and surmounted by a rude wooden cross. The hermit of the
Thebaid made his appearance; he was an honest peasant,
whose long white beard contrasted happily with his ruddy
and youthful countenance. He delivered a handsome
address (of which his master corrected the errors), pronounced his benediction, and offered roots and a bowl of
milk to Consuelo.

"Your hermit seems to me rather young," said Baron
de Kreutz; you should have put a real old man here."

"That would not have pleased the margravine,"
observed Count Hoditz, ingenuously. "She thinks very
reasonably that old age is not attractive, and that in a fête
none but young actors are suitable."

I shall spare the reader the rest of the excursion. I
should never have done if I were to describe the different countries, the Druidical altars, Indian pagodas,
canals and covered passages, virgin forests, subterranean
caverns, artificial mines, with ball rooms, elysian fields,
tombs, cascades, naiads, serenades, and the *six thou-*

sand fountains which Porpora afterwards alleged he had to *swallow*. There were innumerable other inventions which the memoirs of the day speak of with admiration, even to the minutest details, such as a dim grotto in the depths of which you were infallibly terrified by your own image in a looking-glass; a convent where, under pain of imprisonment for life, you were forced to pronounce vows of eternal submission and adoration to the margravine; a rainy tree, which by means of a pump concealed in the branches, deluged you with ink, blood, or rosewater, accordingly as it was intended to compliment or mystify you; in short, a thousand ingenious, novel, incomprehensible, and above all, expensive secrets, which Porpora was rude enough to find scandalous, stupid, and intolerable. Night alone put an end to this excursion round the world, in the course of which they had traveled sometimes on horseback, sometimes on donkeys, in litters, carriages, or open boats, fully three leagues.

Insensible to cold and fatigue, the two Prussian officers, although they laughed at such of the amusements as seemed rather too puerile, were not so much struck as Consuelo with the absurdity of this marvelous abode. She was a true child of nature, accustomed to the open air, and, from the time that she could see, to look at the works of God without screen or opera-glass. But Baron de Kreutz, although perhaps not altogether fascinated with this thoroughly artificial aristocracy, was influenced by the ideas and manners of the age. He by no means hated grottoes, hermitages, and symbols, and in short he was amused, showed much wit and humor in his remarks, and on entering the dining-hall said to his companion, who was respectfully expressing sympathy for his weariness:

"Weary? not at all. I have taken exercise, I have gained an appetite, seen a thousand follies, relieved my mind from dwelling on serious thoughts; I have neither lost my time nor trouble."

They were surprised to find in the dining-room only a circle of chairs set round an empty space. The count begged them to be seated, and ordered dinner.

"Alas! my lord," responded the major-domo, "we had nothing worthy of so honorable a company, and we did not even attempt to lay the table."

"This a pretty affair!" cried the host in a pretended

fury. Then when the jest had lasted some seconds,
"Well," said he, "since men refuse us some refreshments,
I invoke the regions of Pluto to send something worthy of
such guests." So saying, he struck the floor three times,
which glided to one side, and odorous flames were visible
from below. Then to the sound of wild and joyous music,
a table magnificently decorated rose before the guests.
' That is not so bad,' said the count, lifting the cloth, and
speaking under the table. "Only I am surprised that
Master Pluto, who knows that there is not even a drop of
water in the house, has not favored us with a single
goblet."

"Count Hoditz," replied a hoarse voice from the depths,
"water is scarce in Tartarus; all our streams are dried up
since the eyes of her Highness the Margravine have penetrated the entrails of the earth. Nevertheless, if you command it, we shall send a Danaide to the Styx, and see if
she can procure some."

"Let her hasten, then," continued the count; "and see
that you give her a vessel which will not leak."

At this instant a jet of rock water issued from a jasper
tazza in the center of the table, and continued to play during the rest of the entertainment, sparkling like a sheaf of
diamonds in the light of the numerous wax tapers. The
whole was a masterpiece of extravagance and bad taste;
and the waters of the Styx and the gifts of Pluto furnished
the count with opportunities for a thousand stupid jests
and plays upon words, which his childish eagerness and
good nature caused to be readily forgiven. The rich repast, during which the guests were waited upon by youths
and gay shepherdesses, put the Baron de Kreutz in excellent
spirits. He paid little attention, however, to his amphi-
tryon's handsome female slaves. These poor peasant-girls
were at once the servants, singers, and actresses of the
count, who was their professor of music, singing, dancing,
and declamation. Consuelo had had a sample of his demeanor toward them at Passau, and when she thought of
the glorious lot which this noble lord then offered her, she
could not help admiring his present easy and respectful
manner toward her, which betrayed neither surprise nor
confusion. She knew that matters would assume an entirely different aspect on the arrival of the margravine the
ensuing day, and that then she would have to dine with

the maestro in her own apartment, and would no longer have the honor of being admitted to the table of her highness. This gave her no concern, although she was ignorant of one thing which would have infinitely amused her, and that was that she was then supping with a person far more illustrious, and who would not for any consideration have supped next day with the margravine.

Baron de Kreutz, who, as we have said, smiled somewhat coldly on these sylvan nymphs, paid more attention to Consuelo, especially when, after having succeeded in causing her to break silence, he induced her to speak upon music. He was an enlightened and passionate amateur of this divine art; at least he spoke of it in a manner which, together with the good cheer and warmth of the apartments, softened the rugged temper of Porpora.

"It is much to be wished," said he at last to the baron, who had just managed to praise his style indirectly without naming him, "that the sovereign whom we are going to serve, was as good a judge as you !"

"Oh !" replied the baron, " public report bespeaks him very enlightened on this subject, and asserts that he has a real love for the fine arts."

"Are you very sure of that, baron ? " returned the maestro, who could not converse without contradicting every person on every subject. "For my part, I doubt it very much. Kings are always first in every thing, if you believe their courtiers; but it often happens that these courtiers know much more than they do themselves."

"In war, as in science and engineering, the King of Prussia knows much more than either of us," replied the lieutenant with zeal ; "and as to music, it is very certain——"

"That you know nothing about it, nor I either," drily interrupted Captain de Kreutz ; "Master Porpora is absolute authority on the latter subject."

"As for me," returned the maestro, "royal dignity has never imposed upon me in matters of music ; and when I had the honor of giving lessons to the electoral princess of Saxony, I did not pass over her false notes any more than another's."

"What !" said the baron, looking at his companion with an ironical expression, "do crowned heads ever make false notes ?"

"Just like simple mortals, sir!" replied Porpora. "Still I must confess that the electoral princess did not long continue to make them with me, and that she had a refined and cultivated intellect to second my efforts."

"So you would graciously pardon a few false notes to our Fritz, should he have the impertinence to make them in your presence?"

"On condition that he would correct them."

"But you would not wash your hands of him," said Count Hoditz, smiling.

"I would do it, were he to cut off my head," replied the old professor, elevated by the champagne he had drunk.

Consuelo had been duly informed by the canon that Prussia was one huge police-office, where every word, were it even spoken on the frontiers, was echoed to the very cabinet; and that no one should say to any Prussian—a soldier or official especially—even "How do you do?" without first weighing every word. She was not pleased therefore to see her master indulge his cynical humor, and she endeavored by a little stroke of policy to do away with the effect of his imprudence.

"Even were the King of Prussia not the first musician of his time," she said, "he might well be permitted to despise an art so trivial in comparison with his other acquirements."

She was ignorant, however, that Frederick attached as much importance to his flute as to his magazine or his philosophy. The Baron de Kreutz assured her that, if his majesty considered music worthy of notice, he would certainly give it his most serious study and attention.

"Pshaw!" said Porpora, becoming still more animated; —"time and labor do nothing for those who are not endowed with the sacred fire. Genius and fortune do not go hand in hand; and it is easier to gain battles and pension off men of letters, than to borrow the celestial fire of the muses. Baron Frederick Trenck informed us that when his Prussian majesty missed the time, he took it from his courtiers; but that plan would not go down with me!"

"Did Baron Frederick Trenck say that?" exclaimed Baron Kreutz, his eyes gleaming with sudden and uncontrollable anger. "Well, well!" continued he, assuming, by a violent effort, an air of forced tranquillity, "the poor devil has done with jesting by this time, for he is confined in the fortress of Glatz for the rest of his days."

"Indeed !" exclaimed Porpora ; "and what has he done then ?"

"It is a secret of state," replied the baron ; "but there is every reason to believe that he has betrayed the confidence of his master."

"Yes," added the lieutenant, "in selling to Austria the plans of the fortifications of Prussia, his native country."

"Oh, it is impossible !" exclaimed Consuelo, turning pale ; for, notwithstanding her increasing caution, she was not able to repress this exclamation of surprise and grief.

"It is impossible !—it is false !" exclaimed the indignant Porpora ; "they who have thus imposed on the King of Prussia lie in their teeth !"

"I presume that you do not mean indirectly to charge us with falsehood ?" said the lieutenant, growing pale in his turn.

"It would be indeed a diseased susceptibility which could interpret thus what has been said," replied Baron Kreutz, looking fixedly, and even sternly, at his companion. "What does it concern us that Master Porpora manifests some heat in his friendship for this young man ?"

"Yes, I would do so, even in presence of the king himself !" exclaimed Porpora. "I would tell the king to his face that he had been deceived—that it was wrong of him to believe it—and that Frederick Trenck was a noble, an admirable young man, incapable of anything so infamous as——"

"I fancy, dear master," interrupted Consuelo, growing more and more uneasy at the expression of Baron de Kreutz's countenance, "that when you have the honor to approach the King of Prussia's presence, it will not be after dinner ; and I am well assured that music is the only subject on which you will venture to address him."

"Mademoiselle appears singularly prudent," replied the baron. "It would seem, however, that she was not unacquainted with Baron Frederick at Vienna ?"

"I, sir ?" said Consuelo, with assumed indifference ; "I hardly know him."

"But," continued the baron, with a piercing look, "if the king in person were to inquire of you by chance what you thought of this alleged treason ?"

"Sir," answered Consuelo, calmly though modestly

meeting his inquisitorial gaze, "I should reply that I did not believe in treason, unable as I am to understand what it means."

"A noble sentiment, signora!" said the baron, whose face lighted up all at once, "and spoken from an upright soul!"

He turned the conversation on other subjects, and charmed the guests by his grace and talent. During the rest of the meal he displayed in addressing Consuelo a kindness and confidence of manner which he had not previously manifested toward her.

At the close of the dessert, a figure, entirely clothed in white and closely veiled, presented itself before the guests, saying: "*Follow me!*" Consuelo, still condemned to play the part of the margravine, rose first, and, followed by the other guests, mounted the great staircase of the castle, to which there was access from the door at the end of the saloon. The shadow, on reaching the top of the stairs, pushed open another door, and they found themselves almost in total darkness, in an ancient gallery at the extremity of which appeared a faint gleam. Toward this light they directed their steps to the sound of solemn music, which was supposed to be performed by inhabitants of another world.

"*Per Bacco!*" exclaimed Porpora with ironical enthusiasm; "his excellency the count denies us nothing. First we had nautical, then Turkish, then savage, then Chinese, then Lilliputian, and other extraordinary species of music; but this surpasses all the rest, and may be well termed the music of the other world."

"And you are not at the end yet!" replied the count, enchanted at this eulogium.

"We ought to be prepared for everything on the part of your excellency," said the Baron de Kreutz, with the same irony as the professor; "though after this I know not in truth what we can hope for better."

At the end of the gallery the ghost struck a blow upon a kind of tom-tom, which gave forth a sullen sound, and a vast curtain drawing aside disclosed to view the body of the theater decorated and illuminated as it was to be on the following day. I shall not give a description of it, though it were an inviting occasion for flowery verse or prose,

The curtain rose; the scene represented Olympus—
neither more nor less. The goddesses were busy disputing
the heart of the shepherd Paris, and the competition of the
three principal divinities constituted the main subject of
the piece. It was written in Italian, on hearing which
Porpora whispered to Consuelo : "The Hottentot, the
Chinese and the Lilliputian were nothing; here is the Iro-
quois at last." Verses and music — all were the count's
manufacture. The actors and actresses were quite worthy
of their parts. After half an hour of forced metaphors
and trifling conceits upon the absence of a divinity more
charming and more powerful than all the others, but who
disdained to compete for the prize of beauty, Paris having
decided in favor of Venus, the latter took the apple, and
descending from the stage by a flight of steps, came to lay
it at the feet of the margravine, declaring herself unworthy
to keep it, and apologizing for having aspired to it before
her. It was Consuelo who was to perform this character of
Venus, and as it was the most important (including as it
did a cavatina of great effect), Count Hoditz, not willing to
intrust it to any of his coryphées, undertook to fill it himself, as well to carry on the rehearsal as to make Consuelo
feel the spirit, the intention, the wit and the beauty of the
part. He was so ridiculous while gravely personating
Venus and singing with emphasis the insipid airs pilfered
from all the bad operas then in fashion, and badly stitched
together, out of which he pretended to have composed a
score—that no one could keep his countenance. He was
too much excited by the task of scolding his troop, and too
much inflamed by the divine expression he gave to his acting and singing, to perceive the gaiety of the audience.
They applauded him to the skies, and Porpora, who had
placed himself at the head of the orchestra, and who was
obliged to stop his ears secretly from time to time, declared
that all was sublime—poem, score, voices, instruments, and
the temporary Venus above all!

It was agreed that Consuelo and he should read this
masterpiece attentively together that very evening and the
next morning. It was neither very long nor very difficult
to learn, and they flattered themselves that on the next
evening they would have mastered it completely. They
afterward visited the ball-room, which was not yet ready,
because the dances were not to take place till the second

day after, the fête being intended to last two days, and to offer an uninterrupted succession of diversified entertainments.

It was now ten o'clock. The weather was serene and the moon shone brilliantly. The two Prussian officers insisted on recrossing the frontier that very evening, alleging in excuse a superior order which forbade their passing the night in a foreign country. The count was therefore obliged to yield, and having given orders to get their horses ready, he insisted on their accompanying him to drink the stirrup-cup—that is to say, to partake of coffee and excellent liquors in an elegant boudoir, whither Consuelo thought it best not to follow them. She took leave of them, therefore, and after advising Porpora in a low voice to be more guarded than he had been during supper, proceeded toward her apartment, which was in another wing of the château.

But she soon lost her way in the windings of that vast labyrinth, and at last found herself in a sort of cloister, where, to complete her dismay, a current of air extinguished her taper. Fearful of losing her way still farther, and of falling through one of those *surprise* trap-doors, with which the mansion was filled, she endeavored to return, feeling her way until she could reach the lighted part of the building. In the confusion caused by the numerous preparations for committing absurdities, the comforts of that sumptuous dwelling were entirely· neglected. There were savages, ghosts, gods, hermits, nymphs, laughter and plays, but not a domestic to provide a torch, nor a being in his senses to guide her.

Meantime she heard a person approach, who seemed to walk cautiously and purposely keep in the shade, which did not inspire her with sufficient confidence to call out and pronounce her name, more particularly as it was the heavy step and loud breathing of a man. A little agitated, she advanced, keeping close by the wall, when she heard a door open not far off, and the light of the moon gleaming through the aperture fell upon the lofty figure and brilliant costume of Karl.

She hastened to call him by his name.

" Is it you, signora?" said he, in an altered voice. " Ah! I have been endeavoring for some hours to speak to you, and perhaps it is now too late."

"What have you to say to me, my good Karl? and whence this emotion?"

"Let us leave this corridor, signora; I must speak to you in some place where no one can overhear us."

Consuelo followed Karl, and found herself in the open air on the summit of one of the turrets attached to an angle of the mansion.

"Signora," said the deserter, in a cautious tone, for he had only arrived that morning at Roswald, and was almost as ignorant of the localities as Consuelo herself—"have you said nothing to-day that could excite the anger of the King of Prussia, and which you might afterward have occasion to regret at Berlin, if the king were informed of it?"

"No, Karl, nothing of the kind. I was aware that every Prussian whom one does not know, is a dangerous companion, and I watched every word I uttered."

"Ah! I am so glad to hear you say so, for I was uneasy about you. Two or three times I endeavored to speak to you in the ship, when you were sailing on the lake. I was one of the pirates that pretended to board your vessel, but I was so disguised that you could not know me. I stared and signed at you, but you took no notice of me, and I could not slip in a single word. That officer never left you. During the whole time you continued on the water, he was not once from your side. One would have said he guessed you were a charmed buckler to him, and that he hid behind you, lest a ball should perchance have got into one of our harmless guns."

"What say you, Karl? I do not understand. What officer? I do not know what you mean."

"There is no need to tell you; you will know soon enough. Are you not going to Berlin?"

"And why make a secret of it in the meantime?"

"Because it is a terrible one, and I must keep it for another hour."

"You seem uneasy, Karl—what is passing in your mind?"

"Oh! great deeds! hell burns in my heart!"

"Hell?—one would say that you are meditating some dreadful crime."

"Perhaps so."

"In that case you must speak; you must not keep a

secret from me, Karl. You have promised me unhesitating submission."

"Ah! signora, what is that you say? It is true I owe you more than life; you did what you could to save my wife and child — but they perished and they must be revenged!"

"Karl, in the name of your wife and child who pray for you in heaven, I implore you to speak. You are pondering on some mad and vengeful deed — the sight of these Prussians distracts you."

"Yes, they make me mad—furious. But no; I am calm as a saint. It is heaven, signora, not hell, which leads me on. Come! the hour is at hand; adieu, signora! most probably I shall never see you more. All I ask is when you pass through Prague to pay for a mass for me at the chapel of St. John Népomuck, one among the greatest of the patron saints of Bohemia."

"Karl, you must speak — you must confess the wicked thoughts which torment you, or I will never pray for you. On the contrary, I will invoke on your head the malediction of your wife and child, now angels in the bosom of the merciful Jesus. How do you expect to be forgiven in heaven if you do not forgive upon earth? You have a carbine under your cloak, Karl, and you watch to see these Prussians leave the castle."

"No, not here," said Karl, all trembling and agitated; "I would not shed blood in my master's dwelling, nor before you, my sweet young lady; but yonder, do you see, there is a mountain pass—I know it well, for I was there when they passed this morning—but I was there by chance —I was unarmed, and besides I did not at first know that it was he! By and by, however, he will pass, and I—I will be there! I can soon reach it by crossing the park, and shall get there before him though he be on horseback; and as you have said, signora, I have a carbine, a right good carbine, and in it a ball for his heart. It has been there for some time, for I was in earnest when I acted the pirate. I had a good chance, and leveled at him ten times, but you were always there, and I would not fire. By and by you will not be there, and he will not be able to skulk behind you like a coward as he is—for he is a coward, as I well know. I have seen him grow pale and turn his back on the field of battle. One day when he made us advance against my countrymen, against my brethren of Bohemia, oh, what horror I felt! for I am Bohemian in heart and soul, and that is a deed never to be forgiven. But if I be a poor peasant, having never learned to handle aught but the hatchet in my native forests, he has made me, thanks to his corporals, a Prussian soldier, and I know how to take an aim."

"Karl! Karl! be silent—you rave! You do not know this man, I am sure. He is called the Baron de Kreutz; I wager you did not know his name before. You must mistake him for some one else. He is no recruiter; he never did you any harm."

"It is not the Baron de Kreutz; no, signora, I knew him well. I have seen him a hundred times on parade; he is the grand master of men-stealers, and destroyers of families; he is the scourge of Bohemia; he is my enemy. He is the enemy of our church, our religion, and of all our saints. It is he who profaned by his impious laughter the statue of St. John Népomuck on the bridge of Prague. It is he who stole from the castle of Prague the drum covered with the skin of John Ziska, the greatest warrior of his time—that which was at once the safeguard, the honor, and the object of respect of the whole country! Oh! no, I am not mistaken, and I know him well! Besides St. Wenceslas just now appeared to me as I prayed in the chapel; I saw him as plainly as I see you, signora, and he said to me, 'It is he, strike him to the heart!' I have sworn before the Holy Virgin, on the tomb of my wife, and I must keep my oath. Ah! signora, look! there is his horse at the door! It was that I waited for. I go to my post—pray for me; sooner or later my life must pay the penalty; but it matters little so that God saves my soul!"

"Karl!" exclaimed Consuelo, inspired with superhuman strength, "I believed you generous, sensible, pious, but now I see that you are impious, base, and cowardly. Whoever this man may be whom you would assassinate, I forbid you to follow or to harm him. It is the enemy of man who has taken the form of a saint to pervert your reason; and Heaven permits you to fall into his snares for having sworn an impious oath. You are ungrateful and a coward, I tell you; for you no longer think about your master, who has loaded you with favors, who will be accused for your crime, and who, good and generous as he is, will suffer for it with his life. Go, hide yourself, Karl, you are not worthy of the light. Repent, for merely to harbor such a thought is a deadly crime. Stay, at this moment I see your wife, who weeps beside you, and who vainly tries to hold in her embrace your good angel, ready to abandon you to the wicked one forever."

" My wife! my wife!" exclaimed Karl wildly, now completely vanquished; " I see her not. My wife, if you be there, speak to me—let me see you once again ere I die!"

" You cannot see her, for crime is in your heart, and darkness seals your eyelids. Down on your knees! you may yet redeem your soul. Give me this carbine, which stains your hands, and offer up an humble and contrite prayer."

Thus saying, Consuelo took from his hands the carbine, which he did not seek to retain, and hastened from the deserter, who, as she disappeared, fell on his knees and burst into tears. She left the turret in order to hide the weapon instantly in some other spot. She felt exhausted with the efforts she had made to impress the imagination of the fanatic and influence his mind by means of the chimeras which governed him; for time pressed, and she had no leisure to address him with arguments more humane and enlightened. She uttered what first occurred to her mind, inspired perhaps with somewhat of sympathy for the unhappy man, whom she wished to serve at all risks from an act of insanity, and whom she loaded with feigned reproaches while she really deplored a madness which he was unable to control.

She hastened to lay aside the fatal piece, purposing to return and keep him on the turret till the Prussians were far away, when, just as she opened the door which communicated with the corridor, she met the Baron de Kreutz face to face. He was on his way to his apartment, in order to procure his pistols and his cloak. Consuelo had only time to let the weapon fall in the angle behind the door and to rush into the corridor, closing the door between herself and Karl, lest the sight of the enemy might light up all his fury afresh.

This hurried movement, and the agitation with which she supported herself against the door, as if she were on the point of fainting, did not escape the penetrating gaze of Baron de Kreutz. He carried a taper, and stopped before her, smiling. His countenance was perfectly calm, yet Consuelo thought she saw his hand tremble and the flame of the torch oscillate very sensibly. The lieutenant was behind him, pale as death, and with his sword drawn. These circumstances, as well as the certainty she acquired a little later that a window of the apartment which the baron had occupied opened upon the turret, convinced Consuelo afterward that the two Prussians had not lost a word of her conversation with Karl. Nevertheless the baron saluted her with a courteous and tranquil air, and as the agitation she felt at being placed in such a situation made her forget to return his salutation and deprived her of the power of saying a single word, Kreutz, after having examined her for an instant with a look that expressed rather interest than surprise, said to her in a gentle voice, taking her hand: "Come, my child, recover yourself. You seem very much agitated. We must have frightened you in passing suddenly before this door at the moment you opened it, but be assured we are your servants and your friends. I hope we shall see you again at Berlin, where perhaps we can be of some use to you."

The baron partly drew Consuelo's hand toward him, as if his first impulse had been to carry it to his lips; but he contented himself with pressing it gently, saluted her a second time, and withdrew, followed by his lieutenant, who did not seem even to see Consuelo, so much was he bewildered and agitated. His countenance confirmed the young girl in the opinion that he was aware of the danger which had threatened his master.

But who was this man, the responsibility for whose safety weighed so heavily upon another's shoulders, and whose destruction had seemed to Karl so complete and so intoxicating a revenge? Consuelo returned to the terrace to draw this secret from him, at the same time that she continued to watch him; but she found that he had fainted, and, not able to raise his huge frame, she descended the stairs and called the other domestics to come to his assistance. "Ah! it is nothing," said they as they hastened toward the place she pointed out; "he has merely drunk a little too much hydromel this evening and we will carry him to his bed." Consuelo longed to accompany them, as she feared Karl might betray his secret on returning to consciousness; but she was prevented by Count Hoditz, who was passing, and who took her arm, congratulating himself that she had not yet retired and that he could show her a new spectacle. She was obliged to follow him to the porch, and from thence she saw, relieved against the sky on a lofty hill, and precisely in the direction which Karl had pointed out as the one he intended to take, an immense arch blazing with light, in the midst of which some characters could be distinguished formed of colored lamps.

"Yes," said she, with an absent air, "that is a splendid illumination."

"It is a delicate attention, a respectful adieu, to the guest who has just left us," he replied; "he will pass in a quarter of an hour by the foot of the hill, through a deep gorge which we do not discern from this, where he will find as by enchantment this triumphal arch raised over his head."

"My lord," exclaimed Consuelo, rousing herself from her reverie, "who is this individual who has just now quitted us?"

"You shall know hereafter, my child."

"If it be not right to ask, I am silent; meantime I suspect his real name is not Baron de Kreutz."

"I was not deceived for an instant," replied Hoditz, who in this matter prided himself no little on his penetration. "However, I religiously respected his incognito; I know it is a fancy of his, and that he is offended if you do not take him for what he seems. You saw that I treated him merely as a simple officer and nevertheless——" The count was dying to speak, but etiquette forbade him to utter a name apparently so sacred. He adopted a middle course, and presenting a glass to Consuelo, "Look!" said he, "how well yonder arch has succeeded. It is upward of two miles off, and yet with this excellent glass you will be able to read the inscription on the summit. The letters are twenty feet high, although they are hardly perceptible to the naked eye. Now look attentively!"

Consuelo looked, and easily deciphered this inscription, which revealed the secret:

"*Long live Frederick the Great!*"

"Ah! my lord," she exclaimed, much agitated, "there is great danger in such an exalted personage traveling thus, and it is even more dangerous to receive him."

I do not understand you," said the count ; " we are now at peace; no one in all the empire would think of injuring him, and it could disparage no one's patriotism to treat with honor a guest such as he."

Consuelo remained plunged in thought. Hoditz roused her from her reverie by saying that he had an humble request to make; that he feared indeed to take advantage of her kindness, but the matter was so important that he was obliged to importune her. "The request I have to make," said he, with a grave and mysterious air, "is, that you will kindly perform the part of the Shade."

"What Shade?" asked Consuelo, whose thoughts were solely occupied with Frederick and the occurrences of the evening.

" The Shade which comes at the desert to seek the margravine and her guests, in order to lead them through Tartarus, where I have placed the music of the dead, and conduct them to the theater where Olympus is to receive them. Venus does not immediately appear, and you will have time to throw aside the drapery of woe and display the brilliant costume of the queen of love beneath, that is to say, rose-colored satin, with clasps and tinsels of silver mounted in gold looping up the dress, and powdered hair, with pearls, feathers, and roses. An elegant and most recherché toilet, as you shall see. Come! you consent; for the part requires a dignified carriage, and not one of my liltle actresses would have the courage to say to her Lighness, in a tone sufficiently respectful and imperious— *'Follow me.'* It a phrase not easy to say, and I think it requires genius to give it the desired effect. What think you?"

"Oh, it is admirable; and I shall perform the Shade with all my heart," replied Consuelo, smiling.

" Ah, you are an angel; an angel in truth!" exclaimed the count, kissing her hand.

But alas! the fête, this brilliant fête, this dream, which the count had cherished during the whole winter, and for which he had taken three journeys into Moravia to superintend the preparations, this fête so anxiously expected, was destined, like the stern and fatal vengeance of Karl, to vanish into thin air!

The following day every thing was in readiness. The retainers of Roswald were under arms. Nymphs, genii, savages, dwarfs, giants, mandarins, and shades, waited, shivering at their posts, for the signal to commence their evolutions. The roads leading to the castle were cleared of snow and strewn with moss and violets, numerous guests from the neighboring castles, and even distant towns, formed a respectable assemblage—when, alas! an unexpected calamity upset every thing. A courier dashing up at full gallop, brought the intelligence that the margravine's carriage had been overturned, that her highness had two ribs broken, and was forced to alight at Olmutz, where the count was to join her. The crowd dispersed. The count, followed by Karl, who had now regained his reason, mounted the best of his horses, and set off in haste, after having said a few words to his major-domo.

The Pleasures, the Brooks, the Hours, and the Rivers hastily put on their furred boots and woolen dresses; and together with the Chinese, the Pirates, the Druids, and the Anthropophagi returned pell-mell to their labor in the fields. The guests re-entered their carriages, and the same berlin which had brought Porpora and his pupil was again placed at their disposal. The major-domo, conformably to the orders he had received, handed them the sum agreed upon, and compelled them to accept it, although they had only half earned it. They set out the same day for Prague, the professor enchanted at being freed from the cosmopolitan music and the polyglot cantatas of his host, and Consuelo directing many a sorrowful look in the direction of Silesia, and grieved to the heart at being obliged to turn her back on the captive of Glatz without a hope of rescuing him from his unhappy fate.

That same day the Baron de Kreutz, who had passed the night in a village not far from the Moravian frontier, and who had departed again at dawn in a huge traveling coach, escorted by his pages on horseback and followed by a berlin which carried his secretary and his treasure chest, said to his lieutenant, or rather his aide-de-camp, the Baron of Buddenbrock, as they approached the city of Neïsse (and it must be remarked that, dissatisfied with his awkwardness the day before, this was the first time he had spoken to him since their departure from Roswald)— "What was that illumination which I perceived at a distance upon the hill we must have passed, if we had skirted the park of that Count Hoditz?"

"Sire," replied Buddenbrock, trembling, "I saw no illumination."

"You were in the wrong, then. A man who accompanies me ought to see everything."

"Your majesty must forgive me, but the frightful state of agitation into which I was thrown by that wretch's resolution——"

"You do not know what you are saying! That man was a fanatic, an unhappy Catholic devotee, exasperated by the sermons which the Bohemian clergy preached against me during the war, and driven moreover to extremity by some personal misfortune. He must be some peasant whom my recruiters have carried off; one of those deserters whom we sometimes recapture in spite of all their precautions——"

"Your majesty may rely upon it that to-morrow this man shall be retaken and brought before you."

"You have given orders then to have him carried off from Count Hoditz?"

"Not yet, sire; but as soon as I arrive at Neïsse, I will despatch four skillful and determined men——"

"I forbid you to do so; on the contrary, you will obtain information respecting the man, and if his family have fallen victims to the war, as he seemed to indicate in his incoherent talk, you will see that he be paid the sum of one thousand rix-dollars, and you will have him pointed out to the recruiters of Silesia that he be left forever undisturbed. You understand me? His name is Karl, he is very tall, he is a Bohemian, and in the service of Count Hoditz; that is enough to enable you to identify him and to procure information respecting his family and condition."

"Your majesty shall be obeyed."

"I hope so, indeed! What do you think of that professor of music?"

"Master Porpora? He seemed to me foolish, self-satisfied, and exceedingly ill-tempered."

"And I tell you that he is a man of superior acquirements, full of wit, and a most amusing irony. When he arrives with his pupil at the frontier of Prussia, you will send a comfortable carriage to meet him."

"Yes, sire."

"And you are to hand him into it alone; *alone*, you understand? but, at the same time, you will treat him with every respect."

"Yes, sire."

"And afterward?"

"Afterward your majesty means he shall be carried to Berlin?"

"You have not common sense to-day. I mean that he shall be carried back to Dresden, and from thence to Prague, if he desire it, or even to Vienna, if such be his wish; all at my expense. Since I have taken so worthy a man from his occupations, I ought to replace him in his former position without the change costing him any thing. But I do not wish him to place a foot in my kingdom. He has too much wit for us."

"What does your majesty command respecting the cantatrice?"

"That she be conducted under escort, whether willing or unwilling, to Sans Souci, and that an apartment be prepared for her in the château."

"In the château, sire?"

"Yes! are you deaf? the apartment of the Barberini."

"And the Barberini, sire—what shall we do with her?"

"The Barberini is no longer at Berlin. She has left that. Did you not know it?"

"No, sire."

"What *do* you know then? And as soon as the girl has arrived, I am to be notified of the fact, at whatever hour of the day or night it may happen. Do you understand what I have said? The following are the first orders you are to have inscribed upon register number 1 of the clerk of my treasury: the compensation to Karl, the sending back of Porpora, the succession of the Porporina to the honors and emoluments of the Barberini. Ha! here we are at the gates of the city. Resume your good humor, Buddenbrock, and endeavor to be a little less stupid the next time I take a fancy to travel *incognito* with you."

CHAPTER CIV.

THE cold was intense when Porpora and Consuelo arrived at Prague, as night was closing in. A brilliant moon illumined the ancient city, which preserved in its aspect the religious and warlike character of its history. Our travelers entered it by the gate called Rosthor, and passing through that portion of it which is on the right bank of the Moldaw they reached the middle of the bridge without accident. But there the carriage received a heavy shock, and stopped suddenly. "Holy Virgin!" cried the postilion, "my horse has fallen before the statue! it is a bad omen! May Saint John Népomuck help us!"

Consuelo, seeing that the shaft-horse was entangled in the traces, and that the postilion would require some time to raise him and readjust the harness, of which several buckles had been broken by the fall, proposed to her master to alight in order to warm themselves by a little exercise. The maestro having consented, Consuelo approached the parapet in order to examine the localities around. From the spot on which she stood, the two distinct cities of which Prague is composed—one called *the new*, which was built by the Emperor Charles IV in 1348, and the other which ascends to the remotest antiquity, both constructed in the form of amphitheaters—looked like two black mountains of buildings from which ascended here and there the lofty spires of the antique churches and the somber battlements of the fortifications. The Moldaw flowed dark and rapid beneath the bridge, which was of the simplest construction, and which had been the theater of so many tragical events in the history of Bohemia; and the rays of the moon, which silvered the projecting battlements, streamed full on the head of the revered statue. Consuelo examined long the features of the holy doctor, who seemed to fix a melancholy gaze on the dark and flowing waves.

The legend of Saint Népomuck is a holy and touching story, and his name is venerated by every one who esteems independence and loyalty. Confessor to the empress Jane he refused to betray the secrets of her confession, and the drunkard Wenceslas, eager to discover his wife's secret thoughts but unable to draw any thing from the illustrious doctor, had him drowned under the bridge of Prague. The tradition relates that at the moment when he disappeared beneath the waves, five brilliant stars glittered upon the scarcely closed gulf, as if the martyr had allowed his crown to float for an instant upon the waters. In record of this miracle, five stars of metal have been inlaid in the stone of the balustrade, at the very spot from which Népomuck was hurled.

Rosmunda, who was very devout, had preserved a tender recollection of the legend of John Népomuck; and in the enumeration of the saints whom every evening she taught her child to call upon with lisping accents, she had never forgotten that one, the special patron of travelers, and of people in danger, and above all, *the guardian of a good reputation*. Consuelo therefore recalled at this instant the prayer which she formerly addressed to the apostle of purity, and struck by the sight of the place which had witnessed his tragical end, she knelt instinctively among the devotées who at that epoch still paid, each hour of the day and night, an assiduous court to the image of the saint. They were composed principally of poor women, pilgrims, and aged beggars, with perhaps a few Zingari, children of the mandoline and proprietors of the highway. Their piety did not absorb them so much as to make them forget to hold out their hands as she passed. She gave them liberal alms, happy to recall the time when she was neither better clad nor prouder than they. Her generosity affected them so much that they consulted together in a low voice, and then charged one of their number to tell her that they were going to sing one of the ancient hymns in honor of the blessed Népomuck, that the saint might avert the bad omen which had stopped their progress. According to them, the music and the words dated so far back as the time of Wenceslas the drunkard:

> " Suspice quas dedimus, Johannes beate,
> Tibi preces supplices, noster advocate,
> Fieri dum vivimus, ne sinas infames,
> Et nostros post obitum cœlis infer manes."

Porpora, who took pleasure in listening to them, was of opinion that the hymn could not be more than a century old, but a second which he heard, seemed a malediction

addressed to Wenceslas by his contemporaries, and commenced thus:

> " Sævus, piger imperator,
> Malorum clarus patrator, etc. "

Although the crimes of Wenceslas were of no great importance, the poor Bohemians seemed to take a pleasure in
eternally cursing in the person of this tyrant the abhorred
title of *imperator* which had become synonomous in their
eyes with that of Foreigner. An Austrian sentinel
guarded each of the gates placed at the entrances of the
bridge. It was their duty to march unceasingly from
either end and meet before the statue, when they turned
their backs and resumed their monotonous walk. They
heard the Canticles, but as they were not as well versed in
church Latin as the devout inhabitants of Prague, they
doubtless fancied they were listening to a hymn in praise
of Francis of Lorraine, the husband of Maria Theresa.

Listening to these delightful airs by the light of the
moon in one of the most romantic situations in the world,
Consuelo felt herself overwhelmed with melancholy. Her
journey so far had been gay and happy, and by a natural
reaction she fell all at once into the opposite extreme.
The postilion, who set about repairing his harness with
true German phlegm, kept on repeating so constantly,
" Ha! this is bad business," that poor Consuelo at last became affected by his evil presages. Every painful emotion,
every prolonged reverie, recalled Albert's image. At that
moment she recollected that Albert, hearing the canoness
one evening invoke St. Népomuck, the guardian of good
reputation, aloud in her prayer, had said to her: " That is
all very well in you, aunt, who have taken the precaution
to insure yours by an exemplary life; but I have often seen
souls stained by vice call to their aid the miracles of this
saint, in order the better to conceal from men their secret
iniquities. Thus it is that devout practices serve quite as
often to cloak the grossest hypocrisy as to sustain and for-
tify innocence." At that instant, as Consuelo thought, she
heard Albert's voice sounding at her ear in the evening
breeze and in the dusk of the Moldaw's gloomy waves.
She asked herself what he would think of her, he who perhaps believed her already perverted, if he could see her

prostrate before that image; and, almost terrified, she was rising to retire, when Porpora said to her: " Come, let us get into the carriage again; every thing is repaired."

She followed him and was just entering the carriage, when a cavalier, heavily mounted on a horse still heavier than his rider, stopped abruptly, alighted, and approaching gazed at her with a tranquil curiosity, which appeared to her excessively impertinent. " What are you doing there, sir ?" said Porpora, pushing him back; " ladies are not to be stared at so closely. It may be the custom in Prague, but I warn you I am not inclined to submit to it."

The stout man drew his chin out of the furs which enveloped it, and still holding his horse by the bridle, replied to Porpora in Bohemian, without perceiving that the latter did not understand a word of what he said; but Consuelo, struck by his voice, and leaning forward to look at his features by the moonlight, cried, interposing between him and Porpora: " Do I indeed see the Baron of Rudolstadt?"

" Yes, it is I, signora !" replied Baron Frederick; " it is I, the brother of Christian, the uncle of Albert; oh! it is indeed I. And it is in truth you also ?" added he, uttering a deep sigh.

Consuelo was struck by his dejected air and his cold greeting. He who had always been the mirror of chivalry, did not so much as kiss her hand, or touch his furred cap, but contented himself with repeating with a half-stupid, half-terrified air:

" Yes, it is even so—it is indeed you."

" What news from Riesenburg ?" said Consuelo with emotion.

" Yes, signora, I long to tell it to you."

" Well, then, baron, speak; tell me about Count Christian, about the canoness, and——"

" Yes, I shall tell you all," replied the baron, more and more dejected.

" And Count Albert ?" resumed Consuelo, terrified at the expression of his countenance.

" Yes, oh! yes, Albert—yes—I would speak of him."

But he said not a word, and to all the questions of Consuelo he remained as dumb and motionless as the statue of St. Népomuck.

Porpora began to grow impatient. He was cold and

longed to reach some shelter. Moreover, this meeting, which was so well calculated to make a deep impression on Consuelo, annoyed him hugely.

"My lord baron," said he, "we shall have the honor of paying our respects to you to-morrow, but permit us at present to sup and warm ourselves. That is more important than compliments," he added, pressing into the carriage, and pushing Consuelo unwillingly in before him.

"But, my dear friend," she exclaimed, anxiously, "let me ask——"

"Let me alone," he bluntly added. "This man is mad or dead drunk; and we may spend the entire night upon the bridge without getting a word of sense from him."

Consuelo was a prey to the deepest anxiety.

"You are pitiless," said she, as the carriage passed the bridge and entered the ancient city. "Another moment and I should have learned what I am more interested in than any thing else in the world."

"Oh! ho! are we there still?" said the maestro angrily. "Is this Albert always running through your head? A precious family, forsooth, to judge by this old booby with his cap apparently glued to his head, for he had not even the civility to raise it when he saw you."

"It is a family for which, until lately, you expressed the highest esteem; so much so that you consigned me to its care as to a haven of safety, and enjoined on me the deepest respect, love, and affection for all the members of it."

"The last injunction you have obeyed to the letter, I see."

Consuelo was about to reply, but remained silent when she saw the baron mount his horse with the intention apparently of following the carriage. When she alighted she found the old noble at the entrance, holding out his hand to assist her and doing the honors of his house; for it was there and not at the inn that he had directed the postilion to stop. Porpora in vain refused his hospitality; he was not to be put off, and Consuelo, who burned to clear up her melancholy presentiment, hastened to accept his attentions, and proceeded with him into the saloon, where a huge fire and an excellent supper awaited them.

"You perceive, signora," said the baron, "that I calculated on your arrival."

"That greatly surprises me," replied Consuelo, "for we

mentioned it to no one, and we did not even expect to get here before to-morrow."

" You are not more astonished than I am," said the baron, with a disconsolate air.

" But the Baroness Amelia?" asked Consuela, ashamed of having so long neglected to inquire for her old friend.

A cloud lowered on the baron's brow, and his ruddy hue, chilled by the cold, became so livid that Consuelo was terrified. But he replied with a sort of forced tranquillity, " My daughter is in Saxony with one of her relations; she will be sorry at not having seen you."

" And the other members of your family, my lord," resumed Consuelo; " can you inform me ———"

" Yes, you shall know every thing," replied the baron; " eat, signora, you will require it."

" I cannot eat if you do not relieve my disquietude. In the name of heaven, sir, is there any one dead?"

" No person is dead," replied the baron, in a tone as melancholy as if he were announcing the extinction of his whole race; and he began to carve the meats with the same slow and solemn precision that he was in the habit of observing at Riesenburg. Consuelo had not the courage to question him further. The supper appeared to her dreadfully tedious. Porpora, who was less anxious than hungry, endeavored to converse with his host. The latter attempted, on his side, to reply politely, and even to put some questions to the maestro respecting his affairs and projects; but this mental effort was evidently beyond his strength. He never replied coherently, or else he repeated his questions, though he had just received a reply. He carved huge portions of the meat, and filled his plate and glass most copiously; but it was merely the effect of habit; he neither ate nor drank. and letting his fork fall, he fixed his eyes on the table, and gave way to the deepest dejection. Consuelo looked steadily at him, and saw plainly that he was not intoxicated. She asked herself if this sudden sinking of the system was the result of misfortune, of disease, or of old age. At last, after torturing them in this manner for two hours, the repast being ended, the baron signed to his domestics to retire, and after a long search pulled an open letter out of his pocket, and presented it to Consuelo. It was from the canoness, and was as follows:

"We are lost, my dearest brother—there is no hope! Dr. Supperville has at last arrived here from Bareith, and after putting us off for some days he informed me that it would be necessary to arrange the affairs of the family, since in eight days perhaps Albert would be no more. Christian, to whom I dare not make this disclosure, still entertains some hope; but he is dreadfully downcast, and I do not know whether my nephew's loss be the only stroke which threatens me. Frederick, we are lost! Shall we ever survive such misfortunes? I cannot tell—the will of God be done! That is all I can utter; but I do not think I shall have force to bear up against this heavy trial. Come to us, my brother, and endeavor to sustain our courage, if you have sufficient strength remaining after your own heavy misfortune — that crowning blow to the misery of a family which may well be called accursed! What crimes have we committed to deserve such inflictions? May our Heavenly Parent enable me to regard his dealings toward us with humble faith and submission! and yet at times I feel as if this were more than I could accomplish.

"Come to us, dear brother; we wait anxiously for you, and we require your counsel and assistance. Nevertheless do not quit Prague before the 11th. I have a singular commission to give you. I am mad I think to lend myself to it; but I am completely bewildered, and can only conform blindly to Albert's will. On the 11th, then, at seven o'clock in the evening, be on the bridge of Prague at the foot of the statue. The first carriage that passes you will stop; the first person you see in it you will conduct to your house; and if she can leave for Riesenburg that very evening, Albert will perhaps be saved. At least, he says it will give him a hold on eternal life. What he means by that I do not know; however the revelations he has made during the past week, of events the most unforeseen by us, have been realized in so extraordinary a manner that it is no longer permitted me to doubt. He has the gift of prophecy and the perception of hidden things. He called me to his bedside this evening, and in that faint and inaudible voice, which is all that is now left him, and which must be guessed rather than heard, told me to transmit to you the words which I have now faithfully reported. At seven o'clock then, on the 11th, be at the foot of the statue, and whoever may be the occupant of the carriage, bring her hither with all speed."

Consuelo had hardly finished this letter ere she grew as pale as the baron, rose suddenly, then fell back in her seat, where she remained motionless, with rigid arms and clenched teeth. But immediately rallying, she rose a second time and said to the baron, who had relapsed into his stupor :

"Well then, sir, is the carriage ready? If so, I am ready also, and we can set out instantly."

The baron rose mechanically and left the room. Every thing had been prepared beforehand. Carriage and horses were already in the court-yard ; but, like an automaton moved by springs, without Consuelo the baron would have thought no more of their departure.

Hardly had he left the saloon, when Porpora seized the letter, and hastily glanced over its contents. He too turned pale in his turn, could not utter a word, and paced up and down before the stove greatly agitated. The maestro justly reproached himself for what had happened. He had not foreseen it, it is true, but he now thought that he ought to have foreseen it; and seized with terror and remorse, and bewildered moreover, at the invalid's strange prediction respecting Consuelo, he almost believed himself a prey to some horrible dream.

Nevertheless, as he was both calculating and tenacious of purpose to the highest degree, he reflected on the possible consequences of Consuelo's sudden resolution. He moved nervously through the room, struck his forehead, stamped, made various other manifestations of uneasiness, and at last arming himself with courage, and braving the explosion which he feared, he said to Consuelo, shaking her as he spoke to rouse her from her reverie:

"You wish to go with the baron, then? I consent ; but at the same time I shall follow you. You wish to see Albert, and perhaps deal a death-blow to his enfeebled constitution, but as we cannot now turn back, let us set out at once. We have still two days at our disposal. True, we were to spend them at Dresden, but we shall not now pause there. If we are not in Prussia by the 18th, we fail in our engagement. The theater opens on the 25th, and if you are not ready to appear I shall be subject to a heavy fine. I have not half the sum at my disposal, and in Prussia he who does not pay goes to prison. Once there you are forgotten; it may be for ten or perhaps twenty years, and you may die of hunger or old age, whichever you prefer. This is the fate which awaits me if you forget to leave Riesenburg on the 14th by daybreak."

"Do not be uneasy, my dear master," replied Consuelo firmly, "I have already thought of all that. Do not make me suffer at Riesenburg—that is all I ask of you. We shall set out on the 14th by daybreak."

"You must swear it."

"I swear it," she replied, with a gesture of impatience. "When your life and liberty are at stake, no oath, I should think, is needed from me."

At this moment the baron returned, followed by a faithful and intelligent servant, who, wrapping Consuelo up in a fur pelisse as he would have done an infant, bore her off to the carriage. They were soon at Beraum, and arrived at Pilsen by daybreak.

CHAPTER CV.

Much time was lost in the journey from Pilsen to Tauss (though they proceeded as quickly as possible) from the execrable roads, the unfrequented and almost impassable forests, and the various dangers to which they were subjected in traversing them. At last, after having proceeded at the rate of about a league an hour they arrived at the Castle of the Giants about midnight. Consuelo had never experienced a more dreary or fatiguing journey. The Baron Rudolstadt seemed in a measure paralyzed from the effect of age and gout. But one short year before he had been robust as a giant, but his iron frame was not actuated by a resolute and determined will. He had never yielded obedience but to his instincts, and when the first stroke of misfortune assailed him, his feeble frame sunk beneath the blow. The pity which Consuelo felt for him only added to her uneasiness. "Is it thus," thought she, "that I shall find the rest of the family at Riesenburg?"

The bridge was lowered, the gates opened wide, and servants stood waiting their arrival with lighted torches in the court-yard. None of the three travelers thought of making a remark on this strange scene, and no one seemed able to question the domestics. Porpora, seeing that the baron could hardly walk, took his arm and assisted him along, while Consuelo darted to the entrance and flew up the steps.

She met the canoness in the doorway, who, without losing time in salutation, seized her by the arm, saying:

"Follow me; we have not a moment to lose. Albert begins to grow impatient. He has counted the hours and minutes till your arrival, and announced your approach a moment before we heard the sound of your carriage wheels. He had no doubt in his mind of your coming; but, he said, if any accident should happen to detain you, it would be too late. Come, signora, and in the name of heaven do not oppose any of his wishes; promise all he asks ; pretend to love him; and if it must be, practice a friendly deceit! Alfred's hours are numbered; his life draws to a close. Endeavor to soothe his sufferings; it is all that we ask of you."

Thus saying, Wenceslawa led Consuelo in the direction of the great saloon.

"He is up, then—he is not confined to his chamber?" exclaimed Consuelo, hastily.

"He no longer rises, for he never retires to bed," replied the canoness. "For thirty days he has sat in his armchair in the saloon, and will not be removed elsewhere. The doctor says he must not be opposed on this point, and that he would die if he were moved. Take courage, signora; you are about to behold a terrible spectacle!"

The canoness opened the door of the saloon, and added:

"Fly to him; you need not fear to surprise him, for he expects you, and has seen you coming hours ago."

Consuelo darted toward her betrothed, who, as the canoness had said, was seated in a large arm-chair beside the fireplace. It was no longer a man, it was a specter which she beheld. His face, still beautiful, notwithstanding the ravages of disease, was as a face of marble. There was no smile on his lips—no ray of joy in his eyes. The doctor, who held his arm and felt his pulse, let it fall gently, and looked at the canoness, as much as to say—"It is too late." Consuelo knelt before him ; he looked fixedly at her, but said nothing. At last he signed with his finger to the canoness, who had to interpret all his wishes. She took his arms, which he was no longer able to raise, and placed them on Consuelo's sholders. Then she made the young girl lay her head on Albert's bosom, and as the voice of the dying

man was gone, he was merely able to whisper in her ear—
"I am happy." He remained in this position for about
two minutes, the head of his beloved resting on his
bosom, and his lips pressed to her raven hair. Then he
looked at his aunt, and by some hardly perceptible movement he made her understand that his father and his aunt
were both to kiss his betrothed.

"From my very heart!" exclaimed the canoness, embracing Consuelo with deep emotion. Then she raised her
to conduct her to Count Christian, whom Consuelo had not
hitherto perceived.

Seated in a second arm-chair, placed opposite his son's
at the other side of the fireplace, the old count seemed
almost as much weakened and reduced. He was still able
to rise, however, and take a few steps through the saloon ;
but he was obliged to be carried every evening to his bed,
which had been placed in an adjoining room. At that moment he held his brother's hand in one of his, and Porpora's
in the other. He left them to embrace Consuelo fervently
several times. The almoner of the château came also in
his turn to salute her, in order to gratify Albert. He also
seemed like a spectre, notwithstanding his embonpoint
which had only increased ; but his paleness was frightful.
The habits of an indolent and effeminate life had so enervated him that he could not endure the sorrow of others.
The canoness alone retained energy for all. A bright red
spot shone on each cheek, and her eyes burned with a feverish brightness. Albert alone appeared calm. His
brow was calm as a sleeping infant's, and his physical prostration did not seem to have affected his mental powers.
He was grave, and not, like his father and uncle, dejected.

In the midst of those different victims to disease or sorrow, the physician's calm and healthful countenance offered
a striking contrast to all that surrounded him. Supperville was a Frenchman who had formerly been attached to
the household of Frederick when the latter was only crown
prince. Early aware of the despotic fault-finding turn
which lurked in the prince, he fixed himself at Bareith,
in the service of Sophia Wilhelmina, sister of the King of
Prussia. At once jealous and ambitious, Supperville was
the very model of a courtier. An indifferent physician,
in spite of the local reputation he enjoyed, he was a com-

plete man of the world, a keen observer, and tolerably
conversant with the moral springs of disease. He had
urged the canoness to satisfy all the desires of her nephew,
and had hoped something from the return of her for
whom Albert was dying. But however he might reckon
his pulse and examine his countenance after Consuelo's
arrival, he did not the less continue to reiterate that the
time was past, and he determined to take his departure, in
order not to witness scenes of despair which it was no
longer in his power to avert.

He resolved, however, whether in conformity with some
interested scheme, or merely to gratify his natural taste for
intrigue, to make himself busy in family affairs; and seeing that no person in this bewildered family thought of
turning the passing moments to account, he led Consuelo
into the embrasure of a window, and addressed her as follows :

"Mademoiselle, a doctor is in some sort a confessor, and
I therefore soon became aware of the secret passion which
hurries this young man to the grave. As a medical man,
accustomed habitually to investigate the laws of the physical world which do not readily vary, I must say that I do
not believe in the strange visions and ecstatic revelations of
the young count. As regards yourself, it is easy to ascribe
them to secret communication with you, relative to your
journey to Prague, and your subsequent arrival here."

And as Consuelo made a sign in the negative, he continued :

"I do not question you, mademoiselle, and my conjectures need not offend you. Rather confide in me, and look
upon me as entirely devoted to your interests."

"I do not understand you, sir," replied Consuelo, with
a candor which was far from convincing the court doctor.

"Perhaps you will understand presently, mademoiselle,"
he cooly rejoined. "The young count's relations have
vehemently opposed the marriage up to this day. But
now their opposition is at an end. Albert is about to die,
and as he wishes to leave you his fortune, they cannot object to a religious ceremony that will secure it to you for
ever."

"Alas ! what matters Albert's fortune to me," said the
bereaved Consuelo ; "what has that to do with his present situation ? It was not business that brings me here,

sir ; I came to endeavor to save him. Is there no hope then ?"

"None ! This disease, entirely proceeding from the mind, is among those which baffles all our skill. It is not a month since the young count, after an absence of fifteen days, the cause of which no one could explain, returned to his home attacked by a disease at once sudden and incurable. All the functions of life were as if suspended. For thirty days he has swallowed no sort of food ; and it is a rare exception, only witnessed in the case of the insane, to see life supported by a few drops of liquid daily and a few minutes' sleep each night. His vital powers, as you perceive, are now quite exhausted, and in a couple of days at the farthest he will have ceased to suffer. Arm yourself with courage, then ; do not lose your presence of mind. I am here to aid you, and you have only to act boldly."

Consuelo was still gazing at the doctor with astonishment, when the canoness, on a sign from the patient, interrupted their colloquy by summoning him to Albert's side.

On his approach, Albert whispered in his ear for a longer period than his feebleness would have seemed to permit. Supperville turned red and pale alternately. The canoness looked at them anxiously, burning to know what wish Albert expressed.

"Doctor," said Albert, "I heard all you said just now to that young lady."

The doctor, who had spoken in a low whisper and at the farthest extremity of the saloon, became exceedingly confused at this remark, and his convictions respecting the impossibility of any superhuman faculty were so shaken that he stared wildly at Albert, unable to utter a word.

"Doctor," continued the dying man, "you do not understand that heavenly creature's soul, and you only interfere with my design by alarming her delicacy. She shares none of your ideas respecting money. She never coveted my fortune or my title. She never loved me, and it is to her pity alone you must appeal. Speak to her heart. I am nearer my end than you suppose; lose no time. I cannot expire happy if I do not carry with me into the night of my repose the title of her husband.

"But what do you mean by these last words," said

Supperville, who at that moment was solely busied in analyzing the mental disease of his patient.

"You could not understand them," replied Albert, with an effort, "but she will understand them. You have only to repeat them faithfully to her."

"Count," said Supperville, raising his voice a little, "I find I cannot succeed in interpreting your ideas clearly; you have just spoken with more force and distinctness than you have done for the last eight days, and I cannot but draw a favorable augury from it. Speak to mademoiselle yourself; a word from you will convince her more than all I could say. There she is; let her take my place and listen to you."

Supperville in fact found himself completely at fault in an affair which he thought he had understood perfectly; and thinking he had said enough to Consuelo to insure her gratitude in the event of her realizing the fortune, he retired, after Albert had further said to him:

"Remember what you promised. The time has arrived, speak to my relatives. Let them consent, and delay not. The hour is at hand."

Albert was so exhausted by the effort he had just made, that he leaned his forehead on Consuelo's breast when she approached him, and remained for some moments in this position, as if at the point of death. His white lips turned livid, and Porpora, terrified, feared that he had uttered his last sigh. During this time Supperville had collected Count Christian, the baron, the canoness, and chaplain, round the fire-place, and addressed them earnestly. The chaplain was the only person who ventured on an objection, which although apparently faint was in reality as powerful as the old priest could urge.

"If your excellencies demand it," said he, "I shall lend my sacred functions to the celebration of this marriage. But Count Albert, not being at present in a state of grace, must first through confession and extreme unction make his peace with the church."

"Extreme unction!" said the canoness, with a stifled groan. "Gracious God! is it come to that?"

"It is even so," replied Supperville, who as a man of the world and a disciple of the Voltaire school of philosophy, detested both the chaplain and his objections; "yes, it is even so, and without remedy; if his reverence

the chaplain insists on this point, and is bent on tormenting Count Albert by the dreary apparatus of death."

"And do you think," said Count Christian, divided
between his sense of devotion and his paternal tenderness,
"that a gayer ceremony, and one more congenial with his
wishes might prolong his days?"

"I can answer positively for nothing," replied Supperville, "but I venture to anticipate much good from it.
Your excellency consented to this marriage formerly——"

"I always consented to it. I never opposed it," said the
count, designedly raising his voice; "it was master
Porpora who wrote to say that he would never consent,
and that she likewise had renounced all idea of it. Alas!"
he added, lowering his voice, "it was the death-blow to
my poor child."

"You hear what my father says," murmured Albert in
Consuelo's ear, "but do not grieve for it. I believed you
had abandoned me, and I gave myself up to despair; but
during the last eight days I have regained my reason,
which they call my madness. I have read hearts as others
open books—I have read, with one glance, the past, the
present, and the future. I learned, in short, that you
were faithful, Consuelo; that you had endeavored to love
me; and that you had, indeed, for a time succeeded. But
they deceived us both; forgive your master, as I forgive
him!"

Consuelo looked at Porpora, who could not indeed
catch Albert's words, but who on hearing those of Count
Christian was much agitated, and walked up and down
before the fire with hurried strides. She looked at him
with an air of solemn reproach; and the maestro understood her so well that he struck his forehead violently with
his clenched hand. Albert signed to Consuelo to bring
the maestro close to his couch, and to assist him to hold
out his hand. Porpora pressed the cold fingers to his lips,
and burst into tears. His conscience reproached him with
homicide; but his sincere and heartfelt repentance palliated in some measure his fatal error.

Albert made a sign that he wished to listen what reply
his relations made to the doctor, and he heard it, though
they spoke so low that Porpora and Consuelo who were
kneeling by his side could not distinguish a word.

The chaplain withstood, as well as he could, Supperville's bitter irony, while the canoness sought by a mixture of superstition and tolerance, of Christian charity and maternal tenderness, to conciliate what was irreconcilable to the Catholic faith. The question was merely one of form—that is to say, whether the chaplain would consider it right to administer the marriage sacrament to a heretic, unless indeed the latter would conform to the Catholic faith immediately afterward. Supperville indeed did not hesitate to say that Count Albert had promised to profess and believe anything after the ceremony was over; but the chaplain was not to be duped. At last, Count Christian, calling to his aid that quiet firmness and plain good sense with which, although after much weakness and hesitation, he had always put an end to domestic differences, spoke as follows:

"Reverend sir," said he to the chaplain, "there is no ecclesiastical law which expressly forbids the marriage of a Catholic to a schismatic. The church tolerates these alliances. Consider Consuelo then as orthodox, my son as heretic, and marry them at once. Confession and betrothal, as you are aware, are but matters of precept, and in certain cases may be dispensed with. Some favorable change may result from this marriage, and when Albert is cured it will then be time to speak of his conversion."

The chaplain had never opposed the wishes of Count Christian, who was in his eyes a superior arbiter in cases of conscience even to the pope himself. There only now remained to convince Consuelo. This Albert alone thought of, and drawing her toward him, he succeeded in clasping the neck of his beloved with his emaciated and shadowy arms.

"Consuelo," said he, "I read at this hour in your soul that you would give your life to restore mine. That is no longer possible; but you can restore me forever by a simple act of your will. I leave you for a time, but I shall soon return to earth under some new form. I shall return unhappy and wretched if you now abandon me. You know that the crimes of Ziska still remain unexpiated, and you alone, my sister Wando, can purify me in the new phase of my existence. We are brethren; to become lovers, death must cast his gloomy shadow between us. But we must, by a solemn engagement, become man and wife, that in my new birth I may regain my calmness and strength, and become, like other men, freed from the dreary memories of the past. Only consent to this engagement; it will not bind you in this life, which I am about to quit, but it will unite us in eternity. It will be a pledge whereby we can recognize each other, should death affect the clearness of our recollections. Consent! it is but a ceremony of the church which I accept, since it is the only one which in the estimation of men can sanction our mutual relation. This I must carry with me to the tomb. A marriage without the assent of my family would be incomplete in my eyes. Ours shall be indissoluble in our hearts, as it is sacred in intention. Consent!"

"I consent," exclaimed Consuelo, pressing her lips to the pale cold forehead of her betrothed.

These words were heard by all.

"Well!" said Supperville, "let us hasten," and he urged the chaplain vigorously, who summoned the domestics and gave them instructions to have every thing prepared for the ceremony. Count Christian, a little revived, sat close beside his son and Consuelo. The good canoness thanked the latter warmly for her condescension, and was so much affected as even to kneel before her and kiss her hands. Baron Frederick wept in silence, without appearing to know what was going on. In the twinkling of an eye an altar was erected in the great saloon. The domestics were dismissed; they thought it was only the last rights of the church which were about to be administered, and that the patient required silence and fresh air. Porpora and Supperville served as witnesses. Albert found strength sufficient to pronounce a decisive *yes* and the other forms which the ceremony required, in a clear and sonorous voice, and the family from this conceived a lively hope of his recovery. Hardly had the chaplain recited the closing prayer over the newly-married couple, ere Albert arose, threw himself into his father's arms, and embraced him, as well as his aunt, his uncle, and Porpora, earnestly and rapidly; then seating himself in his arm-chair, he pressed Consuelo to his heart and exclaimed:

"I am saved!"

"It is the final effort, the last convulsion of nature," said Supperville, who had several times examined the features, and felt the pulse of the patient, while the marriage ceremony was proceeding.

In fact, Albert's arms loosed their hold, fell forward, and rested on his knees. His aged and faithful dog, Cynabre, who had not left his feet during the whole period of his illness, raised his head and uttered thrice a dismal howl. Albert's gaze was riveted on Consuelo; his lips remained apart as if about to address her ; a faint glow animated his cheek; and then gradually that peculiar and indescribable shade which is the forerunner of death crept from his forehead down to his lips, and by degrees overshadowed his whole face as with a snowy veil. The silence of terror which brooded over the breathless and attentive group of spectators was interrupted by the doctor, who, in solemn accents, pronounced the irrevocable decree: "It is the hand of Death!"

CHAPTER CVI.

Count Christian fell back senseless in his chair. The canoness, sobbing convulsively, flung herself on Albert's remains, as if she hoped by her caresses to rouse him to life again, while Baron Frederick uttered some unmeaning words with a sort of idiotic calm. Supperville approached Consuelo, whose utter immobility terrified him more than the agitation of the others.

"Do not trouble yourself about me, sir," she said, "nor you either, my friend," added she, addressing Porpora, who hastened to add his condolence, "but remove his unhappy relatives and endeavor to sustain and comfort them; as for me, I shall remain here. The dead need nothing but respect and prayers."

The count and the baron suffered themselves to be led away without resistence; as for the canoness, she was carried, cold and apparently lifeless, to her apartment, where Supperville followed to lend assistance. Porpora, no longer knowing where he was or what he did, rushed out and wandered through the gardens like an insane person. He felt as if suffocated. His habitual insensibility was more apparent than real. Scenes of grief and terror had excited his impressionable imagination, and he hastened onward by the light of the moon, pursued by gloomy voices which chanted a frightful *Dies iræ* incessantly in his ears.

Consuelo remained alone with Albert; for hardly had the chaplain begun to recite the prayers for the dead, than he fainted away and was borne off in his turn. The poor man had insisted on sitting up along with the canoness during the whole of Albert's illness, and was utterly exhausted. The Countess of Rudolstadt, kneeling by the side of her husband and holding his cold hands in hers, her head pressed against his which beat no longer, fell into deep abstraction. What Consuelo experienced at this moment was not exactly pain; at least it was not that bitter regret which accompanies the loss of beings necessary to our daily happiness. Her regard for Albert was not of this intimate character, and his death left no apparent void in her existence. The despair of losing those whom we love, not infrequently resolves itself into selfishness, and abhorrence of the new duties imposed upon us. One part of this grief is legitimate and proper; the other is not so, and should be combated, though it is just as natural. Nothing of all this mingled with the solemn and tender melancholy of Consuelo. Albert's nature was foreign to her own in every respect, except in one—the admiration, respect, and sympathy with which he had inspired her. She had chalked out a plan of life without him, and had even renounced the idea of an affection which, until two days before, she had thought extinct. What now remained to her was the desire and duty of proving faithful to a sacred pledge. Albert had been already dead as regarded her; he was now nothing more, and was perhaps even less so in some respects; for Consuelo, long exalted by intercourse with this lofty soul, had come in her dreamy reverie to adopt in a measure some of his poetical convictions. The belief in the transmission of souls had received a strong foundation in her instinctive repugnance toward the idea of eternal punishment after death, and in her Christian faith in the immortality of the soul. Albert, alive, but prejudiced against her by appearances, seemed as if wrapped in a veil, transported into another existence incomplete in comparison with that which he had proposed to devote to pure and lofty affection and unshaken confidence. But Albert, restored to this faith in her and to his enthusiastic affection, and yielding up his last breath on her bosom—had he then ceased to exist as regarded her? Did he not live in all the plenitude of a cloudless existence in passing under the triumphal arch of a glorious death, which conducted him either to a temporary repose, or to immediate consciousness in a purer and more heavenly state of being? To die struggling with one's own weakness, and to awake endowed with strength; to die forgiving the wicked, and to awake under the influence and protection of the upright; to die in sincere repentance, and to awake absolved and purified by the innate influence of virtue—are not these heavenly rewards? Consuelo, already initiated by Albert into doctrines which had their origin among the Hussites of Old Bohemia, as well as among the mysterious sects of preceding ages, who had humbly endeavored to interpret the words of Christ—Consuelo, I repeat, convinced, more from her gentle and affectionate nature than by the force of reasoning, that the soul of her husband was not suddenly removed from her forever and carried into regions inaccessible to human sympathies, mingled with this belief some of the superstitious ideas of her childhood. She had believed in spirits as the common people believe in them, and had more than once dreamed that she saw her mother approach to protect and shield her from danger. It was a sort of belief in the eternal communion of the souls of the living and the dead —a simple and childlike faith, which has ever existed to protest as it were against that creed which would forever separate the spirits of the departed from this lower world, and assign them a perfectly different and far distant sphere of action.

Consuelo, still kneeling by Albert's remains, could not bring herself to believe that he was dead, and could not comprehend the dread nature either of the word or of the reality. It did not seem possible that life could pass away so soon, and that the functions of heart and brain had ceased forever. "No," thought she, "the Divine spark still lingers, and hesitates to return to the hand who gave it, and who is about to resume his gift in order to send it forth under a renewed form into some loftier sphere. There is still, perhaps, a mysterious life existing in the yet warm bosom; and besides, wherever the soul of Albert is, it sees, understands, knows all that has taken place here. It seeks perhaps some aliment in my love—an im-

pulsive power to aid it in some new and heavenly career."
And, filled with these vague thoughts, she continued to
love Albert, to open her soul to him, to express her
devotion to him, to repeat her oath of fidelity — in
short, in feeling and idea, to treat him, not as a departed
spirit for whom one weeps without hope, but as a sleeping
friend whose awakening smiles we joyfully await.

When Porpora had become more composed, he thought
with terror of the situation in which he had left his pupil,
and hastened to rejoin her. He was surprised to find her
as calm as if she had watched by the bedside of a sleeping
friend. He would have spoken to her and urged her to
take some repose:

"Do not utter unmeaning words," said she, "in presence
of this sleeping angel. Do you retire to rest, my dear
master; I shall remain here."

"Would you then kill yourself?" said Porpora, in despair.

"No, my friend, I shall live," replied Consuelo; "I
shall fulfill all my duties toward *him* and toward you, but
not for one instant shall I leave his side this night."

When morning came, all was still. An overpowering
drowsiness had deadened all sense of suffering. The physician, exhausted by fatigue, had retired to rest. Porpora
slumbered in his chair, his head supported on Count Christian's bed. Consuelo alone felt no desire to abandon her
post. The count was unable to leave his bed, but Baron
Frederick, his sister, and the chaplain, proceeded almost
mechanically to offer up their prayers before the altar;
after which they began to speak of the interment. The
canoness, regaining strength when necessity required her
services, summoned her women and old Hans to aid her in
the necessary duties. Porpora and the doctor then insisted on Consuelo taking some repose, and she yielded to
their entreaties, after first paying a visit to Count Christian, who apparently did not see her. It was hard to say
whether he waked or slept, for his eyes were open, his
respiration calm, and his face without expression.

When Consuelo awoke, after a few hours' repose, she returned to the saloon, but was struck with dismay to find it
empty. Albert had been laid upon a bier and carried to
the chapel. His arm-chair was empty, and in the same
position where Consuelo had formerly seen it. It was all
that remained to remind her of him, in this place where

every hope and aspiration of the family had been centered for so many bitter days. Even his dog had vanished. The summer sun lighted up the somber wainscoting of the apartment, while the merry call of the blackbirds sounded from the garden with insolent gayety. Consuelo passed on to the adjoining apartment, the door of which was half open. Count Christian, who still kept his couch, lay apparently insensible to the loss he had just sustained, and his sister watched over him with the same vigilant attention that she had formerly shown to Albert. The baron gazed at the burning logs with a stupefied air; but the silent tears which trickled down his aged cheeks showed that bitter memory was still busy with his heart.

Consuelo approached the canoness to kiss her hand, but the old lady drew it back from her with evident marks of aversion. Poor Wenceslawa only beheld in her the destroyer of her nephew. At first she had held the marriage in detestation, and had opposed it with all her might; but when she had seen that time and absence alike failed to induce Albert to renounce his engagement, and that his reason, life, and health, depended on it, she had come to desire it as much as she had before hated and repelled it. Porpora's refusal, the exclusive passion for the theater which he ascribed to Consuelo, and in short all the officious and fatal falsehoods which he had despatched in succession to Count Christian, without ever adverting to the letters which Consuelo had written, but which he had suppressed — had occasioned the old man infinite suffering, and aroused in the canoness' breast the bitterest indignation. She felt nothing but hate and contempt for Consuelo. She could pardon her, she said, for having perverted Albert's reason through this fatal attachment, but she could not forgive her for having so basely betrayed him. Every look of the poor aunt, who knew not that the real enemy of Albert's peace was Porpora, seemed to say "you have destroyed our child; you could not restore him again; and now the disgrace of your alliance is all that remains to us."

This silent declaration of war hastened Consuelo's resolve to comfort, so far as might be, the canoness for this last misfortune. "May I request," said she, "that your ladyship will favor me with a private interview? I must leave this to-morrow ere daybreak; but before setting out I would fain make known my respectful intentions."

"Your intentions! Oh, I can easily guess them," replied the canoness, bitterly. "Do not be uneasy, mademoiselle, all shall be as it ought to be, and the rights which the law yields you shall be strictly respected."

"I perceive you do not comprehend me, madam," replied Consuelo; "I therefore long——"

"Well! since I must drain the bitter cup to the dregs," said the canoness, rising, "let it be now, while I have still courage to endure it. Follow me, signora. My eldest brother appears to slumber, and Supperville, who has consented to remain another day, will take my place for half an hour."

She rang, and desired the doctor to be sent for, then turning to the baron:

"Brother," said she, "your cares are useless, since Christian is still unconscious of his misfortune. He may never be otherwise—happily for him, but most unhappily for us! Perhaps insensibility is but the forerunner of death. I have now only you in the world, my brother; take care of your health, which this dreary inaction has only too much affected already. You were always accustomed to air and exercise. Go out, take your gun, the huntsman will follow with the dogs. Do, I entreat you, for my sake; it is the doctor's orders, as well as your sister's prayer. Do not refuse me; it is the greatest consolation you can bestow on my unhappy old age."

The baron hesitated, but at last yielded the point. The servants led him out, and he followed them like a child. The doctor examined Count Christian, who still seemed hardly conscious, though he answered any questions which were put to him with gentle indifference, and appeared to recognize those around him. "After all," said Supperville, "he is not so ill; and if he pass a good night, it may turn out nothing after all."

Wenceslawa, a little consoled, left her brother in the doctor's care, and conducted Consuelo to a large apartment, richly decorated in an antique fashion, where she had never been before. It contained a large state-bed, the curtains of which had not been stirred for more than twenty years. It was that in which Wanda Prachalitz, the mother of Count Albert, had breathed her last sigh, for this had been her apartment. "It was here," said the canoness with a solemn air, after having closed the door, "that we found Albert; it is now two-and-thirty days since, after an absence of thirteen. From that day to this he never entered it again ; nor did he once quit the armchair where yesterday he expired."

The dry, cold manner with which the canoness uttered this funereal announcement struck a dagger to Consuelo's heart. She then took from her girdle her inseparable bunch of keys, walked toward a large cabinet of sculptured oak, and opened both its doors. Consuelo saw that it contained a perfect mountain of jewels tarnished by age, of a strange fashion, the larger portion antique and enriched by diamonds and precious stones of considerable value. "These," said the canoness to her, "are the family jewels which were the property of my sister-in-law, Count Christian's wife, before her marriage ; here, in this partition, are my grandmother's, which my brothers and myself made her a present of ; and lastly, here are those which her husband bought for her. All these descended to her son Albert, and henceforth belong to you as his widow. Take them, and do not fear that any one here will dispute with you these riches, to which we attach no importance, and with which we have nothing more to do. The title-deeds of my nephew's maternal inheritance will be placed in your hands within an hour. All is in order, as I told you ; and as to those of his paternal inheritance, you will not, alas! have probably long to wait for them. Such were Albert's last wishes. My promise to act in conformity with them had, in his eyes, all the force of a will."

"Madam," replied Consuelo, closing the cabinet with a movement of disgust, "I should have torn the will had there been one, and I pray you now to take back your word. I have no more need than you for all these riches. It seems to me that my life would be forever stained by the possession of them. If Albert bequeathed them to me, it was doubtless with the idea that, conformably to his feelings and habits, I would distribute them to the poor. But I should be a bad dispenser of these noble charities ; I have neither the talents nor the knowledge necessary to make a useful disposition of them. It is to you, madam, who unite to those qualities a Christian spirit as generous as that of Albert, it belongs to employ this inheritance in works of charity. I relinquish to you my rights (if indeed I can be said to have any), of which I am ignorant and wish always to remain so. I claim from your goodness only one favor, viz: that you will never wound my feelings by renewing such offers."

The canoness changed countenance. Forced to esteem, but unwilling to admire, she endeavored to persist in her offer.

"But what do you mean to do?" said she, looking steadily at Consuelo; "you have no fortune?"

"Excuse me, madam, I am rich enough. I have simple tastes and a love for labor."

"Then you intend to resume — what you call your labor?"

"I am compelled to do so, madam, and for reasons which prevent my hesitating, notwithstanding the dejection in which I am plunged."

"And you do not wish to support your new rank in the world in any other manner?"

"What rank, madam?"

"That which befits Albert's widow."

"I shall never forget, madam, that I am the widow of the noble Albert, and my conduct shall be worthy of the husband I have lost."

"And yet the Countess of Rudolstadt intends once more to appear on the stage!"

"There is no other Countess of Rudolstadt than yourself, madam, and there never will be another after you, except the Baronesss Amelia, your niece."

"Do you mean to insult me by speaking of her, signora?" cried the canoness, who started at that name as if seared with a red-hot iron.

"Why that question, madam?" returned Consuelo, with an astonishment which Wenceslawa saw at once was not feigned. "In the name of heaven, tell me why I have not seen the young baroness here? Oh, heavens! can she be dead also?"

"No," said the canoness bitterly. "Would to heaven she were! Let us not speak of her; what we have said has no reference to her."

"I am nevertheless compelled, madam, to recall to your mind what only now strikes me. It is, that she is the only and legitimate heiress of the property and titles of your family. This must put your conscience at rest respecting the deposit which Albert has confided to you, since the laws do not permit you to dispose of it in my favor."

"Nothing can deprive you of a dowry and title which Albert's last will has placed at your disposal."

"Then nothing can prevent me renouncing them, and I do renounce them. Albert knew well that I neither wished to be rich nor a countess."

"But the world does not authorize you to renounce them."

"The world, madam! Well, that is precisely what I wished to speak to you about. The world would not understand the affection of Albert, nor the condescension of his family toward a poor girl like me. They would consider it a reproach to his memory and a stain upon your life. They would esteem it both ridiculous and shameful on my part; for, I repeat it, the world would understand nothing of what has here passed between us. The world, therefore, ought always to remain ignorant of it, madam, as your domestics are ignorant of it; for my master and the doctor, the only confidants, the only witnesses of that secret marriage, who are not of your own family, have not yet divulged it and will not divulge it. I can answer for the former; you can and ought to assure yourself of the discretion of the latter. Live tranquil then, madam, on this point. It will depend upon yourself alone to bury this secret in the tomb, and never by my act shall the Baroness Amelia suspect that I have the honor to be her cousin. Forget, therefore, the last hour of Count Albert's existence; it is for me to remember it, to bless him and be silent. You have tears enough to shed without my adding to them the mortification you must feel in recalling my existence as the widow of your admirable child!"

"Consuelo! my daughter!" cried the canoness, sobbing, "remain with us! You have a lofty soul and a great heart! Do not leave us again!"

"That would be the dearest wish of this heart which is all devotion to you," replied Consuelo, receiving her caresses with emotion; "but I could not do it without our secret being betrayed or guessed, which is the same thing, and I know that the honor of your family is dearer to you than life. Allow me, by tearing myself from your arms without delay and without hesitation, to render you the only service in my power."

The tears which the canoness shed at the termination of this scene, relieved her from the dreadful weight that oppressed her. They were the first that she had been able to shed since the death of her nephew. She accepted the sacrifice which Consuelo made, and the confidence which she placed in her resolutions proved that she at last appreciated that noble character. She left it to her to communicate them to the chaplain and to come to an understanding with Supperville and Porpora upon the necessity of forever keeping silence on the subject.

CONCLUSION.

CONSUELO, finding herself at perfect liberty, passed the day in wandering about the château, the garden, and the environs, in order to revisit all the places that recalled to her Albert's love. She even allowed her pious fervor to carry her as far as the Schreckenstein, and seated herself upon the stone, in that rightful solitude which Albert had so long filled with his grief. But she soon retired, feeling her courage fail her, and almost imagining that she heard a hollow groan issuing from the bowels of the rock. She dared not admit even to herself that she heard it distinctly; Albert and Zdenko were no more, and the allusion, therefore, for it was plainly such, could not prove otherwise than hurtful and enervating. Consuelo hurriedly left the spot.

On returning to the château toward evening she saw the Baron Frederick, who had by degrees strengthened himself on his legs and had regained some animation in the pursuit of his favorite amusement. The huntsmen who accompanied him started the game, and the baron, whose skill had not deserted him, picked up his victims with a deep sigh.

"He, at least, will live and be consoled," thought the young widow.

The canoness supped, or pretended to sup, in her brother's chamber. The chaplain, who had been praying beside the dead body in the chapel, endeavored to join them in their evening meal. But he felt feverish and ill, and after the first few mouthfuls was obliged to desist. This provoked the doctor a good deal. He was hungry, and, now compelled to let his soup cool in order to conduct the chaplain to his chamber, he could not help exclaiming

—" These people have no strength or courage! There are only two men here—the canoness and the signora !"

He soon returned, resolved not to trouble himself much about the indisposition of the poor priest, and made a hearty supper, in which he was imitated by the baron. Porpora, deeply affected, though he did not display it, could not unclose his lips either to speak or to eat. Consuelo's thoughts were occupied with the last repast she had made at that table between Albert and Anzoleto.

After supper she proceeded along with her master to make the necessary preparations for her departure. The horses were ordered to be in readiness at four in the morning. Before separating for the night, she repaired to Count Christian's apartment. He slept tranquilly, and Supperville, who wished to quit the dreary abode, asserted that he had no longer any remains of fever.

" Is that perfectly certain, sir ?" said Consuelo, who was shocked at his precipitation.

" I assure you," said he, " it is so. He is saved for the present, but I must warn you that it will not be long. At his time of life grief is not so deeply felt at the crisis, but the enemy merely gives way, to return with greater force afterward. So be on the watch, for you are not surely serious in determining to surrender your rights."

" I am perfectly serious, sir," said Consuelo, " and I am astonished that you do not believe in so simple a matter."

" Permit me to doubt, madame, until the death of your father-in-law. Meantime, you have made a great mistake in not taking possession of the jewels and title-deeds. No matter; you have doubtless your reasons, which I do not seek to know; for a person so calm as you are does not act without motives. I have given my word of honor not to disclose this family secret, and I shall keep my promise till you release me from it. My testimony may be of service to you when the proper time comes, and you may rely on my zeal and friendship. You will always find me at Bareith, if alive; and in this hope, countess, I kiss your hand."

Supperville took leave of the canoness, and having assured her of his patient's safety, written a prescription, and received a large fee—small, however, he trusted, in comparison with that which he was to receive from Consuelo—and quitted the castle at ten o'clock, leaving the latter indignant at his sordidness.

The baron retired to rest better than he had been the night before; as for the canoness, she had a bed prepared for herself beside Count Christian's. Consuelo waited till all was still; then when twelve oclock struck she lighted a lamp and repaired to the chapel. At the end of the cloister she found two of the servants, who at first were frightened at her approach, but afterward confessed why they were there. Their duty was to watch a part of the night beside the young count's remains, but they were afraid, and preferred watching and praying outside the door.

"And why afraid?" asked Consuelo, mortified to find that so generous a master inspired only such sentiments in the breast of his attendants.

"What would you have, signora?' replied one of these men, unaware that he was addressing Count Albert's widow; "our young lord had mysterious relations and strange acquaintances among the world of spirits. He conversed with the dead, he found out hidden things, never went to church, ate and drank with the gypsies—in short, no one could say what might happen to any one who would pass the night in this chapel. It would be as much as our lives were worth. Look at Cynabre there ! They would not let him into the chapel, and he has lain all day long before the door without moving, without eating, without making the least noise. He knows very well that his master is dead, for he has never called him once, but since midnight has struck, see how restless he is, how he smells and whines, as if he was aware that his master was no longer alone."

"You are weak fools!" replied the indignant Consuelo. "If your hearts were warmer, your minds would not be so feeble !" and she entered the chapel, to the surprise and consternation of the timid domestics.

"Albert lay on a couch covered with brocade, with the family escutcheons embroidered at the corners. His head reposed on a black velvet cushion, sprinkled with silver tears, while a black velvet pall fell in sable folds around him. A triple row of waxen tapers lit up his pale face, which was so calm, so pure, so manly, that a spectator would have said that he slept peacefully. The last of the Rudolstadts was clothed, according to family custom, in the ancient costume of his fathers. The coronet of a count was on his head, a sword was by his side, a buckler at his feet, and a crucifix on his breast. With his long black hair and beard, he seemed one of the ancient warriors whose effigies lay thickly scattered around. The pavement was strewn with flowers, and perfumes burned slowly in silver censers, placed at each corner of his last sad resting-place.

During three hours Consuelo prayed for her husband and contemplated him in his sublime repose. Death, in spreading a graver shade over his features, had altered them so little, that often, in admiring his beauty, she forgot that he had ceased to live. She even imagined that she heard the sound of his respiration, and when she withdrew for an instant to renew the perfume of the censers and trim the flames of the tapers, it seemed to her that she heard slight rustlings and perceived almost imperceptible undulations in the curtains and draperies. She re-approached him immediately, but on perceiving his frozen lips and silent heart, she renounced her fleeting and insensate hopes.

When three o'clock struck, Consuelo rose, and pressed upon the lips of her spouse her first kiss of love.

"Adieu, Albert!" said she, aloud, carried away by her religious enthusiasm; "you can now read without uncertainty all the emotions of my heart. There is no longer a cloud between us, and you know how I love you. You know that if I abandon your precious remains to the care of a family who to-morrow will return and look upon you with calmness, I shall not the less remember you and your unfaltering love forever. You know that it is not a heedless widow, but a faithful wife that leaves your last abode, and that she shall never cease to bear your memory in her heart. Adieu, Albert! As you have said, death severs us in seeming only, and we shall meet again in eternity. Faithful to the convictions which you have implanted in me, certain that you have merited God's blessing and approval, I weep not for you, and nothing will present you before my thoughts under the false and cruel image of death. You were right, Albert, I feel it in my heart, where I shall ever love you—there is no real death!"

As Consuelo finished these words, the curtains behind the bier were perceptibly moved, and, suddenly opening, presented to view the pale features of Zdenko. She was terrified at first, accustomed as she was to look upon him as her mortal enemy, but there was an expression of gentleness in his eyes which reassured her, and, stretching over the bed of death a rough hand which she did not hesitate to grasp in hers, he exclaimed with a smile—"Let us be at peace, my poor girl, here by his bed of rest. You are the good child of God, and Albert is well pleased with you. Ah! he is nappy now; Albert sleeps well! I have pardoned him as you see! When I learned that he slept, I came; and now I shall never leave him more. To-morrow I snall bring him to the grotto, and there we shall still converse about Consuelo—*Consuelo de mi alma!* Rest then, my child; Albert is no longer alone. Zdenko is there—always there! He wants nothing more—his friend will provide for him! The misfortune is averted; evil is destroyed; death is overcome. The thrice glorious day has risen. *May he whom they have wronged salute you!*"

Consuelo could support no longer this poor fool's childish joy. She bade him a tender adieu; and when she opened the chapel door she allowed Cynabre to enter and bound forward toward his old friend, whom, with his unerring instinct, he had already long perceived. "Poor Cynabre! Come! come! I shall hide you under my master's couch," said Zdenko, caressing him as he spoke with as much tenderness as if he had been his own child. "Come! my Cynabre; we are all three once more united, and never shall we be separated again."

Consuelo hastened to awaken Porpora, and then entered on tiptoe into Count Christian's apartment and glided between his bed and that of the canoness.

"It is you, my daughter?" said the old man, without evincing any surprise; "I am happy to see you. Do not waken my sister, who sleeps well, thank God! Go and do likewise; I feel quite easy. My son is saved, and I shall soon be well."

Consuelo kissed his white hair and his wrinkled hands, and succeeded in stifling her tears which would perhaps have dissipated his illusion. She dared not disturb the canoness, who reposed at last after watching for thirty nights. "God," she thought, "has placed bounds to grief, even in its paroxysm. May the rest of these unhappy souls be long!"

Half an hour afterward Consuelo, who felt her heart wrung with grief on leaving these noble-minded friends, crossed the drawbridge of the castle with Porpora, without once recollecting that the frowning stronghold, whose moats and bars enclosed such riches and such suffering, had become the property of the Countess of Rudolstadt.